SEASON OF THE SPELLSONG

ALAN DEAN FOSTER

SEASON OF THE SPELLSONG

SPELLSINGER
THE HOUR OF THE GATE
THE DAY OF THE DISSONANCE

Nelson Doubleday, Inc.
Garden City, New York

Maps by Richard Oriolo.

Published by arrangement with
Warner Books, Inc.
666 Fifth Avenue
New York, New York 10103

Printed in the United States of America

CONTENTS

SPELLSINGER

For Richard Corben,
Vaughn Bode,
Jimi Hendrix,
and Kitten-cat

PROLOGUE

Discontent ruled the stars, and there were portents in the heavens.

On the fourth day of Eluria, which follows the Feast of Consanguinity, a great comet was seen in the night sky. It crossed east to west over the Tree and lasted for half a fortnight. It left a black scar on the flesh of existence, a scar that glowed and lingered.

Faces formed within the timescar. Only a very few were capable of discerning their existence. None understood their implication. The faces danced and leered and mocked their ignorant observers. Frustrated or simply terrified, the few who could see turned away or deliberately placed a calming interpretation on what had troubled their minds.

One did not. He could not, for those visions haunted his sleep and tormented his days. He dropped words from formulae, bollixed simple conjurations, stuttered in his reading and rhyming studies.

A great evil was afoot in the world, an evil encountered twice before in the wizard's own long lifetime. But never before had it seemed so potent in its anticipation of coming death and destruction. Its core remained just beyond perception; but he knew it was something he did not understand, something fresh and threatening which shattered all the rules known to commonsense magic. It was rank, alien, shudderingly devoid of emotion and meaning. It horrified him.

Of one thing only was he certain. He would need assistance this time—only another attuned to the same unknown could understand it. Only another could save the world from the horror that threatened to engulf it.

For those who know the secret ways, the tunnels between realities, the crossings between universes are no more difficult to pass than the barriers that separate one individual from another. But such passages are of rare occasion, and once the proper formula is invoked, it can rarely be repeated.

Yet it was time to take the risk.

So the wizard heaved and strained, threw out the request carefully roped to his consciousness. It sailed out into the void of space-time, propelled by a mind of great if aging power. It sought another who could help him understand this fresh darkness that threatened his world. Dimensions slid aside, cleaving around the searching thought and giving it passage.

The wizard trembled with the massive effort. Sentient winds howled about his Tree, plucking dangerously at the thin lifeline within. It had to happen quickly, he knew, or the link would fade without attaching to an ally. And this was a link he might not hope to generate again.

Yet still the void yielded nothing and no one. The . . . the writhing tentacle of wizardness caught a mind, a few thoughts, an identity. Uncertain but unable to hunt further, he plunged inward. Surprisingly, the mind was pliable and open, receptive to invasion and manifestation. It almost seemed to welcome being grasped, accepting the tug with a contented indifference that appalled the wizard, but which he was grateful for nonetheless. This mind was detached, drifting. It would be easy to draw it back.

Easy save for the aged enchanter's waning strength. He locked and pulled, heaved with every ounce of power in him. But despite the subject's lack of resistance the materialization was not clean. At the last instant, the link snapped.

No, no . . . ! But the energy faded, was lost. An infrequent but damaging senility crept in and imposed sleep on that great but exhausted mind. . . .

And while he slumbered, the contented evil festered and planned and schemed, and a shadow began to spread over the souls of the innocent. . . .

The citizens of Pelligrew laughed at the invaders. Though they lived nearest of all the civilized folk to the Greendowns, they feared not the terrible inhabitants of those lands. Their town was walled and hugged the jagged face of a mountain. The only approach was up a single narrow path which could be defended against attack, it was said, by five old women and a brace of infants.

So when the leader of the absurdly small raiding party asked for their surrender, they laughed and threw garbage and night soil down on him.

"Go home!" they urged him. "Go back to your stinking homes and your shit-eating mothers before we decorate the face of our mountain with your blood!"

Curiously, this did not enrage the leader of the raiders. A few within the town remarked on this and worried, but everyone else continued to laugh.

The leader made his way back through the tents of his troops, his dignity unimpaired. He knew what was promised to him.

Eventually he reached a tent larger and darker than any of the others. Here his courage faltered, for he did not enjoy speaking to the one who dwelt within. Nevertheless, it was his place to do so. He entered.

It was black inside, though it was mid-morning without, black and heavy with the stench of unwholesome things and the nearness of death. In the back of the tent was the wizard, awash in attendants. In back of him stood the Font of Evil.

"Your pardon, Master," the leader of the soldiers began, and proceeded to tell of his disdainful reception at the hands of the Pelligrewers.

When he had finished, the hunched form in the dark of the tent said, "Return to your soldiers, good Captain, and wait."

The leader left hurriedly, glad to be out of that unclean place and back among his troops. But it was hard to just wait there, helpless before the unscalable wall and restrained by command, while the inhabitants of the town mocked and laughed and exposed their backsides to his angry soldiers.

Suddenly, a darkening turned the sky the color of lead. There was a thunder, yet there were no clouds. Then the great wall of Pelligrew vanished, turned to dust along with many of its shocked defenders. For an instant his own warriors were paralyzed. Then the blood lust renewed them and they swarmed into the naked town, shrieking in gleeful anticipation.

The slaughter was thorough. Not a soul was left alive. Those who disdained meat relaxed and sipped the pooled blood of the still living.

There was some question as to whether or not to keep the children

of the town alive for breeding. Upon consideration, the captain declined. He did not wish to convoy a noisy, bawling lot of infants back
to Cugluch. Besides, his soldiers deserved a reward for the patience
they had displayed beneath the barrage of verbal and physical refuse
the annihilated townsfolk had heaped on them. So he gave his assent
for a general butchering of the young.

That night the fire was put to Pelligrew while her children made
the soldiers a fine supper. The wood of the houses and the thatch of
the roofs burned all night and into the following morning.

The captain watched the last of the flames die out, nodding approvingly as recently dressed meat was loaded for the journey back
home. He sucked the marrow from a small arm as he addressed the
flier.

"Take the swiftest currents of the air, Herald," he instructed the
winged soldier. "Go quickly to the capital. Inform everyone that
taunting Pelligrew, thorn in our side for a thousand years, is no more.
Tell the people and the court that this first small success is complete
and that all the softness of the Warmlands westward shall soon be
ours, and soon all the worlds beyond that!"

The flier saluted and rose into the mountain air. The captain
turned, saw the occupants of the dark tent packing their own
noisome supplies. He watched as the wizard supervised the careful
loading of the awful apparition which had destroyed Pelligrew, and
shuddered as he turned away from it.

On the strength of that vileness and the wizard's knowledge they
might truly march to mastery over the entire Universe, if the wizard
was to be believed. But as for himself, he was personally inclined to
stay as far away from it as possible.

He loved anything which could find new ways to kill, but this had
a reach that spanned worlds. . . .

I

Size and attire alone would have made the giant otter worthy of notice, even if he hadn't tripped over Meriweather's feet. Sprawled whiskers down in the grass, the creature was barely a foot shorter than the lanky youth's own six feet two.

It was by far the largest otter Jon Meriweather had ever seen. Although he was a student of history and not zoology, he was still willing to bet that five and a half feet was somewhat more than otters normally reached. Despite the haze still fogging his brain, he was also fairly certain that they didn't run around in green felt peaked hats, snakeskin vests, or maroon velveteen pants puffed at the ankles. Very deliberately, Jon rose, regarded the stub of the joint he held tightly in his right hand, and flicked it distastefully away. The problem of the moment was not the existence of the utterly impossible otter, but of what his friend Shelly had cut the weed with.

Nevertheless, Jon couldn't take his eyes off the creature as it rolled over onto its rump. The velveteen pantaloons impressed on him a fact he'd never had much reason to consider before: otters have very low waistlines.

This one tugged its feathered cap down firmly over cookie-shaped ears and commenced gathering up the arrows that had spilled from the quiver slung across his back. The task was complicated by the short sword and scabbard strapped across his chest, which kept getting in the way whenever he bent over. An occasional murderous stare directed toward Jon gave him the feeling that the animal would enjoy putting one of the foot-long shafts into him.

That was no reason for concern. He swayed and relished the hallucination. Cannabis had never generated hallucinations in him before, but there was always a first time. What *had* Shelly been cutting their stash with?

Proof that it was cut with something powerful was stumbling about the grass before him, muttering under its breath and gathering arrows.

Doubtless his overtaxed brain was suffering from the long hours of study he'd been putting in lately, coupled with his working from nine at night until three in the morning. The work was necessary. Finals were due in seven weeks, and then presentation of his master's thesis. He savored the title once more: *Manifestations and prefiguring of democratic government in the Americas, as exemplified by the noble-sun king relationships of the Inca, 1248–1350.* It was a great title, he felt, and in presenting a thesis a good title was half the fight. No matter how brilliant the research or the writing, you were doomed without a title.

Having placed the last arrow in its quiver, the otter was carefully sliding it around to his back. This done, he gazed across the meadow. His sharp black eyes took in every tree and bush. Eventually the alert gaze came around to rest on the dreamy figure of Jon Meriweather.

Since the vision appeared to be waiting for some sort of comment, the good-natured graduate student said, "What can I do for you, offspring of my nighttime daydreaming?"

By way of reply the animal again directed its attention across the meadow, searched briefly, then pointed to a far copse. Jon lazily followed the otter's gesture.

Disappearing beneath a mossy boulder the size and shape of a demolished Volkswagen was a bright yellow lizard slightly larger than a chicken. It darted along on its hind legs, the long whiplike tail extended out behind for balance. Once it stared back over its shoulder, revealing a double row of pink dots running down its throat and chest. Then it was gone into the safety of its burrow.

Reality began to rear its ugly head. Jon was slowly taking note of his surroundings. His bed and room, the rows of books on concrete-block-supported shelves, the pinups, the battered TV, had been replaced by an encircling forest of oaks, sycamores, birch, and pine. Tuliplike flowers gleamed nearby, rising above thick grass and clover, some of which was blue. A faint tinkling, as of temple bells, sounded from the distant trees.

Jon held both hands to his head. Lucidity continued to flee laugh-

ingly just ahead of his thoughts. He remembered a pain, a pulling
that threatened to tear his brain out of his skull. Then he'd been
drifting, a different drift from the usual relaxing stupor that enveloped him during an evening of hard study and heavy smoking. His
head throbbed.

"Well?" asked the otter unexpectedly, in a high-pitched but not
really squeaky voice.

"Well what?" Soon, he told himself frantically, soon I'll wake up
and find myself asleep on the bed, with the rest of the Mexia *History
of All the Roman Emperors* still to be finished. Not hash, he thought.
Something stronger. God, my head.

"You asked what you could do for me." The otter gestured again, a
quick, rapid movement in the general direction of the boulder at the
edge of the woods. "As your damned great foot caused me t' fall and
lose the granbit, you can bloody well go and dig it out for me."

"What for? Were you going to eat it?"

"Nay." The otter's tone was bitterly sarcastic. "I were goin' t' tie
the bloody two-legs 'round me neck and wear it as a bloody pendant,
I was." His whiskers quivered with his rage. "Try t' play the smarty-
arse with me, will you? I suppose you be thinkin' your size will
protect you?"

Casually adjusting his bow across his back and chest, the animal
drew his short sword and approached Jon, who did not back away.
How could he, being deep asleep?

"I know what happens now." He shifted his feet, almost fell.
"You'll kill me, and I'll wake up. It's about time. I've got a whole
damn book to finish."

"Be you daft!" The otter's head cocked nervously to one side and a
furry paw scratched a cheek. " 'Cor, I believe you are." He looked
around warily. "I know not what influences are bein' brought t' bear
in this place, but it's cost me a granbit. I'm for leavin'. Will you not
at least apologize?"

"You mean for tripping you?" Jon considered. "I didn't do a damn
thing. I'm asleep, remember?"

"You're a damn sight worse than asleep, man. The granbit choke
you and make you throw up your bowels, if you be lucky enough t'
catch it. I'm finished with it, if it means encounterin' the likes o' you.
And if you follow me, I'll slit you from mouth to arse and hasten the
process. Keep your damned apology then, and take this parting gift
in return."

So saying, he jabbed the dream sword at Jon. It sliced his shirt and knicked his left side just above the belt holding up his jeans. A blinding pain exploded in his side, dampened only slightly by the lingering effects of the evening's smoking. His mouth opened to form a small "O" of surprise. Both hands went to his ribs.

The otter withdrew his sword, the tip now stained red, and slipped it back in its scabbard after cleaning it with tall grass. He turned and started away, muttering obscenities. Jon watched it waddle off across the grass, heading toward the trees.

The pain in his side intensified. Red stained his blue T-shirt. A warm wetness trickled cloyingly down inside his underwear and started down the left leg of his jeans. Superficial wounds bleed way out of proportion to their seriousness, he told himself. But it hurts, he thought despairingly.

I hope to God I wake up soon.

But if he was asleep . . . the pain was too real, far more so than trees or otter. Blood staining the grass, he limped after his assailant.

"Wait a minute . . . please, wait!" The words were thick in his dry throat, and he was ravenously hungry. Holding his wounded side with his left hand and waving his right, he stumbled after the otter. Clover broke fragrantly under his sandals and small flying things erupted in panic from the grass under his feet, to conceal themselves quickly in other pockets of protective green.

Bright sunlight filled the meadow. Birds sang strange songs. Butterflies with stained-glass wings crowned the tulips.

Having reached the outer rank of trees the otter hesitated under an umber sycamore and half drew his sword. "I'm not afeard o' you, daemon-man. Come closer and I'll stick you again." But even while he uttered this brave challenge the animal was backing slowly into the woods, looking to left and right for an avenue of escape.

"I don't want to hurt you," Jon whispered, as much from the agony in his side as from a desire not to panic the creature. "I just want to wake up, that's all." Tears started from his eyes. "Please let me wake up. I want to leave this dream and get back to work. I'll never take another toke, honest to God. It hurts."

He looked back over his shoulder, praying for the sight of his dumpy, cramped room with its cracked ceiling and dirty windows. Instead, he saw only more trees, tulip things, glass butterflies. A narrow brook ran where his bed should have been.

Turning back to the otter he took a step forward, tripped over a rock, and fell, weakened by loss of blood. Peppermint and heather smells filled his nostrils.

Please God, don't let me die in a dream. . . .

Details drifted back to him when he reopened his eyes. It was light out. He'd fallen asleep on his bed and slept the whole night, leaving the Mexia unread. And with an eight o'clock class in Brazilian government to attend.

Judging from the intensity of the light, he'd barely have enough time to pull himself together, gather up his books and notes, and make it to campus. And he'd have words with Shelly for not warning him about the unexpected potency of the pot he'd sold him.

And it was odd how his side hurt him.

"Got to get up," he mumbled dizzily.

" 'Ere now, guv'nor," said a voice that was not his own, not Shelly's, but was nonetheless familiar. "You take 'er easy for a spell. That was a bad knock you took when you fell."

Jon's eyelids rolled up like cracked plastic blinds. A bristled, furry face framing dancing black eyes stared down at him from beneath the rim of a bright green, peaked cap. Jon's own eyes widened. Details of dream slammed into his thoughts. The animal face moved away.

"Now don't you go tryin' any of your daemonic tricks on me . . . if you 'ave any."

"I"—Jon couldn't decide whether to pay attention to the bump on his head or the pain in his side—"I'm not a daemon."

The otter made a satisfied chittering sound. "Ah! Never did think you were. Knew it all along, I did. First off, a daemon wouldn't let hisself be cut as easy as you did and second, they don't fall flat on their puss when they be in pursuit of daemonic prey. Worst attempt at levitation ever I saw.

"Thinkin' I might 'ave misjudged you, for bein' upset over losin' me supper, I bandaged up that little nick I gifted you with. Guess you're naught but a man, what? No hard feelin's, mate?"

Jon looked down at himself. His shirt had been pulled up. A crude dressing of some fibrous material was tied around his waist with a snakeskin thong. A dull ache came from the bandaged region. He felt as though he'd been used as a tackling dummy.

Sitting up very slowly, he again noted his surroundings. He was not in his apartment, a tiny hovel which now seemed as desirable and unattainable as heaven.

Dream trees continued to shade dream flowers. Grass and blue clover formed a springy mattress beneath him. Dream birds sang in the branches overhead, only they were not birds. They had teeth, and scales, and claws on their wings. As he watched, a glass butterfly lit on his knee. It fanned him with sapphire wings, fluttered away when he reached tentatively toward it.

Sinewy muscles tensed beneath his armpits as the otter got behind him and lifted. "You're a big one . . . give us a 'and now, will you, mate?"

With the otter's aid, Jon soon found himself standing. He tottered a little, but the fog was lifting from his brain.

"Where's my room? Where's the school?" He turned a circle, was met by trees on all sides and not a hint of a building projecting above them. The tears started again, surprising because Jon had always prided himself on his emotional self-control. But he was badly, almost dangerously disoriented. "Where am I? What . . . who are you?"

"All good questions, man." This is a funny bloke, the otter thought. Watch yourself, now. "As to your room and school, I can't guess. As to where we are, that be simple enough to say. These be the Bellwoods, as any fool knows. We're a couple days' walk out o' Lynchbany Towne, and my name be Mudge. What might yours be, sor, if you 'ave a name?"

Jon answered numbly, "Meriweather. Jonathan Thomas Meriweather."

"Well then, Jnthin Tos Miwath . . . Joneth Omaz Morwoth . . . see 'ere, man, this simply won't do! That's not a proper name. The sayin' of it ud give one time enough to dance twice widdershins 'round the slick thighs o' the smooth-furred Felice, who's said t've teased more males than there be bureaucrats in Polastrindu. I'll call you Jon-Tom, if you don't mind, and if you will insist on havin' more than one name. But I'll not give you three. That clatters indecently on the ears."

"Bellwoods," the lanky, disoriented youth was babbling. "Lynchbany . . . Lynchbany . . . is that near Culver City? It's got to be in the South Bay somewhere."

The otter put both hands on Jon-Tom's wrists, and squeezed. Hard. "Look 'ere, lad," he said solemnly, "I know not whether you be balmy or bewitched, but you'd best get hold of yourself. I've not the time t' solve your problems or wipe away those baby-bottom tears you're spillin'. You're as real as you feel, as real as I, and if you don't start lookin' up for yourself you'll be a real corpse, with real maggots feedin' on you who won't give a snake fart for where you hailed from. You hearin' me, lad?"

Jon-Tom stopped snuffling, suddenly seemed his proper age. Easy, he told himself. Take this at face value and puzzle it through, whatever it is. Adhere to the internal logic and pray to wake up even if it's in a hospital bed. Whether this animal before you is real or dream, it's all you've got now. No need to make even an imaginary asshole of yourself.

"That's better." The otter let loose of the man's tingling wrists. "You mumble names I ain't never heard o'." Suddenly he slapped small paws together, gave a delighted spring into the air. "O' course! Bugger me for a rat-headed fool for not thinkin' of it afore! This 'as t' be Clothahump's work. The old sot's been meddlin' with the forces of nature again." His attitude was instantly sympathetic, whiskers quivering as he nodded knowingly at the gaping Jon-Tom.

" 'Tis all clear enough now, you poor blighter. It's no wonder you're as puzzled and dazed as you appear, and that I couldn't fathom you a'tall." He kicked at the dirt, boot sending flowers flying. "You've been magicked here."

"Magicked?"

"Aye! Oh, don't look like that, guv'nor. I don't expect it's fatal. Old Clothahump's a decent docent and wily enough wizard when he's sober and sane, but the troublemaker o' the ages when he lapses into senility, as 'e's wont t' do these days. Sometimes it's 'ard to tell when 'e's rightside in. Not that it be 'is fault for turnin' old and dotty. 'appens t' us all eventually, I expect.

"I stay away from 'is place, I do. As do any folk with brains enough. Never know what kind o' crazed incantation you might get sucked up in."

"He's a wizard, then," Jon-Tom mumbled. Trees, grass, the otter before him assumed the clarity of a fire alarm. "It's all real, then."

"I told you so. There be nothin' wrong with your ears, lad. No need t' repeat what I've already said. You sound dumb enough as it is."

"Dumb? Now look," Jon-Tom said with some heat, "I am confused. I am worried. I'll confess to being terrified out of my wits." One hand dropped reflexively to his injured side. "But I'm not dumb."

The otter sniffed disdainfully.

"Do you know who was president of Paraguay from 1936 to 1941?"

"No." Mudge's nose wiggled. "Do you know 'ow many pins can dance on the 'ead of an angel?"

"No, and"—Jon-Tom hesitated; his gaze narrowed—"it's 'how many angels can dance on the head of a pin.' "

Mudge let out a disgusted whistle. "Think we're smart, do we. I can't do fire, but I'm not even an apprentice and I can pindance."

His paw drew five small, silvery pins from a vest pocket. Each was about a quarter of an inch long. The otter mumbled something indistinct and made a pass or two over the metal splinters. The pins rose and commenced a very respectable cakewalk in his open palm.

"Allemande left," the otter commanded. The pins complied, the odd one out having some trouble working itself into the pattern of the dance.

"Never can get that fifth pin right. If only we 'ad the 'ead o' an angel."

"That's very interesting," Jon-Tom observed quietly. Then he fainted. . . .

"You keep that up, guv, and the back o' your nog's goin' to be as rough as the hills of Kilkapny Claw. Not t'mention what it's doin' t' your fur."

"My fur?" Jon-Tom rolled to his knees, took several deep breaths before rising. "Oh." Self-consciously he smoothed back his shoulder-length locks, leaned against the helpful otter.

"Little enough as you 'umans got, I'd think you'd take better care o' it." Mudge let loose of the man's arm. "Furless, naked skin . . . I'd rather 'ave a pox."

"I have to get back," Jon-Tom murmured tiredly. "I can't stay here any longer. I've got a job, and classes, and a date Friday night, and I've got to . . ."

"Your otherworldly concerns are of no matter to me." Mudge gestured at the sticky bandage below the man's ribs. "I didn't spear you bad. You ought t' be able to run if you 'ave t'. If it's 'ome you want, we'd best go call on Clothahump. I'll leave you t' 'im. I've work of me own t' do. Can you walk?"

"I can walk to meet this . . . wizard. You called him Clothahump?"

"Aye, that's it, lad. The fornicating troublemakin' blighter, muckin' about with forces 'e can't no longer control. No doubt in my mind t' it, mate. Your bein' 'ere is 'is doin'. 'E be bound to send you back to where you belong before you get 'urt."

"I can take care of myself." Jon-Tom had traveled extensively for his age. He prided himself on his ability to adapt to exotic locales. Objectively considered, this land he now found himself in was no more alien-appearing than Amazonian Peru, and considerably less so than Manhattan. "Let's go and find this wizard."

"That's the spirit, guv'nor!" Privately Mudge still thought the tall youth a whining, runny-nosed baby. "We'll 'ave this 'ere situation put right in no time, wot?"

Oak and pine dominated the forest, rising above the sycamore and birch. In addition, Jon-Tom thought he recognized an occasional spruce. All coexisted in a botanistic nightmare, though Jon-Tom wasn't knowledgeable enough to realize the incongruity of the landscape.

Epiphytic bushes abounded, as did gigantic mushrooms and other fungi. Scattered clumps of brown and green vines dripped black berries, or scarlet, or peridot green. There were saplings that looked like elms, save for their iridescent blue bark.

The glass butterflies were everywhere. Their wings sent isolated shafts of rainbow light through the branches. Yet everything seemed to belong, seemed natural, even to the bells formed by the leaves of some unknown tree, which rang in the wind and gave substance to the name of this forest.

The cool woods, with its invigorating tang of mint ever present, had become almost familiar when he finally had his first close view of a "bird." It lit on a low-hanging vine nearby and eyed the marchers curiously.

Bird resemblance ended with the feathers. A short snout revealed tiny sharp teeth and a long, forked tongue. The wings sprouted from a scaly yellow body. Having loosened its clawed feet from the vine, the feathered reptile (or scaly bird?) circled once or twice above their heads. It uttered a charming trill that reminded the astonished Jon-Tom of a mockingbird. Yet it bore closer resemblance to the creature he'd seen scamper beneath the boulder in the meadow than to any bird, and was sooner cousin to a viper than a finch.

A small rock whizzed through the air. With an outraged squawk the feathered apparition wheeled and vanished into the sheltering trees.

"Why'd you do that, Mudge?"

"It were circlin' above us, sor." The otter shook his head sadly. "Not entirely bright you are. Or don't the flyers o' your own world ever vent their excrement upon unwary travelers? Or is it that you 'ave magicked reasons o' your own for wishin' t' be shat upon?"

"No." He tried to regain some of the otter's respect. "I've had to dodge birds several times."

The confession produced a reaction different from what he'd hoped for.

"BIRDS?" The otter's expression was full of disbelief, the thin whiskers twitching nervously. "No self-respectin' bird would dare do an insult like that. Why, 'ed be up afore council in less time than it takes t' gut a snake. D'you think we're uncivilized monsters 'ere, like the Plated Folk?"

"Sorry." Jon-Tom sounded contrite, though still puzzled.

"Mind you watch your language 'ere, lad, or you'll find someone who'll prick you a mite more seriously than did I."

They continued through the trees. Though low and bandy-legged like all his kind, the otter made up for his slight stride with inexhaustible energy. Jon-Tom had to break into an occasional jog to keep pace with him.

Seeds within belltree leaves generated fresh music with every varying breeze, now sounding like Christmas chimes, now like a dozen angry tambourines. A pair of honeybees buzzed by them. They seemed so achingly normal, so homey in this mad world that Jon-Tom felt a powerful desire to follow them all the way to their hive, if only to assure himself it was not equipped with miniature windows and doors.

Mudge assured him it was not. "But there be them who are related to such who be anything but normal, lad." He pointed warningly eastward. "Many leagues that way, past grand Polastrindu and the source o' the River Tailaroam, far beyond the Swordsward, on the other side o' great Zaryt's Teeth, lies a land no warmblood has visited and returned to tell o' it. A land not to look after, a country in'abited by stinks and suppurations and malodorous creatures who are o' a vileness that shames the good earth. A land where those who are not animal as us rule. A place called Cugluch."

"I don't think of myself as animal," Jon-Tom commented, momentarily forgetting the bees and wondering at what would inspire such loathing and obvious fear in so confident a creature as Mudge.

"You're not much of a human, either." Mudge let out a high-pitched whistle of amusement. "But I forget myself. You're a stranger 'ere, plucked unwillingly from some poor benighted land o' magic. Unwillingly snookered you've been, an' I ought by right not t' make sport o' you." Suddenly his face contorted and he missed a step. He eyed his taller companion uncertainly.

"You 'ave the right look 'bout you, and you feel right, but with magic one can never be sure. You *do* 'ave warm blood, don't you, mate?"

Jon-Tom winced, listed to his left. A powerful arm steadied him. "Thanks," he told the otter. "You should know. You spilled enough of it."

"Aye, it did seem warm enough, though my thoughts were on other matters at the time." He shrugged. "You've proved yourself harmless enough, anyway. Clothahump will know what he's called you for."

What could this wizard want with me, Jon-Tom wondered? Why is this being done to me? Why not Shelly, or Professor Stanhope, or anyone else? Why me? He noticed that they'd stopped.

"We're there?" He looked around, expecting maybe a quaint thatched cottage. There was no cottage in sight, no house of any kind. Then his eyes touched on the dull-paned windows in the flanks of the massive old oak, the wisp of smoke rising lazily from the chimney that split the thick subtrunks high up, and the modest door scrunched in between a pair of huge, gnarly roots.

They started for the doorway, and Jon-Tom's attention was drawn upward.

"Now what?" wondered Mudge, aware that his entranced companion was no longer listening attentively to his description of Clothahump's growing catalog of peculiarities.

"It's a bird. A real one, this time."

Mudge glanced indifferently skyward. "O' course it's a bird. What, now, did you expect?"

"One of those hybrid lizard things like those we passed in the forest. This looks like a true bird."

"You're bloody right it is, and better be glad this one can't 'ear you talkin' like that."

It was a robin, for all that it had a wingspan of nearly a yard. It wore a vest of kelly green satin, a cap not unlike Mudge's, and a red and puce kilt. A sack was slung and strapped across its chest. It also sported a translucent eyeshade lettered in unknown script.

Three stories above ground a doweled landing post projected from the massive tree. Braking neatly, the robin touched down on this. With surprisingly agile wing tips it reached into the chest sack, fumbled around, and withdrew several small cylinders. They might have been scrolls.

These the bird shoved into a dark recess, a notch or small window showing in the side of the tree. It warbled twice, piercingly, sounding

very much like the robins who frequented the acacia tree outside
Kinsey Hall back on campus.

Leaning toward the notch, it cupped a wing tip to its beak and was
heard to shout distinctly, "Hey, stupid! Get off your fat ass and pick
up your mail! You've got three days' worth moldering up here, and if
I come by tomorrow and it's still piled up I'll use it for nest lining!"
There followed a string of obscenities much out of keeping with the
bird's coloring and otherwise gentle demeanor. It turned from the
notch with a gruff chirp, grumbling under its breath.

"Horace!" shouted the otter. The bird looked downward and
dropped off the perch to circle above them.

"Mudge? Whatcha doin'?" The voice reminded Jon of one he'd
heard frequently during a journey to another exotic section of the real
world, a realm known as Brooklyn. "Ain't seen ya around town
much lately."

"Been out 'untin', I 'ave."

"Where'd ya pick up the funny-looking bozo?"

"Long story, mate. Did I 'ear you right when you said the old
geezer hain't been 'ome in three days?"

"Oh, he's inside, all right," replied the bird. "Mixing and sorcering
as usual. I can tell because there's a different stink blowing out that
mail drop every time I fly in. You wouldn't happen to have a worm
on ya, would ya?"

"Sorry, mate. Crayfish and oysters run more t' my taste."

"Yeah, I know. No harm in asking." He cocked a hopeful eye at
Jon-Tom. "How 'bout you, buddy?"

"Afraid not." Anxious to please, he fumbled in his jeans' pockets.
"How about a Juicyfruit?"

"Thanks, but I've had all the berries I can stand for now. I'm up to
my ass feathers in berries." He stared at Jon a moment longer, then
bid them a civil good-bye.

"Always did envy them birds." Mudge looked envious. "Wings are
so much faster than feet."

"I think I'd rather have real feet and hands."

Mudge grunted. "That's a point t' reckon with, guv'nor." They
moved to the doorway. " 'Ere goes now. Mind," he whispered, "you
be on your best behavior, Jon-Tom. Old Clothahump's got the reputation o' bein' fair-tempered for a wizard, but they're a cranky group.
Just as soon turn you into a dung beetle as look at you. It ain't good
policy t' provoke one, 'specially one as powerful and senile as Clothy-
nose 'ere."

The otter knocked on the door, nervously repeated it when no reply was forthcoming. Jon-Tom noted the animal's tenseness, decided that for all his joking and name-calling he was deeply fearful of wizards or anything having to do with them. He twitched and shifted his feet constantly while they waited. It occurred to Jon-Tom that at no time had he actually seen the otter standing motionless. Trying to ignore the pain pounding in his side he struggled to stand straight and presentable.

In a moment the door would creak inward and he would be standing face to face with what was, at least to Mudge's mind, a genuine magic-making wizard. It was easy enough to visualize him: six and a half feet tall, he would be garbed in flowing purple robes enscribed with mystic symbols. A bestarred pointy hat would crown the majestic head. His face would be wrinkled and stern—what wasn't hidden beneath a flowing white beard—and he would very likely be wearing thick glasses.

The door opened inward. It creaked portentously. "Good morning," he began, "we . . ."

The rest of the carefully rehearsed greeting shattered in his throat as he stumbled backward in panic, tripped, and fell. Something tore in his side and he sensed dampness there. He wondered how much longer he could tolerate the wound without having it properly treated, and if he might die in this falsely cheerful place, as far from home as anyone could be. The monstrosity that had filled the open doorway drifted toward him as he tried to crawl, to scramble away. . . .

II

Mudge stared disgustedly down at his charge, sounded both angry and embarrassed. "Now wot the bloody 'ell's the matter with you? It's only Pog."

"P-p-pog?" Jon-Tom was unable to move his eyes from the hovering horror.

"Clothahump's famulus, you colossal twit! He . . ."

"Never mind," rumbled the gigantic black bat. "I don't mind." His wing tips scraped the jambs as he fluttered back into the portal. Oversized pink ears and four sharp fangs caught the light. His voice was incredibly rough, echoing from a deep gravel mine. "I know I'm not pretty. But I never knocked anyone down because of it." He flew out now to hover nearer Jon.

"You're not very handsome yourself, man."

"Go easy on 'im, Pog." Mudge tried to sound conciliatory. " 'E's been magicked from 'is world into ours, and 'e's wounded besides." The otter diplomatically avoided mentioning that he'd been the cause of the injury.

Jon-Tom struggled unsteadily to his feet. Claret ran from the left leg of his pants, thick and warm.

"Clothahump been workin' up any otherworldly invokings?"

"He is soberer dan usual, if dat's what you mean." The bat let loose a derisive snort.

A rich, throaty voice called from the depths of the tree, an impressive if slightly wavering voice that Jon-Tom instinctively knew belonged to the master sorcerer. "Who's there, Pog?"

"Mudge, da otter hunter, Master. And some damaged, dopey-looking human."

"Human, you say?" There was an excited edge to the question. "In then, bring them in."

"Come on," ordered Pog curtly. "His nibs'll see you." The bat vanished into the tree, wings larger than the robin's barely clearing the entrance.

"You all right, mate?" Mudge watched the swaying form of his unwanted companion. "Why'd you 'ave a fit like that? Pog be no uglier than any other bat."

"It wasn't . . . wasn't his countenance that upset me. It was his size. Most of the bats where I'm from don't grow that big."

"Pog be about average, I'd say." Mudge let the thought slide. "Come on, now, and try not to bleed too much on the floor."

Refusing the otter's support, Jon-Tom staggered after him. The hallway was a shock. It was far too long to fit inside the oak, despite its considerable diameter. Then they entered a single chamber at least twenty-five feet high. Bookshelves lined the walls, filled with tomes of evident age and all sizes and bindings. Incense rose from half a dozen burners, though they could not entirely obliterate the nose-nipping miasma which filled the room.

Scattered among books lay oddly stained pans and bowls, glass vials, jars filled with noisome objects, and other unwholesome paraphernalia. Skulls variously treated and decorated were secured on the walls. To Jon-Tom's horror, they included a brace that were obviously human.

Windows offered ingress to topaz light. This colored the high chamber amber and gold and made live things of the dust motes pirouetting in the noxious air. The floor was of wood chips. A few pieces of well-used furniture made of heavy wood and reptile skin dominated the center of the room.

Two doors ajar led to dimly glimpsed other rooms.

"This is impossible," he said to Mudge in a dull whisper. "The whole tree isn't wide enough to permit this one room, let alone others and the hallway we just came through."

"Aye, guv'nor, 'tis a neat trick it is." The otter sounded impressed but not awed. "Sure solves the space problem, don't it? I've seen it in towns in a few wealthy places. Believe me, the initial spell costs plenty, not t'mention the frequent renewals. Permanently locked hyperdimensional vortical expansions don't come cheap, wot?"

"Why don't they?" Jon-Tom asked blankly, unable to think of a more sensible comment in the face of spatial absurdity.

Mudge looked up at him conspiratorially. "Inflation."

They looked around to see Pog returning from another room. "He says he'll be along in a minute or two."

"What kind of mood is he in?" Jon-Tom looked hopefully at the bat.

"Comprehensible." Keeping his balance in midair, the bat reached with a tiny clawed hand set halfway along his left wing into a pouch strapped to his chest. It was much smaller than the robin's. He withdrew a small cigar. "Gotta light?"

"I'm out o' flints, mate."

"Just a second." Jon-Tom fumbled excitedly in his jeans. "I do." He showed them his cheap disposable lighter.

Mudge studied it. "Interestin'."

"Yeah." Pog fluttered close. Jon-Tom forced himself to ignore the proximity of those gleaming, razor-sharp fangs. "Never saw a firemaker like it." He swung the tiny cigar around in his mouth.

Jon-Tom flipped the wheel. Pog lit the cigar, puffed contentedly.

"Let's 'ave a look, lad." Jon-Tom handed the lighter over. The otter turned it around in his paws. " 'Ow's it work?"

"Like this." Jon-Tom took it back, spun the wheel. Sparks, but no flame. He studied the transparent base. "Out of fluid."

"Got stuck wid a bum spell?" Pog sounded sympathetic. "Never mind. And thanks for da light." He opened his mouth, blew smoke squares.

"It has nothing to do with spells," Jon-Tom protested. "It works on lighter fluid."

"Get my money back if I were you," advised the otter.

"I'd rather get me back." Jon-Tom studied his wrist. "My watch has stopped, too. Battery needs replacing." He held up a hand. "And I don't want to hear anything more about spells." Mudge shrugged, favoring Jon-Tom with the look one would bestow on an idiot relation. "Now where's this lazy old so-called wizard of yours?" Jon-Tom asked Pog.

"OVER HERE!" a powerful voice thundered.

Shaking lest his discourteous remark had been overheard, Jon turned slowly to confront the renowned Clothahump.

There were no flowing robes or white beard, no peaked hat or cryptically marked robe. But the horn-rimmed glasses were present. Somehow they remained fixed above a broad, rounded beak, just above tiny nostrils. The glasses did not have arms extended back and behind ears, since a turtle's ears are almost invisible.

A thick book clutched in one stubby-fingered hand, Clothahump waddled over to join them. He stood a good foot shorter than Mudge.

"I mean no disrespect, sir," Jon had the presence of mind to say. "I didn't know you were in the room and I'm a stranger here and I . . ."

"Tosh, boy." Clothahump smiled and waved away the coming apology. His voice had dropped to normal, the wizardly thunder vanished. "I'm not easily offended. If I were I wouldn't be able to put up with *him.*" He jerked a thumb in Pog's direction. "Just a moment, please."

He looked down at himself. Jon followed the gaze, noticing a number of small knobs protruding from the wizard's plastron. Clothahump tugged several, revealing tiny drawers built into his front. He hunted around for something, mumbling apologies.

"Only way I can keep from losing the really important powders and liquids," he explained.

"But how can you . . . I mean, doesn't that hurt?"

"Oh heavens no, boy." He let loose an infectious chuckle. "I employ the same technique that enables me to enlarge the inside of my tree without enlarging the outside."

"Bragging," grumped Pog, "when da poor lad's obviously in pain."

"Hold your tongue!" The bat whirled around in tight circles, but went silent. "I have to watch his impertinence." Clothahump winked. "Last time I fixed him so he could only sleep right side up. You should have seen him, trying to hang from his ears." He chuckled again.

"But I don't like to lose my temper in front of guests. I cultivate a reputation for mildness. Now then," he said with a professional air, "let's have a look at your side."

Jon-Tom watched as the turtle gently eased aside the crude bandage concocted by Mudge. Stubby fingers probed the glistening, stained flesh, and the youth winced.

"Sorry. You'd best sit down."

"Thank you, sir." They moved to a nearby couch, whose legs were formerly attached to some live creature of unimaginable shape. He lowered himself carefully, since the cushions were barely half a foot off the floor, at a level designed to accommodate the turtle's low backside.

"Stab wound." Clothahump regarded the ugly puncture thoughtfully. "Shallow, though. We'll soon have you fixed."

" 'Ere now, your wizardship," Mudge broke in. "Beggin' your pardon, but I've always 'eard tell 'twas sorceral procedure to seek payment for magicking services in advance."

"That's not a problem here . . . what did you say your name was?"

"I didn't, but it's Mudge."

"Um. As I said, payment will be no problem for this lad. We'll simply consider this little repair as an advance against his services."

"Services?" Jon-Tom looked wary. "What services?"

"He ain't much good for anything, from what I've seen," Mudge piped up.

"I would not expect a mere scavenger such as yourself, Mr. Mudge, to understand." The wizard adjusted his glasses haughtily. "There have been forces at work in the world only I could fully comprehend, and only I am properly equipped to deal with them. The presence of this lad is but a small piece of a dangerously complex puzzle."

There, Mudge thought triumphantly. Knew he'd been muckin' about.

"It is obvious he is the one I was casting for last night. You see, he is a wizard himself."

"Who . . . 'im?" Mudge laughed in the manner of otters, high and squeaky, like the laughter of wise children. "You're jokin', mate."

"I do not joke in matters of such grave import." Clothahump spoke somberly.

"Yeah, but 'im . . . a wizard? He couldn't even put a new spell on 'is firemaker."

The turtle sighed, spoke slowly. "Coming as he does from a world, from a universe, other than our own, it is to be expected that some of his magic would differ from ours. I doubt I would be able to make use of my own formidable talents in his world. But there is an awesome interdimensional magic abroad in the world, Mudge. To cope successfully with it we require the aid and knowledge of one accustomed to its workings." He looked troubled, as though burdened by some hidden weight he chose to keep hidden from his listeners.

"He is the magician I sought. I used many new and unproven words, many intergrams and formulae rare and difficult to blend. I cast for hours, under great strain. I had given up hope of locating anyone, and then chanced upon this drifting spirit, so accessible and free."

Jon-Tom thought back to what he'd been smoking; he'd been drifting, no doubt of that. But what was all this about him being a wizard-magician?

Sharp eyes were staring into his own from behind thick lenses. "Tell me, boy. Are not the wizards and magicians of your world known by the word En'geeniar?"

"En'gee . . . engineer?"

"Yes, that is the proper sounding of it, I think."

"I guess that's as good an analogy as any."

"You see?" He turned knowingly back to Mudge. "And it is through his service he will pay us back."

"Uh, sir . . . ?" But Clothahump had disappeared behind a towering stack of books. Clinking noises sounded.

Mudge was now convinced he'd have been much better off had he never tracked that granbit or set eyes on this particular gangling young human. He studied the slumping form of the injured youth. Jon-Tom was spritely enough of word . . . but a wizard? Still, one could never be certain of anything, least of all appearances, when dealing with wizardly doings. Common folk did well to avoid such.

How could anyone explain a wizard who could not spell a simple firemaker, much less fix an injury to himself? The lad's disorientation and fear were real enough, and neither spoke of the nature of wizards. Best to wait, perhaps, and see what concealed abilities this Jon-Tom might yet reveal. Should such abilities suddenly surface, it might also be best to insure that he forgot who put the hole in his ribs.

"Now lad, don't pay no mind t' what Clothahump says about payments and such. No matter what the final cost, we'll see it's taken care of. I feel sort o' responsible t' make certain o' that."

"That's good of you, Mudge."

"Aye, I know. Best not even t' mention money to 'is nibs."

Laden with bottles and odd containers fashioned of ceramic, the turtle waddled back toward them. He arranged the collection neatly on the wood chips in front of the couch. Choosing from several, he mixed their contents in a small brass bowl set between Jon-Tom's legs. A yellow powder was added to a murky pool in the bowl and was followed by a barely audible mumbling. Mudge and Jon-Tom clutched suddenly at their nostrils. The paste was now emitting an odor awful in the extreme.

Clothahump added a last pinch of blue powder, stirred the mixture, and then began plastering it directly on the open wound. Thoughts of infection faded when it became clear to Jon that the paste was having a soothing effect on the pain.

"Pog!" Clothahump snapped short fingers. "Bring a small crucible. The one with the sun symbols engraved on the sides."

Jon-Tom thought he might have heard the bat mumble, "Why don't ya get it yourself, ya lazy fat cousin to a clam." But he couldn't be sure.

In any case, Pog did not speak when he returned with the requested crucible. He deposited it between Jon-Tom and the wizard, then flapped back out of the way.

Clothahump measured the paste into the crucible, added a vile-smelling liquid from a tall, waspish black bottle, then a pinch of something puce from a drawer near his right arm. Jon-Tom wondered if the wizard's built-in compartments ever itched.

"What the devil did I do with that wand . . . ah!" Using a small ebony staff inlaid with silver and amethyst, he stirred the mixture, muttering continuously.

Within the crucible the paste had gained the consistency of a thick soup. It began to glow a rich emerald green. Tiny explosions broke its surface, were reflected in Jon-Tom's wide eyes. The mixture now smelled of cinnamon instead of swamp gas.

Using the wand, the wizard dipped out some of the liquid and tasted it. Finding it satisfactory, he gripped the wand at either end with two fingers of each hand and began passing it in low swoops over the boiling crucible. The sparks on the liquid's surface increased in intensity and frequency.

> "Terra bacteria,
> Red for muscle, blue for blood,
> Ruination, agglutination, confrontation,
> Knit Superior.
> Pyroxine for nerves, Penicillin for curds.
> Surgical wisps, solvent site, I bid you complete
> your unquent fight!"

Jon-Tom listened in utter bewilderment. There was no deep-throated invocation of tail of newt, eye of bat. No spider's blood or ox eyes, though he remained ignorant of the powders and fluids the wizard had employed. Clothahump's mystic singsong chatter of pyroxine and agglutinating and such sounded suspiciously like the sort of thing a practicing physician might write to amuse himself in a moment of irrepressible nonsense.

As soon as the recital had been completed, Jon-Tom asked about the words.

"Those are the magic words and symbols, boy."

"But they actually mean something. I mean, they refer to real things."

"Of course they do." Clothahump stared at him as if concerned more about his sanity than his wound. "What is more real than the components of magic?" He nodded at the watch. "I do not recognize your timepiece, yet I accept that it keeps true time."

"That's not magical, though."

"No? Explain to me exactly how it works."

"It's a quartz-crystal. The electrons flow through . . . I mean . . ." He gave up. "It's not my specialty. But it runs on electricity, not magic formulae."

"Really? I know many electric formulae."

"But dammit, it runs on a battery!"

"And what is inside this thing you call a battery?"

"Stored electric power."

"And is there no formula to explain that?"

"Of course there is. But it's a mathematical formula, not a magic one."

"You say mathematics is not magic? What kind of wizard are you?"

"I keep trying to tell you, I'm . . ." But Clothahump raised a hand for silence, leaving a frustrated Jon-Tom to fume silently at the turtle's obstinacy.

Jon-Tom began to consider what the wizard had just said and grew steadily more confused.

In addition to the firefly explosions dancing on its surface, the paste-brew had changed from green to yellow and was pulsing steadily. Clothahump laid his wand aside ceremoniously. Lifting the crucible, he offered it to the four corners of the compass. Then he tilted it and drained the contents.

"Pog." He wiped paste from his beak.

"Yes, Master." The bat's voice was subservient now.

Clothahump passed him the crucible, then the brass bowl. "Scullery work." The bat hefted both containers, flapped off toward a distant kitchen.

"How's that now, my boy?" Clothahump eyed him sympathetically. "Feel better?"

"You mean . . . that's it? You're finished?" Jon-Tom thought to look down at himself. The ugly wound had vanished completely. The flesh was smooth and unbroken, the sole difference between it and the surrounding skin being that it wasn't suntanned like the rest of his torso. It occurred to him that the pain had also left him.

Tentatively he pressed the formerly bleeding region. Nothing. He turned an open-mouthed stare of amazement on the turtle.

"Please." Clothahump turned away. "Naked adulation embarrasses me."

"But how . . . ?"

"Oh, the incantations healed you, boy."

"Then what was the purpose of the stuff in the bowl?"

"That? Oh, that was my breakfast." He grinned as much as his beak would allow. "It also served nicely to distract you while you healed. Some patients get upset if they see their own bodies healing . . . sometimes it can be messy to look upon. So I had the choice of putting you to sleep or distracting you. The latter was safer and simpler. Besides, I was hungry.

"And now I think it time we touch on the matter of why I drew you into this world from your own. You know, I went to the considerable trouble, not to mention danger, of opening the portals between dimensions and bending space-time. But first it is necessary to seal this room. Move over there, please."

Still wordless at his astonishing recovery, Jon-Tom obediently stepped back against a bookcase. Mudge joined him. So did the returning Pog.

"Scrubbing crucibles," the bat muttered under his breath. Clothahump had picked up his wand and was waving it through the air, mumbling cryptically. "Dat's all I ever do around here; wash da dishes, fetch da books, clean da dirt."

"If you're so disgusted, why stick around?" Jon-Tom regarded the bat sympathetically. He'd almost grown used to its hideousness. "Do you want to be a wizard so badly?"

"Shit, no!" Pog's gruffness gave way to agitation. "Wizarding's mighty dangerous stuff." He fluttered nearer. "I've indentured myself to da old wreck in return for a major, permanent transmogrification. I only got ta stick it out another few years . . . I tink . . . before I can demand payment."

"What kind o' change you got in mind, mate?"

Pog turned to face the otter. "Y'know da section o' town at da end of da Avenue o' da Pacers? Da big old building dere dat's built above da stables?"

"Cor, wot be you doin' thereabouts? You don't rate that kind o' trade. That's a high-rent district, that is." The otter was grinning hugely under his whiskers.

"I know, I know," confessed the disconsolate Pog. "I've a friend who made a killing on da races who took me dere one night ta celebrate. He knows Madam Scorianza, who runs da house for arboreals. Dere's a girl who works up dere, not much more dan a fledgling, a full flagon o' falcon if ever dere one was. Her name's Uleimee and she is," he fairly danced in the air as he reminisced, "da most exquisite creature on wings. Such grace, such color and power, Mudge! I thought I'd die of ecstasy." The excitement of the memory trembled in the air.

"But she won't have a thing ta do wid me unless I pay like everyone else. She dotes on a wealthy old osprey who runs a law practice over in Knotsmidge Hollow. Me she won't do much more dan loop da loop wid, but whenever dis guy flicks a feather at her she's ready ta fly round da world wid him."

"Forget 'er then, mate," Mudge advised him. "There be other birds and some of 'em are pretty good-lookin' bats. One flyin' fox I've seen around town can wrap 'er wings 'round me any time."

"Mudge, you've never been in love, have ya?"

"Sure I 'ave . . . lots o' times."

"I thought dat much. Den I can't expect ya ta understand."

"I do." Jon-Tom nodded knowingly. "You want Clothahump to transform you into the biggest, fastest falcon around, right?"

"Wid da biggest beak," Pog added. "Dat's da only reason why I hang around dis hole waitin' wing and foot on da doddering old curmudgeon. I could never afford ta pay for a permanent transmogrification. I got ta slave it out."

Jon-Tom's gaze returned to the center of the room. Having miraculously cured the stab wound, the doddering old curmudgeon was beckoning for them to rejoin him. The windows were dimming rapidly.

"Come close, my friends." Mudge and Jon-Tom did so. Pog hung himself from the upper rim of a nearby bookcase.

"A great crisis threatens to burst upon us," the wizard said solemnly. It continued to darken inside the tree. "I can feel it in the movement of worms in the earth, in the way the breezes whisper among themselves when they think no one else is listening. I sense it in the pattern formed by raindrops, in the early flight of leaves this past autumn, in the call of reluctant winter seedlings and in the nervous belly crawl of the snake. The clouds collide overhead, so intent are they on the events shaping themselves below, and the earth itself sometimes skips a heartbeat.

"It is a crisis of our world, but its crux, its center, comes from another . . . from *yours*," and he stabbed a stubby finger at a shocked Jon-Tom.

"Be calm, boy. You yourself have naught to do with it." It was dark as night inside the tree now. Jon-Tom thought he could feel the darkness as a perceptible weight on his neck. Or were the other things crowding invisibly near, fighting to hear through the protective cloak the sorcerer had drawn tight about the tree?

"A vast malevolence has succeeded in turning the laws of magic and reason inside out, to bring spells of terrible power from your world into ours, to threaten our peaceful land.

"It lies beyond my meager skills to determine what this power is, or to cope with it. Only a great en'geeneer-magician from your own world might supply the key to this menace. Woeful difficult it be to open the portal between dimensions, yet I had to cast out for such a person. It can be done only once or twice in a year's time, so great is the strain on parts of the mind. That is why you are come among us now, my young friend."

"But I've been trying to tell you. I'm not an engineer."

Clothahump looked shaken. "That is not possible. The portals would open *only* to permit the entrance of an en'geeneer."

"I'm truly sorry," Jon-Tom spread his hands in a gesture of helplessness. "I'm only a prelaw student and would-be musician."

"It can't be . . . at least, I don't think it can." Clothahump abruptly looked very old indeed.

"Wot's the nature o' this 'ere bloomin' crisis?" the irrepressible Mudge demanded to know.

"I don't precisely know. I know for certain only that it is centered around some powerful magic drawn from this lad's world-time." A horny hand slammed a counter, rocking jars and cannisters. Thunder flooded the room.

"The conjuration could not have worked save for an en'geeneer. I was casting blind and was tired, but I cannot be wrong in this." He took a deep breath. "Lad, you say you are a student?"

"That's right."

"A student en'geeneer, perhaps?"

"Sorry. Prelaw. And I don't think amateur electric guitar qualifies me, either. I also work part time as a janitor at . . . wait a minute, now." He looked worried. "My official title is *sanitation engineer.*"

Clothahump let out a groan of despair, sank back on the couch. "So ends civilization."

Pog let loose of the bookcase shelf and flew high above them, growling delightedly. "Wonderful, wonderful! A wizard of garbage!" He dove sharply, braked to hover in front of Jon. "Welcome oh welcome, wizard most high! Stay and help me make all da dirt in dis dump disappear!"

"BEGONE!" Clothahump thundered in a tone more suited to the throat of a mountain than a turtle. Jon-Tom and Mudge shook as that unnatural roar filled the room, while Pog was slammed up against the far side of the tree. He tumbled halfway to the floor before he could right himself and get shaky wings working again. He whipped out through a side passage.

"Blasphemer of truth." The turtle's normal voice had returned. "I don't know why I retain him. . . ." He sighed, adjusted his spectacles, and looked sadly at Jon-Tom.

" 'Tis clear enough now what happened, lad. I was not precise enough in defining the parameters of the spell. I am an old turtle, and very tired. Sloppy work has earned its just reward.

"Months it took me to prepare the conjuration. Four months' careful rune reading, compiling the requisite materials and injunctives, a full cauldron of boiled subatomic particles and such—and I end up with you."

Jon-Tom felt guilty despite his innocence.

"Not to trouble yourself with it, lad. There's nothing you can do now. I'll simply have to begin again."

"What happens if you don't succeed in time, sir? If you don't get the help you think you'll need?"

"We'll probably all die. But it's a small matter in the universal scheme of things.

"That's all?" asked Jon-Tom sarcastically. "Well, I do have work to get back to. I'm really sorry I'm not what you expected, and I do thank you for fixing my side, but I'd really appreciate it if you could send me back home."

"I don't think that's possible, lad."

Jon-Tom tried not to sound panicked. "If you open this portal or whatever for me, maybe I could find you the engineer you want. Any kind of engineer. My university's full of them."

"I am sure of that," said Clothahump benignly. "Otherwise the portal would not have impinged on the fabric of your world at the place and time it did. I was in the proper fishing ground. I simply hooked the wrong subject.

"Sending you back is not a question of choice, but of time and preparation. Remember that I told you it takes months to prepare such a conjuration, and I must rest as near to a year as possible before I risk the effort once more. And when I do so, I fear it must be for more important things than sending you back. I hope you understand, but it will not matter if you do not."

"What about another wizard?" Jon-Tom asked hopefully.

Clothahump sounded proud. "I venture to say no other in all the world could manipulate the necessary incantations and physical distortings. Rest assured I will send you back as soon as I am able." He patted Jon-Tom paternally with one hand and wagged a cautionary finger at him with the other.

"Never fear. We will send you back. I only hope," he added regretfully, "I am able to do so before the crisis breaks and we are all slaughtered." He whispered some words, absently waved his wand.

"Dissemination vanish,
Solar execration banish.
Wormwood high, cone-form low,
Molecules resume thy flow."

Light returned, rich and welcome, to the dimensionally distorted interior of the tree. With the darkness went the feeling of unclean things crawling about Jon-Tom's back. Lizard songs sounded again from the branches outside.

"If you don't mind my saying so, your magic isn't at all what I expected," Jon-Tom ventured.

"What did you expect, lad?"

"Where I come from, magic formulae are always done up with potions made from things like spiders' legs and rabbits' feet and . . . oh, I don't know. Mystic verbs from Latin and other old languages."

Mudge snorted derisively while Pog, peering out from a doorway, allowed himself a squeaky chuckle. Clothahump merely eyed the pair disapprovingly.

"As for spiders' legs, lad, the little ones underfoot are no good for much of anything. The greater ones, on the other hand . . . but I've never been to Gossameringue, and never expect to." Clothahump gestured, indicating spiders as long as his arm, and Jon-Tom held off inquiring about Gossameringue, not to mention the whereabouts of spiders of such magnitude.

"As for the rabbits' feet, I'd expect any self-respecting rabbit to cut me up and use me for a washbasin if I so much as broached the idea. Words are time-proven by experimentation, and agreed upon during meetings of the sorcerers' grand council."

"But what do you use then to open a passage from another dimension?"

Clothahump edged conspiratorially close. "I'm not supposed to give away any Society secrets, you understand, but I don't think you'd even remember. You need some germanium crystals, a pinch of molybdenum, a teaspoon of californium . . . and working with those short-lived superheavies is a royal pain, I'll tell you. Some regular radioactives and one or two transuranics, the acquisition of which is a task in itself."

"How can you locate . . . ?"

"That's other formulae. There are other ingredients, which I definitely can't mention to a noninitiate. You put the whole concatenation into the largest cauldron you've got, stir well, dance three times moonwise around the nearest deposit of nickel-zinc and . . . but enough secrets, lad."

"Funny sort of magic. Almost sounds like real science."

Clothahump looked disappointed in him. "Didn't I already explain that to you? Magic's pretty much the same no matter what world or dimension you exist in. Only the incantations and the formulae are different."

"You said that a rabbit would resist giving up a foot. Are rabbits intelligent also?"

"Lad, lad." Clothahump settled tiredly into the couch, which creaked beneath him. "All the warm-blooded are intelligent. That is as it should be. Has been as far back as history goes. All except the four-foot herbivores: cattle, horses, antelopes, and the like." He shook his head sadly. "Poor creatures never developed useful hands from those hooves, and the development of intelligence is concurrent with digital dexterity.

"The rest have it, though. Along with the birds. None of the reptiles save us turtles, for some reason. And the inhabitants of Gos-

sameringue and the Greendowns, of course. The less spoken about
them, the better." He studied Jon-Tom.

"Now since we can't send you home, lad, what are we going to do
with you . . . ?"

III

Clothahump considered several moments longer. "We can't just abandon you in a strange world, I suppose. I do feel somewhat responsible. You'll need some money and a guide to explain things to you. You, otter, Mudge!"

The otter was intent on a huge tome Pog was avidly displaying. "Both of you get away from the sex incantations. You wouldn't have the patience to invoke the proper spirits anyhow. Serve you both right if I let you make off with a formula or two and you messed it up right clever and turned yourselves neuter."

Mudge shut the book while Pog busied himself dusting second-story windows.

"What d'you want o' me, your wizardness?" an unhappy Mudge asked worriedly, cursing himself for becoming involved.

"That deferential tone doesn't fool me, Mudge." Clothahump eyed him warningly. "I know your opinion of me. No matter, though." Turning back to Jon-Tom he examined the young man's attire: the poorly engraved leather belt, the scuffed sandals, the T-shirt with the picture of a hirsute human wielding a smoking instrument, the faded blue jeans.

"Obviously you can't go tramping around Lynchbany Towne or anywhere else looking like that. Someone is likely to challenge you. It could be dangerous."

"Aye. They might die alaughin'," suggested Mudge.

"We can do without your miserable witticisms, offspring of a spastic muskrat. What is amusing to you is a serious matter to this boy."

"Begging your pardon, sir," Jon-Tom put in firmly, "but I'm twenty-four. Hardly a boy."

"I'm two hundred and thirty-six, lad. It's all relative. Now, we must do something about those clothes. And a guide." He stared meaningfully at Mudge.

"Now wait a minim, guv'nor. It were your bloomin' portal 'e stumbled through. I can't 'elp it if you pinched the wrong chap."

"Nevertheless, you are familiar with him. You will therefore assume charge of him and see that he comes to no harm until such time as I can make other arrangements for him."

Mudge jerked a furry thumb at the watching youth. "Not that I don't feel sorry for 'im, your wizardship. I'd feel the same way toward any 'alf mad creature . . . let alone a poor, furless human. But t' make me responsible for seein' after 'im, sor? I'm a 'unter by trade, not a bloody fairy godmother."

"You're a roustabout by trade, and a drunkard and lecher by avocation," countered Clothahump with considerable certitude. "You're far from the ideal guardian for the lad, but I know of no scholars to substitute, feeble intellectual community that Lynchbany is. So . . . you're elected."

"And if I refuse?"

Clothahump rolled up nonexistent sleeves. "I'll turn *you* into a human. I'll shrink your whiskers and whiten your nose, I'll thin your legs and squash your face. Your fur will fall out and you'll run around the rest of your life with bare flesh showing."

Poor Mudge appeared genuinely frightened, his bravado completely gone. "No, no, your sorcererness! If it's destined I take the lad in care, I ain't the one t' challenge destiny."

"A wise and prosaic decision." Clothahump settled down. "I do not like to threaten. Now that the matter of a guide is settled, the need of money remains."

"That's so." Mudge brightened. "Can't send an innocent stranger out into a cruel world penniless as well as ignorant."

"Mind you, Mudge, what I give the lad is not to be squandered in wining and wenching."

"Oh, no, no, no, sor. I'll see the lad properly dressed and put up at a comfortable inn in Lynchbany that accepts humans."

Jon-Tom sounded excited and pleased. "There are people like me in this town, then?"

Mudge eyed him narrowly. "Of course there are people in

Lynchbany Towne, mate. There are also a few humans. None your
size, though."

Clothahump was rummaging through a stack of scrolls. "Now
then, where is that incantation for gold?"

" 'Ere, guv'nor," said Mudge brightly. "Let me 'elp you look."

The wizard nudged him aside. "I can manage by myself." He
squinted at the mound of paper.

"Geese . . . gibbering . . . gifts . . . gneechees . . . *gold*, there we
are."

Potions and powders were once more brought into use, placed in a
shallow pan instead of a bowl. They were heaped atop a single gold
coin that Clothahump had removed from a drawer in his plastron.
He noticed Mudge avidly following the procedure.

"Forget it, otter. You'd never get the inflection right. And this coin
is old and special. If I could make gold all the time, I wouldn't need
to charge for my services. This is a special occasion, though. Think
what would happen if just any animal could wander about making
gold."

"It would ruin your monetary system," said Jon-Tom.

"Bless my shell, lad, that's so. You have some learning after all."

"Economics are more in my line."

The wizard waved the wand over the pan.

> "Postulate, postulate, postulate.
> Heavy metal integrate.
> Emulate a goldecule,
> Pile it high, shape it round,
> I call you from the ground.
> Metal weary, metal sound, formulate thy wondrous
>   round!"

There was a flash, a brief smell of ozone. The powders vanished
from the pan. In their place was a pile of shining coins.

"Now, that's a right proper trick," Mudge whispered to Jon-Tom,
"that I'd give a lot to know."

"Come help yourself, lad." Clothahump wiped a hand across his
forehead. "That's a short spell, but a rough one."

Jon-Tom scooped up a handful of coins. He was about to slip them
into a pocket when their unusual lightness struck him. He juggled
them experimentally.

"They seem awfully light to be gold, sir. Meaning no disrespect, but . . ."

Mudge reached out, grabbed a coin. "Light's not the word, mate. It looks like gold, but 'tis not."

A frowning Clothahump chose a golden disk. "Um. Seems to be a fine edge running the circumference of the coin."

"On these also, sir." Jon-Tom picked at the edge. A thick gold foil peeled away, to reveal a darker material underneath. High above, Pog was swimming air circles and cackling hysterically.

"I don't understand." Clothahump finished peeling the foil from his own specimen. He recognized it at the same time as Jon-Tom took an experimental bite.

"Chocolate. Not bad chocolate, either."

Clothahump looked downcast. "Damn. I must have mixed my breakfast formula with the transmuter."

"Well," said the starving youth as he peeled another, "you may make poor gold, sir, but you make very good chocolate."

"Some wizard!" Pog shouted from a sheltered window recess. "Gets chocolate instead of gold! Did I mention da time he tried ta conjure a water nymph? Had his room all laid out like a beaver's lair, he did. Incense and perfume and mirrors. Got his water nymph all right. Only it was a Cugluch dragonfly nymph dat nearly tore his arm off before . . ."

Clothahump jabbed a finger in Pog's direction. A tiny bolt of lightning shot from it, searing the wood where the bat had been only seconds before.

"His aim's always been lousy," taunted the bat.

Another bolt missed the famulus by a greater margin than the first, shattered a row of glass containers on a high shelf. They fell crashing, tinkling to the wood-chip floor as the bat dodged and skittered clear of the fragments.

Clothahump turned away, fiddling with his glasses. "Got to conjure some new lenses," he grumbled. Reaching into his lower plastron, he drew out a handful of small silvery coins, and handed them to Jon-Tom. "Here you are, lad."

"Sir . . . wouldn't it have been simpler to give me these in the first place?"

"I like to keep in practice. One of these days I'll get that gold spell down pat."

"Why not make the lad a new set of clothes?" asked Mudge.

Clothahump turned from trying to refocus a finger on the jeering famulus and glanced angrily at the otter. "I'm a wizard, not a tailor. Mundane details such as that I leave to your care. And remember: no care, no fur."

"Relax, guv'nor. Let's go, Jon-Tom. 'Tis a long walk if we're to make much distance before dark."

They left Clothahump blasting jars and vials, pictures and shelving in vain attempts to incinerate his insulting assistant.

"Interesting character, your sorcerer," said Jon-Tom conversationally as they turned down a well-trod path into the woods.

"Not my sorcerer, mate." A brightly feathered lizard pecked at some bananalike fruit dangling from a nearby tree. " 'Ave another chocolate coin?"

"No thanks."

"Speakin' o' coins, that little sack o' silver he gave you might as well be turned over t' me for safe keepin', since you're under me protection."

"That's all right." Jon-Tom patted the pocket in which the coins reposed. "It's safe enough with me, I think. Besides, my pockets are a lot higher than yours. Harder to pick."

Instead of being insulted, the otter laughed uproariously. He clapped a furry paw on Jon-Tom's lower back. "Maybe you're less the fool than you seem, mate. Frost me if I don't think we'll make a decent animal out o' you yet!"

They waded a brook hauntingly like the one that ran through the botanical gardens back on campus. Jon-Tom fought to keep his mind from melancholy reminiscence. "Aren't you the least bit curious about this great crisis Clothahump was referring to?" he asked.

"Bosh, that's probably just a figment o' 'is sorceral imagination. I've heard tell plenty about what such chaps drink and smoke when they feels the mood. They calls it wizardly speculatin'. Me, I calls it gettin' well stoked. Besides, why dwell on crises real or imagined when one can 'ave so much fun from day t' day?"

"You should learn to study the thread of history."

Mudge shook his head. "You talk like that in Lynchbany and you *will* 'ave trouble, mate. Thread o' 'Istory now, is it? Sure you won't trust me with that silver?" Jon-Tom simply smiled. "Ah well, then."

Any last lingering thoughts that it might all still be a nightmare from which he'd soon awake were forever dispelled when they'd come within a mile of Lynchbany, following several days' march. Jon-Tom couldn't see it yet. It lay over another rise and beyond a dense grove of pines. But he could clearly smell it. The aroma of hundreds of animal bodies basking in the warmth of mid-morning could not be mistaken.

"Something wrong, mate?" Mudge stretched away the last of his previous night's rest. "You look a touch bilious."

"That odor . . ."

"We're near Lynchbany, like I promised."

"You mean that stench is normal?"

Mudge's black nose frisked the air. "No . . . I'd call 'er a mite weak today. Wait until noontime, when the sun's at its 'ighest. Then it'll be normal."

"You have great wizards like Clothahump. Haven't any of them discovered the formula for deodorant?"

Mudge looked confused. "What's that, mate? Another o' your incomprehensible otherworldly devices?"

"It keeps you from smelling offensive," said Jon-Tom with becoming dignity.

"Now you do 'ave some queer notions in the other worlds. How are you t' know your enemies if you can't smell 'em? And no friend can smell offensive. That be a contradiction, do it not? If 'e was offensive, 'e wouldn't be a friend. O' course you 'umans," and he sniffed scornfully. " 'ave always been pretty scent-poor. I suppose you'd think it good if people 'ad no scent a'tall?"

"It wouldn't be such a bad idea."

"Well, don't go propoundin' your bizarre religious beliefs in Lynchbany, guv'nor, or even with me t' defend you you won't last out the day."

They continued along the path. This near to town it showed the prints of many feet.

"No scent," Mudge was muttering to himself. "No more sweet perfumes o' friends and ladies t' enjoy. Cor, I'd rather be blind than unable t' smell, mate. What senses do they use in your world, anyway?"

"The usual ones. Sight, hearing, touch, taste . . . and smell."

"And you'd wish away a fifth o' all your perception o' the universe for some crazed theological theory?"

"It has nothing to do with theology," Jon-Tom countered, beginning to wonder if his views on the matter weren't sounding silly even to himself. "It's a question of etiquette."

"Piss on your etiquette. No greetin' smells." The otter sounded thoroughly disgusted. "I don't think I'd care t' visit long in your world, Jon-Tom. But we're almost there. Mind you keep control o' your expressions." He still couldn't grasp the notion that anyone could find the odor of another friendly creature offensive.

"You 'old your nose to someone and they'll likely spill your guts for you."

Jon-Tom nodded reluctantly. Take a few deep breaths, he told himself. He'd heard that somewhere. Just take a few deep breaths and you'll soon be used to it.

They topped the little hill and were suddenly gazing across tree-tops at the town. At the same time the full ripeness of it struck him. The thick musk was like a barnyard sweltering in a swamp. He was hard pressed not to heave the contents of his stomach out the wrong orifice.

" 'Ere now, don't you go be sick all over me!" Mudge took a few hasty steps backward. "Brace up, lad. You'll soon be enjoyin' it!"

They started down the hill, the otter trotting easily, Jon-Tom staggering and trying to keep his face blank. Shortly they encountered a sight which simultaneously shoved all thought of vomiting aside while reminding him this was a dangerous, barely civilized world he'd been dragged into.

It was a body similar to but different from Mudge's. It had its paws tied behind its back and its legs strapped together. The head hung at an angle signifying a neatly snapped neck. It was quite naked. Odd how quickly the idea of clothing on an animal grew in one's mind, Jon-Tom thought.

Some kind of liquid resin or plastic completely encased the body. The eyes were mercifully closed and the expression not pleasant to look upon. A sign lettered in strange script was mounted on a post driven into the ground beneath the dangling, preserved corpse. He turned questioningly to Mudge.

"That's the founder o' the town," came the reply.

Jon-Tom's eyes clung to the grotesque monument as they strolled around it. "Do they always hang the founders of towns around here?"

"Not usually. Only under special circumstances. That's the corpse o' old Tilo Bany. Ought t' be gettin' on a couple 'undred years old now."

"That body's been hanging there like that for hundreds of years?"

"Oh, 'e's well preserved, 'e is. Local wizard embalmed 'im nice and proper."

"That's barbaric."

"Want to hear the details?" asked Mudge. Jon-Tom nodded.

"As it goes, old Tilo there, 'e's a ferret you see—and they come o' no good line t' start with—'e was a confidence man. Fleeced farmers 'ereabouts for years and years, takin' their money most o' the time and their daughters on occasion.

"Well, a bunch of 'em finally gets onto 'im. 'E'd been buyin' grain from one farmer, sellin' it t' another, borrowin' the money, and buyin' more. It finally came t' a 'ead when a couple o' 'is former customers found out that a lot o' the grain they'd been buyin' afore'and existed only in Tilo's 'ead.

"They gets together, cornerin' 'im in this 'ere grove, and strings 'im up neat. At that point a couple o' travelin' craftsmen . . . wood-worker and a silversmith, I think, or maybe one was a cobbler . . . decided that this 'ere valley with its easy water would be a nice place t' start a craft's guild, and the town sort o' grew up around it.

"When folks from elsewhere wanted t' locate the craftsmen, every-one around told 'em t' go t' the place where they'd lynched Tilo Bany, the confidence ferret. And if you 'aven't noticed yet, guv, you're breathin' right easy now."

Much to his surprise, the queasiness had receded. The smell no longer seemed so overpowering. "You're right. It's not so bad any-more."

"That's good. You stick near t' me, mate, and watch yourself. Some o' the local bully-boys like t' toy with strangers, and you're stranger than most. Not that I'd be afraid t' remonstrate with any of 'em, mind now."

They were leaving the shade of the forest. Mudge gestured ahead. His voice was full of provincial pride.

"There she be, Jon-Tom. Lynchbany Towne."

IV

No fairy spires or slick and shiny pennant-studded towers here, Jon-Tom mused as he gazed at the village. No rainbow battlements, no thin cloud-piercing turrets inlaid with gold, silver, and precious gems. Lynchbany was a community built to be lived in, not looked at. Clearly, its inhabitants knew no more of moorish palaces and pea-cock-patrolled gardens than did Jon-Tom.

Hemmed in by forest on both sides, the buildings and streets meandered down a narrow valley. A stream barely a yard wide trickled through the town center. It divided the main street, which, like most of the side streets he could see, was paved with cobblestones shifted here from some distant riverbed. Only the narrow creek channel itself was unpaved.

They continued down the path, which turned to cobblestone as it came abreast of the rushing water. Despite his determination to keep his true feelings inside, the fresh nausea that greeted him as they reached the first buildings generated unwholesome wrinkles on his face. It was evident that the little stream served as community sewer as well as the likely source of potable water. He reminded himself firmly not to drink anything in Lynchbany unless it was bottled or boiled.

Around them rose houses three, sometimes four stories tall. Sharp-peaked roofs were plated with huge foot-square shingles of wood or gray slate. Windows turned translucent eyes on the street from second and third floors. An occasional balcony projected out over the street.

Fourth floors and still higher attics displayed rounded entrances open to the air. Thick logs were set below each circular doorway. Round windows framed many of these aerial portals. They were obviously home to the arboreal inhabitants of the town, cousins of the red-breasted, foul-mouthed public servant they had met delivering mail to Clothahump's tree several days ago.

The little canyon was neither very deep nor particularly narrow, but the houses still crowded together like children in a dark room. The reason was economic; it's simpler and cheaper to build a common wall for two separate structures.

A few flew pennants from poles set in their street-facing sides, or from the crests of sharply gabled rooftops. They could have been family crests, or signals, or advertisements; Jon-Tom had no idea. More readily identifiable banners in the form of some extraordinary washing hung from lines strung over narrow alleyways. He tried to identify the shape of the owners from the position and length of the arms and legs, but was defeated by the variety.

At the moment furry arms and hands were working from upper-floor windows, hastily pulling laundry off the lines amid much muttering and grumbling. Thunder rumbled through the town, echoing off the cobblestone streets and the damp walls of cut rock and thick wooden beams. Each building was constructed for solidity, a small home put together as strongly as a castle.

Shutters clapped hollowly against bracings as dwellers sealed their residences against the approaching storm. Smoke, ashy and pungent, borne by an occasional confused gust of wet wind, drifted down to the man and otter. Another rumble bounced through the streets. A glance overhead showed dark clouds clotting like black cream. First raindrops slapped at his skin.

Mudge increased his pace and Jon-Tom hurried to keep up. He was too fascinated by the town to ask where they were rushing to, sufficiently absorbed in his surroundings not to notice the isolated stares of other hurrying pedestrians.

After another couple of blocks, he finally grew aware of the attention they were drawing.

"It's your size, mate," Mudge told him.

As they hurried on, Jon-Tom took time to look back at the citizens staring at him. None stood taller than Mudge. Most were between four and five feet tall. It did not make him feel superior. Instead, he felt incredibly awkward and out of place.

He drew equally curious stares from the occasional human he

passed. All the locals were similarly clad, allowing for personal differences in taste and station. Silk, wool, cotton, and leather appeared to be the principal materials. Shirts, blouses, vests, and pants were often decorated with beads and feathers. An astonishing variety of hats were worn, from wide-brimmed seventeenth-century-style feathered to tiny, simple berets, to feathered peaked caps like Mudge's. Boots alternated with sandals on feet of varying size. He later learned one had a choice between warm, filthy boots or chilly but easily cleanable sandals.

Keeping clean could be a full-time trial. They crossed the main street just in time to avoid a prestorm deluge when an irritable and whitened old possum dumped out a bucket of slops from a second-floor porch into the central stream, barely missing the pair below.

"Hey . . . watch it!" Jon-Tom shouted upward at the closing shutters.

"Now wot?"

"That wasn't very considerate," Jon-Tom mumbled, his nose twisting at the odor.

Mudge frowned at him. "Stranger and stranger sound your customs, guv. Now wot else is she supposed t' do with the 'ouse'old night soil?" With a hand he traced the winding course of the steady stream that flowed through the center of the street.

"This time o' year it rains 'ere nigh every day. The rain washes the soil into the central flue 'ere and the stream packs it off right proper."

Jon-Tom let out fervent thanks he hadn't appeared in this land in summertime. "It wasn't her action I was yelling about. It was her aim. Damned if I don't think she was trying to hit us."

Mudge smiled. "Now that be a thought, mate. But when you're as dried up and 'ousebound as that faded old sow, I expect you grab at every chance for amusement you can."

"What about common courtesy?" Jon-Tom muttered, shaking slop from his shoes.

"Rely on it if you wants t' die young, says I."

Shouts sounded from ahead. They moved to one side of the street and leaned up against a shuttered storefront. A huge double wagon was coming toward them, one trailing behind another. The vehicle required nearly the entire width of the street for passage.

Jon-Tom regarded it with interest. The haggard, dripping driver was a margay. The little tiger cat's bright eyes flashed beneath the wide-brimmed floppy felt hat he wore. Behind him, riding the second half of the wagon, was a cursing squirrel no more than three feet tall.

His tail was curled over his head, providing extra protection from the now steadily falling rain. He was struggling to tug heavy canvas or leather sheets over the cargo of fruits and vegetables.

Four broad-shouldered lizards pulled the double wagon. They were colored iridescent blue and green, and in the gloom their startlingly pink eyes shone like motorcycle taillights. They swayed constantly from side to side, demanding unvarying attention from their yowling, hissing driver, who manipulated them as much with insults as with cracks from his long thin whip.

Momentarily generating a louder rumble than the isolated bursts of thunder, the enormous wagon slid on past and turned a difficult far corner.

"I've no sympathy for the chap who doesn't know 'is business," snorted Mudge as they continued on their way, hugging the sides of buildings in search of some protection from the downpour. "That lot ought long since to 'ave been under cover."

It was raining quite heavily now. Most of the windows had been closed or shuttered. The darkness made the buildings appear to be leaning over the street.

From above and behind came a distant, sharp chirping. Jon-Tom glanced over a shoulder, thought he saw a stellar jay clad in yellow-purple kilt and vest alight on one of the fourth-floor landing posts and squeeze through an opening. There was a faint thump as the circular door was slammed behind him.

They hurried on, sprinting from one rickety wooden porch covering to the next. Once they paused in the sheltering lee of what might have been a bookstore. Scrollstore, rather, since it was filled with ceiling-high wooden shelves punched out like a massive wine rack. Each hole held its thick roll of paper.

As Mudge had indicated, the rain was washing the filth from the cobblestones and the now swollen central creek carried it efficiently away.

The front moved through and the thunder faded. Instead of the heavy, driving rain the clouds settled down to shedding a steady drizzle. The temperature had dropped, and Jon-Tom shivered in his drenched T-shirt and jeans.

"Begging your pardon, sir."

Jon-Tom uncrossed his arms. "What?" He looked to his right. The source of the voice was in a narrow alley barely large enough to allow two people to pass without turning sideways.

A gibbon lay huddled beneath a slight overhang, curled protectively against several large wooden barrels filled with trash. His fuzzy face was shielded by several large scraps of wrapping paper that had been wound together and tied with a knot beneath his chin. This crude hat hung limp in the rain. Badly ripped trousers of some thin cotton material covered the hairy legs. He had no shirt. Long arms enfolded the shivering chest, and large circular sores showed where the hair had fallen out. One eye socket was a dark little hollow.

A delicately fingered hand extended hopefully in Jon-Tom's direction. "A silverpiece, sir. For one unlucky in war and unluckier still in peacetime? It was a bad upbringing and a misinformed judiciary that cost me this eye, sir. Now I exist only on the sufferance of others." Jon-Tom stood and gaped at the pitiful creature.

"A few coppers then, sir, if you've no silver to give?" The gibbon's voice was harsh with infection.

Suddenly he shrank back, falling against the protective trashcans. One fell over, spilling shreds of paper, bones, and other recognizable detritus into the alley. Dimensional dislocation does not eliminate the universality of garbage.

"Nay, sir, nay!" An arm shook as the simian held it across his face. "I meant no harm."

Mudge stood alongside Jon-Tom. The otter's sword was halfway clear of its chest scabbard. "I'll not 'ave you botherin' this gentleman while 'e's in my care!" He took another step toward the ruined anthropoid. "Maybe you mean no 'arm and maybe you do, but you'll do none while I'm about."

"Take it easy," murmured Jon-Tom, eyeing the cowering gibbon sympathetically. "Can't you see he's sick?"

"Sick be the word, aright. D'you not know 'ow to treat beggars, mate?" He pulled on his sword. The gibbon let out a low moan.

"I do." Jon-Tom reached into his pocket, felt for the small linen purse Clothahump had given him. He withdrew a small coin, tossed it to the gibbon. The simian scrambled among the stones and trash for it.

"Blessings on you, sir! Heaven kiss you!"

Mudge turned away, disgustedly sliding his sword back in place. "Waste o' money." He put a hand on Jon-Tom's arm. "Come on, then. Let's get you t' the shop I 'ave in mind before you spend yourself broke. It's a hard world, mate, and you'd better learn that soonest. You never saw the blighter's knife, I take it?"

"Knife?" Jon-Tom looked back toward the alley entrance. "What knife?" He felt queasy.

"Aye, wot knife indeed." He let out a sharp squeek. "If I 'adn't of been with you you'd 'ave found out wot knife. But I guess you can't 'elp yourself. Your brains bein' up that 'igh, I expect they thin along with the air, wot? 'Wot knife' . . . pfagh!" He stopped, glared up at the dazed Jon-Tom.

"Now if 'twere just up t' me, mate, I'd let you make as much the idiot of yourself as you seem to 'ave a mind t'. But I can't risk offendin' 'is wizardship, see? So until I've seen you safely set up in the world and on your own way t' where I think you might be able t' take some care for yourself, you'll do me the courtesy from now on o' takin' me advice. And if you'll not think o' yourself, then 'ave some pity for me. Mind the threats that Clothahump put on me." He shook his head, turned, and started on down the street again. "Me! Who was unlucky enough to trip over you when you tripped into my day."

"Yeah? What about me, then? You think I like it here? You think I like you, you fuzz-faced little fart?"

To Jon-Tom's dismay, Mudge smiled instead of going for his sword. "Now that's more like it, mate! That's a better attitude than givin' away your money." He spat back in the direction of the alley. "God-rotted stinkin' layabout trash as soon split your gut as piss on you. D'you wonder I like it better in the forest, mate?"

They turned off the main street into a side avenue that was not as small as an alley, not impressive enough to be a genuine street. It boasted half a dozen shopfronts huddled together in the throat of a long cul-de-sac. A single tall oil lamp illuminated the street. Cloth awnings almost met over the street, shutting out much of the lamp-light as well as the rain. A miniature version of the central stream sprang from a stone fountain at the end of the cul-de-sac.

Jon-Tom shook water from his hands, and squeezed it from his long hair as he ducked under the cover of one awning. It was not designed to shield someone of his height. He stared at the sign over the large front window of the shop. It was almost comprehensible. Perhaps the longer he spent here the more acclimated his brain be-came. In any case, he did not have to understand the lettering to know what kind of shop this was. The window was filled with vests and shirts, elaborately stitched pantaloons, and a pair of trousers with bells running the length of the seams. Some lay on the window counter, others fitted dressmaker dummies that sometimes boasted ears and usually had tails.

A bell chimed brightly as Mudge pushed open the door. "Mind

your 'ead now, Jon-Tom." His tall companion took note of the warning, and bowed under the eave.

The interior of the shop had the smell of leather and lavender.
There was no one in sight. Several chairs with curved seats and backs
were arranged neatly near the center of the floor. Long poles supported cross-racks from which clothing had been draped.

"Hoy, Proprietor!" Mudged whooped. "Show yourself and your
work!"

"And work you shall have, my dear whoever-you-ares." The reply
issued from the back of the shop. "Work only of the finest quality and
best stitchery, of the toughest materials and prettiest . . ." The voice
trailed off quickly.

The fox had come to a halt and was staring past Mudge at the
dripping, lanky shape of Jon-Tom. Silk slippers clad the owner's feet.
He wore a silk dressing gown with four matching ribbons of bright
aquamarine. They ran around his tail in intersecting loops to meet in
a bow at the white tip. He also wore a more practical-looking belt
from which protruded rulers, marking sticks, several pieces of dark
green stone, and various other instruments of the tailor's craft. He
spoke very deliberately.

"What . . . is *that?*" He gestured hesitantly at Jon-Tom.

"That's the work we're chattin' about, and a job it's goin' t' be, I'd
wager." Mudge flopped down in one of the low-slung chairs with
complete disregard for the upholstery and the fact that he was dripping wet. He put both short legs over one arm of the chair and
pushed his feathered cap back on his forehead. "Off to it now, that's a
good fellow."

The fox put both paws on hips and stared intently at the otter. "I
do *not* clothe monsters! I have created attire for some of the best-
dressed citizens of Lynchbany, and beyond. I have made clothing for
Madam Scorianza and her best girls, for the banker Flaustyn Wolfe,
for members of the town council, and for our most prominent merchants and craftsmen, but I do *not* clothe monsters."

Mudge leaned over in the chair and helped himself to a long thin
stick from a nearby tall glass filled with them. "Look on it as a
challenge, mate." He used a tiny flinted sparker to light the stick.

"Listen," said Jon-Tom, "I don't want to cause any trouble." The
fox took a wary step backward as that towering form moved nearer.
"Mudge here thinks that . . . that . . ." He was indicating the otter, who was puffing contentedly on the thin stick. Smoke filled the
room with a delightfully familiar aroma.

"Say," said Jon-Tom, "do you suppose I could have one of those, uh, sticks?"

"For the convenience o' the customers, lad." Mudge magnanimously passed over a stick along with his sparker. Jon-Tom couldn't see how it worked, but at this point was more than willing to believe it had been treated with a good fire spell.

Several long puffs on the glowing stick more than relaxed him. Not everything in this world was as horrible as it seemed, he decided. It was smoking that had made him accessible to the questing thoughts of Clothahump. Perhaps smoking would let something send him home.

Ten minutes later, he no longer cared. Reassured by both Mudge and the giant's dreamy responses, the grumbling fox was measuring Jon-Tom as the latter lay quite contentedly on the carpeted floor. Mudge lay next to him, the two of them considerably higher mentally than physically. The tailor, whose name was Carlemot, did not object to their puffing, which indicated either an ample supply of the powerful smokesticks or a fine sense of public relations, or both.

He left them eventually, returning several hours later to find otter and man totally bombed. They still lay on the floor, and were currently speculating with great interest on the intricacies of the wormholes in the wooden ceiling.

It was only later that Jon-Tom had recovered sufficiently for a dressing. When he finally saw himself in the mirror, the shock shoved aside quite a bit of the haze.

The indigo silk shirt felt like cool mist against his skin. It was tucked neatly into straight-legged pants which were a cross between denim and flannel. Both pants and shirt were secured with matching buttons of black leather. The jet leather vest was fringed around the bottom and decorated with glass beadwork. The cuffs of the pants were likewise fringed, though he couldn't tell this at first because they were stuffed into calf-high black leather boots with rolled tops. At first it seemed surprising that the tailor had managed to find any footgear at all to fit him, considering how much larger he was than the average local human. Then it occurred to him that many of the inhabitants were likely to have feet larger in proportion to their bodies than did men.

A belt of metal links, silver or pewter, held up the pants, shone in sharp contrast to the beautifully iridescent hip-length cape of some green lizard leather. A pair of delicate but functional silver clips held the cape together at the collar.

Despite Mudge's insistence, however, he categorically refused to don the orange tricornered cap. "I just don't like hats."

"Such a pity." Carlemot's attitude had shifted from one of distress to one of considerable pride. "It really is necessary to complete the overall effect, which, if I may be permitted to say so, is striking as well as unique."

Jon-Tom turned, watched the scales of the cape flare even in the dim light. "Sure as hell would turn heads in L.A."

"Not bad," Mudge conceded. "Almost worth the price."

" 'Almost' indeed!" The fox was pacing round Jon-Tom, inspecting the costume for any defects or tears. Once he paused to snip a loose thread from a sleeve of the shirt. "It is subdued yet flashy, attention-gathering without being obtrusive." He smiled, displaying sharp teeth in a long narrow snout.

"The man looks like a noble, or better still, a banker. When one is confronted with so much territory to cover, the task is at first daunting. However, the more one has to work with, the more gratifying the end results. Never mind this plebian, my tall friend," the fox continued, gazing up possessively at Jon-Tom, "what is your opinion?"

"I like it. Especially the cape." He spun a small circle, nearly fell down but recovered poise and balance nicely. "I always wanted to wear a cape."

"I am pleased." The tailor appeared to be waiting for something, coughed delicately.

"Crikey, mate," snapped Mudge, "pay the fellow."

Some good-natured haggling followed, with Mudge's task made the more difficult by the fact that Jon-Tom kept siding with the tailor. A reasonable balance was still struck, since Carlemot's natural tendency to drive a hard bargain was somewhat muted by the pleasure he'd received from accomplishing so difficult a job.

That did not keep Mudge from chastising Jon-Tom as they left the shop behind. The drizzle had become a heavy mist around them.

"Mate, I can't save you much if you're goin' t' take the side of the shopkeeper."

"Don't worry about it." For the first time in a long while, he was feeling almost happy. Between the lingering effects of the smoke session and the gallant appearance he was positive his new attire gave him, his mood was downright expansive. "It was a tough task for him and he did a helluva job. I don't begrudge him the money. Besides," he jingled the purse in his pocket, "we still have some left."

"That's good, because we've one more stop t' make."

"Another?" Jon-Tom frowned. "I don't need any more clothing."

"That so? Far as I'm concerned, mate, you're walkin' around bloody naked." He turned right. They passed four or five storefronts on the wide street, crossed the cobblestones and a little bridge arcing over the central stream, and entered another shop.

It possessed an entirely different ambiance from the warm tailor shop they'd just left. While the fox's establishment had been spotless, soft-looking, and comfortable as an old den, this one was chill with an air of distasteful business.

One entire wall was speckled with devices designed for throwing. There were dozens of knives; ellipsoidal, stiletto, triangular, with or without blood gutters grooved nastily in their flanks, gem-encrusted little pig-stickers for argumentative ladies, trick knives concealed in eyeglass cases or boot soles . . . all the deadly variety of which the honer was capable.

Throwing stars shone in the lamplight like decorations plucked from the devil's Christmas tree. A spiked bolo hung from an intricate halberd. Maces and nunchaku alternated wall space with spears and shields, pikes and war axes. Near the back of the shop were the finer weapons, long bows and swords with more variety of handle (to fit many different size and shape of hand) than of blade. One particularly ugly half-sword looked more like a double scythe. It was easy to envision the damage it could do when wielded by a knowledgeable arm. That of a gibbon with a deceptive reach, for example.

Some of the swords and throwing knives had grooved or hollow handles. Jon-Tom was at a loss to imagine what sort of creature they'd been designed for until he remembered the birds. A hand would not make much use of such grips, but they were perfect for, say, a flexible wing tip.

For a few high moments he'd managed to forget that this was a world of established violence and quick death. He leaned over the counter barring the back of the shop from the front and studied something that resembled a razor-edged frisbee. He shuddered, and looked around for Mudge.

The otter had moved around the counter and had vanished behind a bamboolike screen. When Jon-Tom thought to call to him, he was already returning, chatting with the owner. The squat, muscular raccoon wore only an apron, sandals, and a red headband with two feathers sticking downward past his left ear. He smelled, as did the back of the shop, of coalsmoke and steel.

"So this is the one who wants the mayhem?" The raccoon pursed his lips, looked over a black nose at Jon-Tom.

"Mudge, I don't know about this. I've always been a talker, not a fighter."

"I understand, mate," said the otter amiably. "But there are weighty arguments and there are weighty arguments." He hefted a large mace to further illustrate his point. "Leastways, you don't have to employ none of these tickle-me-tights, but you bloody well better show something or you'll mark yourself an easy target.

"Now, can you use any of these toys?"

Jon-Tom examined the bewildering array of dismembering machinery. "I don't . . ." he shook his head, looking confused.

The armorer stepped in. " 'Tis plain to see he's no experience." His tone was reproving but patient. "Let me see, now. With his size and reach . . ." He moved thoughtfully to a wall where pikes and spears grew like iron wheat from the floor, each set in its individual socket in the wooden planks. His right paw rubbed at his nose.

With both hands he removed an ax with a blade the size of his head. "Where skill and subtlety are absent, mayhap it would be best to make use of the other extremes. No combat or weapons training at all, young lad?"

Jon-Tom shook his head, looked unencouraging.

"What about sports?"

"I'm not bad at basketball. Pretty good jump shot, and I can—"

"Shit!" Mudge kicked at the floor. "What the devil's arse is that? Does it perhaps involve some hittin'?" he asked hopefully.

"Not much," Jon-Tom admitted. "Mostly running and jumping, quick movements. . . ."

"Well, that be something," Mudge faced the armorer. "Something less bull-bright than that meat cleaver you're holdin', then. What would you recommend?"

"A fast retreat." The armorer turned dourly to another rack, preening his whiskers. "Though if the man can lay honest claim to some nimbleness, there ought to be something." He put up the massive ax. "Mayhap we can give him some help."

He removed what looked like a simple spear, made from the polished limb of a tree. But instead of a spearpoint, the upper end widened into a thick wooden knob with bumps and dull points. It was taller than Mudge and reached Jon-Tom's ears, the shaft some two inches in diameter.

"Just a club?" Mudge studied the weapon uncertainly.

" 'Tis the longest thing I've got in the shop." The armorer dragged a clipped nail down the shaft. "This is ramwood. It won't snap in a fight. With your friend's long reach, he can use it to fend an opponent off if he's not much interested in properly disposing of him. And if things get tight and he's still blood-shy, why, a good clop on the head with the business end of this will make someone just as dead as if you'd split his skull. Not as messy as the ax, but just as effective." He handed it to the reluctant Jon-Tom.

"It'll make you a fine walking stick, too, man. And there's something else. I mentioned giving you some help." He pointed at the middle of the staff. Halfway up the shaft were two bands of inlaid silver three inches apart. The space between was decorated with four silver studs.

"Press any one of those, man."

Jon-Tom did so. There was a click, and the staff instantly grew another foot. Twelve inches of steel spike now projected from the base of the staff. Jon-Tom was so surprised he almost dropped the weapon, but Mudge danced about like a kid in a candy shop.

"Bugger me mother if that ain't a proper surprise for any discourteous dumb-butt you might meet in the street. A little rub from that'll cure 'em right quick, I venture!"

"Aye," agreed the armorer with pride. "Just tap 'em on the toe and press your release and I guarantee you'll see one fine wide-eyed expression." Both raccoon and otter shook with amusement.

Jon-Tom pushed down on the shaft and the spear-spike retracted like a cats-claw up inside the staff. Another experimental grip on the studs, and it shot out once more. It was clever, but certainly not amusing.

"Listen, I'd rather not fool with this thing at all, but if you insist . . ."

"I do." Mudge stopped laughing, wiped tears from his eyes. "I do insist. Like the master armorer 'ere says, you don't 'ave t' use that toe-chopper if you've no mind t', but there'll likely be times when you'll want t' keep some sword-swingin' sot a fair few feet from your guts. So take claim to it and be glad."

Jon-Tom hefted the shaft, but he wasn't glad. Merely having possession of the deceptive weapon was depressing him.

Outside they examined the contents of the little purse. It was nearly empty. A few small silver coins gleamed forlornly like fish in a dark tank from the bottom of the sack. Jon-Tom wondered if he hadn't been slightly profligate with Clothahump's generosity.

Mudge appraised the remnants of their fortune. Mist continued to dampen them, softening the lamplight that buttered the street and shopfronts. With the easing of the rain, other pedestrians had reappeared. Animal shadow-shapes moved dimly through the fog.

"Hungry, mate?" asked the otter finally, black eyes shining in the light.

"Starving!" He was abruptly aware he hadn't had a thing to eat all day. Mudge's store of jerked meat had given out the previous evening.

"I also." He clapped Jon-Tom on his cape. "Now you looks almost like a real person." He leaned conspiratorially close. "Now I know a place where the silver we 'ave left will bring us as fat a feast as a pregnant hare could wish. Maybe even enough t' fill your attenuated belly-hollow!" He winked. "Maybe some entertainment besides. You and I 'ave done our duty for the day, we 'ave."

As they strolled further into town, they encountered more pedestrians. An occasional wagon jounced down the street, and individuals on saddled riding lizards hopped or ran past. Long pushbrooms came into play as shopkeepers swept water from porches and storefronts. Shutters snapped open. For the first time Jon-Tom heard the wails of children. Cubs would be the better term, he corrected himself.

Two young squirrels scampered by. One finally tackled the other. They tumbled to the cobblestones, rolling over and over, punching and kicking while a small mob of other youngsters gathered around and urged them on. To Jon-Tom's dismay their initial cuteness was muted by the manner in which they gouged and scratched at each other. Not that his own hometown was devoid of violence, but it seemed to be a way of life here. One cub finally got the other down and was assiduously making pulp of his face. His peers applauded enthusiastically, offering suggestions for further disfigurement.

"A way of life, mate?" Mudge said thoughtfully when Jon-Tom broached his thoughts. "I wouldn't know. I'm no philosopher, now. But I know this. You can be polite and dead or respected and breathin'." He shrugged. "Now you can make your own choice. Just don't be too ready to put aside that nice new toy you've bought."

Jon-Tom made sure he had a good grip on the staff. The increasing crowd and lifting of the fog brought fresh stares. Mudge assured him it was only on account of his unusual size. If anything, he was now clad far better than the average citizen of Lynchbany Towne.

Five minutes later he was no longer simply hungry, he was ravenous.

"Not much longer, mate." They turned down a winding side street. There was an almost hidden entrance on their left, into which Mudge urged him. Once again he had to bend nearly double to clear the overhang.

Then he was able to stand. The ceiling inside was a good two feet above his head, for which he was more than slightly grateful.

"The Pearl Possum," said Mudge, with considerably more enthusiasm than he'd displayed toward anything else so far. "Me, I'm for somethin' liquid now. This way, mate. 'Ware the lamps."

Jon-Tom followed the otter into the bowels of the restaurant, elbowing his way through the shoving, tightly packed crowd and keeping a lookout for the occasional hanging lamps Mudge had warned him about. From outside there was no hint of the considerable, sweaty mob milling inside.

Eight feet inside the entrance, the ceiling curved upward like a circus tent. It peaked a good two and a half stories above the floor. Beneath this central height was a circular counter dispensing food and brew. It was manned by a small battalion of cooks and mixologists. A couple were weasels. There was also a single, nattily dressed rabbit and one scroungy-looking bat, smaller and even uglier than Pog. Not surprisingly, the bat spent most of his time delivering food and drink to various tables. Jon-Tom knew of other restaurants which would have been glad of an arboreal waiter.

What tables there were spotted the floor like fat toadstools in no particular order. On the far side of the Pearl Possum were partially enclosed booths designed for discussion or dalliance, depending on the inclination of the inhabitants.

They continued to make their way through the noisy, malodorous crowd. Isolated ponds of liquor littered the floor, along with several splinters from smashed wooden mugs. The owners had sensibly disdained the use of glass. Numerous drains pockmarked the wooden planking underfoot. Occasionally someone would appear with a bucket of water to wash down a section of floor too slippery with booze, sometimes of the partially digested variety.

He was easily the tallest man—the tallest animal—in the room, though there were a couple of large wolves and cats who were built more massively. It made him feel only a little more confident.

" 'Ere lad, over 'ere!" Following the triumphant shout Jon-Tom felt himself yanked down to a small but abandoned table. His knees pressed up toward his chest—the chairs were much too low for comfortable seating.

Furry bodies pressed close on all sides, filling his nostrils with the stink of liquor and musk. Supporting the table was the sculpted plaster figure of a coquettishly posed female opposum. It had been scratched and engraved with so many lewd comments that the sheen was almost gone.

Somehow a waiter noticed that their hands and table were empty, shoved his way through to them. Like the armorer he was wearing an apron, only this one was filthy beyond recognition, the pattern beneath obliterated by grease and other stains. Like the armorer he was a black-masked raccoon. One ear was badly mangled, and a white scar ran boldly from the ear down the side of his head, just past the eye, and on through the muzzle, but particularly noticeable where it crossed the black mask.

Jon-Tom was too busy observing the life and action swirling around them to notice that Mudge had already ordered.

"Not t' worry, mate. I ordered for you."

"I hope you ordered food, as well as liquor. I'm hungrier than ever."

"That I 'ave, mate. Any fool knows 'tis not good t' drink on an empty belly. 'Ere you, watch yourself." He jabbed an elbow into the ribs of the drunken ocelot who'd stumbled into him.

The animal spun, waving his mug and sending liquor spilling toward the otter. Mudge dodged the drink with exceptional speed. The feline made a few yowling comments about the rib jab, but was too sloshed to pick a serious fight. It lurched helplessly off into the crowd. Jon-Tom followed the pointy, weaving ears until their owner was out of sight.

Two large wooden mugs of something highly carbonated and smelling of alcohol arrived. The hardwood mug looked oversized in Mudge's tiny hand, but it was just the right size for Jon-Tom. He tried a sip of the black liquid within, found it to be a powerful fermented brew something like a highly alcoholic malt liquor. He determined to treat it respectfully.

The waiter's other hand deposited a large platter covered by a badly dented and scratched metal dome. When the dome was removed, Jon-Tom's nose was assailed by a wonderfully rich aroma. On the platter were all kinds of vegetables. Among strange shapes were comfortingly familiar carrots, radishes, celery, and tiny onions. A raft of potatoes supported a huge cylindrical roast. A single center bone showed at either end. It was burnt black outside and shaded to pink near the bone.

He hunted in vain for silverware. Mudge pointed out that the restaurant would hardly provide instruments for its patrons to use on one another. The otter had a hunting knife out. It was short and triangular like the tooth of a white shark and went easily through the meat.

"Rare, medium, or well burnt?" was the question.

"Anything." Jon-Tom fought to keep the saliva inside his mouth. Mudge sliced off two respectable discs of meat, passed one to his companion.

They ate as quietly as smacking fingers and gravy-slick lips would permit. Jon-Tom struggled to keep the juice off his freshly cut clothes. Mudge was not nearly so fastidious. Gravy ran down his furry chin onto his vest, was sopped up by vest and chest fur.

They were halfway full when a partially sated Jon-Tom relaxed long enough to notice that in addition to the center bone running through the roast, there were thin, curving ribs running from the bone to meet like the points of calipers near the bottom.

"Mudge, what kind of meat is this?"

"Not tasty enough, mate?" wondered the otter around a mouthful of vegetables.

"It's delicious, but I don't recognize the cut or the flavor. It's not any kind of steak, is it? I mean, beef?"

"Beef? You mean, cattle?" Mudge shook his head. "They may not be smart, but we're not cannibals 'ere, we're not." He chewed appraisingly. "O' course, it ain't king snake. Python. Reticulated, I'd say."

"Wonderful." Why be squeamish in the face of good taste, Jon-Tom mused. There was no reason to be. He never had understood the phobia some folk had about eating reptile, though he'd never had the opportunity to try it before. After all, meat was meat. It was all muscle fiber to the tooth.

He did not think he'd care to meet a snake of that size away from the dinner plate, however.

They were dismembering the last of the roast when the waiter, unbidden, appeared with a small tray of some fat puff pastries seared black across their crowns. Though he was no longer hungry, Jon-Tom sampled one, soon found himself shoveling them in as fast as possible. Despite their heavy appearance they were light and airy inside, full of honey and chopped nuts and encrusted with burnt cinnamon.

Later he leaned back in the short chair and picked at his teeth with a splinter of the table, as he'd seen some of the other patrons doing.

"Well, that may take the last of our money, but that's the best meal I've had in years."

"Aye, not bad." Mudge had his short legs up on the table, the boot heels resting indifferently in the pastry tray.

A band had begun playing somewhere. The music was at once light and brassy. Jon-Tom took a brief professional interest in it. Since he couldn't see the players, he had to be satisfied with deciding that they employed one or two string instruments, drums, chimes, and a couple of oddly deep flutes.

Mudge was leaning across the table, feeling warm and serious. He put a cautionary paw on Jon-Tom's wrist. "Sorry t' shatter your contentment, mate, but we've somethin' else t' talk on. Clothahump charged me with seein' t' your well-bein' and I've a mind t' see the job through t' the end.

"If you want t' continue eatin' like that, we're goin' to 'ave t' find you some way t' make a living, wot . . . ?"

V

Reality churned in Jon-Tom's stomach, mixed unpleasantly with the pastry. "Uh, can't we just go back to Clothahump?" He'd decided he was beginning to like this world.

Mudge shook his head slowly. "Not if 'e don't get that gold spell aright. Keep in mind that as nice and kindly as the old bugger seemed a few days ago, wizards can be god-rotted temperamental. If we go back already and pester 'im for money, 'e's not going t' feel much proud o' you. Not to mention wot 'is opinion o' *me* would be. You want to keep the old twit feelin' responsible for wot 'e's done t' you, mate.

"Oh, 'e might 'ave a fair supply of silver tucked away neat and pretty somewhere. But 'is supply of silver's bound to be limited. So long as 'e's got 'is feeble old mind set on this dotty crisis of 'is, 'e's not goin' to be doin' much business. No business, no silver. No silver, no 'andouts, right? I'm afraid you're goin' t' 'ave t' go t' work."

"I see." Jon-Tom stared morosely into his empty mug. "What about working with you, Mudge?"

"Now don't get me wrong, mate. I'm just gettin' t' where I can tol'rate your company."

"Thanks," said Jon-Tom tartly.

"That's all right, it is. But huntin's a solitary profession. I don't think I could do much for you there. You don't strike me as the type o' chap who knows 'is way 'round a woods. You'd as soon trip over a trap as set one, I think."

"I won't deny that I feel more at home around books, or a basketball court."

"Otherworldly sports won't do you ant's piss good 'round 'ere, lad. As far as the learnin' part of it . . . wot was it then you were acquiring?"

"I'm into prelaw, Mudge."

"Ah, a barrister-t'-be, is it? Never 'ad much use for the species meself," he added, not caring what Jon-Tom might think of his detrimental opinions of the legal profession. "Wot did you study besides the law itself, for the laws 'ere as you might imagine are likely a mite different from those o' your own."

"History, government . . . I don't guess they'd be much use here either."

"I suppose we might get you apprenticed to some local barrister," Mudge considered. He scratched the inside of one ear, moved around to work on the back. "I don't know, mate. You certain there's nothin' else? You ever work a forge, build furniture? Do metalwork, build a house, cure meat . . . anythin' *useful?*"

"Not really." Jon-Tom felt uncomfortable.

"Huh!" The otter let loose a contemptuous whistle. "Fine life you've led for a so-called wizard."

"That's Clothahump's mistake," Jon-Tom protested. "I never claimed to be that. I've never claimed to be anything other than what I am."

"Which don't appear to be much, as far as placin' you's concerned. Nothin' more in the way of skills, is it?"

"Well . . ." Another ambition flooded through him. With it came the laughs of his friends and the condemnations and horrified protests of his family. Then they were drowned by a vision of himself with a guitar and by the memories of all the groups, all the performances he'd collected and mimicked in his less intellectual, more emotional moments of introspection. Memories and sounds of Zepplin and Harum, of Deep Purple and Tangerine Dream and Moody Blues and a thousand others. Electric melodies tingled in his fingertips. Logic and reason vanished. Once more good sense and truth clashed within him.

Only here good sense did not serve. Heart's desire again took control of him.

"I play a g . . . an electric bass. It's a kind of a stringed instrument. It's only a hobby. I thought once I *might* try to make a career out of it, only . . ."

"So you're a musician then!" Consternation vanished as understanding filled the otter. He pushed back his chair, let his feet down
on the floor, and stared with new interest at his companion. "A
minstrel. I'll be bloody be-damned. Aye, there might be a way there
for you t' make some coppers, maybe even some silver. You'd be a
novelty, anyways. Let me 'ear you sing something."

"Right here?" Jon-Tom looked around nervously.

"Aye. No one's goin' to 'ear you anyway. Not between the babble
and band."

"I don't know." Jon-Tom considered. "I need to warm up. And I
don't have my guitar with me."

"A pox on your bleedin' instrument," growled the otter. " 'Ow do
you expect t' act a proper minstrel if you can't sing on demand, when
someone requires it o' you? Now don't mind me, mate. Get on with
it." He sat expectantly, looked genuinely intrigued.

Jon-Tom cleared his throat self-consciously and looked around. No
one was paying him the least attention. He took a fortifying swallow
from Mudge's mug and considered. Damn silly, he thought. Oh well,
best try an old favorite, and he began "Eleanor Rigby." Am I one of
all the lonely people now? he thought as he voiced the song.

When he'd finished, he looked anxiously at the otter. Mudge's expression was fixed.

"Well? How was I?"

Mudge leaned back in his seat, smiled faintly. "Maybe you were
right, Jon-Tom. Maybe it 'twould be better with some instrumental
accompaniment. Interestin' words, I'll grant you that. I once knew a
chap who kept several faces in jars, though 'e didn't 'ave 'em up by 'is
door."

Jon-Tom tried not to show his disappointment, though why he
should have expected a different reaction from the otter than from
previous audiences he couldn't imagine.

"I'm really much more of an instrumentalist. As far as voice goes,"
he added defensively, "maybe I'm not smooth, but I'm enthusiastic."

"That's so, mate, but I'm not so sure your listeners would be. I'll
try t' think on what else you might do. But for now, I think maybe it
would be a kindness t' forget about any minstrelin'."

"Well, I'm not helpless." Jon-Tom gestured around them. "I don't
want to keep imposing on you, Mudge. Take this place. I'm not
afraid of hard work. There must be hundreds of mugs and platters to
wash and floors to be mopped down, tables to be cleaned, drains to be
scoured. There's a helluva lot of work here. I could . . ."

Mudge reached across the table and had both paws digging into Jon-Tom's indigo shirt. He stared up into the other's surprise and whispered intently.

"You can't do that! That's work for mice and rats. Don't let anyone 'ear you talk like that, Jon-Tom." He let go of the silk and sat back in his chair.

"Come on now," Jon-Tom protested softly. "Work is work."

"Think you that now?" Mudge pointed to his right.

Two tables away from theirs was a rat about three feet tall. He was dressed in overalls sewn from some heavy, thick material that was badly stained and darkened. Thick gloves covered tiny paws, and knee-high boots rested on the floor as the rodent scrubbed at the planking.

The others nearby completely ignored his presence, dropping bones or other garbage nearby or sometimes onto his back. As Jon-Tom watched, the rodent accidentally stumbled across the leg of a drunken gull hunting a table with perches to accommodate ornithological clients. The big bird cocked a glazed eye at him and snapped once with its beak, more taunting than threatening.

Stumbling clear, the rat fell backward, tripped over his own feet, and brought his bucket of trash and goo down on himself. It ran down his boots and over the protective overalls. For a moment he lay stunned in the heap of garbage. Then he slowly struggled to his knees and began silently gathering it up again, ignoring but not necessarily oblivious to the catcalls and insults the patrons heaped on him. A thick bone bounced off his neck, and he gathered it up along with the rest of the debris. Soon the watchers grew bored with the momentary diversion and returned to their drinking, eating, and arguing.

"Only rats and mice do that kind of work?" Jon-Tom inquired. "I used to do something like it all the time. Remember, that's what confused Clothahump into bringing me here in the first place."

"What you do elsewhere you'd best not try 'ere, mate. Any self-respectin' animal would sooner starve before doin' that, or go t' beggin' like our sticker-hiding friend, the gibbon."

"I don't understand any of this, Mudge."

"Don't try t', mate. Just roll with the waves, wot? Besides, those types are naturally lazy and dumb. They'd rather lie about and guzzle cheese all day than do any honest work, they would. Spend all their time when not eatin' in indiscriminate screwing, though you wouldn't think they'd 'ave enough brains t' know which end to work with."

Jon-Tom was fighting to control his temper. "There's nothing wrong with doing menial work. It doesn't make those who do it menial-minded. I . . ." He sighed, wondered at the hopelessness of it all. "I guess I just thought things would be different here, as far as that kind of thing goes. It's my fault. I was imagining a world that doesn't exist."

Mudge laughed. "Little while back I recall you insistin' that this one didn't exist."

"Oh, it exists all right." His fists rubbed angrily on the table as he watched the subservient rat suddenly go down on his chest. A turtle with a disposition considerably less refined than Clothahump's had stuck out a stubby leg and tripped the unfortunate rodent. Once more the laboriously gathered garbage went flying while a new burst of merriment flared from the onlookers.

"Why discrimination like that here?" Jon-Tom muttered. "Why here too?"

"Discrimination?" Mudge seemed confused. "Nobody discriminates against 'em. That's all they're good for. Can't argue with natural law, mate."

Jon-Tom had expected more from Mudge, though he'd no real reason to. From what he'd already seen, the otter was no worse than the average inhabitant of this stinking, backward nonparadise.

There were a number of humans scattered throughout the restaurant. None came near approaching Jon-Tom in height. Nearby a single older gentleman was drinking and playing cards with a spider monkey dressed in black shot through with silver thread. They paired off against a larger simian Jon-Tom couldn't identify and a three-foot-tall pocket gopher wearing a crimson jumpsuit and the darkest sunglasses Jon-Tom had ever seen.

No doubt they were as prejudiced and bigoted as the others. And where did he come off setting himself up as arbiter of another world's morals?

"There ain't nothin' you can do about it, mate. Why would anyone want t' change things? Cor now, moppin' and sweepin' and such are out, unless you want t' lose all respect due a regular citizen. Politickin' you're also qualified for, but that o' course ranks even lower than janitorial-type drudgeryin'. I'd hope you won't 'ave t' fall back on your abilities for minstrelin'." His tone changed to one of hope mixed with curiosity.

"Now ol' Clothahump, 'e was bloody well sure you were some sort of sorcerer, 'e was. You sure you can't work no magic? I 'eard you questioning 'is wizard-wart's own special words."

"That was just curiosity, Mudge. Some of the words were familiar. But not in the way he used them. Even you did the business with the dancing pins. Does everyone practice magic around here?"

"Oh, everyone practices, all right." Mudge swilled down a snootful of black brew. "But few get good enough at it to do much more than a trick or two. Pins are my limit, I'm afraid. Wish to 'ell I knew 'is gold spell." His gaze suddenly moved left and he grinned broadly.

"Course now, when the situation arises I ain't too bad at certain forms o' levitation." His right hand moved with the speed of which only otters are capable.

How the saucily dressed and heavily made up chipmunk managed to keep from dumping the contents of the six tankards she was maneuvering through the crowd was a bit of magic in itself, Jon-Tom thought as he ducked to avoid the few flying suds.

She turned an outraged look on the innocent-seeming Mudge. "You keep your hands to yourself, you shit-eating son of a mud worm! Next time you'll get one of these up your furry backside!" She threatened him with a tankard.

"Now Lily," Mudge protested, " 'aven't you always told me you're always 'untin' for a way t' move up in the world?"

She started to swing an armful of liquor at him and he cowered away in mock fear, covering his face with his paws and still smiling. Then she thought better of wasting the brew. Turning from their table she marched away, elbowing a path through the crowd. Her tail switched prettily from side to side, the short dress barely reaching from waist to knee. It was gold with a gray lining that neatly set off her own attractive russet and black and white striping.

"What did I tell you, mate?" Mudge grinned over his mug at Jon-Tom.

He tried to smile back, aware that the otter was trying to break the glum mood into which Jon-Tom had fallen. So he forced himself to continue the joke.

"Mighty short levitation, Mudge. I don't see how it does her any good."

"Who said anything about her?" The otter jabbed himself in the chest with a thumb. "It's *me* the levitatin' benefits!" He clasped both furry arms around his chest and roared at his own humor, threatening to upset table and self.

Wooden shades were rolled down to cover the two windows, and someone dimmed the oil lamps. Jon-Tom started to rise, felt a restraining paw on his wrist.

"Nay, guv, 'tis nothing t' be concerned about." His eyes were sparkling. "Quite the contrary. Did I not promise you some entertainment?" He pointed to the circular serving counter and up.

What looked like an upside-down tree was slowly descending from a gap in the center of the peaked ceiling. It was green with fresh growth, only the foliage had been tacked on and doubtless was periodically renewed. The still unseen band segued into an entirely new tune. The percussionist was doing most of the work now, Jon-Tom noted. The beat was heavy, slow, and sensuous.

The yelling and shouting that filled the establishment changed also. Barely organized chaos faded to a murmur of anticipation spotted with occasional roars of comment, usually lewd in nature.

Mudge had shifted his seat, now sat close to Jon-Tom. His eyes were on the fake tree as he elbowed his companion repeatedly in the ribs.

"Eyes at the alert now, mate. There's not a fairer nor more supple sight in all Lynchbany."

An animal appeared at the dark opening in the ceiling, prompting a bellow from the crowd. It vanished, then teasingly reappeared. It was slight, slim, and made its way very slowly from the hidden chamber above down into the branches of the ersatz conifer. About three and a half feet in length, it displayed another half foot of active tail and was completely, almost blindingly covered in snow-white fur save for a few inches of black at the tip of the tail.

Its costume, if such so lithe a wrapping could be called, consisted of many layers of black veils of some chiffonlike material through which the brilliant white fur showed faintly. Its face was streaked with red painted on in intricate curlicues and patterns that ran from face and snout down onto shoulders, chest, and back before vanishing beneath the airy folds. A turban of matching black was studded with jewels. The final touch, Jon-Tom noted with fascination, were long false eyelashes.

So absorbing was this glittering mammalian vision that for several moments identification escaped him. That slim form and muscular torso could only belong to some member of the weasel family. When the apparition smiled and displayed tiny sharp teeth he was certain of it. This was an ermine, still in full winter-white coat. That confirmed the time of year he'd arrived, though he hadn't thought to ask anyone. About the creature's femininity he had no doubt whatsoever.

A hush of interspecies expectancy had settled over the crowd. All attention was focused overhead as the ermine ecdysiast began to toy with the clasps securing one veil. She unsnapped one, then its companion. Cries of appreciation started to rise from the patrons, an amazing assortment of hoots, whistles, squeaks, yowls, and barks. She began to uncoil the first veil with snakelike motions.

Jon-Tom had never had occasion to imagine an animal executing anything as erotic as a striptease. After all, beneath any clothing lay another layer of solid fur and not the bare flesh of a human.

But eroticism has little to do with nudity, as he soon discovered. It was the movement of the creature, a supple twisting and turning that no human female could possibly match, that was stimulating. He found himself thoroughly engrossed by the mechanics of the dance alone.

To rising cries of appreciation from the crowd one veil followed another. The cool indifference Jon-Tom had intended to affect had long since given way to a distinct tingling. He was no more immune to beauty than any other animal. The ermine executed a series of movements beyond the grasp of the most talented double-jointed human, and did so with the grace and demeanor of a countess.

There was also the manner in which she oozed around the branches and leaves of the tree, caressing them with hands and body in a way only a chunk of cold granite could have ignored. The room was heavy with musk now, the suggestiveness of motion and gesture affecting every male within sight.

The last veil dropped free, floated featherlike to the floor. The music was moving almost as fast as the performer. That white-furred derrière had become a gravity-defying metronome, a passionate pendulum sometimes concealed, sometimes revealed by the position of the twitching tail, all vibrating in time to the music.

The music rose to a climax as the ermine, hanging by her arms from the lowermost branches, executed an absolutely impossible series of movements which incidentally revealed to Jon-Tom the reason for the circular, central nature of the main serving counter. It served now as fortress wall behind which the heavily armed cooks and bartenders were able to fend off the hysterical advances of the overheated patrons.

One long-eared rabbit which Jon-Tom supposed to be a jack actually managed to grab a handful of black-tipped tail which was coyly but firmly pulled out of reach. A burly bobcat dumped the rabbit back among the surging patrons as the ermine blew a last kiss to her audience. Then she slithered back through branches and leaves to disappear inside the ceiling with a last fluid bump and grind.

Shades and tree were promptly rolled up. Conversation resumed and normality returned to the restaurant. Waitresses and waiters continued to wend their way through the crowd like oxygen in the bloodstream.

"D'you see now wot I mean, mate?" Mudge said with the contentment of one who'd just cashed a very large check, "when I say that there's no one who—" He stopped, stared strangely across the table.

"What's wrong?" asked Jon-Tom uncomfortably.

"'Ave me for breakfast," was the startled reply, "if you ain't blushin'! You 'umans . . ."

"Bull," muttered Jon-Tom, turning angrily away.

"Nope." The otter leaned over the table, peering closely at Jon-Tom despite his attempts to keep his face concealed. "Blimey but it's true . . . you're as red as a baboon's behind, lad." He nodded upward, toward the peak of the roof. "'Ave you ne'er seen such a performance before, then?"

"Of course I have." He turned forcefully back to face his guardian, rocked a little unsteadily. It seeped into his brain that he might have become a little bit tipsy. How much of that black booze had he downed?

"That is, I have . . . on film."

"What be that?"

"A magic apparition," Jon-Tom explained facilely.

"Well if you've gazed upon such, though not, I dare to say," and he gazed admiringly ceilingward, "of such elegance and skill, then why the red face?"

"It's just that," he searched for the right words to explain his confusion, "I shouldn't find the actions of . . ." How could he say, "another animal" without offending his companion? Desperately he hunted for an alternate explanation.

"I've never seen anything done with quite that . . . well, with quite that degree of perverse dexterity."

"Ah, I understand now. Though perverse I wouldn't call it. Crikey, but that was a thing of great beauty."

"If you say so, I guess it was." Jon-Tom was grateful for the out.

"Aye." Mudge growled softly and smiled. "And if I could once get my paws on that supple little mother-dear, I'd show 'er a thing of beauty."

The thick, warm atmosphere of the restaurant had combined with the rich food and drink to make Jon-Tom decidedly woozy. He was determined not to pass out. Mudge already did not think much of him, and Clothahump's warnings or no, he wasn't ready to bet that the otter would stay with him if he made a total ass of himself.

Determinedly he shoved the mug away, rose, and glanced around.

"What be you searchin' for now, mate?"

"Some of my own kind." His eyes scanned the crowd for the sight of bare flesh.

"What, 'umans?" The otter shrugged. "Aw well, never 'ave I understood your peculiar affinity for each other's company, but you're free enough to choose your own. Espy some, do you?"

Jon-Tom's gaze settled on a pair of familiar bald faces in a booth near the rear of the room. "There's a couple over that way. Two men, I think."

"As you will, then."

He turned his attention down to the otter. "It's not that I'm not enjoying your companionship, Mudge. It's just that I'd like one of my own kind to talk to for a while."

His worries were groundless. Mudge was in entirely too good a mood to be offended by anything.

"Wotever you like, mate. We'll go and 'ave a chat then, if that's wot you want. But don't forget we've still the little matter o' settlin' you on some proper course o' employment." He shook his head more to clear it than to indicate displeasure.

"Minstrel . . . I don't know. There might still be the novelty factor." He scratched the fur just under his chin. "Tell you what. Give us another song and then we'll go over and see if we can't make the acquaintance o' those chaps."

"I thought you'd heard enough the first time."

"Never go on first appearances, mate. Besides, 'twas a damn blue and gloomy tune you let out with. Try somethin' different. Many's the minstrel who well mangles one type o' tune yet can warble clearly another."

Jon-Tom sat down again, linked his fingers, and considered. "I don't know. What would you like to hear? Classical, pop, blues, jazz?" He tried to sound enthusiastic. "I know some classical, but what I really always wanted to do was sing rock. It's a form of popular music back where I come from."

"I don't know either, mate. 'Ow 'bout ballads? Everyone likes ballads."

"Sure." He was warming again to his true love. "I know a number of 'em. What subject do you like best?"

"Let me think on it a minute." Actually, it was only a matter of seconds before a gleam returned to the black eyes, along with a smile.

"Never mine," Jon-Tom said hastily. "I'll think of something."

He thought, but it was hard to settle on any one song. Maybe it was the noise and smell swirling around them, maybe the aftereffects of the meal, but words and notes flitted in and out of his brain like gnats, never pausing long enough for him to get a grip on any single memory. Besides, he felt unnatural singing without his trusty, worn Grundig slung over his shoulder and across his stomach. If he only had something, even a harmonica. But he couldn't play that and sing simultaneously.

"Come on now, mate," Mudge urged him. "Surely you can think o' something?"

"I'll try," and he did, launching into a cracked rendition of "Strawberry Fair," but the delicate harmonies were drowned in the bellowing and hooting and whistling that filled the air of the restaurant.

Nonetheless, he was unprepared for the sharp blow that struck him between the shoulderblades and sent him sprawling chest-down across the table.

Angry and confused, he turned to find himself staring into a ferocious dark brown face set on a stocky, muscular body as tall as Mudge's but more than twice as broad. . . .

VI

The snakeskin beret and red bandana did nothing to lessen the wolverine's intimidating appearance.

"Sorry," Jon-Tom mumbled, uncertain of what else to say.

The face glared down at him, powerful jaws parting to reveal sharp teeth as the lips curled back. "You ban not sorry enough, I think!" the creature rumbled hollowly. "I ban pretty sorry for your mother, she having much to listen to a voice like that. You upset my friends and my meal."

"I was just practicing." He was beginning to feel a mite indignant at the insults. The warmth of the roast was still with him. He failed to notice the queasy expression that had come over Mudge's face. "It's difficult to sing without any music to accompany me."

"Yah, well, you ban practice no more, you hear? It ban hurt my ears."

Mudge was trying and failing to gain Jon-Tom's attention. Jon-Tom rose from his seat to tower over the shorter but more massive animal. It made him feel better, giving proof once again to the old adage about the higher, the mightier. Or as the old philosopher said, witness the pigeon's tactical advantage over man.

However the wolverine was not impressed. He gazed appraisingly up and down Jon-Tom's length. "All that voice tube and no voice. Maybe you ban better at singing in harmony, yah? So maybe I put one half neck here and the other half across the table," and powerful clawed hands reached for Jon-Tom's face.

Dodging nimbly, Jon-Tom slipped around the table, brought up his staff, and swung the straight end down in a whistling arc. Having had plenty to consume himself, the wolverine reacted more slowly than usual. He did not quite get both hands up in time to defend himself, and the staff smacked sharply over one set of knuckles. The creature roared in pain.

"Look, I don't want any trouble."

"You stick up for your rights, mate!" Mudge urged him, beginning a precipitous retreat from the vicinity of the table. "I'll watch and make sure it be a fair fight."

"Like hell you will!" He held the staff tightly, trying to divide his attention between the wolverine and the otter. "You remember what Clothahump said."

"Screw that!" But Mudge hesitated, his hand fumbling in the vicinity of his chest sword. Clearly he was sizing up the tense triangle that had formed around the table and debating whether or not he stood a better chance of surviving Clothahump's vengeful spell-making than the wolverine and his friends. The latter consisted of a tall marten and a chunky armadillo who displayed a sword hanging from each hip belt. Of course, carrying weapons and knowing how to use them were two different matters.

They were rising and moving to flank the wolverine and gazing at Jon-Tom in a decidedly unfriendly manner. The wolverine himself had regained his composure and was sliding an ugly-looking mace from the loop on his own belt.

"Steady on, mate," the otter urged his companion, sword out and committed now.

The wolverine was bouncing the spiked iron head of the mace up and down in one palm, gripping the handle with the other. "Maybe I ban wrong about that harmony." He eyed the man's throat. "Maybe I ban eliminate that voice altogether, yah?" He started forward, encountered a waiter who started to curse him, then saw the mace and fled into the crowd.

"Is too crowded in here though. I tink I meet you outside, hokay?"

"Hokay," said Jon-Tom readily. He moved as if to leave, got his right hand under the edge of the table, and heaved. Table, drinks, remnants of their greasy meal and platterware showered down on the wolverine, his companions, and several unsuspecting occupants of other tables. The innocent bystanders took exception to the barrage. One of the wolverine's associates side-stepped the flying table and jabbed his sword at the otter's face. Mudge ducked under the marten's thrust and kept his sword ready to challenge the emerging ar-

madillo while neatly kicking the bellicose marten in the nuts. The
stricken animal grabbed himself and went to his knees.

Among those who had received the dubious decorations proferred
by Jon-Tom's action were a pair of female coatis whose delicacy of
shape and flash of eye were matched by the outrage in their voices.
They had drawn slim rapiers and were struggling to join the fray.

Jon-Tom had moved backward and to his left, this being the only
space still not filled with potential combatants, and was quickly
joined by Mudge. They continued backing until they upset another
table and its patrons. This instituted a chain reaction which led with
astonishing rapidity to a general mayhem that threatened to involve
every one in the establishment.

Only the chefs and bartenders kept their calm. They remained
invulnerable behind their protective circular counter, defending liquor and food as assiduously as they had the honor and person of
their gleaming white star performer. Only when some stumbling bat-
tler intruded on their territorial circle did their heavy clubs come into
play. Waiters and waitresses huddled behind this front line of defense,
casually making book on the outcome of the fight or downing drinks
intended for otherwise occupied patrons.

The fight whirlpooled around this central bastion of calm as the
room was filled with yelps and meows, squeaks and squeals and
chirps of pain and outrage.

It was an arboreal that almost got Jon-Tom. He was effectively if
unartistically using his long staff to fend off the short sword thrusts of
an outraged pika when Mudge yelled, "Jon-Tom . . . duck!"

As it was, the bola-wielding mallard missed his neck but got his
weapon entangled in the club end of Jon-Tom's staff. He shoved
down hard on it. In order to remain airborne the fowl had to surrender his weapon, but not without dropping instead a stream of insults
on the tall human. Jon-Tom had time to note the duck's kilt of orange and green. He wondered if the different kilt colors signified
species or some sort of genus-spanning clan equivalent.

There was little time for sociological contemplation. The marten
had recovered from Mudge's low blow and was moving to put the
sharp edge of his blade through Jon-Tom's midsection. Instinctively
he tilted the staff crosswise. The club end came over and around. It
missed the agile marten, but the entangled bird's bola caught around
the weasel's neck.

Dropping his sword, he pulled the device free of the staff and
stumbled away, fighting to free his neck from the strangling cord.

Jon-Tom, momentarily clear of attackers, hunted through the crowd for his companion.

Mudge was close by, kicking furniture in the way of potential assailants, throwing mugs and other eating utensils at them whenever possible, avoiding hand-to-hand combat wherever he could.

Jon-Tom took no pride, felt no pleasure in his newfound capacity for violent self-defense. If he could only get out of this dangerous madhouse and back home to the peace and quiet of his little apartment! But that distant, familiar haven had receded ever farther into memory, had reached the point where it existed only as misty history compared to the all too real blood and fury surrounding him.

Thank God, he thought frantically, fending off another attacker, for Clothahump's ministrations. Even a well-bandaged wound would have broken open again by now, but he felt nothing in his formerly injured side. He was well and truly healed.

That would not save him if one of many sword or pike thrusts punctured him anew. The indiscriminate nature of the fighting was more frightening than anything else now. It was impossible to tell potential friend from foe.

In vain he looked across the milling crest of the fight for the entrance. It was seemingly at least a mile away across an ocean of battling fur and steel. A desperate examination of the room seemed to show no other exit save via the central bastion of the bar and food counter, whose defenders were not admitting refugees. That left only the windows, an idea the panting Mudge quickly quashed.

"Blimey, mate, you must be daft! That glass be 'alf an inch thick in places and thicker where 'tis beveled. I'd sooner take a sword thrust than slice meself t' bloody ribbons on that.

"There be an alley out back. Let's make our way in that direction."

"I don't see any doors there," said Jon-Tom, straining to see past the rear booths.

"Surely there's a service entryway. I'll settle now meself for a garbage chute."

Sure enough, they eventually discovered a single low doorway hidden by stacks of crates and piles of garbage. The close-packed mob made progress difficult, but they forced their way slowly toward the promise of freedom and safety. Only Jon-Tom's overbearing height enabled them to keep their goal in view. To the other brawlers he must have looked like an ambling lighthouse.

Already his shining snakeskin cape was torn and bloodstained.

Better it than me, he thought gratefully. It was not a pretty riot. The only rules were those of survival.

He passed one squirrel prone on the floor, tail sodden and matted with blood. His left leg was missing below the knee. So much blood and spilled drink and food had accumulated on the floor, in fact, that one of the greatest dangers was losing one's footing on the increasingly treacherous planking.

Jon-Tom watched as a cape-clad coyote picked over the unconscious form of a badly bleeding fox. While his attention was thus temporarily diverted, someone grabbed his left arm. He turned to swing the staff one-handed or jab as was required. So far he hadn't been forced to utilize the concealed spearpoint and hoped he'd never have to.

The figure that had grabbed him was completely swathed in maroon and blue material. He could discern little of the figure save that the mostly hidden face seemed to be human. The short figure tugged hard and urged him back behind a temporary wall formed by a trio of fat porcupines, who, for self-evident reasons, were having little trouble fending off any combatant foolish enough to come close.

He decided there was time later for questions, since the figure was pulling him toward the haven promised by the back door, and that was his intended destination anyway.

"Hurry it up!" Though muffled by fabric the voice was definitely human. "The cops have been called and should be here any second." There was a decided undertone of real fear in that warning, the reason for which Jon-Tom was to discover soon enough.

Visions of hundreds of furry police swarming through the crowd filled his thoughts. From the size and breadth of the conflict he guessed it would take at least that number several more hours to quell the fighting. He was reckoning without the ingenuity of Lynchbany law enforcement.

Mudge, upon hearing of the incipient arrival of the gendarmes, acted genuinely terrified.

"That's fair warnin', mate," he yelled above the din, "and we'd best get out or die trying." He redoubled his efforts to clear a path to the door.

"Why? What will they do?" He swung his staff in a short arc, brought it up beneath the chin of a small but gamely threatening muskrat who was swinging at Jon-Tom's ankles with a weapon like a scythe. Fortunately, he'd only nicked one trouser leg before Jon-Tom knocked him out. "Do they kill people here for fighting in public?"

"Worse than that." Mudge was nearly at the back door, fighting to keep potential antagonists out of sword range and the invulnerable porcupines between himself and the rest of the mob. Then he shouted frantically.

"Quickly—quick now, for your lives!" Jon-Tom thought it peculiar the otter had not sought the identity of their concealed compatriot. "They're here!"

From his position head-and-shoulders high above the crowd Jon-Tom could see across to the now distant main entrance. He also noted with concern that the chefs and bartenders and waiters had vanished, abandoning their stock to the crowd.

Four or five figures of indeterminate furry cast stood inside the entryway now. They wore leathern bonnets decorated with flashing ovals of metal. Emblems on shoulder vests glinted in the light from the remaining intact lamps and the windows. There was a crash, and he saw that unmindful of the danger Mudge had outlined, the appearance of the police had actually frightened one of the fighters into following a chair out through a thick window pane. Jon-Tom wondered what horrible fate was in store for the rest of the still battling mob.

Then he was following the strange figure and Mudge out through the door. As they turned to slam and bar it with barrels behind them he had a last glimpse across the room as the police took action against the combatants within. This was accompanied by a whiff of something awful beyond imagining and concentrated beyond the power of man or beast to endure.

It weakened him so badly that he barely had strength enough to heave his not-yet-digested dinner all over the far wall. It helped his pride if not his stomach to see that the momentary smell had produced the same effect on Mudge and the maroon-clad stranger. As he knelt in the alley and emptied his nausea-squeezed guts, the pattern he'd glimpsed on the arriving police came back to him.

Then they were all up and stumbling, running down the cobblestoned alley, the mist still dense around them and the smell of garbage like perfume compared to that which was fading with merciful speed behind them.

"Very . . . efficient, though I'm not so sure I'd call it humane, even if no one is killed." He clung tightly to his staff, using it for support as they slowed a little.

"Aye, mate." Mudge jogged steadily alongside him, behind the long-legged stranger. Occasionally he gave a worried, disgusted glance back over a shoulder to check for possible pursuit. None materialized.

"Indecent it is. You only *wish* you were dead. It be that way in every town, though. 'Tis clean and there's no after caterwaulerin' about accidental death or police brutalness and such. There's worse things than takin' an occasional sword in the side, though. Like puking to death.

"Makes it a good thing for the skunks, though. I've never seen a one of those black and white offal that lacked a good job in any township. 'Tis a brother and sisterhood sort of comradeship they 'ave, which is well for 'em, since none o' the common folk care for their companionship. They keep the peace, I suppose, and keep t' themselves." He shuddered. "And keep in mind, mate, that we were clean across the room from 'em. Those by the front will likely not touch food for days." Several small lizards left their claimed bit of rotting meat, skittered into a hole in the wall while the refugees hurried past, then returned to their scavenging.

"Never could stand 'em myself, either. I don't like cops and I cannot abide anyone who fights with 'is rear end."

Noises reached them from the far end of the alley and vestiges of that ghastly odor materialized to stab at Jon-Tom's nostrils and stomach.

"They're followin'," said a worried Mudge. "Save us from that. I'd far rather be cut."

"This way!" urged the cloaked figure. They turned up a branch of the alleyway. Mist covered everything, slickened walls and cobblestones and trash underfoot. They plunged onward, heedless of falling.

Gradually the smell began to recede once more. Jon-Tom was grateful for the time he'd spent on the basketball court, and for the unusual stride that enabled him to keep up with the hyperactive Mudge and their racing and still identityless savior.

"They took the main passage," said that voice. "This should be safe enough."

They had emerged on a small side street. Dim will-o'-the-wisp glows came from the warm globes of the street lamps overhead. It was quite dark otherwise, and though the mist curtained the sky Jon-Tom was certain that sunset had come and gone while they'd been dining in the restaurant.

The stranger unwrapped the muffler covering face and neck and let it hang across shoulders and back. Cloak, shirt, and pants were made of the same maroon material touched with silver thread. The material was neither leather nor cotton but some mysterious organic hybrid. Pants, boots, and blouse had further delicate designs of copper thread worked through them, as did the high, almost Napoleonic collar.

A slim blade, half foil, half saber, was slung neatly from the waist. She stood nearly as tall as Mudge's five foot six, which Jon-Tom had been given to understand was tall for a human woman hereabouts. She turned, still panting from the run, to study them. He was glad of the opportunity to reciprocate.

The maroon clothing fit snugly without binding and the face above it, though expectedly petite, was hard and sharp-featured. The green eyes were more like Mudge's than his own. They moved with almost equal rapidity over street and alleyway, never ceasing. Her shoulder-length curls were flame-red. Not the red-orange of most redheads but a fiery, flashing crimson that looked in the lamplight like kinky blood.

Save for her coloring and the absence of fur and whiskers she displayed all the qualities of an active otter. Only the pale green eyes softened the savage image she presented, standing there nervously by the side of a building that seemed to swoop winglike above them in the mist.

As for the rest of her, he had the damndest feeling he was seeing a cylindrical candy bar well packed with peanuts. Her voice was full of hints of clove and pepper, as active as her eyes and her body.

"Thought I'd never get you out of there." She was talking to Mudge. "I tried to get you separated but," she glanced curiously up at Jon-Tom, "this great gangling boy was always between us."

"I'd appreciate it," said Jon-Tom politely, "if you wouldn't refer to me as a 'boy'." He stared unblinkingly at her. "You don't look any older than me."

"I'll change my tune," she shot back, "when you've demonstrated the difference to my satisfaction, though I hope more time isn't required. Still, I have to admit that you handled yourself well enough inside the Possum. Clumsy, but efficient. Size can make up for a helluva lot."

Clove and pepper, he thought. Each word was snapped off sharply in the air like a string of firecrackers.

She turned distastefully away from his indelicate stare and asked Mudge wth disarming candor, "How soon can we be rid of it?" She jerked a thumb in Jon-Tom's bemused direction.

"I'm afraid we can't, m'love. Clothahump 'imself 'as entrusted 'im t' me tender care."

"Clothahump, the wizard of the Tree?" Again she looked curiously at Jon-Tom.

"Aye. It seems 'e was castin' about for an otherworldly wizard type and 'e came up with this chap Jon-Tom instead. As I said, because I 'appened t' be unlucky enough to stumble into this manifestation, I've been ordered t' take care of 'im. At least until 'e can take better care of 'imself." Mudge raised a paw.

"On penalty o' curses too 'orrible t' explain, luv. But it 'ain't been too bad. 'E's a good enough lad, if a trifle naïve."

Jon-Tom was beginning to feel a resurgence of the volatility that had set off the riot in the Pearl Possum. "Hey now, people, I'm getting a little tired of everyone continually running off my list of disabilities."

"Shut up and do as you're told," said the woman.

"Fuck you, sister," he spat back angrily. "How'd you like your backside the same color as your hair?"

Her right hand suddenly sported a sixth finger. The knife gleamed in the dim light. It was no longer than her middle finger but twice as broad and displayed an unusual double blade.

"And how'd you like to sing about three octaves higher?"

"Please now, Talea." Mudge hurriedly interposed himself between them. "Think of me, if naught else. 'E's me responsibility. If any 'arm comes to 'im while 'e's in my care, Clothahump'll 'ave me 'ide. As to 'is singin' I've 'ad more than enough for one night. That's wot started the trouble in the Possum in the first place."

"More's the pity for you then, Mudge." But the blade disappeared with a twist of the wrist, vanishing back inside her right sleeve. "I'll truce on it for you . . . for now."

"I'm not taking any orders from her," Jon-Tom said belligerently.

"Now, now, mate." Mudge made placating gestures. "No one's said that you must. But you're willin' to accept advice, ain't you? That's what I'm 'ere for, after all."

"That's true," Jon-Tom admitted. But he couldn't keep his eyes off the lethal little lady Mudge had called Talea. Her temper had considerably mitigated his first feelings toward her. She was no less beautiful for their argument, but it had become the beauty of a rose sealed in glass. Delicacy and attractiveness were still there, but there was no fragrance, and both were untouchable.

"That's the second time tonight you've shown concern for me, luv." Mudge looked at her uncertainly. "First by 'elpin' us flee that unfortunate altercation back in the Pearl Possum and now again by respectin' me wishes and makin' peace with the lad. I've never known you t' be so solicitous o' my 'ealth or anyone else's exceptin' your precious own. So wot's behind the sudden nursemaidin'?"

"You're right about the first, Mudge. Most of the time you can find your own way to hell for all I care." Her voice finally mellowed, and for the first time she sounded vulnerable and human.

"Truth is that I needed some help, fast. The Pearl Possum was the nearest and most likely place in which to find it. You were the first one I saw that I knew, and considering what was going on in there I didn't have a whole hell of a lot of time to be picky. I do need your help." She looked hesitantly past him at Jon-Tom. "And so I guess I have to put up with him, too." She walked over to Jon-Tom, looked him over sharply.

"In truth, he's an impressive physical speciman." Jon-Tom stood a little taller. "What I need now are strong backs, not brains." He lost an inch.

"I knew you were needin' something, dear," said Mudge knowledgeably. "I couldn't see you givin' yourself over t' philanthropy. Jon-Tom, meet Talea. And widdershins likewise."

"Charmed," said Jon-Tom curtly.

"Yeah, me too." She paused thoughtfully. "So the old magic bugger-in-the-shell was looking around for an other-world wizard and got you instead. I can imagine what his reaction must have been."

"I don't need this." Jon-Tom turned away, spoke almost cheerfully. "I don't need this at all. I'll make my own damn way!"

" 'Old on now, mate," said Mudge desperately. "You think o' me, too. Everyone think o' poor old Mudge for a change."

"When did you ever think of anything else?" snorted Talea.

"Please, luv. Go easy on the poor lad. 'Tis right that you owe 'im nothing and likewise meself. But consider, 'e's a whole new world t' try and cope with, and you're not makin' it any easier."

"What have his problems to do with me?" she replied indifferently, but for a change left off adding any additional insults.

"You said that you needed our help," Jon-Tom reminded her. "And I suppose we owe you a favor for helping us out of that mess back there." He jerked a hand back toward the now distant restaurant. "Or at least for warning us about the police. You can have the use of my back without my affection. At least I can use that without running my mouth."

She almost smiled, flipping away hair from her eyes. The oil lamps set her curls on fire. "That's fair enough. We've wasted enough time here, and I suppose I've wasted most of it. Follow me. . . ."

They trailed her down the street. No strollers were out this time on so miserable a night. Rain dripped off tile and wood roofs, trickled metallically down drainpipes and into gutters. Sometimes they passed a sharper, richer echo where dripwater plunged into a collection barrel.

They'd walked several blocks before she turned into another alleyway. Several yards into the narrow passage he began to hear a strange yet somehow familiar snuffling noise. It sounded like a drunk hog.

Almost stumbling over something firm and heavy, he looked down and saw to his considerable dismay that it was an arm, badly decomposed and with the fur falling from forearm and paw. Nude bone projected like soap from one end.

Mudge and Talea were just ahead. The otter was bending over and examining something on the stones. Jon-Tom hurried to join them.

Two bodies lay sprawled awkwardly across the damp paving, necklaced by puddles of rainwater. One was that of a squirrel he assumed by attire to be female. She was richly dressed in a pleated gown puffed up like a cloud by a series of lace petticoats. Long ruffled sleeves covered each gray-furred arm. Nearby lay a feathered, broad-rimmed hat, torn and broken. She was half a foot shorter than Talea and her carefully applied face powder and paint were smeared like mud across her cheeks.

Nearby was a fat furry form that he at first thought might be a small beaver but that turned out to be another muskrat. An oddly creased tricornered hat still rested on the motionless head, though it was tilted over the hidden eyes. A pair of cracked pince-nez spectacles, much like those worn by Clothahump, reflected the still, small pools between the cobblestones. The iridescent blue silk suit he wore was rich enough to shine even in the dim light of the alley.

One boot had come off and lay limply near a naked foot. Its rhinestone-inlaid mate lay up against the far wall. Talea ignored it as she rechecked the body with professional speed.

"Blimey, luv, what's all this now?" Mudge's attention was directed nervously back toward the narrow plank of light from the street. "I ain't so sure we want to be compromisin' ourselves with business of this disreputable nature."

"Shit, you're compromised just by standing there." Talea heaved at the thick silk jacket. "Not that your reputation would suffer. Who are you lying to, Mudge; yourself, me, or him?" and she nodded briefly toward the self-conscious Jon-Tom. "You know what the cops will do if they find you standing here flapping your whiskers."

"Now Talea, luv—" he began.

"I think we've exchanged enough pleasantries, otter. I need you for muscle, not platitudes.

"Now I don't object to an occasional mugging, especially when the apple stands around begging to be plucked." She was pulling gold buttons off the comatose muskrat's trousers. "But murder's not my style. This fat little twerp decided to show off and resist, and I'll be damned if that fuzzy harridan he was with didn't try to help him. Between the two of them I didn't have much time to get selective with the hilt of my sword. So I bashed him proper and then she just sort of fainted."

Mudge moved over to study the fallen lady. While Jon-Tom watched, the otter knelt and moved her head. There was a dark stain on the stones and a matching one at the back of the furry skull.

"This one's still bleedin', you know."

"I didn't mean to hurt anyone." Talea did not sound particularly contrite. "I was just trying to keep them off. I told you, she fainted. What the hell was I supposed to do, dive underneath and break her fall?"

Mudge moved away and performed a similar examination of the muskrat. "Now why would you 'ave t' do that, luv, when these gentle rocks 'ave done such a neat job of it for you?" he said sardonically. His paws moved over the muskrat's face. "Still breathin', the two of 'em. Bloody lucky you are." He looked up at her.

"Right then. What is it you want of us?"

She finally finished her scavenging, gestured back toward the street. "I've got a wagon tied around the corner on Sorbarlio Close. If I'd left it alley-opposite it would've blocked traffic and worse, drawn attention to this little drama. Besides, it's too wide to fit in the alley entrance.

"Now, I can't carry that fat little bugger by myself. By the time I could drag the two of them to the Close some nosy-body's sure to notice me and ask questions I couldn't answer. Even if I got lucky I'm not sure I could heave these two bloated pumpkins up into the wagon."

Mudge nodded sagely. "That's for us, then. Jon-Tom?"

Jon-Tom's head had finally cleared of smoke and drink, but plenty of confusion still remained. Things had happened awfully fast and his thoughts were running into one another.

"I don't know." He was also worriedly watching the street. Foul-fighting police might appear at any minute, and what Talea had told Mudge about them being guilty by their mere presence at the scene of the crime had a transworldly ring of truth to it.

"I'm not sure this is what Clothahump had in mind when he asked you to educate me."

" 'Tis a fine innocent you are, mate. As you of all people ought t' know, life's incidents are dictated by fate and not neat plannin'. We can't stay 'ere jabberin' all night, lest some idle patrol stumble on us. If you think the copfolk were hard on those poor innocent brawlers, consider wot they're likely t' do t' those they think 'ave assaulted respectable citizens. Or be it then so much different where you come from?"

"No," he replied, "I think they'd react about the same as here."

Mudge had moved to slip an arm around the waist of the uncon-scious squirrelquette, then flipped her with a whistle over his shoul-ders. "I'll take charge o' this one," he said, stumbling.

"Thought you might," snorted Talea. "Here, let me help." She caught the lady's legs just as the overburdened Mudge was about to lose his balance completely, the looked back at Jon-Tom.

"Don't just stand there gawking like a kid at a treepeep nook. Put that great gangling self of yours to work."

Jon-Tom nodded, knelt, and managed to get his arms underneath the snoring, bubbling muskrat shape. The creature was as heavy as he appeared, and the weight made Jon-Tom stagger. Working the mass around he finally got the rotund burden in a fireman's carry.

"Truth, 'tis muscles the lad 'as, if not yet overmuch common sense," Mudge observed. "Does 'e not, lass?"

"Let's get on with it," she said curtly.

On reaching the end of the alley they hesitated. Talea studied the street to the right while Mudge cautiously checked out the other end. Nothing was visible in the nebulous lamplight save cobblestones and lonely clumps of garbage. The night mist had thickened somewhat from earlier in the evening and bestowed on the fugitives a blessing beyond price.

Jon-Tom hurried out after them, the globular body of the muskrat bouncing slightly on his shoulders. He felt something warm on his cheek. At first he thought it was blood, but it turned out to be only saliva dripping from the victim's gaping mouth. He pushed the drool-ing head farther aside and concentrated on keeping close enough to the others to insure he wouldn't lose track of them in the fog.

His feet were carrying him along a course of events he seemed powerless to alter. As he jogged up the street, he considered his present condition.

In the short time he'd been in Lynchbany he'd nearly been assaulted by a beggar, had taken part in a distressingly violent riot, and was presently serving as an accessory to assault, robbery, and possibly murder. He decided firmly that as soon as circumstances permitted he would have to make his way back to Clothahump's Tree, with or without Mudge's assistance. There he would plead with the wizard to try sending him home, no matter the cost. He could not stand another day of this.

But though he did not know it, he was destined to spend rather more time than that. Forces far greater than anything he could imagine continued to gather, the little sounds his boots made in the street puddles faint echoes of the thunder to come. . . .

VII

Eventually they turned a corner onto another street. Mudge and Talea heaved the motionless form of the squirrelquette onto the back of a low-slung buckboard. Clicking sounds like thick wire brushing against glass came to them. They froze, waited in damp silence. But the wagon they heard did not turn down their street.

"Hurry up!" Talea urged Jon-Tom. She turned and snapped at Mudge, "Quit that and let's get out of here."

Mudge removed his hand from beneath the squirrelquette's dress as Jon-Tom bent his head and shoulders to dump the muskrat. That unfortunate landed with a dull thump in the wagon. Despite Mudge's insistence that both victims were still alive and breathing, the muskrat felt very dead to the worried Jon-Tom.

That was now a major concern. He thought he might be able to talk his way out of being in the same wagon with a couple of robbery victims, but if either one of them died and they were stopped by the police he doubted even Clothahump would be able to help him.

Talea was rapidly pulling a thick blanket of some woven gray material over the bodies. Then the three of them were running around to the front seat of the wagon.

There wasn't enough room there for all of them on the down-sized platform. Talea had grabbed the reins and Mudge had already mounted alongside her, so Jon-Tom had no choice but to vault the wagon rail and sit in the bed behind them.

" 'Tis best anyway, mate." Mudge smiled sympathetically. "I know the wood's 'ard, but as big as you are we don't want to draw any more attention than we can get away with. Snuggle yourself down low and we won't."

Talea gave a flip of the reins and shouted a soft "Hup!" and they were on their way. Just in time, too. As they rumbled down the street another rider passed them close.

Despite his exhaustion and confusion Jon-Tom's interest was aroused. He barely had time for a glance at the mist-shrouded rider.

A white-faced, leather-clad rabbit was mounted on a slim lizard traveling on all fours. The reptile had a long snout with two short tusks protruding upward from just back of the nostrils. Its eyes were searchlight bright and yellow with black slit pupils.

The rider sat in a saddle that was securely attached by multiple straps to the lizard's neck and belly, the extra ties necessary because of the animal's peculiar twisting, side-to-side method of travel. It gave a snakelike appearance to the motion. The long tail was curled up in a spiral and fastened to the reptilian rear with a decorative silver scroll. Blunt claws appeared to have been trimmed close to the quick.

As he watched them vanish down the street, he thought that the rider must be getting a smoother ride than any horse could provide, since all the movement was from side to side instead of up and down.

That inspired him to inspect their own team. Shifting around on the wood and trying to avoid kicking the terribly still forms beneath the gray blanket, he peered ahead beneath the raised wagon seat.

The pair of creatures pulling the wagon were also reptilian, but as different from the rabbit's mount as he was from Mudge. Harnessed in tandem to the wagon, they were shorter and bulkier than the single mount he'd just seen. They had blunt muzzles and less intelligent appearances, though that evaluation was probably due more to his unfamiliarity with the local reptilian life than to any actual physiologic difference.

They trudged more slowly over the cobblestones. Their stride was deliberate and straightforward instead of the unusual twisting, side-to-side movement of the other. Stumpy legs also covered less ground, and leathery stomach folds almost scraped the pavement. Obviously they were intended for pulling heavy loads rather than for comfort or speed.

Despite their bovine expressions they were intelligent enough to respond to Talea's occasional tugs on the reins. He studied the process of steering with interest, for there was no telling when such knowledge might prove useful. He was a good observer, one of the hallmarks of both lawyer and musician, and despite his discouragement about his surroundings he instinctively continued to soak up local information.

The reins, for example, were not attached to bits set in the lizard's mouths. Those thick jaws could have bitten through steel. Instead, they were joined to rings punched through each nostril. Gentle tugs at these sensitive areas were sufficient to guide the course of the lumbering dray.

His attention shifted to a much closer and more intriguing figure. From his slouched position he could see only flaming curls and the silver-threaded shape of her blouse and pants, the latter curving deliciously over the back edge of the wooden seat.

Whether she felt his eyes or not he couldn't tell, but once she glanced sharply back down at him. Instead of turning embarrassedly away he met her stare. For a moment they were eye to eye. That was all. No insults this time. When he stepped further with a slight smile, more from instinct than intent, she simply turned away. She had not smiled back, but neither had that acid tongue heaped further abuse on him.

He settled back against the wooden side of the wagon, trying to rest. She was under a lot of pressure, he told himself. Enough to make anyone edgy and impolite. No doubt in less dangerous surroundings she was considerably less antagonistic.

He wondered whether that was likely or if he was simply rationalizing away behavior that upset him. It was admittedly difficult to attribute such bellicosity to such a beautiful lady. Not to mention the fact that it was bad for a delicate male ego.

Shut up, he told himself. You've got more important things to worry about. Think with your head instead of your gonads. What are you going to tell Clothahump when you see him again? It might be best to . . .

He wondered how old she actually was. Her diminutive size was the norm among local humans and hinted at nothing. He already knew her age to be close to his own because she hadn't contradicted his earlier comment about it. She seemed quite mature, but that could be a normal consequence of a life clearly somewhat tougher than his own. He also wondered what she would look like naked, and had reason to question his own maturity.

Think of your surroundings, Meriweather. You're trapped, tired, alone, and in real danger.

Alone . . . well, he would try his best to be friends with her, if she'd permit it. It was absurd to deny he found her attractive, though every time she opened her mouth she succeeded in stifling any serious thoughts he might be developing about extending that hoped-for friendship.

They *had* to become friends. She was human, and that in itself was enough to make him homesick and desperate. Maybe when they'd deposited the bodies at whatever location they were rolling toward she would relax a little.

That prompted him to wonder and worry about just where they *were* taking their injured cargo, and what was going to be done with it when they got there.

A moan came from beneath the blanket behind him, light and hesitant. He thought it came from the squirrelquette, though he couldn't be certain.

"There's a doctor out on the edge of town," Talea said in response to his expression of concern.

"Glad to hear it." So there was at least a shred of soul to complement the beauty. Good. He watched in silence as a delicately wrought two-wheeled buggy clop-clopped past their wagon. The two moon-eyed wallabies in the cab were far too engrossed in each other to so much as glance at the occupants of the wagon, much less at the lumpy cargo it carried.

Half conscious now, the little squirrel was beginning to kick and roll in counterpoint to her low moans. If she reawakened fully, things would become awkward. He resolved that in spite of his desire to make friends with Talea, he would bolt from the wagon rather than help her inflict any more harm. But after several minutes the movement subsided, and the unfortunate victim relapsed into silence.

They'd been traveling for half an hour and were still among buildings. Despite their plodding pace, it hinted that Lynchbany was a good-sized community. In fact, it might be even larger than he supposed, since he didn't know if they'd started from the city center or its outskirts.

A two-story thatched-roof structure of stone and crisscrossed wooden support beams loomed off to their left. It leaned as if for support up against a much larger brooding stone building. Several smaller structures that had to be individual homes stretched off into the distance. A few showed lamps over their doorways, but most slept peacefully in the clinging mist.

No light showed in the two thick windows of the thatched building as Talea edged their wagon over close to it and brought it to a halt.

The street was quite empty. The only movement was from the mouths and nostrils of lizards and passengers, where the increasing chill turned their exhalations to momentarily thicker, tired fog. He wondered again at the reptiles. Maybe they were hybrids with warm blood; if not, they were being extremely active for cold-blooded creatures on such a cold night.

He climbed out of the back of the wagon and looked at the doorway close by. An engraved sign hung from two hooks over the portal. Letters painted in white declaimed:

NILANTHOS—PHYSICIAN AND APOTHECARY

A smaller sign in the near window listed the ailments that could be treated by the doctor. Some of them were unfamiliar to Jon-Tom, who knew a little of common disease but nothing whatsoever of veterinary medicine.

Mudge and Talea were both whispering urgently at him. He moved out of the street and joined them by the door.

It was recessed into the building, roofed over and concealed from the street. They were hidden from casual view as Talea knocked once, twice, and then harder a third time on the milky bubble-glass set into the upper part of the door. She ignored the louder bellpull.

They waited nervously but no one answered. At least no one passed them in the street, but an occasional distinct groan was now issuing from the back of the wagon.

" 'E's not in, 'e ain't." Mudge looked worried. "I know a Doctor Paleetha. 'E's clear across town, though, and I can't say 'ow trustworthy 'e be, but if we've no one else t' turn t' . . ."

There were sounds of movement inside and a low complaining voice coming closer. It was at that point that Jon-Tom became really scared for the first time since he'd materialized in this world. His first reactions had been more disbelief and confusion than fear, and later ones were tied to homesickness and terror of the unknown.

But now, standing in an alien darkened street, accomplice to assault and battery and so utterly, totally *alone,* he started to shake. It was the kind of real, gut-chilling fear that doesn't frighten as much as it numbs all reality. The whole soul and body just turn stone cold—cold as the water at the bottom of a country well—and thoughts are fixated on a single, simple, all-consuming thought.

I'm never going to get out of this alive.

I'm going to die here.

I want to go HOME!

Oddly enough, it was a more distant fear that finally began to return him to normal. The assault of paranoia began to fade as he considered his surroundings. A dark street not unlike many others, pavement, mist chill inside his nose; no fear in any of those. And what of his companions? A scintillating if irascible redhead and an oversized but intelligent otter, both of whom were allies and not enemies. Better to worry about Clothahump's tale of coming evil than his own miserable but hardly deadly situation.

"What's the matter, mate?" Mudge stared at him with genuine concern. "You're not goin' t' faint on me again, are you?"

"Just queasy," said Talea sharply, though not nearly as sharply as before. "It's a nasty business, this."

"No." Jon-Tom shook away the last clinging rags of fear. They vanished into the night. "It's not that. I'm fine, thanks." His true thoughts he kept to himself.

She looked at him uncertainly a moment longer, then turned back to the door as Mudge said, "I 'ear somethin'."

Footsteps sounded faintly from just inside. There was a rattling at the doorknob. Inside, someone cursed a faulty lock.

Their attention directed away from him, Jon-Tom dissected the fragment of Clothahump's warning whose import had just occurred to him.

If something could bring a great evil from his own world into this one, an evil which none here including Clothahump could understand, why could not that same maleficent force reverse the channel one day and thrust some similar unmentionable horror on his own unsuspecting world? Preoccupied as it was with petty politics and intertribal squabbles between nations, could it survive a powerful assault of incomprehensible and destructive magic from this world? No one would believe what was happening, just as he hadn't believed his first encounters with Clothahump's magic.

According to the aged wizard, an evil was abroad in this place and time that would make the minions of Nazism look like Sunday School kids. Would an evil like that be content at consuming this world alone, or would it reach out for further and perhaps simpler conquests?

As a student of history that was one answer he knew. The appetite of evil far exceeds that of the benign. Success fed rather than sated its appetite for destruction. That was a truth that had plagued mankind throughout its entire history. What he had seen around him since coming here did not lead him to think it would be otherwise with the force Clothahump so feared.

Somewhere in this world a terror beyond his imagining swelled and prepared. He pictured Clothahump again: the squat, almost comical turtle shape with its plastron compartments; the hexagonal little glasses; the absentminded way of speaking; and he forced himself to consider him beyond the mere physical image. He remembered the glimpses of Clothahump's real power. For all the insults Pog and Mudge levied at the wizard, they were always tinged with respect.

So on those rounded—indeed, nonexistent—shoulders rested possibly not only the destiny of one, but of two worlds: this, and his own, the latter dreaming innocently along in a universe of predictable physics.

He looked down at his watch, no longer ticking, remembered his lighter, which had flared efficiently one last time before running out of fuel. The laws of science functioned here as they did at home. Mudge had been unfamiliar with the "spell," the physics, which had operated his watch and lighter. Research here had taken a divergent path. Science in his own, magic in this one. The words were similar, but not the methodology of application.

Would not evil spells as well as benign ones operate to bewildering effect in his own world?

He took a deep breath. If such was the case, then he no longer had a safe place to run to.

If that was true, what was he doing here? He ought to be back at the Tree, not pleading to be sent home but offering what little help he could, if only his size and strength, to Clothahump. For if the turtle was not senile, if he was correct about the menace that Jon-Tom now saw threatened him anywhere, then there was a good chance he would die, and his parents, and his brother in Seattle, and . . .

The enormity of it was too much. Jon-Tom was no world-shaker. One thing at a time, boy, he told himself. You can't save worlds if you're locked up in a filthy local jail, puking your lunch all over yourself because the local cops don't play by the rules. As you surely will if you don't listen to Mudge and help this lovely lady.

"I'm all right now," he muttered softly. "We'll take things easy, pursue the internal logic. Just like researching a test case for class."

"Wot's that, mate?"

"Nothing." The otter eyed him a moment longer, then turned back to the door.

Life is a series of tests, Jon-Tom reminded himself. Where had he read that? Not in the laws of ancient Peru, or in Basic Torts or California Contracts. But he was ready for it now, for whatever sudden turns and twists life might throw at him.

Feeling considerably more at peace with himself and the universe, he stood facing the entrance and waited to be told what to do next.

The stubborn knob finally turned. A shape stood inside, staring back at them. Once it had been massively proportioned, but the flesh had sagged with age. The arms were nearly as long as the otter's whole body. One held a lantern high enough to shower light down even on Jon-Tom's head.

The old orangutan's whiskers shaded from russet to gray. His glasses were round and familiar, with golden metal rims. Jon-Tom decided that either wizardly spells for improving eyesight were unknown or else local magic had not progressed that far.

A flowing nightgown of silk and lace and a decidedly feminine cast clad that simian shape. Jon-Tom was careful not to snicker. Nothing surprised him anymore.

"Weel, what ees eet at thees howar?" He had a voice like a rusty lawnmower. Then he was squinting over the top rims of the glasses at Talea. "You. Don't I know you?"

"You should," she replied quickly. "Talea of the High Winds and Moonflame. I did a favor for you once."

Nilanthos continued to stare at her, then nodded slowly. "Ah yes. I reemeember you now. 'Taleea off thee poleece records and thee dubeeous reeputation,' " he said with a mocking smile.

Talea was not upset. "Then along with my reputation you'll recall those six vials of drugs I got for you. The ones whose possession is frowned upon by the sorceral societies, an exclusion extended even to," she coughed delicately, "physicians."

"Yees, yees, off course I reemeember." He sighed resignedly. "A deebt ees a deebt. What ees your probleem that you must call mee op from sleep so late?"

"We have two problems, actually." She started for the wagon. "Keep the door open."

Jon-Tom and Mudge joined her. Hastily they threw aside the blanket and wrestled out the two unlucky victims of Talea's nighttime activities. The muskrat was now snoring noisily and healthily, much to Jon-Tom's relief.

Nilanthos stood aside, holding the lamp aloft while the grisly delivery was hauled inside. He peered anxiously out into the street.

"Surgeree ees een back."

"I . . . remember." Talea grunted under her half of squirrelquette burden. Blood dripped occasionally onto the tiled floor. "You offered me a free 'examination,' remember?"

The doctor closed and locked the door, made nervous quieting motions. "Sssh, pleese. If you wakeen thee wife, I weel not bee able to canceel my half off thee deebt. And no talk off exameenations."

"Quit trembling. I just like to see you sweat a little, that's all."

Nilanthos followed them, his attention now on the limp form slung over Jon-Tom's shoulders. "Eef eether off theese pair are dead, wee weel all sweat a leetle." Then his eyes widened as he apparently recognized the blubbering muskrat.

"Good God, eet's Counceelman Avelleeum! Couldn't you have peeked a leess dangerous veecteem? He could have us all drawn and quarteered."

"He won't," she insisted. "I'm depending on you to see to that."

"You and your good nature." Nilanthos closed the door behind them, moved to spark the oil lamps lining the surgery. "You might have been beetter off leeting theem die."

"And what if they hadn't? What if they'd lived and remembered who attacked them? It was dark, but I can't be sure they'd never recognize me again."

"Yees, yees, I see what you mean," he said thoughtfully. He stood at a nearby sink and was washing long-fingered hands carefully.

"Weel then, what story should I geeve theem wheen they are brought around?" He was pulling on gloves and returning to the large central table on which the two patients had been deposited.

Jon-Tom leaned back against a wall and watched with interest. Mudge paced the surgery and looked bored. Actually, he was keeping one eye on Nilanthos while searching for anything he might be able to swipe undetected.

With a more personal interest in the welfare of the two victims, Talea stood close to the table as Nilanthos commenced his preliminary examination.

"Tell them they had an accident," she instructed him.

"What kind off acceedent?"

"They ran into something." He looked over at her skeptically and she shrugged. "My fist. And the iron chain I had wrapped around it. And maybe a wall. Look, you're a doctor. Think of something reasonable, convince them. Some passersby found them and brought them to you."

He shook his head dolefully. "Why a primate as attracteeve as yourseelf would eendulge een such neefarious doings ees more than I can fathom, Taleea."

She moved back from the table. "You fix them up, and let me take care of me."

Several minutes passed and the examination continued. "Thee Counceelman weel bee fine. Hee has onlee a mild concussion and minor cuts and bruises. I know. I weel make arrangements to have heem deeposited on hees front doorstep by a couple off rats I know who weel do that sort off work weethout letting cureeosity get een their way." He turned his gaze on the squirrelquette, long fingers moving carefully through her hair.

"Theese one ees not as good. There ees a chance off a skull fracture." He looked up at Talea. "That means posseeble eenternal eenjuries." The subject of the examination moaned softly.

"She seems lively enough," Talea commented.

"Appeerances can deeceive, eespecially weeth head eenjuriees." He was applying disinfectant and then bandaging to the wound. The bandage promptly began to show a dark stain. "I'll just have to watch her carefullee. Do you by any chance know her?" Talea shook her head.

"Neither do I. The Counceelman's lady for thee evening. Probably lady *off* thee eevening, too. Shee'll bee angry when shee regains consciousness, but no dangeer. I'll see to that, too."

"Good." Talea started for the exit, hesitated, put a hand on the orang's broad shoulder. "Thanks, Nilanthos. You've more than canceled out our debt. Now I owe you. Call on me if you need *my* services."

The physician replied with a wide simian leer.

"Professionally, I mean." The leer broadened. "You are impossible, Nilanthos!" She feigned a swing at him.

"Do not strike thee doctor while hee ees een thee process off performing hees heeling duties."

"That's a laugh! But I still owe you."

"Honor among theeves, ees that eet?" He looked seriously down at the squirrelquette and the now badly stained bandage wrapped around her skull. "Veree weel. For now eet's best eef you all geet out off heer." He said it while staring at Mudge.

The otter nodded, moved away from the slipcatch-latched drug-and-narcotics case where he'd been idling the past several minutes.

"What's the hurry?" Jon-Tom wanted to know.

Mudge put a hand on his arm, pulled him along. "Be you daft, mate? We've got t' get out o' town."

"But I don't . . . I thought . . ." He barely remembered to duck as they exited the surgery. "If Doctor Nilanthos is going to take care of things as he said, why do we have to run?"

"Cor, he can take away the worries as far as those two in there be concerned, but someone else might 'ave seen us. They might even now be reportin' us t' the police. Your size makes us too conspicuous, lad. We 'ave t' leave, especially after that fight in the Pearl Possum."

"But I still don't see . . ."

"Not *now,* mate." Mudge was insistent. They were out in the dark street again.

"Come on, Jon-Tom," said Talea. "Don't make trouble."

He halted, stared open-mouthed at her. *"Me* make trouble? I've been the innocent victim of trouble ever since I set foot in this stinking, lousy excuse for a world."

"Easy now, mate." Mudge looked sideways at him. "Don't be sayin' somethin' you may be sorry for later."

Jon-Tom's carefully constructed calm had lasted about ten minutes. His voice rose unreasonably, echoing in the mist. "I don't regret anything I have to say!" Talea was looking back toward town, clearly upset. "I want to see some of the goodness, the kindness that this world should have."

"Should 'ave?" Mudge looked confused. "By who's determination?"

"By the . . ." His voice trailed off. What could he say? By the rights of legend. What legend? By logic? Mudge was right.

"Oh, never mind." The anger and frustration which had flared inside faded quickly. "So we're fugitives. So I make us conspicuous. That's the way it is." He nodded at nothing in particular. "Let's get going, then."

He vaulted into the back of the wagon. Mudge climbed into the front seat, caught Talea's questioning glance, and could only shrug blankly. She hefted the reins and let out a vibrant whistle. The somnolent lizards came awake, leaned forward into their reins. The wagon resumed its steady forward motion, the thick feet of its team sounding like sacks of flour landing on the damp pavement.

Jon-Tom noted that they were headed out of town, as Mudge had insisted they must. Houses decorated with little gardens slipped past. No lights showed in their windows at this stygian hour.

They passed the last street lamp. Here the road turned from cobblestone to gravel. Even that gave way to a muddy track only a little while later. All light had vanished behind them.

It was deep night of early morning now. The mist continued to dog them, keeping them wet and chilled. Never is the winter so cloying as at night.

Among the occupants of the wagon only Jon-Tom had a lingering concern for the greater night that threatened to do more to the world than chill it. Talea and Mudge are creatures of the moment, he thought. They cannot grasp the significance of Clothahump's visions. He huddled deeper under the gray blanket, ignoring the persistent aroma of the squirrelquette's perfume. It clashed with the smell of dried blood.

Thunder crossed the sky overhead, oral signatory to the last distant vestiges of the night storm. It helped them bid farewell to Lynchbany. He was not sorry to leave.

Soon they were in the woods. Oaks and elms showed familiar silhouettes against the more melodious boles of belltree and coronet vine. The latter generated an oboesque sob as if pleading for the advent of day and the refreshing heat of the sun.

For hours they plodded steadily on. The road wound like a stream around the hills, taking advantage of the lowest route, never cresting more than an occasional rise. Small lakes and ponds sometimes flanked the trail. They were inhabited by a vast assortment of aquatic lizards who meeped and gibbered in place of frogs. Each glowed a different color, some green, others red or pink, still others a rich azure. Each bubble of sound was accompanied by an increase in light. The ponds were full of chirping searchlights that drifted from branch to bank.

Jon-Tom watched the water and its luminescent reptilians fade behind them. The ponds became a brook which ran fast and friendly alongside the rutted wagon track. Unlike the other travelers it was indifferent to who might overhear its conversation, and it gurgled merrily while teasing their wheels.

Resignation gave way once more to his natural curiosity.

"Well, we're long out of town." He spoke to Talea. "Where are we going?" Rising to his knees he reached out a hand to steady himself in the jouncing wagon. It gave an unexpected lurch to the right, and he caught her side instead of the back of the seat. Hastily he moved his fingers, but she had neither moved away nor protested.

"Somewhere where we can't be trapped," she replied. "For God knows even a blithering Lynchbany cop could piss and track the ruts of this wagon at the same time. Like any other creature we retreat to a lair and we don't fight unless we're cornered. And where we're going not even the police will dare come."

"I ain't sure I'd agree to that." Mudge sounded more hopeful than assured. " 'Tis more of an uneasy truce."

"Nonetheless," she countered, "we're far more likely to be safe there than anyplace else." Jon-Tom still gazed questioningly at her.

"We're going to the local branch of the intracounty association of disadvantaged self-employed artisans and underachievers," she explained.

"Thieves' Hall," Mudge grunted. . . .

VIII

They spent the rest of the night curled beneath the thick blanket in the back of the wagon. Mudge and Talea were soon as motionless as her former victims, but Jon-Tom was too keyed up to sleep. Talea was silent as a stone, but a steady snoring in the form of a high-pitched whistle came from the gray-clad lump that was Mudge.

Jon-Tom lay on his back and studied the night sky, framed by the overhanging branches of the trees. Some of the constellations overhead were familiar, though out of place. Location as well as season was different here. It was a great comfort, however, to see the easily recognizable shape of Orion standing stalwart as ever against the interstellar vastness.

Once something with ghostly gray fluorescent wings passed between him and the moon, a delicate crinoid shape that might have been a reptile, or bird, or something unimaginable. It trailed thin yellow streamers behind it, and for an instant it glittered in the sky.

Then it was gone behind the trees. A low hiccoughing came from some concealed arboreal thing.

Tiny feet sounded like twigs on the road. Their owner paused to sniff at the wagon wheels before skittering onward. Sycamores and gingkos conversed in low philosophical woodtones. They lulled him finally into a deep, dreamless sleep. . . .

He awoke to a welcome sun filtering down through the leaves and a weight on his left shoulder. Turning his head, he saw Talea snuggled up against him. She was sleeping on her side, resting on his shoulder, one arm thrown limply across his chest. He had mixed feelings about disturbing the sculpture.

However . . . they had a destination. He moved a little. Her eyes fluttered, body stirred. She blinked, simultaneously taking note of both him and proximity. As she pulled away, she rubbed sleep from her eyes.

"Easy night," she murmured thickly, "though I've had softer beds."

"Me too." To his surprise he saw that Mudge was already wide awake. He had no idea how long the otter had lain there watching them.

"Best we be on about our business," the otter said brightly. "The Lynchbany lockups ain't particularly persistent, but if it was a slow night a few ambitious types might've elected to come follow." He stood up, gestured back down the road.

"Personally I think we're well clear of 'em, but you never can be sure."

"Right." She was climbing into the driver's seat. "Best never to take chances with a skunk."

Shortly they were trundling once more down a road that had become hardly more than a trail. They'd turned off, he noted, on a branch that was almost devoid of wagon ruts. Their absence was compensated for by large rocks that did nothing to help his kidneys.

They paused later for a Spartan breakfast of bread, jerky, and a kind of dried fruit that resembled lime but tasted much better. Then off again.

It was noon when Talea indicated they'd arrived. Jon-Tom peered ahead between her and the otter. "I don't see anything."

"What did you think?" she asked archly. "That a place like the local branch of the intracounty . . . a place like Thieves' Hall would announce itself with flying banners and a brass band?"

They turned down a still narrower path and penetrated as deeply into the dense woods as trees would allow. After a half-mile walk they came to a crude corral filled with an astonishing assortment of reptilian mounts. Several hundred yards off to the right of this open-air stable Talea located a metal doorway. It lay half hidden beneath the roots of several massive oaks and was set directly into the rock face of a low-browed cliff.

She rapped hard on the metal three times with her open palm, waited, then repeated the knock.

Presently a small window opened in the top of the door. No face showed itself. It was easy enough for whoever was within to see outside without placing an eye invitingly near a possible knife thrust.

"Succor and surcease, comfort and respite to those who know how to live," said a voice from within.

"T' practice usury without interference," Mudge responded promptly. "T' get one's fair share. T' never givin' a sucker an even break."

There was a pause and then the door swung outward on rusty hinges. Talea entered first, followed by Mudge. Jon-Tom had to bend almost double to clear the ceiling.

Inside they confronted a muscular otter a couple of inches taller than Mudge. He inspected them cautiously, reserving particular attention for Jon-Tom.

"That one I don't know."

" 'E's a friend." Mudge smiled as he spoke. "An acquaintance from a far province, wot?" He did not elaborate on that, nor did he mention Clothahump.

The other otter blew his nose on the floor and turned perfunctorily away. They followed. Before long they passed a series of interlocking tunnels. These all seemed to devolve into a much larger central cavern. It was filled with a noisy, raunchy, squalling crowd that made the patrons of the Pearl Possum look like nursery schoolers their first day away from home.

There was enough sharpened steel in that one room to fight a small war. A fair amount of dried blood on the stone floor showed that those instruments were frequently in use. In the enclosed area the noise was close to deafening. Not to mention the odor. He'd almost come to ignore the animal smells, but in that tight, poorly ventilated chamber, populated as it was by a less than usually hygienic assembly, it was overpowering.

"What do we do now?"

"First we find the president of the local chapter," Talea explained, "and pay our protection money. That allows us to stay here. Then we find a piece of unoccupied tunnel. There are hundreds of them honeycombing this hillside. We set up temporary housekeeping and lie low until the councilman has a chance to forget what happened to him.

"Of course, he may buy Nilanthos' explanation, but I wouldn't put it past his type to check out any citizen's reports for that night. That's where we could have trouble, remember. We'll wait here a couple of weeks until it all turns to memory-mush. Then we can safely leave."

At his look of distress, Mudge said, "Don't look so ill, mate. Crikey, 'tis only for a couple o' weeks." He grinned. "Lynchbany cops 'ave mem'ries as brief as their courage. But it do behoove us t' stay out o' sight o' casual travelers for a while. None save the completely daft are likely t' come within leagues o' this spot."

Jon-Tom focused on well-used swords and knives. "I can't imagine why not," he said drily, trying to hold his breath.

As it turned out they did not utilize Thieves' Hall for two weeks. It was less than a day before Jon-Tom made his mistake. It didn't seem like a mistake at the time, and afterward he was too confused to be sorry.

There was a game. It was common in Lynchbany and well known among those who preyed upon the townsfolk. It involved the use of triangular dice and a circle. There were no hidden complexities.

A good student like Jon-Tom had no trouble picking it up, after a few hours of careful study. He was still a mite hesitant about actually participating, but Talea was off somewhere chatting with friends and Mudge had simply disappeared. Left on his own and mentally exhausted, he was both bored and irritable. A little game playing would be good for him.

Clothahump's purse still contained a few tiny copperpieces, the remnants of the Mudge-directed spending spree that had enriched several of Lynchbany's merchants. Cutting an impressive figure in his flashing green cape, Jon-Tom leaned on his club-staff and studied one of the several continuous games before finally deciding to join.

The particular game he'd selected seemed to be the largest. With the greater number of participants he would have more opportunities between throws to study the play. No one objected to or commented on his joining. It was simply a matter of taking the place of a distraught lynx when the latter ran out of money and dropped out.

Through no particular skill (the fickleness of dice being everywhere constant) he did quite well. Dutifully, he concentrated on doing still better. So intent on the game did he become that he failed to notice that he was drawing something of a crowd of onlookers.

Players angrily left and were replaced by eager newcomers, full of fresh spirit and fresh cash. There were always nine or ten throwers seated or squatting around the circle.

The rock was cold against his backside, even through the leather pants. Not quite as chilled were the well-traveled coins beginning to stack up in front of him. For the first time in a long while he was not only relaxed but enjoying himself.

Much to the delight of the crowd, which always pulls for a big winner, he hit two nines in a row. Mutterings of magic came from a few of the other players. They remained mere mutterings. An aged bat named Swal hung himself from the overhead lamps. From there he could watch all the players. His opinion was well respected, Jon-Tom could tell, and his knowledge of magic extensive though he was no wizard himself. Very poor basketball players can make very fine coaches. Swal had a detailed knowledge of magic though he couldn't work any himself.

Nevertheless, one of the other players tried to turn the tide in his own favor, attempting to magic the dice before his turn to throw came up. Neither Jon-Tom nor any of the other players or onlookers caught the unnatural vibration, but the outraged Swal noticed it immediately.

"He muttered it softly, but I tasted the end of it," Swal explained to the crowd.

At that point Jon-Tom had a sampling of thieves' justice in a world where normal justice was not known for its temperance. A group of angry spectators hauled the screaming, protesting gopher out of sight. This was followed by a brief pause, then a single nerve-twisting screech. Wiping their paws and looking grimly satisfied, the vigilantes soon returned.

Another member of the game was throwing, and Jon-Tom had time to turn and ask an onlooker what had happened.

The tall rabbit leaned low on his shoulder. "Swal say that one mutter it softly. You no cheat in Thieves' Hall. Like cheat you brother, you know? I expect they make punishment fit the crime." Jon-Tom continued to stare questioningly up at the other.

The rabbit shrugged. "Since he whisper the formula, others probably cut out his tongue. If he done divinations with his hands, they would have cut them off. Same for eye, and so on."

"Isn't that kind of extreme? It's only a friendly game."

Oddly milky pink eyes looked down at him. "This an extreme business we all in, man. You know that. Difficult enough to get by without having to cope with cheating courts and sly lawyers. We can't stand backstabbingers among own family. Fair punishments like that," and he jerked a thumb back toward the region of the scream, "make sure fairness good sense. You stay healthy, hear; that one was lucky. What line you in?"

"Sorry . . . my dice," Jon-Tom said quickly.

The game continued. Sometimes he lost, more often he won. Now the continued absence of Talea and Mudge was making him nervous. He wondered if he dare take his winnings and drop out. Might not one of the game's big losers have a friend or associate in the crowd, ready to stick a small knife in Jon-Tom's back or accuse him of magic in order to protect his friend or boss?

But the tall rabbit remained close by, reassuring and urging him on. That was only natural, since he was betting along with Jon-Tom's rolls. Yet Jon-Tom's thoughts kept returning to that horrible scream, kept imagining the knife coming down, the blood spurting. . . .

Swal the bat kept his post. Occasionally he would shift his perch on the hanging lamps or tug at the green-feathered cap secured by a strap to his head. His eyes roved steadily over the players.

There were no more cries of cheating. The pile of coins in front of Jon-Tom continued its steady growth.

Then there was an unexpected pause in the action. A very sleek, lupine figure stumbled into the playing circle. The players scrambled to protect their coins from uncertain feet. She seemed outraged and embarrassed, a condition not helped by the catcalls and hoots from the male and female spectators. The bitch replied to the insinuations with a rustle of petticoats and some choice execrations of her own.

Jon-Tom looked to his rabbit friend for an explanation.

"Sorry, man. I wasn't paying attention. But I think I see what's going on. See that fox over there?" He pointed to a tired but well-dressed thrower seated across the circle. Only two or three small silver coins lay on the stone in front of him.

"He out of money I see, but he want to stay in. You know the type. So he bet the girl."

Jon-Tom frowned. "Is she a slave?"

That prompted a mildly angry response. "What you think we are here, barbarians? Only the Plated Folk keep slaves. No, most likely he gotten her to agree to temporary contract." The rabbit winked. "Most likely a couple of nights or so."

"She doesn't look very willing," said Jon-Tom critically.

"Hard to say. Maybe she is, maybe not."

"Then why is she doing it?"

"Because she in love. Can't you see that?" The rabbit sounded surprised at Jon-Tom's evident naïveté.

"Hey . . . I can't play this round."

"Why not, man?" Suddenly the rabbit sounded considerably less friendly.

"I just think I've had enough." He was starting to gather up his winnings, looking for pockets in pants and shirt to shove handfuls of coins into. The other players looked upset and there were some movements in his direction.

But there was honor among thieves here, too. For every angry grumbling from the players there were cries from the onlookers of, "He won fair. . . . The man can pull out any time! . . . Let him leave if he wants. . . . You can't stop him. . . ." and so forth. But some of the comments were accompanied by eager looks at the pile of coins in front of him. It occurred to Jon-Tom that winning the money was no assurance he'd leave with it. Of course, no one would think of making an outright attack on an honest winner. But Thieves' Hall was full of tunnels and dark cul-de-sacs.

He looked helplessly up at the rabbit, whispered, "What should I do?"

The other's attitude softened, turned friendly once again.

"Well first thing, pay attention to you own clothing." He laughed and reached for Jon-Tom's throat. Jon-Tom instinctively started to pull away, but the rabbit only paused and grinned hugely at him. "With you permission?"

Jon-Tom hesitated, then nodded. There was no reason to assume the animal had turned suddenly hostile.

Unclipping the cape while the rest of the players waited impatiently, the rabbit spread it out on the floor. "Ah, I thought right so. Good tailor you got," and he pointed out the hidden stitching and buttons lining the bottom hem of the cape.

This he carefully unsnapped. With Jon-Tom's help, he filled the hidden compartment with handfuls of coins. When it was full to the snaps they sealed it tight again. Jon-Tom clipped it back around his neck. The weight was a tolerable drag.

"There," said the rabbit with satisfaction, "that be more better. No one think to pickpocket a cape. Only these few here, and I see no skilled one among them. Others who see will think only rocks in there."

"Why would I fill my cape with rocks?"

"To keep it from blow over you head and blind you in a fight, or while riding in a storm. Also to use in a fight. You may look weaponless, but what you got now is five-foot flexible club to complement long staff." He turned his gaze skyward. "That how I like to go,

though. Beaten to death with somebody's money. Or perhaps . . ."
He looked back over at Jon-Tom. "It no matter my problems."

"Maybe it does." Jon-Tom reached into the still sizable pile of
coins in front of him and selected three large gold circles. "These are
for your problems. And for your good advice and counsel."

The rabbit took them gratefully, slipped them in a vest pocket, and
sealed it. "That kind of you, man. I take because I need the money.
Under better circumstances I refuse. More advice: don't go passing
around gold too much like this. You attract attention of some not so
noble as I.

"Now as to what you should do, you pull out now if you really
want. But you in middle of round. It be better if you finish this one
go-round. Then no one can say shit to you."

"But what about the girl?" The bitch was tapping feet clad in
pastel blue ballet slippers and looking quite put out.

"Well, I tell you man," and he winked significantly, "you finish out
this round. I have three goldpieces you know. You have place in
circle to finish. If you win, I give you back gold circle for her." He
eyed the muscular, tawny form of the she-wolf. "Maybe two."

"Oh, all right." He looked a last time at the ring of spectators. Still
no sign of Mudge or Talea.

The dice were passed as the watchers nudged one another, muttered, made side bets, or simply stared curiously. A ferret on the far
side rolled a seven, moaned. Next to him was a mole wearing immensely thick dark glasses and a peaked derby. He dumped an eight,
then a six, then a seven, and finally a losing three.

The dice came around to Jon-Tom. He tossed them into the circle.
Two fours and a two. Then a ten. The dice went to the fisher on his
right. He rolled a ten. Cries went up from the crowd, which pushed
and shoved discourteously at the circle of players. Jon-Tom rolled a
six. Back to the fisher, who looked confident. Over went the three
dice, came up showing a one, a two, and a three. The fisher kicked
dirt into the circle. The shouts were ear-shaking.

Jon-Tom had won again.

He spoke as he turned. "There you go, friend. It's time to . . ."
He stopped. There was no sign of the rabbit.

Only a smartly dressed howler monkey nearby had noted the disappearance of Jon-Tom's advisor. "The tall fella? White with gray
patches?" Jon-Tom nodded, and the simian gestured vaguely back
down a main passage.

"He went off that way a while ago. So little golden ground squirrel came up to him . . . delicate little bit of fluff she was . . . and he went off with her."

"But I can't . . ."

A hand touched his shoulder. He turned, found himself staring across into aluminum-like eyes, glistening and penetrating. "I have not done it with many humans, man. I understand some of you are fond of strange practices." The voice was low, husky, and not altogether uninterested. "Is that true also with you?"

"Listen, I don't think you understand."

"Try me."

"No, no . . . that's not what I meant. I mean . . ." He was more flustered than at any time since they'd entered the hall. "It's just that I can't, I don't want you. Go back there." He waved across the circle. "Go back to him."

"Just what the hell are you implying, man?" Her eyes flashed and she stepped back.

The fox was suddenly standing next to her, angry at something other than his losing. "Something wrong with Wurreel? Do you think I need your charity?"

"No, it's not that at all." He slowly climbed to his feet, kept a firm grip on the staff. Around him the crowd was murmuring in an unfriendly manner. The looks he was receiving were no longer benign.

"Please," he told the bitch, "just go back to your master here, or friend, or whatever."

The fox moved nearer, jabbed a clawed finger in Jon-Tom's stomach. "Just what kind of fellow are you? Do you think I don't pay my debts? Do you think I'd renege on my obligations?"

"Screw your obligations, Mossul," said the wolf haughtily, "What about my honor?" Her tone and gaze were now anything but interested. "See how he looks at me, with disgust. I am insulted."

That brought a nasty series of cries from the crowd. "Shame, shame! . . . down with him!"

"It's not that. I just . . . don't want you."

She made an inarticulate growl, hit him in the chest with a fist. "That does it!" She looked around at the shifting circle of spectators. "Is there a male here who will defend my reputation? I demand satisfaction . . . of this kind if not the other!"

"Your reputation . . ." Jon-Tom was becoming badly tongue-tied. "I didn't insult . . . what about him?" He pointed at the fox. "He was the one selling you."

"Loaning, not selling," countered the fox with dignity. "And it was mutually agreed upon."

"That's right. I'd do anything for Mossul. Except be insulted, like this, in public." She put an affectionate arm around the fox's silk-clad shoulders.

"Turn him out, turn him out!" came the rising shouts.

"Wot's 'appening 'ere, mate. I leave you alone for a bit and you manage t' upset the 'ol 'all." Mudge was at Jon-Tom's back and Talea nearby.

"I don't understand," Jon-Tom protested. "I've been winning all day."

"That's good."

"And I just won that," and he indicated the she-wolf, "for a couple of nights."

"That's very good. So what's your problem, mate?"

"I don't want her. Don't you understand? It's not that she's unattractive or anything." The subject of that appraisal growled menacingly. "It's just that . . . I can't do it, Mudge. I'm not prejudiced. But something inside me just . . . can't."

"Easy now, mate. I understand." The otter sounded sympathetic. " 'Tis part o' your strange customs, no doubt, and you're the loser for it."

"Well, tell them that. Tell them where I'm from. Explain to them that I'm . . ."

Mudge put a hand momentarily over Jon-Tom's mouth. "Hush, lad. If they think that you're from some other land, no matter 'ow alien, you won't longer 'ave their protection. As it be, they think you're a local footpad like Talea and meself." His eyes noted the weight dragging down the hem of Jon-Tom's cape. "And judgin' from wot you've won from some 'ere, they'd be more than 'appy to see you made fair game. You wouldn't last twenty seconds." He pulled at an arm. "Come on now. Quiet and confident's the words, while they're still arguin' wot t' do."

They were bumped and even spat upon, but Mudge and Talea managed to hustle their thoroughly confused friend out of the gambling chamber, through the tunnels, and back out the iron door that sealed off the hall from the outside world.

It was mid-morning outside. Jon-Tom suddenly realized how exhausted he was. He must have played through the night. That explained why he hadn't seen Talea or Mudge. They'd been sleeping. But it was time-deceptive inside Thieves' Hall, where the lamps burned round the clock, much in keeping with the activities of the members.

"Why didn't you go with her?" Talea sounded bitter. "Now look at us! Forced out of the one refuge where we'd be impregnable." She stalked on ahead, searching the nearby corral for their team and wagon.

"I suppose I should have lost." He and Mudge had to hurry to keep pace with her. "That would have made you happy, wouldn't it?"

"It would be better than this," she snapped back. "Where do we go now? When you're turned out of Thieves' Hall, there's no place else to run to, and we haven't been in hiding near long enough. We'll still be fresh in the minds of citizens and police, if anyone noticed us. Damn it all!" She jumped the fence, kicked at the flank of an innocent riding lizard. It hissed and scuttled out of her way.

"It's too bad you weren't around, Mudge. You could have played that last round for me."

"It don't work that way, mate. You 'ad t' play it out yourself, from what I 'eard. 'Tis a pity your peculiar customs forced you t' insult that lovely lady's honor. You refused 'er. I couldn't 'ave substituted meself for you thatawise, much willin' as I would've been."

Jon-Tom stared morosely at the ground. "I can't believe she was trading herself willingly like that."

"Blimey lad, 'tis bloody ignorant you be about women. She did it for love of 'er fox-chap. Couldn't you see that? And so when you refused 'er, you insulted 'im as well. You don't know much about the leanin's o' ladies, do you?"

"That's ridiculous. Of course I . . . ." He looked away. "No. No, not a great deal, Mudge. My energies have been pretty much focused on intellectual pursuits. That's one reason why I wanted to be a musician so badly. Musicians don't seem to have to worry about women."

"There not be much pleasure in ignorance, mate. You're a damnsight better off understandin' the whys and wherefores o' what's goin' on." He nodded ahead.

"Now 'ave a look at dear Talea there. Don't tell me you don't find 'er attractive."

"I'd by lying if I said otherwise."

"Well then? Close enough quarters we've been living in these past few days and I 'aven't seen you so much as lean close t' 'er. Me she knows and won't let near, but you're a new factor."

"You've got to be kidding." He watched that mane of red hair bob and weave its way among the herd. "If I so much as touched her she'd split me from brain to belly."

"Don't be so sure, mate. You've already confessed your ignorance, you know."

"And you're the expert, I suppose?"

"I get by on experience, yes. Not much time for that now. But think on what I've said."

"I will. Mudge, what she said about us having no place to go, are we that desperate?"

" 'Ard to say, mate. Depends on whether anyone reported our late-night doin's in Lynchbany. But we'd best move on t' somewhere else for a while."

"I know where I want to go." He looked longingly skyward, though he knew that his world was beyond even the stars that lay hidden behind the sunlight.

Something stung the side of his face. He turned and looked in shock at Mudge.

"A long way to reach with an open palm," the otter said tightly. "Now you listen well, mate. I've told you before and I don't aim to waste time on it again. These maudlin sorrowings for yourself 'ave to stop. You're 'ere. We can't get you back where you belong. Clotha-hump can't or won't get you back t' where you belong. That's bloody well it, and the sooner you get used t' it, the better it'll go for you. Or do you expect me t' wet-nurse you through your next sixty years?"

Jon-Tom, still stunned, didn't reply. Sixty years . . . odd how he hadn't thought of his stay here in terms of years, much less decades. There was always the thought that he could be going home tomorrow, or the next day.

But if Clothahump's genius was as erratic as Mudge insisted, he might never be going home. The wizard could die tomorrow. That night in Lynchbany outside Dr. Nilanthos' he'd reached a temporary accommodation with his situation. Maybe Mudge was right, and it was time he made that accommodation permanent.

Try to regard it like negative thinking for an exam. That way you're only satisfied if you fail, happy with a fifty, and ecstatic with a hundred. That's how you're going to have to start thinking of your life. Right now he was living a zero. The sooner he got used to it, the less disappointed he'd be if Clothahump proved unable to send him back. Back to the lazy mental meanderings of school, the casual tripe mumbled by directionless friends, the day-to-day humdrum existence he'd been leading that inaccessibility now made so tempting.

Zero, he told himself firmly. Remember the zero.

"Goddam rotten son-of-a-bitch! Shit-holes, all of 'em!"

The cry came from the other side of the corral. He and Mudge hurried through the packed animals. But Talea was not in danger. Instead she sat tiredly on a smooth rock while riding lizards of varying size and shape milled nervously around her.

"Stinking sneaky bastards," she rumbled. Jon-Tom started to say something but turned at a touch on his arm. Mudge put a finger to his whiskers, shook his head slowly.

They waited while the bile burned itself up. She finally looked up and seemed to take notice of them. Then she rose and swept an arm around the corral.

"Our wagon's gone. I've been through the whole glade and it's not here. Neither's our team. Do you know what I went through to steal that team?"

"Mossul's friends might have slipped out and run it off to help him cover 'is losses. Or it might 'ave been done as punishment for the insult we did the she-wolf," Mudge said thoughtfully, caressing his whiskers.

"I'll fry the gizzards of whoever's responsible!" She started back toward the hall. Mudge intercepted her quickly. She pushed at him, tried to dodge around, but he was as heavy as she and far faster. Eventually she just stood there, glaring at him.

"Be reasonable, luv. We barely slipped out of there without 'avin' to cut anyone. We can't go back in. Anger's no substitute for another sword. Even if we did get back in clear and free we're just guessin' as to who's responsible. We can't be sure it's Mossul or 'is friends."

The glare softened to a look of resignation. "You're right, otter. As usual." She slumped down on the mossy earth and leaned back against a fence rail. "So much, then, for 'honor among thieves.' "

"I'm sorry." Jon-Tom sat down next to her. "It was my fault. If it means anything, I'll be happy to pay you back for the cart." He jiggled the clinking hem of his cape meaningfully.

"Don't be ridiculous. I stole it. You needn't worry about paying back what you don't owe."

They considered their situation. "We could buy someone else's cart," he suggested.

Mudge looked doubtful. "Good transportation's dearer to a thief than any amount o' money. We could buy such in town, but not 'ere."

"Well then, why don't we steal some of these?"

"Now that's not a bad idea, mate. You're startin' to adapt. Save for one little complication." He looked to his right. At first Jon-Tom saw nothing. Then he noticed the little knot of figures that had appeared outside the Hall entrance. Puffs of smoke rose from the small crowd, and he could see an occasional glance in their direction.

"But they don't know which cart or steeds are ours," Jon-Tom protested. "If we acted like we knew what we were doing, they couldn't tell we were up to anything."

Mudge smiled slightly. "On the other 'and, we don't know that we might not pick on one o' their mounts. A single shout could bring the whole o' Thieves' 'All out on us."

"A pox on this!" said Talea abruptly, springing to her feet. "So we walk, but we're going back to see this wizard of yours. He's bound to put us up for a few days. Might even be safer than the Hall. And we can even pay him." She indicated Jon-Tom's winnings.

"Now 'old on a minim, luv." Mudge looked worried. "If we return there so soon, I'll 'ave t' admit I've run into some difficulties in educatin' this lad."

"Difficulties!" Jon-Tom laughed aloud. "You've already managed to involve me in a local tavern brawl, a police matter, and you," he looked at Talea, "in a mugging and robbery. Two robberies. I suppose I have to count in the cart and team, now."

"Count it any way you like, Jon-Tom." She gestured to the west. "But we can't go to town just yet, and we can't use the hall. I'm not about to strike off into the forest toward somewhere distant like Fifeover or Timswitty. Besides, they cooperate with the Lynchbany cops."

"Be that as it may," said Mudge, folding his arms, "I'm not goin' back t' Clothahump's. The old bugger's too unpredictable for my comfort."

"Suit yourself." She looked up at Jon-Tom. "I think you know the way. You afraid of Clothahump, too?"

"You bet your ass I am," he replied promptly, "but I don't think he's the vengeful type, and I can't think of anything else to do."

She gestured expansively. "After you, Jon-Tom."

He turned and started out of the corral, heading south and hoping his sense of direction wasn't too badly distorted by the time they'd spent riding the night. Mudge hesitated until they were nearly out of sight. Then he dropped a few choice words to the indifferent lizards and sprinted anxiously after the retreating humans. . . .

IX

Thieves' Hall was southeast of Lynchbany Towne. They had to cross the local roads carefully, for according to Talea you never knew when you might encounter a police patrol out for bandits. They also had to take time to hunt and gather food.

It was three days of hard walking before some of the forest started to look familiar to Mudge. They were standing by the side of a muddy, narrow road when Jon-Tom noticed the large sack that had been caught in the crook of a pair of boulders. There was the sparkle of sunlight on metal.

"Your eyes are good, Jon-Tom," said Talea admiringly, as they fell on the sack like three jackals on the half-gnawed carcass of a zebra.

The sack was full of trade goods. Glass beads, some semiprecious gems that might have been garnets or tourmalines, and some scrolls. Talea threw the latter angrily aside as they searched the sack for other valuables. There were more scrolls, some clothing, and several musical instruments. Jon-Tom picked up a set of pipes attached to a curved gourd, puffed experimentally at the mouth openings.

"Hell." Talea sat back against the rocks. She picked up the empty sack and threw it over her shoulder. "Double hell. Even when we find some lucky, it turns out to be deceptive."

Mudge was inspecting the jewelry. "These might fetch two or three golds from a fair fence."

"How delightful," Talea said sarcastically. "You just whistle up a fair fence and we'll have a go at it." The otter let out a long, sharp whistle no human could duplicate, then shrugged.

"Never know till you try." He tucked the jewelry into the pouch at his waist, caught Talea eyeing him. "You don't trust me t' share out." He pouted.

"No, but it's not worth fighting over." She was rubbing her left calf. "My feet hurt."

Jon-Tom had set down the gourd flute and picked up the largest of the three instruments. This one had six strings running in a curve across a heart-shaped resonator. Three triangular openings were cut into the box. At the top of the curved wires were tuning knobs. Near the base of the heartbox resonator was a set of six smaller metal strings, a miniature of the larger, upper set. Twelve strings altogether.

He considered the arrangement thoughtfully. Let's see, the smaller set wouldn't be much good except for plucking the more delicate, higher notes. So the larger sextet is probably strummed. Except for the extra set of tiny strings it looked something like a plastic guitar left too long in an oven.

Talea had picked up one of the flute-things. She tried to blow a tune, produced only a few sour notes that faded quickly, and tossed it away. The second was apparently more to her liking. She finished testing it, slipped it into her belt, and started off back into the forest. Mudge followed, but Jon-Tom, absorbed in the peculiar guitar, hung behind.

Eventually she paused, turned to face him, and waited until he caught up with them. "What's holding you back, larklegs?" He smiled as though he hadn't heard her, turned his attention back to the instrument. A few notes from the small strings filled the air.

"That's a duar. Don't tell me you can play that?"

"Actually, the lad 'as made claims to bein' somethin' of a musician." Mudge studied Jon-Tom's obvious interest hopefully. "You always 'ave said that you sounded better with instrumental accompaniment, mate."

"I know. I remember." Jon-Tom ran his fingers over the upper-level strings. The sound was much softer than he was used to. Almost lyrelike, but not very alien. He plucked once again at the lower strings. They echoed the upper, deeper tones.

The curved arm running out from the heart-shaped box was difficult to cradle. The instrument had been designed to fit around a much broader chest than his own. The short strap that ran from the top of the arm to the base of the resonator helped a little, however. Letting the instrument hang naturally, he found that by leaning forward he could get at both sets of strings. It hurt his back a little, but he thought he could get used to it. He used both hands, trying to strum the upper strings while plucking in counterpoint at the lower.

Talea sighed, turned away, and started off again, Mudge in tandem and Jon-Tom bringing up the rear. His heart still hurt more than his feet, but the music helped. Gradually he discovered how to swing his arm in an arc instead of straight down in order to follow the curve of bar and strings. Soon he was reproducing familiar chords, then snatches of song. As always the tranquilizing sounds made him feel better, lifting his spirits as well as his adrenaline level.

Some of the songs sounded almost right. But though he tuned and retuned until he was afraid of breaking the strings or the tuning knobs, he couldn't create the right melodies. It wasn't the delicate instrument, either, but something else. He still hadn't discovered how to tune it properly.

It was late afternoon when Talea edged closer to him, listening a while longer to the almost music he was making before inquiring, with none of her usual bitterness or sarcasm, "Jon-Tom, are you a spellsinger?"

"Hmmm?" He looked up at her. "A what?"

"A spellsinger." She nodded toward the otter, who was walking a few yards ahead of them. "Mudge says that the wizard Clothahump brought you into our world because he thought you were a wizard who could help him in sorceral matters."

"That's right. Unfortunately, I'm in prelaw."

She looked doubtful. "Wizards don't make those kinds of mistakes."

"Well, this one sure did."

"Then you're not. . ." She eyed him strangely. "A spellsinger is a wizard who can only make magic through music."

"That's a nice thought." He plucked at the lower strings and almost-notes danced with dust motes in the fading daylight. "I wish it were true of me." He grinned, slightly embarrassed. "I've had a few people tell me that despite my less than mesmerizing tenor, I can make a little music-magic. But not the kind you're thinking of."

"How do you know you can't? Maybe Clothahump was right all along."

"This is silly, Talea. I'm no more a magician than I am any other kind of success. Hell, I'm having a hard enough time trying to play this thing and walk at the same time, what with that long staff strapped to my back. It keeps trying to slide free and trip me.

"Besides," he ran his fingers indifferently along the upper strings,

"I can't even get this to sound right. I can't play something I can't even tune."

"Have you used all the dutips?" When he looked blank, she indicated the tuning knobs. He nodded. "And what about the dudeeps?" Again the blank gaze, and this time he had a surprise.

Set into a recess in the bottom of the instrument were two knobs. He hadn't noticed them before, having been preoccupied with the strings and the "dutips," as she'd called them. He fiddled with the pair. Each somehow contracted tiny metal and wood slats inside the resonator. One adjusted crude treble, the other lowered everything a couple of octaves and corresponded very roughly to a bass modulator. He looked closely at them and then looked again. Instead of the usual "treble" and "bass," they read "tremble" and "mass."

But they definitely improved the quality of the duar's sound.

"Now you should try," she urged him.

"Try what? What kind of song would you like to hear? I've been through this with Mudge, so if you want to take the risk of listening to me. . . ."

"I'm not afraid," she replied, misunderstanding him. "Try not for the sound. Try for the magic. It's not like a wizard as great as Clothahump, even if his powers are failing, to make such a mistake."

Try for the magic, he thought. Huh . . . try for the sound. That's what the lead bass player for a very famous group had once told him. The guy had been higher than the Pope when Jon-Tom had accidentally run into him in a hall before a concert playing to twenty thousand. Stuttering, hardly able to talk to so admired a musician, he'd barely been able to mumble the usual fatuous request for "advice to a struggling young guitarist."

"Hey, man . . . you got to try for the sound. Hear? Try for the sound."

That hastily uttered parable had been sufficiently unspecific to stick in his mind. Jon-Tom had been trying for the sound for years, but he hadn't come close to finding it. Most would-be musicians never did. Maybe finding the sound was the difference between the pro and the amateur. Or maybe it was only a matter of getting too stoked to notice the difference.

Whatthehell.

He fiddled a little longer with the pseudo-treble/bass controls. They certainly improved the music. Why not play something difficult? Stretch yourself, Jon-Tom. You've nothing to lose. These two critics can't change your career one way or t'other. There was only one sound he'd ever hoped to reach for, so he reached.

"Purple haze . . ." he began, and thereafter, as always, he lost himself in the music, forgetting the watching Talea, forgetting Mudge, forgetting the place and time of where he was, forgetting everything except reaching for the sound.

He played as hard as he could on that strange curved instrument. It lifted him, juiced him with the natural high playing always brought him. As he played it seemed to him that he could hear the friendly prickling music of his own old electric guitar. His nerves quivered with the pleasure and his ears rang with the familiarity of it. He was truly happy, cradling and caressing that strange instrument, forgetting his surroundings, his troubles, his parents.

A long time later (or maybe it was only a couple of minutes) he became aware that someone was shaking him. He blinked and stopped playing, the last rough chord dying away, soaked up by the earth and trees. He blinked at Talea, and she let loose of his arms, backed away from him a little. She was looking at him strangely.

Mudge also stood nearby, staring.

"What's going on? Was I that bad?" He felt a little dizzy.

" 'Tis a fine chap you are, foolin' your mate like this," said the otter with a mixture of awe and irritation. "Forgive me, lad. I'd no idea you'd been toyin' with me all this time. Don't go too harsh on me. I've only done what I thought best for you and . . ."

"Stop that, Mudge. What are you blubbering about?"

"The sounds you made . . . and something else, spellsinger." He gaped at her. "You're still trying to fool us, aren't you? Just like you fooled Clothahump. Look at your duar."

His gaze dropped and he jumped slightly. The last vestiges of a powerful violet luminescence were slowly fading from the edges of the instrument, slower still from the lambent metal strings.

"I didn't . . . I haven't done anything." He shoved at the instrument as though it might suddenly turn and bite him. The strap kept it secure around his neck and it swung back to bounce off his ribs. The club-staff rocked uncomfortably on his back.

"Try again," Talea whispered. "Reach for the magic again."

It seemed to have grown darker much too fast. Hesitantly (it was only an instrument, after all) he plucked at the lower strings and strummed again a few bars of "Purple Haze." Each time he struck a string it emitted that rich violet glow.

There was something else. The music was different. Cold as water from a mountain tarn, rough as a file's rasp. It set a fire in the head like white lightning and sent goosebumps down his arms. Bits of thought rattled around like ball bearings inside his skull.

My oh, but that was a fine sound!

He tried again, more confidently now. Out came the proper chords, with a power and thunder he hadn't expected. All the time they reverberated and echoed through the trees, and there was no amplifier in sight. That vast sound was pouring purple from the duar resting firm on his shoulder and light beneath his dancing fingers.

Is it the instrument that's transformed, he thought wildly, or something in me?

That was the key line, of course, from another song entirely. But it rationalized, if not explained, he thought, what was happening there in the forest.

"I'm not a spellsinger," he finally told them. "I'm still not sure what that is." He was surprised at the humbleness in his voice. "But I always thought I had something in me. Every would-be musician does. There's a line that goes, 'The magic's in the music and the music's in me.' Maybe you're right, Talea. Maybe Clothahump was more accurate than even he knew.

"I'm going to do what I can, though I can't imagine what that might be. So far all I know I can do is make this duar shine purple."

"Never mind 'ow you do it, mate." Mudge swelled with pride at his companion's accomplishment. "Just don't forget 'ow."

"We need to experiment." Talea's mind was working furiously. "You need to focus your abilities, Jon-Tom. Any wizard . . ."

"Don't . . . call me that."

"Any spellsinger, then, has to be able to be specific with his magic. Unspecific magic is not only useless, it's dangerous."

"I don't know any of the right words," he protested. "I don't know any songs with scientific words."

"You've got the music, Jon-Tom. That's magic enough to make the words work." She looked around the forest. Dusk was settling gently over the treetops. "What do we need?"

"Money," said Mudge without hesitation.

"Shut up, Mudge. Be serious."

"I'm always serious where money be concerned, luv."

She threw him a sour look. "We can't buy transportation where none exists. Money won't get us safely and quickly to Clothahump's Tree." She looked expectantly at Jon-Tom.

"Want to try that?"

"What? Transportation? I don't know what kind . . ." He broke off, feeling drunk. Drunk from the after effects of the music. Drunk from what it seemed he'd done with it. Drunk with the knowledge of an ability he hadn't known he'd possessed, and completely at a loss as to what to make of it.

Make of it some transportation, dummy. You heard the lady.

But what song to play to do so? Wasn't that always the problem? No matter whether you're trying to magic spirits or an audience.

Beach Boys . . . sure, that sounded right. "Little Deuce Coupe." What would Talea and Mudge make of *that!* He laughed wildly and drew concerned looks from his companions.

His hands moved toward the strings . . . and hesitated. "Little Deuce Coup"? Now as long as we're about this, Meriweather, why fool around with small stuff? Try for some *real* transportation.

He cleared his throat self-consciously, feeling giddy, and started to sing. "She's real fine, my four-oh-nine."

In his cradling arms the duar began to vibrate and glow mightily. This time the luminescence spread from the strings to encompass the entire instrument. It was like a live thing in his hands, struggling to break free. He hung on tight while awkwardly picking out the notes. Rising chords sprang from his right fingers.

Talea and Mudge stepped back from him, their eyes wide and intent on the open grass between. A pulsing, yellow ball of light had tumbled from the duar to land on the earth. It grew and twisted, swollen with the music. Jon-Tom was facing away from it, preoccupied with his playing.

When Talea's cry finally made him turn the glowing shape had grown considerably. It was working, he told himself excitedly! The shape was beginning to assume a roughly cylindrical outline. He hoped the lemon-yellow convertible would materialize with a full tank of gas (he didn't know any songs about gasoline). Then they would continue in luxury through the forest in a vehicle the likes of which this world had never imagined.

He really was a little drunk now. Too much pride can stupefy the brain as readily as alcohol. He began to improvise stanzas about AM/FM radios, CB's, racing stripes and mags and slicks. After all, as long as he was conjuring up a vehicle he might as well do it up right.

Abruptly there was a loud bang, a toy thunderbolt like a thousand capguns all going off simultaneously. It knocked him back on his butt. The duar flopped against his stomach.

There was something long and powerful where the contorting yellow cylinder had been. It did not boast slicks, but of its traction there could be no doubt. There were no racing stripes and certainly nothing electronic.

The headlights turned to look at him. They were a bright, rich red save for the black slashes in the centers. A long tongue emerged from the front and flicked questioningly at his sprawled form.

There was a noise from the "vehicle." He looked frantically over at it, and it back at him.

In contrast to his evident terror, both Talea and Mudge appeared anything but cowed. They were inspecting the vehicle casually, admiringly. That gave him the courage to sit up and take a closer look at his conjuration.

It was sight of the reins that brought understanding. There was no bit in the enormous snake's mouth. No living thing could control that single mass of muscle by pulling on its mouth. Instead, the reins were linked to the two ear openings set just in back of the eyes.

Talea moved around in front of the snake and gathered in the reins. She gave a short, sharp tug and barked a single word. Twice as thick as Jon-Tom was tall, the immense reptile turned and docilely dropped its head to the ground. Red eyes stared blankly straight ahead.

Jon-Tom had climbed to his feet and allowed himself to be pulled along by an exuberant Mudge. "Come on then, mate. 'Tis one hellaciously fine wizard you be! Sorry I am that I made fun o' you."

"Forget it." He shook himself out of his mental stupor, allowed himself to be led toward the great snake. It was at least forty feet long, though its immense bulk made it appear shorter. Four saddles were mounted on its back. They were secured not by straps around the belly as with a horse but by a peculiar suction arrangement that held the seats tight to the slick scales.

Having calmed down a little, he had to admit that the snake was quite lovely, clad as it was in alternating bands of red, blue, and bright orange that ran like tempera around its girth. This then was the "vehicle" his song had called up. The magic had worked, but translated into this world's terms. Apparently his abilities weren't quite powerful enough for the forces of magic to take his words literally.

"Is it poisonous?" was the first thing he could think to ask.

Mudge let out his high, chirping otter-laugh, urged Jon-Tom toward one of the rear saddles. "Cor, you're a funny one, mate." Talea had already taken the lead position. She was waiting impatiently for her companions to mount up.

" 'Tis a L'borean riding snake, and what pray tell would it need poison for t' defend itself against? 'Cept one o' its own relatives, and its teeth are plenty big enough t' 'andle that occasional family chore."

"What the devil does something this size feed on?"

"Oh, other lizards, most. Any o' the large nonintelligent herbivores it can find in the wild."

"Even so, some of them are tamed for riding?"

Mudge shook his head at the obvious joke. "Now what were you imaginin' these were for?" He rapped the leather saddle loudly. The stirrups were a bit high for him, but strong arms pulled him to where he could get his feet into them.

"Climb aboard, then, mate, and ride."

Jon-Tom moved to the last saddle. He got a good grip on the pommel, put his right boot in the stirrup, and pulled. His left foot dragged against the side of the creature, which took no notice of the contact. It was like kicking a steel bar.

He found himself staring past Mudge at the beacon of Talea's hair. She uttered a low hiss. The snake started forward obediently, and Jon-Tom reached down and used the curved handle-pommel to steady himself.

The movement was unlike anything he'd ever experienced. Not that he'd ever ridden any animal other than the ponies who once frequented his hometown, but it still seemed incredibly gentle. He was put in mind of the stride of the lizards who had pulled their lost wagon; only having no legs, the snake produced an even smoother ride. Technically, it had no gait at all.

There was no jouncing or bouncing. The snake glided like oil over bumps and boulders. After a few minutes of vibration-free ride Jon-Tom felt confident in letting loose of the handle. He relaxed and enjoyed for a change the passing sights of the forest. It was amazing how relaxed the mind could become when one's feet no longer hurt.

He made certain the duar was secured across his belly and his fighting staff was still tight on his back, then settled back to enjoy the ride.

The only thing difficult to get used to was the feeling of not knowing where they were headed, since the snake's slithering, rippling method of making progress was quite deceptive. Eventually he learned to keep a close eye on the reptile's head. It was more like traveling in a tacking sailboat than on a horse.

Smooth as the ride was, the constant moving from right to left in order to proceed forward was making him slightly queasy. This was solved when he directed his attention sideways instead of trying to stare straight ahead.

"I didn't mean to call this monster up, you know," he said to Mudge. "I was trying for something completely different."

"And what might that 'ave been?" A curious Mudge looked back over his shoulder, content to let Talea lead now that he'd given her a heading.

"Actually, I was sort of hoping for a Jeep Wagoneer, or maybe a Landcruiser. But I didn't know any songs—any spells—for them, so I tried to come as close as I could with what I had."

"I don't know wot the first might be," replied Mudge, meticulously preening his whiskers and face, "but a 'landcruiser' be wot we 'ave, if not just precisely the variety you'd 'oped for."

"I guess." Jon-Tom sounded thoughtful. "I suppose it's a good thing I didn't know any songs about tanks. No telling what we might have ended up with."

Mudge frowned. "Now that's a peculiar thing t' say. Wot would we 'ave needed with extra water, wot with streams aboundin' throughout this part o' the Bellwoods?"

Jon-Tom started to explain, decided instead that this was not the time to launch into a complicated explanation of otherworldly technologies. Mudge and Talea appeared quite pleased with the snake. There was no reason for him not to be equally satisfied. Certainly its ride was far smoother than any mechanized vehicle's would have been.

Idly he ran his fingers over the small strings of the duar. Delicate harplike notes sauntered through the forest air. They still possessed the inexplicable if familiar electronic twang of his old Grundig. Blue sparks shot from beneath his fingers.

He started to hum a few bars of "Scarborough Fair," then thought better of it. He didn't want anything to divert them from their intended rendezvous with Clothahump. Who knew what some casually uttered words might conjure up? Possibly they might suddenly find themselves confronted with a fair, complete with food, jugglers and minstrels, and even police.

Play to amuse yourself if you must, he told himself, but keep the words to yourself. So he kept his mouth shut while he continued to play. His fingers stayed clear of the longer upper strings because no matter how softly he tried to strum those, they generated a disconcertingly vast barrage of sound. They remained linked to some mysterious magickry of amplification that he was powerless to disengage.

He'd hoped for a four-wheel drive, tried for two-wheel, and had produced a no-wheel drive that was far more efficient than anything he'd imagined. Now, what else would add to his feeling of comfort in the forest? An M-16 perhaps, or considering the size of the riding snake and its as yet unseen but possibly belligerent relatives, maybe a few Honest John Rockets.

What'd he'd likely get would be a sword or something. Better to rely on his wits and the war staff bouncing against his spine. Or he might produce the weapon in the firing stage. He would have to be very, very careful indeed if he tried to sing up anything else, he decided. Perhaps Clothahump would have some good advice.

He continued to play as they slithered on through increasing darkness. When asked about why they were continuing, Talea replied, "We want to make as much distance as we can tonight."

"Why the sudden rush? We're doing a helluva lot better than we did when we were walking."

She leaned to her left, looked past him, and pointed downward. "We weren't leaving this kind of trail, either." Jon-Tom looked back and noted the wake of crushed brush and grass the snake was producing. "Outriders from Thieves' Hall will surely pick it up."

"So? Why should they connect that up with us?"

"Probably they won't. But L'borean riding snakes are available only to the extremely wealthy. They'd follow any such track, especially one not leading straight for town, hoping to run down a fat prize. Their disappointment in finding us instead of some rich merchant wouldn't bode well for our futures."

"Bloody well right," agreed Mudge readily. "There's a disconcertin' and disgustin' tendency toward settlin' discontents without resortin' to words."

"Beg your pardon?" said Jon-Tom with a frown.

"Kill first and ask questions afterward."

He nodded grimly. "We have some of those where I come from, too."

He turned moodily back to the duar. It was barely visible in the intensifying night. He fiddled with the bottom controls, and the strings fluttered with blue fire as he played. Carefully he kept his lips closed, forced himself not to voice the words of the song he was playing. It was hard to remember the melody without voicing the words. A silver-dollar moon was rising in the east.

Once he caught himself softly singing words and something green was forming alongside the snake. Damn, this wasn't going to work. He needed to play something without words in order to be completely safe.

He changed the motion of his fingers on the strings. Better, he thought. Then he noticed Mudge staring at him.

"Something wrong?"

"Wot the 'ell is goin' on with you, Jon-Tom?"

"It's a Bach fugue," he replied, not understanding. "Quite a well-known piece where I come from."

" 'Ell with that, mate. I wasn't referrin' t' your music. I was referrin' t' your company."

His voice was oddly muted, neither alarmed nor relaxed. Jon-Tom looked to his right . . . and had to grab the saddle handle to keep from falling out of his seat. . . .

X

He found himself staring directly at a huge swarm of nothing. That is, it seemed that there was definitely something present. Hundreds of somethings, in fact. But when he looked at them, they weren't there.

They had moved to his left. He turned to face them, and as he did so, they moved somewhere else.

"Above you, mate . . . I think." Jon-Tom's head snapped back, just in time to espy the absence of whatever it had been. They'd moved down and to his right, behind a large gingko tree where he couldn't see them because they'd shifted their position to his left, where they no longer were and . . .

He was getting dizzy.

It was as if he were hunting a visual echo. He was left teasing his retinas; every time he turned there were the shadows of ghosts.

"I don't see a thing. I almost do, but never quite."

"Surely you do." Mudge was grinning now. "Just like meself, we're seeing them after they aren't there any more."

"But you were looking at them a moment ago," said Jon-Tom, feeling very foolish now because he knew there was definitely *something* near them in the forest. "You told me where to look, where they'd moved to."

"You're 'alf right, mate. I told you where t' look, but not where they were. You can only see where they've been, not where they are." He scratched one ear as he stared back over a furry shoulder. "It never works. You never can see 'em, but those folks who are lucky enough not t' almost see 'em never stop from tryin'. There!"

He gestured sharply to his right. Jon-Tom's head spun around so fast a nerve spasmed in his neck and he winced in pain. Visual footprints formed in afterimage in his brain.

"They're all around us," Mudge told him. "Around you, mostly."

"*What* are?" His brain was getting as twisted as his optic nerves. It was bad enough not to be able to see something you knew was present without having to try and imagine what they were. Or weren't. It was like magnets. You could get the repelling poles close to each other, but at the last possible instant, they'd always slide apart.

"Gneechees."

Jon-Tom turned sharply to his left. Again his gaze caught nothing. He was positive if he shifted his eyes just another quarter inch around he'd have whatever was there in clear focus. "What the hell are gneechees?"

"Blimey, you mean you don't 'ave 'em where you come from?"

"Where I come from we don't have a lot of the things you're used to, Mudge."

"I always thought . . ." The otter shrugged. "The gneechees be everywhere around us. Some times they're more visible than at others, or less invisible 'ud be a better way o' puttin' it. Millions and millions of 'em."

"Millions? Then why can't I see just one?"

Mudge threw up his paws. "Now that's a fine question, ain't it? I don't know. Nobody knows. Not even Clothahump, I'd wager. As to wot they be, that's another nice little mystery. 'Bout the best description I ever 'eard of 'em was that they're the things you seen when you turn your 'ead and there's nothin' there, but you're sure there was *somethin'*. Gneechees are wot you almost see out o' the corner o' your eye, and when you turn to look at it, it's gone. They're the almost-wases, the nearly theres, the maybe-couldbes. They're always with us and never there."

Jon-Tom leaned thoughtfully back in his saddle, fighting the urge to glance constantly to right or left. "Maybe we do have them. But they seem to be just slightly more visible, just a touch more substantial here than back home." He wondered if there were millions of gneechees swarming around the university. They might be the explanation for a lot of things.

"How can you be so sure they're real, if you can never see one?"

"Oh, they're real enough, mate. You know they're real just as I do, because your noggin tells you there's somethin' there. It's foolin' your mind and not quite completely foolin' your eyes. Not that I care much 'bout 'em. My concerns are more prosaic, they are.

" 'Tis mighty frustratin' t' them who worry about such things, though. See, they're immune t' magic. There's not the wizard been who could slow down a gneechee long enough t' figure exactly what one was. Not Clothahump, not Quelnor, not the legendary sorceress Kasadelma could do it.

"They be 'armless, though. I've never 'eard o' anyone bein' affected by 'em one way or t'other."

"How could you tell?" Jon-Tom wondered. "You can't see them."

"Cor, but you could sure enough see the victim, if they took a notion to go to troublin' someone."

"They give me the crawlies." He tried not to look around, and found himself hunting all the harder. It was one thing to think you were seeing things that weren't, quite another to learn for a fact that millions and millions of minute creatures of unknown aspect and intent were occupying the air around you.

"Why are they hanging around me?"

"Who knows, mate. 'Cept that I've 'eard gneechees are attracted t' worried folk. People who be frettin', or upset. Same goes for magickers. Now, you fit both categories. 'Aven't you ever noticed somethin' around you when you've been like that?"

"Naturally. You always tend to imagine more when you're upset or stressed."

" 'Cept you're not imaginin' them," Mudge explained. "They're 'angin' about all right. 'Tis not their fault. I expect that's just wot they're sensitive to, not t' mention the fact that your emotions and feelin's are otherworldly in nature."

"Well, I wish they'd go away." He turned and shouted, "Go on, go away! All of you!" He waved his hands as though it were a flock of flies he could shoo from his psyche. "Harmless or otherwise, I don't want you around. You're making me nervous!"

"Now that won't do, Jon-Tom." Talea had twisted around in her lead saddle and was staring back at him. "The more angry you become the more the gneechees will cling to your presence."

He continued swatting sideways. "How come I can't hit one? I don't have to see one to hit one. If there's something there, surely I ought to get in a lucky swipe sooner or later."

Mudge let out a sigh. "Crikey, lad, sometimes I think whoever set you out on the tightrope o' life forgot t' give you your balancin' pole. If the gneechees be too fast for us t' see, 'ow do you expect t' fool one with somethin' as slow as the back o' your 'and? I expect we must seem t' be swimmin' through a vat o' blackstrap molasses from their point o' view. Maybe we don't seem t' be movin' at all they just consider us parts o' the landscape. 'Cept we're the parts that generate the emotions or forces or wotever it is that occasionally attracts 'em in big numbers. Just thank wotever sign you were born under that they *are* 'armless."

"I don't believe in astrology." Maybe it was time to change the subject. Continued talk of gneechees was frustrating as well as fruitless.

"Now who said anything about astrology?" The otter eyed him in puzzlement. "Now meself was born beneath a cobbler's sign in the riverbank community o' Rush-the-Rock. 'Ow about you?"

"I don't know . . . oh heck, I guess I was born under the sign of L.A. County General."

"Military family, wot?"

"Never mind." His tone was resigned, and he was a little worn out from his experiments with his newfound abilities, not to mention the discovery that millions of not quite physical creatures found him attractive. In order to get rid of them it seemed he was going to have to cease worrying so much, relax, and stop being strange.

He would work on the first two, but he didn't know if he could do anything about the third.

He spent an uneasy night. Mudge and Talea slept quietly, save for a single incident involving a muffled curse followed by the sound of a fist striking furry flesh.

No matter how hard he tried he could not go to sleep. Trying not to think of the gneechees' presence was akin to not thinking of a certain word. What happened was that one couldn't think of anything *except* the forbidden word or, in this case, the gneechees.

His gaze hunted the dark, always aware of minuscule not-quite-luminescent sparks that darted tantalizingly just out of view. But there are parts of the mind that make their own demands. Without being aware of it, his eyes slowly grew as tired as the rest of his body and he fell into a soft, deep sleep serenaded by the dull cooing of giant walking ferns, night-flying reptiles, and a pool full of harmonizing water bugs who managed a marvelous imitation of what sounded like the journey movement from Prokofiev's Lieutenant Kije Suite.

When he woke the next morning, the bright sunlight helped push thoughts of gneechees from his mind. The reciprocal nature of their existence was instantly apparent. The more you searched for them the more of them you attracted. In contrast, the less you cared and the more you accepted their existence as normal, the less they swarmed. With practice it seemed that the honey could will away the bees.

Before afternoon the tireless riding snake was slithering uphill. They had entered a region of familiar hills and low valleys. Off to the east was something Jon-Tom had not seen on his previous march through this section of the Bellwoods. He and Mudge had not climbed quite this high.

A distant rampart of mountains ragged and rough as the Grand Tetons lay swathed in high clouds and haze. It stretched unbroken from north to south.

Mudge had taken a turn at guiding their mount, and Talea had moved in behind him. She turned as she replied to Jon-Tom's question.

"Those? Zaryt's Teeth." She was gesturing across the treetops as they began to descend again into concealing forest. "That great massif there just to the north is Brokenbone Peak, which holds up this part of the world and whose slopes are littered with the dead bones of would-be climbers."

"What's on the other side?"

There was a tremor in her reply and, startlingly for the redoubtable Talea, a hint of fear. "The Greendowns, where reside the Plated Folk."

"I've heard of them." Childishly, he pounced on the rare hint of weakness. "You sound scared of them."

She made a face, brows narrowing, and idly shook aside red hair, ran a hand through the glowing curls. "Jon-Tom," she said seriously, "you seem to me to be a brave if occasionally foolish man, but you know nothing of the Plated Folk. Do not dismiss so lightly that which you are unfamiliar with.

"Your words do not insult me because I am not afraid to confess my fear. Also, I know that you speak from ignorance, or you would not say such things. So I am not upset."

"I might say such things even if I knew." He was properly abashed. But now he stared at her openly.

"Why are you doing that?" Green eyes stared curiously at him.

"Because I want to upset you."

"I don't understand, Jon-Tom."

"Look, you've been taunting me, chiding me, and generally making fun of me ever since we met. I wanted to strike back at you. Not that

I've given you much reason to think better of me. I've probably given you more ammunition than you need. The trouble I caused back at Thieves' Hall is a good example. I'm sorry about things like that, but I can only learn by experience, and if some of those experiences don't work out very well there's not a whole hell of a lot I can do about it.

"I mean you no harm, Talea. I'd like to be more than just allies. I want to be friends. If that's going to come about then I need a little more understanding and a lot less sarcasm from you. How about it?"

He relaxed in his saddle, more than a little surprised at his lengthy speech.

Talea just stared at him while the snake slid down into a meadow alive with green and pink glass butterflies and sunflowers blinking their cyclopean amber eyes.

"I thought we were already friends, Jon-Tom. If I seem to have been brusque with you it was from frustration and impatience, not from dislike."

"Then you do like me?" He couldn't repress a hopeful grin.

She almost smiled back. "If you prove as quick with your new-found magic as you are with your words, then we will be safe indeed." She turned away, and as she did so he caught a glimpse of an expression midway between amusement and genuine interest. He couldn't be certain it reflected either, for Talea's true feelings could be as not-there as the gneechees.

So he said nothing further, let the brief exchange pass. It was enough that he now felt better about their relationship, even if it was no more than an assurance she was not openly hostile to him. At the same time he discovered a surefire way for pushing thoughts of the gneechees completely from his mind. All he had to do was concentrate on the gentle, subtle rolling action of Talea's derrière on the smoothly undulating snake-saddle. . . .

Another day done. Another day of roots, nuts, berries, and the reptilian meat which proved considerably tenderer and sweeter than he had any right to expect. Skillful hunter and braggart that Mudge was, they now had lizard venison or snake fillet at every meal.

Another day done and a familiar glade came into view. The massive, ancient oak in its center seemed not to have shed a single leaf since last he saw it.

They dismounted tiredly. Talea secured the riding snake so that it could move around in a modest circle. It would not do, she explained, simply to turn it out to hunt, since without constant attention a L'borean riding snake could revert rapidly to the wild.

"Shit, you back again?" griped the black-winged shape that opened the Tree door. "You're either not very bright, man, or else just downright dumb." He looked appreciatively past Mudge and Jon-Tom. "Now who's dat? Nice lookin' dame."

"My name is Talea. And that's enough for you, slave."

"Slave? Who's a slave? I'll show ya who's a slave!"

"Easy now, Pog old chap." Mudge had moved forward to block the bat's egress by waving short arms. "She's a friend, even if her tongue be a bit tart at times. Just tell Clothahump that we're back." He cast a cautioning glance at Jon-Tom. "We've 'ad some bad luck, we 'ave, that's necessitated us returnin' a mite early."

"Bet you did," said the bat expectantly, "or ya wouldn't be here now. I bet ya fouled up real good. It gonna be interesting ta see the old bugger turn ya into a human." His gaze dropped. "You'll make a funnier lookin' one than normal, wid dose legs."

"Now is that any way t' greet a friend, Pog? Don't say such 'orrible things or you'll 'ave me befoulin' me pants and embarrassin' meself in front o' the lady. We did nothin' we couldn't avoid. Isn't that the truth, lad?" He looked concernedly back at Jon-Tom.

It took a moment of internal wrestling to go along with the statement. Maybe Mudge was something less than the most altruistic of teachers, but he'd tried. The otter was the closest time he had in this world to a real friend, barring development of his relationship with Talea. Though he had to admit honestly to himself that if things ever got really tough he was not sure he could depend on the otter, and certainly not on Talea.

However, there was no point in detailing any of those feelings to Pog. "Yeah. We had a rough time of it in Lynchbany. And we have other reasons for coming back to see His Wizardness."

"Well, all right. Come on in. Damn fools . . . I suppose your presence will make more work for me again." He flapped on ahead, grumbling steadily in his usual broken-engine tone.

Jon-Tom stayed a step back of Mudge and the bat. "Be careful about what you say, Talea. This Clothahump's the one who brought me here, remember. He's a very powerful wizard and although I found him to be concerned and even kindly, he's obsessed with this crisis he dreams about, and I've seen him come near to frying that bat."

"Don't worry," she replied with a tight smile. "I know who he is, and what he is. He's a borderline senile who ought to have enough sense to retract into his shell and stay there. Do you think I'm an ignorant country sodder? I follow current rumors and talemonger-ings. I know who's in power and who's doing what, and to whom. That's how I know he's responsible for the mess he's made of your life, Jon-Tom." She frowned at him.

"You're the weirdest sorcerer I've ever encountered or heard tell of, except *maybe* for this Clothahump. In that respect it's a good match, and I can see how in his searching he seized on you." The comparison startled Jon-Tom. He hadn't considered that he and the turtle might have personal affinities, or that they might be responsible for his presence here.

"That's okay," he replied readily. "You're the most interesting mugger I've ever run into."

"Better not do it on a dark street or you're liable to find out just how interesting I am," she said warningly.

"Really? I've never done it on a dark street, and I would like to find out how interesting you are."

She started to snap out a reply, looked uncertain, and then acceler-ated. "Oh, come on." There was exasperation in her voice and just possibly something else. "You're a funny one, Jon-Tom. I'm never quite sure about you."

And you, he thought as he watched her hurry on ahead of him, are maybe not as hopeless as I once thought.

It was quite astonishing, he thought as he followed her, how the sight of a beautiful figure teasingly wrapped in snug clothes could shove aside all worries about such picayune matters as survival. Base animal nature, he mused.

But if he was going to survive in this world, he would have to revert to basics. Wasn't that just what Clothahump and, in different ways, Mudge had both told him? Maybe by keeping his thoughts focused on those basics he could keep a firmer grip on his sanity.

All assuming that Talea didn't change her mind as fast as she seemed able to and didn't decide to shove a sword through his belly. That thought cooled his ardor, if not his long-term interest.

Slowing, he found himself standing close to her in the central chamber of the tree. Her perfume was in his nose, her presence a constant comfort in alien surroundings. Yes, they would have to re-main friends, if naught else. She was too familiar, too human for him to abandon that.

Pog directed them out of the central room and into a work area he and Mudge hadn't visited before. The bat hovered nearby while all four watched in silence as the wizard Clothahump fumbled awkwardly among bottles and vials.

Thoroughly engrossed in his work, the wizard failed to notice his visitors. After a proper pause, Pog fluttered forward and said deferentially, "Pardon da intrusion, Master, but dey have returned."

"Um . . . what? Who's returned?" He looked around and his gaze fell on Jon-Tom. "Oh yes, you. I remember you, boy."

"Not too well, it seems." It was something less than the exuberant welcome he'd hoped for.

"I have a lot on my mind, boy." He slid off the low bench and sought out the gray figure of Mudge, who was partly hidden behind Jon-Tom. "Back early, I see. Well, you lazy, foul-mouthed, slanderous mammal, what have you to say for yourself? Or is this merely a courteous visit and I should assume you've encountered no troubles?" The last sentence was spoken with false sweetness.

" 'Tis not like you're thinkin' at all, Your Worshipfulness," the otter insisted. "I was showin' the lad the ways o' Lynchbany and we ran into some unforeseen problems, we did. They weren't no more my fault than they was 'is," and he jerked a short thumb in Jon-Tom's direction.

Clothahump looked up at the tall young man. "Is what he says true, boy? That's he's done his best and taken good care of you? Or is he the outright liar he looks?"

"Wot a thing to say," muttered Mudge, but not too loudly.

"It's hard to lay responsibility for what we've been through lately at anyone's feet, sir." He was aware of black otter eyes hard on his back. "On the one hand, it certainly seems as though I . . . as though we've been the victims of a really unlikely sequence of unfortunate happenings. On the other. . . ."

"No, mate," interrupted Mudge hurriedly, "there be no need t' go into such silliness now." He looked back to the wizard. "I did me best for the lad, Your Highestness. Why, I venture t' say nary a stranger's 'ad quite such fullness o' experience o' local customs as 'e 'as in these past several days."

Jon-Tom kept his expression carefully neutral. "I certainly can't argue with that, sir."

Clothahump considered while he inspected Jon-Tom. "At least the laggard has clothed you properly." He took note of the war staff and the duar. Then his attention shifted to the third member of the little group.

"And who might you be, young lady?"

She stepped proudly forward. "I am Talea of Wuver County, of the Brightberries that mature at Night, third on my mother's side, first of red hair and green eyes, and I am afraid of neither man, woman, beast . . . nor wizard."

"Hmph." Clothahump turned away from her, then suddenly seemed to slump in on himself. Sitting back down on the workbench he leaned his shell against the table. Fingers rubbed tiredly at his forehead as he smiled almost apologetically at his visitors.

"Pardon my tone, my friends. You especially, Jon-Tom. I forget common courtesy myself these days, as I forget many other things too easily. Responsible as I am for your inconveniencing, I owe you more than a curt interrogation concerning your recent activities. If I seemed brusque it was only out of worry for your welfare. But you see, things are growing worse and not better."

"The coming crisis you told us about?" Jon-Tom wondered sympathetically.

The turtle nodded. "It turns my sleep into a cauldron of black distress. I dream of nothing save darkness and death. Of an ocean of putrification about to drown the worlds."

"Ahhh, I don't see why ya worry yourself so much," said Pog from a nearby rafter. "You knockin' yourself out fer noddin', boss. Everybody else scoffs at ya, taunts ya behind your shell. Ya know some of da names dey call ya? 'Senile' is da best o' them."

"I am aware of the local opinion." Clothahump grinned slightly. "In order for one to be affected by insults, one must have some respect for their source. I've told you that before, Pog. The comments of the rabble are of no import, even if they are the rabble one is trying to save. You'll never make a decent peregrine unless you change your attitude in such matters. Hawks and falcons are a haughty folk. You need to cultivate more mental and social independence."

"Yeah, tell me about it," the bat muttered.

Jon-Tom was fascinated by the still unspecified threat, despite his own personal problems. "So you haven't learned anything new about this evil since we left? Or about its source, or when it will come?"

The wizard shook his head dolefully. "It remains as nebulous in nature, as tenuous of touch as before, boy. Nor am I any nearer concocting a methodology to combat it with."

Jon-Tom tried to cheer the despondent turtle. "I've a surprise for you, Clothahump. It was a surprise to me, also."

"What are you riddling me with, boy?"

"I think I may be able to help after all." Clothahump looked up at him curiously.

"Aye, 'tis true, Your Geniusness," said Mudge excitedly. "Why, 'twas meself who first suggested that . . ." He broke off, thinking better of the incipient lie. "No. No, dammit, I cannot take any o' the credit. The lad did it all on 'is own."

"Did *what* on his own?" asked the exasperated wizard.

"We'd been tryin' 'ard t' discover some useful skill for 'im, Your Mastership. 'Is range o' experience matches 'is youthfulness, so wasn't much in the way o' things 'e was practiced at. 'E 'as 'is natural size and reach, and some agility. At first I thought 'e might make a good mercenary. But 'e kept insistin' 'e wanted t' be either a lawyer or a musician." Jon-Tom nodded in confirmation.

"Well, Your Lordship can imagine wot I thought o' the first suggestion. Concernin' 'tother, while the lad's voice is o' considerable volume, it leaves somethin' t' be desired as far as carryin' the tune, if you follow me meaning. But 'is musicianship was another matter, sor. 'E 'as real enthusiasm for music . . . and as it turned out, somethin' more.

"We stumbled, literally stumbled we did, across that fine duar you see 'angin' about 'is neck. And when he got to strummin' on it, well, the most unbelievable things started a-happenin'! You would not believe it 'ad not you been there yourself. All purple and 'azy it started to shine, and its shape a shakin', and the *sounds*, sor." The otter put his hands melodramatically to his ears.

"The sounds this lad can coax out o' that little musicbox. 'E calls it music like 'e's used to playin', but 'tis of a size I never 'eard in me short but full little life."

"I don't know what happened or why, sir." Jon-Tom ran his fingers over the duar. "It vibrates a little when I play it. I think it's trying to become the kind of instrument I'm used to, and can't. As to the magic"—he shrugged—"I'm afraid I'm not very good at it. I only seem to have the vaguest kind of control over what I call up."

"He's too modest, sir," said Talea. "He's a true spellsinger.

"We were tired and worn from our long march through the woods when he started a strange song about some kind of transportation." She looked sideways at Jon-Tom. "I cannot imagine what it was he was singing about, but what he produced was a L'borean riding snake. I do not think it was specified by his song."

"Not hardly," agreed Jon-Tom.

"Nevertheless, that is what he materialized, and a fine ride it provided us, too."

"Nor be that all, sor," said Mudge. "Soon afterward, as we glide through the forest night, 'e's a-strummin' those strings and then . . . why sor, the like's o' so many gneechees was never seen in this country! I swear by me piece they were about us like fleas on a fox followin' a four-day drunk. You never saw the almost-likes o' it."

Clothahump was silent for long moments. Then, "So it seems you've some spellsinging abilities." He scratched at a loose drawer in his plastron.

"It looks that way, sir. I've heard about hidden talent, but I never expected to find any in myself."

"All most interesting." The wizard rose from the bench, put both hands as far behind his back as they'd reach, and scratched at his shell. "It would help to explain so many things. It would explain why in casting I settled upon you and passed over others." There was a touch of resurgent pride in his voice. "So it may be I am not as senile as some say. I thought there was more to this than mere confusion on my part. The talent I sought has been present all along."

"Not exactly, sir. As Talea explained, I can call for something, but I get something quite different. I don't have control over my, uh, magic. Couldn't that be awfully dangerous?"

"My boy, all wizardry is dangerous. So you think you might be able to help now? Well, if we can settle on something for you to help me against, your services will be most welcome."

Jon-Tom shuffled his feet nervously. "Actually, sir, I didn't mean I'd be able to help in that way. Wouldn't you still prefer a real magician, a real 'engineer' from my world to assist you?"

"I expect I would." Clothahump adjusted his spectacles.

"Then send me back and exchange me for another."

"I told you before, boy, that the energies required, the preparations involved need time to . . ." He stopped, squinted upward. "Ah, I believe I follow your meaning now, Jon-Tom spellsinger."

"That's it, sir." He could no longer restrain his excitement. "If we both concentrate, both devote our energies to it, maybe the combination will be powerful enough to work the switch. It's not like you're shoving me back home all by yourself, or pulling a replacement here alone. We'd be complementing each other's talents, and making an exchange all at once. Only a single conjuration would be involved instead of two."

Clothahump looked seriously at his workbench. "It *might* be possible. There are certain shortcuts. . . ." He glanced back at Jon-Tom. "It involves definite risks, boy. You might find yourself stuck halfway between this world and your own. There's no future in limbo. Only eternity, and I can't think of a duller way to spend existence."

"I'll take that chance. I'll take any chances necessary."

"Good for you, but what about whoever you're going to be trading places with?"

"How do you mean?" He looked uncertain.

"This eng'neer that we locate with our thoughts, Jon-Tom, will be as thrown from his familiar time and place as you were. He will likely also be trapped here for considerably longer than yourself, since I will not have the power to try and return him to his normal life for some time. He might not adapt here as well as you have, might not ever be sent home.

"Are you willing to accept the responsibility for doing that to someone else?"

"You have to take the same responsibility."

"My entire world is at stake, possibly your own as well. I know where I stand." The wizard was staring unwinkingly at him.

Jon-Tom forced himself to think back, to remember what his first sight and feelings were like when he'd materialized in this world. Glass butterflies and utter disorientation. A five-foot-tall otter and bellwoods.

How might that affect an older man of forty or fifty, who might find it far harder to cope with the physical hardships of this place, not to mention the mental ones? A man with a family perhaps. Or a woman who might leave children behind?

He looked back down at Clothahump. "I'm willing to try the exchange and . . . if you're as serious about this crisis as you say, then you don't have any choice. Not if you want a real engineer."

"That is so," replied the wizard, "but I have far more important reasons for wanting to make this switch."

"My reasons are important enough to me." He turned away from the others. "I'm sorry if I don't measure up to your heroic standards."

"I expect no heroic stances from you, Jon-Tom," said Clothahump gently. "You are only a man. All I ask now is that you make the decision, and you have. That is enough for me. I will commence preparations." He turned back to his bench, leaving Jon-Tom feeling expectant, pleased, and slightly anxious.

Self-preservation, he told himself angrily. He would wish whoever was to take his place the best of luck, and could do no more than that. He'd never know who was chosen.

Besides, his erratic and possibly dangerous magic could do little to help Talea and Mudge and Clothahump's world. Probably whoever took his place would be able to, if Clothahump's perception of the danger threatening them was accurate. Rationalization or not, that was a comforting thought to cling to.

I didn't ask to be here, he told himself firmly, and if I have a chance to get home, damned if I'm not going to take it. . .

XI

The rest of the preparations took all afternoon. They were not ready until evening.

In the middle of the Tree's central chamber a circle had been painted on the wood-chip floor. It was filled with cryptographic symbols that might have been calculus and might have been nonsense. Talea, Pog, and Mudge had been directed to stay out of the way, an admonition they needed no urging to obey.

Clothahump stood on the opposite side of the circle from Jon-Tom, who tapped nervously at the wood of the duar.

"What do I do when we begin?"

"You're the spellsinger. Sing."

"Sing about what?"

"About what we're going to try and do. I wish I could help you, my boy, but I have other things to worry about. I never did have much of a voice."

"Look," said Jon-Tom worriedly, "the riding snake was an accident. I don't know how I did that. Maybe we should stop and . . ."

"Not now, boy," the wizard told him curtly. "Do the best you can. Sing naturally and the magic will follow. That's the way it is with spellsingers. You do that and I will do my part."

He slipped into a semitrance with startling speed and began to recite formulae and trace symbols in the air. There was a great deal of mumbling about time vortices, dimensional nexi, and controlled catastrophe theory.

In contrast Jon-Tom started to pluck hesitantly at the strings of the duar. They glowed blue as he furiously searched for an appropriate tune. His thoughts were confused enough without his having to recall the specifics of a song.

Eventually though he settled on one (he had to select *something)* and began. It was "California Dreamin'."

He started to feel the rhythm of the song, the deceptive power of the ballad, and his voice rose higher, the chords becoming richer as he put all his homesick feelings and desires into it: "I'd be safe and warm, if I was in L.A." It grew dark in the Tree. Brilliant yellow clouds formed in the center of the circle. They were echoed by a thick emerald fog that coalesced just above the floor.

Yellow drops of swirling energy started to spill from the clouds, while green rain rose skyward from the lazy fog. Where they met they formed a whirlpool-globe that began to swell and spin.

Jon-Tom's voice echoed around the chamber, his fingers flying over the strings. The powerful electronic mimicry thundered off the walls, blending with Clothahump's sonorous and steady chant. A deep, low ringing like the distant sound of a huge bell being played two speeds too slowly on a bad tape recorder began to fill the room. A tingling came over Jon-Tom's entire body, a glittering heat that radiated through him.

He continued to play, though it felt now as though his fingers were passing through the strings instead of striking them. Glass bottles shattered on the workbench and books tumbled from their shelves as the very heart of the Tree quivered with the sound. For all anyone inside knew, the whole forest was shaking.

The climax of the song was nearing, the end of the ballad, and he was still within the Tree. He tried to convey his helplessness to Clothahump, his uncertainty about what to do next. Perhaps the wizard understood his anxious stare. Perhaps it was just that their timing was naturally good.

A violent yellow-green explosion obliterated clouds and fog and whirlpool-globe. A great invisible fist struck Jon-Tom hard in the sternum and sent him stumbling backward. He bounced off the far wall, staggered a couple of steps, and fell to his right. Scrolls, fragments of skull, some stuffed heads mounted on the wall, wood shavings and chips, powders and bits of cloth were raining around him. Within the circle a whitish haze was beginning to dissipate.

He paid it little attention because he could see it, and he should not have been able to. Even through the shock of the explosion and his subsequent fall he knew he oughtn't to be able to see haze or Tree. He should be back home, preferably in his own room, or in class, or even flat in the middle of Wilshire traffic.

Instead he lay on his butt within the same Tree.

"It didn't work," he murmured aloud. "I didn't go back." He felt like the hero of a war movie who'd set off the magazine of his own ship and gone down with his captors.

The last of the haze was fading from the circle. He caught his breath, aware of something besides his own self-pity now.

A tall young woman just a hair short of six feet was sitting spraddle-legged in the center of the circle. Her arms were straight behind her, keeping her in a sitting position as she gazed around with an altogether appropriate air of bewilderment. Long black hair was tied in a single ponytail.

She was clad in an absurdly brief skirt with matching pantyshorts beneath, sneakers and high socks, and a long sweater with four large blue letters sewn on its front. Her face was a stunning cross between that of a Tijuana professional and a Tintoretto madonna. Jet-black eyes, black as Mudge's, and coffee skin.

Shakily she got to her feet, dusted herself off, and looked around.

With Pog's assistance Clothahump was rolling off his back. Once on all fours he was able to stand up. He started hunting around for his glasses, which had been knocked off by the concussion. A curved dent in the Tree wall behind him showed where he'd struck.

"What happened?" Jon-Tom thought to ask, his eyes still mesmerized by the woman. "What went wrong?"

"You, obviously, did not go back," said Clothahump prosaically, "but someone else was drawn to us." He stared at the new arrival, asked solicitously, "Are you by any chance, my dear, an eng'neer? Or wizard, or sorceress, or witch, as they would be known hereabouts?"

"Sangre de Christo," husked the girl, taking a cautious step away from the turtle. Then she stopped. Her confusion and momentary fear were replaced by an expression of outrage.

"What is this place, huh? *Comprende tortuga?* Do you understand?" She turned slowly. "Where the hell am I?"

Her eyes narrowed as they located Jon-Tom. "You . . . don't I know you from someplace?"

"Am I correct then in assuming you are not an eng'neer?" asked Clothahump despondently.

She looked back over a shoulder at him. "Engineer, me? *Infierno,* no! I'm a theater-arts student at the University of California in Los Angeles. I was on my way to cheerleading squad practice when . . ."

when I suddenly find myself in a nightmare. Only . . . you are not very frightening, *tortuga*.

"So if this is no nightmare . . . what is it?" She put a hand to her forehead, staggered a little. *"Madre de dios,* have I got a headache."

Clothahump looked across the demolished circle. Jon-Tom was still staring open-mouthed at the girl, his own failure now forgotten. "You know this young lady, spellsinger?"

"I'm afraid I do, sir. Her name is Flores Quintera."

At the mention of her name the girl spun back to face him. "I thought I recognized you." She frowned. "But I still can't place you."

"My name is Jon Meriweather." When she didn't react to that, he added, "We attend the same school."

"I still can't place you. Have we had a class together, or something?"

"I don't think so," he told her. "I'd remember if we had. I have seen—"

"Wait a minuto . . . *now* I know!" She pointed an accusatory finger at him. "I've seen you working around campus. Sweeping the halls, working the grounds at practice."

"I do that occasionally," he replied, embarrassed. "I always managed to be out gardening whenever the cheer squad had practice." He smiled hesitantly.

Loud, high-pitched feminine laughter came from behind him. Everyone turned to see Talea sitting on the wood-chip floor, holding her sides and roaring hysterically.

"I don't know you," said Flores Quintera. "What's so funny?"

"Him!" She pointed at Jon-Tom. "He was supposed to be helping Clothahump cast for an engineer to switch places with. So he was thinking back to his home, to familiar surroundings. But he couldn't keep his mind on his business. It was drifting while he was spellsinging, from engineering to something more pleasant, I think."

"I couldn't help it," Jon-Tom mumbled. "Maybe it was something about the song. I mean, I don't remember exactly what aspects of home I was concentrating on. I was too busy singing. Maybe it was the line, 'If I had to tell her. . . .' " He was more embarrassed than he'd ever been in his life.

"So you're responsible for my being here," said the raven-haired amazon, "wherever 'here' is?"

"Sort of," he mumbled. "I've kind of admired you from afar and when I should have been thinking of something else, my thoughts sort of . . . drifted," he finished helplessly.

"Sure. That clarifies everything." She fluffed her hair, looked around at man, woman, otter, turtle, bat. "So since this guy is too tongue-tied to explain, please would one of you?"

Clothahump sighed and took her by the hand. She didn't resist as he led her to a low couch and sat her down. "It is somewhat difficult to explain, young lady."

"Try me. When you come from the *barrio,* nothing surprises you."

So the wizard patiently elucidated while Jon-Tom sat off to one side morose and at the same time perversely happy. If he was going to be marooned here, as it seemed he was, there were worse people to be trapped with than the voluptuous Flores Quintera.

Eventually Clothahump concluded his explanation. His intense listener rose from the couch and walked over to confront Jon-Tom.

"Then it wasn't entirely your fault. I think I understand. *El tortuga* was very enlightening." She turned and waved around the chamber. "Then what are we waiting here for? We have to help these people as best we can."

"That is most commendable of you," said an admiring Clothahump. "You are a most adaptable young lady. It is a pity you are not the eng'neer we sought, but you are bigger and stronger than most. Can you fight?"

She grinned wickedly at him, and something went all weak inside Jon-Tom. "I have eleven brothers and sisters, Mr. Clothahump, and I'm the second youngest. The only reason I'm on the cheerleading squad is because they don't let women play on the football team. Not at the university level, anyhow. I grew up with a switchblade in my boot."

"I am not familiar with the weapon," replied a pleased Clothahump, "but I believe we can arm you adequately."

Talea had stifled her amusement and had walked over to gaze appraisingly up at the new arrival. "You're the biggest woman I've ever seen."

"I'm tall even for back home," said Quintera. "It's been a drawback sometimes, except in sports." She smiled dazzlingly down at Talea and extended a hand. "Do you shake hands here?"

"We do." Talea reached out hesitantly.

"Bueno. I'd like for us to be friends."

"I think I'd like that too." The two women shook, each taking the measure of the other without conceding anything.

"It's just like I've always dreamed," Quintera murmured, eyes shining.

"You mean you're not upset?" Jon-Tom gaped at her.

"Oh, maybe a little."

Pog grumbled steadily as he began cleaning up the debris created by the explosive collapse of the interdimensional vortex.

"But I've always wanted to be the heroine in shining armor, ever since I was a little girl," Quintera continued.

"No need to worry, then," said Jon-Tom firmly. "I've learned quite a bit since I've been here. I'll make sure no harm comes to you."

"Oh, don't worry about me," she replied gaily.

Pog appeared with an armful of old weapons. "Got 'em since ya left," he told the curious Jon-Tom. "Boss thought it'd be a good idea t'have a few lizard-stickers around in case his magic really got rusty."

Flores Quintera immediately knelt over the pile of destruction and began sorting through it with something other than doll-like enthusiasm. "Hoy, but I'm looking forward to this."

"It could be very dangerous." Jon-Tom had moved to stand protectively close to her.

"Well, of course it could, from what Clothaheemp . . . Clothahump tells me . . . watch your foot there, that ax is sharp." He took a couple of steps backward. "It wouldn't be any fun if it didn't have any danger," she informed him, as though addressing a complete fool.

"Oh, this looks nice," she said brightly, hefting a saw-edged short sword. "Can I have this one?" It was designed for someone Mudge's size. In her lithe hands it looked like a long, thick dagger.

She moved as if to put it in her belt, became aware she wasn't wearing one.

"I can't go marching around in this," she muttered.

"Oh God!" Mudge threw up his paws and spun away. "Not again. Please, I can't go back to Lynchbany and go through this again."

"Never mind." Talea was studying the towering female form. "If the wizard can conjure up some material, I think the two of us can make you something, Flores."

"Call me Flor, please."

"I don't know about conjuring," said Clothahump carefully, "but there are stores in the back rooms of the Tree. Pog will show you where."

"O' course he will," snorted the bat under his breath. "Don't he always?"

The two young women vanished with the bat into yet another section of the seemingly endless interior of the tree.

"I 'ave to 'and it t' you, mate." Mudge smacked Jon-Tom's back with a friendly whack from one furry paw and leered up at him. "First you make friends with Talea and now you materialize this black-maned gable o' gorgeousness. Would that I were up t' such, wot?"

"I'd rather have switched places with an engineer," Jon-Tom mumbled.

He considered Flor Quintera. Her personality somehow did not seem to match his imagining of same. "This new lady, Flor. I've seen her a lot, Mudge, but I'd always imagined her to be somewhat more, well, vulnerable."

" 'Er? Vulnerable? Kiss me bum, mate, but she seems as vulnerable as an ocelot with six arms."

"I know," said Jon-Tom sadly.

Mudge was looking at the doorway through which the women had disappeared. " 'Crikey but I won't mind unvulnerablin' 'er. It'd be like climbin' a bloomin' mountain. I always did 'ave a 'ankerin' t' go explorin' through the peaks and valleys of a challengin' range, wot." He moved away from the distraught Jon-Tom, chuckling lasciviously.

Jon-Tom shuffled across to the workbench. Clothahump sat there, inspecting his shattered apparatus and trying to locate intact bits and pieces with which to work.

"I'm really sorry, sir," he said a little dazedly. "I tried my best."

"I know you did, boy. It is not your fault." Clothahump patted Jon-Tom's leg reassuringly. "Rare is the man, wizard, warrior, or worker, who can always think with his brains instead of his balls. Not to worry. What is done is done, and we must make the best of it. At least we have added another dedicated fighter and believer to our ranks. And we still have you and your unpredictable but undeniably powerful spellsinger's abilities, and something more."

"I don't suppose we could try again."

The wizard shook his head. "Impossible. Even if I thought I could survive and control another such conjuration, the last of the necessary powders and material have been used. It would take months simply to find enough ytterbium to constitute the necessary pinch the formula requires."

"I hope you're right about my abilities," Jon-Tom mumbled. "I don't seem to be much good at anything here lately. I hope I can think of the right song when the time comes." He frowned abruptly. "You said we have my abilities and 'something more'?"

The wizard nodded, looked pleased with himself. "Sometimes a good shock is more valuable than any amount of concentration. When I was thrown against the Tree wall by the force of the trans-dimension dissipation, I had a brief but ice-clear image. I now know who is behind the growing evil." He gazed meaningfully up at the staring Jon-Tom.

"Tell me, then. Who and what are—"

But the turtle raised a restraining hand. "Best to wait until everyone has returned. There is ample threat to all in this, and I shall not begin to play favorites now."

So they waited while Jon-Tom watched the wizard. Clothahump sat quietly, contemplating something beyond the ken of the others.

The women returned with Pog muttering irritably behind them. Jon-Tom was a little shocked at the transformation that had come over the delicate flower of his postadolescent fantasies.

In place of the familiar cheerleader's sweater and skirt Flor Quintera was clad in pants and vest of white leatherlike material. The sharply cut vest left her arms and shoulders bare, and her dark skin stood out startlingly against the pale cream-colored clothing. A fringed black cape hung from her neck and matched fringe-topped black boots. The long dagger (or short sword) hung from a black metal belt and a double-headed mace hung from her right hand.

"What do you think?" She twirled the mace gracefully and thus indicated to Jon-Tom why she'd selected it. It was not dissimilar to the baton she was so accustomed to. The major difference was the pair of spiked steel balls at one end, lethal rather than entertaining.

"Don't you think," he said uneasily, "it's a mite extreme?"

"Look who's talking. What's the matter, not what you'd like to see?" She turned on her toes and did a mock curtsey. "Is that more ladylike?"

"Yes. No. I mean . . ."

She turned and walked over to him, laughing, and put a comforting hand on his shoulder. It burned him right through his indigo shirt and iridescent green cape.

"Relax, Jon. Or Jon-Tom, as they call you." She smiled, and his initial irritation at her appearance melted away. "I'm still the same person. You forget that you really don't know anything about me. Oh, don't feel bad . . . few people ever really do. I'm the same person I ever was, and now I've been given the chance to enjoy one of my own fantasies. I'm sorry if I don't fulfill yours."

"But the disorientation," he sputtered. "When I first arrived here I was so confused, so puzzled I could hardly think."

"Well," she said, "I guess I've read a little more of the impossible than you, or dreamed a little deeper. I feel very much at home, *compadre mio.*" She clipped the double mace to her link belt, pushed back her cape, and sat down on the floor. Even that simple motion seemed supernaturally graceful.

"I was explaining to Jon-Tom," Clothahump began, "that the shock or the combination of the shock of the explosion and the magic we were working finally showed me the source of the evil that threatens to overwhelm this world. Perhaps yours as well, young lady," he said to Flor, "if it is not stopped here."

Talea and Mudge listened respectfully, Jon-Tom uncertainly, and Flor anxiously. Jon-Tom divided his attention between the wizard's words and the girl of his dreams.

At least, she had been the girl of his dreams. Her instant adaptation to this strange existence made her seem a different person. Moreover, she seemed to welcome their incredible situation. It left him feeling very inadequate. How many days had it taken him to arrive at a mature acceptance of his fate?

The insecurity passed, to be replaced by a burst of anger at the unfairness of it all, and finally by resignation. Actually, as Mudge had indicated, his situation could have been much worse. If Flor was (as yet, he thought yearningly) no more than a friend, she was a damnsight more interesting to have around than a fifty-year-old male engineer. And he'd made a friend of Talea as well.

Decidedly, life could be worse. There was ample time for events to progress in a pleasant and satisfying fashion. He allowed himself a slight inward smile.

After all, Flor's enthusiastic acceptance of the status quo might be momentary posturing on her part. If what Clothahump believed turned out to be true things were going to become much worse. They would all have to depend on each other. He would be around when it was Flor's turn to do some depending. He accepted her as she was and turned his full attention to Clothahump.

"It is the Plated Folk," the wizard was telling them as he paced slowly back and forth before a tall rack of containers that had not been shattered. "They are gathering in all their thousands, in their tens of thousands, for a great invasion of the warmlands. Legions of them swarm through the Greendowns.

"I saw in an instant great battle-practice fields being constructed on the plains outside Cugluch. Burrows for an endless horde are being dug in anticipation of the arrival and massing of still more troops. I saw thousands of the soulless, mindless workers putting down their work tools and taking up their arms. They are preparing such an onslaught as the warmlands have never seen. I saw—"

"I saw a double-jointed margay once, in a bar in Oglagia Towne," broke in Mudge with astonishing lack of tact. For several minutes he'd been growing more and more restless. Now his frustration burst out spontaneously. "No disrespect t' these ominous foretellin's, Your Omnipotentness, but the Plated Folk 'ave attacked our lands too many times t' count. 'Tis expected that they're t' try again, but wot's the fear of it?" Talea's expression indicated that she agreed with him. "They've always been stopped in the Troom Pass behind the Jo-Troom Gate. Always they 'ave the kind o' impressive numbers you be recitin' t' us, but their strategy sucks, and what bravery they 'ave is the bravery o' the stupid. All they ever 'ave ended up doin' is fertili-zin' the plants that grow in the Pass."

"That's true enough," said Talea. "I don't see that we have any-thing unusual to fear, so I don't understand your worry."

The wizard stared patiently at her. "Have you ever fought the Plated Folk? Do you know the cruelties and abominations of which they are capable?"

Talea leaned back in the chair fashioned from the horns of some unknown creature and waved the question away with one tiny hand.

"Of course I've never fought 'em. Their last attack was sixty-seven years ago."

"The forty-eighth interregnum," said Clothahump. "I remember it."

"And what were the results?" she asked pointedly.

"After considerable fighting and a great loss of life to both sides, the Plated Folk armies were driven back into the Greendowns. They have not been heard from since. Until now."

"Meaning we kicked the shit out of 'em," Mudge paraphrased with satisfaction.

"You have the usual confidence of the untested," Clothahump muttered.

"What about the previous battle, and the one before that, and the thirty-fifth interregnum, which the histories say was such a Plated fiasco, and all the battles and fighting back to the beginning of the Gate's foundations?"

"All true," Clothahump admitted. "In all that time they have not so much as topped the Gate. But I fear this time will be far different. Different from anything a warmlander can imagine."

Talea leaned forward in the chair. "Why?"

"Because a new element has been introduced into the equation, my dear ignorant youngling. A profound stress presses dangerously on the fabric of fate. The balance between the Plated Folk and the warmlander has been seriously altered. I have sensed this, have felt it, for many months now, though I could not connect my unease directly to the Plated Ones. Now I have done that, and the nature of the threat at once becomes clear and thrice magnified.

"Hence my desperate casting for one who could divine and perhaps affect this alteration. You, Jon-Tom, and now you, my dear," and he nodded toward a watchful Flores Quintera.

She shook black strands from her face, clasped both arms around her knees as she stared raptly at him.

"Ahhh, I can't believe it, guv'nor," Mudge said with a disdainful sniff. "The Plated Folk 'ave never made it t' the top o' the Gate as you say. If they did, why, we'd annihilate 'em there at our leisure."

"The assurance of the young," murmured Clothahump, but he let the otter have his say.

" 'Tis only because the warmlander fighters o' the past wanted some decent competition that they sallied out from behind the Gate t' meet the Plated Folk in the Pass, or there'd o' been even more unequal combat than history tells us of. I'm surprised they keep a-tryin'."

"Oh, they will keep 'a-tryin', my fuzzy friend, until they are completely obliterated, or we are."

"And you're so sure this great unknown whateveritis that you know nothin' about 'as given those smelly monstrosities an edge they've never 'ad before?"

"I am afraid that is so," said the wizard solemnly. "Yet I am admittedly no more clear as to the nature of that fresh evil now than I was before. I know only that it exists, and that it must be prepared for if not destroyed." He shook a warning finger at Talea.

"And that, my dear, raises the other important advantage the Plated Folk have, one which must immediately be countered. We of the warmlands are divided and independent, while the Plated Folk possess a unity of purpose under their ultimate leader. They have the strength of central organization, which is not magical in nature but deadly dangerous nonetheless."

"That still hasn't kept them from a thousand years of getting the shit kicked out of their common unity," she replied, unperturbed.

"True enough, but this time . . . this time I fear a terrible disaster. A disaster made worse by the centuries of complacency you have just demonstrated, my dear. A disaster that threatens to break the boundaries of time and space and spread to all continuui.

"I fear if this threat is not contained, we face not a losing fight, my friends. We face Armageddon."

XII

It was silent within the Tree for a while. Finally Talea asked, "What word then has come out of the Greendowns to you, honorable magician?" Clothahump's warning had quieted even her usually irrepressible bravado.

"From what I have sensed," he began solemnly, "Skrritch the Eighteenth, Supreme Ruler of Cugluch, Cokmetch, Cot-a-Kruln, and of all the far reaches and lands of the Greendowns, Commander of all Plated Folk and heir to their allegiance, has called upon that allegiance. They have been building their armies for years. That and this new evil magic they have acquired has convinced them that this time they cannot fail to conquer. That self-confidence, that terrible feeling of surety, is what came through to my mind more powerfully than anything else."

"And you learned nothing more about this new magic," said Jon-Tom.

"Only one thing, my boy. That Eejakrat, master sorcerer among the Plated Ones, is behind it. That is something we could have naturally guessed, for he has been behind most of the exceptional awfulness that rumor occasionally carries to us from out of the Greendowns.

"Do not underestimate these opponents set before us, Jon-Tom." He gestured at the indifferent Talea and Mudge. "Your friends talk like cubs, through no fault of their own." He moved closer to the two tall humans.

"Let me tell you, the Plated Folk are not like us. They would as soon cut up one of us to see what's inside as we would a tree. No, I modify that. We would have more concern and respect for the tree."

"You don't have to go into details," Jon-Tom told him. "I believe you. But what can we do from here?" He flicked casual fingers across the duar. "This magic that seems to be in my music is new to me, and I can't control it very well. I don't know what my limits may be. If you can't do anything, I don't see how an ignorant novice like myself could."

"Tut, my boy, your approach is different from mine, the magic words you employ are new and unique. You may be of some use when least you expect it. Both you and your companion," he indicated the attentive Flor, "are impressive specimens. There will be times when I may be required to impress the reluctant or the doubtful."

"We can fight, too," she said readily, eyes sparkling with uncharacteristic bloodthirstiness in that sensual but childlike face.

"Restrain yourself, my dear," the wizard advised her with a fatherly smile. "There will likely be ample opportunity for slaughter. But first . . . you are quite right, Jon-Tom, in saying that there is little we can do here. We must begin to mobilize the warmlanders, to assuage their doubts and disbelief. They must prepare for the coming attack. A letter or two will not convince. Therefore we must carry the alarm in person."

"The 'ell you say," Mudge sputtered. "I'm not trippin' off t' the ends o' the earth on some 'alf-cocked crusade."

"Nor am I." Talea rose and let her left hand drop casually to the dagger at her hip. "We've our own personal business to attend to and care for."

"Children," Clothahump half whispered. Then, more audibly, "What business might that be? The business of being chased and hunted by the police of the Twelve Morgray Counties? The business of thievery and petty con schemes? I offer you instead the chance to embark upon a far grander and nobler business. One that is vital to the future of not one but two worlds. One in which all who participate will assuredly go down in the memories of all those who sing songs, for twice ten thousand years of legend!"

"Sorry," said Talea. "Not interested."

"Nor me, guv'nor," Mudge added.

"Also," said Clothahump with a tired sigh, "I will make it worth your while."

"Cor, now that be more like it, Your Imponderableness." Mudge's attitude changed radically. "Exactly 'ow worth our whiles did you 'ave in mind?"

"Sufficiently," said the wizard. "You have my word on it."

"Now I don't know as that's exactly . . ." Mudge's sentence floundered like a shark in a salt lake as he detected something new and dangerous and very unsenile in the wizard's expression. "Wot I mean to say, sor, is that naturally that's good enough for us. The word o' a great sorcerer like yourself, I mean." He looked anxiously at Talea. "Ain't it, luv?"

"I suppose so," she said carefully. "But why us? If you're going to need an honor guard, or body guard, or whatever, why not seek out some more amenable to your crazy notions?"

Clothahump replied instantly. "Because you two are already here, have already been exposed to my crazy notions, are familiar with the histories of these two," and he indicated Flor and Jon-Tom, "and because I have no more time to waste with others, if we are to make haste toward distant Polastrindu."

"Now, guv'nor," said Mudge reluctantly, "I've agreed I 'ave, and I'll stick by *me* word, but Polastrindu? You want that we should go . . . do you know 'ow far, meaning no disrespect, that be, sor?"

"Quite precisely, my good otter."

"It'd take months!" shouted an exasperated Talea.

"Yes it would . . . if we were to travel overland. But I am not so foolish or so young as to consider such a cross-country hike. We must make speed, for while I know what is going to happen I do not know when; consequently I am ignorant of how much time we may have left to prepare. In such circumstances it is best to be stingy with what we may not possess.

"We shall not trudge overland but instead will make our way up the River Tailaroam."

"*Up* the river?" said Talea, eyebrows raised.

"There are ways of traveling against the current."

"To a certain point, Your Wonderness." Mudge looked skeptical. "But what 'appens when we reach the rapids o' Duggakurra? And I've 'eard many a tale o' the dangers the deep parts o' the river possess."

"All obstacles can be surmounted." Clothahump spoke with confidence if not assurance. "They matter not. Obstacle or no, we must hurry on."

"I think I'd rather go by land after all," said Talea.

"I am sorry, my dear. Tailaroam's secrets might be better concealed, but it will be the cleaner and faster route."

"Easy for you to say," she grumbled. "You'd be right at home in the water if we had any trouble."

"I have not spent more than occasional recreational time in the water for some years, my dear. While I may be physiologically adapted to an aquatic life, my preferences are for breathing and living in air. As just one example, scrolls do not hold up well at all beneath the water.

"Furthermore, we have now an excellent means for making our way to the river."

"The L'borean riding snake." Talea nodded thoughtfully. "Why not take it all the way to Polastrindu?"

"Because the river will be as steady and much faster. Perhaps our young friend Jon-Tom can conjure up an equally efficient form of water travel."

"Conjure up?" The query came from Flores Quintera, and she looked sideways at Jon-Tom. "You mean, like magic?"

"Yes, like magic." He endeavored to stand a little straighter as he held out the duar. "Clothahump was casting about for an otherworldly magician to assist him with his troubles and he got me. It turns out that my singing, coupled with my playing of this instrument, coupled with *something*—I don't know what—gives me the ability to work magic here."

"That's very impressive," she said in a voice that lit a fire high above his boots.

"Yes, it would be, except that it's kind of a shotgun effect. I fire off a song and never manage to hit exactly what I'm aiming at. I was trying for an old Dodge Charger and instead materialized the grandfather of all pythons. It turned out to be tamed to riding, though." He smiled at her. "No need to worry about it."

"I'm not worried," she replied excitedly. "I love snakes. Where is it? It's really big enough to ride?" She was heading for the door at a respectable jog.

Mudge was whispering to him. "Now you'll 'ave to do better than that, mate. That's no ordinary maiden you've brought t' yourself. Now if I were you . . ."

But Jon-Tom didn't hear the rest because he was hurrying after her. Clothahump watched them, frowning.

"I must make ready. Pog!" the wizard yelled.

"Here, Master." The bat moved tiredly to hover over the workbench, knowing what would be expected of him. Together they began assembling several large piles of potions and powders: a traveling sorcerer's work kit.

"Now 'ow did we get ourselves roped into this, luv?"

Talea looked across at the otter. "Don't trouble your furry noggin about it. We're committed. You agreed yourself."

"Yes, yes," he said softly, looking back to see if Clothahump was paying them any attention. He was not. "But it were only to keep the old bugger-nut from puttin' a spell on me. Then I'd never 'ave a chance to slip away when the proper time comes."

"It's better that we go," she told him. "I've been thinking, Mudge. If a wizard as great as Clothahump says that the danger is so great, then we must help fight it if we can."

"I don't think you follow me thoughts, luv. This wizard Clotha-hump, 'e's a brilliant one, all right. But 'e 'as lapses, if you know wot I mean." He tapped his head with one furry fist.

"You're saying he's senile."

"Not all the time, no. But 'e *is* two 'undred and ought odd years old. Even for a wizard o' the hard-shell, that's gettin' on a bit, wot? I'm a thinkin' 'e's overexaggeratin' this 'ere Plated danger."

"Sorry, Mudge, I don't agree with you. I've seen and heard enough to convince me he's more sane than senile. Besides," she added with a disdainful air, "he was right in that we have no immediate prospects. In fact, it would do us good to get out of this area for a while. He'll pay us to do that. So we're doing right if he's mad and right if he's not."

Mudge looked resigned. "Maybe so, luv. Maybe so. Though I wish 'e'd been a bit more specific in spellin' out just wot 'e meant by 'worth our while.' "

"What do you mean?"

"Sorcerers 'ave the use o' words that you and I ain't privy to, luv. So it stands t' reason they could be more subtle when it comes t' the employin' o' more familiar ones."

"Mudge! Are you saying he lied to us?"

"No. 'E couldn't do that, not and keep 'is wizardly powers. But there be direct truth and then there be spiral truth, as me sainted mother used t' tell me."

"You had a mother?"

He took a playful swipe at her with a paw and she stepped lithely out of reach. "I always did think a lot o' you, luv. If you only 'ad a bit more body fur, at least on your chest, say."

"No thanks." She edged toward the door. "We'd better go see how the others are making out."

They started down the hallway. "I'm not worried much about the giantess," Mudge was saying, "but our friend Jon-Tom still displays pangs o' loneliness. I worry that the appearance o' the girl from 'is 'ome may do him more 'arm than good, seein' as how besotted 'e is on her."

"Besotted?" Talea studied the walls. "You think so?"

They had almost reached the doorway. " 'Tis in the lad's voice, in 'is manner and look. I've dodged traps that were better 'idden. But I don't think 'e'll 'ave much luck with this one. She's cheery enough, but I 'ave a 'unch 'er true love's reserved for 'er new sword. She strikes me a proper mate for a wolverine, not our Jon-Tom."

"I don't think he's besotted," Talea murmured. "A boyish attraction, certainly."

"And that be somethin' else. 'E may act boyish, but in a fight 'e's all right. Remember 'is magic, and they also say that those who can draw the gneechees in the numbers 'e can may 'ave greater powers locked within 'em than even they can imagine."

"He's already admitted he doesn't know much about his own magical capabilities," she replied. "I don't think they're so much greater than what we've seen."

"We're likely to find out on this bug-brained journey."

The riding snake would have carried the extra load with ease, but they had only four saddles. They were fashioned of the finest hides and specially worked in far-off Malderpot by the warmland's most skilled leatherworkers.

"Two of us will have to double up," said Clothahump, voicing the obvious as the last of their baggage was secured to the snake's lengthy back. "At least Pog does not present a problem."

"Thank the Design!" agreed the bat, fluttering overhead and adjusting his body and back pouches. "It going to be hard enough ta slow down ta keep up wid ya."

"Jon-Tom and Flor must have saddles to themselves," the wizard pointed out, "they being simultaneously the largest and least experienced of us. Perhaps the two of you . . . ?" He gestured at Talea and Mudge.

"Oh no." She shook her head negatively. "I'm not riding with *him.*" Mudge looked hurt.

"In that case," Clothahump bowed as best he could, considering his short legs and weighty front, "you may join me."

"Fine."

"Cor, now, Talea me luv. . . ."

"Get to your own saddle, you mange-mouthed mucker. D'you honestly think I'd let you sit that close to me?"

"Talea sweets, you 'ave poor Mudge all wrong."

"Sure I do." She mounted the lead saddle, spoke down to Clothahump. "You can ride behind me. I trust your hands, and we've a shell between us."

"I can assure you, my dear," said the wizard, sounding slightly offended, "that I have no intentions in the slightest of . . ."

"Yeah, that's what they all say." She slipped both boots into her stirrups. "But come on and get aboard."

Clothahump struggled with the high seat, puffing alarmingly. His short legs and great weight rendered mounting all but impossible. Jon-Tom moved forward and got his arms and shoulders beneath the considerable bulk. It was against Clothahump's principles (not to mention his ego) to use magic to lift himself into the saddle. With Jon-Tom pushing and Talea pulling he managed to make it with a minimum of lost pride.

When they were all seated Talea tugged lightly back on the reins. Having slept all night and morning as was the habit of its kind, the snake came awake slowly. She let the reins hang loose and the snake started to move forward.

A laugh of surprise and delight came from the third saddle, where Flores Quintera sat. She was clearly enjoying the new sensation provided by an extraordinary means of locomotion. Looking back over her shoulder, she flashed a dazzling smile at Jon-Tom.

"What a wonderful way to travel! *Que magnifico!* You can see everything without having your behind battered." She faced forward again and placed both hands on the pommel of the saddle.

"Giddy up!" Her heels kicked girlishly at the scaly sides. The snake did not notice the minuscule tapping on its flanks, but paid attention only to the steering tugs at its sensitive ears.

"Any particular route you'd like me to follow?" Talea inquired of her fellow saddle-mate.

"The shortest one to the Tailaroam," replied Clothahump. "There we will hire passage."

"What about building our own raft?"

"Impossible. Tacking upstream against the current would be difficult. At the Duggakurra rapids it would become impossible. We must engage professionals with the know-how and muscle to fight such obstacles. I think we should turn slightly to the left here, my dear."

Talea pulled gently on the reins, and the snake obediently altered its slither. "That'll take us a day longer, if I remember the land right. It's been a long time since I've been as far south as the river. Too many nasty types hole out there."

"I agree it may take us a little longer to reach our goal this way, but by doing so we will pass a certain glade. It is ringed with very old oaks and is a place of ancient power. I am going to risk a dangerous conjuration there. It is the best place for it, and will be our last chance to learn the nature of the special corruption the warmlands will have to face.

"To do this involves stretching my meager powers to the utmost, so I will require all the magical support the web of Earthforce can supply me. The web is anchored at Yul, at Koal-zin-a-Mec, at Rinamundoh, and at the Glade of Triane."

"I've never heard of the others."

"They lie far around the world and meet at the center of the earth. The affairs of all sentient beings are interwoven in the web, each individual's destiny tied to its own designated strand. I will stand on one of the four anchors of fate and make the call that I must."

"Call? Who are you going to call?"

But Clothahump's thoughts seemed to have shifted. "The glade is close enough to the river so that we may leave our riding snake before we reach it and walk the rest of the way."

"Why not ride the snake all the way to the river?"

"You do not understand." She could feel his eyes on the back of her neck. "You will not, until you see the result of what I am to attempt. Such as this," and he tapped the riding snake's back with a foot, "is but a dumb creature whose life might not survive even a near confrontation of the sort I have in mind. It is as strong as it is stupid, and in a panic could be the undoing of all of us. So we must leave it a day behind when we give it its freedom."

She shrugged. "Whatever you say. But my feet will argue with you." She urged the snake to a faster pace.

Several days of pleasant travel passed as they journeyed southward. No predator came near the massive snake, and at night they didn't even bother to set a watch.

Flores Quintera was a pleasant companion, but what troubled Jon-Tom was not her dissuasion of his hesitant attempts at intimacy so much as that the excitement of the trip seemed to make her oblivious to anything else.

"It's everything I ever dreamed of when I was a little girl." She spoke to him as they sat around the small cookfire. The flames danced in her night-eyes, prompting thoughts of obsidian spewing from the hearts of volcanoes.

"When I was little I wished I was a boy, Jon-Tom," she told him fervently. "I wanted to be an astronaut, to fly over the poles with Byrd, to sail the unexplored South Pacific with Captain Cook. I wanted to be with the English at Agincourt and with Pizzaro in Peru. Failing a change of gender, I imagined myself Amelia Earhart or Joan of Arc."

"You can't change your sex," he told her sympathetically, "and you can't go back in time, but you could have tried for the astronaut training."

She shook her head sadly. "It's not enough to have the ambition, Jon-Tom. You have to have the wherewithal. *Los cerebros.* I've got the guts but not the other." She looked up at him and smiled crookedly. "Then there is the other thing, the unfortunate drawback, the crippling deformity that I've had to suffer with all my life."

He stared at her in genuine puzzlement, unable to see the slightest hint of imperfection.

"I don't follow you, Flor. You look great to me."

"That's the deformity, Jon-Tom. My lack of one. I'm cursed with beauty. Don't misunderstand me now," she added quickly. "I'm not being facetious or boastful. It's something I've just had to try and live with."

"We all have our handicaps," he said, not very sympathetically.

She rose, paced catlike behind the fire. Talea was stirring the other one nearby. Mudge was humming some ribald ditty about the mouse from Cantatrouse who ran around on her spouse, much to the gruff amusement of Pog. Clothahump was a silent, brooding lump somewhere off in the darkness.

"You don't understand, do you? How could you imagine what it's like to be a beautiful animal? Because that's how the world sees me, you know. I did the cheerleader thing because I was asked to." She paused, stared across the flames at him. "Do you know what my major is?"

"Theater Arts, right?"

"Acting." She nodded ruefully. "That's what everyone expected of me. Well it's easy for me, and it lets me concentrate on the harder work involved in my minor. I didn't have the math for astrophysics or tensor analysis or any of that, so I'm doing business administration. Between that and the theater arts I'm hoping I can get in on the public relations end of the space program. That's the only way I ever thought I'd have a chance of getting close to the frontiers. Even so, no one takes me seriously."

"I take you seriously," he murmured.

She stared at him sharply. "*Do* you? I've heard that before. Can you really see beyond my face and body?"

"Sure." He hoped he sounded sincere. "I don't pretend that I can ignore them."

"Nobody can. Nobody!" She threw up her hands in despair. "Professors, fellow students: it's hell just trying to get through an ordinary class without having to offend someone by turning down their incessant requests for a date. And it's next to impossible to get any kind of a serious answer out of a professor when he's staring at your *tetas* instead of concentrating on your question. You can call it beauty. I call it my special deformity."

"Are you saying you'd rather have been born a hunchback? Maybe with no hair and one eye set higher than the other?"

"No." Some of the anger left her. "No, of course not. I just could have done with a little less of everything physical, I suppose."

"*Asi es la vida,*" he said quietly.

"*Si, es verdad.*" She sat down on the grass again, crossing her legs. "There's nothing I can do about it. But here"—and she gestured at the dark forest and the huge serpentine shape coiled nearby—"here things are different. Here my height and size are helpful and people, furry or human, seem to accept me as a person instead of a sex object."

"Don't rely on that," he warned her. "For example our otter friend Mudge seems to have no compunctions whatsoever about crossing interspecies lines. Nor do very many others, from what I've seen."

"Well, so far they've accepted me as a warrior more than a toy. If that's due to my size more than my personality, at least it's a start." She lay down and stretched langorously. The fire seemed to spread from the burning embers to Jon-Tom's loins.

"Here I have a chance to be more than what heredity seemed to have locked me into. And it's like my childhood dreams of adventure."

"People get killed here," he warned her. "This is no fairyland. You make a mistake, you die."

She rolled over. It was a warm winter night and her cape was blanket enough. "I'll take my chances. It can't be any worse than the *barrio*. Good night, Jon-Tom. Remember, when in Rome . . ."

He kicked dirt over the fire until it subsided and wished he were in Rome, or any other familiar place. All he said was, "Good night, Flor. Pleasant dreams." Then he rolled over and sought sleep. The night was pleasant, but his thoughts were troubled.

The following day found them climbing and descending much hillier terrain. Trees were still plentiful, but on the higher knolls they tended to be smaller and with more land between. Occasionally bare granite showed where the ground cover had thinned, though they were still traveling through forest.

And the gneechees were back. Even when Jon-Tom was not strumming his duar, swarms of almost-theres were clustering thickly around the little party of travelers.

He explained to Flor about gneechees. She was delighted at the concept and spent hours trying to catch one with her eyes. Talea mumbled worriedly about their inexplicable presence. Clothahump would have none of it.

"There is no room in magic for superstition, young lady," the turtle admonished her. "If you would learn more about the world you must disabuse yourself of such primitive notions."

"I've seen primitive notions kill a lot of people," she shot back knowingly. "I don't mean to question you, but I bet you'd be the last person to say that we know everything there is to know."

"That is so, child," agreed the wizard. "If the latter were true we would not be making our way to this glade." He snapped irritably at Pog. The bat was diving and swooping above their heads.

"You know you'll never catch one, Pog. You can't even see one."

"Yeah. Dey don't even react to my headseek either." He snapped at empty air where something might have been.

"Then why do you persist?"

"Gives me somethin' ta do, as opposed ta idly dancin' in da air currents. But dat's a thrill you'll never know, ain't it?"

"Do not be impertinent, Pog." The wizard directed Talea to stop. He dismounted, looked around. "We walk from now on."

Packages and supplies were doled out, stuffed into backpacks. Then they started uphill. The rise they were ascending was slight but unvarying. It grew dark, and for a while they matched strides with the mounting moon. Clouds masked its mournful silver face.

"We are close, close," Clothahump informed them much later. The moon was around toward the west now. "I have sensed things."

"Yeah, I just bet ya have, boss," the bat muttered under his breath. He snapped hungrily at a passing glass moth.

If the wizard had heard, he gave no sign. In fact, he spent the next two hours in complete silence, staring straight ahead. No conversational gambit could provoke a response from him.

A subtle tingling like the purr of a kitten began to tickle Jon-Tom's spine. Tall trees closed tight around them once again, ranks of dark green spears holding off the threatening heavens. Stars peeked through the clouds, looking dangerously near.

A glance showed Talea looking around nervously. She reacted to his gaze, nodded. "I feel it also, Jon-Tom. Clothahump was right. This is an ancient part of the world we are coming to. It stinks of power."

Clothahump moved nearer to Jon-Tom. Clouds of gneechees now dogged the climbers. "Can you feel it, my boy? Does it not tease your wizardly senses?"

Jon-Tom looked around uneasily, aware that something was playing his nerves as he would play the strings of the duar. "I feel something, sir. But whether it's magical influences or just back trouble I couldn't say."

Clothahump looked disappointed. Somewhere an anxious night hunter was whistling to its mate. There were rustlings in the brush, and Jon-Tom noted that the hidden things were moving in the same direction: back the way the climbers had come.

"You are not fully attuned to the forces, I expect," said the wizard, unnaturally subdued, "so I suppose I should not expect more of you." He looked ahead and then gestured pridefully.

"We have arrived. One corner of the subatomic forces that bind the matter of all creatures of all the world lies here. Look and remember, Jon-Tom. The glade of Triane."

XIII

They had crested the last rise. Ahead lay an open meadow that at first glance was not particularly remarkable. But it seemed that the massive oaks and sycamores that ringed it like the white hair of an old man's balding skull drew back from that open place, shunning the grass and curves of naked stone that occasionally thrust toward the sky.

Here the moonlight fell unobstructed upon delicate blue blades. A few darker boulders poked mushroomlike heads above the uneven lawn.

"Stop here," the wizard ordered them.

They gratefully slid free of packs and weapons, piled them behind a towering tree that spread protective branches overhead.

"We have one chance to learn the nature of the great new evil the Plated Folk have acquired. I cannot penetrate all the way to Cugluch with any perceptive power. No magic I know of can do that.

"But there is another way. Uncertain, dangerous, but worthy of an attempt to utilize, I think. If naught else it could give us absolute confirmation of the Plated Folk's intentions, and we may learn something of their time schedule. That could be equally as valuable.

"You cannot help me. No matter what happens here, no matter what may happen to me, you must not go beyond this point." No one said anything. He turned, looked up into the tree. "I need you now, Pog."

"Yes, Master." The bat sounded subdued and quite unlike his usual argumentative self. He dropped free, hovered expectantly above the wizard's head as the two conversed.

"What's he going to try?" Talea wondered aloud. Her red hair turned to cinnabar in the moonlight.

"I don't know." Jon-Tom watched in fascination as Clothahump readied himself. Flor had the collar of her cape pulled tight up around her neck. Mudge's ears were cocked forward intently, one paw holding him up against the tree trunk.

From beneath the leaf-shadowed safety of the ancient oak they watched as the wizard carefully marked out a huge ellipse in the open glade. The fluorescent white powder he was using seemed to glow with a life of its own.

Employing the last of the powder, he drew a stylized sun at either end of the ellipse. Red powder was then used to make cryptic markings on the grass. These connected the two suns and formed a crude larger ellipse outside the first.

"If I didn't know better," Flor whispered to Jon-Tom, "I'd think he was laying out some complex higher equations."

"He is," Jon-Tom told her. "Magic equations." She started to object and he hushed her. "I'll explain later."

Now Clothahump and Pog were creating strange, disturbing shapes in the center of the first ellipse. The shapes were not pleasant to look upon, and they appeared to move across the grass and stone of their own volition. But the double ellipse held them in. From time to time the wizard would pause and use a small telescope to study the cloudy night sky.

It had been a windless night. Now a breeze sprang up and pushed at the huddling little knot of onlookers. It came from in front of them and mussed Jon-Tom's hair, ruffled the otter's fur. Despite the warmth of the night the breeze was cold, as though it came from deep space itself. Branches and leaves and needles blew outward, no matter where their parent trees were situated. The breeze was not coming from the east, as Jon-Tom had first thought, but from the center of the glade. It emerged from the twin ellipses and blew outward in all directions as if the wind itself were trying to escape. Normal meteorological conditions no longer existed within the glade.

Clothahump had taken a stance in the center of the near sun drawing. They could hear his voice for the first time, raised in chant and invocation. His short arms were above his head, and his fingers made mute magic-talk with the sky.

The wind strengthened with a panicky rush, and the woods were full of zephyr-gossip. These moans and warnings swirled in confusion around the watchers, who drew nearer one another without comment.

A black shape rejoined them, fighting the growing gale. Pog's eyes were as wide as his wing beats were strained.

"You're all ta stay right where ya are," he told them, raising his voice to be heard over the frightened wind. "Da Master orders it. He works his most dangerous magic." Selecting a long hanging limb, the famulus attached himself to it and tucked his wings cloaklike around his body.

"What is he going to do?" Talea asked. "How can he penetrate all the way to Cugluch through the walls of sorcery this Eejakrat must guard himself with?"

"Da Master makes magic," was all the shivering assistant would say. A wing tip pointed fretfully toward the open glade.

The wind continued to increase. Flor drew her cape tight around her bare shoulders while Mudge fought to retain possession of his feathered cap. Large branches bent outward, and occasional snapping sounds rose above the gale to hint at limbs bent beyond their strength to resist. Huge oaks groaned in protest all the way down to their roots.

"But what is he trying to *do?*" Talea persisted, huddling in the windbreak provided by the massive oak.

"He summons M'nemaxa," the terrified apprentice told her, "and I don't intend ta look upon it." He drew his wings still closer about him until his face as well as his body was concealed by the leathery cocoon.

"M'nemaxa's a legend. It don't exist," Mudge protested.

"He does, he does!" came the whimper from behind the wings. "He exist and da Master summon him, oh, he call to him even now. I will not look on it."

Jon-Tom put his lips close to Talea in order to be heard over the wind. "Who or what's this 'Oom-ne-maxa'?"

"Part of a legend, part of the legends of the old world." She leaned hard against the bark. "According to legend it's the immortal spirit of all combined in a single creature, a creature that can appear in any guise it chooses. Some tales say he/she may actually have once existed in real form. Other stories insist that the spirit is kept alive from moment to moment only by the belief all wizards and sorceresses and witches have in it.

"To touch it is said to be death, to look upon it without wizardly protection is said to invite a death slower and more painful. The first death is from burning, the second from a rotting away of the flesh and organs."

"We'll be safe, we'll be safe," insisted Pog hopefully. "If da Master says so, we'll be safe." Jon-Tom had never seen the bellicose mammal so cowed.

"But I still won't look on it," Pog continued. "Master says da formulae and time-space ellipsoids will hold him. If not . . . if dey fail and it is freed, Master says we should run or fly and we will be safe. We are not worthy of its notice, Master say, and it not likely to pursue."

A delicate gray phosphorescence had begun to creep like St. Elmo's fire up the trunks and branches of the trees ringing the glade. Argent silhouettes now glowed eerily against the black night. The glade had become a green bowl etched with silver filigree. Earth shivered beneath it.

"Can this thing tell Clothahump what he wants to know?" Jon-Tom was less skeptical of the wizard's abilities than was Pog.

"It know all Time and Space," replied the bat. "It can see what da Master wants to know, but dat don't mean it gonna tell him."

There was a hushed, awed murmur of surprise from the otter. "Cor! Would you 'ave a look at that."

"I won't, I won't!" mewed Pog, shaking behind his wings.

Clothahump still stood erect within his sun symbol. As he turned a slow circle, arms still upraised, he was reciting a litany counterpointed by the chorus of the ground. Earth answered his words though he talked to the stars.

Dark, boiling storm clouds, thick black mountains, had assembled over the glade with unnatural haste. They danced above the wind-bent trees and blotted out the friendly face of the moon. From time to time electric lava jumped from one to another as they talked the lightning-talk.

Winds born of hurricane and confusion now assaulted the ancient trees. Jon-Tom lay on the ground and clung to the arched root of the sage-oak. So did Talea and Mudge, while Pog swayed like a large black leaf above them. Flor nestled close to Jon-Tom, though neither's attention was on the other. Branches and leaves shot past them, fleeing from the glade.

None of the swirling debris struck the chanting wizard. The winds roared down into the double ellipse, then outward, but avoided the sun symbol. Above the center of the glade the billowing storm clouds jigged round and round each other in a majestic whirlpool of energy and moisture.

Lightning leapt earthward to blister the ground. No bolt struck near Clothahump, though two trees were shattered to splinters not far away.

Somehow, above the scream of wind, of too close thunder and the howling vortex that now dominated the center of the glade, they could still hear the steady voice of Clothahump. Trying to shield his eyes from flying dirt and debris, Jon-Tom clung tightly to the tree root and squinted at the turtle.

The wizard was turning easily within his proscribed symbol. He appeared completely unaffected by the violent storm raging all around him. The sun symbol was beginning to glow a deep orange.

Clothahump halted. His hands slowly lowered until they were pointing toward the small heap of powders in the center of the inner ellipse. He recited, slowly and with great care, a dozen words known only to a very few magicians and perhaps one or two physicists.

The ancient oak shuddered. Two smaller trees nearby were torn free of the earth and hurled into the sky. There was a mighty, rumbling crescendo of sound that culminated in a volcanic rumble from the glade, and a brief flash of light that fortunately no one looked at directly.

The shape that appeared out of that flash within the inner ellipse took away what little breath remained to Jon-Tom and his companions. He could not have moved his knuckles to his mouth to chew on them, nor could his vocal cords give form to the feelings surging through him.

Soft, eerie moans came from Flor and a slight, labored whistling from Mudge. All were motionless, paralyzed by the sight of M'nemaxa, whose countenance transfigures continents and whose hoofbeats can alter the orbits of worlds.

Within the inner ellipse was a ferociously burning shape. The form M'nemaxa had chosen to appear in was akin to all the horses that had ever been, and yet was not. He showed himself this time as a stallion with great wings that beat at the air more than sixty feet from tip to body. Even so the spirit shape could not be more than partially solid. It was formed of small solar prominences bound together in the form of a horse. Red-orange flames trailed from tail and mane, galloping hooves and majestic wings, to trail behind the form and flicker out in the night.

Actually the constantly shed shards of sunmeat vanished when they reached the limits imposed by the double ellipse, disappeared harmlessly into a thermonuclear void only Clothahump could understand. Though wings tore at the fabric of space and flaming hooves galloped over the plane of existence, the spirit stallion remained fixed within the boundaries of sorceral art.

There was no hint of fading. For every flaming streamer that fell and curled from the equine inferno, new fire appeared to keep the shape familiar and intact, as M'nemaxa continuously renewed his substance. A pair of fiery tusks descended from the upper jaw of the not quite perfect horse shape, and pointed teeth burned within jaws of flame.

Among all that immense length of horsehell, a living stallion sun whose breath would have incinerated Apollo, there were only two things not composed of the ever regenerating eternal fire—eyes as chillingly cold as the rest was unimaginably hot.

The eyes of the stallion-spirit M'nemaxa were dragonfly eyes, great black curving orbs that almost met atop the skull. They were far too large for a normal horse shape, but that was only natural. Through the still angry cyclone, Jon-Tom thought he could see within those all-seeing spheres of black tiny points of light; purple and red, green, blue, and purest white that stood out even against the perpetual fusion that constituted the body shape.

Though he could not know it, those eyes were fragments of the Final Universe, the greater one which holds within it our own universe as well as thousands of others. Galaxies drifted within the eyes of M'nemaxa.

Now a long snake tongue flicked out, a flare from the surface of a living horse star. It tasted of dimensions no puny creature of flesh could ever hope to sample. It arched back its massive flaming head and whinnied. It stunned the ears and minds of the tiny organic listeners. The earth itself trembled, and behind the clouds the moon drew another thousand miles away in its orbit. Rarely was so immense an eminence brought within touch of a mere single world.

"ONE WHO KNOWS THE WORDS HAS SUMMONED!" came the thunder. Great red-orange skull and galactic eyes looked down upon the squat shape of an old turtle.

But the wizard did not bend or hide his head. He remained safe within his sun symbol. His shells did not melt and crack, his flesh did not sear, and he looked upon the horse-star without fear. It dug at existence and its hooves burned time, but it moved no nearer.

"I would know the new magic that gives so much confidence to the

Plated Folk of the Greendowns as they ready their next war against my peoples!" Clothahump's most sonorous sorceral tone sounded tinny beside the world-shaking whisper of the horse.

"THAT IS OF NO CONSEQUENCE TO ME."

"I know," said Clothahump with unbelievable brashness, "but it is of consequence to me. You have been summoned to answer, not to question."

"WHO DARES . . . !" Then the anger of the stallion spirit faded slightly. "YOU HAVE SPOKEN THE WORDS, MASTER OF A HUMBLE KNOWLEDGE. YOU HAVE DONE THE CALLING, AND I MUST REPLY." The spirit seemed almost to smile. "BEWARE, LEADER OF AN IGNO-RANT SLIME, FOR THOUGH THEY KNOW IT NOT THEMSELVES, I FORESEE THEM DESTROYING YOU WITH MIRRORS OF WHAT IS IN YOUR OWN TINY MIND."

"I don't understand," said Clothahump with a frown.

Again the whinny that frightened planets. "AND WHY SHOULD YOU, FOR YOU HAVE NOTHING TO UNDERSTAND WITH. THE DAN-GER TO YOU IS NOTHING TO ME, AND YOU CANNOT IMAGINE IT."

"When will this take place?"

"THEY ARE UNCERTAIN, AS I MUST BE UNCERTAIN, AS IS EVER THE FUTURE UNCERTAIN. LET ME GO NOW."

Suddenly the flaming hooves were another ten feet above the sur-face. Yet it was not M'nemaxa who had moved, but the earth, which had pulled away in fear at the spirit's rising fury.

"Stay!" Clothahump threw up his hands. "I am not finished."

"THEN BE QUICK, LITTLE CREATURE, OR, WORDS OR NOT, I WILL MAKE OF THIS WORLD WHITE ASHES."

"I still do not understand the Plated Folk's new magic. If you cannot describe it to me any better, at least tell me how to counter it. Then I will let you go."

"I WILL GO ANYWAY, FOR WORDS CAN HOLD ME BUT SO LONG AND NO LONGER. I CAN TELL YOU NO MORE. I CHOSE NOT TO ARBITRATE THE FATE OF THIS WORLD, FOR I HAVE MY OWN JOUR-NEY TO MAKE AND YOU CANNOT STOP ME." There was a vast, roar-ing chuckle. "IF YOU WOULD KNOW MORE, ASK YOUR ENEMY YOURSELF!"

A violent concussion shook Jon-Tom loose from the tree root. Bark came away in his bloody fingertips. But he was blown only a few feet downslope when the wind began to fade from hurricane to mere gale force.

The thermonuclear stallion spirit vanished in an expanding ellipse of brilliant light. As the light faded, it left behind a three-dimensional residue. He saw a wavy image of some huge, sinister chamber. It was decorated with red gems, blue metal . . . and white bone.

Within the bower stood an insect shape ten feet tall. Chains of jewels and cloth and small skulls of horribly familiar design draped the chitin. The nightmare stood next to a throne with a high curving back decorated with larger jewels and skulls. Some of the skulls still had flesh on them.

It was talking to someone out of their view. Then something made it turn, and it saw them. A high, vibrating shriek filled the glade, and made Jon-Tom shiver. No dentist's drill could have made a more excruciating sound.

A far smaller flash, an echo of M'nemaxa's blinding passing, obliterated the awful sight.

And then there was no longer anything within the glade save one very tired wizard, wind, and grass.

The gale had become a breeze. As if confused by its presence, the wind-cloud vortex that had hung above the glade simply dispersed. Silver phosphorescence shimmied down trunks and branches to run like water back into the soil.

A light rain began to fall. Hesitantly, the moon peeked through the intermittent clouds, filling the glade with healthy light.

By the time the panting Jon-Tom and the others had reached the center of the glade the ellipses and suns and arcane symbols and formulae no longer glowed against the ground. Though he sought Clothahump, Jon-Tom's mind still saw the face of the towering praying mantis, heard once more the grating scream that had issued from it just before it vanished.

Pog was hovering nervously above them. The rain was steadily washing the powders and rare essences back into the soil from which they'd been extracted. This corner of the web of the world had held.

They found Clothahump sitting on the grass, his glasses askew on his horned beak.

"Are you all right, sir?" Jon-Tom spoke with a mixture of anxiety and respect.

"Who, me? Yes, my boy, I believe I am."

"You ought not to have tried it, good wizard." Talea studied the empty ellipse warily. "There are extremes of magic which should not be touched."

He shook a finger at her. "Don't try to tell me my business, young lady. Pog, give me a wing up." The bat dipped lower, helped the wizard to his feet.

"I have learned part of what I wished to know, my friends. Though I must confess I did not expect the spirit M'nemaxa to speak in riddles."

"Actually, I don't see that we've learned that much," said Flor.

"We have something to work with, my dear, even if it is only couched as a riddle or metaphor. That is a great deal more than we had before." He sounded pleased. "And if naught else, we have given a scare to the Empress Skrritch that may make her hesitate or delay her attack, for she it was whom we saw in that final moment.

"We can continue our journey, secure now in the knowledge that this will be a full-scale war led by the Empress of all the Plated Folk herself. That should win over some of muddleheads in Polastrindu!"

"I hope we don't have to go through this many more times," Flor muttered. "Santa Cecilia may not have many more blessings left for me."

"Not to worry, child," he assured her. "I will not attempt it again. Such a conjuration cannot be made more than once in a lifetime, and tonight I have used mine. I employed incantations I will never employ again, spoke words I may not safely speak henceforth.

"From now on, each day on earth will be one twenty-two thousandth of a day shorter than previously, for in order to draw the immortal from the far depths of his journey I had to utilize the soul-strength of the earth itself."

Jon-Tom walked out into the inner ellipse. Every blade of grass within the marked shape had been vaporized. So had the soil. All that remained was a perfect ellipsoidal shape of melted stone. The white granite had been twisted like taffy.

"You spoke of its journey, sir, and so did it. I . . . I heard it."

"Did you see how furiously it soared, how steadily it galloped, though it did not move beyond my confinement?" Jon-Tom nodded.

"It was at once here with us and holding its place in its journey." He checked to make certain his plastron compartments were still tightly closed. "If the legends of wizards and the admonitions of necromants are correct, the spirit M'nemaxa has traveled approximately a thirtieth of its journey. The journey began at the beginning of the first life, life which in making its journey M'nemaxa strews across the worlds behind it.

"It is galloping around the circumference of the Universe. It is said that when it meets itself coming it will annihilate purpose. Then it can finally rest. 'Tis no surprise it was irritated at our interruption. With a journey of several trillion years still to make, even a little pause is unwelcome.

"Yet despite all that, the formulae worked. The ellipse held." He glowed a little bit himself, with pride. "It was contained, and It answered when It was called." He blinked and slowly sat down on the grass again. "I'm a little tired, all of a sudden."

"I think we're all a little tired," said Jon-Tom knowingly.

"Aye, I'll not argue that, mate." The afterimage of the enormous winged flame-horse still lingered on the otter's outraged retinas. "I think we could all do with a bit o' sleep 'ere."

Everyone agreed. After a brief mutual examination to insure that no injuries had been sustained, they began to make camp. Sleep finally came to all, but fiery images alternated with visions of a tall green-black horror to provoke less than benign dreams.

Far above and away a distant pinprick of light flared briefly across the cosmos. The tiny burst faded quickly. It came from the vicinity of NGC 187, where M'nemaxa angrily kicked aside a star or two as he raced back to where he'd left off his eternal race around the infinite bowl of existence. . . .

XIV

There was panic in Cugluch Keep.

Word of the troubles seeped down from servitors to attendants to workers and even to the lowly apprentice workers who toiled in the deepest burrows and worked endlessly to keep the omnipresent ooze from flooding the undertunnels.

Rumors abounded. Workers whispered of a flaming rain that had fallen from the sky and destroyed hundreds of brood platforms. Or they told of tons of carefully hoarded foodstuffs invaded and ruined by spore rot. Or that the sun had appeared for three consecutive days, or that several of the Royal Court had been discovered feeding on the corpse of a mere worker and had been summarily dismissed.

The truth was far worse than the rumors. Those who knew hid in fear and went about their daily business always looking over their shoulders (those who could look over their shoulders, for some had no necks . . . and some no shoulders).

Hunter packs took every opportunity to get away from the capital city, on the pretext of adding still further to the enormous stocks of supplies. Official auditors bent low over their tallies. All were affected by the panic, a panic that reached beyond sense, beyond normal fears of mortality, to affect even quivering grubs within their incubation cocoons.

The Empress Skrritch was on a rampage. Blood and bits of loose flesh trailed in her wake as she stormed through the rooms and chambers of the labyrinthine central palace.

Safe from her wrath, endless legions of mandibled, facet-eyed troops drilled mechanically on the mossy plains outside the city. As if fearful of reaching the ground, the rays of the sun penetrated the dun-colored sky only feebly.

Guards and servants, scurrying messengers and bureaucrats alike felt the Empress' temper. Eventually the rage spent itself and she settled herself down in one of the lesser audience chambers.

Her thoughts were on her own fear. Idly she nibbled the headless corpse of a still twitching blue beetle chamberlain who'd been too slow to get out of her way. Chitin crunched beneath immensely powerful jaws.

It was some time before Kesylict the Minister dared to stick fluttery antennae around the arched doorway into the chamber. Sensing only simmering anger and the absence of blind fury he poked first his head and then the rest of his antlike body into the room.

A glance revealed a ruby the size of a man's head and redder than his blood. In the top facet Kesylict saw the reflection of the Empress. She was squatting on four legs. The body of the unfortunate chamberlain dangled loosely from one hand while the beautifully symmetrical porcelain-inlaid face of the Empress stared out without seeming to see him.

Though not as lavishly decorated as the main audience chamber or the sinister den of death designated as the royal bedroom, this chamber was still lush with gems and precious metals. The Greendowns were rich in such natural wealth, as though the earth had compensated the land for its noisome, malodorous surface and eternal cloud cover.

They were much appreciated by the hard-shelled denizens of those lands. In the absence of the sun, their sparkle and color provided much beauty. All the varieties of corundum were mined in great quantities: beryl, sapphire, ruby. Rarer diamond framed the windows in the chamber, and thousands of lesser gems, from topaz to chrysoberyl, studded furniture and sculpture and the ceiling itself.

But Kesylict had not kept his head by mooning like a bemused grub at commonplace baubles. He waited and was ready when the triangular emerald green skull jerked around and huge multifaceted eyes dotted with false black pupils glared down at him.

Kesylict debated whether it might not be prudent to retire and wait a while longer before attending his Empress. However, cowardice could cause him to go the way of the chamberlain. That former servitor was now only an empty husk that had been neatly scraped clean by the voracious Empress.

"Why do you cower in the doorway, Kesylict? Yes, I recognize you." Her voice was thick and raspy, like sandpapered oil. Useless wings twitched beneath a long flowing cape of pure silk inlaid with ten thousand amethysts and morions shaped by the empire's finest gem-cutters and polishers, and attached to the cape by a dozen royal seamstresses.

"Pardon, Your Majesty," said the hopeful Kesylict, "but I do not cower. I only hesitate because while I have hoped to talk with you for the past several hours, your mood recently has not been conducive to conversation." He gestured at the corpse-shell of the chamberlain. "Mutual conversation is difficult when one of the participants is forced to function minus his head."

That glowering, fixed skeleton shape could not twist her mouth parts into a smile, and such an expression would have been foreign to her anyway. Nonetheless, Kesylict felt some of the tension depart the room.

"A sense of humor when one's own possible demise is at stake is a finer recommendation of courage than the most dry and somber brilliance, my Kesylict." She tossed the empty shell of the chamberlain into a far corner, where it shattered like an old dish. A couple of legs fell away and rolled up against a far door. The corner was rounded, as were all in the room. The inhabitants of the Greendowns disliked sharp angles.

She turned away from the window. "Anyway, I am full, and tired. But there is more than that." Both knife-edged arms crossed in front of the green thorax, and the decorated head rested on the crux they formed, producing a frozen image of an insectoid odalisque.

"I am worried."

"Worried, Your Majesty?" Kesylict scuttled into the chamber, though taking care to try and remain unobtrusively out of her reach. One could not escape the lightning-swift grasp of the mantis unless one remained beyond its range. So Kesylict approached no closer than protocol demanded. None could tell when the mercurial desires of the Empress might change from a request for advice to a craving for dessert.

"What could possibly be enough to worry Your Majesty? The preparations?" He waved toward the far window. Outside and below were the busy streets of Cugluch, capital of the Empire of the Chosen, their most powerful city. Teeming thousands of dedicated citizens dutifully slaved for the glory of their Empress and their society. Their own lives were filled with the shared glory of their race, and each lowly worker was ready to share in the coming conquests. Preparations were proceeding with the usual efficiency.

"We ready ourselves better than ever before in the history of the Empire, and this time we cannot fail, Majesty."

"There has been no trouble with the stores?"

"None, Majesty." Kesylict sounded genuinely concerned. Though fearful for his personal safety, he was nevertheless a loyal and devoted servant of his Empress, and she did indeed seem worried.

"The training and mobilization also proceeds smoothly. Every day more grubs shed their larval skin and develop arms and the desire to bear weapons. Never has our army been as powerful, never has the desire of its troops been greater. Not one but three great armies stand ready and anxious for the ultimate assault on the lands to the west. Victory is within our grasp. Or so generals Mordeesha and Evaloc have been saying for over a year now. The whole Empire pulses with desire and readiness for battle.

"Yet by wisdom we wait, grow stronger still, so that we can now overwhelm the hated soft ones with but a third of our strength."

She sighed, a low hiss. "Still, we have many thousands of years of failure behind us to show the folly of brave words. I will not give the order to move unless I am certain of success, Kesylict." Her head twitched to one side and she used an arm to clean a bulging eye.

"No trouble then with the Manifestation?"

"Why, no, Majesty." Kesylict was appalled at the thought. For all his talk of strength and desire, he knew that the Empress and general staff were pinning their ultimate hopes on the Manifestation.

"What could be wrong with it?"

She shook a cautionary claw at him. "Where magic is involved, anything is possible. This development is so different it frightens even Eejakrat, who is responsible for it. The greatest care must be exercised to insure its safety and surroundings."

"So it has been, Majesty. Any unauthorized who have come within a hundred zequets of it have been killed, their bodies buried without even the meat being consumed. Greater security has never been exercised in the whole history of the Empire." He peered hard at her.

"Even still, my Majesty worries?"

"Even still." She made as if to rise from her squat. Kesylict took a nervous step backward. She gestured casually, slowly, with an armored arm.

"Be at ease, my valued servant. I am sated physically. It is my mind that hungers for surcease, and your counsel that I require. Not your meat."

"Gladly will I offer my poor advice to Your Majesty."

"This is not for you alone, Kesylict. Summon High General Mordeesha and the sorcerer Eejakrat. I have need of their thoughts as well."

"It will be done, Your Majesty." The Minister turned, his cushioned shoes scraping on the extruded stone floor. He was grateful for the respite but at the same time concerned for the health of his Empress.

Everything was going so well. What could possibly have happened to upset her to the point where she was worried about the outcome of the Great Enterprise?

Later, squatting with the others, Kesylict felt by far the most vulnerable, to both physical abuse and criticism.

To his left rested the heavily armored and aged beetle shape of High General Mordeesha. Battle armor drooped from his soft underbody. Insignia of rank and the less symmetrical wounds of war were cut into his thick dorsal wing covers. Sharp curving horns made of metal protruded from the helmet that fit over his own horny skull. Sweeping metal flanges shielded his eyes.

From his neck hung tiny skulls and teeth taken from the corpses of those the General had personally vanquished. They clanked hollowly against his metal thorax plate as he shifted his position.

Nearby was the Grand Sorcerer Eejakrat, a thin, delicate insect-specter. Pure white enamel decorated his wing cases and chitin. Strings of long white and silver beads dangled fringelike from both sides of his maxilla. An artificial white and silver crest ran from his forehead down between the dark compound eyes to disappear in the middle of his back. It included his insignia of office, of wisdom and knowledge, and marked him as the manipulator of magic most exalted.

Alongside the General, whose great physical skills could crush him easily, and Eejakrat, whose arcane abilities could turn him back into a grub, the Minister felt very inadequate indeed. Yet he squatted in the audience chamber amid the glittering gems and thousand shafts of light they threw back from the dozens of candles and the crystal candelabra overhead, as an equal with the others. For Kesylict possessed an extraordinary reservoir of common sense, an ability most Plated Folk lacked. It was for this that the Empress valued him so much, as a counterweight to the blind drive of the General and the intricate machinations of the Sorcerer.

"We've heard about your distress, Majesty," said the General tactfully. "Is it so important that you must summon us to council now? The critical time nears. Drill and redrill are required more than ever."

"I wish, though," responded Eejakrat in a voice that was almost a whisper between his mandibles, "I could persuade you to wait at least another year, General. I am not yet confident enough master over the Manifestation."

"Wait and wait," grumbled the General, skulls tinkling against his thorax. "We've waited more than a year already. Always building, always preparing, always strengthening our reserves. But there comes a time, good brother, much as I respect your learning, when even a soldier as unthinkingly devoted as those of the Empire grows over-drilled and loses that keen edge for slaughter his officer has worked so long and hard to instill in him. The army cannot retain itself at fever-ready forever.

"Probably we will overwhelm the soft ones by sheer weight of numbers this time, and will have no need of your obscure learning. You can then relax in your old age and toy with this wonder you have conjured up. The final victory shall be ours no matter what."

The General's voice trembled at the thought of the Great Conquest awaiting him, a conquest that would alter forever the history of the world.

"Even so," said the Sorcerer softly, "you are glad to have both my old age and my wonder in reserve, since in twenty thousand years we have shown ourselves unable to defeat the soft ones, despite all our preparations and boastings."

As always, the General was ready to reply. Skrritch waved a knife-studded green arm. The movement was slow to her, awesomely fast to her attendants. They quieted, waited respectfully for what she might say.

"I have not called you here to discuss timing or tactics, but to listen to a memory of a dream." She gazed at Mordeesha. "In dreams, General, it is Eejakrat who is master. But I may want your opinion nonetheless." Obediently the General bowed low.

"I am no jealous fool, Majesty. Now, of all times, we must put aside petty rivalries to work for the greater glory of Cugluch. I will give my opinion if it is asked for, and I will defer to my colleague's ancient wisdom." He nodded to Eejakrat.

"A wise one knows his own limitations," observed a satisfied Eejakrat. "Describe the dream, Majesty."

"I was resting in the bedchamber," she began slowly, "half asleep from the orgy of mating and conversing with my most recent mate preparatory to his ritual dispatching, when I felt a great unease. It was as if many hidden eyes were spying upon me. They were alien eyes, and they burned. Hot and horribly moist they felt. I believed they were seeing into my very insides.

"I gave a violent start, or so my attending mate later said, and struck violently, instinctively, at the empty air. The cushions and pillows of my boudoir are flayed like the underbellies of a dozen slaves because I struggled so fiercely against nothingness.

"For an instant I seemed to see my tormentors. They had shape and yet no shape, form without substance. I screamed aloud and they vanished. Awake, I flew into a frustrated rage from which I have only just recovered." She looked anxiously at Eejakrat.

"Sorcerer, what does this portend?"

Eejakrat located a clean place amid the royal droppings and rested on his hind legs. The tip of his abdomen barely touched the floor. Minims, foot-long subservitors, busied themselves cleaning his chitin.

"Your Majesty worries overmuch on nothing." He shrugged and waved a thin hand. "It may only have been a bad hallucination. You have so much on your mind these days that such upsets are surprising only in that you have not experienced many before this. In the afterdaze of postcoital subsidence such imaginings are only to be expected."

Skrritch nodded and began to clean her other eye, shooing away the distraught minims. "Always the soft ones have managed to defeat us in battle." General Mordeesha shifted uncomfortably.

"They are fast and strong. Most of all, they are clever. We lose not because our troops lack strength or courage but because we lack imagination in war. Perhaps my imagining is, after all, a good sign. Do not look so uncomfortable, General. You are about to receive the word you have waited for for so long."

"I believe the time has come to move." Mordeesha looked excited. "Yes, General. You may inform the rest of the staff to begin final preparations."

"Majesty," put in Eejakrat, "I would very much like another six months to study the ramifications of the Manifestation. I do not understand it well enough yet."

"You will have some time yet, my good advisor," she told him, "because it will take a while to get so vast an enterprise in motion. But General Mordeesha's words concerning the morale and readiness of the troops must be acknowledged. Without that, all your magic will do us no good."

"I will give you all the time I can, wizard," said Mordeesha. "I wish your support." His eyes glittered in the candlelight as he rose to a walking position. He bowed once more.

"By your leave, Majesty, I will retire now and initiate preparations. There is a great deal to do."

"Stay a moment, General." She turned her attention to the sorcerer. "Eejakrat, I like not rushing the wise ones among us who serve with you in this great undertaking. We have been defeated in the past because we acted without patience or stealth. But I feel the time is right, and Mordeesha concurs. I want you to understand I am not favoring his advice over yours." She looked at Kesylict.

"I am neither general nor wizard, Majesty," the Minister told her, "but my instincts say, 'act now.' It is the mood of the workers as well."

Eejakrat sighed. "Let it be so, then. As to the dream-hallucination, Majesty . . . there are many masters of magic among the soft ones. We can despise them for their bodies but not for their minds. Perhaps I am paranoid with our plans so near fruition, but it is not inconceivable that the shapes you think were watching you were knowledgeable ones among the soft folk. Though," he admitted, "I know of no wizardly power strong enough to reach all the way from the warmlands to Cugluch and then penetrate the Veils of Confusion and Conflict I have drawn about the Manifestation. Nevertheless, I shall try to learn more about what occurred.

"If that happened to be true, however, it means that the sooner we act the surer we shall be of surprise and victory." He turned to the General. "See, Mordeesha, how my thoughts give support to your desires against my own hopes. Perhaps it is for the best. Perhaps I grow overcautious in my old age.

"If you are ready, if the armies are ready, then I will force myself to be ready also. To the final glory, then?"

"To the final glory," they all recited in unison.

Skrritch turned, pulled a cord. Three servitors appeared. Each carried a freshly detached, dripping limb from some unfortunate, unseen source. These were distributed. The four in council sucked out the contents of the arms by way of mutual congratulations.

They then took their leave, the General to his staff meeting,

Eejakrat to his quarters to ponder a possible impossible mental intrusion into Cugluch, and Kesylict to arrange the mundane matters of mealtimes and official appointments for the following day.

The Minister had good reason to ponder the Empress' words concerning the notorious cleverness of the soft ones. By such similar adroitness had he retained his head upon his neck, even to agreeing with the others that the time to move had arrived. Privately he thought Eejakrat should be given all the time he wished. Kesylict had read the forbidden records, knew the litany of failure of past battles with the soft ones. So while he was as ignorant of the complexities of the Manifestation as any of the Royal Council, he knew that in Eejakrat's manipulation of it lay the Plated Folk's hopes for final victory over their ancient enemies, and not in General Mordeesha's boasts of superior military strength.

Alone, Skrritch pulled a second call cord. A servitor appeared with a tall, narrow-spouted drinking vessel. The Empress washed down the remnants of the recent toast, then turned and stared once more out the window.

Thickening mist obscured even the ramparts of the Keep. The city of Cugluch and its milling thousands were blotted out as though they did not exist. Day turned toward night as the mist and fog grew darker, indicating the down passage of the sun.

Mordeesha and his fellow generals had been chafing at the bit for several laying periods. She had held off as long as possible in order to give Eejakrat still more time to study his Manifestation. But knowing the wizard, such study could go on forever.

The elastic of patience had been broken now. Soon the word would spread throughout the Greendowns that the war had begun.

For an instant she thought again of the disturbing dream. Perhaps it had been no more than a daymare. Even empresses were subject to strain. Eejakrat did not seem overly concerned about it, so there was no reason for it to continue to trouble her thoughts.

There were promotions and demotions to be bestowed, executions to order, punishments to decide, and rewards to be handed out. Tomorrow's court schedule, so ably organized by the prosaic Kesylict, was quite full.

Such everyday activities seemed superfluous, now that the first steps toward final victory had been initiated. She savored the thought. Of all the emperors and empresses of the far-flung Empire she would be the first to stride possessively through the gentle lands of the soft ones, the first to bring back plunder and thousands of slaves from the other side of the world.

And after that, what might she not accomplish? Even Eejakrat had voiced thoughts about the possibilities the Manifestation might create. Such possibilities extended beyond the bounds of a single world.

She turned on her side and leaned back against a hundred glowing red rubies and crimson cushions. Her ambition was as boundless as the universe, as far-reaching as Eejakrat's magic. She could hardly wait for the war to begin. Glory would accrue to her and to Cugluch. With the wizard's assistance why should she not become Empress of the Universe, supreme ruler of as yet unknown beyonds and their inhabitants?

Yes, she would have the exquisite pleasure of presiding over destruction and conquest instead of records and stupid, fawning, peaceful citizens. Cugluch was on the march, as it should be. Only this time it would swell and grow instead of sputtering to an ignominious halt!

The hallucination faded until it was only an amusing and insignificant memory. . . .

XV

Jon-Tom was split down the middle. Half of him was cool and damp from the early morning mist. The other side was warm and dry, almost hot with the weight leaning against it.

He opened his eyes with that first lethargic movement of awakening and saw a white-and-black-clad form snuggled close against his own. Flor's long black hair lay draped over his shoulder. Her head was nestled in the crook of his left arm.

Instead of moving and waking her, he used the time to study that perfect, silent face. She looked so different, so childlike in sleep. Further to his left slumbered the silent shape of the wizard.

With his head and limbs retracted Clothahump was a boulderish form near a clump of bushes. Jon-Tom started to look back down at his sleeper when he became aware of movement just behind him. Startled, he reached automatically for his war staff.

"Rest easy, Jon-Tom." The voice was less reassuring than the words it spoke. Talea moved down beside him, staring morosely at the recumbent couple. "If I murder you, Jon-Tom, it won't ever be in your sleep." She stepped lithely over them both and trotted over to Clothahump.

She bent and rapped unceremoniously on the shell. "Wake up, wizard!"

A head soon appeared, followed by a pair of arms. One hand held a pair of spectacles which were promptly secured before the turtle's eyes. Then the legs appeared. After resting a moment on all fours, the wizard pushed back into a squat, then stood.

"I am not accustomed," he began huffily, "to being awakened in so brusque a fashion, young lady. If I were of less understanding a mind . . ."

"Save it," she said, "for him." She pointed to the unsteady shape of Pog. The sleepy bat was fluttering awkwardly over to attend to his master's early morning needs. He'd been sleeping in the branches of the great oak overhead.

"What's da matter?" he asked tiredly. "What's all da uproar? Can't ya let a person sleep?"

"C'mon," Talea said curtly, "everybody up." She looked back at Jon-Tom, and he wondered at something he thought he saw in her gaze. "Well," she asked him, "are you two going to join this little session or aren't you? Or do you intend to spend the rest of your life practicing to be a pillow?"

"I might," he shot back, challenging her stare and not moving. She looked away. "What's the trouble, anyway? Why the sudden fanaticism for an early start? I've never noticed you passing up any chance for a little extra sleep."

"Ordinarily I'd still be asleep, Jon-Tom," she replied, "but what made me wake up wasn't too much sleep but the lack of something else. Isn't it obvious to any of you yet?" She spread both hands and turned a half circle. "Where's Mudge?"

Jon-Tom eased Flor off his shoulder. She blinked sleepily and then, becoming aware of her position, slid to one side. Her cat stretch made it difficult for him to concentrate on the problem at hand.

"Mudge is gone," he told her as he rose, trying to work the kinks out of shoulders and legs.

"So da fuzzy little bugger up and split." Pog used the tip of one wing to clean an ear, grimacing as he did so. "Don't surprise me none. He as much as said he was gonna do it first chance he got."

"I thought better of him." Jon-Tom looked disappointedly at the surrounding woods.

Talea laughed. "Then you're a bigger fool than you seem. Don't you realize, the only thing that kept him with us this far was wizardly threats." She jabbed a thumb toward Clothahump.

"I am most upset," said the wizard quietly. "Despite his unfortunate predilection for illegal activities, I rather liked that otter." Jon-Tom watched the turtle's expression change. "Well, I cannot bring him back, but I can fix him, where he is. I'll put a seekstealth on him."

Inquiry revealed that a seekstealth was something of a magical delayed-action bomb. Possessed of its own ethereal composition, it would drift about the world invisibly until it finally tracked down its assigned individual. At that point the substance of the spell would take effect. Jon-Tom shook at how devastating such a Damoclean conjuration could be. The unfortunate subject could successfully elude the seekstealth for years, only to wake up one morning having long since forgotten the original incident to discover that he now had, for example, the head of a chicken. How could this happen to his friend Mudge? Wait one hour, he begged the wizard, who reluctantly agreed.

One hour later Clothahump commenced forming the complex spell. He was halfway through it when a figure appeared out of the forest. Jon-Tom and Flor turned from preparing breakfast to observe it.

Several small, bright blue lizard shapes dangled from its belt, their heads scraping the ground. In all other respects it was quite familiar.

Mudge detached the catch from his waist and tossed the limp forms near the cookfire. Then he frowned curiously at the half circle of gaping onlookers.

" 'Ere now, wot's with all the fish-faces, wot?" He bent over the lizards, pulled out his knife, and inserted it in one of the bodies. "Take me a moment, mates, t' gut these pretties and then we can set t' some proper fryin'. Takes a true gourmet chef, it does, t' prepare limnihop the right way."

Clothahump had ceased his mumbling and gesticulating. He looked quite angry.

"Nice mornin' for huntin'," said the otter conversationally. "Ground's moist enough t' leave tracks everwhere, so wakin' up early as I did, I thought I'd 'ave a go at supplementin' our larder." He finished the last lizard, began to skin them. Then he paused, whiskers twitching a touch uncertainly as he noticed everyone still staring at him.

"Crikey, wot's the bloomin' matter with you all?"

Jon-Tom walked over, patted the otter on the back. "We thought for a moment that you'd run out on us. I knew you wouldn't do that, Mudge."

"The 'ell I wouldn't," came the fervent reply. Mudge gestured toward Clothahump with the knife. "But I've no doubt 'Is Brainship 'ere would keep his wizardly word t' do somethin' rotten t' meself, merely because I might choose t' exercise me own freedom o' will. Might even do me the dirty o' puttin' a seekstealth on me."

"Oh, now I don't know that I would go that far," muttered Clotha-hump. Jon-Tom looked at him sharply.

"Now don't get me wrong, mate," the otter said to Jon-Tom. "I like you, and I like the two dear ladies, even if they are a bit stand-offish, and even old Pog 'ere can be good company when 'e wants to." The bat looked down from his branch and snorted, then returned to preening himself.

"It's just that I'm not lookin' forward t' the prospect o' possible dismemberment. But then, I've said all this before, 'aven't I." He smiled beatifically. " 'Tis the threat that keeps me taggin' along. I know better than t' try and run off."

"It is not that we believed you had actually done that. Which is to say, we were not entirely certain that . . ."

"Stow it, guv'nor. I don't pay it no mind." He set the fillets on the fire, moved to a mossy log, and pulled off one boot. Furry toes wiggled as he turned the boot upside down and tapped the heel with a paw. Several small pebbles tumbled out.

"Some bloody deep muck I 'ad t' slop through t' run that set down. 'Twas worth it, I think. They're young enough t' be sweet and old enough t' be meaty. Truth t' tell, I was gettin' tired o' nuts and berries and jerky." He shoved his foot back into the boot.

"Come on, now. Surely none o' you seriously thought I'd taken the long hike? Let's get t' some serious business, right? Breakfast!" He ambled toward the fire. "I may be ignorant, foul-mouthed, lecherous, and disreputable," he reached for the proximate curves of Talea's derrière and she jumped out of the way, "but there be one thing I am that's good. I'm the best camp cook this side o' the Muddletup Moors." He winked at Jon-Tom.

"Comes from 'avin' t' eat on the run all your life."

There was no more talk of desertion. The lizards looked rather more ghastly than the average hunk of cooked meat. Flor bit into her section with obvious gusto, so Jon-Tom could hardly show queasiness. Meat was meat, after all, and he'd eaten plenty of reptile in the past weeks. It was just that they'd been such cute little blue things.

"Muy bueno," Flor told Mudge, licking her fingers. "Maybe one of these days I'll have a chance to make you my *quesadillas."*

Mudge was repacking his gear. "Maybe one o' these days I'll 'ave a chance to sample some *quintera."*

"No, no. *'Quesadilla.' Quintera* is my . . ." She gaped, and then to Jon-Tom's considerable surprise, she blushed. The flush was very becoming on her dark skin. He wanted to say something but somehow the idea of admonishing an otter about a ribald remark upset him. He simply could not visualize the furry joker as a rival. It was inhuman. . . .

They shouldered their packs and started across the glade. Jon-Tom chatted with Mudge and Clothahump while Flor engaged the gruff but willing Pog in conversation. She was curious about the functions of a famulus, and he readily supplied her with a long list of the mostly unpleasant activities he was regularly required to perform. He spoke softly, out of the wizard's hearing.

Water occasionally lapped at their boots. The night's rain had littered the glade with little pools. They avoided the largest without anyone noticing that several of the depressions were identical in outline: the shape of hooves had been melted into the rock.

Jon-Tom was not prepared for his first sight of the river. The Tailaroam was anything but the modest stream he'd expected.

It was broad and wild, with an occasional flash of racing white water showing where the current ran from east to west. He had no way of knowing its depth, but it seemed substantial enough to support a very large vessel indeed. It reminded him of pictures he'd seen of the Ohio in colonial times. Not that he expected to see anything as technologically advanced as a steamship or sternwheeler.

Possibly it was the contrast that made the river seem so big. This was the first time he'd seen anything larger than a rivulet or creek, and the Tailaroam was enormous in comparison. Willow and cypress clustered thickly along the banks. Here and there, scattered stands of birch thrust thin skeletal fingers toward a cloud-flecked sky.

They turned eastward and moved steadily upstream. The dense undergrowth that hugged the river made progress slow. Tangled clumps of moonberry bushes often forced them to change direction, and brambles stuck to their capes and tried to work their way to the skin beneath.

Eventually they found what Clothahump had been searching for: a flat peninsula of sand and gravel that jutted out into the water. Only a few bushes clung tenaciously to the poor soil. In high-water weather the little spit would be submerged. For now it formed a natural landing place and a good one, the wizard explained, from which to hail a passing ship.

Day slid into day, however, without any sign of river travel.

"Commerce is thin this time of year," Clothahump told them apologetically. "There are more ships in the spring when the river is higher and the upper rapids more navigable. If we do not espy transport soon, we may be reduced to constructing our own." He sounded irritated and perhaps a little peeved that Talea might have been right in suggesting they travel overland.

The next two days offered only hopeful signs. Several boats passed them, but all were traveling downstream toward the Glittergeist Sea and distant Snarken.

Jon-Tom used the time to practice his duar, working to master the difficult double-string arrangement. He was careful only to play soft music and not to sing any songs for fear of accidentally conjuring something distressing. Clouds of gneechees seemed to swarm about him at such times. He was learning to resist the constant temptation to spend all his time trying to catch one in his gaze.

Once something like a foot-long glowworm crawled out of the shallows to dance and writhe near his feet. It did nothing else, and shot back into the water the instant he stopped playing.

Flor was fascinated by the instrument. Despite Jon-Tom's initial worries she insisted on trying it herself. She succeeded only in strumming a few basic chords, and went back to listening to him play.

She was doing so one morning when a cry came from Talea.

"A ship!" She stood on the end of the sandy point and gestured to the west.

"How big?" Clothahump puffed his way over to stand next to her. Jon-Tom slipped the duar back across his chest, and he and Flor moved to stand behind them.

"Can't tell." Talea squinted, shielded her eyes. The cloud cover now restricted the sunlight, but the glare from the surface of the river was still strong enough to water unwary eyes.

Soon the vessel hove into full view. It was stocky and pointed at both ends. Two square-rigged sails were mounted on separate masts set fore and aft. There was a central cabin abovedeck and a narrow high poop from which a figure was steering the ship by means of an enormous oar.

There were also groups of creatures moving from east to west along the sides of the ship. They shoved at long poles. Jon-Tom thought he could make out at least a couple of humans among the fur.

"Looks like a cross between a miniature galleon and a keelboat," he murmured thoughtfully. Wetting a finger, he tested the wind. It was blowing upstream. That would propel a sailboat against the current, and the ship could then down sail and take the current back downstream. Except on days such as today. The breeze was weak, and the keel poles had been brought into play to keep the vessel moving.

"Are they flying a merchant's pennant?" Clothahump fiddled with his spectacles. "One of these days I really *must* try and master that spell for myopia."

"Hard to tell," Talea said. "They're flying something."

"There seem to be an awful lot of people on deck." Jon-Tom frowned. "Not all of them are pushing on those poles. Some of them seem to be running around the edge of the ship. Could they be exercising?"

"Are you more than 'alf mad, mate? Anyone not workin' 'is arse off would be below decks restin' out o' the way."

"They're running nonetheless." Jon-Tom frowned, trying to make some sense out of the apparently purposeless activity taking place on the ship.

"Pog!"

The bat was instantly at Clothahump's side. "Yes, Master?" He hastily tossed away the lizard leg he'd been gnawing on.

"Find out who they are, how far upstream they are traveling, and if they will take us as passengers."

"Yes, Master." The bat soared out over the water, heading for the boat. Jon-Tom followed the weaving shape.

Pog appeared to circle above the vessel. It was now almost opposite their little beach, though on the far side of the river. It wasn't long before the famulus came speeding back.

"Well?" Clothahump demanded as the bat fluttered to a resting stance on the ground.

"Boss, I don't think dey're much in the mood for talking business." He raised a wing and showed them the shaft of the arrow protruding from it. Plucking it free, he threw it into the water and studied the wound. "Shit! Needle and thread time again."

"Are you certain they were shooting at you?" asked Flor.

Pog made a face, which on a bat can be unbearably gruesome. "Yes, I'm sure dey were shooting at me!" he said sarcastically, mimicking her voice. "So sorry I couldn't bring more proof back wid me, but unfortunately I managed ta dodge da other dozen or so bellysplitters dey shot at me."

He was fumbling in his backpack. Out came a large needle and a spool of some organic material that Jon-Tom knew could not be catgut. As the bat sewed, he spoke.

"Dere seemed ta be some kind of riot or fight taking place on da deck. I just kinda circled overhead trying ta make some sense outta what was going on. Eventually I gave up and drifted over da poop deck. Tings were quieter dere and it's where I'd expected ta find da captain. I tink one of 'em was, because he was better dressed dan any of da odders, but I couldn't be sure, ya know?" He pushed the needle through the membrane without any sign that it pained him, stuck it around and in again, and pulled smoothly. The hole was beginning to close.

"So I shout down at dis joker about us needing some transportation upstream. First ting he does is call me a black-winged, gargoyle-faced, insect-eating son-of-a-bitch." He shrugged. "Da conversation went downhill from dere."

"I don't understand such hostility," murmured Clothahump, watching as their hoped-for transport began to slip out of sight eastward. No telling how long it might be before another going that way might pass them.

"I just got da impression," continued Pog, "that da captain and his crew were pretty fucking mad about someting and was in no mood to talk polite to anyone including dere own sweethearts, if dey got any, which I doubt. Why dey were so mad I don't know, an' I wasn't about ta hang around an make no pincushion of my little bod ta find out."

"We might find out anyway." Everyone looked toward Mudge. The otter was staring out across the river.

"How do you mean?" asked Flor.

"I believe they just threw somebody overboard."

Distant yelling and cursing came from the fading silhouette of the ship. Several splashes showed clearly now around the ship's side. Even Jon-Tom saw them.

"Somebody's jumped in after the first," said Talea. "I don't think anyone's been thrown, Mudge. There! The three that just jumped are being pulled back aboard. The first is swimming this way. Can you make out what it is?"

"No, not yet, luv," replied the otter, "but it's definitely comin' toward us."

They waited curiously while the ship slowly receded from sight, trailing a philologic wake of insult behind it.

Several long minutes later they watched as a thoroughly drenched figure nearly as tall as Flor emerged dripping from waist-deep water and slogged toward them. It was a biped and clad in what when dry would be an immaculate silk dressing jacket lined with lace at cuffs and neck. A lace shirt protruded wetly from behind the open jacket, the latter a green brocade inlaid with gold thread. The white lace was now dim with river muck.

Matching breeches blended into silk knee-length stockings which rose from enormous black shoes with gold buckles. The shoes, Jon-Tom estimated hastily, were comparable to a size twenty-two narrow for a human, which the damp arrival was not.

It stopped, surveyed them with a jaundiced eye, and began wringing water from its sleeves. A monocle remained attached to the jacket by means of a long gold chain. After adjusting it in his right eye, the rabbit said with considerable dignity: "Surely you would not set upon a traveler in distress. I am the victim of antisocial activities." He gestured tiredly upstream to where the boat had vanished.

"I cast myself on your mercies, being too exhausted to fight or flee any farther."

"Take it easy," said Talea. "You play square with us and we'll be square with you."

"An estimable offer of association, beautiful lady." Bending over, the rabbit shook his head and ran a clutching paw down each long white and pink ear. Water dripped from their ends.

A few isolated patches of brown and gray spotted the otherwise white fur. Nose and ears were partly pink. From a hole in the back of his breeches protruded a white tail. At the moment it resembled a soggy lump of used cotton.

Mudge had been assisting Pog in trimming and tying off the end of his stitchery. At first he'd paid the new arrival only cursory attention. Now he left the bat and moved to join his companions. As he did so he had a better view of the bedraggled but still unbowed refugee, and he let out an ear-splitting whistle.

Expecting the worst, the rabbit flinched back, thinking he was now about to be attacked despite Talea's announcement of assistance. But when he got his first look at the otter he let out a sharp whistle of his own. Mudge flung himself into the taller animal's arms and the two spent several minutes apparently trying to beat each other to death.

"Bugger me for a fag ferret!" Mudge was shouting gleefully. "Imagine seein' you 'ere!" He turned, panting, to find his friends staring dumbfoundedly at him. " 'Ere now, you chaps don't know who this be, do you?" He whacked the rabbit on the back once more. "Introduce yourself, you vagrant winter coat!"

The rabbit removed his monocle carefully and cleaned it with a dry sleeve. "I am Caspar di Lorca di l'Omollia di los Enansas Giterxos.

However," and he slipped the now sparkling eyepiece back in place, "you may all call me Caz."

He frowned as he examined his silk stockings and pants. "You must please excuse my dreadful appearance, but circumstances compelled that I exit hastily and by unexpected aquatic route from my most recent method of conveyance."

"Good riddance ta 'em," snorted Pog, giving the horizon the finger.

"Ah, the aerial disruption that facilitated my departure." The rabbit watched as Pog tested his repaired wing. "It was because of your arrival that I was able to take leave so unbloodily, my airborne friend. Though I had little time for extraneous observation I saw the disgusting manner in which you were treated. It was rather like my own situation."

Clothahump had little time for individual tales of woe, no matter how nicely embroidered. "Talea said that we would treat you fairly, stranger. So we shall. I must tell you immediately that I am a wizard and that," he pointed at Jon-Tom, "is an otherworldly wizard. With two wizards confronting you, you dare not lie. Now then, be good enough to tell us exactly why you jumped off that boat and why several members of its crew chased you into the water themselves?"

"Surely the sad details of my unfortunate situation would only bore you, wizened sir."

"Try me." Clothahump wagged a warning finger at the rabbit. "And remember what I said about telling the truth."

Caz looked around. He was cut off from the rest of the shore. Two humans of enormous size towered expectantly over him. If the turtle was no wizard, he was clearly convinced he was one.

"Best do as 'Is Smartship says, mate," Mudge told him. " 'E's a true wizard as 'e says. Besides," the otter hunkered down on his haunches against a smooth section of sand, "I'm curious meself."

"There's not much to relate." Caz moved over to their smoking camp fire and continued to dry himself. "It was in the nature of a childish dispute over a game of chance."

"That sounds about right." Talea grinned tightly. "They did throw you overboard, then?"

The rabbit smiled slightly, turned, and shoved his tail end toward the fire. "Sadly, they would not have been content with that. I fear they had somewhat more lethal designs on my person. I was forced to fend them off until your friend with the wings momentarily distracted them, thus enabling me to enter the river intact. Though I first tried my best to reason with them."

"Yeah," said Pog from nearby, "I saw how ya was reasoning wid dem." He flapped experimentally, rose a few feet into the air. "Dey reasoned ya all over da ship!"

"Ignorant peddlars of trash and quasi-pirates," said Caz huffily. He studied his sodden lacework in evident distress. "I fear they have caused me to ruin my attire."

"What did they catch you cheating at," asked Flor casually, "cards?"

"I beg your pardon, vision of heaven, but that is an accusation so vile I cannot believe it fell from the lips of one so magnificent as to constitute a monument to every standard of beauty in the universe."

"It fell," she told him.

"I never cheat at cards. I have no need to, being something of an expert at their manipulation."

"Which means they caught you cheating at dice," Talea said assuredly.

"I fear so. My expertise with the bones does not match my skill at cards."

Talea laughed. "Meaning it's a damnsight harder to hide a die up your sleeve than a card. No wonder your shirt boasts so much lace."

The rabbit looked hurt, ran fingers through the fur on his forehead and then up one ear. "I had hoped to find refuge. Instead I am subject to constant ridicule."

"Truth, you mean."

Caz readied another reply, but Flor interrupted him. "Never you mind. We're all busy showing each other how tough we can be. We'll just have to make sure not to gamble with you."

"Where such loveliness is present, I never gamble," he informed her. Flor looked nonplussed.

"Well, you're well out o' it, mate," observed Mudge. "From the look o' you, squelchy as a fish or not, you've done right well since the last we met."

"I recall that encounter clearly." Now the rabbit was cleaning his buckled shoes. "If I remember correctly, that was also an occasion that demanded a hasty departure."

High otter-laugh whistled over the water. "I'll never forget it, guv. The look on that poor banker clerk's face when 'e found out 'ow 'e'd been duked!" Their voices blended as they reminisced.

Talea listened for a few minutes, then walked to the water's edge. Flor was sitting there, watching the two furry friends converse.

"Otherworlder," Talea began, "that Caz had a certain look in his eye when he was talking to you. I know his type. Fast talk, fast action, fast departure. You watch yourself."

Flor looked up, then stood. She shaded the comparatively diminutive Talea.

"Thanks for the advice, but I'm a big girl now. I can take care of myself. *Comprende?*"

"Size and wise don't necessarily go together," the redhead said. "I was just giving you fair warning."

"Thanks for your concern."

"Just remember one thing about him." Talea nodded toward the chattering Caz. "He'll probably screw anything that walks and likely a few things that don't. Old Mudge is a talker, but this one's a doer. You can tell."

"I'm sure I can rely on your experienced judgment," replied Flor evenly. She moved away before Talea could ask exactly what the last comment meant.

"That is my recent history," the rabbit was saying. He examined the otter's companions. "What then are you bound to, old friend? This does not appear to me to be a typical robber band, though if such is their wont I daresay they would be efficient at it. Those are two of the biggest humans I've ever seen. And the turtle called the man an 'otherworldly' wizard."

"I don't wonder at your wonderin', mate," said Mudge. " 'Tis all part o' the strangest tale ever a 'alf-senile wizard wove. I'd give me left incisor if I'd never o' become involved with this bunch." His voice had dropped to a whisper.

"Now don't you go botherin' yourself about it. You can't 'elp me. You get on your way afore 'is 'ard-shelled and 'ard-'eaded wizardship there conscripts you also. 'E's a no-nonsense sorcerer 'e is, and 'e's dragged us all off on some bloody crusade to save the world. Don't think o' doubtin' 'is magic, for 'e's the real article, 'e is, not some carnival fakir. The tall 'uman man with the slightly stupid expression, 'im I still ain't figured out. 'E seems as naïve sometimes as a squallin' cub, but I've seen with me own eyes the magic 'e can work. 'E's a spellsinger."

"What about the tall human woman. Is she a sorceress?"

"Not that she's shown so far," said Mudge thoughtfully. "I don't think she is. Sure is built, though."

"Ah, my friend, you have no appreciation for the arts of higher learning. Even in our brief exchange I could tell that she is of a noble order of initiates on whom high intellectual honors are bestowed."

"Like I said," reiterated the otter, "she sure is built."

Caz shook his head dolefully. "Will you never lift your thoughts from the gutter, friend Mudge?"

"I like it in the gutter," was the response. " 'Tis warm and friendly down there, and you meet up with all manner o' interestin' folk. What's 'appened t' me since I made the mistake o' temporarily comin' out o' the gutter is that I was stuck as wet-nurse t' the lad, and now I've got meself sort o' swept along a course I can't change or swim out of. As I've said afore, mate, the company is nice but the situation sucks. Shssh, be quiet, an' watch your words. 'Ere 'e comes now."

Clothahump had waddled over to them. Now he looked sorrowingly down at Mudge. "My dear otter," he said, peering over his spectacles, "do you never stop to consider that one who is capable of calling up elemental forces from halfway across the universe is also quite able to hear what is being said only a few yards behind him?"

Mudge looked startled. "You 'eard everythin', then?"

"Most everything. Oh, don't look like a frightened infant. I'm not going to punish you for expressing in private an opinion you've made no secret of in public." The otter relaxed slightly.

"I didn't imagine you might 'ave a 'earin' spell set on yourself, Your Niceness."

"I didn't," explained the wizard. "I simply have very good hearing. A compensation perhaps for my weak eyesight." He regarded the watchful Caz. "You, sir, you have heard what our mutual friend thinks. Allow me to explain further, and then see if you think our 'crusade' is so insane."

He proceeded to give the rabbit a rundown on both their purpose and progress.

When he'd finished, Caz looked genuinely concerned. "But of course if what you say is imminent, then I must join your company."

"*Wot?*" Mudge looked stunned, and his whiskers twitched uncontrollably.

"That's damn decent of you," said Jon-Tom. "We can use all the help we can get."

"It simply seems to me," said the rabbit slowly, "that if the sorcerer here is correct, and I have no reason to doubt him, then the world as we know it will be destroyed unless we do our best to help prevent the coming catastrophe. That strikes me as quite an excellent cause to commit oneself to. Yes, I shall be honored to join your little expedition and give what assistance I may."

"You're daft!" Mudge shook his head in despair. "Downright balmy. The water's seeped into your brain."

"Idiot," was all Pog said, confirming Mudge's assessment of Caz's action. But there were congratulations and thanks from Clothahump and the two otherworldly humans.

Even Talea ventured a grudging kind of admiration. "Not many people around who'll do the honorable thing these days."

"That's true of at least one other world, too," added Flor tentatively.

"It is sad, but honor is a dying attribute." Caz put a paw over his heart. "I can but do my slight best to help restore it."

"We're certainly glad to have you with us." Clothahump was clearly overwhelmed by this first voluntary offer to help. "Do you have a sword or something?"

"Alas," said the rabbit, spreading his paws, "I have nothing but what you see. If I can procure a weapon I will naturally carry it, though I have found that my most efficient methods of disarming an opponent involve the employment of facile words and not sharp points."

"We need sword arms, not big mouths," grumbled Talea.

"There are times, head and heart of fire, when a large mouth can smother the best attack an antagonist can mount. Do not be so quick to disparage that which you do not possess."

"Now look here, are you calling me dumb, you fuzz-faced son of . . . !"

Clothahump stepped between them. "I will not tolerate fighting among allies. Save your fury for the Plated Folk, who will absorb all you can muster." He suddenly looked very tired.

"Please, no more insult-mongering. Not direct," and he glared at Talea, "or veiled," and he glanced over his shell at Caz.

"I shall endeavor to control an acid tongue," said the rabbit dutifully.

"I'll keep my mouth shut if he does the same," Talea muttered.

"Good. Now I suggest we all relax and enjoy the midday meal. Have you eaten recently, sir?"

The rabbit shook his head. "I fear I had to depart before lunch. This has not been my day for timing."

"Then we will eat, and wait. . . ."

XVI

But no other vessel appeared while they ate. Nor all the rest of that day or the morning of the next.

"In truth, we passed much commerce moving downstream toward the Glittergeist," Caz informed them, "but practically none save ourselves moving in the other direction. The winds are capricious this time of year. Not many shipowners are willing to pay the expense of poling a cargo all the way up the Tailaroam. Good polers are too expensive. They make profit most uncertain.

"We shall be fortunate to see another ship moving upstream, and even if we should, there's no guarantee they'd have room aboard for so many passengers. My vessel was quite crowded and I was the only noncrewmember aboard." He spat delicately at the sand. "A distinction I should have avoided."

Clothahump sighed. He struggled to his feet and trundled to the water's edge. After a long stare at the surface, he nodded and told them, "This part of the Tailaroam is wide and deep. It should be full of docile but fast-swimming salamanders. They will be safer and cheaper than any ship." He cleared his throat. "I will call several from the deeps to carry us."

He raised short arms over the gently lapping water, opened his mouth, and looked very confused. "At least, I believe I will. That spell . . ." He began searching the drawers in his plastron. "Salamanders . . . salamanders . . . Pog!"

The bat appeared, hovered in front of him. "Don't ask me, boss. I don't know where ya put it, either. I don't tink I ever remember hearin' about it. When was da last time ya had ta use it? Maybe ya can goose me memory if not your own."

The wizard looked thoughtful. "Let me see . . . oh yes, it was about a hundred years ago, I think."

Pog shook his head. "Sorry, Master. I wasn't around."

"Damn it," Clothahump muttered in frustration, still sorting through his shell, "it has to be in here someplace."

Jon-Tom turned his attention to the water. Everyone's attention was on the wizard. He swung the duar around from his back, experimented with the strings. Notes floated like Christmas ornaments over the surface.

"Allow me, sir," he said importantly, watching out of the corner of an eye to see if Flor was paying attention.

"What, again?"

He waded ankle-deep out into the water. It swirled expectantly about his boots. "Why not? Didn't I do well the last time we needed transportation?" Yes, Flor was definitely watching him now.

"You did well indeed, boy, but by accident."

"Not entirely accident. We needed transportation, I called for it, we got it. The outlines were a little different, that's all. I should have more control over it this time."

"Well . . . if you think you're ready." Clothahump sounded uncertain.

"Ready as I can be."

"Then you know a proper salamander song?"

"Uh . . . not exactly. Maybe if you'd describe one."

"We should need six of them," the turtle began. "Pog has his own transportation. Salamanders are about twelve feet long, including tail. They have shiny gray bodies tending to white on their bellies, and their backs and sides are covered with red and yellow splotches. They have small but sharp teeth, long claws on webbed feet, and are dangerous only when threatened. If you can induce them up, I can put a control spell on them that will allow us to manage them all the way to Polastrindu." He added under his breath, "Know that stupid thing's around here somewhere."

"Twelve feet long, gray to white with red and yellow spots, claws and teeth but dangerous only when threatened," Jon-Tom muttered. He was stalling for time, aware of everyone's eyes on him. "Let's see . . . something by Simon and Garfunkle maybe? No, that's not right. Zepplin, Queen, Boston . . . damn. There was a song by the Moody Blues . . . no, that's not right."

Flor leaned close to Talea. "What's he doing?"

"Preparing the proper spellsong, I suppose."

"He sounds confused to me."

"Wizards often sound confused. It's necessary to the making of magic."

Flor looked doubtful. "If you say so."

Eventually Jon-Tom reached the conclusion that he'd have to play something or admit defeat. That he would not do, not with Flor watching him. He fiddled with the mass and tremble controls, ran fingers over both sets of strings, strumming the larger and plucking at the smaller. No doubt he'd have been better off asking Clothahump for help, but the fear of self-failure pushed him to try.

Besides, what could go wrong? If he conjured up fish instead of salamanders they might not be on their way any sooner, but at least they would eat well while waiting.

Let's see . . . why should he not modify a song to fit the need of the moment? Therefore, ergo, and so forth. . . . "Yellow salamander" didn't scan the same as "yellow submarine," but it was close enough. "We all live on a yellow sal'mandee, yellow sal'mandee, yellow sal'mandee. . . ."

At the beginning of the chorus there was a disturbance in the water. It broadened into a wide whirlpool.

"They're down there, then," murmured Clothahump excitedly, peering at the surface. He tried to divide his attention between the river and the singer. "Maybe a little longer on the verbs, my boy. And a little more emphasis on the subjects of seeking. Sharply on the key words, now."

"I don't know what the key words are," Jon-Tom protested between verses. "But I'll try."

What happened was that he sang louder, though his voice was not the kind suited to shouting. He was best at gentle ballads. Yet as he continued the song became easier. It was almost as if his brain knew which of the words catalyzed the strange elements of quasi-science Clothahump called magic. Or was the wizard right, and science really quasi-magic?

This was no time, he told himself furiously as he tried to concentrate on the song, for philosophizing. A couple of jetboats might be even more useful. . . .

Careful, remember the riding snake! Ah, but that was a fluke, the natural result of an uncertain first-time try at a new discipline. Sheer accident. At the time he'd had no idea of what he'd been doing or how he'd been doing it.

Salamanders Clothahump wanted and salamanders he'd get.

Now the water in the vicinity of the whirlpool was beginning to bubble furiously.

"There they are!" yelled Talea.

"Blimey but the lad's gone an' done it." Mudge looked pridefully at his wailing ward.

For his part Jon-Tom continued the song, sending notes and words skipping like pebbles out across the disturbed river. Water frothed white at the center of the whirlpool, now bubbling to a respectable height. Occasionally it geysered twenty feet high, as if something rather more massive than a lowly salamander was stirring on the river bottom.

Talea and Caz were the first to frown and begin backing away from the shore. "Jon-Tom," she called to him, "are you sure you know what you're doing?"

Oblivious now to outside comments, he continued to sing. Clothahump had told him that a good wizard or spellsinger had to always concentrate. Jon-Tom was concentrating very hard.

"My boy," said Clothahump slowly, rubbing his lower jaw with one hand, "some of the words you're using . . . I know context is important, but I am not sure . . ."

Bubbles and froth rose three times the height of a man. There was a watery rumble and it started moving toward shore. If there were any amphibians out there, it was apparent they now likely numbered more than half a dozen.

The violence finally penetrated Jon-Tom's concentration. It occurred to him that perhaps he might be better off easing back and trying a new song. But Flor was watching, and it was the only watery song he knew. So he continued on despite Clothahump's voiced uncertainty.

At least something was out there.

There was thunder under the water now. Suddenly, a head broke the froth, a head black as night with eyes of crimson. There was a long narrow snout, slightly knobbed at the tip and crowded with razor ivories. Bat-wing ears fluttered at the sides and back of the skull. The head hooked from a thickly muscled, scaly neck and ran into a massive black chest shot through with lines of iridescent purple and azure. Red gills ran half the length of the neck.

A forefoot rose up out of the water. It was bigger than Jon-Tom, whose fingers had frozen on the strings of the duar as completely as the remaining words of the stanza had petrified in his mouth.

The sun continued to shine. Only a few dark clouds pockmarked the sky, but around them the day seemed to grow darker. The thick, leathery foot, dripping moss and water plants from black claws the length of a man's arm, moved forward to land in a spray of water. Webbing showed between the digits.

The elegant nightmare opened its mouth. A thin stream of organic napalm emerged in a spray that turned the water several yards short of the sandy peninsula into instant cloud.

"Ho!" said a distinct, rumbling voice that made Pog sound positively sweet by comparison, "who dares to disturb the hibernation of Falameezar-aziz-Sulmonmee? Who winkles me forth from my home inside the river? Who seeks," and the great toothy jaws curved lower on the muscular neck-crane, "to join great Falameezar for lunch?"

Mudge had scuttled backward and was nearing the edge of the forest. The dragon tilted its head, sighted, and closed one eye. His mouth tightened and he spat. A tiny fireball landed several feet ahead of Mudge, incinerating some bushes and a medium-sized birch. Mudge halted instantly.

"You have summoned me . . . but I have not dismissed you." The head was now almost drooping directly over Jon-Tom, who was developing a crick in his neck from looking up at it.

"Know that I am Falameezar-aziz-Sulmonmee, Three Hundred and Forty-Sixth of the line of Sulmonmeecar, Dragons of all the River, who guard the fast depths of all the rivers of all the worlds! Who, practitioner of rashness, might you be?"

Jon-Tom tried to smile. "Just a stranger here, just passing through, just minding my own business. Look now, uh, Falameezar, I'm sorry I disturbed you. Sometimes I'm not too prudent in certain things. Like, my elocution never seems able to keep up with my enthusiasm. I was really trying to summon some salamanders and—"

"There are no salamanders here," thundered the voice from behind the teeth. The dragon made a reptilian smile. A black gullet showed beyond the teeth. "I have already eaten all who swam hereabouts. The others have fled to safer waters, where I must soon follow." The smile did not fade. "You see, I am often hungry, and must take sustenance where I can find it. To each according to his needs, isn't that right?"

Clothahump raised his hands.

"Ancestor of the lizard neat,
Troubler of our tired feet,
On your way I bid you go,
Lest we your internal temp'rature low."

The dragon glanced sharply at the turtle. "Cease your mumblings, old fool, or I'll boil you in your shell. I can do that before you finish that incantation."

Clothahump hesitated, then fell silent. But Jon-Tom could see his mind working furiously. If someone could give him a little more time . . .

Without thinking, he took several steps forward until the water was lapping at the tops of his boots. "We mean you no harm," there was a faint dragon-chuckle and puffs of smoke drifted from scaly nostrils, "and I'm sorry if we disturbed you. We're on a mission of great importance to—"

"The missions and goings and comings of the warmlanders are of no interest to me." The dragon sounded disgusted. "You are all economically and socially repressive." His head dipped again and he moved closer, a black mountain emerging from the river. Now Falameezar was close enough to smash the duar player with one foot.

Somewhere behind him he could hear Flor whispering loudly, "A *real dragon!* How wonderful!" Next to her, Talea was muttering sentiments of a different kind.

"You live or become food," said the dragon, "at my whim. That is the way of dragons who chance upon travelers. As is our way, I will offer you the chance to win your freedom. You must answer a riddle."

Jon-Tom sloshed water with one foot. "I'm not much at riddles."

"You have no choice. In any case, you need not worry yourself much." Saliva was trickling from his lower jaw. "Know that not one who has come my way has been able to answer my riddle."

" 'Ere now, mate," Mudge called to him encouragingly, "don't let 'im intimidate you. 'E's just tryin' t' frighten you out o' careful consideration o' your reply."

"He's succeeding," Jon-Tom snapped back at the foolhardy otter. He looked back up at the mouth waiting to take him in one bite. "Isn't there some other way we can settle this? It's not polite to eat visitors."

"I did not invite you," growled the dragon. "Do you prefer to end it now by passing over your right to try and answer?"

"No, no!" He glanced sideways at Clothahump. The wizard was clearly mumbling some sort of spell soft enough so the dragon could not overhear, but either the spell was ineffective or else the wizard's capricious memory had chosen this inopportune moment to turn to mush.

"Go ahead and ask," he said, still stalling. Sweat was making his indigo shirt stick to his back.

The dragon smelled of mud and water and pungent aquatic things. The thick smell gave Jon-Tom something to concentrate on besides his fear.

"Then riddle me this," rumbled the dragon. He lolled in the shallow water, keeping a sharp, fiery eye on the rest of the frightened group.

"What is the fundamental attribute of human nature . . . and of all similar natures?" He puffed smoke, hugely enjoying Jon-Tom's obvious confusion.

"Love!" shouted Talea. Jon-Tom was shocked at the redhead's uncharacteristic response to the question.

"Ambition," suggested Flor.

"Greed." No need to see who'd said that. It could only have come from Mudge.

"A desire to better one's self without harming one's fellows." That was Caz's graceful offering. At least, it was graceful until he added, "Any more than necessary."

"Fear," said the stuttering Pog, trying to find a tree to hide behind without drawing the dragon's attention.

"The wish to gain knowledge and become wise," said Clothahump, momentarily distracted from his spell weaving.

"No, no, no, no, and no!" snorted the dragon contemptuously, searing the air with a gout of flame. "You are ignorant as all. All that fools have to recommend themselves is their taste."

Jon-Tom was thinking hectically about something the dragon had said before. Yes . . . his comment about the warmlanders being "economically and socially repressive." Now the riddle sounded almost familiar. He was sure he recognized it, but where, and was there more to it that might be the answer? His brain fumbled and hunted desperately for the distant memory.

Falameezar hissed, and water boiled around Jon-Tom's boots. He could feel the heat even through the thick leather. He wondered if he would turn red, like a lobster . . . or black, like burnt toast.

Perhaps the dragon could read minds as well as he could pose riddles. "I will now give you another choice. I can have you steamed or broiled. Those who would prefer to be steamed may step into the river. Those who prefer broiling remain where you are. It is of no matter to me. Or I can eat you raw. Most meals find precooking preferable, however."

Come *on*, meal, he chided himself. This is just another test, but it may be the last one if you don't . . .

"Wait. Wait a minute! I know the answer!"

The dragon cocked a bored eye at him. "Hurry up. I'm hungry."

Jon-Tom took a deep breath. "The fundamental attribute of human nature is . . . productive labor." For good measure he added casually, "Any fool knows that."

The dragon's head reared back, dominating the sky. Batwing ears fluttered in confusion, and for a moment he was so startled he choked on his own smoke.

Still menacingly, but uncertain now, he brought his massive jaws so near that Jon-Tom could have reached out and caressed the shiny black scales. The air was full of dampness and brimstone.

"And what," he rumbled, "determines the structure of any society?"

Jon-Tom was beginning to relax a little. Unbelievable as it seemed, he felt safe now. "Its economic means of production."

"And societies evolve . . . ?"

"Through a series of crises caused by internal contradictions," Jon-Tom finished for him.

The dragon's eyes flashed and his jaws gaped. Though confident he'd found the answer, Jon-Tom couldn't help but back away from those gnashing teeth. A pair of gigantic forefeet rose dripping from the water. Tiny crustaceans scrambled frantically for cover.

The feet lunged toward Jon-Tom. He felt himself being lifted into the air. From somewhere behind him Flor was yelling frantically and Mudge was muttering a dirge.

An enormous forked tongue as startlingly red as the slitted eyes emerged from the mouth and flicked wetly at Jon-Tom's face.

"Comrade!" the dragon declaimed. Then Jon-Tom was gently deposited back on dry land.

The dragon was thrashing at the water in ecstasy. "I *knew* it! I knew that *all* the creatures of this world could not exist ignorant of the true way." He was so happy he blew fire simply from pure joy, though now he carefully directed it away from his stunned audience.

The otter ran out onto the sand, sidled close to the tall human. "Crikey, mate, be this more o' your unexpected wizardry?"

"No, Mudge." He wiped dragon spit from his cheeks and neck. It was hot to the touch. "Just a correct guess. It was sparked by something he'd said to us earlier. Then it came back to me. What I don't understand is how this bonafide dragon was transformed into a dedicated Marxist."

"Maziwhich? Wot's that? Some otherworldly magickin', maybe?"

"Some people think so. Others would regard it more as pure superstition. But for God's sake, don't say anything like that to him or we'll all find ourselves in the soup, literally."

"Pardon my curiosity," he called to the dragon, "but how did you happen to stumble on the," he hesitated, " 'true way'?"

"It happens on occasion that dragons stumble into interdimensional warps," Falameezar told him as he calmed himself down. "We seem prone to such manifestations. I was suspended in one for days. That is when it was revealed to me. I have tried to make others see but," he shrugged massive black shoulders, "what can but one do in a world aswarm with voracious, ravenous capitalists?"

"What indeed?" murmured Jon-Tom.

"Even if one is a dragon. Oh, I try now and then, here on the river. But the poor abused boatmen simply have no comprehension of the labor theory of value, and it is quite impossible to engage even the lowliest worker in an honest socialist dialectic."

"I know the problem," said Jon-Tom sympathetically.

"You do?"

"Yes. As a matter of fact, we're all embarked on a journey right now, we seven comrades, because this land which you say is filled with capitalists is about to be invaded and overrun by an entire nation of totalitarian capitalists, who wish to enslave completely the, uh, local workers to a degree the primitive bosses hereabouts can't begin to match."

"A terrible prospect!" The dragon's gaze turned to the others. "I apologize. I had no idea I was confronting fellow crusaders of the proletariat."

"Dead right," said Mudge. "You ought t' be ashamed o' yourself, mate." He began cautiously moving back toward the sand. Clothahump looked at once intrigued and puzzled, but for the moment the wizard was quite content to let Jon-Tom do the talking.

"Now then, comrade." The massive black shape folded its forelegs and squinched down in the sandy shallows. "What can I do to help?"

"Well, as you would say, from each according to his ability to each according to his need."

"Just so." The dragon spoke in a tone usually employed for the raising of saints.

"We need to warn the people against the invasion of the bosses. To do so we must warn the local inhabitants of the most powerful center of government. If we could get upstream as quickly as possible—"

"Say no more!" He rose majestically on hind legs. A great surge of water nearly washed away their packs. As the dragon turned, his thick black and purple tail, lined with rigid bumps and spinal plates, stretched delicately onto the sand.

"Allow me the honor. I will take you wherever you wish, and far more quickly than any capitalist pig of a boat master could manage. On one condition." The tail slipped partway back into the river.

Jon-Tom had been about to start up the tail and now hesitated warily. "What's that?"

"That during the course of our journey we can engage in a decent philosophical discussion of the true nature of such matters as labor value, the proper use of capital, and alienation of the worker from his output. This is for my own use. I need all the ammunition I can muster for conversing with my fellows. Most dragons are ignorant of the class struggle." He sounded apologetic. "We tend to be solipsists by nature."

"I can understand that," said Jon-Tom. "I'll be happy to supply whatever arguments and information I can."

The tail slid back onto the sand. Jon-Tom began the climb up the natural ladder and glanced back at his companions.

"What are you all waiting for? It's safe. Falameezar's a fellow worker, a comrade."

The dragon positively beamed.

When they had all mounted and found seats and had secured their baggage, the dragon moved slowly out into the water. In a few minutes they had reached the center of the river. Falameezar turned upstream and began to swim steadily and without apparent effort against the considerable current.

"Tell me now," he said by way of opening conversation, "there is a thing I do not understand."

"There are things none of us understand," said Jon-Tom. "Just now I'm not too sure I understand myself."

"You are introspective as well as socially conscious. That's nice."

The dragon cleared his throat, and smoke drifted back over the riders.

"According to Marx, the capitalists should long since have been swept away and the world should now exist in a stateless, classless society. Yet nothing could be further from the truth."

"For one thing," Jon-Tom began, trying not to sound too much like a tutor, "this world hasn't yet fully emerged from the feudal stage. But more importantly . . . surely you've heard of Rosa Luxemburg's *Accumulation of Capital?*"

"No." A crimson eye blinked curiously back at him. "Please tell me about it."

Jon-Tom proceeded to do so, with caution and at length.

They had no problems. Falameezar could catch more fish in one snap than the entire party could in a day's trying, and the dragon was quite willing to share his catch. Also to cook it.

The assured, easy supply of fresh food led Mudge and Caz to grow exceedingly lazy. Jon-Tom's biggest worry was not occupying Falameezar but that either of the two dragon-borne lotus-eaters might let something slip in casual conversation which would tell the dragon that they were no more Marxists than they were celibate.

At least they were not merchants or traders. Mudge, Caz, and Talea qualified as free agents, though Jon-Tom couldn't stretch the definition of their erstwhile professions far enough to consider them craftsmen. Clothahump could be considered a philosopher, and Pog was his apprentice. With a little coaching from Jon-Tom, the turtle was able to acquire a semantic handle on such concepts as dialectical materialism and thus assist with some of the conversational load.

This was necessary because while Jon-Tom had studied Marxism thoroughly it had been over three years ago. Details returned reluctantly. Each was challenged by the curious Falameezar, who had evidently committed to memory every word of both *The Communist Manifesto* and *Das Kapital.*

There was no talk of Lenin or Mao, however, for which Jon-Tom was thankful. Any time the subject of revolution arose the dragon was apt to wonder if maybe they oughtn't to attack this or that town or cluster of traders. But without much of a practical base on which to operate he grew confused, and Jon-Tom was able to steer their debate to less violent aspects of social change.

Fortunately, there were few traders plying the river to stimulate the dragon's ire, and the moment they spotted the black silhouette of Falameezar they hastily abandoned both their boats and the water.

The dragon protested that he would like to talk with the crews as much as he would like to cremate the captains, but sadly admitted he did not seem to have the ability to get close to people.

"They don't understand," he was saying softly one morning. "I merely wish to be accepted as an equal member of the proletariat. They will not even stop to listen. Of course, most of them do not have the necessary grasp and overview of their society's socioeconomic problems. They rant and rave and are generally so abusive that they give me heartburn."

"I remember what you said about your fellow dragons' independent natures. Can't you organize them at all?"

Falameezar let out a disgusted snort, sending orange fire across the water's surface. "They will not even stop to listen. They do not understand that to be truly happy and successful it is necessary for all to work together, each helping his comrade as we march onward toward the glorious, classless, socialist future."

"I didn't know dragons had classes."

"It embarrasses me to admit it, but there are those among us who hold themselves better than their fellows." He shook his great head dolefully. "It is a sad, confused world we live in, comrade. Sad and exploitative."

"Too true," agreed Jon-Tom readily.

The dragon brightened. "But that makes the challenge all the greater, does it not?"

"Absolutely, and this challenge we go to confront now is the most dangerous one ever to face the world."

"I suppose." Falameezar looked thoughtful. "But one thing puzzles me. Surely among all these invaders-to-come there must be *some* workers? They cannot all be bosses."

Oh, lord, now how, Jon-Tom? "That's the case, I suppose," he replied as quickly as he could, "but they're all irrevocably imbued with the desire to be bigger bosses than those they now serve." Falameezar still seemed unsure.

Inspiration served. "And they also believe implicitly that if they can conquer the rest of the world, the warmlands and the rest, then they will become capitalist bosses over the workers here, and their old bosses will remain master over them. So they will give rise, if successful, to the most implacable class of capitalists the world has ever known, a class of bosses' bosses."

Falameezar's voice echoed like an avalanche across the water. "This must be stopped!"

"I agree." Jon-Tom's attention for the past hour had been more and more on the shoreline. Hills had risen in place of low beaches. On the left bank they merged into sheer rock walls almost a hundred feet high, far too high for even the powerful Falameezar to negotiate. The dragon was swerving gradually toward his right.

"Rapids ahead," he explained. "I have never traveled beyond this point. I dislike walking and would much rather swim, as befits a river dragon. But for the cause," he said bravely, "I will of course dare anything, so I will walk the rapids."

"Of course," Jon-Tom murmured.

It was growing dark. "We can camp the first place you can easily climb ashore, comrade Falameezar." He looked back in distaste. Mudge and Caz were playing at dice on a flat section of the dragon's back. "For a change maybe our 'hunters' can find us something to eat besides fish. After all," he murmured with a wicked grin, "everyone must contribute to the welfare of the whole."

"How very true," said the dragon, adding politely, "not that I mind catching you fish."

"It's not that." Jon-Tom was enjoying the thought of the two somnolent gamblers slogging through the muck to find enough meat to feed the voracious dragon. "It's time some of us did some real work for you. You've sure as hell done enough for us."

"Well put, comrade," said the dragon. "We must bow to social decorum. I would enjoy a change from fish."

The hilly shore bordered a land of smaller trees, narrower of bole and widely scattered amid thick brush. Despite his insistence that he preferred water to land, the dragon had no trouble smashing his way through the foliage bulwarking the water's edge.

A small clearing close to the river was soon located. They settled into camp to the accompaniment of rising moonlight. Ahead was the steady but soothing roar of the rapids Falameezar would have to negotiate the next day.

Jon-Tom dumped a load of wood by the fire, brushed bark and dirt from his hands, and asked Caz, "What do ships traveling past this point do about the rapids?"

"Most are constructed and designed so as to make their way safely through them when traveling down to the Glittergeist," the rabbit explained. "When traveling upstream it is necessary to portage around. There are places where it can be done. Logs have been laid across ancient, well-known paths. The ships are then dragged across this crude cellulose lubrication until quieter water is reached." He

nodded curiously toward the dragon. Falameezar lay contentedly on
the far side of the clearing, his tail curled across his jaws.

"How did you ever manage to talk the monster into conveying us
atop his belly instead of inside it? I understood nothing of his riddle
or your reply, nor of the lengthy talk you have engaged in subse-
quently."

"Never mind," said Jon-Tom, stirring the fire with a twig. "I'll
take care of the dialectic. You just try to say as little as possible to
him."

"No fear of that, my friend. He is not my idea of a scintillating
conversationalist. Nor do I have any desire to become someone's
supper through misapplication of a word or two." He patted Jon-
Tom on the back and grinned.

Despite the rabbit's somewhat aloof bearing, Jon-Tom couldn't
help liking him. Caz was inherently likable and had already proven
himself a willing and good-natured companion. Hadn't he volunteered to come on what was likely to be a dangerous journey? To be
quite fair, he was the only true volunteer among them.

Or was there some other motive behind the rabbit's participation
that so far he'd kept well hidden? The thought gave Jon-Tom an
unexpected start. He eyed the retreating ears. Maybe Caz had reasons
of his own for wanting to travel upstream, reasons that had nothing
to do with their mission. He might desert them at the first convenient
opportunity.

Now you're thinking like Clothahump, he told himself angrily.
There's enough for you to worry about without trying to analyze
your companion's thoughts.

Speaking of companions, where the devil had Mudge got himself
to? Caz had returned a few moments ago with a fat, newtlike creature. It drew deprecatory comments from Talea, the designated chef
for the evening, so they'd given it to the delighted Falameezar.

But Mudge had been gone a long time now without returning. Jon-
Tom didn't think the mercurial otter would try to split on them in so
isolated a place when he'd already passed up excellent opportunities
to do so in far more familiar surroundings.

He walked around the fire, which was now crackling insistently for
fuel, and voiced his concern to Clothahump. As usual, the wizard sat
by himself. His face shone in the firelight. He was mumbling softly to
himself, and Jon-Tom wondered at what lay behind his quiet talk.
There was real magic in the sorcerer's words, a source of never ending amazement to Jon-Tom.

The wizard's expression was strained, as befitted one on whose shoulders (or shell) rested the possible resolution of a coming Armageddon.

Clothahump saw him without having to look up. "Good eve to you, my boy. Something troubles you." Jon-Tom had long since overcome any surprise at the wizard's sensitivity.

"It's Mudge, sir."

"That miscreant again?" The aged face looked up at him. "What has he done now?"

"It's not what he's done so much as what he hasn't done, sir, which is come back. I'm worried, sir. Caz returned a while ago, but he didn't go very far into the forest and he hasn't seen Mudge."

"Still hunting, perhaps." Most of the wizard's mind seemed to be on matters far off and away.

"I don't think so, sir. He should have returned by now. And I don't think he's run off."

"No, not here, my boy."

"Could he have tried to catch something that caught him instead? It would be like Mudge to try and show off with a big catch."

"Not that simpleton coward, boy. But as to something else making a meal of him, that is always a risk when a lone hunter goes foraging in a strange forest. Remember, though, that while our otter companion is somewhat slow upstairs, there is nothing sluggish about his feet. He is lightning fast. It is conceivable that something might overpower him, but it would first have to surprise him or run him down. Neither is likely."

"He could have hurt himself," persisted a worried Jon-Tom. "Even the most skillful hunter can't outrun a broken leg."

Clothahump turned away from him. A touch of impatience crept into his voice. "Don't belabor it, boy. I have more important things to think upon."

"Maybe I'd better have a look for him." Jon-Tom glanced speculatively at the silent ring of thin trees that looked down on the little clearing.

"Maybe you had." The boy means well, Clothahump thought, but he tends not to think things through and to give in to his emotions. Best to keep a close watch on him lest he surrender to his fancies. Keep him occupied.

"Yes, that would be a prudent thing to do. You go and find him. We've enough food for the night." His gaze remained fixed on something beyond the view of mere mortals.

"I'll be back with him soon." The lanky youth turned and jogged off into the woods.

Clothahump was fast sinking into his desired trance. As his mind reeled, something pricked insistently at it. It had to do with this particular section of Tailaroam-bordered land. It was full night now, and that also was somehow significant.

Was there something he should have told the boy? Had he sent him off unprepared for something he should expect to encounter hereabouts? Ah, you self-centered old fool, he chided himself, and you having just accused *him* of not thinking things through.

But he was far too deeply entranced now to slip easily back into reality. The nagging worries fell behind his probing, seeking mind.

He's a brave youngster, was his fading, weak appraisal. He'll be able to take care of himself. . . .

Untold leagues away, underneath the infectious mists of the Greendowns in the castle of Cugluch, the iridescent Empress reclined on her ruby pillows. She replayed her sorcerer's words mentally, lingering over each syllable with the pleasure that destruction's anticipation sent through her.

"Madam," he had bowed cautiously over this latest pronouncement, "each day the Manifestation reveals powers for which even I know no precedent. Now I believe that we may be able to conquer more thoroughly than we have ever dreamed."

"How is this, Sorcerer?—and you had better be prepared to stand by any promises you make me." Skrritch eyed his knobby legs appraisingly.

"I will give you a riddle instead of a promise," Eejakrat said with untoward daring. Skrritch nodded.

"When will we have completed the annihilation of the warmlands?" he asked her.

"When every warmlander bows to me," she answered without hesitation.

The wizard did not respond.

"When every warmlander has been emptied to a dead husk?"

Still he did not reply.

"Speak, Sorcerer," Skrritch directed testily.

"The warmlands will be ours, my lady, when every warm-blooded slave has been returned to the soil and in his place stands a Plated subject. When the farmlands, shops, and cities of the west are repopulated with Plated Folk your empire will know no limit!"

Skrritch looked at him as if he'd gone mad and began to preen her claw tips. Eejakrat took a prudent step backward, but his words held the Empress in mid-motion.

"Madam, I assure you, the Manifestation has the power to incinerate entire races of warmlanders. Its death-power is so pervasive that we shall not only crush them, we will obliterate their memory from the earth. Your minions will march into their cities to find the complete welcome of silence."

Now Skrritch smiled her weird, omnivorous smile. The wizard and his queen locked eyes, and though neither really understood the extent of the destruction at their disposal, the air reverberated with their insidious obsession to find out. . . .

It was very dark in the forest. The moon made anemic ghosts of the trees and turned misshapen boulders to granite gargoyles. Bushes hid legions of tiny clicking things that watched with interest and talked to one another as the tall biped went striding past their homes.

Jon-Tom was in fair spirits. The nightly rain had not yet begun. Only the usual thick mist moistened his face.

He carried a torch made from the oil rushes that lined the river's edge. Despite the persistent mist the highly combustible reeds readily caught fire when he applied the tip of the well-spelled sparker Caz had lent to him. The torch lit readily and burned with a satisfying slowness.

For a moment he had thoughts of swinging round his duar and trying to conjure up a flashlight or two. Caution decided him against the attempt. The torch would serve well enough, and his accuracy where conjuration was involved thus far left something to be desired.

The ground was damp from the mist-caress of late evening, and Mudge's tracks stood out clearly. Occasionally the boot marks would cross each other several times in one place, indicating where the otter had rested behind a large boulder or fallen log.

Once the gap between the prints abruptly lengthened and became intermixed with tiny polelike marks, evidence that Mudge had given chase to something. The pole prints soon vanished and the otter marks shortened in stride. Whether the otter had made a successful kill or not Jon-Tom couldn't tell.

Oblivious to the fact that he was moving steadily deeper into the woods, he continued to follow the tracks. Unexpectedly the brush gave way to an open space of hard-packed earth that had been raised several inches above the level of the surrounding surface. The footprints led up to the platform and disappeared. It took Jon-Tom long minutes before he could locate traces of them, mostly scuffs from the otter's boot heels. They indicated he'd turned off to his right along the artificial construct.

"Come on back, Mudge!" There was no reply, and the forest swallowed any echo. "Caz brought in something already, and everyone's getting worried, and my feet are starting to hurt!" He started jogging down the platform.

"Come on out, damn you! Where the hell have—?"

The "you" was never uttered. It was replaced by a yelp of surprise as his feet went out from under him. . . .

XVII

He found himself sliding down a gentle incline. It was slight enough and rough enough so that he was able to bring himself to a halt after having tumbled only a few yards. The torch bumped to a stop nearby. It had nearly gone out. Flames still flickered feebly at one corner, however. Leaning over, he picked it up and blew on it until it was once more aflame. Try as he would, though, he couldn't induce it to provide more than half the illumination it had supplied before.

The reduced light was barely sufficient to show that he'd stumbled into an obviously artificial tunnel. The floor was flat and cobbled with some dully reflective stone. Straight walls rose five feet before curving to a slightly higher ceiling.

Having established that the roof was not about to fall in on him, he took stock of himself. There were only bruises. The duar was scratched but unbroken. Ahead lay a blackness far more thorough and intimidating than friendly night. He wished he hadn't left his staff back in camp. There was nothing but the knife strapped to his belt.

He stood, and promptly measured the height of the ceiling. Carefully turning around, he walked awkwardly back toward the circle of moonlight he'd fallen through. Nothing materialized from the depths of the tunnel to restrain him, though his neck hairs bristled. It is always easier to turn one's back on a known enemy than on an unknown one.

He crawled up the slight incline and was soon staring out at the familiar forest. The lip of the gap was lined with neatly worked stone engraved with intricate designs and scrollwork. Many twisted in upon themselves and were set with the same dimly reflective rock used to pave the tunnel.

He started to leave . . . and hesitated. Mudge's last boot prints had been moving in this direction. A close search of the rim of the hole showed no such prints, but the earth there was packed hard as concrete. A steel rod would not have made much of an impression upon it, much less the boot of an ambling otter.

The paving of the slope and tunnel was of still tougher material, but when he waved the torch across it the light fell on something even more revealing than a boot print. It was an arrow of the kind Mudge carried in his hunting quiver.

Crawling back inside, he started down the tunnel. Soon he came across another of the orphaned shafts. The first had probably fallen from the otter's quiver, but this one was cleanly broken. He picked it up, brought the torch close. There was no blood on the tip. It might have been fired at something and missed, to shatter on the wall or floor.

It was possible, even likely, that Mudge was pursuing some kind of burrow-dwelling prey that had made its home in the tunnel. In that case Jon-Tom's worries might prove groundless. The otter might be just ahead, busily gutting a large carcass so that he'd have to carry only the meat back to camp.

The thought of traveling down into the earth and leaving the friendly exit still further behind appalled him, but he could hardly go back and say truthfully he'd been able to track Mudge but had been too afraid to follow the otter the last few yards.

There was also the possibility that his first assumption might prove correct, that the creature Mudge had been pursuing had turned on him and injured him. In that case the otter might lie just a little ways down the tunnel, alive but helpless and bleeding.

In his own somewhat ambivalent fashion Mudge *had* looked out for him. Jon-Tom owed him at least some help, with either bulky prey or any injuries he might have suffered.

With considerable trepidation he started moving down the tunnel. The slope continued to descend to the same slight degree. From time to time torchlight revealed inscriptions on the walls. There also were isolated stone tablets neatly set into recesses. Directions perhaps . . . or warnings? He wondered what he would do if he reached a place where the tunnel split into two or more branches. He was too intent on the blackness to study the revealing frescoes overhead.

He had no desire to become lost in an underground maze, far from surface and friends. No one knew where he was, and when the night rain began it would obliterate both Mudge's tracks and his own.

Holding the torch ahead and to one side, he continued downward. Mmmmmm-m-m-m-m-m . . .

He stopped instantly. The eerie moaning came clearly to him, distorted by the acoustics of the tunnel. He knelt, breathing hard, and listened.

Mmmm-lllll-l-l-l-l . . .

The moan sounded again, slightly louder. What unimaginable monster might even now be treading a path toward him? His torch still showed only blackness ahead. Had the creature already devoured the poor otter?

He drew the knife, wishing again for the staff and its foot-long spear point. It would have been a particularly effective weapon in the narrow tunnel.

There was no point in needlessly sacrificing himself, he thought. He'd about decided to retreat when the moan unexpectedly dissolved into a flurry of curses that were as familiar as they were distinct.

"Mmmm-l-l-l-let me go or I'll slice you into stew meat! I'll fillet you neat and make wheels out o' your 'eads! I'll pop wot little eyeballs you've got out o' their sockets, you bloody blind-faced buggerin' ghouls!"

A loud *thump* sounded, was followed by a bellow of pain and renewed cursing from an unfamiliar source. The source of the first audible imprecations was no longer in doubt, and if Mudge was cursing so exuberantly it was most likely for the benefit of an assailant capable of reason and understanding and not blind animal hatred.

Jon-Tom hurried down the corridor, running as fast as possible with his hunched-over gait. There were still no lights showing ahead of him, so he had burst around a bend and was on top of the busy party before he realized it.

Letting out an involuntary yell at the sight, he threw up his arms and fell back against a wall, waving knife and torch to keep his balance. The effect produced among Mudge's attackers was unexpected, but highly satisfactory.

"Lo, a monster! . . . Daemon from the outer world! . . . Save yourselves! . . . Every mole for hisself . . . !"

Amid much screaming and shrieking he heard the sounds of tiny shoes slapping stone racing not toward but away from him. This was mixed with the noise of objects (weapons, perhaps) being thrown away in great haste by their panicky owners.

It occurred to him that the sight of a gigantic human clad entirely in black and indigo, flashing a reflective green lizardskin cape and brandishing a flaming torch and knife, might be something which could truly upset a tunnel dweller.

When the echoes of their flight had finally faded away, he regained control of his own insides and lowered the torch toward the remaining shape on the floor.

" 'Ad enough, then, you bloomin' arse'oles?" The voice was as blustery as before, if softer from lack of wind. "Be that you, mate?" A pause while otter eyes reflected the torchlight. "So 'tis, so 'tis! Untie me then mate, or give me the knife so's I can cut—"

"If you make a move, outworlder," said a new voice, "I will slit what I presume to be your friend's throat. I can get to it before you can reach me."

Jon-Tom raised the torch higher. Two figures lay on the floor of the tunnel. One was Mudge. His feet were bound at the ankles and knees and his arms done up similarly at wrists and elbows. A carrying pole had been slipped neatly between the bindings.

Leaning over the otter was a furry creature about four feet tall. His attire was surprisingly bright. He wore a yellow vest studded with blue cabochons and held together across the chest with blue laces. Additional lacings held the vest bottom securely to what looked like lederhosen.

A ringlet much like a thin tiara sat askew on the brown head. It was fastened under the chin by yellow straps. Broad sandals were laced across its feet. The sandals were pointed at toe and heel, possibly a matter of design, perhaps to aid in digging, giving freedom to the long thick claws on each hind foot.

One hand was fitted with a yellow metallic glove. This covered the creature's face as he squinted sideways through barely spread fingers, though he was trying hard to look directly at Jon-Tom and his torch.

The other hand held the sickle-shaped weapon that was resting on the otter's throat. Mudge's own weapons lay scattered on the floor nearby, even to his secret heel-boot knife. His arrows, sword, and bow shared space with the spears and wicked-looking halberds abandoned by those who had fled at Jon-Tom's appearance.

"I say to you again," repeated the determined gopher, his grip tightening on the sickle-knife, "if you move I'll open this thief's neck and let out his life among the stones."

"Thief?" Jon-Tom frowned as he looked back down at the tightly trussed otter.

"Ah, you fart-faced worm eater, that's the biggest lie since Esaticus the eagle claimed to 'ave done it flyin' underwater!"

Jon-Tom settled back against the cool wall and deliberately lowered his knife, though he didn't go so far as to replace it in its sheath. The gopher watched him uncertainly.

"What has been going on here, Mudge?" he asked the otter quietly.

"I'm tellin' you, mate! I was out huntin' for our supper when I tripped while chasin' a fine fat broyht. I fell down into this pit o' 'orrors, where I was promptly set upon by this 'orde o' rabid cannibals. They're blood-drinkers, lad. You'd best take care o' this one with your magical powers afore—"

"That's enough, Mudge." He looked up at the gopher. "You can put up your sickle, or knife, or whatever you call it, sir. That position can't be too comfortable." He set the torch down on the floor. "I'm sorry if my light hurts your eyes."

The gopher was still wary. "Are you not this one's friend?"

"I'm his associate in travel. I'm also a believer in the truth. I promise not to attack you while we talk, or make a hostile move of any kind."

"Lad, you don't know wot you're sayin'! The minute you put up your knife 'e's likely to—"

"Mudge . . . shut up. And be glad I'm here instead of Clothahump. He'd probably just leave you." The otter went quiet, muttering under his breath.

"You have my word," Jon-Tom informed the gopher, "as a traveler in your country and as a," he thought rapidly, "as a wizard who means you no harm. I swear not to harm you on my, uh, sacred oath as a spellsinger."

The gopher noted the duar. "Wizard it may be, though it was more of a daemonic effect you had upon my men." Reluctantly the scythe blade moved away from Mudge's throat.

"I'm Jon-Tom."

"And I am called Abelmar." The gopher moved his hand away from his eyes and squinted painfully at the man. "It was your light as well as your appearance which startled my troop. Most of them are moles and the light is far more hurtful to them than to me, for my kind occasionally make daytime forays when the city so requires it. Some daytime activity is necesary for the maintenance of normal commerce, much as we of Pfeiffunmunter prefer to keep to ourselves." He looked meaningfully down at Mudge.

"Except when we are intruded upon by cutthroats and thieves."

" 'Tis all a bloody lie!" Mudge protested. "When I get out o' these blinkin' ropes I'll do some intrudin' you'll never forget. Come on now, mate," he said to Jon-Tom, "untie me."

Jon-Tom ignored the twisting, writhing otter. "I meant no intrusion, Abelmar. My friend says that you attacked him. You've called him a thief."

"I am in charge of the east-end morning patrol," explained the gopher. He looked worriedly back down the tunnel. "Citizens will soon be appearing on nightly business, awakening from the day's sleep. It would be embarrassing for them to see me this way. Yet I must carry out my duty." He stiffened.

"Your associate is guilty of attempted theft, a sadly common crime we must continually face when we deal with outlanders. Yet it is not the theft that troubles us so much as the vandalism."

"Vandalism?" Jon-Tom looked accusingly at Mudge.

"Yes. It is not serious, but if left unchecked could become a serious threat to our neatly built community. Do you have any idea, Jon-Tom, how taxes go up when the public thoroughfares are torn to pieces by strangers?"

" 'E's lying through those oversized teeth o' 'is again, mate," Mudge protested, though with less conviction this time. "Why would I want t' go around rippin' up 'is blinkin' street?"

Abelmar sighed. "I suppose it is our own fault, but we are aesthetes by nature. We enjoy a bit of brightness in our city, for all that it gives us problems with ignorant travelers such as this," and he kicked Mudge in the back. "But I see you still do not understand." He'd grown accustomed enough to Jon-Tom's torch to look without blinking now.

"Look," and he bent toward Mudge.

"Careful!" Jon-Tom took a step forward and raised his knife.

"Easy move, Jon-Tom stranger," said the gopher. "If you are suspicious of my movements, then look instead at your own feet. Or can it be in truth you have not looked closely at our fine streets?"

Jon-Tom knelt cautiously, still keeping an eye on the gopher. Moving the torch, he stared intently at the closely laid bricks. They gleamed as dully as those he'd encountered near the tunnel entrance, only with the torch resting directly on them the glow intensified. They threw back a half-familiar, reddish-yellow light.

"Gold?" he asked uncertainly.

"Common enough below Pfeiffunmunter," said the gopher with a trace of bitterness, "but not to those who come along and try ripping it out of our beautiful pathways and boulevards. It makes for pretty paving, don't you think?"

"Surely now that you understand you can excuse me the temptation, mate," said Mudge defensively. "You wouldn't think these grave diggers would be so greedy they'd resent a poor visitor a few cobblestones."

"Excuse me." Jon-Tom rose and almost cracked his head again on the low ceiling. "I apologize to you for any damage, Abelmar."

"It's not too bad. You have to understand," the gopher told him, "that if we let this sort of thing persist and word of it spread 'round the outworld, before too long we'd have mobs of sunlifers down here destroying all our public thoroughfares, our roads, and our very homes. It would be the end of civilization as we know it."

He paused. Noise was growing behind him, moving up from the depths of the tunnel. "Travelers out for an evening walk," the gopher surmised, "or else my men, the cowardly bastards, coming back to see if anything's left of me." He sighed. "I have my duty, but I can face reality as well. We have something of a standoff here, friend spellsinger. I must confess I am now more interested in punishing my men than in your pitiful petty thief of a friend.

"If you will get him out of here and promise not to let him return, and will do so without disturbing any municipal construction, I won't report this incident to the Magistrates, or cut your friend's throat. Well though he deserves it!"

"I'd appreciate that, and I agree," said Jon-Tom.

"So do I, guv'nor." Mudge smiled toothily up at the gopher.

Abelmar hesitated, then used the curved blade on the otter's ropes before slipping it through a catch in his lederhosen straps. Mudge scrambled across the floor until he was standing next to Jon-Tom. He stretched luxuriously, working the kinks out of his muscles and joints.

"Now mate, quick now, while there still be time!" He bent and hefted one of the loose golden bricks. "Cover me with the knife while I slip a few o' those into me quiver an' pants." He hurried to recover his own weapons. "You're bigger than 'im, and you've got the light."

When the otter had finished gathering up his possessions, Jon-Tom said tiredly, "All right, Mudge. Put down the gold and let's go."

The otter stared at him, both arms now full of gleaming paving-stones. "You gone daft, mate? I'm 'oldin' a bloody fortune right now. We've got us a chance t'—"

"Put it down, Mudge!" The knife moved threateningly, not at the gopher now. "Or I swear I'll leave you the way I found you."

"Cor," muttered the otter. Reluctantly he opened his arms.

There was a heavy clattering as the gold bricks dented the pavement. Abelmar was nodding and looking satisfied. The cries of the approaching patrol were intelligible now. He peered down the tunnel and thought he could see dim, snouty shapes approaching. They wore gold earrings, clothing similar to Abelmar's, and very dark sunglasses. Their newly acquired weapons shone in the faint torchlight. Jon-Tom idly noted that the gopher's sickle-knife was made of gold.

"You're a man of your word," said the gopher, "which is rare among sunlifers. Go in peace." He glared at Mudge. "If I ever run across your flea-flecked body again, sir, I'll see you skinned and thrown to the carrion herds."

Mudge made quick use of the middle digit of his right hand. "Up yours, shit face!" He turned to Jon-Tom. "Right, then. It's done. You've kept your part o' the bloody bargain, but you've no guarantee 'is men will keep theirs."

"Let's get going, then." They started back up the tunnel.

"No need to worry," Abelmar shouted to them, "my men will be busily engaged." He turned to face down the tunnel.

"So, you cowards have come back, have you?"

Angry mutterings sounded from the ranks of armed moles. A few gophers were scattered among them.

"They're getting away, sir!" shouted one of the moles, pointing up the tunnel.

"When I'm finished with you lot you'll wish you'd gone with them!" roared Abelmar, letting loose a string of curses that reverberated around the tunnel. Their echoes followed Jon-Tom and Mudge out.

"Keep going, Mudge." Jon-Tom gave the otter a gentle but insistent shove.

" 'Ere now, mate, let's not panic, shall we? That officer's stopped t' give 'is troop a thorough bastin'. There's still plenty o' pavin' 'ereabouts." He stomped on the bricks with one boot. "It wouldn't 'urt no one if we took a few minims 'ere and did a nice little bit o' work. There be no way that buck-toothed flat-faced cop would know we were the ones responsible. Perhaps if I just—"

"Perhaps if I just stick this torch up your ass," Jon-Tom told him firmly.

"All right, all right. It were only a thought, lad."

The moon was bright when they emerged again into the forest. There were no indications of pursuit, though he had a feeling of movement from behind them. It was a distant rumbling, the sounds carried through the earth that indicated the burrow city of Pfeiffunmunter was coming awake for another busy night.

"Just be thankful I got there when I did," he told the otter. "He might've cut your throat without waiting to present you to the Magistrates."

"Poppycock," snorted Mudge. "I could've made me way loose eventual-like." He straightened his vest and tugged his cap tight on his head. "All that beautiful gold!" He shook his head regretfully. "More gold than even wizards can make! An' those bloody dirt-eaters defile it by usin' it just t' walk upon."

"That's better than the other way around."

"Huh?" Mudge eyed him perplexedly. "Are you wizard riddlin' me, mate?"

"Not at all." They turned off into the woods.

The otter looked bemused. "You be either the sharpest spellsinger that ever came up the river, mate, or else the biggest fat'ead."

Jon-Tom smiled faintly. "Hardly much thanks for the one who saved your life." He pushed at the clinging brush.

"Better to die tryin' for wealth than to live on in poverty," the otter grumbled.

"Okay. Go on back to the entrance, then. I won't try to stop you. See if you can help yourself to some pavement. I'm sure Abelmar and his troops will be happy to welcome you. Or do you think him fool enough to trust us to the point of leaving the gateway unguarded?"

"On the other 'and," Mudge said, without breaking stride, " 'tis a wise chap who bides 'is time and rates 'is chances. I told you once I ain't no gambler, not like old Caz. But if you'd come back an' give me a 'and, lad. . . ."

"No way." He shook his head. "I gave my word."

The otter looked crushed, shoved aside a branch, and cursed his foul luck as he stumbled over a projecting root.

"If you expect to make anythin' o' yourself 'ere, mate, you're goin' to 'ave to discard these otherworldly ethical notions."

"That sounds funny coming from you, Mudge. If you'll think a moment, you'll remember that you're embarked on an ethical sort of journey."

"Under duress," Mudge insisted.

Jon-Tom looked back and smiled at him. "You know, I think you use that as an excuse to keep from having to admit your real feelings." The otter grumbled softly.

"We'll tell them you had an unsuccessful hunt, which is hardly a lie. That'll do you better than telling them what a greedy, self-centered little prick you really are."

"Now that 'urts me to me 'eart, lad," Mudge said in mock pain.

"It would have hurt you a lot more if you'd returned with your arms full of gold and Falameezar saw you. Or hadn't you stopped to consider that? Considering the strength of his feelings where personal accumulation of wealth is concerned, I don't think even I could have argued him out of making otter chips out of you."

Mudge appeared genuinely startled. "You know wot, mate? I truly 'adn't given the great beastie a thought. 'E is a mite quick-tempered, even for a dragon."

"Not quick-tempered at all," Jon-Tom argued. "He simply believes in his own ethical notions. . . ."

The beginnings of real distress were stirring through the camp when they finally walked into the glow of the camp fire. Falameezar was vowing he'd burn down the entire forest to find Jon-Tom, while Pog had volunteered to lead a night search party.

It was difficult for Jon-Tom to restrain himself from telling them the truth as he watched Talea and Flor fawn over the otter.

"Are you all right?" asked Flor, running concerned fingers through the fur of his forehead.

"What happened out there?" Talea was exhibiting more concern than she had for anyone since the journey'd begun.

" 'Twas a chameleon," said Mudge bravely, sitting down on a rock near the fire with the look of one who'd run far and hard. "You know 'ow dangerous they can be, Talea. Blendin' their colors in with the landscape and waitin' with those great sticky tongues o' theirs for some unwary travelersby."

"Chameleons?" Flor looked confusedly over at Jon-Tom. He muttered something about much of the reptilian life growing to the size of buffaloes and why should chameleons be any exception.

"I just 'ad crept up on 'im and was drawin' back me bow," said Mudge tensely, warming to his story, "when the brute saw me against a light-barked tree. Turned on me right there, 'e did, with all three horns a flashin' in the moonlight an 'im so close I could smell 'is fetid breath."

"What happened then?" wondered Flor, leaning close. The exhausted otter rested the back of his head against the cushion of her bosom and tried with difficulty to concentrate on his spellbinding invention, while Talea soothingly stroked one limp arm.

"I 'eard that slick raspy noise they make when they open their jaws just afore the strike, so I dove right back between two trees. That tongue came after me so fast you'd o' swore it 'ad wings o' its own. Came right between the trees after me an' went over me 'ead so near it took off the top o' me cap.

"I started runnin' backward, just to keep 'im in sight. The damn persistent cham followed 'is tongue right through those trees. I tell you, 'is nose 'orn 'twere no farther from me 'eart than you are from me now." He patted the cushion against which he rested.

"Then how did you get away?" asked the rapt Flor, her black hair mixing in his short fur.

"Well, 'e charged so fast and reckless, so 'ungry was 'e for me flesh, that 'e gets 'imself pinned between the trunks, 'is top right 'orn pierced 'alfway through one. For all I know 'e's still there a-tuggin' and a-pullin', tryin' to free 'imself." Whiskers twitching, the otter wiped a hand across his forehead.

" 'Twere a near thing, luv."

A disgusted Jon-Tom was angrily tossing twigs into the fire. A warm paw came down on his shoulder. He looked up to see Caz, the orange firelight sparkling on his monocle, grinning down at him around a pair of blunt white incisors.

"Something less than the truth to our friend's tale, Jon-Tom?" Another twig bounced into the flames. "I know, I've heard him spin stories before. What he lacks in literacy he compensates for with a most fecund imagination. By the time he finishes he will half believe it actually happened."

"I don't mind him spinning a yarn," Jon-Tom said, "it's the way those two are lapping it up."

"Don't let it dig at you, my friend," said the aristocratic lepus. "As I said, it is his enthusiasm that carries his storytelling. Before very long cleverness instinctively gives way to a natural lack of subtlety coupled with an inability to let well enough alone."

In confirmation, a startled yelp came from the other side of the fire, followed by the sound of a hand striking furry flesh. An argument filled the misty night air. Jon-Tom saw both Flor and Talea stalking angrily away from the recumbent and protesting otter.

"You see?" Caz sounded disapproving. "Mudge is a good fellow, but at heart he is crude. No style."

"What about you?" Jon-Tom looked curiously up at his companion. "What's your style? What do you expect to get out of this journey?"

"My style . . . is to be myself, friend." It was spoken with dignity. "To be true to myself, my friends, and forgiving to my enemies."

"Including those who chased you off the boat?"

"Tut! They were justified in their feelings, if not the extremity of their reaction." He winked with his unglassed eye. "I was doubtless guilty of some indelicate prestidigitation of the dice. My mistake was that I was found out.

"If they had actually caught and killed me, of course, I would have been somewhat more upset."

Jon-Tom couldn't help breaking into a grin.

"As to what I expect to 'get out of this journey,' I have already stated that I feel assisting this worthy cause is reason and therefore satisfaction enough. You have been too long in the company of likable but amoral types such as Mudge and Talea. I believe implicitly everything our currently comatose wizard leader says.

"I have been studying him closely these past few days. Any idiot can see plainly that all the woes of the world weigh squarely upon his head. I am no hero, Jon-Tom, but neither am I such a fool that I cannot see that the destruction of the world as it currently exists would mean the end of my pleasant manner of living. I'm quite fond of it.

"So you see, it is in my own best interest to go along with and to help you, as it would be for any warmlander satisfied with his existence. I will help Clothahump in any way I can. I am not much for soldiering, but I have some skill in the use of words. Even he realizes, I think, that he has a tendency to be impatient with fools. On the other hand I am quite used to dealing with them."

"This group could sure use a diplomat," agreed Jon-Tom. "I've tried my best at mediating but . . . I guess I just don't have the experience for it."

"Do not belittle that which you have no control over, which is your youth, my friend. You strike me as wise for your years. That's more than anyone could ask, from what I've learned of your unwilling presence here. It strikes me you want not for ability but for goals.

"Though I have more experience than you, I am always willing to listen to others. And I could never do what you've done with the dragon. There is experience and there is experience. You handle him who breathes fire and I will take care of those who breathe insults and threats. We will complement each other. Agreed?"

"Fair enough." Man and rabbit shook hands warmly. The sensation no longer surprised Jon-Tom. It was like shaking hands with someone wearing mittens.

Camp was growing quiet and the nightly rain had hesitantly begun a late fall.

"You see?" Caz pointed to the motionless figure of Clothahump, still seated on his log. He seemed not to have moved since Jon-Tom left the camp to search for Mudge. Now he sat glaze-eyed and indifferent to the falling rain.

"Our friend broods on larger matters. Yet often is the greater lost for lack of attention to the lesser."

"Meaning what?"

"Meaning that we have posted no sentries. This is strange country to all of us."

"In this case I don't think we have to worry. You're forgetting something." He pointed.

" 'Pon my soul," laughed the rabbit, "so I have." He sounded embarrassed. "It is not easy to forget a dragon. How quiet he is, though."

"Dreaming sweet dreams of a classless society, no doubt."

Caz removed his monocle, absently polished it with the hem of his beautiful shirt. "Then it seems we can sleep soundly ourselves. The dragon's presence is worth more than any hundred sentries. I will enjoy the security of sleeping near to so powerful an ally."

"Just be careful he doesn't turn in his sleep." Caz waved smilingly back to him, and Jon-Tom watched the bobbing white tail recede toward the black bulk shielding their camp.

A gentle voice reached back to him. "Dragons don't toss and turn in their sleep, my friend. They're not built that way. But I surely hope he does not snore. I wouldn't enjoy waking up with my pants on fire."

Jon-Tom laughed with him. Pog was asleep, dangling like a dark decoration from the branch of an overhanging oak. Talea and Flor were chatting quietly beneath bedrolls on the other side of the fire. He thought of joining them, shrugged, and spread out his own blanket. He was dead tired, and it would soon be morning.

Right then his body needed comforting more than his ego. . . .

XVIII

Two days of climbing the rapids followed, during which the only danger they had to cope with was the burning in Jon-Tom's ears as he was compelled to endure Mudge's reciting and embroidering of the story of his escape from the monstrous chameleon. When the horned color-changer grew to twice the size of Falameezar, even Flor threatened to beat the glib otter.

On the fourth day they encountered signs of habitation. Plowed fields, homes with neatly thatched or slate-tiled roofs, smoking chimneys, and small docks with boats tied to them began to slip past.

Falameezar would glide deeper in the water, keeping only his eyes, ears, and passengers above the surface as he breathed through his gills. Anyone on shore watching would think the several travelers were floating atop a peculiarly low boat.

On the tenth day Clothahump noted a group of low hills off to their left. Rapids lay directly ahead, though they were not nearly as swift as those that cut through the Duggakurra hills close by buried Pfeiffunmunter.

"You may put us ashore here, friend dragon. We are quite close to the city."

"But why?" Falameezar sounded disappointed. "The river is still deep and the current not too strong." He puffed smoke ahead. "I can pass on easily."

"Yes, but your presence with us might panic the inhabitants."

"I know." The downcast dragon let out a sigh. "I shall put you in to land, then. What shall I do next?"

Jon-Tom threw Clothahump a look, and the wizard subsided in the youth's favor. "I'll talk to the commissars of the Polastrindu commune. Perhaps they might accept you as a member."

"Do you think so? I had no idea so enlightened a community existed." Fiery eyes stared back down at Jon-Tom hopefully. "That would be wonderful. I'm certainly willing to do my share of the work."

"You've already done more than that this trip, comrade Falameezar. Clothahump is right, though, in suggesting you wait here in the river. Even the most educated comrades can sometimes react thoughtlessly when confronted by the unfamiliar." He leaned forward, and the dragon bent his neck back and down as Jon-Tom whispered to him, "There are counterrevolutionaries everywhere!"

"I know. Be on your guard, comrade Jon-Tom."

"I will."

The dragon eased into shore. They marched down his back and tail, passing supply packs from hand to hand. A well-used track halfway between a wide trail and a small road led over the hills. Jon-Tom looked back for a moment. The others had already started up the road. Flor was alive with excitement at the prospect of entering the strange city. Her enthusiasm made her glow like the lining of clouds after a storm.

He waved to the dragon. "Be well, comrade. Up the revolution."

"Up the revolution!" the dragon rumbled back, saluting him with a blast of fire and smoke. Then the ferocious head dipped beneath the surface. A flurry of bubbles and some fading, concentric ripples marked with a watery flower the place where the dragon sank. Then they too were gone.

Jon-Tom waded, his long legs and walking staff soon bringing him up alongside his companions, despite the burden of guilt he carried. Falameezar was far too nice a dragon to have been so roundly deceived. Perhaps they'd left him happier than he'd been before, though.

"What do you think he'll do?" Caz moved next to Jon-Tom. "Will he stay and wait for you to return?"

"How should I know? I'm no expert on the motivations of dragons. His political beliefs seem unshakable, but he tends more to philosophizing than action, I think. He might simply grow bored and swim back downstream to his familiar feeding grounds." He looked sharply at the rabbit. "Why? Do you expect trouble in Polastrindu?"

"One never knows. The larger the city, the more arrogant the citizens, and we're not exactly the bearers of good news. We shall see."

An hour's hike had brought them to the crest of the last hill. Finally the destination of so many days' traveling lay exposed to their sight.

It was wonderful, yes, but it was a flawed wonderment. They started down the hill. Why should a city here be so very different from any other? he thought sardonically.

There was a massive stone wall surrounding the city. It was intricately decorated with huge bas-reliefs and buttressed at ground level. Several gates showed in the wall, but the traffic employing them was sparse.

It was not a market day, Caz explained. Farmers were not bringing produce into the city, nor distant craftsmen and traders their wagon-borne wares.

There was somewhat more activity to the south of the city. The great wall ran almost to the river there. At least a dozen vessels were tied to the rotting docks. Some were similar to the sail-and-oar-powered keel-type boat that Caz had fled from that day on the river. Jon-Tom wondered if that very same ship might be among those bobbing gently at anchor below them. Barges and fishing vessels comprised the rest of the motley but serviceable flotilla.

"The main gate is on the opposite side of the city, to the northwest and facing the Swordsward."

"What's that?" Flor wondered aloud. "Have you been there? It seems like you've been everywhere."

Caz cleared his throat. "No, I have not. I've been no farther than anyone else, I should say. It is a vast, some say endless, ocean of vegetation inhabited by vile aborigines and dangerous creatures.

"We have no need to march around the whole city. The harbor gate should be a quite satisfactory ingress."

They continued down the winding path, which had now expanded to road size. Curious fellow travelers let their gaze linger long on the unusual group.

Lizard-drawn wagons and carts trundled past them. Sometimes riders on individual mounts would run or hop past. There was even a wealthy family on a small riding snake.

Clothahump was enjoying himself. He moved with much less effort downhill than up. His glance turned upward. "Pog! Anything to report, you useless miscreant?"

The bat yelled down to them as he dipped lower in the sky. "Da usual aerial patrol. A couple o' armed jays overflew us a few minutes ago. I don't tink dey saw us wid da dragon, though. Dey've long since turned 'round and flown back to report. Dey didn't act excited."

Clothahump appeared satisfied. "Good. I have no time for intermediaries. Polastrindu is too big for them to bother with every odd group of visitors, even if we are a bit odder than most."

"We may not seem so from the air, sir," Jon-Tom pointed out.

"Quite so, my boy."

They strolled into the docks without anyone challenging them. They watched as busy stevedores, mostly broad-shouldered wolves, margays, and lynxes, laboriously loaded and unloaded stacks of crates and bales. Exotic goods and crafts were stacked neatly on shore or loaded carefully onto dray wagons for transport into the city.

Along the docks the aroma was pungent but something less than exotic. Even the river was darker here than out in midstream. The gray coloration derived not from some locally dark soil, as Jon-Tom first thought, but from the effluent pouring out of pipes and gutters. The raw sewage abraded much of the initial glamor he'd come to associate with Polastrindu.

Flor's expression twisted in disgust. "Surely it's not this bad in the city."

"I sure hope not." Talea sniffed once, tried to close down her sense of smell.

"It is said that the larger the town, the dirtier the habits of its citizens." Caz trod lightly on the filthy paving lest it sully the supple leather of his enormous shoes. "This derives from the concentration of the inhabitants on the making of money. Fastidiousness follows financial independence, not hard work."

One narrow stone arch bridged an open trench. As they crossed, the stench nearly knocked Flor unconscious. Jon-Tom and Caz had to help her across. Once past she was able to stand by herself and inhale deep drafts of only partly tainted air.

"Mierda, what a smell!"

"It should be less overwhelming once we are inside the city gate." Clothahump did not sound particularly apologetic. "There we will be away from the main sewer outfalls."

A rattling warning fell on them as Pog dipped close. "Master, soldiers come from da gate. Maybe dat overfly patrol wasn't so indifferent as it seemed. Maybe we in for some trouble."

Clothahump waved him away as one might a large housefly. "Very good, Pog, but you worry overmuch. I will deal with them."

It was a well armed if motley-looking knot of soldiers that soon came into view, marching toward them. Between twenty and thirty, Jon-Tom guessed. He slipped his club-staff from its lacings and leaned on it expectantly. Other hands drifted in the vicinity of sheathed swords. Mudge made a show of inspecting his bow.

The troop was led by a heavily armored beaver, a thickset individual with a no-nonsense gleam in his eyes. Catching sight of the column, sailors and stevedores scattered for cover. While at first they had ignored the newcomers, they now shied from them as if they carried plague.

Boots, sandals, and naked feet generated a small rumble of retreat as other onlookers scurried for safety. Ten soldiers detached themselves with forced casualness from the main body. They quick-marched to the left to get behind the newcomers and cut off any possible retreat.

"That doesn't look promising." Jon-Tom's grip tightened on the staff as he watched the maneuver.

"Easy, my friend." The imperturbable Caz stepped forward. "I will handle this."

"They would not dare to attack us," said an outraged Clothahump. "I am an emissary to the Council of Wizards and as such my person is inviolable and sacred."

"Don't tell me, good sir," said Caz, gesturing at the nearing troops. "Tell them."

Now the walls had become menacing instead of beautiful. Their stone towers cast threatening shadows over the travelers. From ships and other places of concealment the mutterings of watchful sailors and merchants could be heard.

Finally the main body of soldiers drew up in a crescent facing them. Their leader stepped forward, pushed his helmet back on his furry forehead with a muscular paw, and studied them curiously. In addition to his chain mail, helmet, and thicker steel plates protecting particularly vulnerable places there was an unusual moon-shaped iron plate strapped to the thick, broad tail. It was studded with sharp spikes and would make a devastating weapon if it came to close-quarter fighting.

"Well," he said, speaking with a distinct lisp, "what have we here? Two gianth, a tough-looking little female"—Talea spat at the ground

—"a dithreputable otter type, a fop, and an elderly gentleman of the amphibian perthuathion."

"Good sir." Caz bowed slightly. "We are travelers from downriver on a mission that is of great importance to Polastrindu and the world."

"Thath motht interethting. Whom do you reprethent?"

"By and large we represent ourselves for now, primarily in the person of the great wizard Clothahump," and he gestured toward the impatient turtle. "He carries information vital to our survival that he must present to the city council."

The beaver was casually twirling an ugly skull-splitter of a mace, indifferent to where the spike-studded ball might land.

"Thath all very nice, but it remainth that you're not citithenth of thith city or county. At leatht, I athum you are not. Unleth of courth you can produth your identity chith."

"Identity chits?"

"Everyone who liveth in the county or thity of Polathrindu hath an identity chith."

"Well, since we don't come from the county or city of Polastrindu, as you've just been informed, obviously we don't have any such thing," Jon-Tom said in exasperation.

"That doth not nethetherily follow," said the beaver. "We get many vithitoth. They all have properly thtamped identity chith. To be freely admitted to the thity all you have to do ith apply for and rethieve your proper chith." He smiled around enormous teeth. "I will be happy to provide you with thom."

Jon-Tom relaxed a little. "Good. We'll need theven."

"You very funny, big man. Thinth you have thuch a good thenth of humor, for your party it will cotht only"—the beaver performed some silent cogitation—"theven hundred silver pietheth."

"Seven hundred . . . !" Clothahump sputtered all over the pavement. "That's extortion! Outright robbery! I am insulted. I, the great and wise and knowing Clothahump, have not been so outraged in a hundred years!"

"I believe that our leader," said Caz quietly, "is somewhat disinclined to pay. Now if you will just convey word of our arrival to your superiors, I am sure that when they know why we have come—"

"They won't hear why you have come," broke in the beaver, "until you pay up. And if you don't pay up, they won't hear why you were overcome." He grinned again. His huge teeth were badly stained by some dark brown liquid. "Actually, ith eighty silver pietheth per party for identity cardth, but my men and I have to make a living of thom kind, don't we? A tholdierth pay ith pretty poor."

There were angry murmurs of agreement from the troops standing behind him.

"We will depart peacefully then," said Caz.

"I don't think tho," said the beaver. The ten soldiers who had detached themselves earlier now moved in tightly behind the travelers, blocking their path. "I don't want you going around to the other gateth."

Flor whispered to Mudge, "Are all your cities so hospitable?"

Mudge shrugged. "Where there's wealth, luv, there's corruption. There's a lot of wealth in Polastrindu, wot?" He eyed the soldiers nervously.

Some of them were already fingering swords and clubs in anticipation of a little corrective head-bashing. They looked healthy and well fed, if not especially hygienic.

" 'Ere now, your wizardship, why don't we just pay up? These blokes look as though they'd rather 'ave themselves a good massacre than anythin' else. If we wait much longer we won't 'ave ourselves much o' a choice."

"I will not pay." Clothahump obstinately adjusted his spectacles. "Besides, I can't remember that asinine silver spell."

"You won't pay, eh?" The beaver waddled over until he was glaring eye to eye with the turtle. "Tho you're a great withard, eh? Leth thee how much of a withard you really are," and he flipped the mace around, snapped his wrist, and struck Clothahump square on the beak.

The sorcerer let out a startled cry and sat down hard. "Why you impudent young whelp!" He fumbled for his glasses, which had been knocked loose but not broken. "I shall show you who is a wizard. I will disembowel you, I'll . . . !"

"Port armth!" the beaver barked. Instantly a cluster of spears and clubs was pointed at the travelers. The officer said sourly, "I've had jutht about enough of thith foolithneth. I don't know who you are, where you come from, or what kind of game you're trying to play with me, but we don't take kindly to vagranth here. Ith dragged off to the thellth you're to be, and methily, too, unleth you come up with thom cash."

There was stone wall to his right and sharp steel ahead and behind, but nothing blocked Jon-Tom's path as he'd worked his way to the water's edge. He cupped his hands and yelled desperately, "Falameezarrrr!"

"What, thereth more of you then?" The beaver's whiskers twitched as he turned to face the stagnant water. "Where ith thith one? Hiding on a boat? Ith going to cotht you another hundredth silver piethes. I'm growing tired of thith. You'll pay me right now or elth . . ." and he twirled the mace menacingly.

A great tired creaking drowned out the last words of the threat as two ships were bodily shouldered aside. Dock planking gave under irresistible pressure from below. A huge black head emerged from beneath, trailing water and shattered boards. Great claws dug into broken stone, and coal-eyes glared down at the group.

The beaver stared open-mouthed up at the wet, shiny teeth clashing just above him. "D-d-d-d—!" He never did get the whole word out, but managed to outwaddle half his subordinates in the race for the main gate.

Sailors hastily abandoned their ships in the mad rush for the gate. Vendors and merchants abandoned their stocks and wharfside businesses in favor of drier territory. There was panic on the city wall as rudely awakened troops ran into one another in their rush to take up defensive positions.

The now solitary band of travelers put up their own weapons.

"A timely appearance, comrade," said Jon-Tom. "I'd hoped you might still be nearby, but I had no idea it would be quite this near."

Falameezar gazed at the terrified faces peeking over the top of the wall. "What is wrong with them?" He was more curious than angry. "I heard your call and came as promised, but I thought they surely would treat you as fellow comrades-in-arms in the great struggle to come."

"Yes, but you recall what I told you about the presence of counter-revolutionaries?" Jon-Tom said darkly.

"Oho, so that's it!" Falameezar let out a furious hiss and a trio of small shops burst into flame.

"Careful. We just want to get inside, not burn the city down."

A massive tail lashed at the water and instantly put out the small fires, though he did the innocent shops no more good than had the flames.

"Keep your anger in check, Falameezar," Jon-Tom advised. "I'm sure we'll have this all straightened out as soon as we can get to talk with the city's commissars."

"I should certainly think so!" said the dragon huffily. "The idea of letting counterrevolutionaries interdict innocent travelers."

"It's hard to tell the true revolutionaries from their secretive enemies."

"I suppose that's so," the dragon admitted.

"There might be even worse yet to come," Jon-Tom informed him as they all sashayed across the stones toward the now tightly barred wooden gate.

"Like what, comrade?"

Jon-Tom whispered, "Revisionists."

Falameezar shook his head and muttered tiredly, "Is there no decency left in the world?"

"Just keep your temper under control," Jon-Tom told him. "We don't want to accidentally incinerate any honest proletarians."

"I will be careful," the dragon assured him, "but inside I am trembling with outrage. Yet even a filthy revisionist can be reeducated."

"Yes, it's clear that the formation of instructional cadres should be a priority here," Jon-Tom agreed.

The city of Polastrindu had suddenly taken on the aspect of a ghost town. At the dragon's continued approach all interested faces had vanished from the wall. Only an occasional spear showed itself, and that was the only sign of movement.

Jon-Tom could feel the eyes of hidden sailors and stevedores on his back, but there was nothing to worry about from that quarter. In fact, so long as Falameezar remained with them there was little to fear from anywhere.

He glanced at Caz. The rabbit smiled and nodded back at him. Being the one in control of the dragon, it behooved Jon-Tom to do the talking. So he marched up to the gate and rapped arrogantly on the wood.

"Captain of the Gate, show yourself!" When there was neither a reply nor hint of movement from within, he added, "Show yourself or we'll burn down your gate and make you Captain of Ashes!"

There were sounds of argument from within. Then a slight groaning of wood as the massive portal opened just wide enough to permit the egress of a familiar figure. The gate shut quickly closed behind him.

"That's better." Jon-Tom eyed the beaver, who looked considerably less belligerent now. "We were discussing something about 'identity chits'?"

"They're being prepared right now," the officer told him, his gaze continually darting up at the glowering crimson-eyed face of the dragon.

"That's nice. There was also the matter of a large number of silver pieces?"

"No, no, no. Don't be ridiculouth. And abthurd mithunderthanding!"

A moment later a grateful expression came over his face as the gate opened again. He disappeared inside and came back with a handful of tiny metal rectangles. Each was stamped with tiny symbols and a few words.

"Here we are." He passed them out quickly. "You are to have your own nameth engraved here." He indicated a wide blank place on each chit. "At your leithure, of courth," he added obsequiously.

"But there are only seven chits here." The beaver looked confused. "Remember, by your own recognition there are now eight in our party."

"I don't underthand," said the nervous officer. He nodded slightly in Falameezar's direction. "Thurely *that* ith not coming into the thity?"

"A bourgeois statement if ever I heard one!" The dragon leaned close enough for the smell of brimstone and sulfur to overpower the odor of spilling sewage. That he could swallow the officer in one snap was a fact not lost on that worthy.

"No, no . . . a mithunderthanding, thath all. I . . . I'm truly thorry, thir dragon. I didn't realize you were a part of thith party . . . not jutht . . . if you'll excuth me, pleath!" He back-pedaled through the opening faster than Jon-Tom would have believed those bandy legs could carry him.

Several minutes went by this time before he reappeared. "The latht chit," he said, panting as he proferred the freshly stamped metal plate.

"I'll take charge of it." Jon-Tom slipped it into a shirt pocket. "And now if you'd be so kind as to open the gate?"

"Open up in there!" yelled the officer. The newcomers strolled through. Falameezar had to duck his head and barely succeeded in squeezing through the opening.

They found themselves in a deserted courtyard. Hundreds of anxious eyes observed them from behind dozens of barely opened windows.

Huge stone structures marched off in all directions. As in Lynchbany, they gave the impression of dozens of smaller buildings that had grown together, only here the scale was larger. The city had the appearance of a gray sand castle. Some of the structures were six and seven stories tall. Ragged apartment buildings displayed odd windows and individual balconies.

The streets they could see were much wider than in provincial Lynchbany, though overhanging porches and window boxes made them appear narrower. The street that opened into their courtyard led to the harbor gate. It was only natural that it be wider than most. Undoubtedly the city possessed its share of alleys and closes.

Evidence of considerable traffic abounded, from the worn domes of the cobblestones that projected like the bald skulls of buried midgets to the huge piles of discarded trash. Several dozen stalls ringed the courtyard square.

Jon-Tom suspected that until a little while ago these had been crowded with busy vendors hawking wares to sailors and shoppers alike. A few salespeople still cowered within, too weak or too greedy to flee. Some of the frightened faces were furry, a few humanly smooth.

"Look at 'em, ashrinkin' behind their bellies." Mudge made insulting faces at the half-hidden onlookers, feeling quite invulnerable with the bulk of Falameezar immediately behind him. "Welcome to wonderful Polastrindu. Pagh! The streets stink, the people stink. Sooner we've done with this business and can get back to the clean forest, the better this 'ere otter'll like it." He cupped his hands and shouted disdainfully.

"You 'ear me, you quiverin' cowardly buggers! Yer 'ole city sucks! Want to argue about it?"

No one did. Mudge looked satisfied, turned to face Jon-Tom. "What now, mate?"

"We must meet with the local sorcerers and the city council," said Clothahump firmly, "during which meeting you will do me the pleasure of restraining your adolescent outpourings."

"Ah, they deserve it, guv."

"Council?" That ominous rumble came from a quizzical Falameezar.

"Council of commissars," explained Jon-Tom hastily. "It's all a matter of semantics."

"Yes, of course." The dragon sounded abashed.

Looking around, Jon-Tom spotted the beaver hovering uncertainly in a nearby doorway. "You there, come here." The officer hesitated as long as possible.

"Yes, you!"

Reluctantly he emerged. Halfway across the square, perhaps conscious of all the eyes watching him from numerous windows, he seemed to regain some of his former pride and dignity. If he was going to his death, seemed to be his thinking, then he might as well make a good showing of it. Jon-Tom had to admire his courage, belated though it might be.

"Very well," the beaver told him calmly. "You've bullied your way into my city."

"Which was necessary only because you tried to bully us outside," Jon-Tom reminded him. "Let's say we're even now. No hard feelings."

The beaver shot a whiskery glance at the quiescent form of Falameezar before staring searchingly back at Jon-Tom.

"You mean that, thir? You are not going to take your revenge on me?"

"No. After all," Jon-Tom added, hoping to gain a local ally, "you were only doing your duty as you, uh, saw it."

"Yeth. Yeth, thath right." The officer was still reluctant to believe he wasn't being set up and that Jon-Tom's offer of friendship was genuine.

"We have no grudge against you, nor against any citizen of Polastrindu. We're here to help you."

"And every sentient inhabitant of our warmland world," Clothahump added self-importantly.

The officer grunted. Clearly the beaver preferred talking with Jon-Tom, though staring up at the towering human hurt his short neck.

"What then can I do to be of thervith to you, my friend?"

"You could arrange for us to meet with the city council and military administrators and the representatives of the wizards of this region," Jon-Tom informed him.

The beaver's eyes widened. Massive incisors clicked against lower teeth. "Thath quite a requetht, friend! Do you have any idea what you're athking?"

"I'm sorry if it's going to be difficult for you, but we can't settle for anything less. We would not have traveled all this way unless it was on a matter of critical importance."

"I can believe that. But you got to underthand I'm jutht a thuboffither. I'm not in a pothition to—"

Shouts came from behind him. Several of his soldiers were emerging from the door behind which they'd taken refuge and pointing up the main street.

An elaborate sedan chair was approaching. It was borne aloft by six puffing mice. They hesitated at their first view of Falameezar, but shouts from inside the chair and the crack of the shrewish driver's whip forced them onward. The shrew was elegantly dressed in lace and silk, complete to lace cap.

The chair halted a modest distance away. The three-foot-tall driver descended rapidly and opened the door, bowing low. The abused bearers slumped in their harnesses and fought to catch their breath. They'd apparently run most of the way.

The individual who emerged from the vehicle was clad in armor more decorative than functional. It was heavily gilded, befitting its owner's high station and haughty demeanor. He appraised the situation in the square and ambled over.

Open paw slapping across his chest, the beaver saluted sharply as the newcomer neared. A faint wave from the other was all the acknowledgment he gave the officer.

"I am Major Ortrum, Commandant of the City Guard," the raccoon said unctuously. He managed the considerable feat of ignoring Falameezar as he talked to the rest of the arrivals.

The dragon caught Jon-Tom's attention. The youth edged back alongside the black bulk while the raccoon recited some sort of official greeting in a bored voice.

"Those poor fellows there," said the dragon angrily, nodding toward the exhausted bearers of the sedan chair, "appear to me the epitome of the exploited worker. And I don't care for the looks of this one now talking."

Jon-Tom thought very fast. "I expect they take turns. That's only fair."

"I suppose," said the dragon doubtfully. "But those workers," and he indicated the panting mice, "are all of the same kind, while the speaker is manifestly different."

"Yeah . . . but what about the driver? He's different, too."

"Yes, but . . . oh, never mind. It is my suspicious nature."

Too suspicious by half, Jon-Tom thought, breathing a mental sigh of relief at having once again buffaloed the dragon. He hoped to God the Major didn't take his leave by kicking one or two of the bearers erect.

"I gather," the raccoon was saying, inhaling a choice bit of snuff, "that you are here on some silly sort of important mission?"

"That's true." Clothahump eyed the Major distastefully.

"Ah, you must be the wizard who was mentioned to me." Ortrum performed a smooth, aristocratic bow. "I defer to one who has mastered the arcane arts, and to whom all must look up to." There was a short, sharp guffaw from the bat fluttering overhead, but Clothahump's opinion of the Major underwent a radical change.

"At last, someone who recognizes the worth of knowledge! Maybe now we will get somewhere."

"That will depend," said the Major. "I am told you seek an audience of the council, the military, and the sorceral representatives as well?"

"That's right," said Mudge, "an' if they know wot's good for them they'll give us a hard listen, they will."

"Or . . . ?"

"Or . . ." Mudge looked helplessly at Clothahump.

"A crisis that threatens the entire civilized world looms closer every day," said the wizard. "To counter it will require all the resources of the warmlands."

"Understand that I do not dispute your word, knowledgeable sir," the Major said, closing his silver snuffbox, "but I am ill prepared to consider such matters. Therefore I suppose you must have your audience. You must realize how difficult it will be to gather all the notables you require in a brief period of time."

"Nevertheless, it must be done."

"And at the audience you will of course substantiate all your claims."

"Of course," said the turtle irritably.

Jon-Tom took note of the implied threat. There was more to Major Ortrum than met the eye, or the nose. It took considerable bravery to stand there showing apparent disregard for the massive presence of Falameezar. Even Jon-Tom himself, at first sight, made many of the locals pause.

Then it occurred to him that bravery might have nothing to do with it. He wondered at the contents of the snuffbox. Major Ortrum might be stoned out of his socks.

"It will take a little time."

"As soon as possible, then," said Clothahump with a harrumph of impatience.

"Naturally, you will give me the particulars of this supposed threat, so that the sorcerers at least will know, excuse my boldness sir, that they are not being dragged from their burrows and dens to confront only the ravings of a senile fraud." He put up a mollifying hand. "Tut, tut, sir. Think a moment. Surely you yourself would want some assurance if the positions were reversed?"

"That seems reasonable enough. The wizards of the greater territories are a supercilious bunch. They must be made to understand the danger. I will give you such information as will be sufficient to induce them to attend the audience." He hunted through his plastron.

"Here, then." He removed a handful of tiny scrolls. "These are curse-sealed."

"Yes, I see the mark," said the raccoon as he carefully accepted them.

"Not that it would matter if you saw their contents," Clothahump told him. "All the world will know soon enough. But there are certain snobbish types who would resent the intrusion of mere laymen into sorceral affairs."

"Rest assured they will not be tampered with," said the Major with a fatuous smile. He placed the scrolls in his side purse.

"Now to less awesome matters. It is growing late. Surely you must be tired from the day's work"—he eyed the unfortunate beaver sharply—"and from your extensive journeying. Also, it would help settle the populace if you would retire."

Caz brushed daintily at his lace cuffs and silk stockings. "I for one could certainly use a bath. Not to mention something more elaborate than camp cuisine. Ah, for an epinard and haricot salad with spiced legume dressing!"

"A gourmet." Major Ortrum looked with new interest at the rabbit. "You will pardon my saying so, sir, but I do not understand you falling in with this kind of company."

"I find my present company quite satisfactory, thank you." Caz smiled thinly.

Ortrum shrugged. "Life often places us in the most unexpected situations." It was clear he fancied himself something of a philosopher. "We will find you your bath, sir, and lodgings for you all."

The beaver leaned close, still stiffly at attention, and jerked his head toward the dragon. "Lodgings, thir? Even for that?"

"Yes, what about Falameezar?" Jon-Tom asked. "Comrades are not to be separated." The dragon beamed.

"No trouble whatsoever," the raccoon assured him. He pointed behind them. "That third large structure there, behind you and to your left, is a military barracks and storehouse. At present it is occupied only by a small maintenance crew, who will be moved. Should your substantial reptilian friend desire to return to his natural aquatic habitat, whether permanently or merely for a washup, he will find the river close at hand. And there is ample room inside for all of you, so you will be able to stay together.

"If you will please follow me?" He returned to his chair. Curses and urgings came from the driver. Though high-pitched and squeaky, they were notable for their exceptional vileness.

Divide and promote a selected few, Jon-Tom thought angrily. That's how to keep the oppressed in line. The treatment of the smaller rodents was a source of continuing unease to him.

They followed the chair to the entrance of a huge wooden building. A pair of towering sliding doors were more than large enough to admit Falameezar.

"This building is often used to house large engines," Ortrum explained. "Hence the need for the oversized portal.

"I will leave you here now. I must return to make my report and set in motion the requests you have made. If you need anything, do not hesitate to ask any of the staff inside for assistance. I welcome you as guests of the city."

He turned, and the chair shuffled off under the straining muscles of the mice. . . .

XIX

Their quarters were Spartan but satisfactory. Falameezar declared himself content with the straw carried in from the stables, the consistency being drier but otherwise akin to the familiar mud of his favorite riverbottom.

"There are some ramifications of communal government I would like to discuss with you, comrade," he said to Jon-Tom as the youth was walking toward his own quarters.

"Later, Falameezar." He yawned, nearly exhausted by the hectic day. It had turned dark outside. The windows of Polastrindu had come alive like a swarm of fireflies.

Also, he was plain tired of keeping the dragon's insatiable curiosity sated. His limited store of knowledge about the workings of Marxism was beginning to get a little threadbare, and he was growing increasingly worried about making a dangerous philosophical mistake. Falameezar's friendship was predicated on a supposedly mutual affinity for a particular socioeconomic system. A devastating temper lay just beneath those iridescent scales.

A hand clutched his arm and he jumped. It was only Mudge.

"Take 'er a mite easier, mate. Yer more knotted up than a virgin's girdle. We've made it 'ere, an' that were the important thing, wot? Tonight we'll go out an' find ourselves a couple of less argumentative ladies than the pair we're travelin' with and 'ave ourselves a time of it, right?"

Jon-Tom firmly disengaged his arm. "Oh no. I remember the last tavern you took me into. You nearly got my belly opened. Not to mention abandoning me in Thieves' Hall."

"Now that were Talea's doin', not mine."

"What was my doing?" The redhead had appeared in the doorway ahead.

"Why nothin', luv," said Mudge innocently.

She eyed him a moment longer, then decided to ignore him. "Anybody noticed that there are dormitories at each end of this mausoleum? They're full of soldiers. We've been given the officer's quarters, but I don't like being surrounded by the others."

"Afraid of being murdered in your sleep?" Flor had joined the discussion.

Talea glared at her. "It's been known to happen, usually to those who think their beds safe. Besides, that Major Maskface said there was normally only a 'maintenance crew' living here. Then where'd all the bully-boys come from, and why?"

"How many are there?" inquired Caz.

"At least fifty at each end. Possums, weasels, humans; a nice mix. They looked awfully alert for a bunch of broom-pushers. Well armed, too."

"It's only natural for the city to be nervous at our presence," Jon-Tom argued. "A few guards are understandable."

"A few yes, a hundred I'm not so sure."

"Are you saying we're prisoners?" said Flor.

"I'm saying I don't sleep well knowing that over a hundred 'nervous' and well-armed soldiers are sleeping on either side of me."

"Wouldn't be the first time," Mudge murmured.

She looked at him sharply. "What? What did you say, you fuzz-faced little prick?"

"That it wouldn't be the first time we've been surrounded, luv."

"Oh."

"There's one way to find out." Caz moved to the small door set in one of the huge sliding panels hung from the west wall. He opened it and conversed with someone unseen. Presently the beaver officer they'd first encountered outside the city appeared. He looked unhappy, tried to avoid their stares.

"I underthand you would like an evening meal."

"That's right," said Caz.

"They will be brought in immediately. The betht the city can offer." He started to leave. Caz restrained him.

"Just a moment. That's a very kind offer, but some of us would prefer to find our own dinery." He picked absently at his tail, whiskers twitching. "That's all right, isn't it?" He took a step toward the open door.

The officer reluctantly moved to block his path. "I'm truly thorry, thir." He sounded as if he meant it. "But Major Ortrum gave thrict inthructions on how you were to be quartered and fed. Your thafety ith of much conthern to the authoritieth. They are worried that thertain radical foolth among the population might try to attack you."

"Their concern for our health is most kind," replied Caz, "but they needn't worry. We can take care of ourselves."

"I know that, thir," admitted the officer, "but my thuperiorth think otherwithe. Ith for your own protecthion." He backed out, closing the door tightly behind him.

"That's it, then," snapped an angry Talea. "We're under house arrest. I knew they were up to something."

Flor was playing with her knife, cleaning her long nails and looking quite ravishing as she leaned against a wall, legs crossed and her black cape framing her figure.

"That's easily fixed. *Un poco sangre* and we'll go where we please, *¿no es verdad?* Or we could wake up Jonny-Tom's fire-breathing *compadre* and make charcoal of that door." She gestured at the huge sliding panels with the knife.

"These aren't the enemy, Flor. Now is a time for diplomacy," he told her. "In any case, I can't risk leaving Falameezar."

Black eyes flashed at him and she stood away from the wall, jabbed the knife into the wood. "Maybe so, but I'm like Talea in this. I don't like being told where I can and can't go even if it supposedly is for my own 'protection'! I had twenty years of older brothers and sisters telling me that. I'll be damned if I'm going to let some oversized stuffy coon dictate the same thing to me now."

"Tch, tch . . . children, children."

They all turned. The squat figure of Clothahump was watching them, clucking his tongue in disapproval.

"You will all be valuable on the battlefield in the war to come, but that war is not yet, nor here. The fleshpots of the city do not interest me in the least, so," and he smiled up at Jon-Tom, "I will remain here to satisfy our large companion's desire for conversation."

"Are you sure . . . ?" Jon-Tom began.

"I have listened closely to much of your chatter, and you have instructed me well. The underlying principles to which this dragon adheres so fanatically are simple enough to manipulate. I can handle him. Besides, it is the nature of wizards and dragons to get along with one another. There are other things we can talk about.

"But you should all go, if you so desire. You have done all I have asked of you so far and deserve some relaxation. So I will occupy the attention of the dragon when required, and will aid you in slipping away."

"I don't know." Jon-Tom studied the snoring figure of the dragon. "He has a pretty probing, one-track mind."

"I will endeavor to steer our talk away from economics. That seems to be his main interest. After you have departed I shall bar the door from the outside . . . a simple bit of levitation. With the bars in place and the sounds of conversation inside, the other guards will assume all are still here.

"That shouldn't be too 'ard to do, wot?"

Mudge jumped. The wizard had mimicked his voice perfectly.

A dark form descended from the rafters. "What about me, Master?" Pog looked imploringly at him.

"Go with them if you will. I will have no need of you here tonight. But stay away from the brothels. That's what got you into this in the first place, remember. You will end up indenturing yourself to a second master."

"Not ta worry, boss. And thanks!" He bowed in the air, dipping like a diving plane.

"I don't believe you, but I will not hold you back and let the others go. Moral desiccation," he muttered disgustedly. Pog simply winked at Jon-Tom.

"You said you'd help us get out. What are you going to do," Flor wondered, "dissolve the wall?"

Clothahump frowned at her as much as his hard face would allow. "You underestimate the resources available to a sophisticated worker of miracles such as myself. If I were to do as you suggest, it would be immediately evident to those watching us what had taken place. Your temporary departure must go unnoticed.

"When it is but a little darker I will allow you to pass safely and unseen into the city."

So it was that several hours later the little group of sightseers stood clustered in a narrow side street. Oil lamps flickered in the night mist. Light struggled to escape from behind closed shutters. Around them drifted the faint sounds of a city too big and bustling to go to sleep at night.

Behind them, across the deserted square, bulked the shadowy, barnlike barracks in which they'd been confined only moments earlier.

Jon-Tom had expected Clothahump to do something extraordinary, such as materializing them inside another building.

Instead, the wizard had moved to another small side door. His gift for mimicry, magical or otherwise, had been used to throw the studied voice of one snoozing guard. Through the use of ventriloquism he had cast rude aspersions on the ancestry of the other guard. Violently waking up his supposedly insulting companion, this victim and his associate soon fell to more physical discussion.

At that point it was a simple matter for Caz and Talea to slip up behind them and via the judicious application of some loose cobblestones, settle the argument for the duration of the evening.

It was not quite the miraculous manipulation of magic Jon-Tom had expected from Clothahump, but he had to admit it was efficient.

No one troubled them or challenged them as they walked down the deserted thoroughfare. Citizens were voluntarily or else by directive giving the barracks area a wide berth.

Soon they began encountering evening pedestrian traffic, however, and despite the size of Jon-Tom and Flor, they attracted little attention. Talea and Mudge had never been inside a city the size of Polastrindu. They were trying hard to act blasé, but their actual feeling was awe.

Jon-Tom and Flor were equally ignorant of the city's customs, though not of its size, and so was Pog. So it was left unspoken that Caz would lead them. After a while Jon-Tom felt almost comfortable walking the rain-soaked streets, his cape up over his head. With its overhanging balconies and flickering oil lamps it was not unlike Lynchbany. The principal difference was the increased volume of bickering and fighting, of the sounds of loving and playing and cursing and crying cubs that issued from behind doors and windows.

As in Lynchbany the uppermost garret levels were inhabited by the various arboreal citizens. Bats like Pog, or kilt-clad birds. Night-fliers filled the sky and danced or fought in silhouette against the cloud-shrouded moon.

A group of drunken raccoons and coatis ambled past them. Their capes and vests were liquor-stained. One inebriated bobcat tottered in their midst. She was magnificently dressed in a long flowing skirt and broad-rimmed hat. With short tail switching and cat-eyes piercing the night she looked as if she might just have emerged from a stage

version of *Puss n' Boots,* though the way her companion coati was
pawing her was anything but fairytalish.

They encountered a group of voles and opossums on their way to
work. Having just arisen from a long day's sleep, the workers were
anxious to reach their jobs. The revelers would not let them pass.
There was shoving and pushing, much of it good-natured, as the
workers made their way at last up the street.

"Down this way," Caz directed them. They turned down a narrow,
winding road. The lighting was more garish, the noise from busy
establishments more raucous. Heavily made-up faces boasting extreme coloration of fur and skin only partly due to cosmetics beckoned to them from various windows. By no means were all of them of
a female cast. Flor in particular studied them with as much interest
as ever she'd devoted to a class in the sociology of nineteenth-century
theater.

Occasionally these faces would regard them with more than usual
intent. These stares were reserved primarily for the giants Flor and
Jon-Tom. Some of the comments that accompanied these looks were
as appreciative as they were ribald.

"My feet are beginning to hurt," Jon-Tom told Caz. "How much
farther? You know where you're taking us?"

"In a nonspecific way, yes, my friend. We are searching for an
establishment that combines the best of all possible worlds. Not every
tavern offers sport. Not every gaming house supplies refreshment.
And of the few that offer all, not many are reputable enough to set
foot in."

Still another corner they turned. To his surprise Jon-Tom noted
that Talea had sidled close to him.

"It's nice to be out," he said conversationally. "Not that I was so
uncomfortable back there in the barracks, but it's the principle of the
thing. If they think they can get away with restricting our movements, then they'll be more inclined to do so, and less respectful of
Clothahump's information."

"That's so," she said huskily. "But that's not what concerns me
now."

"No?" He put his arm around her experimentally. She didn't resist. He thought back to that morning in the forest when he'd awakened to find her curled up against his shoulder. That warmth commu-
nicated itself now through her shirt and cape. It traveled through his
fingers right up his arm and down toward nether regions.

"What does concern you, then?" he asked affectionately.

"That for the past several minutes we've been followed." Startled, Jon-Tom started to look back over his shoulder when a hand jabbed painfully into his ribs.

"Don't look at them, you idiot!" He forced his eyes resolutely ahead. "There are six or seven of them, I think."

"Maybe it's just another group of party-goers," he said hopefully.

"I don't think so. They've neither fallen behind us, turned off on a different street, nor come any nearer. They've kept too consistent a gap between us to mean well."

"Then what should we do?" he asked her.

"Probably turn into the next tavern. If they mean us any harm, they'll be more reluctant to try anything in front of a room full of witnesses."

"We can't be sure of that. Why not send Pog back to check 'em out," he suggested brightly, "before we jump to any conclusions? At the least he can tell us exactly how many of them there are and how heavily armed they are."

She looked up at him approvingly. "That's more like it. The more suspicious you become, Jon-Tom, the longer you'll live. Pog! *Pog?*" The others looked back at her curiously.

"Pog! Good-for-nothing parasitic airborne piece of shit, where the hell—?"

"Stow it, sister!" The bat was abruptly fluttering in front of them. "I've got some bad news for ya."

"We already know," Talea informed him.

He looked puzzled, remained hovering a couple of feet in front of them as they walked. "You *do?* But how could you? I flew on ahead because I was getting bored, and surely ya can't see . . . ?"

"Wait . . . wait a second," muttered Jon-Tom. *"Ahead?* But," and he jerked a thumb back over his left shoulder, "we were talking about the group that's be—"

"That's far enough!" declaimed a strange voice.

"Whup . . . see yas." Pog suddenly rocketed straight up into the darkness formed by garrets and overhanging beams.

Jon-Tom hastily searched the street. The nearest open doorway from which music and laughter emerged was at least half a block ahead of them on the left. At the moment there was nothing flanking them save a couple of dark portals. One led into a close that pierced a labyrinth of stairways. The other was heavily barred with iron-studded shutters.

There was no one else in sight. Not a single stray celebrant, or better still, any of the city's night patrol.

In front of them waited perhaps a dozen heavily armed humans. Most boasted long scraggly hair and longer faces. They hefted clubs, maces, quarterstaffs, and bolas. It was an impressive assortment of armament. Not until much later did he have time to reflect on the fact that there was not a single serious killing weapon, not one knife or spear or sword, among them.

The humans had spread themselves into a semicircle across the street, blocking it completely. Jon-Tom considered the narrow close a last time. It had more the look of a trap than a means of escape.

Two-thirds of the humans were male, the rest female. None wore decent clothes or pleasant looks. All were roughly Talea's height. Even Caz was taller than most of them. Their attention was on Jon-Tom and Flor, whom they regarded with unconcealed interest.

"We'd appreciate it if you'd come along with us." This request was made by a stocky blond fellow in the middle of the group. His beard seemed to continue right down into his naked chest, as did the drooping mustache. In fact, he displayed so much hair that Jon-Tom wondered in the darkness if he really was human and not one of the other furry local citizens.

That led him to consider the unusual homogeneity of the group. Up till now, every gathering of locals he'd encountered, whether diners or merchants, sailors or pedestrians, had been racially mixed.

He looked backward. The lot who'd been trailing them had spread out to block any retreat back up the street and yes, they were also wholly human, and similarly armed.

"That's nice of you," Caz said, replying to the invitation, "but we have other plans of our own." He spoke for all his companions. Jon-Tom casually swung his staff around from his back, slipped the duar out of the way. Talea's hand dropped to her sword. There was some uneasy shuffling among the humans confronting them.

"I'm sorry. We insist."

"I wish you would encyst," said Flor cheerfully, "preferably with something cancerous."

The insult was lost on the man, who simply blinked at her. Both clusters began to crowd the travelers, edging in from front and back.

There was a light metallic sound as Talea's sword appeared in her hand. "First one of you rodents lays a hand on me is cold meat."

In the dim light from the oil lamps Jon-Tom thought she looked lovelier than ever. But then, so did Flores Quintera.

She'd assumed an amazonian stance with her own short sword and mace held expectantly in front of her, the light gleaming off the saw teeth lining the steel.

"*Ovejas y putas,* come and take us . . . if you can."

"Ladies, please!" protested Caz, aghast at the manner in which his attempted diplomacy was being undermined from behind. "It would be better for all of us if . . . excuse me, sir." He'd been glancing back at Talea and Flor but had not lost sight of their opponents. One of them had jumped forward and attempted to brain the rabbit with a small club, whereupon Caz had hopped out of the way, offered his apologies, and stuck out a size twenty-two foot. His assailant had gone tumbling over it.

"Dreadfully sorry," murmured Caz. His apology did nothing to stem the rush which followed as the two groups of encircling humans attacked.

The narrowness of the street simplified defensive tactics. The set-upon arranged themselves back to back in a tight circle and hacked away at their antagonists, who threw themselves with shocking reck-lessness against swords and knives. The light and sweat and scream-ing swam together around Jon-Tom. The duar was a heavy weight bouncing under his arm as the blunt end of his staff-club sought out an unprotected face or groin.

It occurred to him that a little magic might have frightened off their assailants. He cursed himself for not thinking of it earlier. It was too late now for singing. He couldn't stop defending himself long enough to swing the duar around.

Three frustrated attackers were trying to get beneath his enormous reach. He held them off with the club. One slipped underneath the staff and raised a mace. Jon-Tom thumbed a stud on the staff and flipped it around in an arc as he'd been shown. The spring-loaded spearpoint sliced across the mace-wielder's thighs. He collapsed, moaning and holding his legs.

Something dark covered Jon-Tom's eyes as he was hit from below and behind. Flailing wildly with the staff, he went over backward. The staff intercepted something yielding, which yelped once.

A heaviness pressed down on his senses as well as his eyes. Then everything turned to mush, including the noise of fighting. His thoughts swam sluggishly as though he were trying to think through Jell-O. Dimly he could still make out shrieks and screams from the continuing battle, but they sounded faint and far away.

He recognized the high-pitched challenge of Talea alternating with

Mudge's taunts and curses. Flor was yowling war cries in an interesting mixture of English and Spanish. The last sight he'd glimpsed before the black cloth or bag or whatever it was had been slipped over his head showed a starlit sky mottled with clearing rain clouds and a sickle moon beaming bluely down between peaked roofs that overhung the street like cupped hands. He hoped they were formed in prayer for him.

Then even that wish faded, along with the remnant of his consciousness. . . .

CODE NAME

XX

At first he thought a fly had somehow tumbled into his brain. It was beating against the sides, trying to get out. When the fly-feeling gave way to a certainty that the buzzing came from elsewhere, he opened his eyes and hunted for its source.

An oil lamp burned on a simply hewn wood table. A gruff announcement came from someone unseen.

"He's awake!"

This was followed by the pad-padding of many feet. Jon-Tom struggled to a sitting position. Gravity, or something, tried to pull off the back of his head. He winced at the pain. It slowly dribbled away, down his neck and into oblivion.

He discovered he was sitting on the edge of a cot. In the dim lamplight he could now make out the familiar shapes of his staff and duar leaning against the far wall of the room.

Flanking his possessions were two of the humans who'd attacked him. One wore a bandage across his forehead and over one ear. The other exhibited a deep purple bruise and knot over his right eye. His mouth also showed signs of having been cut.

Normally an exceptionally pacific person, Jon-Tom experienced an uncharacteristic surge of pleasure at this evidence of the damage he and his companions had done. He'd made up his mind to make a rush for the club-staff when a door opened on his left and half a dozen people marched in.

Leaning forward, he was disappointed to discover he could see nothing past the door except a dimly lit corridor, though he could hear distant conversation.

The new arrivals stationed themselves around the room. Three of them took up positions in front of the door while another closed it behind them. Two additional lamps were lit. Everyone in the room looked very determined. Another trio sat down at the table. Someone brought a few roughly forged goblets and a couple of plates piled high with steaming meat and a close relative of boiled potatoes.

There were no windows in the room. The only light came from the three oil lamps and the crack beneath the door. Captors and captive examined each other with interest for long minutes.

Then one of the three seated at the table spoke to him, and Jon-Tom recognized the blond spokesman who had confronted him in the street.

"You hungry?" Jon-Tom shook his head. "Thirsty?" Again the negative motion, accompanied by a smile and an obscene gesture. Jon-Tom was not thinking like a would-be lawyer now. He was still light-headed and maybe just a little crazy.

His actions and silence did not seem to upset his interrogator, who shrugged and said, "Suit yourself. I am." He picked up a potato-thing and spread some sort of transparent glaze over it, using a spoon set in a small jar. Taking a bite out of it, he chewed noisily. Glaze slid down his chin and onto his chest.

When he'd finished half the tuber he looked again at Jon-Tom. Then he asked bluntly, "Head hurt?"

"You know goddam well it does," Jon-Tom told him, feeling of the lump that was maturing on the back of his skull.

"We're sorry about that." And to Jon-Tom's surprise the man sounded honestly contrite. "But you wouldn't come with us voluntarily, and we didn't have much time to talk. Patrol could've come along."

"If you've been facing twelve armed people in an unfamiliar street, would you have gone along?"

The blond smiled wryly. "I suppose not. We're not much on tact, I guess. But it was imperative you come with us, and we had to get you away from the animals."

That made Jon-Tom take another anxious look around the room. No question about it, he was the sole captive present.

"Where are the others? Where are my friends?"

"Where we left them. Scattered around the alleys of the Loose Quarter. Oh, they didn't seem badly hurt," he added when Jon-Tom looked ready to rise from the cot. "Far less so than our own people. We simply led the fight away from you once we had you drugged and under control."

"Why me?" He leaned back against the rock wall. "What's so interesting about me?"

The stocky speaker peered hard at him. "It is said that you are a wizard, a spellsinger, from another world." He seemed at once skeptical and yet anxious to have that skepticism disputed.

"Yes . . . yes, that's right." Jon-Tom stretched out his arms and waved his fingers. "And if you don't let me out of here in ten seconds I'm going to turn you all into mushrooms!"

The leader shook his head, looking down at the floor and then up again to smile at Jon-Tom. He clasped both hands together on his lap.

"Any spellsinger requires his instrument to make magic." He nodded in the direction of the closely guarded duar. "You threaten emptily. I had heard that you controlled a river dragon. That plus your admission just now is proof enough for me."

"How do you know that I'm controlling the dragon? Maybe I'm just trying to frighten you into releasing me. Clothahump the turtle is still back at our barracks, and he's a powerful wizard, much more powerful than I am. Maybe he's controlling the dragon and even now setting up a spell to dissolve all of you like so much tea."

"We know of the hard-shelled bumbler who accompanied you. We know also that he and the great dragon are even now arguing absurdities back in the harbor barracks. We know this not through magic but through our well-organized and loyal network of observers and spies." Again the smile. "Sometimes that is worth more than magic."

Network, Jon-Tom thought? What's this talk of spies and networks? Something else, something about the attitude of the people in the room, their attacking with nonlethal weapons, all bespoke something deeper than your everyday garden-variety robbers.

"Who do you spy for? Aren't you all citizens of the city or county of Polastrindu?"

"By birth," admitted the man, and there were murmurs of agreement from the others in the room, "but not by inclination, or belief."

"You're losing me."

"We don't want to do that," said the man, unclasping his hands. "We want you to join us."

"Join you? In what? I haven't got time to join anything else. I'm already into something vitally important to your whole world." He started to recite Clothahump's warning about the coming cataclysm.

"The Plated Folk are readying their greatest invasion of these lands in their history, and they have—"

"We know all that," said one of the other guards impatiently.

Jon-Tom gaped at the woman who'd spoken. She was one of the trio blocking the doorway. "You know?" Nods of assent came from several of the others.

"But I thought . . . Clothahump said he was the only one perceptive enough to . . . but *how* do you know?"

"Patience," the blond urged him. "All will be explained."

"You asked if we were not citizens of the city, and what we wanted you to join us for. We are citizens of this city, yes, and we are something more, we believe. As for what we want you to join, I have already told you. We want you to join us."

"What the hell do you mean by 'us'? Some kind of political organization?"

The man shook his head. "Not really. Us. *Us* . . . we humans." He spoke patiently, as though explaining to a child.

"I still don't follow you."

The man looked in exasperation at his companions, then once more back at Jon-Tom. "Listen to me carefully, spellsinger. For tens of thousands of years mankind has been compelled to exist as a lowly equal with the animals. With the hordes of stinking, smelly, hairy beasts who are obviously our inferiors." This was said with casual disregard for his own unkempt mat of fur. "With those who are destined to be damned together with the rats and mice they so readily discriminate against themselves."

Jon-Tom didn't reply. The man almost pleaded with him. "Surely you have felt the inequality, the unnaturalness of this situation?" He paced in front of Jon-Tom's cot, occasionally shaking clenched fists at him.

"We are more than animals, are we not? Clearly nature has intended us to be superior, yet some unnatural force or circumstance has held us back from achieving our birthright. The time to change that is near. Soon mankind shall inherit this world, as nature intended him to!"

"You're talking, then," said Jon-Tom slowly, "about a race war?"

"No!" The stocky leader turned angrily on him. "This is to be a war for the race, for the human race, to place it in its rightful position as leader of civilization." He leaned near, stared searchingly into Jon-Tom's face. "Tell me then, spellsinger: do the humans of your other-world exist equally with the animals?"

My God, Jon-Tom thought in panic. What do I say? How percep-tive are they? Can they detect, through magic or otherwise, if I lie? And if so, and they learn the truth, will they use that to gather support among the humans here for their own hateful plans?

But are they after all so hateful? Do you hate what this man is saying, Jon-Tom, or do you hate the thought that you might agree with him?

"Well?" the man prompted.

No reply was worse than anything he might say, he decided. "The humans I've met are no more than the equal of the other animals here in size and intelligence. Some have shown themselves to be a damnsight less so. What makes you think you're so superior?"

"Belief, and inner knowledge," came the instant reply. "This can-not be the way nature meant things to be. Something is wrong here. And you have not yet answered my question about the relationship between humans and animals in your world."

"We're all animals together. Intelligence is the determining factor, and the other *persons* I've met here have been pretty much equal in intelligence."

"Ah . . . the other animals you've met *here*. What about your own world's 'animals'?"

Jon-Tom's voice rose in frustration. "God damn you, shape and size has nothing to do with it!"

"It confirms what the dream raiders told us," murmured someone in the back of the room. There were other unintelligible whispers, smug and self-satisfied. Jon-Tom found them unsettling.

"Anyway, I won't join you." He folded his arms. "I doubt that many will. I know plenty of humans already who can tell the differ-ence between civilized and uncivilized, between intelligent and igno-rant, without having to think about it, and it hasn't a fucking thing to do with body odor. So you can take your 'belief' and 'inner knowl-edge' and stuff it! Those are the kinds of groundless, half-assed rea-sons dictators have used throughout history for discriminating against others, and I don't want anything to do with it.

"Besides, humans are just another mammalian minority here. Even if they all went nuts and joined you, you're far too outnumbered to even think the kind of genocide you're contemplating has a chance of success."

"You're right on all counts," agreed the leader, "except one."

"I don't think I overlooked anything."

"Perhaps it would be better if *I* explained." The voice had a hoarseness to it that suggested a severe cold or laryngitis. The man who'd spoken stepped out into the light. He was as thickset as the leader and even more hirsute. Long black hair flowed below his shoulders, and his beard almost obscured his face. Brown and blue leathers were draped tentlike on his body.

Jon-Tom was by now almost too furious to think straight. "Who the hell are you, jack?" He was thinking of Mudge and Clothahump, of the aristocratic but friendly Caz, and the acerbic Pog. The idea that this motley mob of near barbarians considered themselves good enough to lord it over his new-won furry friends was almost more than he could stomach.

"My identity is perhaps better shown than stated," said the black-haired shape as he reached up and carefully removed his head.

The skull thus revealed was smaller than a human head, but occupied almost as much volume because of the bulging, bright green compound eyes. The chitin was bright blue spotted with yellow patches. A slash of maroon decorated the mandibles. Antennae drooped toward Jon-Tom. They were constantly in motion, alternating like a swimmer's arms.

It spoke again, the same harsh, rasping tone. The mouth did not move. Jon-Tom realized the insect was generating a crude approximation of normal speech by controlling the flow of air through its breathing spicules.

"I am Hanniwuz," said the apparition huskily. "This suit I wear is necessary lest the locals kill me on sight. They bear an unreasoning hatred for my people and have persecuted us for thousands of years."

Jon-Tom had recovered from the initial shock of the revelation. "The way I hear it, it's your people who have been doing the hating, trying to invade and enslave the locals for millennia."

"I will not deny that we seek control, but we do not seek conquest. It is for our protection. We require security of some kind. The warm-landers grow constantly stronger. One day their hatred will overwhelm their lethargy and they will arise en masse to massacre the Plated Folk. Do we not have the right to self-defense?"

Oh boy, Jon-Tom thought: history and legalisms. He felt suddenly at home. "Don't try and bullshit me. Whenever one nation claims it requires 'secure borders' with another, that border is usually the far border of the neighboring country and not the common one. That 'border' country gets swallowed up, and the secure borders have to be moved outward again, and then again. It's a never ending process. Security may never be satisfied that way, but greed usually is."

The insect's head swiveled to look up at the blond man. "Spellsinger or not, I think this one more dangerous than useful. I do not think he will be of use to us." Jon-Tom went cold and still.

"No, he's not as positive as he sounds." The leader turned imploringly, smilingly back to the lanky youth. "Please tell Hanniwuz you'll join us."

"I don't see the connection between you two."

"The Plated Folk recognize that among the warmlanders only we humans think like they do. Only we have the ability to make war with detachment and then to govern properly. That's our natural right, and the Plated Folk are willing to recognize that. If we help them, they will allow us to rule in their stead. That will give them the security they seek."

"You really believe that? Then you people are either dumb or morally bankrupt. You have no 'natural right' to rule anything. Genetics has worked out differently here."

One of the other guards said worriedly, "Careful, he speaks magic words." Candlelight glinted on swords and spears, a sparkling forest of death suddenly aimed threateningly at Jon-Tom.

"Watch your mouth, stranger! . . . Don't try magicking us!"

"See the effect he has?" The leader turned to Hanniwuz. "Consider how important an ally he could be to the cause."

" 'Could be' are the key words, my friend." The insect envoy lifted a hand, turned his head sideways, and preened his ommatidia. "He remains violently opposed."

The stocky chieftain walked up to Jon-Tom, who tensed, but the man only put his hands on the youth's shoulders.

"Listen to me, spellsinger. You have the size and bearing of a warrior along with your gift for magicking. You could be a leader among us, one of those who lord it over these lands. The climate here suits not the Plated Folk. They have need of our services now and they will have need of them when the war is done."

"So they say." Jon-Tom eyed the impassive insect. "It's astonishing how fast a conquerer can get acclimated."

"Control your first reactions, spellsinger. Think rationally and without bitterness on what I say. With your stature and abilities you could rule whole counties, entire reaches of the Lands. A dozen or more cities like Polastrindu could be under your absolute control. Anything you wanted could be yours for the asking: riches, fine goods, slaves of any species or sex.

"You are a young man still. What future does your mentor Clothahump offer you in comparison? A chance to go to an unpleasant death? Is it so very wrong that humans rule over the animals? So you do not agree with the moral justification of our cause. Can you not rationalize what it would bring to you personally?

"Think hard, spellsinger, for the Plated Folk are destined to conquer this time, no matter who or what opposes them. It is easy to support a martyr's death for others . . . but what about for yourself? Is that what you have hoped for all your life, to die young and bravely?" His hand slashed at the air. "That is stupid."

"I don't think your victory is assured just yet," Jon-Tom said quietly, "despite your"—he caught himself just in time, having been on the verge of saying "despite your secret magic," and instead finished —"despite all the quislings you can recruit, and I don't think there'll be all that many."

"Then there are no circumstances under which you would consider joining us? Think hard! The world can be yours."

"Shit, I wouldn't know what to do with it. I don't . . ." He stopped.

Seriously now, what did he owe to this world into which he'd been rudely, unwillingly, and perhaps permanently yanked? If he ever succeeded in returning to his own place and time, what would he become? A corpulent attorney, fat and empty of real life? Or a sour, doped-up musician playing cheap bars and sweet-sixteen parties?

Here he could be one step above a mayor and one step below a god. Weren't all of them, for all their veneer of civilization and intelligence, nothing more than oversized animals? Mudge, Caz, Pog, all of them? He considered the way Flor had occasionally looked at Caz. Was it right that he should consider himself, even momentarily, in competition for the love of his life with an oversized hare? Was that less repugnant than cooperation with these people?

Why shouldn't he join them. then? Why should he not look out for himself for a change?

"That's very good, man," whispered Hanniwuz. "You think. Death, or ascension to a throne we will create for you. It seems an easy choice to make, does it not? The day we attack there will be uprisings of humans throughout the warmlands. They will flock to our cause. Together we shall force these bloated, soft, smelly creatures back into the dirt where they belong . . . aahhh-chrriick!"

"I'm not sure—" Jon-Tom began.

Yells and shouts from the other side of the door and all eyes turned in that direction. Then the opening was full of flying bodies, blood, and steel. Talea darted in and out of the crowd, her sword taking bites out of larger and more muscular bodies. Caz wielded a rapier with delicacy but far more ferocity than Jon-Tom had suspected him of possessing, a furry white demon in the candlelight. Mudge charged into the thick of the fray, his energy and activity compensating for his usual lack of good judgment.

Dim light was reflected from fast-moving metal. There were screams and curses and the sound of flesh hitting stone. Blood hit Jon-Tom in the face, temporarily blinding him. Flores Quintera towered above the mob, her black mane flailing the air as she cut with mace and her small saw edge at anyone who tried to get near her.

Above them all, clinging precariously to a chink in the roof and occasionally tossing a knife down into the milling cluster below, was Pog.

That explained how the others had tracked him. When the fight in the street had broken away from Jon-Tom, Pog had thoughtfully left the battle to shadow Jon-Tom and his captors. Then he'd returned to lead the others to the rescue.

A large, spiked mace rose in front of Jon-Tom's gaze. The man hefting it was bleeding badly from the neck and sanity had left his face.

"Die then, otherworld thing!"

Jon-Tom closed his eyes and readied himself for oblivion. There was the shock of concussion, but it was in his right shoulder instead of his forehead. Opening his eyes he found the mace-wielder sprawled across his legs. As he watched, the dying man slid to the floor.

Talea stood above the corpse, a knife in each hand, her clothes splattered with the darker stains of blood. She looked back into the room. Another door had opened in the far corner. His few surviving captors were retreating via the new exit. Of Hanniwuz there was no sign.

The redhead was breathing heavily, her chest heaving beneath the shirt. She had a wild look in her eyes. It became one of concern as she focused on the slumped shape of Jon-Tom. He blinked at her as he held his throbbing shoulder.

"I'm all right. But just barely. Thanks." He looked past her. "Pog? You responsible for this?"

"Dat a fact. Sometimes da coward's course is da best. When I saw da fight all revolving around you, I knew it was you dey were after. So I held myself in reserve in case I had ta follow or bring help."

"I'll bet you 'eld yourself in 'reserve,' you sanctimonious 'ypocrite!" bellowed Mudge from across the room. The last of Jon-Tom's captors had fled or been dispatched, and the otter was walking toward the table, wiping at a cut across his chest.

"Near ruined me best vest, bugger it! Cost me thirty coppers in Lynchbany." He smiled then at Jon-Tom and let out a pleased whistle-whoop. "But it don't matter much, mate, because you're awright."

"Your vest's in better shape than my shoulder." Jon-Tom sat up with Talea's help. She felt of it ungently, and he yelped.

"Don't be such a cub. It's not broken, but I wager you'll have the devil of a bruise for a few weeks." She cleaned one knife on a pants leg and used it to point at an overhead set of iron bars. Jon-Tom walked beneath them. They'd been invisible from his seat on the cot.

"Crawl space up there. We heard you talking with this bunch before we interrupted the party." She looked back at him interestedly. "What were you talking about?"

"Nothing much." He looked away. "They wanted me to join them."

"Huh! Join them in what?"

"Sort of an outlaw band," he muttered uncomfortably.

"And what were you going to do?"

He looked angrily at her. "I didn't give it a thought, of course!" He hoped he appeared suitably outraged. "What do you take me for?"

She regarded him silently for a moment before saying, "A confused, stubborn, naïve, brilliant, and I hope sensible guy."

With that she left him, joined Flor in inspecting the escape door to see if any wounded remained.

Caz was at his back, undoing his bonds. "Rather awkward situation, my friend."

" 'Ere now, it were bloody well more than 'awkward,' flagears!" Mudge had adopted a familiar swagger, now that the fight was won. "When I shot into the room and saw that mace comin' down I was afraid we were goin' t' be a second too late. Good thing sweet flametop's as fast with 'er 'ands as she is with 'er 'ips," and he glanced around quickly to make certain Talea hadn't overheard him.

"I'm okay, Mudge." The ropes came loose. Circulation stabbed back into his wrists. Rubbing them, he stood, towering once more over his rescuers.

Mudge, Caz, Pog. Not only were they not "animals," he decided, they were a hell of a lot more "human" than the so-called humans who'd kept him prisoner. The thought of betraying their trust on behalf of the Plated Folk now made him almost physically ill. As for dreams of power and mastery, they vanished from his thoughts. Not because they were unattainable, not because they were morally repugnant, but because Jon-Tom had always been utterly unable to do less than the Right Thing.

I'd make a lousy lawyer, he thought. And if I can't help thinking about power and mastery, well hell, I'm only human.

Maybe if I work real hard, he told himself, I can manage to overcome that.

"There was an insect envoy with them," he said. "One of the Plated Folk. They're trying to find allies among the locals. We have to inform the authorities."

"We'll do that for a fact, mate," said a startled Mudge. "Cor, t' think o' one o' them great ugly bugs a-sneakin' about in this part o' the world!"

"How could he get in here?" Caz wondered.

"He looked as human as any of the others," Jon-Tom told them. "Clothahump should know."

Talea and Flor crawled back out of the secret doorway. "No sign of the one Jon-Tom says he saw here, nor the scum that got away."

They moved cautiously to the main door. Jon-Tom gathered up his belongings. It felt good to have the smooth bulk of the duar under his arm and the staff in his hands. While his companions formed a protective cordon around him, Mudge checked the stairway. It was empty now.

Then they were racing up the hallway toward the street, Jon-Tom and Flor taking the steps two at a time. Mudge and Talea burst outward into the mist, one looking right, the other left.

"All clear," Talea called back. The others soon stood on the cobblestones.

They started back up the street. Eyes searched windows for drawn bows as they walked rapidly between dark buildings. Pog overflew alleys in search of ambush. But there was no sign of any attempt to block their progress.

Jon-Tom stumbled once as his shoulder flared with pain. Talea was alongside. She remained there despite his insistence that he was all right.

"This outlaw band," she inquired, still warily inspecting the street ahead, "you sure you didn't consider joining up with them? They might do real well if they have Plated Folk support."

"Why would I do an asinine thing like that?" he snapped. "I've no love for the insects."

"They've done nothing to you or yours. Why should you not be as willing to join with them as with us?"

How much did she overhear through that grating? he wondered. Then it occurred to him that she was nervous, not angry. The unaccustomed expression of vulnerability made him feel suddenly and oddly warm inside.

"I didn't like those people," he told her calmly. "I didn't like that envoy Hanniwuz. And I do like you. And Caz, and Mudge, and the others."

"As simple as that?"

"As simple as that, Talea."

She seemed about to say something more, lengthened her stride instead. "Let's hurry it up." She moved out in front of them and the others, even the long-limbed spellsinger, had to hurry to keep pace.

A disturbed Pog suddenly dipped low overhead. "Jon-Tom, Jon-Tom! There's something wrong up ahead!"

"What? What's wrong, Pog?"

"Big commotion, boss. Many people running like da Naganuph's after dem. I can't see a cause yet."

They turned a corner and were nearly trampled. Dozens of citizens poured down the wide street, bumping into the new arrivals and each other. Anxious raccoons cuddled masked infants in their arms, squirrel tails bobbed hysterically, and nightgown-clad anteaters stumbled into panicky simians. All were screeching and yelling and bawling in fear, and all were obviously running away from something utterly terrifying.

"What's wrong, what's the matter?" Talea demanded of one of the fleeing inhabitants.

The elderly bobcat beat feebly at her with her cane. "Let me go, woman. He's gone mad, he has. He'll kill us all! Let me go!"

"Who's gone mad? What . . . ?"

In her other hand the feline carried a heavy purse, weighed down perhaps with the family gold horde. She struck at Talea's wrist with it and tore free of her grasp.

Humans in night clothes and sleeping caps were among the mob. With their smooth strides they were outdistancing some of their shorter-legged neighbors, but they were equally panicked. Only the occasional roos and wallabies bounded past them.

"Falameezar. It's got to be," Jon-Tom said fearfully. "Something's gone wrong at the barracks."

"Maybe it would be better," Mudge said, slowing slightly, "if some of us waited 'ere. Pog and I could stay in reserve in case of . . ."

"Not me," said the bat forcefully. "My master may be in trouble. I've got ta help him if he is."

"Loyalty from you, Pog?" Jon-Tom couldn't help saying aloud.

"Loyalty my airborne arse!" the bat snorted derisively. "Dat hard-shelled senile old turd and I have a contract, and he's not gonna get out of it by getting himself stepped on by some berserk overheated lizard!" He soared on ahead above the foot traffic, darting and weaving his way around the panicked birds and bats that flew toward him.

For a while it seemed as if they'd never make it back to the courtyard. Eventually the crowds of refugees started to thin, however. Soon they'd vanished altogether.

Ahead the evening sky was glowing brightly, and it wasn't from a rising moon. They turned a last corner and found themselves in the open square on the opposite side from the barracks. That massive structure was a mass of flame. Orange fire licked at the sky from several smaller buildings nearby, but the blaze had not yet spread to the large, closely packed residential structures lining the courtyard. The city wall was solid rock and immune to the flames, though tents and banners and other flammables stacked near it were twisting skeletons of orange-lipped black ash that writhed and shrank in the night.

Close by the main harbor gate stood several clusters of nervous animals. Some were in uniform, others only partially so. Behind them were several large wagons, three axled, sporting hand pumps. The rudely awakened soldiers waited and held tight to their axes and spears while handlers behind them tried frantically to control the baying, hissing lizards yoked to the wagons.

Tubes trailed like brown snakes from each wagon back through the partly opened gate and doubtless from there out into the river. It was clear that the Polastrindu fire department was equipped to fight fires, but not the black and purple-blue behemoth they could hear raging and roaring behind the wall of flame that had engulfed the barracks.

"Clothahump! Where's Clothahump?" Pog yelled as the little group raced across the cobblestones toward the gate.

The leader of one of the fire teams gazed at the bat uncomprehendingly for a moment before replying. "The wizard turtle, you mean?" He gestured indifferently to his left. Then he returned his attention to the spreading conflagration, obviously debating in his mind if it was worth the risk of attracting the dragon's attention in order to try to at least contain the vanguard of the blaze.

They found Clothahump seated nearby on a low hitching bench contemplating the fire. From time to time thunderous bellows and Hephaestean threats could be heard from somewhere inside the blazing barracks.

They clustered around the motionless wizard, looked at him helplessly. He appeared to be deep in thought.

"What happened, sir?" asked Flor concernedly.

"What?" He looked around, frowned at some private thought. "Happened? Oh yes. The dragon. The dragon and I were talking pleasantly. I was doing quite well, boy." The wizard's glasses were bent and dangled precariously on his beak. His carapace was black with soot and he looked very old, Jon-Tom thought.

"I was rationalizing my end of the discussion efficiently when a pair of our guards joined us unexpectedly. They wondered where you were and I informed them you were all asleep, but they remained. I think they were attempting to prove their bravery by remaining in the dragon's presence.

"Falameezar greeted them as comrades, a word I explained to them. We all began to talk. I would have made excuses, but the dragon was enthusiastic about the chance to have a serious talk with members of the local proletariat." Despite the proximity of the blaze, a cold chill traveled down Jon-Tom's spine.

"The beast inquired about their aspirations for their huge commune and their eventual hopes for strengthening proletarian solidarity. None of that made any sense to the guards, of course, but then it doesn't make any sense to me either, so I was hard put to rationalize their replies.

"But that was not what ignited, so to speak, the problem. Soon both guards were boasting uncontrollably about their plans for leaving the army and getting rich. I tried to quiet them, but between explaining to the dragon and attempting to silence them, I got confused. I could not work any magic to shut them up.

"They went on and on about their supposedly wealthy friends, one of whom was a merchant who had a hundred and sixty people working for him, slaving away making garments for the trade. They boasted about how cheaply he paid them, how enormous his profits were, and how they hoped they would be as fortunate some day.

"I think what finally set the dragon off was the offer one of them made to employ him to work in a foundry, helping to make weapons so the local police could clear the streets of 'the pitiful beggars who infest decent neighborhoods.' That appeared to send him beyond reason. I could no longer communicate with him.

"He started raving about revolutions betrayed and capitalist moneymongers and began spewing fire in all directions. It was only by tucking my head into my shell and scrambling as fast as I could that I escaped. The two rabbit guards, I fear, exploded like torches when the dragon exhaled at them." He sighed heavily.

"Now he insists he will burn down the entire city. I'm afraid the only thing that has kept him from destroying more of the town thus far is his own rage. It chokes him so severely he cannot concentrate on generating fire."

"Why don't you make him stop, wizard?" Talea was leaning close to his face and practically shouting into it. "You're the all-powerful sorcerer, the great master of magic. Make him stop!"

"Stop, yes? I was trying to think." Clothahump leaned his chin on stubby fingers. "Dragon spells are as complicated as their subjects, you know. The right ingredients are required for a truly effective cast. I don't know . . ."

"You've got to do something!" She looked back at the searing blaze. Then she looked at Jon-Tom. So did everyone else.

"Now the lad's willin' and good-natured," said Mudge cautioningly, "but 'e ain't no fool. Are you, mate?" The otter was torn between common sense and the desire to save his own highly flammable skin.

But Jon-Tom already had the duar swung around against his belly and was trying to think of something to sing. He could remember several rain songs, but that might only anger the dragon and certainly wouldn't solve the problem. Falameezar might not burn Polastrindu down, but from the smashing and crunching sounds issuing from behind the flames Jon-Tom judged him quite capable of tearing it down physically.

He marched out toward the barracks, ignoring the single plea that came from Flor. None of the others tried to dissuade him. They had not the right, and they knew he had to try. They wanted him to try.

The near barracks' wall suddenly collapsed in a Niagara of flaming embers and hot coals. He shielded himself with the duar and his green cape. There was a roaring in his ears from the flames, and wood exploded from the heat ahead.

"*You!* Deviationist! Counterrevolutionary!" The epithets emerged fast and accusing from the fire, though so far without accompanying arcs of flame. Jon-Tom looked up from beneath his cape and found himself only a couple of yards away from the glowering visage of Falameezar. Red eyes burned down into his own, and plate-sized teeth gleamed in the orange light as the dragon-skull dipped down toward him. . . .

XXI

"Lies, lies, lies! You lied to me." A massive clawed foot gestured toward the inner city. "This is no commune, not even in part, but instead a virulent nest of capitalistic vice. It needs not to be reformed, for it is beyond that. It needs to be *cleansed!*"

"Now hold on a minute, Falameezar." Jon-Tom tried hard to sound righteous. "What gives you the right to decide what should happen to all these workers?"

"Workers . . . pagh!" Fire scorched the cobblestones just to Jon-Tom's right. "They have the tasks of workers, but the souls of imperialists! As for my right, I am pure of philosophy and dedicated in my aims. I can tell when a society is capable of achieving a noble state . . . or is beyond redemption! And besides," he spat a petulant burst of fire at a nearby market stall, which immediately burst into flame, "you lied to me."

Since indecision was clearly the path leading to imminent incineration, Jon-Tom replied boldly. "I did *not* lie to you, Falameezar. This is a commune-to-be, and most of the population are workers."

"It means naught if they willingly condone the system which exploits them."

"How much choice does an oppressed worker have, comrade? It is easy to speak of revolution when you're twenty times bigger than anyone else and can spit fire and destruction. You expect an awful lot of some poor worker with a family to take care of. You don't have those kinds of responsibilities, do you?"

"No, but . . ."

"Then don't condemn some poor bear for protecting his family. You're asking them to sacrifice cubs and children. And besides, they don't have your education. You're expecting revolutionary sophistication from uneducated workers. Shouldn't you try and educate them first? Then if they reject the True Path and continue to accept the capitalistic evils they live with, then it will be time for cleansing."

And by that time, he thought hopefully, we'll be safely away from Polastrindu.

"They still willingly countenance an antibourgeois life," said Falameezar grumblingly, but with less certainty.

Meanwhile Jon-Tom was still furiously trying to recall an anti-dragon song. He didn't know any. "Puff the Magic Dragon" was pleasant but hardly restrictive. Think, man, think!

But he had no time to think of songs. He was too busy trying to tie the dragon's tale into semantic knots.

"But would it not be best for all concerned if a warning was to be given?"

Falameezar's head rose high against the glowing night. "Yes, a warning! Burn out the evil influences so that the new order can be installed. Down with the exploiting industries and the factories of the capitalists! Build the commune anew, beneath the banner of true socialism."

"Didn't you hear what I just said?" Jon-Tom took a worried step backward. "You'll destroy the homes of the innocent, ignorant workers."

"It will be good for them," Falameezar replied firmly. "They will have to rebuild their homes with their own hands, cooperatively, instead of living in those owned by landlords and the bosses. Yes, the people must have the opportunity to begin afresh." He turned his attention speculatively to the nearest multistoried building, considering how most efficiently to commence "cleansing" it.

"But they already hate their bosses." Jon-Tom ran parallel to the loping dragon. "There's no reason to put them out in the rain and cold. What's needed here now isn't violence but a sound revolutionary dialectic!"

Falameezar's claws scraped on the cobblestones like the wheels of a vast engine.

"Remember the workers!" He shook his fist at the unresponsive dragon. "Consider their ignorance and their personal plights." Then, without thinking, his fingers were flying over the duar, the necessary words and music having come to him abruptly and unbidden.

"Arise ye pris'ners of starvation!
Arise, ye wretched of the Earth.
For justice thunders condemnation, a better world in birth.
No more tradition's chains shall bind us.
Arise, you slaves, no more in thrall!"

At the first stirring words of the *"Internationale,"* Falameezar halted as if shot. Slowly his head swung around and down to stare blankly at Jon-Tom.

"Watch 'im, mate!" sounded the faint voice of Mudge. Similar warnings came from Caz and Flor, Talea and Pog.

But the dragon was utterly mesmerized. His ears remained cocked attentively forward as the singer's voice rose and fell.

Finally the anthem was at an end. As Jon-Tom's fingers trailed a last time over the duar's strings, Falameezar slowly emerged from his stupor, nodding slowly.

"Yes, you are right, comrade. I will do what you say. For a moment I forgot what is truly important. Compassion was lost in my desire to establish proper dogma among the proletariat. I had forgotten the more important task before us in my rage at petty injustice." His head drooped low.

"I lost control of myself, and I apologize for the damage."

Jon-Tom whirled and frantically waved his arms, shouting the all-clear. Immediately the wagons of the Polastrindu fire brigade trundled forward, trailing hoses like brown slugtracks. Hands and paws were laid to pumps, and water was soon attacking the burning barracks. Thicker dark smoke filled the sky as the flames were pushed back and hot embers sizzled.

"I shall cause no more trouble," said the downcast dragon. "I will not forget again." Then the great lean skull turned to one side, and a crimson eye locked on Jon-Tom. "But before long we *will* make revolutionary progress here, and the bosses will be thrown out."

Jon-Tom nodded rapidly. "Of course. Remember that first we have to defeat the most repressive, most brutal bosses of all."

"I will remember." Falameezar sighed and a puff of smoke emerged from his mouth. Jon-Tom winced instinctively, but there was no flame. "We will strike to protect the workers." He curled up like a great cat, laid his head across his right foreleg.

"I'm very tired now. I leave the night in your hands, Comrade." With that he closed his eyes, oblivious to the activity and smoke and yelling all around him, and went peacefully to sleep.

"Thank you, Comrade Falameezar." Jon-Tom turned away. He was starting to shiver now, recalling the feel of heat on his face and the fury in the dragon's gaze when he'd first confronted him.

His friends were cautiously running to him. Their expressions were a mixture of relief and awe.

"What in hell did you sing? . . . What spell did you use? . . . How did you do it?" were some of the amazed comments.

"I don't know, I'm not sure. The words just came to me. Old studies that stick," he muttered as they walked back toward the city gate.

Clothahump was waiting there to greet him. The old turtle solemnly offered his hand. "A feat worthy of a true wizard, whether you believe yourself that or not, my boy. I salute you. You have just saved our journey."

"I'm afraid my principal motivation was to save myself, there at the last." He couldn't meet the wizard's eyes.

"Tut, motivation! It is accomplishment and result that count. I welcome you to the brotherhood of magicians." Jon-Tom found his fingers clasped in the cool but emphatic grasp of the elderly sorcerer.

"Perhaps it would be a good thing if you were to teach me the words to that spellsong, in case something were to happen to you. My voice is not particularly melodious, but at least I would have the words. It sounded especially powerful, and may serve to control the beast another time."

"It specializes in control, for all sorts of beasts," Jon-Tom replied.

The others listened as well, but the words had no special effect on them. Across the courtyard the fire brigade was bringing the last of the blaze under control. Falameezar snored unconcernedly nearby, his rage spent, his conscience assuaged.

Possibly it was because of Falameezar's tantrum, but in any case the summons to council came the following day. A much subdued beaver informed them that the representatives they'd wished to meet were already assembled and waiting for them.

Jon-Tom had spent much of the previous night coaching Caz in socialist jargon, realizing that Clothahump could not remain behind this time. The fact that the rabbit had volunteered to remain behind and keep a watch on the still somnolent dragon pleased Jon-Tom.

The fact that Talea and Flor had decided to remain and assist him did not. So he was in a foul mood as they neared the city hall.

"My boy," Clothahump was telling him, "if ever you live to be half my age you will learn that love is a lasting thing, while lust is but transitory. Are you so sure that you've sorted out the degree and direction of your feelings? Because if you are drowning in the former, then you have my wholehearted support. If merely the latter, then I can only sympathize with your subservience to the follies of youth, which are locked to but physical matters."

"It's just physical to *me*." He slammed the butt end of his staff angrily into the road with each stride. "Anyhow, you can't be objective about it. Aren't turtles by nature sluggish in such matters?"

"Occasionally yes, sometimes no. What is important is one's mental reaction, since it is the mind that makes the separation between love and lust, not the body. You let your gonads do your thinking, my boy, and you're no better than a lizard."

"That's easy for you to say. I'd imagine the internal fires are barely simmering after two hundred and a few odd years."

"We are not talking about my situation but of yours."

"Well, I'm trying to control myself."

"That's the good lad. Then I suggest you stop trying to find water beneath the street."

Jon-Tom eased up on his staff.

Mudge strode cockily alongside the youth. He was basking in the attention of the pedestrians who stopped on the street to stare at them, in the curious looks of others peering down from windows. Pog fluttered and soared majestically overhead, darting past aerial abodes with seeming indifference to their feathered inhabitants. While Clothahump did not anticipate treachery, he'd still insisted the bat remain safely out of arrow shot. Pog was their link with the unspoken dragonthreat sleeping back by the harbor gate.

"We're here, thirth." The beaver came to a halt, and directed them onward. They climbed a series of stone steps. Two guards stood on either side of the arched entrance. They snapped to attention, ceremonial armor shining in the sun and giving evidence of much laborious polishing. Dents in the metal were testimony to other activities.

Life quickly returned to normal around the fountain that dominated the small square in front of the city hall. Jon-Tom paused to study the peaceful scene.

A young wolf bitch nursed two cubs. Young hares and muskrats played a crude variety of field hockey with sticks and the battered skull of a recent guillotine victim. Two grizzled oldsters chatted casually about weather and politics. The aged possum hung from an oak tree branch while his corpulent companion, a fat fox clad in heavy overcoat, sat beneath him on a bench. The fact that one was upside down and the other rightside up had no effect on their conversation.

A clockmaker and candleshop owner stood in their doorways and argued business in the warmth of the unusually benign winter day. A customer entered the clock shop and the proprietor, an aproned gibbon, returned reluctantly to ply his trade.

Maybe the warm day was a good omen, Jon-Tom thought as he turned away from the peaceful scene. It was hard to imagine that all who frolicked or chattered in the square might soon be dead or locked in slavery.

It looked heartbreakingly normal. He felt that if he could only blink, refocus his mind, when he opened his eyes again there would be old men sitting and talking, boys and girls running and playing. And yet they were old men, boys and girls, for all their shapes were different and they were covered with warm fur. It was the warm blood that mattered. Everything else was superficial.

He turned to gaze into the hallway before them. They would have to face and convince a hostile, suspicious Council of the danger that was imminent. Somehow he would have to master the magic inherent in his duar and in his voice. He was not going to confront a group of teachers now, not about to present a scholarly master's thesis on some obscure portion of history. Millions of lives were at stake. The future of this world and maybe his own.

Except . . . this was his world now, and the dark future foreseen by Clothahump had become his future. His friends stood alongside him, ready to offer support and comfort. Flor Quintera never looked as beautiful shouting inanities beside a field of false combat. He would talk loud and hope silently.

"Let's go, and may the strength of our ancestors go with us," announced Clothahump, trundling up the last steps.

Jon-Tom could only agree, though as they passed beneath the appraising stares of the soldiers lining the hallway, he wished fervently for a little grass, and not the kind that grew in the courtyard outside.

THE HOUR OF THE
GATE

To

the trio that never was
But should have been.

Janis
Aretha
Billie

The ladies, bless 'em all.

I

Jon-Tom reeled dizzily at the top of the steps. All wrong, he knew. Out of place, out of time. He was *not* standing before the entrance to this strange Council Building in a city named Polastrindu. A five-foot tall otter in peaked green cap and bright clothing was *not* eying him anxiously, wondering if he was about to witness a fainting spell. A bespectacled bipedal turtle was *not* staring sourly at him, waiting for him to regain his senses so they could be about the business of saving the world. An enormous, exceedingly ugly black bat was *not* hovering nearby, muttering darkly to himself about dirty pots and pans and the lack of workman's comp a famulus enjoyed while in a wizard's employ.

Sadly, saying these things were *not* did *not* transform the reality.

" 'Ere now, mate," the otter Mudge inquired, "don't you be sick all over us, wot?"

"Sorry," Jonathan Thomas Meriweather said apologetically. "Oral exams always make me queasy."

"Be of good cheer, my young friend," said the wizard Clothahump. He tapped his plastron. "I shall do the necessary talking. You are here to add credence to what I will say, not to add words. Come now. Time dies and the world draws nearer disaster." He ambled through the portal. As he had now for many weeks, the transposed Jon-Tom could only long for his own vanished world, hope desperately that once this crisis had passed Clothahump could return him to it, and follow the turtle's lead.

Inside they marched past scribes and clerks and other functionaries, all of whom turned to look at them in passing. The hall itself was wood and stone, but the bark-stripped logs that supported this structure had been polished to a high luster. Rich reds faded into bright, almost canary-yellow grains. The logs had the sheen of marble pillars.

They turned past two clusters of arguing workers. The arguing stopped as they passed. Apparently everyone in Polastrindu now knew who they were, or at least that they controlled the dragon who'd almost burned down the city the previous night.

Up a pair of staircases they climbed. Clothahump puffed hard to keep up with the rest. Then they passed through a set of beautiful black and yellow buckeye-burl doors and entered a small room.

There was a single straight, long table on a raised dais. It curved at either end, forming horns of wood. To the right a small bespectacled margay sat behind a drafting table. He wore brown shirt, shorts, boots, and an odd narrow cap. The quill pen he was writing with was connected by wooden arms to six similar pens hovering over a much larger table and six separate scrolls. It was a clever mechanism enabling the scribe to make an original and six copies simultaneously. An assistant, a young wolf cub, stood nearby. He was poised to change the scrolls or unroll them as the occasion demanded.

Seated behind the raised table was the Grand Council of the City, County, and Province of Greater Polastrindu, the largest and most influential of its kind in the warmlands.

Jon-Tom surveyed the councillors. From left to right, he saw first a rather foppishly clad prairie dog draped in thin silks, lace, neck chains, and a large gold earring in his right ear. Next came a corpulent gopher in pink, wearing the expected dark wraparound glasses. This redoubtable female likely represented the city's nocturnal citizens. His eyes passed impatiently over most of the others.

There were only two truly striking personalities seated behind the table. At its far right end sat a tall, severely attired marten. If not actually a military uniform, his dress was very warlike. It was black and blue and there were silver epaulets crusting his shoulders and chevronlike ripples on his sleeves. Double bandoliers of small stilettoes formed a lethal "X" across his chest. His clothing was so spotless Mudge whispered that it must have a dirt-repellent spell cast on it.

His posture matched his attire. He sat rigidly erect in his low chair, his high torso not bending even slightly across the table. His attitude was also much more attentive than that of any of the other council members.

Jon-Tom tried to analyze their states of mind as they took stock of the tiny group waiting before the long table. Their expressions conveyed everything from fear to amusement. Only the marten seemed genuinely interested.

The other imposing figure on the dais sat in the middle of the table. He was flanked by two formal perches on which rested the representatives of Polastrindu's arboreal population.

One was a large raven. At the moment he was picking his beak with a silver pick held easily in his left foot. He wore a red, green, and ocher kilt and matching vest. On the other perch was the smallest intelligent inhabitant of the warmlands Jon-Tom had yet encountered. The hummingbird was no larger than a man's head. It had a long beak, exquisite plumage, and heavily jeweled kilt and vest. It might have flown free from the treasure vaults of Dresden.

Gold trim lined the kilt, and a necklace of the finest gold filigree hung around the ruby-throated neck. He also wore a tiny cap similar to an Australian bush hat. It was secured on the iridescent head with a gold strap.

Jon-Tom marveled at the hat. Slipping it on over that curving beak would be a considerable project, unless the strap joined at a tiny buckle he couldn't see.

All inhabitants and stretches of the province were thus represented. They were dominated by the motionless figure of the marten on the far right, and by the stocky individual in their center.

It was that citizen who commanded everyone's attention as he pushed back his chair and stood. The badger wore spectacles similar to Clothahump's. His fur was silvered on his back, indicating age. He had very neatly trimmed claws. Despite his civilized appearance Jon-Tom was grateful for the manicure, knowing the reputation badgers had for ferocity and tenacity in a fight. Deep-set black eyes stared out at them. He wore a stiff, high-collared suit marked only by a discreet gold flower on his lapel. One paw slammed down hard on the table. Jon-Tom hadn't known what to expect, but the instant angry outburst was not the greeting he'd hoped for.

"Now what do you mean by bringing this great narsty fire-breathing beastie into the city limits and burning down the harbor barracks, not to mention disrupting the city's commerce, panicking its citizenry, and causing disruption and general dismay among the populace?!?" The voice rose immediately to an angry pitch as he shook a thick warning finger down at them.

"Give me one reason why I should not have the lot of you run into the lowest jails!"

Jon-Tom looked at Mudge in dismay. It was Clothahump who spoke patiently. "We have come to Polastrindu, friend, in order to—"

"I am Mayor and Council President Wuckle Three-Stripe!" snorted the badger, "and you will address me as befits my titles and position!"

"We are here," continued the wizard, unperturbed and unimpressed, "on a mission of great consequence to every inhabitant of the civilized world. It would behoove you to listen closely to what I am about to tell you."

"Yeah," said Pog, who had settled on one of the numerous empty perches ringing the room, "and if ya don't, our good buddy da dragon will burn your manure pile of a rat-warren down around your waxy ears!"

"Shut up, Pog." Clothahump glared irritably at the bat.

While he was doing so the unctuous gopher leaned over and spoke to the badger in a delicate yet matronly voice. "The creature is undiplomatic, Mayor-President, but he has a point."

"I will not be blackmailed, Pevmora." He looked down the other way and asked in a less belligerent tone, "What do you say, Aveticus? Do we disembowel these intruders now, or what?"

The marten's reply was so quiet Jon-Tom had to strain to make it out. Nevertheless, the creature conveyed an impression of cold power. As would any student interested in the law, Jon-Tom noticed that all the other council members immediately ceased picking their mouths, chattering to each other, or whatever they'd been doing, in order now to pay attention.

"I think we should listen to what they have to say to us. Not only because of the threat posed by the dragon, against whose breath I will not expend my soldiers and whom you must admit we can do nothing about, but also because they speak as visitors who mean us nothing but good will. I cannot yet pass on the importance of what they may say, but I think we can safely accept their professed motivations. Also, they do not strike me as fools."

"Sensibly put, youngster," said Clothahump.

The marten nodded once, barely, and ignored the fact that he was anything but a cub. He smiled as imperceptibly as he'd nodded, showing sharp white teeth.

"Of course, good turtle, if you are wasting our time or do indeed mean us harm, then we will be forced to take other measures."

Clothahump waved the comment away. "You give us credit for being other than fools. I return the compliment. Now then, let us have no more talk of motivations and time, for I have none of the last to spare." He launched into a long and by now familiar explanation of the danger from the Plated Folk and their preparations, from their massed armies to their still unknown new magic.

When he'd finished the badger looked as bellicose as before. "The Plated Folk, the Plated Folk! Every time some idiot seer panics, it's 'the Plated Folk are coming, the Plated Folk are coming!'" He resumed his seat and spoke sarcastically.

"Do you think we can be panicked by tales and rumors that mothers use to scare their cubs into bed? Do you think we believe every claim laid before us by every disturbed would-be leader? What do you think we are, stranger?"

"Stubborn," replied Clothahump patiently. "I assure you on my honor as a wizard and member in good standing of the Guild for nearly two hundred years that everything I have just told you is true." He indicated Jon-Tom, who until now had been silently watching and listening.

"Last night, this young spellsinger actually encountered an envoy of the Plated Folk. He was here to foment trouble among local human citizens, and according to my young associate he was well disguised."

That brought some of the more insipid members of the council wide awake. "One of *them* . . . here, in the city . . . !"

"He was attempting to begin war between the species," reiterated the wizard. More mutters of disbelief from those behind the long table.

"He wanted me to join with his puppets," Jon-Tom explained. "The humans he'd recruited say the Plated Folk have promised to make them the overlords and administrators of all the warmlands the insects conquer. I didn't believe it for a minute, of course, but I think I've studied more about such matters than those poor deluded people. I don't think they have many followers. Nevertheless, the word should be spread. Just letting it be known that you know what the Plated Folk are trying to do should discourage potential recruits to their cause."

The muttering among the councillors changed from nervous to angry. "Where is he?" shouted the hummingbird, suddenly buzzing over the table to halt and hover only inches from Jon-Tom's face. "Where is the insect offal, and his furless dupes?" Tiny, furious eyes stared into larger human ones. "I will put out their eyes myself. I shall . . ."

"Perch down, Millevoddevareen," said Wuckle Three-Stripe, the badger. "And control yourself. I will not tolerate anarchy in the chambers."

The bird glared back at the Mayor, muttered something under his breath, and shot back to his seat. His wings continued to whirr with nervous energy. He forced himself to calm down by preening them with his long bill.

"Such fringe fanatics have always existed among the species," the Mayor said thoughtfully. "Humans have no corner on racial prejudice. These you speak of will be warned, but they are of little consequence. When the time for final choices arrives, common sense takes precedence over emotion. Most people are sensible enough to realize they would never survive a Plated Folk conquest." He smiled and his mask fur wrinkled.

"But no such invasion has ever succeeded. Not in tens of thousands of years."

"There is still only one way through Zaryt's Teeth," proclaimed a squirrel, "and that is by way of the Jo-Troom Pass. Two thousand years ago Usdrett of Osprinspri raised the Great Wall on the site of his own victory over the Plated Folk. A wall which has been strengthened and fortified by successive generations of fighters. The Gate has never been forced open, and no Plated Folk force has ever even reached the wall itself. We've never let them get that far down the Pass."

"They're too stratified," added the raven, waving a wing for emphasis. "Too inflexible in their methods of battle to cope with improvisation and change. They prepare to fight one way and cannot shift quickly enough to handle another. Why, their last attempt at an invasion was among the most disastrous of all. Their defeats grow worse with each attack. Such occasional assaults are good for the warmlands: they keep the people from complacency and sharpen the skills of our soldiers. Nor can we be surprised. The permanent Gate contingent can hold off any sudden attack until sufficient reinforcements can be gathered."

"This is no usual invasion," said Clothahump intently. "Not only have the Plated Folk prepared more thoroughly and in greater numbers than ever before, but I have reason to believe they have produced some terrible new magic to assist them, an evil we may be unable to counter and whose nature I have as yet been unable to ascertain."

"Magic again!" Wuckle Three-Stripe spat at the floor. "We still have no proof you're even the sorcerer you claim to be, stranger. So far I've only your word as proof."

"Are you calling me a liar, sir?"

Concerned that he might have overstepped a trifle, the Mayor retreated a bit. "I did not say that, stranger. But surely you understand my position. I can hardly be expected to alarm the entire civilized warmlands merely at the word of a single visitor. That is scarcely sufficient proof of what you have said."

"Proof? I'll give you proof." The wizard's fighting blood was up. He considered thoughtfully, then produced a couple of powders from his plastron. After tossing them on the floor he raised both hands and turned a slow circle, reciting angrily.

> "Cold front, warm front, counteract my affront.
> Isobars and isotherms violently descend.
> Nimbus, cumulus, poles opposizing,
> Ions in a mighty surge my doubters upend!"

A thunderous roar deafened everyone in the room and there was a blinding flare. Jon-Tom dazedly struggled back to a standing position to see Clothahump slowly picking himself up off the floor and readjusting his glasses.

Wuckle Three-Stripe lay on the floor in front of him, having been blown completely across the council table. His ceremonial chair was a pile of smoking ash. Behind it a neat hole had been melted through the thick leaded glass where the tiny lightning bolt had penetrated. The fact that it was a cloudless day made the feat all the more impressive.

The Mayor disdained the help of one of the other councillors. Brushing himself off and rearranging his clothing, he waddled back behind the table. A new chair was brought and set onto the pile of ash. He cleared his throat and leaned forward.

"We will accept the fact that you are a sorcerer."

"I'm glad that's sufficient proof," said Clothahump with dignity. "I'm sorry if I overdid it a mite. Some of these old spells are pretty much just for show and I'm a little rusty with them." The scribe had returned to his sextupal duplicator and was scribbling furiously.

"Plated envoys moving through our city in human disguise," murmured one of the councillors. "Talk of interspecies dissension and war, great and strange magic in the council chambers. Surely this portends unusual events, perhaps even a radically different kind of invasion."

The prairie dog leaned across the table, steepling his fingers and speaking in high-pitched, chirping tones.

"There are many forms of magic, colleagues. While the ability to conjure thunder and lightning on demand is most impressive, it differs considerably from divination. Do we then determine that on the basis of a flash of power we cease all normal activities and place Polastrindu on war alert?

"Should the call go out on that basis to distant Snarken, to L'bor and Yul-pat-pomme and all the other towns and cities of the warmlands? Must we now order farmers to leave their fields, young men their sweethearts, and bats their nightly hunts? Commerce will come to a halt and fortunes will be lost, lives disrupted.

"This is a massive question, colleagues. It must be answered by more than the words and deeds of one person." He gestured deferentially with both hands at Clothahump. "Even one so clearly versed in the arts of wizardry as you, sir."

"So you want more proof?" asked Jon-Tom.

"More specific proof, yes, tall man," said the prairie dog. "War is no casual matter. I need hardly remind the other participants of this council," and he looked the length of the long table, "that if there is no invasion, no unusual war, then it is our bodies that will provide fertilizer for next season's crops, and not those of our nomadic visitors." He looked back out of tiny black eyes at Jon-Tom. "Therefore I would expect some sympathy for our official positions."

A mild smattering of applause came from the rest of the council, except for Millevoddevareen the hummer. He continued to mutter, "I want those traitorous humans. Put their damn perverted eyes out!" His colleagues paid him no attention. Hummingbirds are notoriously more bellicose than reflective.

"Then you shall have more conclusive proof," said the weary wizard.

"Master?" Pog looked down solicitously at the turtle. "Do ya really tink anodder spell now, so close ta da odder, is a good idea?"

"Do I seem so tired then, Pog?"

The bat flapped idly, said without hesitation, "Yeah, ya do, boss."

Clothahump nodded slowly. "Your concern is noted, Pog. I'll make a good famulus out of you yet." The bat smiled, which in a bat

is no prettier than a frown, but it was unusual to see the pleased
expression on the fuzzy face of the normally hostile assistant.

"I expect to become more tired still." He looked at Jon-Tom, then
around him at Mudge. "I'd say you represent the lower orders accu-
rately enough."

"Thanks," said the otter drily, "Your Sorcererness."

"What would it take to convince you of the reality of this threat?"

"Well, if'n I were ignorant o' the real situation and I needed a good
convincin'," Mudge said speculatively, "I'd say it were up t' you t'
prove it by showin' me."

Clothahump nodded. "I thought so."

"Master . . . ?" began Pog warningly.

"It's all right. I have the capacity, Pog." His face suddenly went
blank, and he fell into a deep trance. It was not as deep as the one he
had used to summon M'nemaxa, but it impressed the hell out of the
council.

The room darkened, and curtains magically drew themselves
across the back windows of the chambers. There was nervous whispering among those seated behind the long table, but no one moved.
The marten Aveticus, Jon-Tom noted, did not seem in the least concerned.

A cloud formed at the far end of the chamber, an odd cloud that
was flat and rectangular in shape. Images formed inside the cloud. As
they solidified, there were gasps of horror and dismay from the council members.

Vast ranks of insect warriors marched across the cloud. They bore
aloft an ocean of pikes and spears, swords and shields. Huge Plated
generals directed the common troops, which stretched across misty
plains as far as the eye could see. Tens of thousands paraded across
that cloud.

As the view shifted and rolled, there was anxious chatter from the
council. "They seem better armed than before . . . look how purposefully they drill. . . . You can feel the confidence in them . . .
never saw that before. . . . The numbers, the numbers!"

The scene changed. Stone warrens and vast structures slid past in
review. A massive, bulbous edifice began to come into view: the towering castle of Cugluch.

Abruptly the view changed to one of dark clouds, fluttered, and
vanished. There was a thump, the cloud dissipated, together with the
view, and light returned to the room.

Clothahump was sitting down on the floor, shaking his head. Pog was hovering above him, fumbling with a vial. The wizard took a long sip of the liquid within, shook his head once more, and wiped the back of his mouth with an arm. With the bat's help he stood and smiled shakily at Jon-Tom.

"Not a bad envisioning. Couldn't get to the castle, though. Too far, and the inhibitory spells are too strong. Lost the damn vertical hold." He started to go down, and Jon-Tom barely got hold of an arm in time to keep the turtle from slumping back to the floor.

"You shouldn't have done it, sir. You're too weak."

"Had to, boy." He jerked his head toward the long table. "Some hardheads up there."

The councillors were babbling among themselves, but they fell silent when Clothahump spoke. "I tried to show you the interior of the castle keep, but its secrets are too well protected by powerful spells I cannot pierce."

"Then how do you know this great new magic exists?" asked the ever skeptical prairie dog.

"I summoned M'nemaxa."

Mutters of amazement mixed with disbelief and awe.

"Yes, I did even that," Clothahump said proudly, "though the consequences of such a conjuration could have been fatal for me and all those in my care."

"If you did so once, could you not summon the spirit once more and learn the true nature of this strange evil you feel exists in Cugluch?" wondered one of the councillors.

Clothahump laughed gently. "I see there are none here versed in wizardly lore. A pity no local sorcerer or ess could have joined us in this council.

"It was remarkable that I was able to conduct the first conjuration. Were I to try it again I could not bind the M'nemaxa spirit within restrictive boundaries. It would burst free. In less than a second I and all around me would be reduced to a crisp of meat and bone."

"I withdraw the suggestion," said the councillor hastily.

"We must rely on ourselves now," said Clothahump. "Outside forces will not save us."

"I think we should . . ." began one of the other members. He fell silent and looked to his left. So did the others.

The marten Aveticus was standing. "I will announce the mobilization," he said softly. "The armies can be ready in a few months' time. I will contact my counterparts in Snarken and L'bor, in all the other towns and cities." He stared evenly at Clothahump.

"We will meet this threat, sir, with all the force the warmlands can bring to bear. I leave it to you to counter this evil magic you speak of. I dislike fighting something I can't see. But I promise you that nothing which bleeds will pass the Jo-Troom Gate."

"But General Aveticus, we haven't reached a decision yet," protested the gopher.

The marten turned and looked down his narrow snout at his colleagues. "These visitors," and he indicated the four strangers standing and watching nearby, "have made their decision. Based upon what they have said and shown us, I have made mine. The armies will mobilize. Whether they do so with your blessing is your decision. But they will be ready." He bowed stiffly toward Clothahump.

"Learned sir, if you will excuse me. I have much work to do." He turned and strode out of the room on short but powerful legs. Jon-Tom watched his departure admiringly. The marten was someone he would like to know better.

After an uncomfortable pause, the councillors resumed their conversation. "Well, if General Aveticus has already decided so easily . . ."

"That's right," said the hummingbird, buzzing above the table. "Our decision has been made for us. Not by these people," and he gestured with a wing, though it was so fast Jon-Tom couldn't swear he'd actually noticed the gesture so much as imagined it, "but by the General. You all know how conservative he is.

"Now that we are committed, there must be no dissension. We must act as one mind, one body, to counter the threat." He soared higher above the floor.

"I shall notify the air corps of the decision so that we may begin to coordinate operations with the army. I will also send out the peregrines with messages to the other cities and towns that the Plated Folk are again on the march, stronger and more voracious than ever. This time, brothers and sisters, we will deal them a defeat, give them a beating so bad they will not recover for a thousand years!"

Words of assent and a few cheers echoed around the council chamber. One came from the cub manipulating the scrolls. His scribe looked at him reprovingly, and the youngster settled back down to his paper shuffling as Millevoddevareen left via an opened window.

"It seems that your appeal has accomplished what you intended," said the gopher quietly, preening an eyelash. Gems sparkled around her thick neck and from the rings on every finger. "At least among the military-minded among us. All the world will react to your cry of alarm." She shook her head and smiled grimly.

"Heaven help you if your prediction turns out to be less than accurate."

"I can only say to that, madam, that I would much rather be proved inaccurate than otherwise in this matter." Clothahump bowed toward her.

There were handshakes and hugs all around as the councillors descended from their dais. In doing so, they left behind a good deal of their pomposity and officiousness.

"We'll finish the slimy bastards this time!"

"Nothing to worry about . . . be a good fight!"

There was even grudging agreement from the Mayor, who was still irked that General Aveticus hadn't waited for the decision of the council before ordering mobilization. But there was nothing he could do about it now. Given the evidence Clothahump had so graphically presented, he wasn't sure he wanted to try.

"You'll advise us immediately, sir," he said to Clothahump, "if you learn of any changes in plan among the Plated Folk."

"Of course."

"Then there remains only the matter of a new and perhaps more elegant habitation for you until it's time to march. We have access to a number of inns for the housing of diplomatic guests. I suppose you qualify as that. But I don't know what we can do with your great flaming friend back in the courtyard, since he so impolitely burned down his quarters."

"We'll take care of him," Jon-Tom assured the Mayor.

"Please see that you do." Wuckle Three-Stripe was recovering some of his mayoral bearing. "Especially since he's the only *real* danger we've been certain of since you've appeared among us."

With that, he turned to join the animated conversation taking place among several members of the council.

Once outside the chambers and back in the city hall's main corridor Jon-Tom and Mudge took the time to congratulate Clothahump.

"Aye, that were a right fine performance, guv'nor," said the otter admiringly. "Cor, you should o' seen some o' those fat faces when you threw that army o' bugs up at 'em!"

"You've done what you wanted to, sir," agreed Jon-Tom. "The armies of the warmlands will be ready for the Plated Folk when they start through the Jo-Troom Pass."

But the wizard, hands clasped around his back, did not appear pleased. Jon-Tom frowned at him as they descended the steps to the city hall courtyard.

"Isn't that what you wanted, sir? Isn't that what we've come all this way for?"

"Hmmm? Oh, yes, my boy, that's what I wanted." He still looked discouraged. "I'm only afraid that all the armies of all the counties and cities and towns of all the warmlands might not be enough to counter the threat."

Jon-Tom and Mudge exchanged glances.

"What more can we do?" asked Mudge. "We can't fight with wot we ain't got, Your Magicalness."

"No, we cannot, good Mudge. But there may be more than what we have."

"Beggin' your pardon, sor?"

"I won't rest if there is."

"Well then, you give 'er a bit of some thought, guv, and let us know, won't you?" Mudge had the distressing feeling he wasn't going to be able to return to the familiar, comfortable environs of Lynchbany and the Bellwoods quite as soon as he'd hoped.

"I will do that, Mudge, and I will let you know when I inform the others. . . ."

II

The quarters they were taken to were luxurious compared to the barracks they'd spent their first night in. Fresh flowers, scarce in winter, were scattered profusely around the high-beamed room. They were ensconced in Polastrindu's finest inn, and the decor reflected it. Even the ceiling was high enough so Jon-Tom could stand straight without having to worry about a lamp decapitating him.

Sleeping quarters were placed around a central meeting room which had been set aside exclusively for their use. Jon-Tom still had to duck as he entered the circular chamber.

Caz was leaning back in a chair, ears cocked slightly forward, a glass held lightly in one paw. The other held a silver, ornately worked pitcher from which he was pouring a dark wine into a glass.

Flor sat on one side of him, Talea on the other. All were chuckling at some private joke. They broke off to greet the newcomers.

"Don't have to ask how it went," said Talea brightly, resting her boots on an immaculate couch. "A little while ago this party of sub-servient flunkies shows up at the barracks and tells us rooms have been reserved for us in this gilded hole." She sipped wine, carelessly spilled some on a finely woven carpet. "This style of crusading's more to my taste, I can tell you."

"What *did* you tell them, Jon-Tom?" wondered Flor.

He walked to an open window, rested his palms on the sill, and stared out across the city.

"It wasn't easy at first. There was a big, blustery badger named Wuckle Three-Stripe who was ready to chuck us in jail right away. It was easy to see how he got to be mayor of as big and tough a place as Polastrindu. But Clothahump scorched the seat of his pants, and after that it was easy. They paid serious attention.

"There was a general named Aveticus who's got more common sense than the rest of the local council put together. As soon as he'd heard enough he took over. The others just slid along with his opinion. I think he likes us personally, too, but he's so cold-faced it's hard to tell for sure what he's thinking. But when he talks everybody listens."

Down below lay a vast black and purple form coiled in the shade of a high stone wall. Falameezar was apparently sleeping peacefully in front of the inn stables. The other stable buildings appeared to be deserted. No doubt the riding lizards of the hotel staff and its guests had been temporarily boarded elsewhere.

"The armies are already mobilizing, and local aerial representatives have been dispatched to carry the word to the other cities and towns."

"Well, that's all right, then," said Talea cheerfully. "Our job's finished. I'm going to enjoy the afterglow." She finished her considerable glass of wine.

"Not quite finished." Clothahump had snuggled into a low-seated chair across from her couch.

"Not quite, 'e says," rumbled Mudge worriedly.

Pog selected a comfortable beam and hung himself above them. "The master says we got ta seek out every ally we can."

"But from what has been said, good sir, we are already notifying all possible allies in the warmlands." Caz sat up in his chair and gestured with his glass. Wine pitched and rolled like a tiny red pond and he didn't spill a drop.

"So long as the city fathers and mothers have seen fit to grant us these delightful accommodations, I see no reason why we should not avail ourselves of the local hospitality. Polastrindu is not so very far from Zaryt's Teeth and the Gate itself. Why not bivouac here until the coming battle? We can offer our advice to the locals."

But Clothahump disagreed. "General Aveticus strikes me as competent enough to handle military preparations. Our task must be to seek out any additional assistance we can. You just stated that all possible warmland allies are being notified. That is so. My thoughts concerned possible allies elsewhere."

"Elsewhere?" Talea sat up and looked puzzled. "There is no elsewhere."

"Try tellin' 'is nib's 'ere that," said Mudge.

Talea looked curiously at the otter, then back at the wizard. "I still don't understand."

"There is another nation whose aid would be invaluable," Clothahump explained energetically. "They are legendary fighters, and history tells us they despise the Plated Folk as much as we do."

Mudge circled a finger near one ear, whispered quietly to Jon-Tom. "Told you 'e was vergin' on the senile. The lightnin' an' the view conjurin' 'as sent him off t' balmy land."

The most unexpected reaction came from Pog, however. The bat left his beam and hovered nervously overhead, his eyes wide, his tone fearful.

"No, Master! Don't tink of it. Don't!"

Clothahump shrugged. "Our presence here is no longer required. We would find ourselves lost among the general staffs of the assembling armies. Why then should we not seek out aid which could turn the tide of battle?"

Jon-Tom, who had returned from his position by the open window, listened curiously and wondered at Pog's sudden fright.

"What kind of allies were you thinking about, sir? I'm certainly willing to help recruit." Pog gave him an ugly look.

"I'm talking about the Weavers, of course."

The violence of the response to this announcement startled Jon-Tom and Flor.

"Who are these 'Weavers'?" she asked the wizard.

"They are thought to be the most ferocious, relentless, and accomplished mountain fighters in all the world, my dear."

"Notice he does not say 'civilized' world," said Caz pointedly. Even his usually unruffled demeanor had been mussed by the wizard's shocking pronouncement. "I would not disagree with that appraisal of Weaver fighting ability, good sir," continued the rabbit, his nose twitching uncontrollably. "And what you say about them hating the Plated Folk is also most likely true. Unfortunately, you neglect the likely possibility that they also despise us."

"That is more rumor and bedtime story than fact, Caz. Considering the circumstances, they might be quite willing to join with us. We do not know for certain that they hate us."

"That's for sure," said Talea sardonically, "because few who've gone toward their lands have ever come back."

"That's because no one can get across the Teeth," Mudge said assuredly. " 'Ate us or not don't matter. Probably none of them that's tried reachin' Weaver lands 'as ever reached 'em. There ain't no way across the Teeth except through the Gate and then the Pass, and the Weavers, if I recall my own bedtimey stories aright, live a bloody good ways north o' the Greendowns."

"There is another way," said Clothahump quietly. Mudge gaped at him. "It is also far from here, far from the Gate, far to the north. Far across the Swordsward."

"Cross the Swordsward!" Talea laughed in disbelief. "He *is* crazy!"

"Across the great Swordsward," the sorcerer continued patiently, "lies the unique cataract known as the Sloomaz-ayor-la-Weentli, in the language of the Icelands in which it arises. It is The-River-That-Eats-Itself, also called the River of Twos, also the Double-River. In the language and knowledge of magic and wizardry, it is known as the SchizoStream."

"A schizoid river?" Jon-Tom's thoughts twisted until the knot hurt. "That doesn't make any sense."

"If you know the magical term, then you know what you say is quite true, Jon-Tom. The Sloomaz-ayor-la-Weentli is indeed the river that makes no sense."

"Neither does traveling down it, if I'm following your meaning correctly," said Caz. Clothahump nodded. "Does not The-River-That-Eats-Itself flow through the Teeth into something no living creature has seen called The Earth's Throat?" Again the wizard indicated assent.

"I see." Caz ticked the relevant points off on furry fingers as he spoke. "Then all we have to do is cross the Swordsward, find some way of navigating an impossible river, enter whatever The Earth's Throat might be, counter whatever dangers may lie within the mountains themselves, reach the Scuttleteau, on which dwell the Weavers, and convince them not only that we come as friends but that they should help us instead of eating us."

"Yes, that's right," said Clothahump approvingly.

Caz shrugged broadly. "A simple task for any superman." He adjusted his monocle. "Which I for one am not. I am reasonably good at cards, less so at dice, and fast of mouth, but I am no reckless gambler. What you propose, sir, strikes me as the height of folly."

"Give me credit for not being a fool with my own life," countered Clothahump. "This must be tried. I believe it can be done. With my guidance you will all survive the journey, and we will succeed." There was a deep noise, halfway between a chuckle and a belch.

Clothahump threw the hanging famulus a quick glare, and Pog hurriedly looked innocent.

"I'll go, of course," said Jon-Tom readily.

The others gazed at him in astonishment. "Be you daft too, mate?" said Mudge.

"Daft my ass." He looked down at the otter. "I have no choice."

"I'll go," announced Flor, smiling magnificently. "I love a challenge."

"Oh, very well." Caz fitted his monocle carefully, his pink nose still vibrating, "but it's a fool's game to draw and roll a brace of twelves after a muntle-star pays out."

"I suppose I'll come too," said Talea with a sigh, "because I've no more good sense than the rest of you."

All eyes turned toward Mudge.

"Right then, quit staring at me, you bloody great twits!" His voice dropped to a discouraged mutter. "I 'ope when we find ourselves served up t' the damned Weavers for supper that I'm the last one on the rottin' menu, so I can at least 'ave the pleasure o' watchin' 'em eat you arse'oles first!"

"To such base uses we all eventually come, Mudge," Jon-Tom told him.

"Don't get philosophical with me, mate. Oh, you've no choice for sure, not if you've a 'ope o' seeing your proper 'ome again. Old Clothahump's got you by the balls, 'e as. But as for me, I can be threatened so far and then it don't matter no more."

"No one is threatening you, otter," said the wizard.

"The 'ell you ain't! I saw the look in your eye, knew I might as well say yes voluntary-like and 'ave done with it. You can work thunder and lightnin' but you can't make the journey yourself, you old fart! You don't fool me. You *need* us."

"I have never tried to deny that, Mudge. But I will not hold you. I have not threatened you. So behind all your noise and fury, why *are* you coming?"

The otter stood there and fumed, breathing hard and glaring first at the turtle, then Jon-Tom, then the others. Finally he booted an exquisite spittoon halfway across the room. It bounced ringingly off the far wall as he sat down in a huff.

"Be billy bedamned if I know!"

"I do," said Talea. "You'd rather travel along with a bunch of fools like the rest of us than stay here and be conscripted into the army.

With Clothahump and Jon-Tom gone, the local authorities will treat you like any other bum."

"That's bloody likely," snorted Mudge. "Leave me alone, then, won't you? I said I'd go, though I'd bet heavy against us ever comin' back."

"Optimism is better than pessimism, my friend," said Caz pleasantly.

"You. I don't understand you at all, mate." The otter shoved back his cap and walked across the carpet to confront Caz. "A minute ago you said you weren't no reckless gambler. Now you're all for agoin' off on this charmin' little suicide trot. And of all o' us, you'd be the one I'd wager on t' stay clear o' the army's clutches."

The rabbit looked unimpressed. "Perhaps I can see the larger picture, Mudge."

"Meanin' wot?"

"Meaning that if what our wise friend Clothahump knows to be true indeed comes to pass, the entire world may be embarking on that 'trot' with us." He smiled softly. "There are few opportunities for gambling in a wasteland. I do not think the Plated Folk will permit recreation as usual if they are victorious. And I have other reasons."

"Yeah? Wot reasons?"

"They are personal."

"The wisdom of pragmatism," said Clothahump approvingly. "It was a beneficial day indeed when the river brought you among us, friend Caz."

"Maybe. But I think I would be still happier if I had not misjudged the placement of those dice and been forced to depart so precipitately from my ship. The happiness of the ignorant is no less so than any other. Ah well." He shrugged disarmingly. "We are all of us caught up in momentous events beyond our ability to change."

They agreed with him, and none realized he was referring as much to his previously mentioned personal reasons as to the coming cataclysm. . . .

The city council provided a three-axle wagon and a dray team of four matched yellow-and-black-striped lizards, plus ample supplies. Some among the council were sorry to see the wizard and spellsinger depart, but there were others who were just as happy to watch two powerful magicians leave their city.

Talea handled the reins of the wagon while Flor, Jon-Tom, Mudge, Clothahump, and Caz sorted living quarters out of the back of the heavily loaded vehicle. Thick canvas could be drawn across the top to keep out the rain. Ports cut in the slanting wooden walls provided ventilation and a means for firing arrows at any attacker.

Aveticus, resplendent in a fresh uniform and as coldly correct as ever, offered to provide a military escort at least part of the way. Clothahump declined gracefully, insisting that the less attention they attracted the better their chance for an uneventful traverse of the Swordsward.

Anyway, they had the best protection possible in the form of Falameezar. The dragon would surely frighten away any possible assailants, intelligent or otherwise.

It took the dray lizards a day or two to overcome their nervousness at the dragon's presence, but soon they were cantering along on their strong, graceful legs. Bounding on six solid rubber wheels the wagon fairly flew out of the city.

They passed small villages and farms for another several days, until at last no sign of habitation lay before them.

The fields of golden grain had given way to very tall light green grasses that stretched to the ends of the northern and eastern horizons. Dark wintry rain clouds hovered above the greenery, and there were rumblings of distant thunder.

Off to their right the immense western mountain range known as Zaryt's Teeth rose like a wall from the plains. Its lowermost peaks rose well above ten thousand feet while the highest towered to twenty-five thousand. Dominating all and visible for weeks to come was the gigantic prong of Brokenbone Peak, looking like the ossified spine of some long-fossilized titan.

It was firmly believed by many that in a cave atop that storm-swept peak dwelt the Oracle of All Knowledge. Even great wizards had been unable to penetrate the winds that howled eternally around that inaccessible crag. For by the time any grew wise enough to possibly make the journey, they had also grown too old, which might explain why isolated travelers sometimes heard monstrous laughter avalanching down Brokenbone's flanks, though most insisted it was only the wind.

The Swordsward resembled a well-manicured field. Patches of other vegetation struggled to rise above the dense grass, were only occasionally successful. Here and there small thickets that were either very thin flowering trees or enormous dandelions poked insolently above the waving green ocean.

Despite Clothahump's protests General Aveticus had given them a mounted escort to the boundary of the wild plains. The soldiers raised a departing cheer as the wagon left them behind and started out through the grass.

There were no roads, no paths through the Swordsward. The grass that formed it grew faster than any bamboo. So fast, according to Caz, that you could cut the same patch bare to the earth four times in a single day, and by nightfall it would be as thick as ever. Fortunately the blades were as flexible as they were prolific. The wagon slid over them easily.

Each blade knew its assigned place. None grew higher than the next and attempted to steal the light from its neighbor. Despite the flexibility of the grass, however, the name Swordsward had not been bestowed out of mischief or indifference. While Falameezar's thick scales were invulnerable, as were those of the dray lizards, the others had to be careful when descending from the wagon least the sharp edges of the tall blades cut through clothing and skin.

Jon-Tom learned quickly enough. Once he'd leaned over the back of the wagon to pluck a high, isolated blue flower. A quick, sharp pain made him pull back his hand. There was a thin line of red two inches long across his palm. It felt as if someone had taken a piece of new paper and drawn it fast across his skin. The wound was narrow and bled only for a minute, but it remained painful for days.

Several times they had glimpses of lanky predators like a cross between a crocodile and a greyhound. They would pace the wagon for hours before slinking off into the green.

"Noulps," Caz told him, peering out the arrowport behind him. "They would kill and eat us if they could, but I don't think that's likely. Falameezar scares them off."

"How can you tell?"

"Because they leave us. A noulp pack will follow its quarry for weeks, I'm told, until they run it down."

Days became weeks that passed without trouble. Each day the black clouds massing in the west would come nearer, their thunder more intimate. They promised more severe weather than the steady, nightly rain.

"It is winter, after all," Clothahump observed one day. "I worry about being caught out here in a really bad storm. This wagon is not the cover I would wish."

But when the full storm finally crested atop them, even the wizard was unprepared for its ferocity. The wind rose until it shook the wagon. Its huddled inhabitants felt like bugs in a box. Rain and sleet battered insistently at the wooden sides, seeking entry, while the lizards lay down in a circle in the grass and closed their eyes against the driving gale.

The wagon was wide and low. It did not leak, did not tip over. Jon-Tom was even growing used to the storm until, on the fourth day, a terrible scream sounded from outside. It faded rapidly, swallowed up by the wind.

He fumbled for a candle, gave up, and used his sparker. Flame flashed off emerald eyes.

"What's the matter?" Talea asked him sleepily. The others were moving about beneath their blankets.

"Someone screamed."

"I didn't hear anything."

"It was outside. It's gone now."

Heads were counted. Flor was there, blinking sleep from her eyes. Nearby Caz leaned up against the inner wall. Mudge was the last to awaken, having displayed the unique ability to sleep soundly through thunder, screaming, and wind.

Only Clothahump looked attentive, sensing the night smells.

"We're all here," said Flor tiredly. "Then who screamed?"

Clothahump was still listening intently, spoke without moving head or body. "The lowliest are always missed the last. Where is Pog?"

Jon-Tom looked toward the back of the wagon. The hanging perch in the upper left corner was empty. Rain stained the wood, showing where the canvas backing had been unsnapped. He moved to inspect it. Several of the sealing snaps had been broken by the force of the gale.

"He's been carried off in his sleep," said Clothahump. "We have to find him. He cannot fly in this."

Jon-Tom stuck his head outside, immediately drew it back in. The ferocity of rain and wind drowned both skin and spirits. He forced himself to try again, called the bat's name several times.

A massive, damp skull suddenly appeared close by the opening. Jon-Tom was startled, but only for a moment.

"What's the matter, Comrade?" Falameezar inquired. "Is there some trouble?"

"We've . . . we've lost one of the group," he said, trying to shield his face against the battering rain. "Pog, the bat. We think he got caught by a freak gust of wind and it's carried him off. He doesn't answer, and we're all worried. He can't walk well in the best of weather and he sure as hell can't fly in this gale. Also, there don't seem to be any trees around he could catch hold of."

"Never fear, Comrade. I will find him." The massive armored body turned southward and bellowed above the wind, "Comrade Pog, Comrade Pog!"

That steady, confident voice echoed back to them until even it was overwhelmed by distance and wind. Jon-Tom watched until the black shadow shape faded into the night, then drew back inside, wiping water from his face and hair.

"Falameezar's gone after him," he told the anxious watchers. "The storm doesn't seem to be bothering him too much, but I doubt he's got much of a chance of finding Pog unless the storm forced him down somewhere close by."

"He may be leagues from here by now," said Caz dolefully. "Damn this infernal wind!" He struck in frustration at the wooden wall.

"He was impertinent and disrespectful, but he performed his duties well for all his complaining," said Clothahump. "A good famulus. I shall miss him."

"It's too early to talk in the past tense, wizard." Flor tried to cheer him up. "Falameezar may still find him. *Quien sabe;* he may be closer than we think."

"Your words are kind, my dear. Thank you for your thoughtfulness."

The wagon rattled as another blast of near hurricane force whistled about them. Everyone fought for balance.

"But as our young spellsinger says, the weather is not encouraging. Pog is not very resourceful. I don't know. . . ."

There was no sign of the bat the next day, nor of Falameezar, and the storm continued without abating. Clothahump worried now not only that Pog might never be found but that the dragon might become disoriented and not be able to relocate the wagon. Or that he might find a river, decide he was bored with the entire business, and simply sink out of sight.

"I don't think the last likely, sir," argued Jon-Tom. "Falameezar's made a political commitment. We're his comrades. He'll be back. It would take some kind of personal crisis to make him abandon us, and there isn't much that can affect him."

"Nevertheless, though I would like to have both of them back with us, time is becoming too important." The turtle let out a resigned sigh. "If the weather breaks tomorrow, as I believe it may, we will wait one additional day. Then we must be on our way or else we might as well forget this entire mission."

"Praise the weather," murmured Mudge hopefully, and turned over in his blankets. . . .

III

When Jon-Tom woke the following morning, his first sight was of the rear canvas panel. It had been neatly pinned up, and sunlight was streaming brilliantly inside. Flor knelt and stared outward, her black hair waterfalling down her back. She seemed to sparkle.

He sat up, threw off his covers. It was eerie after so many days of violence not to hear the wind. Also absent was the persistent drumming of raindrops overhead. He leaned forward and peered out. Only a few scattered storm clouds hung stubbornly in an otherwise clear sky.

He crawled up alongside her. A gentle breeze ruffled the Swordsward, the emerald endlessness appearing as soft and delicate as the down on a young girl's legs. The distant yellow puffballs of dandelion trees looked lonely against the otherwise unbroken horizon.

"Good morning, Jon-Tom."

"Buenos dias. Que pasa, beautiful?"

"Not much. Just enjoying the view. And the sunshine. A week in that damn wagon." She fluffed her hair out. "It was getting a little squirrelly."

"Also smelly." He breathed deeply of the fresh air, inhaled the rich sweet smell of the rain-swept grasses. Then he stepped out onto the rear wagon seat.

Slowly he turned a circle. There was nothing but green sward and blue sky in all directions. Against that background even a distant Falameezar would have stood out like a truckload of coal in a snowbank. But there was no sign of the dragon or of his quarry.

"Nobody. Neither of 'em," he said disappointedly, turning back to look down into the wagon. Talea had just raised her head from beneath a pile of blankets and blinked at him sleepily, her red curls framing her face like the scribbles of a playful artist.

"I am most concerned," said Clothahump. He was seated at the front end of the wagon, stirring a pot of hot tea. The little copper kettle squatted on the portable stove and steamed merrily. "It is possible that—" He broke off, pointed toward Jon-Tom, and opened his mouth. Jon-Tom heard only the first of his comment.

"I do believe there is someone be—"

Something yanked hard at Jon-Tom's ankles. Arms windmilling the air, he went over backward off the platform. He landed hard, the grass cushioning him only slightly.

Blackness and colorful stars filled his vision, but he did not pass out. The darkness was a momentary veil over his eyes. By the time his head cleared his hands had been drawn above his hair, his ankles placed together, and tough cords wrapped around them. Looking down at his feet, he saw not only the bindings but a remarkably ugly face.

Its owner was perhaps two and a half feet tall, very stocky, and a perversion of humanity. Jon-Tom decided it looked like a cross between an elf and a wino. The squat creature boasted an enormous, thick black beard.

Out of this jungle peered two large brown eyes. They flanked a monstrous bulbous nose and were in turn framed by a pair of huge, floppy ears that somehow managed to fight their way out of the wiry hair. There were hints of clothing beneath the effervescent mass.

Thick, stubby fingers made sure of Jon-Tom's bonds. A set of sandals large enough for the recumbent youth floored enormous feet.

Tying the other knots was a slightly smaller version of the first ugly, except he was blond instead of dark-haired and had watery blue eyes.

Something landed on Jon-Tom's chest and knocked the wind out of him. The newcomer was solid as iron and extremely muscular. It was not the build of a body builder but instead the seamlessly smooth and deceptively porcine musculature of the power lifter.

The one on his chest now was female. Only a few red whiskers protruded from her chin. She was no less gruesome in appearance than her male counterparts. She was shaking a fist in his face and jabbering at high speed. For the first time since arriving in Mudge's meadow words had no meaning to him.

He turned his head away from that indifferently controlled fist. Angry noises and thumping sounds came from the wagon. He looked to his right, but the grass hid whatever was happening there.

Of only one thing was he certain: the sward was alive with dozens of the fast-moving, excited creatures.

The dray lizards wheezed and hissed nervously as the little monsters swarmed onto harness and reins. Mixed in with the beelike babbling of their assailants Jon-Tom could make out other voices. Most notable was that of Caz, who was speaking in an unfamiliar language similar to that of their captors. Mudge could be heard alternately cursing and bemoaning his fate, while Talea was railing at an attacker, warning that if he didn't get his oversized feet off her chest she was going to make a candlewick out of his beard.

A pole was brought and neatly slipped between the bindings on Jon-Tom's ankles and the others at his wrists. He was lifted into the air. Clearing the ground by only a few inches, he was borne off at considerable speed through the grass. He could see at least half a dozen of his captors shouldering the pole, three at his feet and three above his head. Although his sense of speed was artificially accelerated by his proximity to the ground, he fervently prayed that his bearers' sense of direction was as efficient as their deltoids. The sharp grass did not seem to bother them.

With a creak he saw the wagon turn and follow.

He had resigned himself to a long period of jouncing and bumping, but it hardly seemed he'd been picked up when he was unceremoniously dumped on the ground. Flor was dropped next to him. One by one he watched as the rest of his companions were deposited alongside. They mashed down the grass so he could see them clearly, lined up like so many kabobs. The similarity was not encouraging.

Clothahump had evidently retreated into his shell in an attempt to avoid being moved. They had simply hefted him shell and all to carry him. When he finally stuck arms and legs out again, they were waiting with lassos and ropes. They managed to snare only a leg before he retreated in on himself.

Mutterings issued from inside the shell. This produced excited conversation among the creatures. They kicked and punched at the impervious body frantically.

The activity was directed by one of their number, who displayed a variety of metal ornaments and decorative bits of bone in hair and beard. Under his direction a couple of the creatures poked around inside the shell. They were soon able to drag the protesting, indignant turtle's head out. With the aid of others they shoved several bunches of dried, balled-up grass into his mouth and secured the gag tightly. Clothahump reached up to pull the stuffing out, and they tied his arms also. At that point he slumped back and looked exhausted.

The creature resplendent in bone and metal jumped up and down happily, jabbing a long feather-encrusted pole at the now safely bound and gagged turtle. Evidently the fashion plate was the local witch doctor or wizard, Jon-Tom decided. He'd recognized that Clothahump had been starting a spell inside his shell and had succeeded in rendering his opponent magically impotent.

Jon-Tom lay quietly and wondered if they would recognize the sorceral potential of his singing, but the duar was inside the wagon and he was firmly tied on the ground.

Moans came from nearby. Straining, he saw another of their captors idly kicking Talea with considerable force. Each time she'd curse her tormentor he'd kick her. She would jerk in pain and it would be several minutes before she regained enough strength to curse him again.

"Knock it off!" he yelled at her assailant. "Pick on somebody your own size!"

The creature responded by leaving Talea and walking over to stare curiously down into Jon-Tom's face. He jabbered at him experimentally.

Jon-Tom smiled broadly. "Same to you, you sawed-off shithead."

It's doubtful the creature followed Jon-Tom's meaning, but he accepted the incomprehensible comment with equanimity and commenced booting the lanky youth in the side instead. Jon-Tom gritted his teeth and refused to give the creature the satisfaction of hearing him groan.

After several kicks produced nothing but a steady glare, his attacker became bored and wandered off to argue with some of his companions.

In fact, there appeared to be as much fighting taking place between members of the tribe as there'd been between them and their captives. Jon-Tom looked around and was astonished to see tiny structures, camp fires, and ugly, hairless smaller versions of the adults, which could only be children. Small green and blue lizards wore backpacks and suggested scaly mules. There was consistent and unrelenting activity taking place around the six bound bodies.

Camp fires and buildings gave every appearance of having been in place for some time. Jon-Tom tried to estimate the distance they'd traveled.

"Christ," he muttered, "we couldn't have been camped more than a couple of hundred yards from this town, and we never even saw them."

"The grass conceals the Mimpa," Caz told him. Jon-Tom looked to his right, saw rabbit ears pointed in his direction. "They move freely among it, completely hidden from most of their enemies."

"Call 'em what you like. They look like trolls to me." His brow twisted in thought. "Except I always thought trolls lived underground. Singularly unlovely bunch, too."

"Well, I know naught of trolls, my friend, but the Mimpa live in the sward."

"Like fleas," Mudge snorted from somewhere nearby. "An' if I could get loose I'd start on a little deinfestation, wot!"

Now Jon-Tom could just see the otter's head. His cap was missing, no doubt knocked off during the struggle for the wagon. The otter was jerking around as if he were wired, trying to break free.

Of them all he was the only one who could match their captors for sheer energy, but he could not break the ropes.

Jon-Tom turned his attention back to the rabbit. "Can you talk to them, Caz?"

"I believe I can understand their language somewhat," was the reply. "A well-traveled animal picks up all sorts of odd knowledge. As to whether I can 'talk' to them, I don't think so. Talking takes two, and they strike me as particularly nonconversant with strangers."

"How is it they speak a language we can't follow?"

"I expect that has something to do with their being violently antagonistic to what we think of as civilized life. They're welcome to their isolation, so far as I am concerned. They are incorrigibly hostile, incorrigibly filthy, and bellicose to the point of paranoia. I sincerely wish they would all rot where they stand."

"Amen to that," said Flor.

"What are they going to do with us, Caz?"

"They're talking about that right now." He gestured with an unbound ear. "That one over there with the spangles, the chap who fancies himself something of a local dandy? The one who unfortunately forestalled Clothahump's spell casting? He's arguing with a couple of his equals. Apparently they function as some sort of rudimentary council."

Jon-Tom craned his neck, could just see the witch doctor animatedly arguing with two equally pretentious and noisy fellows.

One of them displayed the mother of all Fu Manchu mustaches. It drooped almost to his huge splayed feet. Other than that he was entirely bald. The third member of the unkempt triumvirate had a long pointed beard and waxed mustachio, but wore his hair in a crew cut. Both were as outlandishly clad as the witch doctor.

"From what I can make out," said Caz, "Baldy thinks they ought to let us go. The other two, Flattop and Bigmouth, say that since hunting has been poor lately they should sacrifice us to the gods of the Sward."

"Who's winning?" Flor wanted to know. Jon-Tom thought that for the first time she was beginning to look a little frightened. She had plenty of company.

"Can't we talk to them at all?" he asked hopefully. "What about the one who had Clothahump gagged? Do you know his real name?"

"I already told you," said Caz. "His name is Bigmouth. Flattop, Baldy, and Bigmouth: that's how their names translate. And no, I don't think we can talk to them. Even if I knew the right words I don't think they'd let me get a word in edgewise. It seems that he who talks loudest without letting his companions make their points is the one who wins the debate."

"Then if it's just a matter of shouting, why don't you give it a try?"

"Because I think they'd cut out my tongue if I interrupted them. I am a better gambler than that, my friend."

It didn't matter, because as he watched the debate came to an end. Baldy shook a threatening finger less than an inch from Bigmouth's proboscis, whereupon Bigmouth frowned and kicked the overly demonstrative Baldy in the nuts. As he doubled over, Flattop brought a small but efficient-looking club down on Baldy's head. This effectively concluded the discussion.

Considerable cheering rose from the excited listeners, who never seemed to be standing still, a condition duplicated by their mouths.

Jon-Tom wondered at the humanoid metabolism that could generate such nonstop energy.

"I am afraid our single champion has been vanquished," said Caz.

"I don't want to die," muttered Flor. "Not here, not in this place." She started reciting Hail Marys in Spanish.

"I don't want to die either," Jon-Tom yelled at her in frustration.

"This isn't happening," she was saying dully. "It's all a dream."

"Sorry, Flor," he told her unsympathetically. "I've already been

that route. It's no dream. You were enjoying yourself until now, remember?"

"It was all so wonderful," she whispered. She wasn't crying, but
restraining herself required considerable effort. "Our friends, the
quest we're on, when we rescued you that night in Polastrindu . . .
it's been just as I'd always imagined this sort of thing would be. Being
murdered by ignorant aborigines doesn't fit the rest. Can they actually kill us?"

"I think they can." Jon-Tom was too tired and afraid even to be
sarcastic. "And I think we'll actually die, and actually be buried, and
actually be food for worms. If we don't get out from here." He looked
across at Clothahump, but the wizard could only close his eyes apologetically.

If we could just lower the gag in Clothahump's mouth when
they're busy elsewhere, he thought anxiously. Some kind of spell,
even one that would just distract them, would be enough.

But while the Mimpa were uncivilized they were clearly not fools,
nor quite so ignorant as Caz believed. That night they confidently
ignored all their captives except the carefully watched Clothahump.

At or near midnight they were all made the centerpiece of a robust
celebration. Grass was cut down with tiny axes to form a cleared
circle, and the captives were deposited near the center, amid a ground
cover of foul-smelling granular brown stuff.

Flor wrinkled her nose, tried breathing through her mouth instead.
"*Mierda* . . . what have they covered the ground here with?"

"I believe it is dried, powdered lizard dung," said Caz worriedly.
"I fear it will ruin my stockings."

"Part of the ceremony?" Jon-Tom had grown accustomed to
strange smells.

"I think it may be more than that, my friend. It appears to retard
the growth of the Sward grasses. An efficient if malodorous method
of control."

Small fires were lit in a circle, uncomfortably near the bound prisoners. Jon-Tom would have enjoyed the resultant celebration for its
barbaric splendor and enthusiasm, were it not for the fact that he was
one of the proverbial pigs at the center of the banquet table.

"You said they'd sacrifice us to the gods of the Sward." As he
spoke to Caz he fought to retain both confidence and sanity. "What
gods do they have in mind?" His thoughts were of the lithe, long-
limbed predators they'd seen sliding ribbonlike through the grass
their first week out of Polastrindu.

"I have no idea as yet, my friend." He sniffed disdainfully. "Whatever, I'm sure it will be a depressing way for a gentleman to die."

"Is there another way?" Even Mudge's usually irrepressible good humor was gone.

"I had hoped," replied the rabbit, "to die in bed."

Mudge let out a high whistle, some of his good spirits returning. "O' course, mate. Now why didn't I think o' that right off? This 'ole miserable situation's got me normal thinkin' paths crossed whixwize. And not alone, I'd wager."

"Not alone your whixwized thoughts, or dying in bed?" asked Caz with a smile.

"Sort o' a joint occasion is wot I'd 'ave in mind." Again the otter whistle, and they both laughed.

"I'm glad somebody thinks this is funny." Talea glared at them both.

"No," said Caz more quietly, "I don't think it's very funny at all, glowtop. But our hands and feet are bound, I can reach no familiar salve or balm from our supplies though I am bruised all over. I can't do anything about the damage to my body, but I try to medicate the spirit. Laughter is soothing to that."

Jon-Tom could see her turn away from the rabbit, her badly tousled hair even redder in the glow from the multiple fires. Her shoulders seemed to droop and he felt an instinctive desire to reach out and comfort her.

Odd the occasions when you have insights into the personalities of others, he thought. Talea struck him as unable to find much laughter at all in life, or, indeed, pleasure of any kind. He wondered at it. High spirits and energy were not necessarily reflective of happiness. He found himself feeling sorry for her.

Might as well feel sorry for yourself, an inner voice reminded him. If you don't slip loose of these pygmy paranoids you soon won't be able to feel sorry for anyone.

Unable to pull free of his bonds, he started working his way across the circle, trying to come up against a rock sharp enough to cut them. But the soil was thick and loamy, and he encountered nothing larger than a small pebble.

Failing to locate anything else he tried sawing patiently at his ropes with fingernails. The tough fiber didn't seem to be parting in the least. Eventually the effort exhausted him and he slid into a deep, troubled sleep. . . .

IV

It was morning when next he opened his eyes. Smoke drifted into the cloudy sky from smoldering camp fires, fleeing the still, swardless circle like bored wraiths.

Once more the carrying poles were brought into use and he felt himself lifted off the ground. Flor went up next to him, and the others were strung out behind. As before, the journey was brief. No more than three or four hundred yards from the site of the transitory village, he estimated.

Quite a crowd had come along to watch. The poles were removed. Mimpa gathered around the six limp bodies. Chattering among themselves, they arranged their captives in a circle, back to back, their legs stuck out like the spokes of a wheel. Arms were bound together so that no one could lie down or move without his five companions being affected. A large post was placed in the center of the circle, hammered exuberantly into the earth, and the prisoners shoulders bound to it.

They sat in the center of a second clearing, as smelly as the first. The Mimpa satisfied themselves that the center pole was securely in the ground and then moved away, jabbering excitedly and gesturing in a way Jon-Tom did not like at the captives ringing the pole.

Despite the coolness of the winter morning and the considerable cloud cover, he was sweating even without his cape. He'd worked his nails and wrists until all the nails were broken and blood stained the restraining fibers. They had been neither cut nor loosened.

Along with other useless facts he noted that the grass around them was still moist from the previous night's rain and that his feet were facing almost due north. Clothahump was struggling to speak. He couldn't make himself understood around the gag and in any case didn't have the strength in his aged frame to continue the effort much longer.

"We can move our legs, anyway," Jon-Tom pointed out, raising his bound feet and slamming them into the ground.

"Actually, they have secured us in an excellent defensive posture," agreed Caz. "Our backs are protected. We are not completely helpless."

"If any of those noulps show up, they'll find out what kind of legs I have," said Flor grimly, kicking out experimentally with her own feet.

"Lucky noulps," commented Mudge.

"What a mind you have, otter. *La cabeza bizzaro.*" She drew her knees up to her chest and thrust out violently. "First predator that comes near me is going to lose some teeth. Or choke on my feet."

Jon-Tom kicked outward again, finding the expenditure of energy gratifying. "Maybe they'll be like sharks and have sensitive noses. Maybe they'll even turn toward the Mimpa, finding them easier prey than us."

"Mayhap," said Caz, "but I think you are all lost in wishful thinking, my friends." He nodded toward the muttering, watchful nomads. "Evidently they are not afraid of whatever they are waiting for. That suggests to me a most persistent and myopic adversary."

In truth, if they were anticipating the appearance of some ferocious carnivore, Jon-Tom couldn't understand why the Mimpa continued to remain close by. They appeared relaxed and expectant, roughly as fearful as children on a Sunday School picnic.

What kind of devouring "god" were they expecting?

"Don't you hear something?" At Talea's uncertain query everyone went quiet. The attitude of expectancy simultaneously rose among the assembled Mimpa.

This was it, then. Jon-Tom tensed and cocked his legs. He would kick until he couldn't kick any more, and if one of those predators got its jaws on him he'd follow Flor's suggestion and shove his legs down its throat until it choked to death. They wouldn't go out without a fight, and with six of them functioning in tandem they might stand an outside chance of driving off whatever creature or creatures were coming close.

Unfortunately, it was not simply a matter of throats.

By straining against the supportive pole Jon-Tom could just see over the weaving crest of the Sward. All he saw beyond riffling tufts of greenery was a stand of exquisite blue- and rose-hued flowers. It was several minutes before he realized that the flowers were moving.

"Which way is it?" asked Talea.

"Where you hear the noise." He nodded northward. "Over there someplace."

"Can you see it yet?"

"I don't think so." The blossoms continued to grow larger. "All I can see so far are flowers that appear to be coming toward us. Camouflage, or protective coloration maybe."

"I'm afraid it's likely to be rather more substantial than that." Caz's nose was twitching rapidly now. Clothahump produced a muffled, urgent noise.

"I fear the kicking will do us no good," the rabbit continued dispiritedly. "They apparently have set us in the path of a Marching Porprut."

"A what?" Flor gaped at him. "Sounds like broken plumbing."

"An analogy closer to the mark than I think you suspect, nightmaned." He grinned ruefully beneath his whiskers. "As you shall see all too soon, I fear."

They resumed fighting their restraints while the Mimpa jabbering rose to an anticipatory crescendo. The assembled aborigines were jumping up and down, pounding the ground with their spears and clubs, and pointing gleefully from captives to flowers.

Flor slumped, worn out from trying to free herself. "Why are they doing this to us? We never did anything to them."

"The minds of primitives do not function on the same cause-and-effect principles that rule our lives." Caz sniffed, his ears drooping, nose in constant motion. "Yes, it must be a Porprut. We should soon be able to see it."

Another sound was growing audible above the yells and howls of the hysterical Mimpa. It was a low pattering noise, like small twigs breaking underfoot or rain falling hard on a wooden roof or a hundred mice consuming plaster. Most of all it reminded Jon-Tom of people in a theater, watching quietly and eating popcorn. Eating noises, they were.

The row of solid Sward grass to the north began to rustle. Fascinated and horrified, the captives fought to see beyond the greenery.

Suddenly darker vegetation appeared, emerging above the thin, familiar blades of the Sward. At first sight it seemed only another type of weed, but each writhing, snakelike olive-colored stalk held a tiny circular mouth lined with fine fuzzy teeth. These teeth gnawed at the Sward grass. They ate slowly, but there were dozens of them. Blades went down as methodically as if before a green combine.

These tangled, horribly animate stems vanished into a brownish-green labyrinth of intertwined stems and stalks and nodules. Above them rose beautiful pseudo-orchids of rose and blue petals.

At the base of the mass of slowly moving vegetation was an army of feathery white worm shapes. These dug deeply into the soil. New ones were appearing continuously out of the bulk, pressing down to the earth like the legs of a millipede. Presumably others were pulled free behind as the creature advanced across the plain.

" 'Tis like no animal I have ever heard of or seen," said Talea in disgust.

"It's not an animal. At least, I don't think it is," Jon-Tom murmured. "I think it's a plant. A communal plant, a mobile, self-contained vegetative ecosystem."

"More magic words." Talea fought at her bonds, with no more success than before. "They will not free us now."

"See," he urged them, intrigued as he was horrified, "how it constantly puts down new roots in front. That's how it moves."

"It does more than move," Caz observed. "It will scour the earth clean, cutting as neat and even a path across the Swordsward as any reaper."

"But we're not plants. We're not part of the Sward," Flor pointed out, keeping a dull stare on the advancing plant.

"I do not think the Porprut is much concerned with citizenship," said Caz tiredly. "It appears to be a most indiscriminate consumer. I believe it will devour anything unable or too stupid to get out of its path."

Much of the Porprut had emerged into the clearing. The Mimpa had moved back but continued to watch its advance and the effect it produced in its eventual prey. It was much larger than Jon-Tom had first assumed. The front was a good twenty feet across. If the earth behind it was as bare as Caz suggested, then when the creature had finished with them they would not even leave behind their bones.

It was particularly horrible to watch because its advance was so slow. The Porprut traveled no more than an inch or two every few minutes at a steady, unvarying pace. At that rate it would take quite a while before they were all consumed. Those on the south side of the pole would be forced to watch, and listen, as their companions closer to the advancing plant were slowly devoured.

It promised a particularly gruesome death. That prospect induced quite a lot of pleasure among the watchful Mimpa.

Jon-Tom dug his feet into the soft, cleared earth and kicked violently outward. A spray of earth and gravel showered down on the forefront of the approaching creature. The writhing tendrils and the mechanically chewing mouths they supported took no notice of it. Even if the prisoners had their weapons and freedom, it still would have been more sensible to run than to stand and fight.

It was loathesome to think you were about to be killed by something neither hostile nor sentient, he mused. There was nothing to react to them. There was no head, no indication of a central nervous system, no sign of external organs of perception. No ears, no eyes. It ate and moved; it was supremely and unspectacularly efficient. A basic mass-energy converter that differed only in the gift of locomotion from a blade of grass, a tree, a blueberry bush.

In a certain perverse way he was able to admire the manner in which those dozens of insatiable mouths sucked and snapped up even the least hint of growth or the tiniest crawling bug from the ground.

"Fire, maybe," he muttered. "If I could get at my sparker, or make a spell with the duar. Or if Clothahump could speak." But the wizard's struggles had been as ineffective as his magic was powerful. Unable to loosen his bonds or his gag, he could only stare, helpless as the rest, as the thousand-rooted flora edged toward them.

"I don't want to die," Flor whispered, "not like this."

"Now, we been through all that, luv," Mudge reminded her. " 'Tis no use worryin' about it each time it seems about t' 'appen, or you'll worry yourself t' death. Bloody disgustin' way t' go, wot?"

"What's the difference?" said Jon-Tom tiredly. "Death's death, one way or the other. Besides," he grinned humorlessly, "as much salad and vegetables as I've eaten, it only seems fair."

"How can you still joke about it?" Flor eyed him in disbelief.

"Because there's nothing funny about it, that's how."

"You're not making any sense."

"You don't make any sense, either!" he fairly screamed at her. "This whole world doesn't make any sense! Life doesn't make any sense! Existence doesn't make any sense!"

She recoiled from his violence. As abruptly as he'd lost control, he calmed himself. "And now that we've disposed of all the Great Questions pertaining to life, I suggest that if we all rock in unison we might be able to loosen this damn pole and make some progress southwestward. Ready? One, two, three . . .''

They used their legs as best they could, but it was hard to coordinate the actions of six people of very different size and strength and would have been even if they hadn't been tied in a circle around the central pole.

It swayed but did not come free of the ground. All this desperate activity was immensely amusing to the swart spectators behind them. As with everything else it was ignored by the patiently advancing Porprut.

It was only a foot or so from Jon-Tom's boots when the proverbial sparker he'd wished for suddenly appeared. Amid shouts of terror and outrage the Mimpa suddenly melted into the surrounding Sward. Something blistered the right side of Jon-Tom's face. The gout of flame roared a second time in his ears, then a third.

By then the Porprut had halted, its multiple mouths twisting and contorting in a horrible, silent parody of pain while the falsely beautiful red and blue blooms shriveled into black ash. It made not a sound while it was being incinerated.

A winged black shape was fluttering down among the captives. It wielded a small, curved knife in one wing. With this it sliced rapidly through their bonds.

"Damn my ears but I never t'ought we'd find ya!" said the excited Pog. His great eyes darted anxiously as he moved from one bound figure to the next. "Never would have, either, if we hadn't spotted da wagon. Dat was da only ting dat stuck up above da stinking grass." He finished freeing Clothahump and moved next to Jon-Tom.

Missing his spectacles, which remained in the wagon, Clothahump squinted at the bat while rubbing circulation back into wrists and ankles. The woven gag he threw into the Sward.

"Better a delayed appearance than none at all, good famulus. You have by rescuing us done the world a great service. Civilization owes you a debt, Pog."

"Yeah, tell me about it, boss. Dat's da solemn truth, an' I ain't about ta let civilization forget it."

Free again, Jon-Tom climbed to his feet and started off toward the wagon.

"Where are you going, boy?" asked the wizard.

"To get my duar." His fear had rapidly given way to anger. "There are one or two songs I want to sing for our little friends. I didn't think I'd have the chance and I don't want to forget any of the words, not while they're still fresh in my mind. Wait till you hear some of 'em, Clothahump. They'll burn your ears, but they'll do worse to—"

"I do not have any ears in the sense you mean them, my boy. I suggest you restrain yourself."

"Restrain myself!" He whirled on the wizard, waved toward the rapidly carbonizing lump of the Porprut. "Not only were the little bastards going to feed us slowly to that monstrosity, but they were all sitting there laughing and having a hell of a fine time watching! Maybe revenge isn't in the lexicon of wizards, but it sure as hell is in mine."

"There's no need, my boy." Clothahump waddled over and put a comforting hand on Jon-Tom's wrist. "I assure you I bear no misplaced love for our hastily departed aboriginal associates. But as you can see, they *have* departed."

In truth, as he looked around, Jon-Tom couldn't see a single ugly arm, leg, or set of whiskers.

"It is difficult to put a spell on what you cannot see," said the wizard. "You also forget the unpredictability of your redoubtable talents. Impelled by uncontrolled anger, they might generate more trouble than satisfaction. I should dislike being caught in the midst of an army of, say, vengeful daemons who, not finding smaller quarry around, might turn their deviltry on us."

Jon-Tom slumped. "All right, sir. You know best. But if I ever see one of the little fuckers again I'm going to split it on my spearpoint like a squab!"

"A most uncivilized attitude, my friend," Caz joined them, rubbing his fur and brushing daintily at his soiled silk stockings. "One in which I heartily concur." He patted Jon-Tom on the back.

"That's what this expedition needs: less thinking and more bloodthirstiness. Cut and slash, hack and rend!"

"Yeah, well . . ." Jon-Tom was becoming a bit embarrassed at his own mindless fury. It was hardly the image he held of himself. "I don't think revenge is all that unnatural an impulse."

"Of course it's not," agreed Caz readily. "Perfectly natural."

"What's perfectly natural?" Flor limped up next to them. Her right leg was still asleep. Despite the ordeal they'd just undergone, Jon-Tom thought she looked as magnificent as ever.

"Why, our tall companion's desire to barbeque any of our disagreeable captors that he can catch."

"*Si,* I'm for that." She started for the wagon. "Let's get our weapons and get after them."

This time it was Jon-Tom who extended the restraining hand. Now he was truly upset at the manner in which he'd been acting, especially in front of the dignified, sensible Caz.

"I'm not talking about forgiving and forgetting," he told her, shivering a little as he always did at the physical contact of hand and arm, "but it's not practical. They could ambush us in the Sward, even if they hung around."

"Well we can damn well sure have a look!" she protested. "What kind of a man are you?"

"Want to look and see?" he shot back challengingly.

She stared at him a moment longer, then broke into an uncontrollable giggle. He laughed along with her, as much from nervousness and the relief of release as from the poor joking.

"Hokay, hokay," she finally admitted, "so we have more important things to do, *si?*"

"Precisely, young lady." Clothahump gestured toward the wagon. "Let us put ourselves back in shape and be once more on our path."

But Jon-Tom waited behind while the others reentered the wagon and set to the task of organizing the chaos the Mimpa had made of its contents.

Walking back to the cleared circle which had so nearly been their burial place, he found a large black and purple form bending over a burned-out pile of vegetation. Falameezar had squatted down on his haunches and was picking with one massive claw at the heap of ash and woody material.

"We're all grateful as hell, Falameezar. No one more so than myself."

The dragon glanced numbly back at him, barely taking notice of his presence. His tone was ponderously, unexpectedly, somber.

"I have made a grave mistake, Comrade. A grave mistake." The dragon sighed. His attention was concentrated on the crisped, smoking remains of the Porprut as he picked and prodded at the blackened tendrils with his claws.

"What's troubling you?" asked Jon-Tom. He walked close and affectionately patted the dragon's flank.

The head swung around to gaze at him mournfully. "I have destroyed," he moaned, "an ideal communal society. A perfect communistic organism."

"You don't know that's what it was, Falameezar," Jon-Tom argued. "It might have been a normal creature with a single brain."

"I do not think so." Falameezar slowly shook his head, looking and sounding as depressed as it was possible for a dragon to be. Little puffs of smoke occasionally floated up from his nostrils.

"I have looked inside the corpse. There are many individual sections of creature inside, all twisted and intertwined together, intergrown and interdependent. All functioning in perfect, bossless harmony."

Jon-Tom stepped away from the scaly side. "I'm sorry." He thought carefully, not daring to offend the dragon but worried about its state of mind. "Would you have rather you'd left it alone to nibble us to death?"

"No, Comrade, of course not. But I did not realize fully what it consisted of. If I had, I might have succeeded in making it shift its path around you. So I have been forced to murder a perfect natural example of what civilized society should aspire to." He sighed. "I fear now I must do penance, my comrade friend."

A little nervous, Jon-Tom gestured at the broad, endless field of the Swordsward. "There are many dangers out there, Comrade. Including the still monstrous danger we have talked so much about."

It was turning to evening. Solemn clouds promised another night of rain, and there was a chill in the air that even hinted at some snow. It was beginning to feel like real winter out on the grass-clad plain.

A cold wind sprang from the direction of the dying sun, went through Jon-Tom's filthy leathers. "We need your help, Falameezar."

"I am sorry, Comrade. I have my own troubles now. You will have to face future dangers without me. For I am truly sorrowful over what I have done here, the more so because with a little thought it might have been avoided." He turned and lumbered off into the rising night, his feet crushing down the Sward, which sprang up resiliently behind him.

"Are you sure?" Jon-Tom followed to the edge of the cleared circle, put out imploring hands. "We really need you, Comrade. We have to help each other or the great danger will overwhelm all of us. Remember the coming of the bosses of bosses!"

"You have your other friends, your other comrades to assist you, Jon-Tom," the dragon called back to him across the waves of the green sea. "I have no one but myself."

"But you're one of us!"

The dragon shook his head. "No, not yet. For a time I had willed to myself that it was so. But I have failed, or I would have seen a solution to your rescue that did not involve this murder."

"How could you? There wasn't time!" He could barely see the dark outline now.

"I'm sorry, Comrade Jon-Tom." Falameezar's voice was faint with distance and guilt. "Good-bye."

"Good-bye, Falameezar." Jon-Tom watched until the dragon had completely vanished, then looked disappointedly at the ground. "Dammit," he muttered.

He returned to the wagon. Lamps were lit now. Under their familiar, friendly glow Caz and Mudge were checking the condition of the dray team. Flor, Clothahump, and Talea were restocking their scattered supplies. The wizard's glasses were pinched neatly on his beak. He looked out and down as Jon-Tom, hands shoved into his pockets and gaze on the ground, sauntered up to him.

"Problems, my boy?"

Jon-Tom raised his eyes, nodded southward. "Falameezar's left us. He was upset at having to kill the damn Porprut. I tried my best to argue him out of it, but he'd made up his mind."

"You did well even to try," said Clothahump comfortingly. "Not many would have the courage to debate a dragon's decision. They are terribly stubborn. Well, no matter. We shall make our way without him."

"He was the strongest of us," Jon-Tom murmured disappointedly. "He did more in thirty seconds to the Porprut and the Mimpa than all the rest of us were able to do at all. No telling how much trouble just his presence prevented."

"It is true we shall miss his brute strength," said the wizard, "but intelligence and wisdom are worth far more than any amount of muscle."

"Maybe so." Jon-Tom vaulted into the back of the wagon. "But I'd still feel better with a little more brute strength on our side."

"We must not bemoan our losses," Clothahump said chidingly, "but must push ahead. At least we will no longer be troubled by the Mimpa." He let out an unwizardly chuckle. "It will be days before they cease running."

"Do we continue on tonight, then?"

"For a short while, just enough to leave this immediate area behind. Then we shall mount a guard, just in case, and continue on tomorrow in daylight. The weather looks unpleasant and we will have difficulty enough in holding to our course.

"Then too, while I don't know how you young folk are feeling, I'm not ashamed to confess that the body inside this old shell is very much in need of sleep."

Jon-Tom had no argument with that. Falameezar or no Falameezar, Mimpa or no Mimpa, he was dead tired. Which was a good deal better than what he'd earlier thought he'd be this night: plain dead.

The storm did not materialize the next day, nor the one following, though the Swordsward received its nightly dose of steady rain. Flor was taking a turn at driving the wagon. It was early evening and they would be stopping soon to make camp.

A full moon was rising behind layers of gray eastern clouds, a low orange globe crowning the horizon. It turned the rain clouds to gauze as it lifted behind them, shedding ruddy light over the darkening sward. Snowflakelike reflections danced elf steps on the residue of earlier rain.

From the four patient yoked lizards came a regular, heavy swish-swish as they pushed through the wet grasses. Easy conversation and occasional laughter punctuated by Mudge's lilting whistle drifted out from the enclosed wagon. Small things rose cautiously to study the onward trundling wooden beast before dropping down into grass or groundholes.

Jon-Tom parted the canvas rain shield and moved to sit down on the driver's seat next to Flor. She held the reins easily in one hand, as though born to the task, and glanced over at him. Her free hand rested across her thighs. Her long black hair was a darker bit of shadow, like a piece of broken black plate glass, against the night. Her eyes were luminous and huge.

He looked away from their curious stare and down at his hands. They twisted and moved uncomfortably in his lap, as though trying to find a place to hide; little five-footed creatures he could not cage.

"I think we have a problem."

"Only one?" She grinned at him, barely paying attention to the reins now. Without being told, the lizards would continue to plod onward on their present course.

"But that's what life's all about, isn't it? Solving a series of problems? When they're as varied and challenging as these," and she flicked long nails in the air, a brief gesture that casually encompassed two worlds and a shift in dimension, "why, that adds to the spice of it."

"That's not the kind of problem I'm talking about, Flor. This one is personal."

She looked concerned. "Anything I can do to help?"

"Possibly." He looked up at her. "I think I'm in love with you. I think I've always been in love with you. I . . ."

"That's enough," she told him, raising a restraining hand and speaking gently but firmly. "In the first place, you can't have always been in love with me because you haven't known me for always. Metaphysics aside, Jon-Tom, I don't think you've known me long enough.

"In the second place, I don't think you're really in love with me. I think you're in love with the image of me you've seen and added to in your imagination, *es verdad, amigo?* To be crude about it, you're in love with my looks, my body. Don't think I hold it against you. It's not your fault. Your desires and wants are a product of your environment."

This was not going the way he'd hoped, he mused confusedly. "Don't be so sure that you know all about me either, Flor."

"I'm not." She was not offended by his tone. "I mean, how have you 'seen' me, Jon-Tom? How have you 'known' me? Short skirt, tight sweater, always the perfect smile, perfectly groomed, long hair flouncing and pom-poms jouncing, isn't that about it?"

"Don't patronize me."

"I'm not patronizing you, dammit! Use your head, *hombre.* I may look like a pinup, but I don't think like one. You can't be in love with me because you don't know me."

" 'Ere now, wot the 'ell are you two fightin' about?" Mudge stuck his furry face out from behind the canvas. " 'Tis too bloomin' nice a night for such witterin'."

"Back out, Mudge," said Jon-Tom curtly at the interruption. "This is none of your business."

"Oh, now let's not get our bowels in an uproar, mate. Suit yourself." With a last glance at them both, he obligingly retreated inside.

"I won't deny that I find you physically attractive, Flor."

"Of course you do. You wouldn't be normal if you didn't." She stared out across the endless dark plain, kissed with orange by the rising moon. "Every man has, ever since I was twelve years old. I've been through this before." She looked back at him.

"The point is you don't know me, the real Flores Quintera. So you can't be in love with her. I'm flattered, but if we're going to have any kind of chance at a real relationship, we'd best start fresh, here and now. Without any preconceived notions about what I'm like, what you'd like me to be like, or what I represent to you. *Comprende?"*

"Flor, don't you think I've had a look at the real you these past weeks?" Try as he might, he couldn't help sounding defensive.

"Sure you have, but that's hardly long enough. And you can't be certain that's the real me, either. Maybe it's only another facet of my real personality, whose aspects are still changing."

"Wait a minute," he said hopefully. "You said, 'chance at a real relationship.' Does that mean you think we have a chance for one?"

"I've no idea." She eyed him appraisingly. "You're an interesting man, Jon-Tom. The fact that you can work magic here with your music is fascinating to me. I couldn't do it. But I don't know you any better than you know me. So why don't we start clean, huh? Pretend I'm just another girl you've just met. Let's call this our first date." She nodded skyward. "The moon's right for it."

"Kind of tough to do," he replied, "after you've just poured out a deeply felt confession of love. You took that apart like a professor dissecting a tadpole."

"I'm sorry, Jon-Tom." She shrugged. "That's part of the way I am. Part of the real me, as much as the pom-poms or my love of the adventure of this world. You have to learn to accept them all, not just the ones you like." She tried to sound encouraging. "If it's any consolation, while I may not love you, I do like you."

"That's not much."

"Why don't you get rid of that hurt puppy-dog look, too," she suggested. "It won't do you any good. Come on, now. Cheer up! You've let out what you had to let out, and I haven't rebuffed you completely." She extended an open hand. *"Buenos noches,* Jon-Tom. I'm Flores Maria Quintera. *Como 'stas?"*

He looked silently at her, then down at the proferred palm. He took it with a resigned sigh. "Jon-Tom . . . Jon Meriweather. Pleased to meet you."

After that, they got along a little more easily. The puncturing of Jon-Tom's romantic balloon released tension along with hopes. . . .

V

It was a very ordinary-looking river, Jon-Tom thought. Willow and cypress and live oak clustered thirstily along its sloping banks. Small scaly amphibians played in thick underbrush. Reeds claimed the quiet places of the slow-moving eddies.

The bank on the far side was equally well fringed with vegetation. From time to time they encountered groups of animals and humans occupied in various everyday tasks on the banks. They would be fishing, or washing clothes, or simply watching the sun do the work of carrying forth the daytime.

The wagon turned eastward along the southern shore of the Sloomaz-ayor-le-Weentli, heading toward the growing massif of the mountains and passing word of the coming invasion to any warm-lander who would listen. But the River of Twos was a long way from Polastrindu, and the Jo-Troom Gate and the depredations of the Plated Folk only components of legend to the river dwellers.

All agreed with the travelers on one matter, however: the problem of trying to pass downstream and through the Teeth.

"Eh?" said one wizened old otter in response to their query, "ye want to go where?" In contrast to Mudge the oldster's fur was streaky-white. So were his facial whiskers. Arthritis bent him in the middle and gnarled his hands and feet.

"Ye'll never make it. Ye won't make it past the entrance and if ye do, ye'll not find yer way through the rock. Too many have tried and none have ever come back."

"We have resources others did not have," said Clothahump confidentially. "I am something of a formidable conjurer, and my associate here is a most powerful spellsinger." He gestured at the lanky form of Jon-Tom. They had stepped down from the wagon to talk with the elder. The dray lizards munched contentedly on rich river-bank growth.

The old otter put aside his fishing pole and studied them. His short whistle indicated he didn't think much of either man or turtle, unseen mental talents notwithstanding.

"Sorcerers ye may be, but the passage through the Teeth by way of the river is little but a legend. Ye can travel by legend only in dreams. Which is all that's likely to be left of ye if ye persist in this folly. Sixty years I've lived on the banks of the Sloomaz-ayor-le-Weentli." He gestured fondly at the flowing water behind him. "Never have I heard tell of anyone fool enough to try and go into the mountains by way of it."

"Sounds convincin' enough for me, 'e does." Mudge leaned out of the wagon and spoke brightly. "That settles that: time to turn about for 'ome."

Jon-Tom looked over his shoulder at the green-capped face. "That does not settle it."

Mudge shrugged cheerfully. "Can't biff a bloke for tryin', mate. I ought t' know better, I knows it, but somethin' in me insists on tryin' t' fight insanity in the ranks."

"Ya ought ta have more faith in da master." Pog fluttered above the wagon and chided the otter. "Ya oughta believe in him and his abilities and great talents." He drifted lower above Mudge and whispered. "Frankly, we all been candidates for da fertilizer pile since we started on dis half-assed trek, but if da boss tinks we gots to go on, we don't got much choice. Don't make him mad, chum."

But Jon-Tom had overheard. He walked back to stand next to the wagon. "Clothahump knows what he's doing. I'm sure if things turned suicidal he'd listen to reason."

"Ya tink dat, does ya?" Pog's small sharp teeth flashed as he hovered in front of Jon-Tom. One wing pointed toward the turtle, who was still conversing with the old otter.

"Da boss has kept Mudge from runnin' off and abandonin' dis trip wid t'reats. What makes ya tink he'd be more polite where you're concerned?"

"He owes me a debt," said Jon-Tom. "If I insisted on remaining behind, I don't think he'd try to coerce me."

Pog laughed, whirled around in black circles. "Dat's what you tink! Ya may be a spellsinger, Jon-Tom-mans, but you're as naïve as a baby's belly!" He rose and skimmed off over the river, hunting for insects and small flying lizards.

"Is that your opinion too, Mudge? Do you think Clothahump would keep me from leaving if that's what I wanted?"

"I wouldn't 'ave 'alf a notion, mate. But since you say you want to keep on with this madness, there ain't no point in arguin' it, is there?" He retreated back inside the wagon, leaving Jon-Tom to turn and walk slowly back down to the riverbank. Try as he would to shove the thought aside, it continued to nag him. He looked a little differently at Clothahump.

"There be only one way ye might get even partways through," continued the old otter, "and if yer lucky, out again alive. That's to have a damn good boatman. One who knows how to maneuver on the Second river. That's the only way ye'll even get inside the mountain."

"Can you recommend such an individual?" asked Clothahump.

"Oh, I know of several good boatfolk," the oldster boasted. He turned, spat something brown and viscous into the water, then looked from the turtle to Jon-Tom. "Trouble for ye is that ain't none of 'em idiots. And that's going to be as important a qualification as any kind of river skill, because only an idiot's going to try and take ye where ye wants to go!"

"We have no need of your sarcasm, young fellow," said Clothahump impatiently, "only of your advice. If you would rather not give us the benefit of your knowledge, then we will do our best to find it elsewhere."

"All right, all right. Hang onto ye shell, ye great stuffed diviner of catastrophes!

"There's one, just one, who might be willing to help ye out. He's just fool enough to try it and just damnblast good enough to bring it off. Whether ye can talk him into doin' so is something else again." He gestured to his left.

"Half a league farther on you'll find that the riverbank rises steep-like. Still farther you'll eventual come across several large oaks overlooking a notch or drop in the cliffs. He's got his place down there. Goes by the name of Bribbens Oxley."

"Thank you for your help," said Clothahump.

"Would it help if we mentioned your name to him?" Jon-Tom wondered.

The otter laughed, his whistles skipping across the water. "Hai, man, the only place me name would help you is in the better whore-houses in Wottletowne, and that's not where ye are going!"

Clothahump reached into one of his plastron compartments, with-drew a small silver coin, and offered it to the otter. The oldster stepped away, waving his hands.

"No, no, not for me, friend! I take no payment for assisting the doomed." He gathered up his pole and gear and ambled crookedly off upstream.

"Nice of him to give us that name," said Jon-Tom, watching the other depart. "Since he wouldn't take the money, why didn't we try to help his arthritis?"

"Arth . . . his joint-freezes, you mean, boy?" Clothahump ad-justed his spectacles. "It is a long spell and requires time we do not have." He turned resolutely toward the wagon.

Jon-Tom continued to stand there, watching the crippled otter make his loping way eastward. "But he was so helpful."

"We do not know that yet," the turtle insisted. "I was willing to chance a little silver on it, but not a major medical spell. He could simply have told us his stories to impress us, and the name to get rid of us."

"Awfully cynical, aren't you?"

Clothahump gazed up at him as they both scrambled into the wagon. "My boy, the first hundred years of life teaches you that no one is inherently good. The next fifty tells you that no one is inher-ently bad, but is shaped by his surroundings. And after two hundred years . . . give me a hand there, that's a good boy." Jon-Tom helped lug the bulky body over the wooden rail and into the wagon.

"After two hundred years, you learn that nothing is predictable save that the universe is full of illusions. If the cosmos withholds and distorts its truths, why should we expect less of such pitifully minute components of it as that otter . . . or you, or me?"

Jon-Tom was left to ponder that as the wagon once more rolled noisily westward.

Everyone hoped the oldster's recommendation was sounder than his estimate of distance, for it took them two full days of traveling before they encountered three massive oaks dominating a low dip in the riverbank. While still a respectable width, the river had narrowed between the higher banks and ran with more power, more confidence, and occasional flecks of foam.

Still, it didn't appear particularly dangerous or hard to navigate to Jon-Tom. He wondered at the need for a guide. The river was far more gentle than the rapids they had passed (admittedly with Falameezar's muscle) on the journey to Polastrindu.

The path that wound its careful way down to the shore was narrow and steep. The lizards balked at it. They had to be whipped and cajoled downward, their claws shoving at the dirt as they tried to move backward instead of down the slope. Gravel and rocks slid over the side of the path. Once they nearly had a wheel slip over the edge, threatening to plunge wagon and lizards and all ass-over-heels into the tiny chasm. Verbally and physically, however, they succeeded in eventually getting the lizards to the bottom.

Reeds and ferns dominated the little cove in which they found themselves. To the left, hunkered up tight against the cliffs, they found a single low building. It was not much bigger than a shack. A few small circular windows winked like eyes as they approached it, peering out beneath brows of adobe and thatching. Smoke curled lazily from the brown and gray rock chimney made of rounded river stones.

What attracted their attention the most was the boat. It was moored in the shallows. Water lapped gently at its flanks. A well-turned railing ran around the deck, and there was no central cabin.

A heavy steering oar bobbed at the stern. There was also a single mast from which a fore-rigged sail hung limp and tired, loosely draped across the boom.

"I hope our guide is as tough as his boat looks to be," said Talea as they mounted the covered porch fronting the house.

"Only one way to find out." Jon-Tom ducked beneath the porch roof. The door set in the front of the building was cut from aged cypress. There was no window or peephole set into it.

Pog found a comfortable cross-beam, hung head down from it, and let out a relieved sigh. "Not fancy, maybe, but a peaceful place ta live. I've always liked rivers."

"How can you like anything?" Talea chided him as they inspected the house. "You see everything upside down."

"Lizard crap," said the bat with a grunt. "You're da ones dat sees everyting upside down."

Clothahump knocked on the door. There was no response. He rapped again, harder. Still nothing, so he tried the handle.

"Locked," he said curtly. "I could spell it open easily enough, but that would mean naught if the owner is not present." He sounded concerned. "Could he perhaps be off on business with a second boat?"

"If so," Jon-Tom started to say, "it wouldn't hurt us to have a short rest. We could wait until—"

The door opened inward abruptly. The frog that confronted them stood just over five feet tall, slightly less than Talea, a touch more than Mudge. Tight snakeskin shorts stopped just above his knees. The long fringework that lined its hem fell almost to his ankles. It swayed slightly as he stood inspecting them.

The shorts were matched by a fringed vest of similar material. Beneath it he wore a leathern shirt that ended above his elbows. Fringe reached from there to his wrists. He wore no hat, but a single necklace made from the vertebrae of some large fish formed a white collar around his green-and-yellow-spotted neck.

His ventral side was a pale blue that shaded to pink at the pulsing throat. The rest of his body was dark green marked with yellow and black spots. Compared to, say, Mudge or Clothahump, the coloration was somewhat overwhelming. He would be difficult to lose sight of, even on a dark day.

Examining them one at a time, the frog surveyed his visitors. He thoroughly sized up every member of the group, not missing Pog where he hung from the rafter. The bat's head had swiveled around to stare curiously at the boatman.

The frog blinked, spoke in a low monotone distinguished by its lack of inflection, friendly or otherwise.

"Cash or credit?"

"Cash," replied Clothahump. "Assuming that we can work out an agreement to our mutual satisfaction."

"Mutual my ass," said the frog evenly. "I'm the one who has to be satisfied." When Clothahump offered no rebuttal, the boatman expressionlessly stepped back inside. "Come on in, then. No point in standing out in the damp. Sick customers make lousy passengers."

They filed in, Jon-Tom and Flor electing to take seats on the floor rather than risk collision with the low, thick-beamed ceiling. In addition, the few chairs looked too rickety to support much weight.

The frog moved to a large iron stove set against a back wall. A large kettle simmered musically on the hot metal. He removed the cover, stirred the contents a few times, then sampled it with a large wooden ladle. The odor was foul. Taking a couple of large wooden shakers from a nearby wall shelf, he dumped some of their powdered contents into the kettle, stirred the liquid a little more, and replaced the iron cover, apparently satisfied.

Then he sauntered back to the thick wooden table in the center of the room. Boating equipment, hooks, ropes, woodworker's tools, braces and pegs and hammers lined the other two walls.

At the back was a staircase leading downward. Possibly it went to the hold, or to clammier and more suitable sleeping quarters.

Leaning forward across the table, the frog clasped wet palms together and stared across at Clothahump and Jon-Tom. His long legs were bent sideways beneath the wood so as not to kick his guests. Caz was standing near one wall inspecting some of the aquatic paraphernalia. Talea hunted for a suitable chair. She finally found one and dragged it up to the table, where she joined the other three.

"My name's Bribbens Oxley, of the sandmarsh Oxleys," the frog told them. "I'm the best boatman on this or any other river." This was stated quietly, without any particular emphasis or boastfulness.

"I know every loggerhead, every tree stump, every knot, boulder, and rapids for the six hundred leagues between the Teeth and Kreshfarm-in-the-Geegs. I know the hiding places of the mudfishers and the waterdrotes' secret holes. I can smell a storm two days before it hits and ride a wave gently enough not to upset a full teacup. I even know the exact place where ten thousand years ago the witch Wutz tripped over the cauldron full of magic which doubled the river, and I know therefore whence comes the name Sloomaz-ayor-le-Weentli."

Jon-Tom gazed back out the still open door, past the dangling Pog, to what still appeared to be a quite ordinary stream. Somewhere, he imagined, the river had to fork, hence the nicknames River of Twos, Double River, and the others. Since the fork was not here and was unlikely to be between this spot and the mountains, it had to lie upstream. He would soon have the chance to find out, he thought, as he returned his attention to the conversation.

"I can turn my craft circles 'round any other craft and reach my destination in half their time. I can ride out weather that puts other merchantmen and fisherfolk under their beds. I'm not afraid of anything in the river or out of it.

"I personally guarantee to deliver cargo and/or passengers to their chosen destination for the agreed-upon fee, on the date determined in advance, if not earlier, or to forfeit all of my recompense.

"I can outfight anyone, even someone twice my size," he said, glancing challengingly at Jon-Tom, who tactfully did not respond, "outeat any other intelligent amphibian or mammal, and I have twenty-two matured tadpoles who can attest to my other abilities.

"My fee is one goldpiece per league. I'm no cook, and you can provide your own fodder, or fish if you like. As to drink, river water's good enough for me, for I'm as home in it as in this house, but if you get drunk on my craft you'll soon find yourself swimming for shore. Any questions so far?"

No one said anything. "Anyone care to dispute anything I've said?" Still no comment from the visitors. Full of impatient energy, Talea left her seat and stalked to the door, stood there leaning against the jamb and staring out at the river. Bribbens watched her and nodded approvingly.

"Right." He leaned back in his chair, picked idly at the tangled fringe of his right sleeve. "Now then. How many of you are going, is there cargo, and where is it you wish to go?"

Clothahump tapped the table with short fingers. "There is no cargo save our nominal supplies and personal effects, and all of us are going." He added uncertainly, "Does our number affect the fee?"

The frog shoved out his considerable lower lip. "Makes no difference to me. Fee's the same whether one of you goes or all of you. The boat has to travel the same distance upstream and the same distance down again when I return. One goldpiece per league."

"That's part of the reason for my inquiry," said the wizard.

"The goldpiece per league?" Bribbens eyed him archly.

"No. The direction. You see, it's downstream we wish to go, not up."

The frog belched once. "Downstream. It's only three days from here to the base of the Teeth. Not much between. A couple of villages and that's all, and them only a day from here. No one lives at the base of the mountains. They're all afraid of the occasional predator who slinks down out of the Teeth, like the flying lizards, the Ginnentes who nest in the crags and crevices. I hardly ever find anyone who wants to go that way. Most everything lies upstream."

"Nevertheless, we wish to travel down," said the wizard. "Far farther, I dare say, than you are accustomed to going. Of course, if you chose not to go, we will understand. It would only be normal for you to be afraid."

Bribbens leaned forward sharply, was eye to eye with Clothahump across the table, his body stretched over the wood, webbed hands flat on the surface.

"Bribbens Oxley is afraid of nothing in or out of the river. Visitor or not, I don't like your drift, turtle."

Clothahump did not pull away from the batrachian face inches from his own. "I am a wizard and fear only that which I cannot understand, boatman. We wish to travel not to the base of the mountains but through them. Down the river as far as it will carry us and then out the other side of Zaryt's Teeth."

The frog sat back down slowly. "You realize that's just a rumor. There may not be any other side."

"That makes it interesting, doesn't it?" said Clothahump.

Fingers drummed on the table, marking time and thoughts. "One hundred goldpieces," Bribbens said at last.

"You said the fee didn't vary," Talea reminded him from the doorway. "One gold piece a league."

"That is for travel on earth, female. Hell is more expensive country."

"I thought you said you weren't afraid." Jon-Tom was careful to make it sound like a normal question, devoid of taunting.

"I'm not," countered Bribbens, "but neither am I stupid. If we survive this journey I want more in return than personal satisfaction.

"Once we enter the mountains I shall be dealing with unknown waters . . . and probably other unknowns as well. Nevertheless," he added with becoming indifference, "it should be interesting, as you say, wizard. Water is water, wherever it may be."

But Clothahump pushed away from the table, spoke grimly. "I'm sorry, Bribbens, but we can't pay you."

"A wizard who can't transmute gold?"

"I can," insisted Clothahump, looking embarrassed. "It's just that I've misplaced the damn spell, and it's too complicated to try and fake." He checked his plastron again. "I can give you a few pieces now and the rest, uh, later."

Bribbens rose, slapped the table loudly with both hands. "It's been an interesting conversation and I wish you all luck, which you are going to need even more than you do a good and willing boatman. Now if you don't mind excusing me, I think my supper's about ready." He started back toward the stove.

"Wait a minute." Clothahump frowned at Jon-Tom. Bribbens halted. "We can pay you, though I'm not sure how much."

"My boy, there is no point in lying. I don't do business that way. We will just have to—"

"No, we can, Clothahump." He grinned at Mudge. "I'm something of a beggar in wolf's clothing."

"Wot?" Then the otter's face brightened with remembrance. "I'd bloody well forgotten that night, mate."

Jon-Tom unsnapped his cape. It landed heavily on the table, and Bribbens eyed it with interest. As he and the others watched, Jon-

Tom and Mudge slit the cape's lining. Coins poured from the rolled lower edge.

When the counting was concluded, the remnant of Jon-Tom's hastily salvaged gambling winnings totaled sixty-eight gold pieces and fifty-two silver.

"Not quite enough."

"Please," said Flor, "isn't it sufficient? We'll pay you the rest. . . ."

"Later. I know." The boatman would not bend. "Later is a synonym for never, female. Would you wish me to convey you 'almost' to the end of the river and then make you swim the rest of the way? By the same light, I will not accept 'almost' my determined fee."

"If you're as able as you are stubborn, you're for sure the best boatman on the river," grumbled Jon-Tom.

"There's something more." Talea was still leaning in the doorway, but now she was staring outside. "What about our wagon and team?"

"Sure!" Jon-Tom rose, almost bumped his head, and looked down at Bribbens. "We've got a wagon which any farmer or fisherman would be proud to own. It's big enough to carry all of us and more, and sturdy enough to have done it all the way across the Swordsward from Polastrindu. There are harnesses, yokes, four solid dray lizards, and spare wheels and supplies, all made from the finest materials. It was given to us by the city council of Polastrindu itself."

Bribbens looked uncertain. "I'm not a tradesman."

"At least have a look at it," Flor implored him.

The frog hesitated, then padded out onto the porch, ignoring Pog. The others filed out after him.

Tradesman or not, Bribbens inspected the wagon and its team intimately, from the state of the harness buckles to the lizard's teeth.

When he was finished underneath the wagon, he crawled out, stared at Clothahump. "I accept. It will make up the difference."

"How munificent of you!" Caz had taken no part in the bargaining, but his expression revealed he was something less than pleased by the outcome. "The wagon alone is worth twenty goldpieces. You would leave us broke and destitute."

"Perhaps," admitted Bribbens, "but I'm the only one who stands a chance of leaving you broke and destitute at your desired destination. I won't argue with you." He paused, added as an afterthought, "Dinner's about ready to boil over. Make up your minds."

"We have little choice," said Clothahump, "and no further use for the wagon anyway." He glared at Caz, who turned away and studied the river, unrepentant. "We agree. When can we start?"

"Tomorrow morning. I have my own preparations to make and supplies to lay in. Meanwhile, I suggest you all get a good night's sleep." Bribbens looked at the cliffs which rose to the east.

"Into the Teeth." He fixed a bulbous eye on Jon-Tom. "You'll have no need for money in there, nor on the other side, if there is one. My offspring will find it here if I don't come back, and it will do them more good than the dead." Humming to himself, he turned and padded back toward his house.

They slept in the wagon again that night. As Bribbens formally explained, their fee included only his services and transport and did not extend to the use of his home.

But the following morning he was up before the sun and was ready to depart before they'd hardly awakened. "I like to get an early start," he explained as they gathered themselves for the journey. "I give value for money. You pay for a day's travel, you get a day's travel."

Caz adjusted his monocle. "Reasonable enough, considering that we've given a month's pay for every day we're likely to travel."

Bribbens looked unperturbed. "I once saw a rabbit who'd had all his fur shaved off. He was a mighty funny-looking critter."

"And I," countered Caz with equal aplomb, "once saw a frog whose mouth was too big for his head. He experienced a terrible accident."

"What kind of accident?" inquired Bribbens, unimpressed.

"Foot-in-mouth. Worst case I ever saw. It turned out to be fatal."

"Frogs aren't subject to hoof-in-mouth."

The rabbit smiled tolerantly. "My foot in his mouth."

The two held their stares another moment. Then Bribbens smiled, an expression particularly suited to frogs.

"I've seen it happen to creatures other than my own kind, three-eyes."

Caz grinned back. "It's common enough, I suppose. And I see better out of one eye than most people do out of two."

"See your way to moving a little faster, then. We can't sleep here all day." The boatman ambled off.

Talea was leaning out of the wagon, brushing sleepily at reluctant curls tight as steel springs.

"Since you layabouts aren't ready yet, I'm going to take the time to secure my team and wagon and lay out fodder for them," said the frog.

"Possessive little bugger, ain't 'e?" Mudge commented.

"It's his wagon and team now, Mudge." Jon-Tom carefully slipped his staff into the loops crossing his back beneath the flashing emerald cape. "They're in his care. Just like we are."

When they were all assembled on the boat and had tied down their packs and supplies, Bribbens loosed the ropes, neatly coiled them in place, and leaned on the long steering oar. The boat slid out into the river. Pog shifted his grip on the spreaders high up on the mast and watched as silver sky raced past blue ground.

Before very long the current caught them. The cove with its mud-and-thatch house vanished behind. Ahead lay a gray-brown wall of granite and ice; home to arboreal carnivores, undisciplined winds, and racing cloud-crowns.

Jon-Tom lay down on the edge of the craft and let a hand trail lazily in the water. It was difficult to think of the journey they'd embarked upon as threatening. The water was warmed from its long journey down from distant Kreshfarm-in-the-Geegs. The sun often snuck clear of obstructing clouds to lie pleasantly on one's face. And there seemed no chance of rain until the night.

"Three days to get to the base of the mountains, you said?"

"That's right, man," Bribbens replied. The boatman did not look at Jon-Tom when he spoke. His right arm was curled around the shaft of the steering oar, and his eyes were on the river ahead. He sat in a chair built onto the railing at the craft's stern. A long, thin curved pipe dangled from thick lips. River breeze carried the thin smoke from its small white bowl up into the sky.

"How far into the mountains does the river go?" Flor was on her knees, staring over the front of the boat. Her voice was full of expectation and excitement.

"Nobody knows," said Bribbens. "Leagues, maybe weeks worth. Maybe only a few hours."

"Where does it end, do you suppose? In an underground lake?"

"Helldrink," said the boatman.

"And what's Helldrink, *Señor Rana?*"

"A rumor. A story. An amalgam of all the fears of every creature that's ever navigated on the waters in times of trouble, during bad storms or on leaking ships, in foul harbors or under the lash of a drunken captain. I've spent my life on the water and in it. It would be worth the trip to me if we should find it, even should it mean my death. It's where all true sailors should end up."

"Does that mean we're likely to get a refund?" inquired Caz.

The boatman laughed. "You're a sharp fellow, aren't you, rabbit? I hope if we find it you'll still be able to joke."

"There should be no difficulty," said Clothahump. "I, too, have heard legends of Helldrink. They say that you know it is there before you encounter it. All you need do is deposit us safely clear of it and we will continue our journey on foot. You may proceed to your sailor's discovery however you wish."

"Sounds like a fine scenario, sir," the boatman agreed. "Assuming I can make a landing somewhere safe, if there is a safe landing. Otherwise you may have to accompany me on my discovery."

"So you're risking your life to learn the truth about this legend?" asked Flor.

"No, woman. I'm risking my life for a hundred pieces of gold. And a wagon and team. I'm risking my life for twenty-two offspring. I'm risking my life because I never turned down a job in my life. Without my reputation, I'm nothing. I had to take your offer, you see."

He adjusted the steering oar a little to port. The boat changed its heading slightly and moved still further into the center of the stream.

"Money and pride," she said. "That's hardly worth risking your life for."

"Can you think of any better reason, then?"

"You bet I can, *Rana*. One a hell of a lot less brazen than yours." She proceeded to explain the impetus for their journey. Bribbens was not to be recruited.

"I prefer money, thank you."

It was a good thing Falameezar was no longer with them, Jon-Tom thought. He and their boatman were at opposite ends of the political spectrum. Of course, with Falameezar, they would not have required Bribbens' services. He was surprised to discover that despite the archaic, inflexible political philosophy, he still missed the dragon.

"Young female," Bribbens said finally, "you have your romantic ideas and I've got mine. I'm helping you to satisfy your needs and that's all you'll get from me. Now shut up. I dislike noisy chatter, especially from romantic females."

"Oh you *do*, do you?" Flor started to get to her feet. "How would you like—"

The frog jerked a webbed hand toward the southern shore. "It's not too far to the bank, and you look like a pretty good swimmer, for a human. I think you can make it without any trouble."

Flor started to finish her comment, got the point, and resumed her seat near the craft's bow. She was fuming, but sensible. It was Bribbens' game and they had to play with his equipment, according to his rules. But that didn't mean she had to like it.

The boatman puffed contentedly on his pipe. "Interesting group of passengers, more so than my usual." He tapped out the dottle on the deck, locked the steering oar in position, and commenced repacking his pipe. "Wonder to me you haven't killed one another before now."

It was odd, Jon-Tom mused as they drifted onward, to be moving downstream and yet toward mountains. Rivers ran out of hills. Perhaps the Sloomaz-ayor-le-Weentli dropped into an as yet unseen canyon. If so, they would have a spectacular journey through the mountains.

Occasionally they had to set up the canvas roofing that attached to the railings to keep off the nightly rain. At such times Bribbens would fix the oar and curve them to a safe landing onshore. They would wait out the night there, raindrops pelting the low ceiling, until the sun rose and pushed aside the clouds. Then it was on once more, borne swiftly but smoothly in the gentle grip of the river.

Jon-Tom did not fully appreciate the height of Zaryt's Teeth until the third day. They entered the first foothills that morning. The river cut its way insistently through the green-cloaked, rolling mounds. Compared to the nearing mountains, the massive hillocks were merely bruises on the earth.

Here and there great lumps of granite protruded through the brush and topsoil. They reminded Jon-Tom of the fingertips of long-buried giants and brought back to him the legends of these mountains. While not degenerating into rapids, the river nonetheless increased its pace, as if anxious to carry those traveling upon it to some unexpected destination.

Several days passed during which they encountered nothing suggestive of habitation. The hills swelled around them, becoming rockier and more barren. Even wildlife hereabouts was scarce.

Once they did drift past a populated beach. A herd of unicorns was backed up there against the water. Stallions and mares formed a semicircle with the water at their backs, protecting the colts, which snorted and neighed nervously.

Pacing confusedly before the herd's defensive posture was a pack of perhaps a dozen lion-sized lizards. They were sleek as whippets and their red and white scales gleamed in the sunlight.

As the travelers cruised past, one of the lizards sprang, trying to leap over the adults and break the semicircle. Instead, he landed on the two-foot-long, gnarly horn of one of the stallions.

A horrible hissing crackled like fresh foil through the day and blood fountained in all directions, splattering colts and killer alike. Bending his neck, the unicorn used both forehooves to shove the contorted body of the dying carnivore off his head.

The boat drifted around a bend, its passengers ignorant of the eventual outcome of the war. Blood from the impaled predator flowed into the river. The red stain mindlessly stalked the retreating craft. . . .

VI

It was the following afternoon, when they rounded a bend in the river, that Jon-Tom thought would surely be their last.

The foothills had grown steadily steeper around them. They were impressive, but nonexistent compared to the sheer precipices that suddenly rose like a wall directly ahead. Clouds veiled their summits, parting only intermittently to reveal shining white caps at the higher elevations; snow and ice that never melted. The mottled stalks of conifers looked like twigs where they marched up into the mists.

It was a seamless gray cliff which rose up unbroken ahead of the raft. Solid old granite, impassable and cold.

Bribbens was neither surprised nor perturbed by this impassable barrier. Leaning hard on the sweep, he turned the boat to port. At first Jon-Tom thought they would simply ground on the rocks lining the shore, but when they rounded a massive, sharp boulder he saw the tiny beach their boatman was aiming for.

It was a dry notch cut into the fringe of the mountain. Warm water slapped against his boots as the boat's passengers scrambled to pull it onto the sand. Driftwood mixed with the blackened remnants of many camp fires. The little cove was the last landing point on the river.

On the visible river, anyway.

The wind tumbled and rolled down the sheer cliffs. It seemed to be saying, "Go back, fools! There is nothing beyond here but rock and death. Go back!" and a sudden gust would send Talea or Mudge stumbling westward as the wind tried to urge their retreat.

Jon-Tom waded out into the river until the water lapped at his boot tops. Leaning around a large, slick rock, he was able to see why Bribbens had rowed them into the protected cove.

Several hundred yards downstream, downstream was no more. An incessant crackling and grinding came from the river's end. An immense jam of logs and branches, bones, and other debris boiled like clotted pudding against the gray face of the mountain. Foam thundered on rock and wood like cold lava.

He couldn't see where the water vanished into the mountainside because of the obstructing flotsam, but from time to time a log or branch would be sucked beneath the brow of the cliff, presumably into the cavern beyond. The thickness of the jam suggested that the cave opening into the mountain couldn't be more than a few inches above the waterline. If it were higher, he would have been able to see it as a dark stain on the granite, and if lower, the river would have backed up and drowned out, among other things, the cove they were beached upon.

But the opening must be quite deep, because the river had narrowed until it was no more than thirty yards wide where it ground against the mountainside, and the current was no swifter than usual.

"What do we do now?" Flor had waded out to stand next to him. She watched as logs several yards thick spun and bounced off the rock. They must have weighed thousands of pounds and were waterlogged as well.

"There's no way we can move any of that stuff upstream against the current."

"It doesn't matter," he told her. "Even if Clothahump could magic them aside, the opening's still much too low to let the boat through."

"So it seems." Bribbens stood on the sand behind them. He was unloading supplies from the boat. "But we're not going in that way. That is, we are, but we're not."

"I don't follow you," said Jon-Tom.

"You will. You're paying to." He grinned hugely. "Why do you think the Sloomaz-ayor-le-Weentli is called also The Double River, The River of Twos?"

"I don't know." Jon-Tom was irritated at his ignorance. "I thought it forked somewhere upstream. It doesn't tell me how we're going to get through there," and he pointed at the churning, rumbling mass of jackstraw debris.

"It does, if you know."

"So what do we do first?" he said, tired of riddles.

"First we take anything that'll float off the boat," was the boatman's order.

"And then."

"And then we pole her out into the middle of the current, open her stoppers, and sink her. After we've anchored her securely, of course."

Jon-Tom started to say something, thought better of it. Since the frog's statement was absurd and since he was clearly not an idiot, then it must follow that he knew something Jon-Tom did not. When confronted by an inexplicable claim, he'd been taught, it was better not to debate until the supporting evidence was in.

"I still don't understand," said Flor confusedly.

"You will," Bribbens assured her. "By the way, can you both swim?"

"Fairly well," said Jon-Tom.

"I don't drown," was Flor's appraisal.

"Good. I hope the other human is likewise trained.

"For the moment you can't do anything except help with the unloading. Then I suggest you relax and watch."

When the last buoyant object had been removed from the boat, they took the frog at his word and settled down on the beach to observe.

Bribbens guided the little vessel out into the river. On locating a place that suited him (but that looked no different from anywhere else to Jon-Tom and Flor) he tossed over bow and stern anchors. Sunlight glistened off the boatman's now bare green and black back and off the smooth fur of the nude otter standing next to him.

Both watched as the anchors descended. The boat slowly swung around before halting about a dozen yards farther downstream. Bribbens tested the lines to make certain both anchors were fast on the bottom.

Then he vanished belowdecks for several minutes. Soon the boat began to sink. Shortly only the mast was visible above the surface. Then it too had sunk out of sight. Mudge swam above the spot where it had gone under, occasionally dipping his head beneath the surface. The amphibian Bribbens was as at home in the river's depths as he was on land. Mudge was almost as comfortable, being a faster swimmer but unable to extract oxygen from the water.

Soon the otter waved to those remaining on shore. He shouted something unintelligible. They saw his back arch as he dived. He repeated the dive-appear-dive-appear sequence several times. Then

Bribbens broke the surface alongside him and they both swam in to the beach.

They silently took turns convoying the floatable supplies (carefully packed in watertight skins) out to the center of the stream, disappearing with them, and then returning for more.

Finally Bribbens stood dripping on the beach. "Good thing the river doesn't come out of the mountain. Be too cold for this sort of thing."

"What sort of thing?" a thoroughly bemused Flor wanted to know.

"Let's go and you'll find out."

"Go? Go where?"

"Why, to the ship, of course," said Talea. "You don't know, do you?"

"No one explains things to me. They just look." She was almost angry.

"It will all be explained in a minute," said Clothahump patiently.

The boatman held out a watertight sack. "If you'll put your clothes in here."

"What for?" Flor's gaze narrowed.

Bribbens explained patiently, "So they won't get wet." He started to turn away. "It's no difference to me. If you want to spend the journey inside the probably cold mountain in wet clothing, that's your business. I'm not going to argue with you."

Jon-Tom was already removing his cape and shirt. Talea and Caz were doing likewise. Flor gave a little shrug and began to disrobe while the wizard made sure his plastron compartments were sealed tight. Physically he was the weakest of them, but like the boatman, he would have no difficulty going wherever they were going.

There was one problem, though. It took the form of a black lump hanging from a large piece of driftwood.

"Absolutely not! Not on your life, and sure as hell not on mine." Pog folded his wings adamantly around his body and looked immovable. "I'll wait for ya here."

"We may not return this way," explained Clothahump.

"You may not return at all, but dat ain't da point dat's botherin' me," grumbled the bat.

"Come now." Clothahump had elected to try reason on his famulus. "I could make you come, you know."

"You can make me do a lot of tings, boss," replied the bat, "but not you nor anyting else in dis world's going to drag me into dat river!"

"Come on, Pog." Jon-Tom felt silly standing naked on the beach

arguing with the reluctant bat. "Flor, Talea, Caz, and I aren't water
breathers either. But I trust Clothahump and our boatman to know
what they're about. Surely we're going to reach air soon. I can't hold
my breath any longer than you."

"Water's fit for drinking, not for living in," Pog continued to insist.
"You ain't getting me into dat liquid grave and dat's final."

Jon-Tom's expression turned sorrowful. "If that's the way you feel
about it." He'd seen Talea and Mudge sneaking around to get behind
the driftwood. "You might as well wait here for us, I suppose."

"I beg your pardon?" said the wizard.

Jon-Tom put a hand on the turtle's shell, turned him toward the
river. "It's no use arguing with him, sir. His mind is made up and—"

"Hey? Let me loose! Damn you, Mudge, get off my wings! I'll tear
your guts out! I'll, I'll . . . ! Let me up!"

"Get his wings down! . . . Watch those teeth!" Flor and Jon-Tom
rushed to help. The four of them soon had the bat neatly pinned.
Talea located some strong, thin vines and began wrapping the famulus like a holiday package.

"Sorry to do this, old fellow," said Caz apologetically, "but we're
wasting time. Jon-Tom's right though, you know. I'm probably the
worst swimmer of this lot, but I'm willing to give it a go if Clothahump insists there's no danger."

"Of course not," said the wizard. "Well, very little, in any case.
Bribbens knows precisely how far we must descend."

The boatman stood listening. He eyed the bat distastefully. "Right.
Bring him along, then."

They carried the bound and trussed famulus toward the water's
edge.

"Let me go!" Pog's fear of the river was genuine. "I can't do it, I
tell ya! I'll drown. I'm warning ya all I'll come back and haunt ya the
rest of your damn days!"

"That's your privilege." Talea led the way into the river.

"You'll drown all right," Bribbens told him, "if you don't do exactly as I say."

"Where are we going, then?" Jon-Tom asked, a little dazedly.

The frog pointed out and down. "Just swim, man. When we get to
the spot I'll say so. Then you dive . . . and swim."

"Straight down?" Jon-Tom kicked, the water smooth and fresh
around him. A little shiver of fear raced down his back. Clothahump
and Bribbens and to a lesser extent Mudge need have no fear of the
water. It was one of their environments. But what if they were

wrong? What if the underwater cave (or whatever it was they were going down into) lay too deep?

A friendly pat on one shoulder reassured him. " 'Ere now, why the sunken face, mate? There ain't a bloomin' thing t' worry about." Mudge smiled around his wet whiskers. " 'Tain't far down atall, not even for a splay-toed 'uman."

Bribbens halted, bobbing in the warm current. "Ready then? Just straight down. I've allowed for the carry of the current, so no need to worry about that."

Everyone exchanged glances. Pog's protests bordered on hysteria.

"Here, give the flyer over." A disgusted Bribbens gripped one side of the bat, locking fingers tightly in the bindings. Pog resembled a large mouse sealed in black plastic. "You take the other side."

"Righty-ho, mate." Mudge grabbed a handful of vines opposite the frog.

With the two strongest swimmers holding their reluctant, wailing burden, Bribbens instructed the others. "Count to three, then dive." The humans nodded. So did Caz, who was doing a good job of concealing his fears.

"Ready? One . . . two . . . better stop screaming and take a deep breath, bat, or you'll be ballast . . . three!"

Backs arched into the morning air. The howling ceased as Pog suddenly gulped air.

Jon-Tom felt himself sliding downward. Below the surface the water quickly turned darker and cooler. It clutched feebly at his naked body as he kicked hard.

Around him were the dim forms of his companions. A slick palm touched one fluttering foot, pushed gently. Looking back he could make out the plump shape of Clothahump. He was swimming casually around the nonaquatics. The water took a hundred years off his age, and he moved with the grace and ease of a ballet dancer.

The push was more to insure that no one lost his orientation and began swimming sideways than to speed the swimmers in their descent.

Even so, Jon-Tom was beginning to grow a mite concerned. Increasing pressure told him that they'd descended a respectable distance. Both he and Flor were in fairly good condition, but he was less sure of Pog and Caz. If they didn't reach the air pocket they had to be heading toward shortly, he'd have to turn around and swim for the surface.

The surface he broke was unexpected, however. He felt himself falling helplessly, head over heels, windmilling his arms in a desperate attempt to regain his balance.

A loud splash echoed up to him as someone else hit the water. Then he landed with equal force, sank a few feet, and fought his way back to the surface and fresh air.

He broke through and inhaled several deep breaths. Nearby Talea's red curls hung straight and limp as paint from her head. She blinked away water, gasped, and sniffed once.

"Well, that wasn't bad at all. I'd heard it wasn't, but you can't always trust the tales people tell."

Her breasts bobbed easily in the current. Jon-Tom stared at her, more conscious now of her nudity than he'd been when they'd first removed their clothes up above.

But they were above. Weren't they?

Something shoved him firmly between the shoulders.

"Let the current carry you."

Jon-Tom turned in the water, stared into the vast eyes of Bribbens. Looking past him he saw the ship. It was neatly anchored and sat stable in the middle of the stream, perhaps ten yards away. They were drifting toward it.

Following the boatman's advice he relaxed, his body grateful for the respite after the dive, and let the current push him toward the boat. Mudge was already aboard, restocking supplies. He leaned over the side and gave Jon-Tom a hand up, then did the same for Talea.

There was a large, flopping thing on deck that Jon-Tom first thought to be an unfortunate fish. It flipped over, and he recognized the still bound and outraged body of Pog. He accepted Mudge's proferred towel, dried himself, and began to untie the famulus' bonds.

"You okay, Pog?"

"No, *I'm not okay,* dammit! I'm cold, drenched, and sore all over from that fall."

"But you made it through all right." Jon-Tom loosened another slipknot and one wing stretched across the deck. It jerked, sent water flying.

"Not much I can do about it now, I guess," he said angrily.

With the other wing unbound the bat got to his knees, then his feet. He stood there fanning both wings slowly back and forth to dry them.

Mudge joined them. His fur shed the water easily and, almost dry, he was slipping back into his clothes.

"Wot's up, mate?" he asked the bat. "Don't you 'ave no word for your old buddy?"

The large sack of clothing lay opened nearby. Jon-Tom moved to sort his own attire from the wad.

"Yeah, I got something to say ta my old buddy. You can go fuck yourself!" The bat flapped hard, lifted experimentally off the deck, and rose to grip the right spreader. He hung head down from there, his wings still extended and drying.

"Now don't be like that, mate," said the otter, fitting his cap neatly over his ears and fluffing out the feather. "It was necessary. You were 'ardly about t' come voluntarily, you know."

Pog said nothing further. The otter shrugged and left the disgruntled apprentice to his huff.

Jon-Tom buttoned his pants. While the others continued dressing around him, he took a moment to inspect their extraordinary new surroundings.

There was a dull roaring as if from a distant freight train. It sounded constantly in the ears and was a subtle vibration in his own body. His first thought was that they were in a dimly lit tunnel. In a way they were.

The ship rode easily at anchor. On either side were high, moist banks lush with mosses and fungi. That they were not normal riverbanks was proven by the peculiar habits of the higher growths clinging to them. These ferns and creepers put out roots both upward and down, into both running rivers.

Above was a silver-gray sky: the underside of the upper river. Jon-Tom estimated the distance between the two streams at perhaps ten meters. The mast of the boat cleared the watery ceiling easily.

How the two rivers flowed without meeting, without smashing together and eliminating the air space between them, was an interesting bit of physics. More likely of magic, he reminded himself.

"Easy part's over with." Bribbens moved to wind in the bow anchor, using the small winch bolted there.

"The easy part?" Jon-Tom didn't hear the boatman too clearly. Water still sloshed in his ears.

"Yes. This much of the Sloomaz-ayor-le-Weentli is known. Little traveled in its lower portion, but still known." He pointed with a webbed hand over the bow. Ahead of them the river(s) disappeared into darkness.

"What's ahead is not."

Jon-Tom walked forward and gave the boatman a hand with the winch. "Thanks," Bribbens said when they were finished.

A strong breeze blew in Jon-Tom's face. It came from the blackness forward and chilled his face even as it dried his long hair. He shivered a little. The wind came from *inside* the mountain. That hinted at considerable emptiness beyond.

Here there was no mass of water-soaked debris to prevent their continued traveling. The mouthlike opening could easily swallow the logs and branches bunched against the mountainside above. The cliff did not descend this far.

When they had the second anchor up and secured and the boat was drifting downstream once more, Bribbens moved to a watertight locker set in the deck. It offered up oil lamps and torches. These were set in hook or hole and lit.

The wind blew the flames backward but not out. Oil light flickered comfortingly inside conical glass lamps.

"Why didn't you explain it to us?" Flor brushed at her long black mane while she chatted with the boatman.

Bribbens gestured at the squat shape of Clothahump, who rested against the railing nearby. "He suggested back at my cove that it'd be a good idea not to say anything to you."

Jon-Tom and Flor looked questioningly at Clothahump.

"That is so, youngsters." He pointed toward the flowing silver roof. "From there to here's something of a fall. I wasn't positive of the distance or of what your mental reactions to such a peculiar dive might be. I thought it best not to go into detail. I did not wish to frighten you."

"We wouldn't have been frightened," said Flor firmly.

"That may be so," agreed the wizard, "but there was no need to take the chance. As you can see we are all here safe and sound and once more on our way."

A muttered obscenity fell from the form on the right spreader.

They were interrupted by a loud multiple splashing to starboard. As they watched, several fish the size of large bass leaped skyward. Their fins and tails were unusually broad and powerful.

Two of the leapers fell back, but the third intersected the flowing sky, got its upper fins into the water, and wiggled its way out of sight overhead. Several minutes passed, and then it rained minnows. A huge school of tiny fish came shooting out of the upper river to disappear in the lower. The two unsuccessful leapers were waiting for them. They were soon joined by the descending shape of the stronger jumper.

Jon-Tom had grown dizzy watching the up-and-down pursuit. His brain was more confused than his eyes. The new optical information did not match up with stored information.

"The origin of the name's obvious," he said to the boatman, "but I still don't understand how it came to be."

Bribbens proceeded to relate the story of the Sloomaz-ayor-le-Weentli, of the great witch Wutz and her spilled cauldron of magic and the effect this had had upon the river forevermore.

When he'd finished the tale Flor shook her head in disbelief. *"Grande, fantastico.* A schizoid stream."

"What makes the world go 'round, after all, Flor?" said Jon-Tom merrily.

"Gravitation and other natural laws."

"I thought it was love."

"As a matter of fact," said Clothahump, inserting himself into the conversation, "the gravitational properties of love are well known. I suppose you believe its attractive properties wholly psychological? Well let me tell you, my boy, that there are certain formulae which . . ." and he rambled off into a learned discussion, half balderdash and half science: which is to say, fine magic. Jon-Tom and Flor tried to follow, largely in vain.

Talea leaned on the bow railing, her gaze fixed on the blackness ahead and around them. The cool wind continued, ruffling her hair and making her wonder what lay ahead, concealed by the screen of night.

For days they drifted downstream in darkness; water above, water below, floating through an aqueous tube toward an uncertain destination. Jon-Tom was reminded of a corpuscle in the bloodstream. After all the talk of Zaryt's "Teeth" and of traveling into the "belly" of the mountain, he found the analogy disquieting.

From time to time they would anchor in midstream and supplement their supplies from the river's ample piscean population. Occasionally Bribbens and Mudge would make exploratory forays into the upper river. They would climb the mast, Mudge helping the less adapted boatman. A small float attached to an arrow was shot into the underside of the current overhead. The float was inflated until it held securely. Then the cord trailing from it would be tied to the mast. Bribbens and the otter would then shinny up it, to disappear into the liquid ceiling.

With them went small sealed oil lamps fitted with handles. These provided light in the darkness, a necessity since even such agile swimmers as the two explorers could become lost in the deep waters.

On the twelfth day, when the monotony of the trip had become dangerously settled, Bribbens slid down the line in a state of uncharacteristic excitement.

"I think we're through," he announced cheerily.

"Through? Through where? Surely not the mountains." Clothahump frowned. "It could not be. The range is too massive to be so narrow. And the legends . . ."

"No, no, sir. Not through the mountains. But the airspace above the upper river has suddenly expanded from but a few inches to one many feet high. There is a substantial cave, far more interesting to look at than this homogeneous tunnel. We can travel above now, and there's some light as well."

"What kind of light?" Flor wanted to know.

"You'll see."

Preparations were made. Buoyant material did not have to be dragged or shoved downward this time. Instead, they simply had to raise it to the upper stream and insert it, whereupon it would instantly bob to the second surface. Mudge was waiting to slip a line on such packages and drag them to shore.

When all their stores had been transferred, the nonaquatics climbed the mast rope and pushed themselves into the upper river. It was far easier to ascend than that first uncertain dive had been.

Jon-Tom broke the surface with wind to spare. He remained there a while, treading water as he inspected the cavern into which the river emerged.

The boatman had understated its size in his usual phlegmatic fashion. The cave was enormous. Off to his left Jon-Tom could see the abrupt cessation of the solid stone wall that had formed a tight lid on the upper stream for so many days. Little debris drifted this far on the river, and what few pieces and bits of wood tumbled by were worn almost smooth from the continual buffeting against that unyielding overhang.

More amazing were the cavern walls. They appeared to be coated with millions of tiny lights. He swam lazily toward the nearby beach, crawled out and selected a towel with which to dry himself, and moved to inspect the nearest glowing rocks.

The lights were predominantly gold in hue, though a few odd bursts and patches of red, blue, green, and yellow were visible. The bioluminescents were lichens and fungi of many species, ranging from mere colored smears against the rock to elaborate mushrooms and step fungi. Individually their lumen output was insignificant, but in the millions they illuminated the cavern as thoroughly as an evening sun.

He was kneeling to examine a cluster of bright blue toadstools when a vast rush and burble sounded behind him. He turned, instinctively expecting to see some unmentionable river monster rising from the depths. It was only their boat.

The first days on board he'd wondered at the purpose of great collapsed intestines, carefully scraped and dried, that lined the little craft's hold. Now he knew. Having been inflated in turn they'd given the boat sufficient lifting power to rise like a balloon from the lower river right up to the surface of its twin.

Now it bobbed uncertainly as Bribbens rushed to open the valves sealing each inflated stomach before they could lift the ship from its second surface to the ceiling of the cavern. Water ran off the decks and out the seacocks. Mudge pumped furiously to purge the remaining water from the hold.

Dry and dressed, the passengers were soon traveling once more eastward. The scenery had improved greatly. Jon-Tom hoped the cavern would not shrink around them and force them again down to the dull surface of the understream.

He needn't have worried. Instead of compacting, the cavern grew larger. It seemed endless, stretching vast and fluorescent ahead of them.

Phosphorescent growths made the river an artist's palette, oils of many colors all run together and anarchically brilliant. Gigantic stalactites drooped like teeth from the distant ceiling. Some were far larger than the boat. They drifted past huge panels of flowstone, frozen rivers of stained calcite. Helictites curled and twisted from the walls, twitching at gravity like so many crystalline whiskers. Fungi flashed from them all.

On both sides they could see passages branching from the main cavern. Jon-Tom had a powerful urge to grab a lamp and do some casual spelunking. But Clothahump reminded him there would be ample exploring to do without deviating from their course. So long as the river continued to run eastward they would keep to the boat.

The size and magnificence of the cavern kept him from thinking about the composition of the Sloomaz-ayor-le-Weentli. It was disconcerting to sail along a river that flowed not on rock or sand but on air.

"How do you know it even has a solid bottom?" Flor once asked their boatman. "Maybe it's a triple—or quadruple—river?"

Bribbens rested in his seat at the stern, one arm draped protectively across the steering oar.

"Because I've been in and out of it many times, lady. Anyway, no matter where you are on the river the anchors always bite into the second bottom."

Here and there the warm glow of the bioluminescents would fade and then vanish. At such times they had to rely on the lamps for light until they reached another fluorescent section.

It didn't bother Pog. He'd finally recovered from his lengthy grumpiness. To him the darkness was natural, and he enjoyed the stretches of no-light. They could hear him swooping and darting beyond the range of the boat's lamps, playing dodgem with the cave formations. Sometimes he'd leave the boat for long stretches of time, much to Clothahump's displeasure and concern, only to have his internal sonar unerringly bring him back to the ship many hours later.

"Beautiful," Jon-Tom was murmuring as he watched the glowing shapes drift past. "It's absolutely beautiful."

Talea stood next to him and eyed the dark openings that branched off from the main cavern. Sometimes these gaping holes would come right down to the river's edge.

"Funny idea of beauty you have, Jon-Tom. I don't like it at all."

"Humans got no appreciation of caves," said Pog with a snort, weaving in the air above them. "Dis all wasted on ya except da spellsinger dere, an' dat's da truth!"

"Can I help it if I prefer light to dark, freedom to confinement?" she countered.

"Amen," said Flor heartily.

For both women the initial loveliness of the formations had been surrendered to the superstitious dread most people hold of deep, enclosed places. Jon-Tom was the only one with a real interest in caves, and so he was somewhat immune to such fears. To him the immense shapes, laid down patiently over the ages by dripping water and dissolved limestone, were as exquisite as anything the world of daylight had to offer.

Flor and Talea were not alone in their nervousness, however.

"I think I liked it better inside the rivers," Mudge said one morning. "Leastwise there a chap knew where 'e was, wot?" He indicated the darkness of a large, unilluminated side passage with a sweep of one furry arm. "Don't care much for this place atall. I ain't ready t' be buried just yet."

"Superstition," Clothahump muttered. "The bane of civilization."

As for their boatman, he remained as calm as if he'd been sailing familiar waters.

"Does this place have a name?" Jon-Tom asked him, watching a clump of bright azure mushrooms on the shore.

"Only in legend." Bribbens looked away for a moment. An impossibly long tongue flicked out and snared something which Jon-Tom saw only as a ghost of glittering, transparent wings and body.

The frog smacked his lips appraisingly. "No color, but the flavor isn't bad." He nodded at the cavern. "In stories and legends of the riverfolk this is known as the Earth's Throat."

"And where does it go?" Flor asked him.

Bribbens shrugged. "Who knows? Your hard-shelled mentor believes it to travel much of the way through the mountains. Perhaps he's right. I prefer to think we'll come out there instead of, say, the earth's belly."

"That doesn't sound very nice." Nearby Talea fingered the haft of her knife as though she could intimidate the surrounding darkness with it.

Or whatever else might be out there. . . .

VII

They were beginning to think they might complete the passage through the Teeth (or at least to the end of the river) without mishap. Long days of idle drifting, the boat carried smoothly by the current, had lulled the fears they'd acquired on the Swordsward.

Pog, his hearing more acute than anyone else's, was first to note the noise.

"Off key," he explained in response to their queries, "but it's definitely somebody's idea of song. More than one of whatever it is, too."

"I'm sure of it." Caz's long ears were cocked alertly toward the northern shore. They twitched in counterpoint to his busy nose.

It was several minutes more before the humans could hear the subject of their companion's intense listening. It was a rhythmic rising and falling, light and ethereal as an all-female choir might produce. Definitely music, but nothing recognizable as words.

It was occasionally interrupted by a few moments of vivace modulation that sounded like laughter. Jon-Tom could appreciate the peculiar melodies, but he didn't care for the laughter-chords one bit.

Bribbens interrupted their listening, his tone quiet as always but unusually urgent. "Tiller's not answering properly."

Indeed, the boat was drifting steadily toward the north shore. There was a gravel beach and rocks: not much of a landing place. Muscles strained beneath the boatman's slick skin as he fought the steering, but the boat continued to incline landward.

Soon they were bumping against the first rocks. These obstacles poked damp dark heads out of the water around the boat.

Flor stumbled away from the railing on the opposite side and screamed. Jon-Tom rushed to join her. He stared over the side and recoiled instinctively.

Dozens of shapes filled the water. They had their hands on the side of the boat and were methodically pushing at it even though it was already half grounded on the rocky bottom.

"Steady now," said Talea warningly. She stood at the bow, her knife and sword naked in the glow-light, and pointed to the land.

A great number of creatures were marching toward the boat. They were identical to the persistent pushers in the water. All were approximately five feet tall and thin to the point of emaciation. They were faintly human, memories of almost-people parading in unison.

Two legs and two arms. They were nude but smooth-bodied and devoid of external sex organs. For that matter they displayed nothing in the way of differentiating characteristics. They might have been stamped from a single mold.

Their white flesh was truly white, blank-white, like milk and bordering on translucence. Two tiny coal-pit eyes sat in the puttylike heads where real eyes ought to have been. There were no pupils, no ears or nostrils, and only a flat slit of a mouth cutting the flesh below the eye-dots. Hands had short fingers, which along with the legs looked jointless as rubber.

In time to the music they marched toward the ship, waving their arms slowly and hypnotically while singing their moaning, methodical song.

Jon-Tom looked to Clothahump. The wizard looked baffled. "I don't know, my boy. None of the legends says anything about a tribe of albino chanters living in the Throat." He called to the marchers.

"What are you called? What is it you want of us?"

"What can we do for you?" Flor asked, adding something unintelligible in Spanish.

The singers did not respond. They descended the slight slope of the beach with fluid grace. The ones in the lead began reaching, clutching over the railing.

Two of them grabbed Talea's right arm. "Ease back there," she ordered them, pulling away. They did not let go and continued to tug at her insistently.

Several other pale singers were already on the deck and were pulling with similar patient determination at Jon-Tom and Mudge.

" 'Ere now, you cold buggerers, take your bloody 'ands off me!" The otter twisted free.

So did Talea and Jon-Tom. Yet the pale visitors wordlessly kept advancing, groping for the strangers.

Another sound quietly filled the cavern. It seeped across the river and dominated the rise and fall of the expressionless choir. A deep, low moaning, it was in considerable contrast to the melody of the white singers. It was not at all nice. In fact, it seemed to Jon-Tom that it embodied every overtone of menace and malignance one could put into a single moan. It issued from somewhere back in the black depths, beyond where the singers had come from.

"That's about enough," said Bribbens firmly. He hefted his backup steering sweep and began swinging it at the singers stumbling about on deck. Two of them went down with unexpected lack of resistance. Their heads bounced like a pair of rubber balls across the deck. The black eyespots never twitched and they uttered not a word of pain. Their singing, however, ceased. One of the skulls bounced over the railing and landed in the water with a slight splash, to sink quickly out of sight.

A shocked Bribbens paused to stare at the decapitated corpses. There was no blood.

"Damn. They aren't alive."

"They are," Clothahump insisted, struggling awkwardly in the grasp of three singers who were trying to wrestle his heavy body off the ship, "but it is not our kind of alive."

"I'll make them our kind of dead." Talea's sword was moving like a scythe. Three singers fell neatly into six halves. They lay on the deck like so many lumps of white clay, motionless and cold.

Jon-Tom hurried to assist Clothahump. "Sir, what do you think we . . . ?"

"Fight for it, my boy, fight! You can't argue with these things, and I have a feeling that if we're taken from this boat we'll never see it again." He had retreated inside his shell, confounding his would-be abductors.

Above the shouts of the boat's defenders and the singsong of their horribly indifferent assaulters came a reprise of that ominous, basso groaning. It was definitely nearer, Jon-Tom thought, and redoubled his efforts to clear the deck.

He was swinging the club end of his staff in great arcs, indiscriminately lopping off heads, arms, legs. The singers broke like hardened clay, but the dozens dismembered were replaced by ranks of thoughtless duplicates, still droning their eerie anthem.

"Get us out in the current!" Talea was trying to keep the white bodies away from the bow.

With Mudge shielding him from clutching fingers Bribbens put down his oar and returned to the main sweep. Though he leaned on it as hard as he could, and though the current was with them, they still couldn't move away from the shore.

Jon-Tom leaned over the side. Using his reach and the long club he began clearing bodies from the waterline. White hands pulled possessively at him from behind, but Flor was soon at his side swinging her mace, cutting them down like pale shrubs. Most of them ignored her. Possibly it had something to do with her white leather clothing, he mused.

He concentrated on swinging the club in long arcs, knocking away heads or pieces of boneless skull with great rapidity. Their slight resistance barely slowed the force of his swings.

When the heads were knocked loose the bodies simply ceased their shoving and slid below the surface. A few bobbed on the current and drifted like styrofoam down the river.

The singing continued, undisturbed by the bloodless slaughter, by screams of anger or despair. Rising louder around the boat was that rich, bellowing moan. It had become loud enough now to drown out the chorus. A few fragments of rock fell from the cavern roof.

Finally enough of the bodies had been swept from the side of the boat for it to drift once more out into the river. Like so many termites supple white singers continued to march down toward the water. They walked until the water was up to their chests and began swimming slowly after the boat.

Breathing hard, Jon-Tom leaned back against the railing, holding tight to his staff for additional support. All of the original swimmers who'd forced the craft in to shore had been knocked away or decapitated. Now that they were out again in midstream, the current kept them well ahead of their lugubrious pursuers.

"I don't understand what—" He was talking to the boatman, but Bribbens wasn't listening. He'd suddenly locked the steering oar in position and was unbolting smaller ones from the deck.

"Paddle, man! Paddle for your life!"

"What?" Jon-Tom looked back at the shore, expecting to see the horde of singers clumsily stumbling after them across the rocks.

Instead his gaze fastened onto something that stifled the scream welling up in his throat and turned it into that peculiar choking noise people make at times of true horror. A vast, glowing gray mass filled the cavern shore behind them. It came near to touching the ceiling. Where large formations rose the gray substance flowed over or around it, displaying a consistency partly like cloud and then like lard. Its moans rattled the length of the cavern and echoed back from distant walls.

It looked like a fog wrapped with mucus, save for two enormous, pulsing pink eyes. They stared lidlessly down at the tiny fleeing ship and the stick figures frozen on its deck.

Bits of its flanks were in constant motion. These portions of mucus slid toward the ground. As they did so their color paled to a now familiar white. Tumbling like the eggs of some gigantic insect, they dropped off the huge slimy sides onto the rock and gravel. There they rolled over and stood upright on newly formed legs. Simultaneously a section of their smooth faces parted and a fresh voice would join intuitively in the awful mellifluous chorus of its duplicates.

Something hard and unyielding struck Jon-Tom in his midsection. Looking down he saw the hardwood oar Bribbens had shoved at him. The glaring frog face moved away, to pass additional oars to the rest of his passengers.

Then he was back at his sweep, rowing madly and yelling at his companions. "Paddle, damn you all, paddle!"

Jon-Tom's feet finally moved. He leaned over the side and ripped with the oar at the dark surface of the river. It was difficult going and the leverage was bad, but he rowed until his throat screamed with pain and a deep throbbing pounded against his chest.

Yet that horror lurching and tumbling drunkenly along the shore just behind them put strength in weakened arms. Talea, Flor, Caz, and Mudge imitated his efforts. Pog had hidden behind his wings, where he hung from the spreaders, a shivering droplet of black membrane, flesh, and fear. Clothahump stood and watched, watched and mumbled.

A thick gray pseudopod reached across the river, emerging from the slate-covered moving mountain. It slapped violently at the water only yards from the stern of the fleeing vessel. For all its nebulous horror, the substance of the monster was real enough. Water drenched those on board.

Black almost-eyes glistened wetly as white grub-things continued peeling from the pulsating bulk of the beast. Jon-Tom frowned; someone had spoken above the reverberant bellowing. He looked across at Clothahump.

"The Massawrath." The wizard noticed Jon-Tom staring at him, and he repeated the name. "I have seen it in visions, my boy, suspected it in trances, but to have located its lair . . . Is it not appalling and unique? Do you not recognize any of this?"

"Recognize . . . ? Clothahump, have you gone mad? Or have we all? Or is it just that . . . that . . ."

He hesitated. For all its utterly alien appearance, there was truly something almost familiar about the apparition.

Again the pseudopod slapped at them. There was a broken groan from the boat. The tip of the massive appendage had struck just to Clothahump's left, tearing away railing along with a bit of the deck. The turtle had instinctively withdrawn and rolled several yards bowward. There he stuck out arms and legs once more and struggled to his feet while Bribbens rowed harder than ever and quietly cursed the abomination pursuing them.

Several partly formed white shapes had fallen from the end of the pseudopod. They lay on deck, their uncompleted limbs thrashing slowly. Among them was a head that had not grown a proper body and a lower torso the chest region of which tapered to a point.

Jon-Tom pulled in his oar and began kicking the disgusting things over the side. The last one clutched and pulled at him. It had arms but no legs. He was forced to touch it. Somehow he kept down his nausea and pulled it away from his legs. The white, rubbery flesh was cold as ice. He lifted it and heaved it over the railing, its weak grip sliding along his arm. It splashed astern while the Massawrath hunched its way over boulders and stalagmites, pacing just aft of the racing ship and gibbering mindlessly.

"If the river narrows and brings us in reach, we're finished." Talea spoke in a high, nervous voice and wrestled with the long oar.

"What *is* it?" Jon-Tom wiped his hands on his pants but the clamminess he'd picked off the flesh wouldn't dry. He raised his oar and shoved it back into the water.

"The Massawrath," Clothahump repeated. His hurried tumble across the deck apparently hadn't affected him. "She is the Mother of Nightmares This is her lair, her home."

Jon-Tom tried not to watch the loping gray slime. Bits of congealed white, animated puddings, continued to drip from those vast flanks, climb to their feet, and march for the water. They remained at least twenty yards astern though they kept up their pursuit. They did not have the muscular strength (if they had muscles, Jon-Tom thought) to overtake the boat. An army of fellow singers surged and marched around the base of the Massawrath. Some were indifferently squished beneath the vast mass, others shoved aside into the water.

"And what are the white things?" Flor forced herself to ask.

Clothahump peered over his glasses at her in evident surprise. "Why child, what would you expect the Mother of Nightmares to produce, except nightmares? I asked if you recognized them. Having no dreams to invade they are presently unformed, shapeless, incipient. Here in their place of birthing they are partly solid. When they pass out and into the minds of thinking creatures they have become thin as wind. Their lives are brief, empty, and full of torment."

"Wha-at?" Caz swallowed, tried again. "What does the blasted thing want with us?" The fur was as stiff on his neck as the nails of a yogi's board.

"Nightmares need dreams to feed on," explained the wizard. "Minds on which to fasten. What the Massawrath Mother feeds on I can only imagine, but I am not ready to offer myself to find out. I do not think it would be pleasant to be nightmared to death. Mayhap she feeds on the loose minds of the mad, carried back to her by those fragments of nightmare offspring that survive longer than a night. It is said the insane never awaken."

It continued to trail them, roaring and moaning. Pale things fell like white sweat from her back and sides. Occasionally a fresh appendage, gray and wet, would extend out toward them. It did not again come close enough to contact the boat.

Jon-Tom remembered Talea's frantic warning: if anything forced them nearer the Massawrath's shore they would be better off killing each other.

Another worry was the vibration he'd been feeling for more than a few minutes. Though it steadily intensified, it *seemed* to have no connection with the pursuing Mother of Nightmares. Soon a vast thunder filled his ears, powerful enough to reduce even the Massawrath's moan to a faint wailing.

Still it grew in volume. Now the maddened gray hulk struck out at the boat with dozens of pseudopods of many lengths. They raised water from the river and dropped dozens of slimy nightmares behind the boat.

The roaring grew louder still, until it and the vibration underfoot merged and were one. Exhausted from wrestling with the steering sweep, Bribbens leaned across it and tried to catch his breath. Then he frowned, staring over the bow. Several minutes went by and an expression of great calm came over his face.

Jon-Tom relaxed on his own oar and panted uncontrollably. "You
. . . you recognize it?"

"Yes, I recognize it." The boatman looked happy, which was encouraging. He also looked resigned, which was not. "Every boatman
knows the legends of the Sloomaz-ayor-le-Weentli. It could only be
one thing, you know.

"At least the Massawrath will not have us. This will be a cleaner,
surer death."

"What death? What are you talking about?" Talea and the others
had shipped their own oars as their pursuer fell back.

Bribbens reached out with an arm and gestured across the bow.
Ahead of them a thick fog was becoming visible. It boiled energetically and spread a cloud across the roof of the great cavern.

"Clothahump?" Jon-Tom turned back to the wizard. "What's he
raving about?"

"He is not raving, my boy." The stocky sorcerer had also turned
his attention away from the fading horror behind them. "He told you
once, remember? It is why the Massawrath cannot follow and why
she flails in rage at us. She cannot cross Helldrink."

Thunder deafened Jon-Tom, and he had to put his hands to his
ears. He felt the noise through the deck, through his legs and entire
body. It pierced his every cell.

Fog and roaring, mist and thunder drew nearer. What did that say?
It's speaking to you, he told himself, announcing its presence and
declaring its substance. It was familiar to Bribbens, who'd never seen
it. Should it therefore also be recognizable to him?

Waterfall, he thought. He knew it instantly.

Hurrying to the storage lockers, he tried to think of a saving song.
The duar was in his hands, clean and dry, waiting to be stroked to
life, waiting to sing magic. He draped straps over his neck, felt the
familiar weight on his shoulders.

One final time long cables of gray mucus reached out for them. The
Massawrath had extended itself to the utmost, but its reach still fell
short. Quivering with frustration, it hunkered down on the rocks now
well behind the boat, the volcanic pits of its eyes glaring balefully at
those now beyond its grasp.

Ahead fog boiled ceilingward like wet flame.

Jon-Tom stared mesmerized at the mist and hunted through his
repertoire for an appropriate song. What could he sing? That they
were nearing a waterfall was all too clear, but what kind of waterfall?
How high, how wide, how fast or . . . ?

Desperately he belted out several choruses from half a dozen different tunes relating to water. They produced no visible result. The boat's course and speed remained unchanged. Even the gneechees seemed to have deserted him. He'd come to expect their almost-presence whenever he'd strummed magic, and their absence panicked him.

Nothing ahead now but swirling vapor. Then Talea cursed loudly. Caz gave a warning shout and locked his arms around the railing while Mudge put his head on the deck and covered his eyes with his hands, as though by not seeing he might not be affected.

A faint mumbling rose behind Jon-Tom. Helpless and confused, he spared a second to look around.

Clothahump was standing by the steering sweep, next to a stoic Bribbens. The wizard's short, stubby arms were raised, the fingers spread wide on his left hand while those on the right made small circles and traced invisible patterns in the air.

With a snap the mainsail rose taut, the luff rope zipping up the mast with a whirr though no hand had touched the rigging. A terrified Pog reacted to the ascending sail by letting loose the spreader he'd been hanging from. A powerful updraft caught him, and he had to flap furiously to regain his perch. This time he clung flat to the spreader, arms and legs wrapped as tightly about the wooden cross member as his wings were around his body.

Clothahump's murmur changed to a stentorian, wizardly monotone. Now the wind blew hard in their faces, rough and threatening where the gentle on-bow breeze of previous days had been a comfortable companion.

The roar that permeated his entire body had numbed Jon-Tom's hearing completely. But his vision still functioned. They were almost upon a cauldron of spray and fog. Water particles danced in the air and became one with the river. He wanted to close his eyes, but curiosity kept them open. They no longer could see or hear the Massawrath.

A harder gray loomed immediately ahead, a definitive axis around which the mist boiled and fumed: the edge. The little boat crossed it . . . and kept going. All the while Clothahump continued his recitation. Even his charged voice was lost in the aqueous thunder, though Jon-Tom thought he could make out the part of the chant that made mention of "hydrostatic immunatic even keel please." The boat now eased out on the turgid air.

With the cold, distant interest of a parachutist whose chute has failed to open, Jon-Tom let the duar lie limp against him and moved to the railing. He looked over the side.

A thousand feet deep, the waterfall was. No, five thousand. It was hard to tell, since it disappeared into mist-shrouded depths. It might have dropped less than a thousand feet, or for all he could tell it might have plunged straight to the heart of the earth. Or to hell, if its legend-name was accurate.

Instead, the depths seemed to hold a fiery, red-orange glow. It arose from a distant whirlpool point.

As the boat continued to cruise smoothly across emptiness, he finally saw the source of much of the thunder. There was not just one waterfall, but four. Others crashed downward to port and starboard, and the fourth lay dead ahead. These sibling torrents were each as broad and fulsome as the one the boat had just crossed. Four immense cascades converged above the Pit and tumbled to a hidden infinity called Helldrink. They were vast enough to drain all the oceans of all the worlds.

The boat lurched, and everyone grabbed for something solid. They'd reached the middle of the Drink and had encountered the vortex of spray and upwelling air that dwelt there. The little vessel spun around twice, a third time, in that confluence of moist meteorologics, and then was spun free by the vortex's centrifugal power. It continued sailing steadily across the chasm.

Ahead the far waterfall loomed closer. The bow made contact with the water, the keel slipped in. They were sailing steadily now upstream, against the current. Wind rising from the Drink now blew at them from astern instead of in their faces. The sail billowed and filled for the first time since they'd entered the Earth's Throat.

Clothahump suddenly leaned back against the railing. His hands dropped and his voice faltered. The boat slowed. For an awful moment Jon-Tom thought the wind wouldn't be enough to cancel the insistent force of the swift current. Only Bribbens' skill enabled them finally to resume their forward progress.

Gradually they picked up speed, until the awesome pounding of the falls had fallen to a gentle rumbling echo. They were traveling upstream now, the wind steady behind them. The same luminescent growths lined portions of cavern wall and ceiling. They were in a subterranean chamber no different from the one they had fled.

Emotionally wrung, Jon-Tom leaned over the side of the boat and gazed astern. By now the last mists had been swallowed by distance. No Massawrath clone waited here to challenge them.

It did not have to. Never again could it send its pale white children to haunt the sleep of at least one traveler. Having been exposed, Jon-Tom was now immune. The encounter had innoculated him against nightmare. One who has looked upon the Mother of Nightmares cannot be frightened by her mere minions of ill sleep.

Clothahump had slumped to the deck. He sat there rubbing his right wrist. "I am out of shape," he muttered to no one in particular. His attention rose to the mast. Pog was twisted around the upper spreaders like a black coil.

The bat was slowly unwrapping himself. His malaria-like shivers faded, and he spoke in a querulous whisper. "Ointments, Master? Unguents and balms for ya arm, maybe a blue pill for ya head?"

"You okay?" Jon-Tom gazed admiringly down at the exhausted wizard.

"I will be, boy." He spoke hoarsely to his famulus. "Some ointment, yes. No pill for my head, but I will have one of the green ones for my throat. Five minutes of nonstop chanting." He sighed heavily, glanced back to Jon-Tom.

"Keep in mind, my boy, that a wizard's greatest danger is not lack of knowledge nor the onset of senility nor such forgetfulness as I am now prone to. It's laryngitis."

Then everyone was swarming happily around him. Except the unperturbable, steady Bribbens. The boatman remained at his post, eyes directed calculatingly upstream. They had left the boat in his hands, and he left the congratulating in theirs.

It was later that Mudge found Jon-Tom seated near the bow and staring morosely ahead. Strong wind from behind lifted his bright green cape, and he tucked it around and between his upraised knees. The duar lay in his lap. He plucked disconsolately at it as multihued formations passed in glowing revue.

"'Ere now, lad," said the otter concernedly, leaning over and squeak-sniffing, "wot's the matter, then? That Massawatchoris-whatever's behind us now, not comin' down at us."

Jon-Tom drew another chord from the instrument, smiled faintly up at the otter. "I blew it, Mudge." When the otter continued to look puzzled, he added, "I could've done the same thing as Clothahump, but I couldn't come up with the right music." He looked down at the duar.

"I couldn't think of a single appropriate tune, not even a chord. If it had all been up to me," he said with a shrug, "we'd all be dead by now."

"But we ain't," Mudge pointed out cheerfully, "and that be the important thing."

"Our cheeky companion is correct, you know." Caz had come up behind them both. Now he stood opposite Mudge, looking at the seated human. His paws were behind his back and folded just above the puffball of a tail. "It doesn't matter who does the saving. Just as friend Mudge says, the fact that we are saved is the important thing. Remember, it was you who tamed the great Falameezar that fiery night in Polastrindu. Not Clothahump. You want to hold all the glory for yourself?"

When he saw that the irony was lost on Jon-Tom he added, "We all work for the same end. It matters nothing who does what so long as that end is achieved. It shall be, unless some of us put our personal feelings and desires above it."

Mudge looked a little uncomfortable at the rabbit's bluntness. " 'E's right, mate. We can't be thinkin' o' ourselves in this business." The last was said with a straight face. "You'll 'ave plenty o' opportunity t' demonstrate your wonderfulness t' the ladies when this all be done with." He winked and whistled knowingly before leaving for the stern.

Caz considered giving the self-pitying human a comforting pat, decided Jon-Tom might regard it as patronizing, and left to join Mudge.

Jon-Tom, sitting by himself, muttered aloud, "The ladies have nothing to do with it." He watched the cavern walls glide past. Gentle spray licked his face, kicked up from the bow as the boat made its way upstream.

They didn't, he insisted to himself, resting his chin on folded hands. He'd only been worried about the general welfare.

Then he grinned, though there was no one to see him. The trouble with studying law is that you develop a tendency to bullshit yourself as well as your counterparts. What about the theory that all great events, all the turning points of history, had in some measure or another been motivated by matters of passion? Catherine the Great, Napoleon, Hitler, Washington . . . the sexual theory of history explained a hell of a lot of things economics and social migration and such did not.

It was quite a different kind of history that balanced on the outcome of their little expedition. Jon-Tom had never accorded the theory much credit anyway. Yet though meant at least partly in jest, Mudge's words forced home to him how often emotional yearnings coupled with the basic desires of the body could overwhelm those usually thought of as rational creatures.

So he was sitting there moping about nothing except himself. That was selfish and stupid. Maybe it had affected the thinking of Napoleon and Tiberius and others, but it wouldn't affect *him*. It was a damn good thing Clothahump had found the words that had escaped his human companion.

His moroseness fading, he strummed softly on the duar. A flicker of dancing motes haunted his left elbow. When he turned to inspect them, they'd gone. Gneechees.

What still did worry him was the thought that the next time he might be called upon to sing some magic, he might be as mentally paralyzed as he'd been when nearing Helldrink. He would have to fight that.

It wasn't the thought of death or the failure of their mission that troubled him as he sat there and played. It was a fear of personal failure, a fear that had haunted him since he'd been a child. It was the fear which had driven him to pursue two different careers without being able to choose between them.

And though he didn't realize it, it was the fear which had driven more men and women to greatness than far more rational motivations. . . .

VIII

Several days later the cathedral hove into view. It was not a cathedral, of course. But it might have been. No one could say. That turned out not to be as confusing as it seemed.

To Jon-Tom it looked like a cathedral. The ceiling of the great underground chamber in which it rose was several hundred feet high. Towers and turrets nearly touched that far stone roof. At that distance massive stalactites, each weighing many tons, resembled pins hanging from a carpet.

The bioluminescents were especially dense here and the chamber and its far reaches so brightly lit that it took the travelers several minutes to adjust to that unexpectedly vibrant organic glow.

It was more like a hundred cathedrals, Jon-Tom thought, all executed in miniature and piled one atop the other. Care and fine craftsmanship were apparent in every line and curve of the labyrinthine structure. Thousands of tiny colored windows gleamed on dozens of levels. The edifice filled much of the huge chamber.

It was a measure of the distances his mind had crossed that it was only incidental to him that the building shone a rich, metallic gold. Of course, that might only be a result of extensive use of gilt paint. Still, he vowed privately to keep a close watch on their avaricious otter.

The term miniature was applicable to more than just the building. When it became clear to them that the inhabitants of the strange boat were not hostile, the builders began to show themselves.

No more than four inches tall, the little people were covered with a rich umber fur that suggested sable. This fur was quite short, and long, fine hair of the same shade grew on the heads of male and female alike. Hordes of them started emerging from tiny doors and cubbyholes. Most resumed working on the building. Acres of scaffolding bristled on battlements and turrets and towers. One group of several dozen were installing a massive window all of a yard high.

Bribbens eased the boat in toward shore. At closer range they could make out thousands of golden sculptures adorning the building, gargoyles and worm-sized snakes and things only half realized because they originated in other dimensions, from a different biological geometry. Unlike the gneechees, these wonderful creations could be viewed, if not wholly perceived.

As the boat drifted still closer the thousands of tiny workers began milling uncomfortably, clustering close by doorways and other openings. Jon-Tom hailed them from his position at the bow, trying to assuage their worries.

"We mean you no harm," he called gently. "We're only passing through your lands and admire your incredible building. What's it for?"

From the crest of a water-caressed rock a fur-covered nymph all of three and a half inches tall shouted back at him. He had to strain to understand the tiny lady.

"It is the Building," she told him matter-of-factly, as though that should be explanation enough to satisfy anyone.

"Yes," and he lowered his voice still further when he saw that his normal tone was painfully loud to her, "but what is the building for?"

"It is the Building," the sprite reiterated. "We call it 'Heart-of-the-World.' Does it not shine brightly?"

"Very brightly," Talea said appreciatively. "It's very beautiful. But what is it for?"

The down-clad waif laughed delicately. "We are not sure. We have always worked on the Building. We always will work on the Building. What else is there to life but the Building?"

"You say you call it 'Heart-of-the-World.'" Jon-Tom studied the radiant walls and glistening spires. At first he thought it had been made of real gold, then stone covered with gilt paint. Now he wasn't sure. It might be metal of another kind, or plastic, or ceramic, or some unimaginable material he knew nothing of.

"Perhaps it is the very heart of the world itself," the little lady offered in suggestion. She smiled joyfully, showing perfect minuscule teeth. "We do not know. It beats with light as a heart does. If our

work were to be stopped, perhaps the light would go out of the
world."

Jon-Tom considered saying more but found reason and reality at
odds with one another, mixed up like a dog and a cat chasing each
other around a pole, getting nowhere. He looked helplessly to Clothahump for an explanation. So did his companions.

"Who can say?" The wizard shrugged. "If it is truly the architecture of the heart of the world, then at least we can tell others that the
world is well and truly fashioned."

"Thank you, sir." The sprite leaped nimbly to another rock further
upstream to keep pace with them. "We do our best. We have become
very adept at adding to and maintaining the Building."

"Make sure," Jon-Tom called to her, "that its glow never goes
out!" They were passing into a narrower section of the river cavern,
leaving the unnamed little folk and their enigmatic, immense construct behind.

"Who knows," he said quietly to Flor, "if it is the heart of the
world, then they'd better not be disturbed in their work. That's a hell
of a responsibility. And if it's not, if it's only a building, an obsession,
it's too beautiful to let die anyway."

"I never thought the heart of the world would be a building," she
said.

"Aren't we all structures?" With the Massawrath and Helldrink
safely far behind he was feeling alive and expansive. He'd always been
that way: high ups and abyssal downs. Right now he was up.

"Each of us develops piece by piece. We're full of carefully built
rooms and halls, audience chambers and windows, and we're populated with changing individualistic thoughts. I never imagined the
heart of the world would be a building, though." He stared back
down the tunnel. It was growing dark, the radiant growths vanishing
as they were prone to at unexpected intervals.

"In fact, I never thought of the world as having a heart."

The last rich light from the distant chamber was lost to sight as
they rounded a slight bend in the river. Bribbens was lighting the first
lamp.

"That's a nice thought, Jon-Tom. If only having a heart meant you
would be happy."

"I suppose it often means the opposite." But when the import of
her last comment finally penetrated, she had left him to chat with
their stolid steersman.

Jon-Tom hesitated, thought about pursuing it further by rejoining her to say, "Flor, are you trying to tell me something?" But he was as afraid of showing ignorance if he was interpreting her wrongly as he was of failure.

So he sat himself down in the flickering light and began to clean and tune his duar. As he tightened or loosened the strings, a gneechee or two would appear behind him, peering over his shoulder. He knew they were there and did his best to ignore them.

They were compelled to run on lamplight. Gradually the immense cave formations, the helictites and flowstone and such, began to grow smaller. In the narrowing confines of the river channel the rush and roar reverberated louder from the walls. The continuing absence of the familiar fluorescent fungi and their cousins was becoming unsettling.

No one liked the darkness. It reminded them too much of sleep, and that reminded of the now distant but never to be forgotten sight of the Massawrath. More importantly, their lamp oil was running out. Bribbens had prepared well, but he hadn't expected to journey for long in total darkness. The now sorely missed bioluminescents were all that had kept them from traveling in black. Soon it appeared they might have to do so, relying on Pog's abilities to guide them, unless the light-producing vegetation reappeared.

A hand was shaking him. It was too small to be part of the Massawrath, too solid to be one of its children. Nevertheless he had an instant of terror before coming awake.

"Get up, Jon-Tom. Move your ass!" It was the urgent voice of Talea.

"What?" But before he could say anything more she'd moved on to the next sleeping form. He heard her banging on an echoing surface.

"Wake up, wizard. You lazy old wizard, wake up!" She sounded worried.

"I still admit to 'old' but not the other." A grumbling Clothahump clambered to his feet.

Jon-Tom blinked, fought to dig sleep from his eyes. It was hard to see anything in the reduced light from the lamps. Bribbens was trying to conserve their dwindling supply of oil.

Then he saw the cause of her anxiety. In the blackness ahead was a writhing sheet of flame, completely blocking the river. It hung in the air there, a dull, thick orange-silver that did not move. The others awoke and moved to the bow to examine it. All agreed it was a most peculiar kind of fire.

As they cruised closer no rise in temperature or indeed any heat at all could be felt. The orange-silver hue did not change.

"Can it be another structure like the Heart-of-the-World building of the little folk?" Flor licked her lower lip and stared anxiously forward.

"No, no. The color is all wrong, supple shadow, and there is no sign of separation; levels, floors, or windows." Caz faced the wizard. "What is your opinion of it, sir?"

"Just a moment, will you?" Clothahump sounded irritable. "I'm not fully awake yet. Do you children think I have your physical resiliency simply because my brain is so much more active? Now then, this surely cannot be dangerous." He called back to Bribbens. "Steady ahead, my good boatman."

"Don't have much choice." The frog snapped off his reply as he tightened his grip on the steering sweep. "Tunnel's become too narrow for us to turn 'round in. Some of the rocks hereabouts look sharp. I don't want to chance 'em, so it's steady ahead unless it turns desperate."

The boatman was forced to raise his voice to a near shout to make himself understood. The rush of air in the pipe of a cave argued noisily with the increased force of the current.

They watched silently while that cold flame came nearer. Then there was another, dimmer light haloing it, and the orange-silver no longer blocked their progress. The new light came from tiny shining points that flickered unevenly, but not like gneechees. These were both visible and motionless.

"Well, shit." Mudge put hands on hips and sounded thoroughly disgusted with himself. " 'Tis a prize pack o' idiots we be, mates."

Jon-Tom didn't understand immediately, but it didn't take long until he knew the reason for the otter's embarrassment. When he did so he felt equally ashamed of his own fear.

The orange-silvery color was familiar enough. Then they emerged from the cavern. The great rising orb of moon no longer shone directly down into the Earth's Throat.

"We made it." He hugged a startled Talea. "Damned if we didn't!"

The character of the land they had emerged into was very different from that of the Swordsward and the river country of Bribbens' home. It was evident they had climbed a considerable distance.

Behind them towering crags reached for the stars. Clouds capped them, though they were not as thick as those on the eastern flanks of the range. No open plains or low scrub bordered the river here. There was no fragrant coniferous forest or high desert.

Mountains rose all around the little river valley in which they found themselves. Despite the altitude the country displayed the aspect of more tropical climes. It was warm but not hot, nor was it particularly humid. Jon-Tom thought of a temperature-zone climax forest.

Vines and creepers leaped from tree to tree. A thick undergrowth prevented them from seeing more than a few yards inland on either shore.

It was with relief that Jon-Tom inhaled the fresh air, fragrant with the aroma of flowers and green things. Though hardly tropical, the climate was more pleasant despite the altitude than any place he'd yet been. Compared to the bone-rattling winds of the Swordsward it was positively Edenic.

"Fine country," he said enthusiastically. "I'm surprised none of the warmlanders have tried to migrate here."

"Even if they knew this land existed they could not get over the mountains," Clothahump reminded him. "Only a very few in memory have ever made that journey. Even if would-be settlers could survive the trip, kindly keep in mind that this land is already occupied. Legend says the Weavers dislike any strangers. Consider what their opinion would be of potential colonists."

"And these are the people we're trying to make allies of?" Flor wondered.

"They are not overt enemies," Clothahump told her, shaking his head slowly. "Legend says they are content enough here in their land. Yet I admit legend also insists they hold no love for any but their own kind. It is said they like most to keep to themselves and maintain their privacy.

"As near as I know we are the first folk to journey past the mountain barrier in hundreds of years. Perhaps the legends no longer hold true. It may be that in all that time the inhabitants of the Scuttleteau have mellowed."

"They sure sound charming," said Flor apprehensively. "I can't wait to meet them." Her voice rose in tone, and she mimed a sardonic greeting. *"Buenos dias,* Señor Weaver. *Como esta usted,* and please don't eat me, I'm only a tourist." She sighed and grimaced at the wizard. "I wish I were as confident of success as you are."

"I'm 'ardly an optimist, meself," Mudge commented, surveying the near shore and considering a warm swim.

"Oh well. Surely they will see the need," said Caz hopefully, "to stand together against a common threat."

"That is to be hoped," the wizard agreed. "But we cannot be certain. We can only pray for a friendly welcome. Should we actually achieve anything more than that, it would exceed my wildest hopes."

There were some shocked looks in response to that. Jon-Tom spoke for all of them. "You mean . . . you're not sure you can persuade them?"

"My dear boy, I never made any such claim."

"But you gave me the impression . . ."

Clothahump held up a hand. "I made no promises. I merely stated that there was little we could do if we remained in Polastrindu and that we might have some chance of securing another strong ally were we to successfully complete this journey. I never said that reaching the Scuttleteau was a guarantee we could do that. Nor did I ever display any optimism about striking such an alliance. I simply declared that I thought it would be a good idea to try."

"You stiff-backed, bone-brained old fart, you led us on!" Talea was nearly too furious for words. "You cajoled us through all that," and she pointed back toward the mouth of the tunnel they'd recently emerged from, "through everything we've suffered since leaving Polastrindu, without thinking we had any chance to succeed?"

"I did not say we did not have a chance." Clothahump patiently corrected her. "I said our chances were slim. That is different from nonexistent. When I say achieving such an alliance would exceed my wildest hopes, I am merely being realistic, not fatalistic. The chance is there."

"Why the fuck couldn't you have been 'realistic' back in Polastrindu?" she growled softly. "Couldn't you have told us how slight you thought our chances of success were?"

"I could have, but no one thought to ask me. As to the first, if I had been more, shall we say, explicit in my opinions, none of you would have come with me. Those who might have would not have done so with as much confidence and determination as you have all displayed thus far."

Since this logic was irrefutable, no one chose to argue. There was some spirited name-calling, however. The wizard ignored it as one would have the excited chatter of children. Pog found the situation unbearably amusing.

"Now ya see what I have ta deal wid, don'tcha?" He giggled in gravely bat-barks as he swung gleefully from the spreader. "Maybe now ya all'll sympathize wid poor Pog a little bit more!"

"Shut your ugly face." Talea heaved a hunk of torchwood at him. He dodged it nimbly.

"Now, now, Talea-tail. Late for recriminations, don'tcha tink?" Again the rich laughter. "His Bosship has ya all where he wants ya." A series of rapid-fire squeeks seeped out as he delightedly lapped up their discomfort.

"It does seem you've been somewhat less than truthful with us, sir," said Caz reprovingly.

"Not at all. I have not once lied to any of you. And the odds do not lessen the importance of our trying to conclude this alliance. The more so now that we have actually completed the arduous journey through the Earth's Throat and have reached the Scuttleteau.

"Admittedly our chances of persuading the Weavers to join with us are slight, but the chance is real so long as we are real. We must reach for every advantage and assistance we can."

"And if we die on the failure of this slight chance?" Flor wanted to know.

"That is a risk I have resigned myself to accepting," he replied blandly.

"I see." Talea's fingers dug into the wood of the railing. She stared at the river as she spoke. "If we all die, that's a risk *you're* prepared to take. Well, I'm not."

"As you wish." Clothahump gestured magnanimously at the water. "I herewith release you from any obligation to assist me further. You may commence your swim homeward."

"Like hell." She peered back at Bribbens. "Turn this deadwood around."

The boatman threw her a goggle-eyed and mournful look. "How much can you pay me?"

"I . . ."

"I see." He turned his attention back to the river ahead. "I take orders only from those who can pay me." He indicated Clothahump. "He paid me. He tells my boat where it is to go. I do not renege on my business agreements."

"Screw your business agreements, don't you care about your own life?" she asked him.

"I honor my commitments. My honor is my life." This last was uttered with such finality that Talea subsided.

"Commitments my ass." She turned to sit glumly on the deck, glaring morosely at the wooden planking.

"I repeat, I have not lied to any of you." Clothahump spoke with dignity, then added by way of an afterthought, "I should have thought that all of you were ready to take any risk necessary in this time of crisis. I see that I was mistaken."

It was quiet on the boat for several hours. Then Talea looked up irritably and said, "I'm sorry. Bribbens is right. We all made a commitment to see this business through. I'll stick to mine." She glanced back at the wizard. "My fault. I apol . . . I apologize." The unfamiliar word came hard to her. There were murmurs of agreement from the others.

"That's better," Clothahump observed. "I'm glad that you've all made up your minds. Again. It was time to do so because," and he pointed over the bow, "soon there will be no chance of turning back."

Completely spanning the river a hundred yards off the bow was a soaring network of thick cables. They made a silvery shadow on the water, a doomed superstructure of glistening filaments in the intensifying morning light.

Waiting and watching with considerable interest from their resting places high up in the cables were half a dozen of the Weavers.

Clothahump knew what to expect. Caz, Mudge, Talea, Pog, and Bribbens had some idea, if through no other means than the stories passed down among generations of travelers.

But Jon-Tom and Flor possessed no such mental buffering. Primeval fear sent a shudder through both of them. It was instinctive and unreasoning and cold. Only the fact that their companions showed no sign of panic prevented the two otherworlders from doing precisely that.

The six Weavers might comprise a hunting party, an official patrol, or simply a group of interested river gazers out for a day's relaxation. Now they gathered near the leading edge of the cablework.

One of them shinnied down a single strand when the boat began to pass beneath. Under Bribbens' directions and at Clothahump's insistence, Mudge and Caz were taking down the single sail.

"No point in making a show of resistance or attempting to pass uncontested," the wizard murmured. "After all, our purpose in coming here is to meet with them."

Unable to override their instincts, Jon-Tom and Flor moved to the rear of the boat, as far away from their new visitor as they could get.

That individual secured the bottom of his cable to the bow of the little boat. The craft swung around, tethered to the overhead network, until its stern was pointing upstream.

Having detached the cable from the end of his abdomen, the Weaver rested on four legs, quietly studying the crew of the peculiar boat with unblinking, lidless multiple eyes. Four arms were folded across the cephalothorax. His body was bright yellow with concentric triangles decorating the underside of the sternum. His head was a beautiful ocher. The slim abdomen had blue stripes running down both the dorsal and ventral sides.

Complementing this barrage of natural coloration was a swirling, airy attire of scarves and cloth. The material was readily recognizable as pure silk. It was twisted and wrapped sari-style around the neck, cephalothorax, abdomen, and upper portions of the legs and arms. Somehow it did not entangle the Weaver's limbs as he moved.

It was impossible to tell how many pieces of silk the visitor was wearing. Jon-Tom followed one feathery kelly-green scarf for several yards around legs and abdomen until it vanished among blue and pink veils near the head. A series of bright pink bows knotted several of the scarves together and decorated the spinneret area. Mandibles moved idly, and occasionally they could see the twin fangs that flanked the other mouth-parts. The Weaver was a nightmare out of a Max Ernst painting, clad in Technicolor.

The nightmare spoke. At first Jon-Tom had trouble understanding the breathy, faint voice. Gradually curiosity overthrew his initial terror, and he joined his companions in the bow. He began to make sense of the whispery speech, which reminded him of papers blowing across stepping-stones.

As the Weaver talked, he tested the cable he'd spun himself from bridge to boat. Then he sat down, having concluded his prayer or invocation or whatever it had been, by folding his four legs beneath him. His jaw rested on the upper tarsals and claws. The body was three feet long and the legs almost doubled that.

"it has been a long time," said the veiled spider, "far beyond my lifetime, beyond i think the memory of any currently alive, since any of the warmland people have visited the scuttleteau."

Jon-Tom tried to analyze the almost nonexistent inflection. Was the Weaver irritated, or curious, or both?

"no one can cross the mountains." A pair of arms gestured toward the towering peaks that loomed above them.

"We did not come over the mountains," said Clothahump, "but

through them." He nodded toward the river. "We came on this watercourse through the Earth's Throat."

The spider's head bobbed from side to side. "that is not possible."

"Then how the hell do you think we got here?" Talea said challengingly, bravery and bluster overcoming common sense.

"it may be that . . ." The spider hesitated, the whispery tones little louder than the breeze wafting across the ship. Then faint, breathy puffs came from that arachnoid throat. It was a laughter that sounded like the wind that gets lost in thick trees and idles around until it blows itself out.

"ah, sarcasm. a trait of the soft-bodied, i believe. what do you wish here on the scuttleteau?"

Jon-Tom felt himself drawn to the side by Caz while the wizard and Weaver talked. The rabbit gestured toward the sky.

The other five Weavers now hung directly above the boat from short individual cables. It was obvious they could be on the deck in seconds. They carried cleverly designed knives and bolas that could be easily manipulated by the double flexible claws tipping each limb.

"They've been quiet enough thus far," said Caz, "but should our learned leader's conversation grow less than accommodating, we should anticipate confronting more than one of them." His hand slid suggestively over the knife slung at his own hip, beneath the fine jacket.

Jon-Tom nodded acknowledgment. They separated and casually apprised the others of the quintet dangling ominously over their heads.

When Clothahump had finished, the spider moved back against the railing and regarded them intently. At least, that was the impression Jon-Tom received. It was difficult to tell not only how he was seeing them mentally, but physically as well. With four eyes, two small ones and two much larger ones mounted higher on his head, the Weaver would be hard to surprise.

"you have come a long way without being sure of the nature of your eventual reception. to what purpose? you have talked much and said little, the mark of a diplomat but not necessarily of a friend. why then are you here?"

Above, the Weaver's companions swayed gently in the breeze and caressed their weapons.

"I'm sorry, but we can't tell you that," said Clothahump boldly. Jon-Tom moved to make certain his back was against the mast. "Our information is of such vital importance to the Weavers that it can only be related to the highest local authority."

"nothing a warmlander can say is of any importance to the weavers." Again came that distant, whistling laugh, blowing arrogantly across the deck.

"Nilonthom!" roared Clothahump in his most impressive sorceral tone. Vibrations rattled the boat. Whitecaps snapped on the crests of sudden waves, and there was a distant rumble of thunder. The five watchers in the net overhead bounced nervously on their organic tethers while the Weaver in the boat stiffened against the rail.

Clothahump lowered his arms. One had to stare hard at the inoffensive-appearing little turtle with the absurd spectacles to believe that voice had truly issued from that hard-shelled body.

"By my annointment as Sorcerer-Majestic of the Last Circle, by the brow of Elrath-Vune now long dust, by all the oaths that bind all the practitioners of True Magic back to the beginnings of divination, I swear to you that what I have to say *is* vital to the survival of Weaver as well as warmlander, and that it can be imparted only to the Grand Webmistress herself!"

That pronouncement appeared to shake their visitor as badly as had the totally unexpected demonstration of wizardly power.

"most impressive in word and action," the spider husked. "that you are truly a wizard cannot be denied." He recovered some "octupul" poise and executed a short little bow, crossing all four upper limbs across his chest.

"forgive my hesitation and suspicions and accept my apologies should i have offended you. my name is ananthos."

"Are you in charge of the river guards, then?" Flor indicated the five remaining armed Weavers still drifting in the wind overhead.

The spider turned his head toward her, and she fought hard not to shudder. "your meaning is obscure, female human. we do not 'guard' the bridge. there are not any who would harm it, and none until now come out of the hole into which the river dies."

"Then why are you here at all? Why the bridge?" Jon-Tom didn't try to conceal his puzzlement.

"this is," and the Weaver gestured with one limb at the network of silken cables and its watchful inhabitants, "a lifesaving grid. it was erected here to protect those young and ignorant weavers who are fond of playing in the river lamayad and who sometimes tend to drift too close to the hole which kills the water. were they to vanish within they would be forever lost.

"did you think then we were soldiers? there is no need for soldiers on the scuttleteau. we have no enemies."

"Then a revelation is in store," muttered Clothahump so low the Weaver did not hear him.

"the bridge is to help protect infants," Ananthos finished.

"Now don't that soothe a beatin' 'eart!" Mudge whispered disbelievingly to Jon-Tom. "A fearsome lookin' lot like this and 'e says they've no soldiers. Wot a fine pack o' allies they'll make, eh?"

"They've got weapons," his companion argued, "and they look like they know how to use them." He raised his voice and addressed the Weaver. "If this is nothing more than a station for rescuing wayward children, then why do you and your companions carry weapons?"

Ananthos gestured at the surrounding forest. "to protect ourselves, of course. even great fighters may be overwhelmed by a single large and powerful foe. there are beasts on the scuttleteau that would devour all on this craft and the craft itself in a single gulp. because we do not maintain an army to confront nonexistent enemies does not mean we are fleet-limbed cowards who run instead of fight. or did you think we were all eggsuckers?" He bared his respectable fangs.

"the confident and strong have no need of an army. each weaver is an army unto itself."

"It is about armies and fighting that we come," said Clothahump, "and about such matters that we must speak to the Webmistress."

Ananthos appeared as upset as a spider could possibly be. "to bring warmlanders into the capital is a great responsibility. by rights of history and legend i should turn you around and send you back into the hole from whence you emerged. and yet"—he struggled with the conflict between prescribed duty and personal feelings and thoughts —"i cannot dismiss the fact that you have made an impossible journey for reasons i am not equipped to debate. if it is of the importance you insist, i would fail did i not escort you to the capital. but to see the grand webmistress herself . . ."

He turned away from them, whether from embarrassment or indecision or both they could not tell.

"Why don't you," said Caz helpfully, "take us into protective custody, convey us to the capital under guard, and turn us over to your superiors?"

Ananthos looked back at him, his head bobbing in that odd side-to-side motion that was half nod and half shake. He spoke in a whispery, grateful hush.

"you have some understanding of what it means to be responsible to someone placed higher than oneself, warmlander of the big ears."

"I've been in that uncomfortable situation before, yes," Caz admitted drolly, polishing his monocle.

"i bow to your excellent suggestion."

IX

He leaned back and called breathily upward. "arethos, imedshud! *intob coom.*" Two of the watchful Weavers dropped to the deck, their spinnerets snipping off the cables trailing from their abdomens. They studied the warmlanders with interest.

"these will accompany us on the journey, for i can hardly claim to have you in restriction, as your tall white friend has suggested, all by myself. yet i am charged with the watchfulness on this bridge and cannot leave it deserted. so three of us will accompany you and three remain here.

"we shall proceed upstream. a day's journey from here, the river lamayad splits. several days further it splits again. against that divide, set against the breath, is our capital, my home."

He added warningly, "what happens then is no longer my responsibility. i can make no promises as to the nature of your reception, for i am low in the hierarchy, most low, for all that no weaver lies in the mud and none soars above the others. our hierarchy is a convenience and necessary to governing, and that is all.

"as to an audience with the grand webmistress . . ." his voice trailed away meaningfully.

"Diplomacy moves best when it moves cautiously," said Caz, "and not in dangerous leaps."

"For now it will be more than enough if you see us to the capital, Ananthos," Clothahump assured him.

The spider seemed greatly relieved. "then my thoughts are clear. i am neither helping nor hindering you, merely referring you to those in the position to do so." He turned and ceremoniously detached the cable holding the bow of the motionless boat.

Bribbens had remained by his oar during the discussion. Now he leaned gently on it as once again the wind began to fill the sail. The boat turned neatly on its axis as the cry of "ware the boom!" rang out from the steersman. Soon they had passed beneath the intricate webwork spanning the river and were once again traveling upstream.

"i've never seen a warmlander." Ananthos was standing quite close to Jon-Tom. "most interesting biology." Despite ten thousand years of primitive fears, Jon-Tom did not pull away when the spider reached out to him.

Ananthos extended a double-clawed leg. It was covered with bristly hairs. The delicate silk scarves of green and turquoise enveloping the limb mitigated its menacing appearance. The finger-sized claws touched the man's cheek, pressed lightly, and traveled down the face to the neck before withdrawing. Somehow Jon-Tom kept from flinching. He concentrated on those brightly colored eyes studying him.

"no fur at all like the short bewhiskered one, except on top. and soft . . . so soft!" He shuddered. "what a terrible fragility to live with."

"You get used to it," said Jon-Tom. It occurred to him that the spider found him quite repulsive.

They continued studying each other. "That's beautiful silk," the man commented. "Did you make it yourself?"

"do you mean, did i spin the silk or manufacture the scarf? in truth i did neither." He waved a leg at the others. "we differ even more in size than you seem to. some of our smaller cousins produce far finer silk than a clumsy oaf like myself is capable of. they are trained to do so, and others carefully weave and pattern their produce." He reached down and unwrapped a four-foot turquoise length and handed it to Jon-Tom.

A palmful of feathers was like lead compared to the scarf. He could have whispered at it and blown it over the side of the boat. The dye was a faint blue, as rich as the finest Persian turquoise with darker patches here and there. It was the lightest fabric he'd ever caressed. Wearing it would be as wearing nothing.

He moved to hand it back. Ananthos' head bobbed to the left. "no. it is a gift." Already he'd refastened two other long scarves to compensate for the loss of the turquoise. Jon-Tom had a glimpse of the intricate knot-and-clip arrangement that held the quasi-sari together.

"Why?"

Now the head bobbed down and to the right. He was beginning to match head movements to the spider's moods. What at first had seemed only a nervous twitching was becoming recognizable as a complex, highly stylized group of suggestive gestures. The spiders utilized their heads the way an Italian used his hands, for speech without speaking.

"why? because you have something about you, something i cannot define. and because you admired it."

"I'll say we've got something about us," Talea grumbled. "An air of chronic insanity."

Ananthos considered the comment. Again the whispery laughter floated like snowflakes across the deck. "ah, humor! humor is among the warmlander's richest qualities. perhaps the most redeeming one."

"For all the talk of hostility our legends speak of, you seem mighty friendly," she said.

"it is my duty, soft female," the Weaver replied. His gaze went back to Jon-Tom. "please me by accepting the gift."

Jon-Tom accepted the length of silk. He wrapped it muffler-like around his neck, above the indigo shirt. It didn't get tangled in his cape clasp. In fact, it didn't feel as though it was there at all. He did not consider how it might look sandwiched between the iridescent green cape and purple shirt.

"I have nothing to offer in return," he said apologetically. "No, wait, maybe I do." He unslung his duar. "Do the Weavers like music?"

Ananthos' answer was unexpected. He extended two limbs in an unmistakable gesture. Jon-Tom carefully passed over the instrument.

The Weaver resumed his half-sit, half-squat and laid the duar across two knees. He had neither hands nor fingers, but the eight prehensile claws on the four upper limbs plucked with experimental delicacy at the two sets of strings.

The melody that rose from the duar was light and ethereal, alien, atonal, and yet full of almost familiar rhythms. It would begin to sound almost normal, then drift off on strange tangents. Very few notes contributed to a substantial tune. Ananthos' playing reminded Jon-Tom more of samisen music than guitar.

Flor leaned blissfully back against the mast, closed her eyes, and soaked up the spare melody. Mudge sprawled contentedly on the deck while Caz tried, without success, to tap time to the disjointed beat. Nothing soothes xenophobia so efficiently as music, no matter how strange its rhythms or inaudible the words.

An airy wail rose from Ananthos and his two companions. The three-part harmony was bizarre and barely strong enough to rise above the breeze. There was nothing ominous in their singing, however. The little boat made steady progress against the current. In spite of his unshakable devotion to his job, even Bribbens was affected. One flippered foot beat on the deck in a futile attempt to domesticate the mystical arachnid melody.

It might be, Jon-Tom thought, that they would find no allies here, but he was certain they'd already found some friends. He fingered the end of the exquisite scarf and allowed himself to relax and sink comfortably under the soothing spell of the spider's frugal fugue. . . .

It was early in the morning of the fourth day on the Scuttleteau that he was shaken awake. Much too early, he mused as his eyes opened confusedly on a still dark sky.

He rolled over, and for a moment memory lagged shockingly behind reality. He started violently at the sight of the furry, fanged, many-eyed countenance bending over him.

"i am sorry," said Ananthos softly. "did i waken you too sharply?"

Jon-Tom couldn't decide if the Weaver was being polite and offering a diplomatic way out or if it was an honest question. In either case, he was grateful for the understanding it allowed him.

"No. No, not too sharply, Ananthos." He squinted into the sky. A few stars were still visible. "But why so early?"

Bribbens' voice sounded behind him. As usual, the boatman was first awake and at his duties before the others had risen from beneath their warm blankets. "Because we're nearing their city, man."

Something in the frog's voice made Jon-Tom sit up fast. It was not fear, not even worry, but a new quality usually absent from the boatman's plebian monotone.

Pushing aside his blanket, he turned to look over the bow, matching Bribbens' gaze. Then he understood the strange new quality he'd detected in the boatman's voice: wonderment.

The first rays of the sun were arriving, having mounted the mountain shield soaring ahead of the boat. In the distance lay a range of immense peaks more massive than Zaryt's Teeth. Several crags vanished into the clouds, only to reappear above them. Jon-Tom was no surveyor, but if the Teeth contained several mountains higher than twenty thousand feet then the range ahead had to average twenty-five.

More modest escarpments dominated the north and south. Swathed in glaciers and clouds, the colossal eastern range also displayed an additional quality: dark smoke and occasional liquid red flares rose from several of the peaks. The towering range was still alive, still growing.

The sparks and smoke that drifted overhead came from a massif much closer than the eastern horizon, however. Quite close a black caldera rose from surrounding foothills to a height a good ten thousand feet above the river, which banked to the south before it. Ice and snow crowned the fiery summit.

Snow gave way to conifers and hardwoods, they in turn surrendered to the climax vegetation of the variety which flanked the river, and that at last to a city which crept up and clung to the volcano's flanks. Small docks spread thin wooden fingers out into the river.

"my home," said Ananthos, "capital and ancestral settlement from which the first weavers laid claim to the scuttleteau and all the lands that abut it." He spread four forearms. "i welcome you all to gossameringue-on-the-breath."

The city was a marvel, like the scarf. The similarities did not end there, for like the scarf it was woven of fine silk. Morning dew adhered to struts and suspensions and flying buttresses of webwork. Roofs were hung from supports strung lacily above instead of being supported by pillars from beneath. Millions of thick, silvery cables supported buildings several stories high, all agleam with jewels of dew.

Other cables as thick as a man's body, spun from the spinnerets of dozens of spiders, secured the larger structures to the ground.

On the lower, nearer levels they could discern dozens of moving forms. It was clear the city was heavily populated. Spreading as it did around the base of the huge volcano and climbing thousands of feet up its sides, it appeared capable of housing a population in the tens of thousands.

There was enough spider silk in that single city, if it could be unwrapped to its seminal strands, to cocoon the Earth.

Once Jon-Tom had spent an hour marveling at a single small web woven by one spider on an ocean coast. It had been speckled with dew from the morning fog.

Here the dew seemed almost choreographed. As the first rising rays of the sun struck the city, it suddenly turned to a labyrinth of platinum wires and diamond dust. It was too bright to look at, but the effect faded quickly as the dew evaporated. The sun rose higher, the enchanting effect dissipating as rapidly as the sting from a clash of cymbals. Left behind was a spectacle of suspended structures only slightly less impressive.

Gossameringue was all spheres and ellipses, arches and domes. Jon-Tom could not find a sharp angle anywhere in the design. Everything was smooth and rounded. It gave the city a soft feeling which its inhabitants might or might not reflect.

As the sun worked its way up into the morning sky, the little boat put in at the nearest vacant dock. A few early morning workers turned curious multiple eyes on the unique cargo of warmlanders. They did not interfere. They only stared. As befitted their historical preference for privacy, these few Weavers soon turned to their assigned tasks and ignored the arrivals. It troubled Clothahump. A people fanatic about minding its own business does not make a ready ally.

Under Ananthos' escort they left the boat and crossed the docks. Soon they had entered a silk and silver world.

"This mission had best be successful," said Caz as they began to climb. He placed his broad feet carefully. The roadway was composed of a fine checkerboard of silk cables. They were stronger than steel and did not quiver even when Jon-Tom experimentally jumped up and down on one, but if one missed a rung of the gigantic rope ladder and fell through, a broken leg was a real possibility.

After a while caution gave way to confidence and the party was able to make faster progress up the side of the mountain.

"I'll settle for just getting out of here alive," Talea whispered to the rabbit.

"Precisely my meaning," said Caz. He gestured back the way they'd come. The river and docks had long since been swallowed up by twisting, contorting bands of silk and silken buildings. "Because we'd never find our way out of here without assistance."

It was not all silk. Some of the buildings boasted sculptured stone or wood, and there was some use of metalwork. Windows were made of fine glass, and there was evidence of vegetable matter being employed in sofas and other furniture.

Though the Weavers were not arboreal creatures, their construction ignored the demands of gravity. The whole city was an exercise in the aesthetic applications of geometry. It was difficult to tell up from down.

Caz was right, Jon-Tom thought worriedly. Without Weaver help they would never find their way back to the river.

They climbed steadily. Wherever they passed, daily routines

ground to a halt as the populace stared dumbfoundedly at creatures they knew only from legend. Ananthos and his two fellow guards took an aggressive attitude toward those few citizens who tried to touch the warmlanders.

The only ones who weren't shoved aside were the curious hordes of spiderlings who swarmed in fascination around the visitors' legs. Most of these infants had bodies a foot or more across. They were a riot of color underfoot; red, yellow, orange, puce, black, and more in metallic, dull, or iridescent shades. They displayed stripes and spots, intricate patterns and simple solids.

It was difficult to make sense of the extraordinary variety of colors and shapes because the predominant sensation was one of wading through a shallow pond made of legs. With remarkable agility the youngsters scrambled in and between the feet of the visitors, never once having a tiny leg kicked or stepped on.

They reserved most of their attention for Talea, Flor, and Jon-Tom. Bribbens and Clothahump they ignored completely. Nor were they in the least bit shy.

One scrambled energetically up Jon-Tom's right side, pulling thoughtlessly at his fortunately tough cape and pants. It rode like a cat on his right shoulder, chattering breathily to its less enterprising companions. Jon-Tom tried hard to think of it as a cat.

The adolescent displayed a cluster of painted lines that ran from its mandibles back between its eyes and down the back of its head. The cosmetics did not give Jon-Tom a clue as to its sex. He thought of brushing it away, but it behooves a guest to match the hospitality of his hosts. So he left it alone, resolutely ignoring the occasional reflexive flash of poisonous fangs.

The spiderling sat there securely and waved its foot-long legs at disapproving adults and envious brethren. It whispered in a rush to its obliging mount.

"where do you come from? you are warm, not cold like the prey or the creatures of the forest. you are very tall and thin and you have hair only atop your head and there very dense." The youngster's partly clad abdomen brushed rhythmically against the back of Jon-Tom's neck. He assumed it was a friendly gesture. The fur on the spiderling's bottom was as soft as Mudge's.

"you have funny mouths and your fangs are hidden. may i see them?"

Jon-Tom patiently opened his mouth and grimaced to show his

teeth. The spiderling drew back in alarm, then moved cautiously closer.

"so many. and they're white, not black or brown or gold. they are so flat, save two. how can you suck fluids with them?"

"I don't use my fangs—my teeth—to suck fluids," Jon-Tom explained. "What liquid I do ingest I swallow straight. Mostly I eat solid food and use my teeth to chew it into smaller pieces."

The youngster shuddered visibly. "how awful, how gruesome! you actually eat solid, unliquified flesh? your fangs don't look up to the task. i'd think they'd break off. ugh, ugh!"

"It can be tough sometimes," Jon-Tom confessed, recalling some less than palatable meals he'd downed. "But my teeth are stronger than yours. They're not hollow."

"i wonder," said the spiderling with the disarming honesty common to all children, "if you'd taste good."

"I'd hope so. I'd hate to think I've lived all these years just to give some friend an upset stomach. I'd probably be pizza-and-coke flavored."

"i don't know what is a pissaoke." The infant bared tiny fangs. "i don't suppose you'd let me have a taste? your elders aren't watching." He sounded hopeful.

"I'd like to oblige," Jon-Tom said nervously, "but I haven't had anything to eat yet today and might make you sick. Understand?"

"oh well." The youngster didn't sound too disappointed. "i don't guess i'd like you sucking out one of my legs, either." He quivered at the thought. "you're a nice person, warmlander. i like you." Jon-Tom experienced the abdomen caress once again. Then the spiderling jumped down to join his fellow scamperers.

"luck to you, warmlander!"

"And to you also, child," Jon-Tom called hastily back to him. Ananthos and several responsible bystanders were finally shooing the spiderlings away. The children waved and cheered in excited whispers, like any others, their multiple, multicolored legs waving goodbyes.

A greater weight pressured his left arm and he looked around uncertainly. It was no disrespectful spiderling, however. Flor's expression was ashen, and she slumped weakly against him. He quickly got an arm under her shoulders and gave her some support.

"What's wrong, Flor? You look ill."

"What's wrong?" Fresh shock replaced some of the paleness that had dominated her visage. "I've just been poked, probed, and swarmed over by a dozen of the most loathesome, disgusting creatures anyone could . . .''

Jon-Tom made urgent quieting motions. "Jesus, Flor. Keep your voice down. These are our hosts."

"I know, but to have them touch me all over like that." She was trembling uncontrollably. *"Aranas* . . . uckkkk! I hate them. I could never even stand the little ones the size of my thumb, for all that Mama used to praise them for catching the cockroaches. So you can imagine how I feel about these. I could hardly stand it on the boat." She moved unsteadily away from his arm. "I don't know how much more of this I can take, Jon-Tom," and she gestured at Ananthos, who was marching ahead of them.

They turned up another, broader web-road. "What matters isn't what they look like," Jon-Tom told her sternly, "but what's behind their looks. In this case, intelligence. We need their help or Clothahump wouldn't have herded us all this way." He eyed her firmly.

"Think you can manage by yourself now?"

She was breathing deeply. The color was returning to her face. "I hope so, *compadre*. But if they climb over me like that again . . ." A brief reprise of the trembling. "I feel so . . . so icky."

" 'Icky' is a state of mind, not a physiological condition."

"Easy for you to say, Jon-Tom."

"Look, they probably don't think much of the way we look, either. I know they don't."

"I don't care what they think," she shot back. "Santa Maria, I hope we finish with this place quickly."

"Oh, I don't know." He noted the way in which the rising sun, bright despite the intensifying cloudiness, sparkled off the millions of cables and the silken buildings and webwork walkway they were climbing. "I think it's kind of pretty."

"The fly complimenting the spider," she muttered.

"Except that the flies are here hunting for allies."

"Let's hope they are allies."

"Ahhh, you worry too much." He gave her an affectionate pat on the back. She forced a grin in response, thankful for his moral support.

Jon-Tom's attention returned forward, and to his surprise he found himself staring straight into Talea's eyes. The instant their gazes locked she turned away.

He decided she probably hadn't been looking at him. Probably trying to memorize their path in case they had to try and flee. Such preparation and suspicion would be typical of the redhead. It did not occur to him that the glance might have been significant of anything else.

They had climbed several thousand feet by the afternoon. Ahead loomed an enormous structure. How many spiders, Jon-Tom wondered, had labored for how many years patiently spinning the silk necessary to create those massive ramparts of hardened silk and interlaced stone?

The royal palace of Gossameringue was made largely of hewn rock cemented together not with mortar or clay or concrete but layer on layer of spider silk. Turrets of silver bulged from unexpected places. The entire immense structure was suspended from a vast overhang of volcanic rock by cables a yard thick. Those cables would have supported a mountain. Though the wind was stronger here, high up the volcanic flank, the palace did not move. It might as well have been anchored in bedrock.

They entered a round, silk-lined tube and were soon walking through tunnels and hallways. It grew dark only slowly inside since the glassy silk admitted a great deal of light. Eventually torches and lamps were necessary, however, to illuminate the depths.

They confronted a portal guarded by a pair of the largest spiders yet seen. Each had a body as big as Jon-Tom's, but with their loglike legs they spanned eighteen feet from front to back.

They were a rich dark brown, without special markings or bright colors anywhere on their bodies. The multiple black eyes were small in comparison to the rest of the impressive mass. Shocking-pink and orange silks enveloped torsos and legs. There was also a set of white scarves tied around two forelegs and the nonexistent necks. Huge halberds with intricately carved wooden shafts rested between powerful forelegs.

They didn't move, but Jon-Tom knew they were closely scrutinizing the peculiar arrivals. For the first time since they'd entered Gossameringue he was frightened. Thoughts of the friendly spiderlings faded from his mind. It would have been little comfort had he realized that the pair of impressive guards before them were there precisely to intimidate visitors.

Ananthos turned to them. "you will have to wait here." After conversing briefly with the two huge tarantulas he and his two associates disappeared through the round entrance.

While they waited, the visitors occupied themselves by inspecting the now indifferent guards and the gleaming silk walls. The silk had been dyed red, orange, and white in this corridor and shone wetly in the light of the lamps. Jon-Tom wondered how far from the entrance they'd come.

Mudge sauntered over next to him. "I don't know 'ow it strikes you, mate, but seems t' me our eight-legged friends 'ave been gone a 'ell of a long time now."

Jon-Tom tried to sound secure as well as knowledgeable. "You don't just walk in on the ruler of a powerful people and announce your demands. The diplomatic niceties have to be observed. History shows that."

"More o' your studies, wot? Well, maybe it do take some time at that. Never met a lot o' bureaucrats that did move much faster than the dead. I expect they're all like that, slow movin' an' slow thinkin', no matter 'ow many legs they got."

"Here they come," Jon-Tom told him confidently.

But it was not Ananthos and his familiar comrades who emerged from the opening but instead a tall, very thin-legged arachnid with a delicate body and eyes raised high on the front of his skull. His forelegs were tied up in an intricate network of blue silk ribbons and there were matching purple ones on the rearmost limbs.

One wire-thin leg pointed at Caz, who stood nearest the portal, while dozens of spiders of varied size and color suddenly poured from behind him.

"immobilize them and carry them down!"

"Hey, wait a minute." Jon-Tom was unable to get his staff around before he'd been seized by half a dozen hooking legs. Others thrust threatening spears and knives at his belly.

"There has been a mistake." Clothahump was already disappearing around a corner, carried on his back.

"Put me down or I'll cut your smelly heads off!" All fire and helpless frustration, Talea was being carted closely behind the wizard.

Then Jon-Tom felt himself turned on his back and borne on dozens of hairy legs, kicking and protesting with equal lack of effect.

They went down into darkness. How far he couldn't guess, but it wasn't long before they were dumped into a silk-and-stone cell under the imperious direction of the emaciated and beribboned spider in charge.

The silk lining the chamber was old and filthy. There were no windows to let in light, only a few oil lamps in the corridor beyond.

Jon-Tom gathered himself up and moved to inspect the cross-hatched webwork that barred their exit.

It was not sticky to the touch, but was quite invulnerable. He leaned against it and shouted at their retreating captors.

"Stop, you can't put us in here! We're diplomatic visitors. We're here to see the Grand Webmistress and . . . !"

"Save your wind, my friend." Caz stood at the outermost corner of the cell, squinting up the silk ladder-steps. "They've gone."

"Shit!" Jon-Tom kicked at an irregular, flattened piece of shiny material. At first he thought it was a piece of broken pottery. Closer inspection revealed it was a section of chitin. It clattered off a stone set in the far wall.

"God damn that sly-voiced Ananthos. He led us all this way by making us believe he was our friend."

"He never said he was our friend." Bribbens sat against a wall, his head resting on his knees. "Merely that he was doing his duty. Get us this far, then it'd be up to us, he said." The frog chuckled throatily. "Certainly hasn't gone out of his way to make it easy for us, looks like."

Talea was sniffing the air and frowning. "I don't know if any of you have noticed it yet, but—"

There was a startled scream. Jon-Tom looked left. Flor had been standing there. Now she'd fallen forward and landed hard on the floor. Her foot had vanished through an opening in the wall and the rest of her was slowly following. . . .

X

They hadn't noticed the passageway when they'd been chucked into the cell. There was no telling where it ran to or what had hold of Flor. Blood oozed from beneath her nails as she tried to dig her fingers into the floor.

Jon-Tom was first at her side. Without thinking, he leaned over and heaved a head-sized rock at her foot. There was a breathy exclamation of surprise and pain from beyond. She stopped sliding.

Caz and Mudge half dragged, half carried her across the cell. Whatever had hold of her had missed her leg, but her boot was neatly punctured just behind the calf.

As he backed away from the opening several legs scrambled through. They were attached to a two-foot-wide bulbous body of light green with blue stripes and spots. Jon-Tom took note of the fact that it wore only one black silk scarf tied around the left rear leg at the uppermost joint.

The visitor was followed closely by a second, smaller spider. This one was an electric maroon with a single large gray rectangle on its abdomen. A third spider squeezed into their cell, barely clearing the passageway. It was gray-brown with white circles on cephalothorax and abdomen and had shockingly red legs. All wore only the single black scarf on identical limbs.

The three spiders stood confronting the wary knot of warmlanders.

"what the hell," said the first spider who'd entered, in a tone so high and flighty it was barely intelligible, "are you?"

"Diplomatic ambassadors," Clothahump informed them, with as much dignity as he could muster under the circumstances.

The little arachnid bobbed his head in that maybe yes, maybe no movement Jon-Tom had come to recognize. "maybe you're diplomatic ambassadors to you," he said, "but you're just food to us."

"they look nice and soft," said the big one in a slightly deeper but still tenebrous voice. His body was a good three feet across, bulky, and with three foot legs. "diplomats or blasphemers, ambassadors or storage-stealers, what difference does it make?" He displayed bright red fangs. "dinner is dinner."

"You think so? Touch one of us again," said Jon-Tom warningly, "and I'll shove your fangs down your throat."

The first spider cocked multiple eyes at him. "will you now, half-limbed?" The latter was an apparent reference to Jon-Tom's disproportionately fewer number of limbs. "tell you a thing. if you can do that we'll treat you as something more than dinner. if you can't"—he pointed with a leg toward the shivering Flor—"we start with that one for an appetizer."

"Why her, why not me?"

The spider could not grin, but conveyed that impression nonetheless. "almost had a taste. she smells full of fluid."

It was too much for the terrified arachniphobe, that casual talk of being sucked dry like a lemon. She turned and vomited.

"there, you see?" said the spider knowingly.

Jon-Tom quelled his own rising nausea. He ignored the gagging sounds behind him to keep his attention on the big red-legged spider. It had scuttled off to the side, away from its companions.

"you can have me if you can get me," it taunted.

"Same goes for me," said Jon-Tom grimly. "Leave the others out of this."

"we'll do that for a start." The spider was sitting back on his hind legs, waving the four front limbs ritualistically as it bobbed from side to side. Then it brought them down and rushed forward.

It had been a while since Jon-Tom had practiced any karate. Four years, in fact. But he'd become reasonably good before he'd quit. What he hadn't learned was how to attack something with eight limbs. Not that they would matter if the spider got those red fangs into him. Even if this particular arachnid's venom wasn't very toxic, the shock alone might be enough to kill.

The attacker's intent seemed to involve throwing as many legs as possible at its prey in order to distract him while the fangs bit home.

It was possible the spider wouldn't expect an attack. If the eight limbs were confusing to Jon-Tom, then perhaps his human length and long legs might equally puzzle the spider. Besides, the best defense is a good offense, he reasoned.

So he ran at his opponent instead of away from it, keeping his eyes on his target as he was supposed to and trying hard to remember. Up on the opposite foot, kick out with the right, left leg tucked under the other.

Agile claws reacted quickly, but not quickly enough. They scraped at Jon-Tom's neck and arms. They didn't prevent his right foot from landing hard between the eight eyes (there was no chin to aim for).

The impact traveled up Jon-Tom's leg. He landed awkwardly on his left foot, stumbled, and fought desperately to regain his balance.

It wasn't necessary. The spider had stopped in its tracks. Making mewling noises horribly reminiscent of a lost kitten, it sat down, rolled over on its back, and clawed at its face. The leg movements slowed like a clock winding down. Jon-Tom waited nearby, panting hard in a defensive posture.

The leg movements finally ceased. Green goo dripped from between the eyes, which no longer shone in the lamplight. The spider who'd entered the cell first scrabbled over to its motionless, larger companion.

"damme," he breathed in disbelief, "you've killed jogand."

Jon-Tom caught his breath, frowned. "What do you mean, I've killed him? I didn't kick him hard enough to kill him."

"dead for sure, for sure," said the smaller spider, turning a respectful gaze on the man. Blood continued to seep from the wound.

Fragile exoskeleton, Jon-Tom thought in relief and astonishment. Come to think of it, he'd seen a lot of clubs here. They'd be very effective against recalcitrant arachnids. Instead of a glass jaw, the spider possessed a glass body.

Or maybe he'd just slipped in a lucky blow. Either way . . .

He glared warily at the remaining pair. "No hard feelings?"

The first spider gazed distastefully down at his dead companion. "jogand always was the impulsive type."

They were distracted by a clattering in the corridor. A spider they did not recognize approached the webwork silk bars. He was not the skinny one with all the ribbons. As they watched silently, he poured the contents of a pear-shaped bottle on a section of the bars. They began to dissolve like so much hot jelly.

Another figure emerged from the shadows to stand just behind the jailer: Ananthos.

"i am terribly sorry," he told them, waving many legs at the cell. "this was done without higher orders or good knowledge. the individual responsible has already been punished."

"Blimey but if we didn't think you'd sold us over!" said a relieved Mudge.

Ananthos looked outraged. "i would never do such a thing. i take my responsibilities seriously, as you well should know." Then he noticed the corpse on the cell floor, looked back into the cell.

" 'Twere 'is wizardship there," said Mudge, indicating Jon-Tom. Ananthos bowed respectfully toward the human.

"a good piece of work. i am sorrowful for the trouble caused you."

A pathway large enough to allow egress had been made in the bars. Ananthos' companions moved aside as the prisoners exited.

The small spider tried to follow Clothahump out and was promptly clobbered behind the head by one of the guards. The spider shrank back into the cell.

"not you," muttered the guard. "warmlanders only."

"why not? aren't we part of their party now?" He hooked foreclaws over the rapidly hardening new bars two of the guards were spinning.

"you are common criminals," said Ananthos tiredly. "as you must know, common criminals are not permitted audience with the grand webmistress."

The little spider hesitated. His head cocked toward Jon-Tom. "you're going to see the grand webmistress?"

"That's what we've come all this way for."

"then we'll stay right here. you can't force us to come!" And both spiders drew back behind the bleeding corpse of their dead companion, scuttled for the tunnel leading to their own cell.

Their sudden shift sparked uncomfortable thoughts in Jon-Tom's mind as he followed Talea's twisting form up the stairwell they'd so recently been hustled down.

"What do you suppose he meant by that?" She looked back down at him and shrugged.

"i told you i could do nothing for you beyond bringing you to gossameringue," Ananthos explained. "it must be considered that the webmistress not only might not assist you but may condemn you to rejoin those rabble in their hole," and he gestured with a leg back down the stairs.

"So we could find ourselves right back in jail?" asked Flor.

"or worse." He continued to point downward with the waving, silk-swathed leg. "i hope you will not hold what occurred down there against me. a chamberlaine overstepped her authority."

"We know it wasn't your fault," said Clothahump reassuringly. Pog seemed about to add something but kept his mouth shut at a warning glance from the wizard.

Before long they had retraced their ignominious descent and stood before the high, arching doorway flanked by the two immense guards. A small blue spider met them there. He was full of apologies and anxiety.

When he'd finished bobbing and weaving, he beckoned them to follow.

The chamber they entered was high and dark. A few narrow windows were set in the rear wall. Only a couple of lamps burned uncertainly in their wall holders, shedding reluctant amber light on vast lounges and pillows of richly colored silk. It did not occur to anyone to wonder what they were stuffed with.

More surprising was the large quantity of decorative art. There were sculptures in metal and wood, in stone and embalmed spider silk. Gravity-defying mobiles stretched from ceiling to floor. Some were cleverly lit from within by tiny lamps or candles. Some of the sculpture was representational, but a surprising amount was abstract. Silken parallelograms vied with stress patterns for floor space. The colors of both sculptures and furniture were subdued in shade but bright of hue: orange, crimson, black and purple, deep blues and deeper greens. There were no pastels.

"the grand webmistress Oll bids you welcome, strangers from a far land," the little spider piped. "i leave you now." He turned and scurried quickly out the doorway.

"i must go also," said Ananthos. He hesitated, then added, "some of your ideas mark you almost akin to the eternal weave. perhaps we shall meet again some day."

"I hope so," said Jon-Tom, whispering without knowing why. He watched as the spider followed the tiny herald in retreat.

They walked farther into the chamber. Clothahump put hands on nonexistent hips, murmured impatiently, "Well, where are you, madam?"

"up here!" The voice was hardly stentorian, but it was a good deal richer than the breathy weaver whispers they'd had to contend with thus far; chocolate mousse compared to chocolate pudding. It seemed the voice had slight but definite feminine overtones, but Jon-Tom decided he might be anthropomorphizing as he stood there in the near darkness.

"here," said the voice once more. The eyes of the visitors traveled up, up, and across the ceiling. High in the right-hand corner of the chamber was a vast, sparkling mass of the finest silk. It had been inlaid with jewels and bits of metal in delicate mosaic until it sucked all the light out of the two feeble lamps and threw it back in the gaze of any fortunate onlookers. The silk itself had been arranged in tiny abstract geometric forms that fit together as neatly as the pieces of a silver puzzle.

A vast black globe slid over the side of the silken bower. On a thin thread it fell slowly toward the chamber floor, like a huge drop of petroleum. It was not as large as the massive tarantulas guarding the entryway, but it was far bulkier than Ananthos and most of the other arachnid inhabitants of Gossameringue. The bulbous abdomen was nearly three feet across. Save for a brilliant and all too familiar orange-red hourglass splashed across the underside of the abdomen, the body appeared to be encased in black steel.

Multiple black eyes studied the visitors expressionlessly. The spinnerets daintily snipped the abdomen free from the trailing silk cable. Settling down on tiptoe, the eight legs folded neatly beneath the body. Then the enormous black widow was resting comfortably on a sprawling red cushion, preening one fang with a leg tip.

"i am the grand webmistress Oll," the polite horror informed them. "you must excuse the impoliteness of cleaning my mouth, but my husband was in for breakfast and we have only just now finished."

Jon-Tom knew something of the habits of black widows. He eyed the jeweled boudoir above and shuddered.

Clothahump, unfazed by the Grand Webmistress' appearance, stepped briskly to the fore. Once again he laid out the reason for their extraordinary journey. He detailed their experiences on the Swordsward, in the Earth's Throat, related the magical crossing of Helldrink. Even in his dry, mechanical voice the retelling was impressive.

The Grand Webmistress Oll listened intently, occasionally permitting herself a whispered expression of awe or appreciation. Clothahump rambled on, telling of the peculiar new evil raised by the Plated Folk and their imminent invasion of the warmlands.

Finally he finished the tale. It was silent in the chamber for several minutes.

Oll's first reaction was not expected. "you! come a little nearer." She finally had to raise a leg and point, since it was impossible to tell exactly where those lidless black eyes were looking.

She pointed at Jon-Tom.

His hesitation was understandable. After the initial shock of their appearance, he'd been able to overcome his instinctive reactions to the spiders. He'd done so to a point where he'd grown fond of Ananthos and his companions, to a point where he could allow curious spiderlings to clamber over his body. Even the three antisocial types they'd encountered in the cells below had seemed more abhorrent for their viciousness than their shape.

But the dark, swollen body before him was representative of a kind he'd been taught to fear since childhood. It brought to the surface fears that laughed at logic and reason.

A hand was nudging him from behind. He looked down, saw Clothahump staring anxiously at him.

"come, come, fellow," said the Webmistress. "i've just eaten." A feathery, thick laugh. "you look as though you'd be all bone, anyway."

Jon-Tom moved closer. He tried to see the Webmistress in a matronly cast. Still, he couldn't keep his gaze entirely away from the dark fangs barely hidden in their sheaths. Just a graze from one would kill him instantly, even if the widow's venom had been somewhat diluted by her increased size.

A black leg, different from any he'd yet encountered in Gossameringue, touched his shoulder. It traveled down his arm, then his side. He could feel it through his shirt and pants.

Close now, he was able to note the delicate and nearly transparent white silks that encompassed much of the shining black body. They had been embroidered with miniature scenes of Gossameringue life. Attire impressive and yet sober enough for a queen, he thought.

"what is your name, fellow?"

"Jon-Tom. At least, that's what my friends call me."

"i will not trouble you with my entire name," was the reply. "it would take a long time and you would not remember it anyhow. you may call me Oll." The head shifted past him. "so may you all. as you are not citizens of the scuttleteau, you need show no special deference to me."

Again the clawed, shiny leg moved down his front. He did not flinch. "do you also support the claims and statements of the small hard-shelled one?" Another leg gestured at Clothahump.

"I do."

"well, then." She rested quietly for a moment. Then she glanced up once more at Jon-Tom. "why should we care what happens to the peoples of the warmlands?"

"You have to," Clothahump began importantly, "because it is evident that if—"

"be silent." She waved a leg imperiously at the wizard. "i did not ask you."

Clothahump obediently shut up. Not because he was afraid of the large, poisonous body but because pragmatism is a virtue all true wizards share.

"now, you may answer," she said more softly to Jon-Tom.

History, he told himself, trying not to stare at those fangs so near. Try to see in this massive, deadly form the same grace and courtesy you've observed in the other arachnids you've met. To answer the question, remember your history. Because if you don't . . .

"It's quite easily explained. Are not you and the Plated Folk ancient enemies?"

"we bear no love for the inhabitants of the greendowns, nor they for us," was the ready reply.

"Isn't it clear, then? If they are successful in conquering all of the warmlands, what's to prevent them from coming for you next?"

There was dark humor lacing the reply. "if they do there will be such a mass feasting as gossameringue has never seen!"

Jon-Tom thought back to something Clothahump had told him. "Oll, in thousands of years and many, many attempts the Plated Folk have failed even to get past the Jo-Troom Gate, which blocks the Pass leading from the Greendowns to the warmlands."

"that is a name and place i have heard of, though no weaver has ever been there."

"Despite this, Clothahump, who is the greatest of wizards and whose opinion I believe in all such things, insists this new magic the Plated Folk have obtained control of may enable them to finally overthrow the peoples of the warmlands. After hundreds of previous failures.

"If they can do that after thousands of years of failure, why should they not do so to you as well? A thousand swords can't fight a single magic."

"we have our own wizards to defend us," Oll replied, but she was clearly troubled by Jon-Tom's words. She looked past him. "how do i know you are all the wizard this fellow says you are?"

Clothahump looked distressed. "Oh ye gods of blindness that cloud the vision of disbelieving mortals, not another demonstration!"

"it will be painless." She turned and called to the shadows. "ogalugh!"

A frail longlegs came tottering out from behind a high pile of cushions. Jon-Tom wondered if he'd been listening back there all along or if he'd just recently arrived. He barely had the strength to carry the thin silks that enveloped his upper body and ran in spirals down his legs.

He looked at Clothahump. "what is the highest level of the plenum?"

"Thought."

"by what force may one fly through the airs atop a broom?"

"Antigravity."

"what is the way of turning common base metals into gold?"

Clothahump's contemptuous and slightly bored expression suddenly paled.

"Well, uh, that is of course no easy matter. You require the entire formula, of course, and not merely the descriptive term applied to the methodology."

"of course," agreed the swaying inquisitor.

"Base metal into gold, my . . . it has been a while since I've had occasion to think on that."

Quit stalling, Jon-Tom urged the wizard silently. Give them an answer, any answer. Then the truth will come out in the arguing. But say *something*.

"You need four lengths of sea grass, a pentagram with the number six carefully set in each point, the words for shifting electron valences, and . . . and . . ."

The Grand Webmistress, the sorcerer Ogalugh, and the other inhabitants of the chamber waited anxiously.

"And you need . . . you need," and the wizard looked up so assuredly it seemed impossible he'd forgotten something so basic for even a moment, "a pinch of pitchblende."

Ogalugh turned to face the expectant Oll, spoke while bobbing and weaving his head. "our visitor is in truth, a wizard webmistress. how great i cannot say from three questions, but he is of at least the third order." Clothahump harrumphed but confined his protest to that.

"none but the most experienced and knowledgeable among the weavers of magic would know the last formula." He tottered over to rest a feathery leg on the turtle's shoulder.

"i welcome you to gossameringue as a colleague."

"Thank you." Clothahump nodded importantly, began to look pleased with himself.

The longlegs addressed Oll. "it may be that these visitors are all that they claim, webmistress. the fact that they have made so perilous a journey without assurance of finding at its end so much as a friendly welcome is proof alone of high purpose. i fear therefore that the words of my fellow wizard are truth."

"a troublesome thing if true," said the webmistress, "a most troublesome thing if true." She eyed Jon-Tom. "there has been hatred and emnity between the plated folk and the people of the scuttleteau for generations untold. if they can conquer the inhabitants of the warmlands then it may be, as you say, that they can also threaten us." She paused in thought, then climbed lithely to her feet.

"it will be as it must be, though heretofore it has never been." She stood close by Jon-Tom, the hump of her abdomen nearly reaching his shoulder. "the weavers will join the people of the warmlands. we will do so not to help you but to help ourselves. better the children of the scuttleteau have company in dying." She turned to face Clothahump.

"bearer of bad truths, how much time do we have?"

"Very little, I would suspect."

"then i will order the calling put out everywhere on the scuttleteau this very day. it will take time to assemble the best fighters from the far reaches. yet that is not the foremost of our problems. it is one perhaps you might best solve, since the proof of your abilities as travelers is not to be denied." She studied the little group of visitors.

"how in the name of the eternal weave are we to get *to* the jo-troom gate? we know only that it lies south to southwest of the scuttleteau. we cannot go back through the earth's throat, the way you've come to us. even if so large a group could cross helldrink, my people will not chance the chanters."

"Offspring of the Massawrath," Caz murmured to Mudge. "Can't say as I blame them. I'm still not sure it wasn't blind luck that got us through there, not sensible actions."

"I don't want to go back myself," said Talea.

"Nor me, Master," said Pog, hanging from a strand of dry silk overhead.

"Then it follows that if we cannot return by our first route we must make a new one southward."

"through the mountains?" Ogalugh did not sound enthusiastic.

"Are they so impassable then?" Clothahump asked him.

"no one knows. we are familiar with the mountains of the scuttleteau and to some small extent those surrounding us, but we are not fond of sharp peaks and unmelting snows. many would perish on such a journey, unless a good route exists. if one does, we do not know of it."

"so it will be up to you, experienced travelers, to seek out such a path," stated the queen.

"your pardon, webmistress," said the spindly sorcerer, "but there are a people who might know such a way, though they would have no need or use of it themselves."

"why must wizards always talk in riddles? whom do you speak of, ogalugh?"

"the people of the iron cloud."

Rich, whispery laughter filled the chamber. "the people of the iron cloud indeed! they will have nothing to do with *anyone.*"

"that is so, webmistress, but our visitors are experienced travelers of the mind as well as the land, for have they not this very instant convinced us to join with them?"

"we are but independent," Oll replied. "the people of the iron cloud are paranoid."

"rumor and innuendo spread by unsuccessful traders who have returned from their land empty-clawed. it is true they are less than social, but that does not mean they will not listen." He turned to face Jon-Tom.

"they are much like some of you, friend. like yourself, and those two there," he pointed to Mudge and Caz, "and that one above," and he pointed now at Pog.

"They sound most interesting," said Clothahump. "I confess I know nothing of them."

"Are they good fighters?" Flor wondered. "Maybe we can get more out of them than directions."

"they are great warriors," admitted Ogalugh readily. "but you speak so facilely of making allies of them. you do not understand. they are interested in nothing save themselves, will support no causes but their own."

"That's just what we were told to expect of the Weavers," Jon-Tom said with becoming boldness.

"but we are sensible enough to see advantage and necessity where they occur," Oll argued back. "the people of the iron cloud, i am told, are unaffected by events elsewhere. they are protected by their indifference and their isolation."

"Nothing is safe from the evil the Plated Folk build," said Clothahump somberly.

"i am already convinced, wizard," she said. "convince the ironclouders: not me. it will be enough if they can show our fighters the way through the southern peaks."

"I have some small diplomatic skill," said Clothahump immodestly. "I believe we can persuade them to do that, at least."

"perhaps. you must, or we can be of no help to you and your peoples, no matter what the plated ones decide to do. we will march when ready, but if we cannot find a way, we will be forced to turn back.

"i will send from among the weavers a personal representative. perhaps the proof that we have joined with you will help to convince the people of the iron cloud. in any case, someone will be necessary to come back to report on the results of your mission, be it successful or not."

"Not to preempt your prerogatives, Oll," said Caz carefully, "but if we might be permitted to choose the representative . . . ?"

"Sure," said Jon-Tom quickly, turning to face the Webmistress. "Would it be okay if a river guard named Ananthos served as your representative?"

"ananthos . . . i do not know the name. a common river guard, you say?"

"Yes. He's the one who brought us here."

"a common river guard of uncommon discernment, then. but still, it should be someone of higher rank."

"Please, Oll," Jon-Tom said, "rank will mean nothing to these Ironclouders if what you say of their nature is correct. And Ananthos is familiar with us. We know we can get along with one another."

"a sound recommendation, i suppose." She sighed and that whole globular black mass quivered. "it is the common soldiers who will decide this battle to come, as they do all such battles. perhaps it is fitting that one of their rank be our ambassador. as you say, it will likely not matter to the ironclouders.

"very well. you may have this ananthos. he will go with you as would one of my own children. uzmentap!"

"yes my lady, yes my lady?" A tiny adult spider scurried into the chamber, the same one who had admitted them a little while earlier.

"put out the word to all the ends of the scuttleteau, to the uppermost flanks of the mountains and the bottoms of the rivers, to all the believers in the weave and to all who would defend their webs against the plated folk, that a *temporary* alliance has been struck with the people of the warmlands to help them drive the plated beasts back into their putrid hole of a homeland once and for all!"

"it shall be done, my lady," said the herald quickly. She dismissed him with a wave of one leg and he hurried away to do the bidding.

"we will move as soon as we have word from your messenger ananthos," she told them. "we will go hopefully with a known route and will try our best if none such is available. but i will not send the best of the weave over the high snows to a cold death."

"We know that," said Clothahump gratefully. "You can't be expected to sacrifice yourselves to no purpose. But don't worry. We'll convince these people to show us a way."

Jon-Tom did not think it a judicial time to mention the possibility that such a path might not exist.

"it is in your claws now. i will have this ananthos found and will give him my personal instructions and the scarf of ambassadorial rank. will you require an escort?"

"We've gotten this far on our own," Talea pointed out. "From what you say these Ironclouders aren't hostile, just stubborn." She patted the sword at her hip. "We can take care of ourselves."

"i did not mean to imply otherwise. i will see that you are well supplied with food and—" She broke off at the twisted expression on Flor's face, one that was sufficiently intense and abrupt to transcend interspecies differences. "perhaps you had best see to your own provisioning, at that. list what you wish and i will see it is provided. i had forgotten for a moment that you partake of nourishment in a fashion somewhat different from ours."

"Our marital habits are a little different, too." Jon-Tom glanced significantly toward the bejeweled boudoir.

"so i have heard. honor is a strange thing. sometimes it is better to die happy and honored than to live miserably and unrespected. and you do not consider the effects such repeated matings have on my own mind. a burdensome thing. i am not permitted a lifetime of happiness but instead short periods followed by regretful melancholy. tradition must be upheld, however." She waved a leg magnanimously.

"all that is required will be provided. i only hope that we have sufficient time to prepare and that we are granted a path by which to proceed."

"We are most grateful," said Clothahump, bowing slightly. "You are a Grand Webmistress indeed."

"it is no compliment to say that one can see the truth." She waved several legs. "good fortune to you, newfound friends."

The visitors began to file out of the chamber. Jon-Tom got halfway to the portal, then turned and walked back to her.

"the audience is at an end," Oll told him somewhat less than politely.

"I'm sorry. But I have to know something. Then I'll leave you to your privacy."

Fathomless eyes regarded him quietly. "ask then."

"Why did you single me out to talk with, instead of Clothahump or Caz or one of the others?"

"why? oh, because of your delightful and inspiring selection of garb. it marks you clearly as a superior being to your companions, wizardly talents notwithstanding."

Turning, she walked rhythmically back to stand below the royal bower. Reattaching fresh silk to the dangling cable, she promptly climbed up and disappeared behind the barrier of gems and silken embroidery.

Jon-Tom was left to consider his bright black leathern pants, the matching boots and dark shirt.

It was only much later, as they were departing Gossameringue with Ananthos in the lead, that Jon-Tom had the startling and unsettling thought that the Grand Webmistress might have been considering him as material for something besides conversation. . . .

XI

It was terrible in the mountains.

Higher peaks towered to east and west, but as they moved south they were traversing the windswept flanks of Zaryt's Teeth, where they merged with the lower but still impressive mountains from which the greater heights sprang. It was bitingly cold. Soon they were walking not on rock or earth but on snow so dry and fresh it crunched like sugar underfoot.

On the third day after leaving the Scuttleteau and its gentle rivers and warm forests they encountered snow flurries. The day after that they were stumbling through a modest blizzard. Oll's fears that the southern range might prove unnegotiable seemed well founded.

Mudge and Caz suffered least of all, in contrast to their companions who did not enjoy the benefits of a personal fur coat.

Everyone profited from the example set by the stoic Bribbens. Though highly susceptible to the cold he trudged patiently along, silent and uncomplaining. Oftentimes his bulbous eyes were all that could be seen outside the thick clothing the Weavers had provided. He kept his discomforts to himself, and so his companions were shamed into doing the same.

Working with only rumor and supposition, the least reliable of guides, Ananthos somehow managed to pick a path southward.

They had made little progress in five days of hard marching when Jon-Tom had his idea. A temporary camp was established in the shelter of a small cave. Jon-Tom and Flor led the others in the hunt for suitable saplings and green vines. These were then woven together with spider silk dispensed by Ananthos.

With the aid of the new snowshoes their pace improved considerably. So did their spirits, boosted not only by their improved method of travel but by the hysterical image Ananthos presented as he shuffled along on six of the carefully wrought shoes, picking his way as uncertainly and carefully as a water strider trying to cross a pool of mud.

They also improved Bribbens' morale. While they kept him no warmer, the enormous shoes on his webbed feet gave him tremendous stability.

Jon-Tom moved up to march alongside Ananthos. It was the morning of their eighth day in the mountains.

"Could we have missed it?" His breath made a cloud in front of his face. The cold fought implacably for a route through his clothes. The crude parka hastily fashioned by the Weavers was no substitute for a goose-down jacket. There was a real danger of freezing to death if they didn't find warmer country soon.

"i don't think so." Ananthos indicated the precious scroll he kept in a protective, watertight tube strapped to his rear left leg. "i can only rely on the chart the court historians made for us. no weaver has been this far south in many years. there was no reason for doing so and, for obvious reasons, no desire to do so."

"Then how can you be so sure we haven't passed it?"

"i can be only as sure as the charts. but the tales say if one but continues south, as we have, following the lowest route through the mountains, he will come upon the iron cloud. that is, if the tales are true."

"And if there is an iron cloud at all," Jon-Tom mumbled.

A leg touched his waist, but Ananthos' reassurances were stolen by the wind.

Despair is sometimes the preface to hope. On the ninth day the weather took pity on them. The snow ceased, the storm clouds betook themselves elsewhere, and the temperature warmed considerably, though it did not rise above freezing.

As if to compensate they were confronted with another danger: snow blindness. The brilliant Alpine sun ricochetted off snowbanks and glacier fronts, turning everything to shocking, adamantine white.

They managed to fashion crude shades from Ananthos' supply of scarves. Even so they were forced to keep their gaze to the ground and their senses at highest alert, lest the next snowbank turn out to be just the fatal side of some nearly hidden chasm.

Another day and they started downward.

Two weeks after departing Gossameringue they found the iron cloud.

They were climbing a slight rise, bisecting a saddle between two slopes. For days they had seen little color but varying shades of white, so the highly reflective black that suddenly confronted them was physically shocking.

Across a rocky slope of crumbled granite patched with snow was a mountainside that appeared to have been deluged with frozen tar. It was encrusted with ice and snow in occasional crevices.

Clearly the immense, smooth masses of black which jutted like an oily waterfall from the flank of the mountainside were composed of material much tougher than tar. They resembled a succession of monstrous bubbles piled one atop another without bursting. Holes pockmarked the blackness.

It was the metallic luster that led Flor to exclaim in surprise, *"Por dios, es* hematite."

"What?" Jon-Tom turned a puzzled expression on her.

"Hematite, Jon-Tom. It's an iron ore that occurs naturally in formations like that," and she pointed to the mountainside, "though I never learned of any approaching such size. The formation is called mammary, or reniform, I think."

"What is she saying?" asked Clothahump with interest.

"That the 'iron' part of the name Ironcloud is taken from reality and not poetry. Come on!"

They descended the gentle slope on the other side of the saddle and made their way across the stony plateau. The huge black extrusion hung above them, millions of tons of near-iron as secure as the mountain itself. Viewed against the surrounding snow and sky, it did indeed look much like a cloud.

But where were the fabled inhabitants, he wondered? What could they be like? The holes which pierced the masses overhead hinted at their possible abode, but though the party surveyed them intently there was no hint of motion from within.

"It looks abandoned," said Talea, staring upward.

"Don't see a soul," Pog commented from nearby.

They slid their burdensome backpacks off while examining the inaccessible caves above. Climbing the granite wall was out of the question. Not only did the massive formation overhang but the smooth iron offered little purchase. Without sophisticated mountaineering gear there was no way they could reach even the lowest of the caves.

It was clear enough how the invisible inhabitants managed the feat, however. From the rim of each cave opening hung a long vine. Knots were tied in each roughly six inches apart. The profusion of dangling vines, swaying gently in the mountain breeze, gave the formation the look of a dark man with a beard.

The problem arose from the fact that the shortest cable-vine was a good two hundred feet long. No one thought themself capable of the combination of strength and dexterity necessary to make the climb. Talea considered it, but the thinness of the vine precluded the attempt. Whoever used the vines weighed a good deal less than any in the frustrated party of visitors.

Mudge was agile, but he wasn't fond of climbing. Ananthos was clearly too large to enter the hole, though he stood the best chance of rising to the height.

"We waste time on peripheral argument," Clothahump finally snorted at them, when he was at last able to get a word in. "Pog!"

Everyone looked around, but the bat was nowhere to be seen.

" 'Ere 'e is!" Mudge pointed toward a large boulder.

They ran to the spot to find the bat squatting resolutely on the gravel behind the rock. He looked up at them with determined bat eyes.

"No way am I going up dere and sticking my nose in one of dose black pits. No telling what might take a notion to bit it off."

"Come now, mate," said Mudge reasonably, adjusting his parka top, "be sensible. You're the only arboreal among us. If I didn't think that vine'd bust under me weight, I'd give a climb a good try. But why the 'ell should one o' us 'ave t' risk that, when you could be up there and back in a bloody minute or two without so much as strainin' your wings?"

"An accurate evaluation of our situation." Caz positioned his monocle tighter over his left eye. He'd steadfastly refused to surrender the affectation, even at the risk of losing the monocle in the snow. "You know, you really should have been up there and back already, on your own initiative."

"Initiative, hell!" Pog flapped his wings angrily. "One more display of 'initiative' from dis crazy bunch and we'll find ourselves meat on somebody's table."

"Now Pog," Clothahump began warningly.

"Yeah, I know, I know, boss. Go to it or ya'll turn me into a human or worse." He sighed, unfurled his wings experimentally.

"perhaps i could get up there—at least if i can't fit inside, i could attach to a hole above and hang down to look in." Ananthos sounded awkward, wanting to contribute.

"You know that surface is too slick for you to get a hold on, and if you could you probably couldn't get in and move around in there. Your leg span is too wide. Besides, I think Pog should have a chance at this." Clothahump was firm.

"A chance at what? Meeting my maker in a cold hole in da sky?"

Ananthos looked pained, but Jon-Tom gave Pog encouragement with his eyes.

"If you're all determined den to see poor Pog get his t'roat laid open, I expect I'll have ta be about da business. I warn ya, dough, if I don't come back alive I'll come back dead and haunt ya all to an early grave."

"Don't take any chances, Pog," Jon-Tom advised him. "Probably you won't find anything, or anyone. Just fly up and check out one or two caves, see if this place is really as deserted as it looks. If it is, maybe you'll learn the reason why."

"Maybe one of da reasons is hiding in one of dose caves!" snapped the worried bat, gesturing upward with a wing thumb.

"If so then don't hang around to argue with it," said Talea. "You're going up to look, not to fight. Get your butt back down here as fast as you can."

Pog hovered just above the ground, lit on top of the boulder he'd been hiding behind. "No need ta worry 'bout that, Talea lady." He pulled his knife from its back sheath and slipped it between his jaws.

"Wish me luck," he mumbled around the blade.

"There is no need for luck when intelligence and good judgment are exercised," said Clothahump.

Pog made a rude noise, flapped his wings, and launched himself from the crest of the rock. He dropped, skimmed inches above sharp gravel, and then began to climb, using the warm currents rising from the bare plateau to ascend in a steady spiral.

"You think he'll be okay?" Flor shielded her eyes from the glare and squinted at the sky where a black shape was growing gradually smaller. Pog now looked like a toy kite against the pure blue curtain overhead.

"Instinct is a powerful aid to self-preservation."

"Oh?" she said with just a hint of sarcasm. "What book did that come out of?"

Jon-Tom was also leaning back and looking toward the lip of the iron cloud. He just swallowed Flor's remark.

Hemarist, da tall human lady had called it. No, dat wasn't right. Hema . . . Hema*tite*. Like in a tight spot, which is what you gots yourself into, Pog thought to himself. He was high above the rocky plain now. The figures of his companions were sharp and distinct against the gray gravel. He could tell they were watching him.

Waiting ta see how I get it, he thought miserably.

He circled before the lowest of the globular projections. His personal sonar told him nothing moved inside any of the several caves he'd flown past. That at least was a promising sign. Maybe the place *was* deserted.

Black iron, huh? It looked like a vast black face to him, with no eyes but lots of little mouths ready to swallow you, swallow you whole. Pretty soon he was going to have to stick his head into one of 'em.

Why couldn't ya have listened ta your mudder, he berated himself, and gone inta da mail soivice, or crafts transport, or aerial cop work?

But nah, ya had ta fall hard for a pretty piece o' fluff who won't give ya da time o' night, den get stinking drunk and apprentice yourself ta a half senile, sadistic, hard-shelled, hard-headed old fart of a wizard in da faint hope he'll eventually turn ya inta something more presentable ta your lady love.

He thought of her again, of the smoothly elegant blend of feathers from back to tail, of the slightly cruel yet delicate curve of beak, and of those magnificent, piercing yellow eyes which turned his guts to paste when they passed over him. Ah, Uleimee, if ya only knew what I'm suffering for ya!

He caught himself, broke the thought like a ceramic cup. If she knew what you was suffering she wouldn't give a flyin' fuck about it. She's the type who appreciates results, not well-meaning failures.

So gather what's left of your small store of courage, bat, and be about your job. And don't t'ink about whether when your time's up, old Clothamuck will have forgotten da formula for transforming ya.

But, oh my, dat cave mouth looming just ahead is dark! Empty, dough. His eyes as well as his sonar told him that. He fluttered next to the opening for a while, wrestling with the knowledge that if he didn't explore at least one of the caves his mentor would simply force him to return and try again.

He drifted cautiously inside. He sensed the echo of his wing beats pushing air off the tunnel walls. Then he settled down to walk.

The floor of the cave was carpeted with clean straw, carefully braided into intricately patterned mats. They appeared to be in good repair. If this iron warren was abandoned, it hadn't been so for long.

The tunnel soon expanded into a larger, roughly oval-shaped chamber. It was filled with a peculiar assortment of furniture. There were lounges but no chairs, and high-backed perches. The lounges suggested creatures that walked, as did the climbing vines dangling outside each cave opening, but the high-backs pointed to arboreals like himself. He shook his head. Deductive thinking was not his strong suit.

The utensils were also confusing rather than enlightening. A little light reached the chamber from the cave opening, but his sonar was still searching the surroundings as though it were pitch dark. His heart beat almost as rapidly. Finish dis, he told himself frantically. Finish it, and get out.

Several additional chambers branched from the back of the one he was studying. He would begin with the one immediately on his right and work his way through them. Then Clothahump couldn't say he'd made only a superficial inspection and order him to return.

It turned out to be a pantry-kitchen arrangement. It was discouraging to find that whoever had lived in the cave was omnivorous. In addition to instruments for preparing meat and fruit there was also a surprising garbage pile of small insect carcasses and empty nuts.

It was an eclectic and indiscriminate diet. Perhaps it also included bats. He shuddered, drew his wings tighter around his small body. One more room, he told himself. One more, and den if da boss wants more info he can damn well climb up and look for himself.

He entered the next chamber, found more furniture and little else. He was ready to leave when something tickled his sonar. He turned.

A pair of huge, glowing yellow eyes stared down at him. Their owner was at least seven feet tall and each of those luminous orbs was as big around as a human face. Pog stuttered but couldn't squeeze out word or shout.

"Hoooooooo," said the voice beneath those fathomless eyes in a long, querulous, and slightly irritated tone, "the hell are yoooooo?"

Pog was backing toward the chamber exit. Something sharp and unyielding pricked his back.

"Tolafay asked you a question, interloper! Better answer him." The new voice was completely different from the first, high and almost human.

Pog glanced over his shoulder, saw eyes not as large as the first pair he'd encountered but larger still in proportion to the body of their owner. Four yellow eyes, four malevolent little angry suns, swam in a dizzying circle around his head. He started to slump.

The sharp thing moved, poked him firmly in the side. "And don't faint on us, interloper, or I'll see your body leaves your gizzard behind. . . ."

"What the devil's keeping him?" Jon-Tom stared with concern up at the cave where Pog had vanished.

"Maybe they go very deep into the mountainside," Talea suggested hopefully. "It may take him a while to get all the way in and all the way out again."

"Perhaps." Bribbens stared longingly at a small creek that flowed from the base of an icefall across the barren little plateau. "How I long for a boat again." He lifted one of his enormous, snowshoed feet. "Walking's beginning to get to me. No fit occupation for a riverman."

"If it's any consolation I'd rather be on a boat myself just now," said Jon-Tom.

Then Mudge was gesturing excitedly upward. "Ease off it, mates! 'Ere 'e comes!"

"And damned if he hasn't got company." Talea unsheathed her sword, stood ready and waiting for whatever might drop out of the sky.

Pog drifted down toward them, a black crepe-paper cutout against the bright sky. He was paced by a similar silhouette several times more massive, with a distinctly animate lump attached to its back.

Dozens of other fliers poured from the perforated cloud-cliff like water from a sieve. They did not descend but instead blended together to create a massive, threatening spiral above the plateau.

Talea reluctantly placed her sword back in its holder. "Doesn't look like they've hurt Pog. We might as well assume they're friendly, considering how badly we're outnumbered."

"Characteristic understatement, flame-fur." Caz's monocle waltzed with the sun as he craned his neck to inspect the soaring whirlpool overhead. "I make out at least two hundred of them. Size varies, but the shape is roughly the same. I think they're all owls. I've never heard of such a concentrated community of them as this, not even in Polastrindu, which has a respectable population of noctural arboreals."

"It is odd," Clothahump agreed. "They are antisocial and zealously guard their privacy, which fits with what the Weavers told us about the psychology of Ironcloud's inhabitants. Yet they appear to have established a community here."

Pog touched down on the high boulder he'd so recently tried to hide behind. The flier shadowing him braked ten-foot wings. The force of the backed air nearly knocked Flor off her feet.

The creature took a couple of dainty steps, ruffled its feathers, and stood staring at them. The high tufts atop the head identified this particular individual as a Great Horned Owl. Jon-Tom found himself more impressed with those great eyes, like pools of speculative sulfur, than by the creature's size.

The lump attached to its back, which even Caz had not been able to identify, now detached itself from the light, high-backed saddle it had been straddling. It slid decorative earmuffs down to its neck, unsnapped its poncho, and leaned against its companion's left wing.

Now the spiral high above started to break up. Most of the fliers returned to their respective caves in the hematite. A few assumed watchful positions.

Jon-Tom eyed the lemur standing close to the owl. It was no longer a mystery who made use of the thin, knotted vines fringing the cave mouths. With their diminutive bodies and powerful prehensile fingers and toes, the lemurs could travel up and down the cables as easily as Jon-Tom could circle an oval track.

Pog glided down from the crest of his boulder and sauntered over to rejoin his friends. "Dis guy's called Tolafay." He gestured with a wingtip at the glowering owl. "His skymate's named Malu."

The lemur stepped forward. He was barely three feet tall. "Your friend explained much to us."

"Yes. Quite a story it was, tooooo." The owl smoothed the folds of its white, green, and black kilt. "I'm not sure how much of it I believe," he added gruffly.

"We have managed to convince half a world," replied Clothahump impatiently. "Time grows short. Civilization teeters on the edge of the abyss. Surely I need not repeat our whole tale again?"

"I don't think you have to," said Malu. He indicated the watchful Ananthos. "The mere fact that a Weaver, citizen of a notoriously xenophobic state, is traveling as ally with you is proof enough that something truly extraordinary is going on."

"look who is calling another 'xenophobic,' " whispered Ananthos surlily.

"It had better be extraordinary," the owl grumbled. He used a flexible wing tip to wipe one saucer-sized eye. "You've awakened all of Ironcloud from its daily rest. The populace will require a reasonable explanation." He blinked, shielding his face as the sun emerged from behind a stray cloud.

"How you can live with that horrid light burning your eyes is something I'll never understand."

"Oh very well," said Clothahump with a sigh. "You will convey details of our situation to your leader or mayor or—"

"We have no single leader," said the owl, mildly outraged. "We have neither council nor congress. We coexist in peace, without the burdens imposed by noisome government."

"Then how do you make communal decisions?" Jon-Tom asked curiously.

The owl eyed him as though he represented a lower species. "We respect one another."

"There will be a feasting tonight," said Malu, trying to lighten the atmosphere. "We can discuss your request then."

"That's not necessary," said Flor.

"But it is," the lemur argued. "You see, we can welcome you either as enemies or as guests. There will be a feasting either way."

"I believe I follow your meaning." Caz spoke drily, eyeing Tolafay's razor-sharp beak, which was quite capable of snapping him in half. "I sincerely hope, then, that we can look forward to being greeted as guests. . . ."

They gathered that evening in a chamber far larger than any of the others. Jon-Tom wondered at the force, technological or natural, which could have hollowed such a space in the almost solid iron.

It was dimly lit by lamp but more brightly than usual in deference to the Ironclouders' vision-poor visitors. Trophy feathers and lizard skins decorated the curving walls. Nearly a hundred of the great owls of all species and sizes reveled in music and dance along with their lemur companions.

Their guests observed the spectacle of feathers and fur with pleasure. It was comfortably warm in the cave, the first time since departing Gossameringue any of them had been really warm.

The music was strange, though not as strange as its sources. Nearby a great white barn owl stood in pink-green kilt playing a cross between a tuba and a flute. It held the instrument firmly with flexible wing tips and one clawed foot, balancing neatly on the other while pecking out the melody with a precision no mere pair of lips could match.

Owls and lemurs spilled out on the great circular iron floor, dancing and spinning while their companions at the huge curved tables ate and drank their fill. It was wonderful to watch those great wings spinning and flaying at the air as the owls executed jigs and reels with their comparatively tiny but incredibly agile primate companions. Claws and tiny padded feet slipped and hopped in and around each other without missing a beat.

The night was half dead when Jon-Tom leaned over to ask Flor, "Where's Clothahump?"

"I don't know." She stopped sipping from the narrow-mouthed drinking utensil she'd been given. "Isn't he magnificent?" Her eyes were glowing almost as brightly as those of an acrobat performing incredible leaps before their table, his long middle fingers tracing patterns in the air. A beautiful female sifaka joined him, and the dance-gymnastics continued without a pause.

Jon-Tom put the question to the furry white host on his other side.

"I don't know either, my friend," said Malu. "I have not seen the hard-shelled oldster all evening."

"Don't worry yourself, Jon-Tom." Caz looked at him from another seat down. "Our wizard is rich in knowledge, but not rich in the ability to enjoy himself. Leave him to his private meditations. Who knows when again we will have an opportunity for such rare entertainment as this?" He gestured grandly toward the dancers.

But the concern took hold of Jon-Tom's thoughts and would not let go. As he surveyed the room, he saw no sign of Pog, either. That was still more unusual, familiar as he was with the bat's preferences. He should have been out on the floor, teasing and flirting with some lithesome screech owl. Yet he was nowhere about.

Jon-Tom's companions were having too good a time to notice his departure from the table. In response to his questions a potted tarsier with incredibly bloodshot eyes pointed toward a tunnel leading deeper into the mountainside. Jon-Tom hurried down it. Noise and music faded behind him.

He almost ran past the room when he heard a familiar moaning: the wizard's voice. He threw aside the curtain barring the entryway.

Lying on a delicate bunk that sagged beneath his weight was the wizard's bulky body. He'd withdrawn arms and legs into his shell so that only his head protruded. It bobbed and twisted in an unnerving parody of the head movements of the Weavers. Only the whites of his eyes showed. His glasses lay clean and folded on a nearby stool.

"Hush!" a voice warned him. Looking upward Jon-Tom saw Pog dangling from a lamp holder. The flickering wick behind him made his wings translucent.

"What is it?" Jon-Tom whispered, his attention on the lightly moaning wizard. "What's the matter?" The echoes of revelry reached them faintly. He no longer found the music invigorating. Something important was happening in this little room.

Pog gestured with a finger. "Da master lies in a trance I've seen only a few times before. He can't, musn't be disturbed."

So the two waited, watching the quivering, groaning shape in fascination. Pog occasionally fluttered down to wipe moisture from the wizard's open eyes, while Jon-Tom guarded the doorway against interruptions.

It is a terrible thing to hear an old person, human or otherwise, moan like that. It was the helpless, weak sound a sick child might make. From time to time there were snatches and fragments of nearly recognizable words. Mostly, though, the high singsong that filled the room was unintelligible nonsense.

It faded gradually. Clothahump settled like a fallen cake. His quivering and head-bobbing eased away.

Pog flapped his wings a couple of times, stretched, and drifted down to examine the wizard. "Da master sleeps now," he told the exhausted Jon-Tom. "He's worn out."

"But what was it all about?" the man asked. "What was the purpose of the trance?"

"Won't know till he wakes up. Got ta do it naturally. Dere's nothin' ta do but wait."

Jon-Tom eyed the comatose form uncertainly. "Are you sure he'll come out of it?"

Pog shrugged. "Always has before. He better. He owes me. . . ."

XII

Once there were inquiring words at the curtain and Jon-Tom had to go outside to explain them away. Time passed, the distant music faded. He slept.

A great armored spider was treading ponderously after him, all weaving palps and dripping fangs. Run as he might he could not outdistance it. Gradually his legs gave out, his wind failed him. The monster was upon him, leering down at his helpless, pinioned body. The fangs descended but not into his chest. Instead, they were picking off his fingers, one at a time.

"Now you can't play music anymore," it rumbled at him. "Now you'll have to go to law school . . . aha ha ha!"

A hand was shaking him. "Da master's awake, Jon-Tom friend."

Jon-Tom straightened himself. He'd been asleep on the floor, leaning back against the chamber wall. Clothahump was sitting up on the creaking wicker bed, rubbing his lower jaw. He donned his spectacles, then noticed Jon-Tom. His gaze went from the man to his assistant and back again.

"I now know the source," he told them brightly, "of the new evil obtained by the Plated Folk. I know now from whence comes the threat!"

Jon-Tom got to his feet, dusted at himself, and looked anxiously at the wizard. "Well, what is it?"

"I do not know."

"But you just said . . . ?"

"Yes, yes, but I do know and yet I don't." The wizard sounded very tired. "It is a mind. A wonderfully wise mind. An intelligence of a reach and depth I have never before encountered, filled with knowledge I cannot fathom. It contains mysteries I do not pretend to understand, but that it is dangerous and powerful is self-evident."

"That seems clear enough," said Jon-Tom. "What kind of creature is it? Whose head is it inside?"

"Ah, that is the part I do not know." There was worry and amazement in Clothahump's voice. "I've never run across a mind like it. One thing I was able to tell, I think." He glanced up at the tall human. "It's dead."

Pog hesitated, then said, "But if it's dead, how can it help da Plated Folk?"

"I know, I know," Clothahump grumbled sullenly, "it makes no sense. Am I expected to be instantly conversant with all the mysteries of the Universe!"

"Sorry," said Jon-Tom. "Pog and I only hoped that—"

"Forget it, my boy." The wizard leaned back against the black wall and waved a weary hand at him. "I learned no more than I'd hoped to, and hope remains where knowledge is scarce." He shook his head sadly.

"A mind of such power and ability, yet nonetheless as dead as the rock of this chamber. Of that I am certain. And yet Eejakrat of the Plated Folk has found a means by which he can make use of that power."

"A zombie," muttered Jon-Tom.

"I do not know the term," said Clothahump, "but I accept it. I will accept anything that explains this awful contradiction. Sometimes, my boy, knowledge can be more confusing than mere ignorance. Surely the universe holds still greater though no more dangerous contradictions than this inventive, cold mind." He reached a decision.

"Now that I am sensitized to this mind, I am confident we can locate it. We must find out whose it is and destroy him or her, for I had no sense of whether the possessor is male or female."

"But we can't do dat, Master," Pog argued, "because as you say dis brain is under da control of da great sorcerer Eejakrat, and Eejakrat stays in Cugluch."

"Capital city of the Plated Folk," Clothahump reminded Jon-Tom.

"Dat's right enough. So it's obvious dat we can't . . . we can't . . ." The words came to a halt as Pog's eyes grew wide as a lemur's.

"No, Master!" he muttered, his voice filled with dread. "We can't. We can't possibly!"

"On the contrary, famulus, it is quite possible that we can. Of course, I shall first discuss it with the rest of our companions."

"Discuss what?" Jon-Tom was afraid he already knew the answer.

"Why, traveling into Cugluch to find this evil and obliterate it, my boy. What else could a civilized being do?"

"What else indeed." Jon-Tom had resigned himself to going. Could this Cugluch be worse than the Earth's Throat? Pog seemed to think so, but then Pog was terrified of his own shadow.

Clothahump's strength had returned. He slid off the bed, started for the doorway. "We must consult the rest of our party."

"They may not all be in a condition to understand," Jon-Tom warned him. "We have generous hosts, you know."

"A night of harmless pleasure is good for the soul now and then, my boy. Though it should never descend to unconsciousness. I am pleased to see that you have retained control of yourself."

"So far," said Jon-Tom fervently, "but after what you've just proposed, I may change my mind."

"It will not be so bad," said the wizard, clapping him on the waist as they swung aside the concealing curtain and moved out into the tunnel. "There will be some danger, but we have survived that several times over."

"Yeah, but it's not like an inoculation," Jon-Tom muttered. "We haven't become immune. We keep taking risks and sooner or later they've got to catch up with us." He ducked to avoid a low section of iron ceiling.

"We shall do our best, my boy, to see that it is later."

Pog remained behind, hanging quietly from the oil lamp in the now empty room. He considered remaining behind permanently. The Ironclouders would shelter him, he was sure.

That would mean no transformation, of course. All that he'd suffered at the wizard's hands, and mouth, would have been for naught. Also, as the only arboreal of the group, he knew how they depended on him for reconnaissance and such.

Besides, better death than life cursed by unrequited love.

He let free of the lamp, dipped in the air, and soared out into the tunnel after the two wizards.

There was the anticipated debate and argument the next morning. One by one, as before, the various members of the little group were won over by Clothahump's assurances, obstinacy, and veiled threats.

Their course decided, it was time to ascertain the position taken during the night by the inhabitants of Ironcloud. Five of the great owls faced the travelers on the plateau below the cave city. Two were horned, two pale barn, and one a tiny hoot, who was smaller than Pog but equal in dignity to his massive feathered brothers. With them were five lemurs. The sun was not yet up.

"We do not doubt your seriousness nor the truth you tell," Tolafay was saying, "nor the worth of your mission, but still we doubted whether it was worth breaking a rule of hundreds of years of noninvolvement in the arguments of others." He gestured at Ananthos.

"Yet we share such feelings with the inhabitants of the Scuttleteau and they have nonetheless agreed to help you. So we will help, too." Murmurs of agreement came from his companions.

"That's settled, then," said a satisfied Clothahump. "You will be valuable allies in the coming war and—"

"A moment, please." One of the lemurs stepped forward. He had a high, stiff collar and light vest above billowing pantaloons of bright yellow. "We did not say that we'd be your allies. We said we'd help.

"You asked us to give the Weavers permission to travel through our country and to provide a route southward through the mountains so they can reach the Swordsward and then make their way to the Jo-Troom Gate you speak of. That's what we'll do. We'll also try and find you a way to the Greendowns. But we won't fight."

"But I thought—" Jon-Tom began.

"No!" snapped one of the other owls. "Absolutely no. We simply can't do any more for yoooooo. Don't ask it of us."

"But surely—" A restraining hand touched Talea and she quieted.

"It is more than we'd hoped for, friends. It will suffice." Clothahump turned to face Ananthos. "We have the allies we came to find."

"so you do," said the spider at last, "provided the army can be assembled in time to make the march."

"I can only hope that it does," the wizard told him solemnly, "because the fate of several worlds may depend on it."

"Not Ironcloud," said another of the owls smugly. "Ironcloud is impregnable to assault by land or air."

"So it is," agreed Caz casually, "but not by magic."

"We'll take our chances," said Tolafay firmly.

"Then there's nothing more to be said." Clothahump nodded.

Wordlessly the Ironclouders departed, owl and primate soaring to join their brethren high in the night sky. Great wings and glowing eyes shone as the night hunters returned in twos and threes to their black home. They filled the air between earth and moon.

Another pair lifted from the plateau, heading for interior darkness and a good, warm day's sleep. Jon-Tom could only hope those homes would be as invulnerable as their inhabitants believed from the eventual attacks of the Plated Folk.

The last of the lemurs stared at them curiously while her companion owl kicked impatiently at the ground. The sun had peeked over the eastern crags and those great eyes were three-quarters closed in half sleep.

"There's one thing I'd like to know. How do you warmlanders expect to penetrate Cugluch?"

"Disguise," Cothahump told her confidently.

"You do not look much like Plated Folk," replied the lemur doubtfully.

Clothahump shook a finger at her, spoke knowingly. "The greatest disguise is assurance. We will be protected because no Plated One would believe our presence. And where assurance operates, magic is not far behind."

The lemur shrugged. "I think you are all fools, brave fools, and soon-to-be-dead fools. But we will show the Weavers the path they require and you the path to your deaths." She looked upward. "Your guides come."

Two owls descended to join them. One motioned to the waiting Ananthos. The Weaver trembled slightly as he made his farewells.

"we shall meet at the gate," he told them. "that is, if I survive this journey. i am not afraid of heights, but I have never been in a high place where i could not break a fall by attaching silk to some solid object. you cannot spin from a cloud."

He climbed on the owl's back, waved legs at them. The owl took a few steps, flapping mighty wings, and then soared into the air of morning. He wore dark shades to protect him from the sunlight.

They watched until the wings became a black line on the horizon. Then the pair faded even from Caz's view.

The small hoot owl stood muttering to herself nearby. Her kilt was black, purple, and yellow. "I'm Imanooo," she informed them brusquely. "Let's get on with this. I'll point you the way for two days, but that's all. Then you're on your own."

The remaining lemur mounted his saddle. "I still think you're all fools, but," he smiled broadly, "many a brave fool has succeeded where a cautious genius has failed. Fly well." He saluted with an arm wave as he and his friend rose skyward.

Alone in their cold-weather garb, the travelers watched until the last pairing vanished into the hematite. Then Imanooo rose and started off to the south, and they followed.

The path where there was no path carried them steadily lower. The unvarying downhill hike was a welcome change from the tortuous march to Ironcloud. The day after Imanooo left them they began to discard their heavy clothing. Soon they were down among trees and bushes, and snow was only a fading memory.

Jon-Tom slowed his pace to stay alongside Clothahump. The wizard was in excellent spirits and showed no ill effects from the past weeks of marching.

"Sir?"

"Yes, my boy?" Eyes looked up at him through the thick glasses. Abruptly Jon-Tom felt uncomfortable. It had seemed so simple a while ago when he'd thought of it, a mere question. Now it fought to hide in his throat.

"Well, sir," he finally got out, "among my people there's a certain mental condition."

"Go on, boy."

"It has a common name. It's called a death wish."

"That's interesting," said Clothahump thoughtfully. "I presume it refers to someone who wishes to die."

Jon-Tom nodded. "Sometimes the person isn't aware of it himself and it has to be pointed out to him by another. Even then he may not believe it."

They walked on a while longer before he added, "Sir, no disrespect intended, but do you think you might have a death wish?"

"On the contrary, my boy," replied the wizard, apparently not offended in the least, "I have a life wish. I'm only putting myself into danger to preserve life for others. That hardly means I want to relinquish my own."

"I know, sir, but it seems to me that you've taken us from one danger to another only to take successively bigger risks. In other words, the more we survive, the more you seem to want to chance death."

"A valid contention based solely on the evidence and your personal interpretation of it," said Clothahump. "You ignore one thing: I wish to survive and live as much as any of you."

"Can you be certain of that, sir? After all, you've already lived more than twice a normal human lifetime, a much fuller life than any of the rest of us." He gestured at the others.

"Would it pain you so much to die?"

"I follow your reasoning, my boy. You're saying that I am willing to risk death because I've already had a reasonable life and therefore have less than you to lose."

Jon-Tom didn't reply.

"My boy, you haven't lived long enough to understand life. Believe me, it is more precious to me now because I have less of it. I guard every day jealously because I know it may be my last. I don't have less to lose than you: I have more to lose."

"I just wanted to be sure, sir."

"Of what? The reasons for my decisions? You can be, boy. They are founded upon a single motivation: the need to prevent the Plated Masses from annihilating civilization. Even if I did want to die, I would not do so until I had expended every bit of energy in my body to prevent that conflagration from destroying the warmlands. I might kill myself if I suffered from the aberration you suggest, but only after I'd saved everyone else."

"That's good to hear, sir." Jon-Tom felt considerably relieved.

"There is one thing that has been troubling me a little, however."

"What's that, sir?"

"Well, it's most peculiar." The wizard looked up at him. "But you see, I'm not at all certain that I remember the formula for preparing our disguises."

Jon-Tom hesitated, frowned. "Surely we can't enter Cugluch without them, sir?"

"Of course not," agreed Clothahump cheerfully. "I suggest therefore that you consider some appropriate spellsongs. You have seen one of the Plated Folk. That is what we must endeavor to look like."

"I don't know if . . ."

"Try, my boy," said the wizard in a more serious tone, "for if you cannot think of anything and I cannot remember the formula, then I fear we will be forced to give up this attempt."

Though he worked at it for the next several days, Jon-Tom was unable to think of a single appropriate tune. Insects were not a favorite subject for groups whose music he knew by heart, such as Zepplin or Tull, Queen or the Stones or even the Beatles, who, he felt sure, had written at least one song about everything. He searched his memory, went through the few classical pieces he knew, jumped from Furry Lewis to Ferlin Husky to Foreigner without success.

The dearth of material was understandable, though. Love and sex and money and fame were far more attractive song subjects than bugs. The thinking helped to kill the time and made the march more tolerable.

Never once did it occur to him that Clothahump might have invented the request simply in order to keep Jon-Tom's mind on harmless matters.

Three more days passed before they reached the outskirts of the vast, festering lowlands that formed the Greendowns. They rested on a slope and munched nuts, berries, and lizard jerky while studying the fog and mist that enshrouded the lands of the Plated Folk.

Conifers had surrendered the soil to hardwoods. These now fought to assert their dominance over palms and baobabs, succulents and creepers. Occasionally a strange cry or whistle would rise from the mist.

Jon-Tom finished his meal and stood, his leathern pants sticking to his legs from the humidity. To the west towered the snow-crowned crags of Zaryt's Teeth. It was difficult to believe that a pass broke that towering rampart. It lay somewhere to the southwest of their present position. At its far end was the Jo-Troom Gate and beyond that, a section of Swordsward and bustling, friendly Polastrindu.

His own home was somewhat more distant, a trillion miles away on the other side of time, turn right at the rip in the fabric of space and take the fourth-dimensional offramp.

He turned. Clothahump was busy with wizard's business. Pog assisted him.

"We'd better come up with something." Talea had moved to stand next to him, stood looking down into the mist. "We go down there looking like ourselves and we'll be somebody's supper before the day's out."

"Aye, that's the truth, lass," agreed Mudge. " 'E'll 'ave t' make us look like a choice slice o' 'ell."

"He already has, I think," was Caz's comment. "You'd better straighten your antenna. The left one is pointing backward instead of forward."

"I'll do that." Mudge reached up and was in the middle of straightening the errant sensor when he suddenly realized what had happened. " 'Cor, but that was quick!"

Clothahump rejoined them. Rather, they were joined by a squat, pudgy beetle that sounded something like Clothahump. Pale red compound eyes inspected them each in turn. Four arms crossed over the striated abdomen.

"What do you think, my friends? Have I solved the problem and allayed your fears, or not?"

When the initial shock finally wore off, they were able to take more careful stock of themselves. The disguises seemed foolproof. Talea, Flor, Mudge, and the rest now resembled giant versions of things Jon-Tom usually smashed underfoot. The middle set of arms moved in tandem with their owners actual ones. Pog had turned into a giant flying beetle.

"Is that really you in there, Jon-Tom?" The thing with Flor's voice ran a clawed hand over the pale blue chitin encasing him.

"I think so." He looked down at himself, noted with astonishment the multijointed legs, the smooth undercurve of abdomen, the peculiar wave-shaped sword at his hip.

"Not too uncomfortable, my boy?"

Jon-Tom looked admiringly at the squat beetle. "It's a wonderful job, sir. I feel like I'm inside a suit of armor, yet I'm cooler than I was a few moments ago without it."

"Part of the spell, my boy," said the wizard with pride. "Attention to detail makes all the difference."

"Speakin' o' attention t' detail, Your Masterness," Mudge said, " 'ow do I go about takin' a leak?"

"There are detachable sections of chitin in the appropriate places, otter. You must take care to conceal bodily functions of any kind from those we will be among. I could not imagine Plated Folk jaws through which we might eat, for example. Hopefully we can finish our business in Cugluch and be out of it and these suits before very long."

"You remembered the formula well," Jon-Tom told the wizard.

"Well enough, my boy." They left their packs and started down the slope into the steaming lowlands. "One key phrase eluded me for a time.

> "Multioptics, eyes of glass,
>   sextupal reach in fiberglass,
>   hot outside but cool within,
>   suit of polymers I'll spin."

He proceeded to detail the formula that had provided such perfectly fitted disguises.

"So these are foolproof, then?" Talea asked hopefully from just ahead of them. It was difficult to think of the black-and-brown-spotted creature as the beautiful, feisty Talea, Jon-Tom mused.

"My dear, no disguise is foolproof," Clothahump replied somberly.

"Dat's for damn sure." Pog fluttered awkwardly overhead on false beetle wings.

"We are entering the Greendowns from the northern ranges," the wizard reminded them. "The Plated Folk cannot imagine someone intentionally entering their lands. The only section of their territories which might be even lightly watched is that near the Pass. We should be able to mingle freely with whoever we chance to encounter."

"That'll be the true test of these suits, won't it?" said Caz. "Not whether we look believable to each other, but whether we can fool them."

"The formula was as all-encompassing as I could fashion it," said Clothahump confidently. "In any case, we shall know in a moment."

They turned a bend in the animal path they'd been following and came face to face with a dozen workers of that benighted land. The Plated Folk were cutting hardwood and loading the logs on a lizard-drawn sled. Unable to retreat, the travelers marched doggedly ahead.

They were nearly past when one of the cutters, a foreman perhaps, walked over on short spindly legs and gestured with two of his four limbs. Jon-Tom marked the gesture for future use.

"Hail, citizens! Whence come you, and wither go?"

There was an uncomfortably long silence until Caz thought to say, "We've been out on patrol."

"Patrol . . . in the mountains?" The foreman looked askance at the snows beyond the forest's edge. He made a clicking sound that might have passed for laughter. "What were you patrolling for? Nothing comes from the north."

"We do not," said Caz, thinking furiously, "have to provide such information to hewers of wood. However, there is no harm in your knowing." His disguise gave his voice a raspy tone.

"In her wisdom the Empress has decreed that every possible approach be inspected at least once in a while. Surely you do not question her wisdom?" Caz put his hand on his scimitar, and two limbs gripped the strange weapon.

"No, no!" said the insect foreman hastily, "of course not. Now, of all times, the greatest secrecy must be preserved." He still sounded doubtful. "Even so, nothing has come out of these mountains in years and years."

"Of course not," said Caz haughtily. "Does that not prove the effectiveness of these secret patrols?"

"That is sensible, citizen," agreed the foreman, his confusion overcome thanks to Caz's inexorable logic.

The others had continued past while the rabbit had been conversing with the foreman. That worthy snapped to attention and offered an interesting salute with both arms on his left side. Caz mimicked it in return, his false middle arm functioning smoothly in tandem with the real one.

"The Empress!" said the foreman with praiseworthy enthusiasm.

"The Empress," Caz replied. "Now then, be on about your business, citizen. The Empire needs that wood." The foreman executed a sign of acknowledgment and returned to his work. Caz tried not to move too hastily down the slope after his companions.

The foreman returned to his cutters. One of the laborers glanced up and asked curiously, "What was that all about, citizen foreman?"

"Nothing. A patrol."

"A patrol, up here?"

"I know it is odd to find one in the mountains."

"More than odd, I should think." His antennae pointed downhill toward the retreating travelers. "That is a peculiar grouping for a patrol of any kind."

"I thought so also." The foreman's tone stiffened. "But it is not our place to question the directives of the High Command."

"Of course not, citizen foreman." The laborer returned quickly to his work.

Wooded hillsides soon gave way to extensive cultivated fields cleared from bog and jungle. Most were planted with a tall, flexible growth about an inch in diameter that looked like jaundiced sugar cane. Swampy plantings alternated with herds of small six-legged reptiles who foraged noisily through the soft vegetation.

They also encountered troops on maneuver, always marching in perfect time and stride. Once they were forced off the raised roadway by a column twelve abreast. It took an hour to pass, trudging from east to west.

They passed unchallenged among dozens of Plated Folk. No one questioned their disguises. But Clothahump grew uneasy at their progress.

"Too slow," he muttered. "Surely there is a better way than this, and one that will have the extra advantage of concealing us from close inspection."

"What've you got in mind, guv'nor?" Mudge wanted to know.

"A substitute for feet. Excuse me, citizen." The wizard stepped out into the road.

The wagon bearing down on him pulled to a halt. It was filled with transparent barrels of some aromatic green liquid. The driver, a rather bucolic beetle of medium height, leaned over the side impatiently as Clothahump approached.

"Trouble, citizen? Be quick now, I've a schedule to keep."

"Are you by chance heading for the capital?"

"I am, and I've no time for riders. Sorry." He lifted his reins preparatory to chucking the wagon team into motion again.

"It is not that we wish a ride, citizen," said Clothahump, staring hard at the driver, "but only that we wish a ride."

"Oh. I misunderstood. Naturally. Make space for yourselves in the back, please."

As they climbed into the wagon, Jon-Tom passed close by the driver. He was sitting stiffly in his seat, eyes staring straight ahead yet seeing very little. Seeing only what Clothahump wanted them to see, in fact.

Under the wizard's urging, the rustic whipped the team forward. The mesmerization had taken only a moment, and no one else had observed it.

"Damnsight better than walking." Talea reached awkwardly down to draw one foot toward her, wishing she could massage the aching sole but not daring to remove even that small section of the disguise.

"Sure is," agreed Jon-Tom. He balanced himself in the swaying, rocking wagon as he made his way forward. Clothahump sat next to the driver. The insect ignored his arrival.

"A great deal happening these days," Jon-Tom said by way of opening conversation.

The driver's gaze did not stray from the road. His voice was oddly stilted, as though a second mind were choosing the words to answer with.

"Yes, a great deal."

"When is it to begin, do you think, the invasion of the warmlands?" Jon-Tom made the question sound as casual as he could.

A movement signifying ignorance from the driver. "Who is to know? They do not permit wagon masters to know the inner workings of the High Military. But it will be a great day when it comes. I myself have four nestmates in the invasion force. I wish I could be among them, but my district logistician insists that food supplies will be as important as fighting to the success of the invasion.

"So I remain where I am, though it is against my desires. It will be a memorable time. There will be a magnificent slaughter."

"So they claim," Jon-Tom murmured, "but can we be so certain of success?"

For a moment, the shocked disbelief the driver felt nearly overcame the mental haze into which he'd been immersed. "How can anyone doubt it? Never in thousands of years has the Empire assembled so massive a force. Never before have we been as well prepared as now.

"Also," he added conspiratorially, "there is rumor abundant that the Great Wizard Eejakrat, Advisor to the Empress herself, has brought forth from the realms of darkness an invincible magic which will sweep all opposition before it." He adjusted the reins running to the third lizard in right line.

"No, citizens, of course we cannot lose."

"My feelings are the same, citizen." Jon-Tom returned to the rear of the wagon. Clothahump joined him a moment later, as he was chatting softly to the others.

"If confidence is any indication of battleworthiness, we're liable to be in for a bad time."

"You see?" said Clothahump knowingly as he leaned up against a pair of green-filled barrels, "that is why we must find and destroy this dead mind that Eejakrat somehow draws knowledge from, or die in the attempt."

"Speak for yourself, guv'," said Mudge. " 'E wot fights an' runs away lives t' fight another day."

"Unfortunately," Clothahump reminded the otter quietly, "if we fail, like as not there will not be another day."

XIII

Several days passed. Farms and livestock pastures began to give way to the outskirts of a vast metropolis. Fronted with stone or black cement, tunnels led down into the earth. On the surface row upon row of identical gray buildings filled the horizon, a vast stone curve that formed the outer wheel of the capital city of Cugluch.

As they entered the first gate of many, they encountered larger structures and greater variety. Faint pulses of light from within cast ambivalent shadows on the travelers while the echoes of hammerings resounded above the babble of the chitinesque crowd. Once they passed a wagon emerging from a large, cubical building. It was piled high with long spears and pikes and halberds bound together like sheaves of grain. The weapon-laden vehicle moved westward. Westward like the troops they'd passed. Westward toward the Jo-Troom Gate.

It had rained gently every day, but was far warmer than in the so-called warmlands. Fat, limpid drops slid off their hard-shelled disguises, only occasionally penetrating the well-fashioned false chitin. Cooled by spell, those inside the insect suits remained comfortable in spite of the humidity. Clothahump, as a good wizard should, had foreseen everything except the need to scratch the occasional itch.

Only an isolated clump of struggling trees here and there brought color to the monotonous construction of the city. It was an immense warren, much of it out of sight beneath the surface of the earth.

They pushed their way through heavier and heavier traffic, increasingly military in nature. Clothahump guided the driver smoothly, directing them deeper into the city.

Wagonloads of troops, ant- and beetle-shapes predominant, shoved civilian traffic aside as they made their way westward. Enormous beetles eight and nine feet long displayed sharpened horns to the travelers. Three or four armed soldiers rode on the backs of these armored behemoths.

Once a dull *thump* sounded from behind a large oval structure. Jon-Tom swore it sounded like an exploding shell. For an awful moment he thought it was the result of Eejakrat's unknown magic and that the Plated Folk had learned the use of gunpowder. His companions, however, assured him it was only a distant rumble of thunder.

Buildings rose still higher around them. They were matched by roads that widened to accommodate the increased traffic. Weaving ribbons of densely populated concrete and rock rose six and seven stories above the streets, hives of frenetic activity devoted now to destruction and death.

Sleep was in snatches and seconds that night. Clothahump woke them to a soggy sunrise.

Ahead in the morning mist-light lay a great open square paved with triangular slabs of gray, black, purple, and blue stone. Across this expansive parade ground, populated now only by early risers, rose a circular pyramid. It consisted of concentric ring shapes like enormous tires. These tapered to a smooth spire hundreds of feet high that pierced the mist like a gray needle.

Half a dozen smaller copies of the central structure ringed it at points equidistant from one another. There was no wall around any of them, nor for that matter around the main square itself.

Despite this the driver refused to go any further. His determination was so strong even Clothahump's hypnotic urgings failed to force him and his wagon onto the triangular paving.

"I have no permit," he said raspily, "to enter the palace grounds. It would be my death to be found on the sacred square without one."

"This is where we walk again, my friends. Perhaps it is best. I see only one or two wagons on the square. We do not want to attract attention."

Mudge let himself over the back of the wagon. "Cor, ain't that the bloody ugliest buildin' you ever saw in your life?"

They abandoned the wagon. Clothahump was last off. He whispered a few words to the driver. The beetle moved the reins and the wagon swung around to vanish up the street down which they'd come. Jon-Tom wondered at the excuse the unfortunate driver would offer when he suddenly returned to full consciousness at his delivery point after nearly a week of amnesia.

"It seems we need a permit to cross," said Caz appraisingly. "How do we go about obtaining one?"

Clothahump sounded disapproving. "We need no permit. I have been observing the pedestrians traversing the square, and none has been stopped or questioned. It seems that the threat is sufficient to secure the palace's exclusiveness. The permit may be required within, but it does not seem vital for walking the square."

"I hope you're right, sir." The rabbit stepped out onto the paving, a gangling, thoroughly insectoid shape. Together they moved at an easy pace toward the massive pyramidal palace.

As Clothahump had surmised, they were not accosted. If anything, they found the square larger than it first appeared, like a lake that looks small until one is swimming in its center.

From this central nexus the spokes of Cugluch radiated outward toward farmland and swamp. The city was far larger than Polastrindu, especially when one considered that much of it was hidden underground.

Thick mist clung to the crests of the seven towers and completely obscured the central one. Nowhere did they see a flag, a banner, any splash of color or gaiety. It was a somber capital, dedicated to a somber purpose.

And the massive palace was especially dark and foreboding. Here at least Jon-Tom had expected some hint of brightness. Militaristic cultures were historically fond of pomp and flash. The palace of the Empress, however, was as dull as the warrens of the citizen-workers. Different in design but not demeanor, he decided.

The lowest level of the circular pyramid was several stories high. It was fashioned, as the entire palace complex no doubt was, of close-fitting stone mortared over with a gray cement or plaster. Water dripped down its curves to vanish into gutters and drains lining the base. There was a minimum of windows.

The triangular paving of the square ceased some fifteen yards from the base of the palace. In its place was a smooth surface of black cement. That was all; no fence, no hidden alarms, no hedgerows or ditches. But on that black fifteen yards, which encircled the entire palace, nothing moved save the stiffly pacing guards.

They formed a solid ring, ten yards from the palace wall, five yards apart. They marched in slow tread from left to right, keeping the same distance between them like so many wind-up toys. As near as Jon-Tom could tell they ringed the entire palace, a moving chain of guards that never stopped.

At Clothahump's urging they turned southward. The guards never looked in their direction, though Jon-Tom was willing to wager that if so much as a foot touched that black cement, the trespasser would suddenly find himself the object of considerable hostile attention.

Eventually they stood opposite an arched triangular portal cut from the flank of the palace. The entryway was three stories high. At present its massive iron gates were thrown wide. A line of armed beetles extended from either open gate out across the cement to the edge of the paving. The unbroken ring of encircling guards passed through this intercepting line with precision. The moving guards never touched any of the stationary ones.

"Now wot, guv'nor?" Mudge whispered to the wizard. "Do we just walk up t' the nearest bugger an' ask 'im polite-like if the Empress be at 'ome an' might we 'ave 'is leave t' skip on in t' see the old dear?"

"I have no desire to see *her*," Clothahump replied. "It is Eejakrat we are after. Rulers survive by relying on the brains of their advisors. Remove Eejakrat, or at least his magic, and we leave the Empress without the most important part of her collective mind."

He gazed thoughtfully at Caz. "You have laid claim to a working knowledge of diplomacy, my boy, and have shown an aptitude for such in the past. I am reluctant to perform a spell among so many onlookers and so near to Eejakrat's influence. I've no doubt he has placed alarm spells all about the palace. They would react to my magicking, but not to your words. We must get inside. I suggest you employ your talent for extemporaneous and convincing conversation."

"I don't know, sir," replied the rabbit uncertainly. "It's easy to convince people you're familiar with. I don't know how to talk to these."

"Nonsense. You did well with that curious woodcutter whom we encountered during our descent. If anything, the minds you are about to deal with are simpler than those you are more familiar with. Consider their society, which rewards conformity while condemning individuality."

"If you want me to, sir, I'll give it a try."

"Good. The rest of you form behind us. Pog, you stay airborne and warn us if there is sudden movement from armed troops in our direction."

"What does it matter?" said the sorrowful bat from inside his disguise. "We'll all be dead inside an hour anyway." But he spiraled higher and did as he was told, keeping a watchful eye on the guards and any group of pedestrians who came near.

Following Caz and Clothahump, the travelers made their way toward the entrance. There was an anxious moment when they stepped from paving to cement, but no one challenged them. The guards flanking the approach kept their attention on a point a few inches in front of their mandibles.

Then it was through the encircling ring, which likewise did not react. They were a couple of yards from the entrance.

Jon-Tom had the wild notion that they might simply be able to march on into the palace when a massive beetle slightly taller but much broader than Caz lumbered out of the shadows to confront them. He was flanked by a pair of pale, three-foot-high attendants of the mutated mayfly persuasion. One of them carried a large scroll and a marking instrument. The other simply stood and listened.

"State your business, citizens," demanded the glowering hulk in the middle. He reminded Jon-Tom of a gladiator ready to enter the arena, and pity be on the lions. The extra set of arms ruined the illusion.

With the facility of an established survivor, Caz replied without hesitation. "Hail, citizen! We have special, urgently requested information for the sorcerer Eejakrat, information that is vital to our coming success." Not knowing how to properly conclude the request he added blandly, "Where can we find him?"

Their interrogator did not reply immediately. Jon-Tom wondered if his nervousness showed.

After a brief conversation with the burdenless mayfly the beetle gestured backward with two hands. "Third level, Chamber Three Fifty-Five and adjuncts."

Politely, he stepped aside.

Caz led them in. They walked down a short hallway. It opened into a hall that seemed to run parallel to the circular shape of the building. Another, similar hall could be seen further ahead. Evidently there was a single point from which the palace and thence the entire city of Cugluch radiated in concentric circles, with hallways or streets forming intersecting spokes.

Jon-Tom leaned over and whispered to Clothahump. "I don't know how you feel, sir, but to me that was much too easy."

"Why shouldn't it have been?" said Talea, feeling cocky at their success thus far. "It was just like crossing the square outside."

"Precisely, my dear," said Clothahump proudly. "You see, Jon-Tom, they are so well ordered they cannot imagine anyone stepping out of class or position. They cannot conceive, as that threatening individual who confronted us outside cannot, that any of their fellows would have the presumption to lie to gain an audience with so feared a personality as Eejakrat. If we did not deserve such a meeting, we would not be asking for it.

"Furthermore, spies are unknown in Cugluch. They have no reason to suspect any, and traitorous actions are as alien to the Plated Folk as snow. This may be possible after all, my friends. We need only maintain the pretext that we know what we are doing and have a right to be doing it."

"I'd imagine," said Caz, "that if the spoke-and-circle layout of the city and palace is followed throughout, the center would be the best place to locate stairways. Third level, the fellow said."

"I agree," Clothahump replied, "but we do not wish to find Eejakrat except as a last resort, remember. It is the dead mind he controls that must remain our primary goal."

"That's simple enough, then," said Mudge cheerfully. "All we 'ave t' do now is ask where t' find a particularly well-attended corpse."

"For once, my fuzzy fuzz-brained friend, you are correct. It will likely be placed close by Eejakrat's chambers. Let us proceed quickly to the level indicated, but not to him."

They did so. By now they were used to being ignored by the Plated Folk. Busy palace staff moved silently around them, intent on their own tasks. The narrow hallways and low ceilings combined with the slightly acidic odor of the inhabitants made Jon-Tom and Flor feel a little claustrophobic.

They reached the third level and began to follow the numbers engraved above each sealed portal. Only four chambers from the stairway they'd ascended was a surprise: the corridor was blocked. Also guarded.

Instead of the lumbering beetle they'd encountered at the entrance to the palace they found a slim, almost effeminate-looking insect seated behind a desk. Other armed Plated Folk stood before the temporary barrier sealing off the hall beyond. Unlike their drilling brothers marching single-mindedly outside, these guards seemed alert and active. They regarded the new arrivals with unconcealed interest.

There was no suspicion in their unyielding faces, however. Only curiosity.

It was Clothahump who spoke to the individual behind the desk, and not Caz.

"We have come to make adjustments to the mind," he told the individual behind the desk, hoping he had gauged the source correctly and hadn't said anything fatally contradictory.

The fixed-faced officer preened one red eye. He could not frown but succeeded in conveying an impression of puzzlement nonetheless.

"An adjustment to the mind?"

"To Eejakrat's Materialization."

"Ah, of course, citizen. But what kind of adjustment?" He peered hard at the encased wizard. "Who are you, to be entrusted with access to so secret a thing?"

Clothahump was growing worried. The more questions asked, the more the chance of saying something dangerously out of sync with the facts.

"We are Eejakrat's own special assistants. How else could we know of the mind?"

"That is sensible," agreed the officer. "Yet no mention was made to me of any forthcoming adjustments."

"I have just mentioned it to you."

The officer turned that one over in his mind, got thoroughly confused, and finally said, "I am sorry for the delay, citizen. I mean no insult by my questions, but we are under extraordinary orders. Your master's fears are well known."

Clothahump leaned close, spoke confidentially. "An attribute of all who must daily deal with dark forces."

The officer nodded somberly. "I am glad it is you who must deal with the wizard and not myself." He waved aside the guards blocking the doorway in the portable barrier. "Stand aside and let them pass."

Caz and Talea were the first through the portal when the officer suddenly put out an arm and touched Clothahump. "Surely you can satisfy the curiosity of a fellow citizen. What kind of 'adjustment' must you make to the mind? We all understand so little about it and you can sympathize with my desire to know."

"Of course, of course." Clothahump's mind was working frantically. How much did the officer actually know? He'd just confessed his ignorance, but mightn't it be a ploy? Better to say anything fast than nothing at all. His only real worry was that the officer might have some sorceral training.

"Please do not repeat this," he finally said, with as much assurance as he could muster. "It is necessary to apfrangle the overscan."

"Naturally," said the officer after a pause.

"And we may," the wizard added for good measure, "additionally have to lower the level of cratastone, just in case."

"I can understand the necessity for that." The officer grandly waved them through, enjoying the looks of respect on the faces of his subordinates while praying this visitor wouldn't ask him any questions in return.

They proceeded through the portal one by one. Jon-Tom was last through and hesitated. The officer seemed willing enough.

"It's still in the same chamber, of course."

"Number Twelve, yes," said the officer blandly.

Clothahump fell back to match stride with Jon-Tom. "That was clever of you, my boy! I was so preoccupied with trying to get us in that I'd forgotten how difficult it would be to sense past Eejakrat's spell guards. Now that is no longer a constraint. You cannot teach deviousness," he finished pridefully. "That is instinctive."

"Thank you, sir. I think. What kind of corpse do you think it is?"

"I cannot imagine. I cannot imagine a dead brain functioning, either. We shall know soon enough." He was deciphering the symbols engraved above each circular doorway. The guarded barrier had long since disappeared around the continuous curve of the hallway.

"There is number ten . . . and there eleven," he said excitedly, pointing to the door on their right.

"Then this must be twelve." Talea stopped before the closed door.

It was no larger than any of the others they'd passed. The corridor nearby was deserted. Clothahump stepped forward and studied the wooden door. There were four tiny circular insets midway up the left side. He inserted his four insect arms into them and pushed.

The spring mechanism that controlled the door clicked home. The wood split apart and inward like two halves of an apple.

There was no light in the chamber beyond. Even Caz could see nothing. But Pog saw without eyes.

"Master, it's not very large, but I think dat dere's someting . . ." He fluttered near a wall, struck his sparker.

A lamp suddenly burst into light. It revealed a bent and very aged beetle surrounded by writhing white larval forms. Startled, it glared back at them and muttered an oath.

"What is it now? I've told Skrritch I'm not to be disturbed unless

. . . unless . . ." His words trailed away as he stared fixedly at Clothahump.

"By the Primordial Arm! A warmlander wizard!" He turned to a siphon speaker set in the wall nearby. "Guards, guards!" The maggots formed a protective, loathesome semicircle in front of him.

"Quick now," Caz yelled, "where is it?" They fanned out into the chamber, hunting for anything that might fit Clothahump's description.

One insectoid, one mammalian, the two wizards faced each other in silent summing up. Neither moved, but they were battling as ferociously as any two warriors armed with sword and spear.

"We've got to find it fast," Flor was muttering, searching a corner. "Before . . ."

But hard feet were already clattering noisily in the corridor outside. Distant cries of alarm sounded in the chamber. Then the soldiers were pouring through the doorway, and there was no more time.

Jon-Tom saw something lying near the back wall that might have been a long, low corpse. An insect shape stepped up behind him and raised a cast-iron bottle high. Just before the bottle came down on his head it occurred to him that the shape wielding it was familiar. It wasn't one of the insect guards who'd just arrived. Before he blacked out under the impact he was positive the insectoid visage was that concealing Talea's. The realization stunned him almost as badly as the bottle, which cracked his own false forehead and bounced off the skull beneath. Darkness returned to the chamber.

When he regained consciousness, he found he was lying in a dimly lit, spherical cell. There was a drain in the center, at the bottom of the sphere. The light came from a single lamp hanging directly over the drain. It was windowless and humid. Moss and fungi grew from the damp stones, and it was difficult to keep from sliding down the sloping floor. Compared to this, the cell they'd been temporarily incarcerated in back in Gossameringue had been positively palatial.

No friendly Ananthos would be appearing here to rectify a mistaken imprisonment, however.

"Welcome back to the world of the living," said Bribbens. Good times or bad, the boatman's expression never seemed to change. The moisture in the cell did not bother him, of course.

"I should've stayed on my boat," he added with a sigh.

"Maybe we all ought to 'ave stayed on your boat, mate," said a disconsolate Mudge.

It occurred to Jon-Tom that Bribbens looked like himself. So did Mudge, and the other occupants of the cell.

"What happened to our disguises?"

"Stripped away as neatly as you'd peel an onion," Pog told him. He lay morosely on the damp stones, unwilling to hang from the fragile lamp.

Clothahump was not in the cell. "Where's your master?"

"I don't know, I don't know," the bat moaned helplessly. "Taken away from us during da fight. We ain't seen him since, da old fart." There was no malice in the bat's words.

"It was Eejakrat," Caz said from across the cell. His clothing was torn and clumps of fur were missing from his right cheek, but he still somehow had retained his monocle. "He knew us for what we were. I presume he has taken special care with Clothahump. One sorcerer would not place another in an ordinary cell where he might dissolve the bars or mesmerize the jailers."

"But what he doesn't know is that we still have the services of a wizard." Flor was looking hopefully at Jon-Tom.

"I can't do anything, Flor." He dug his boot heels into a crack in the floor. It kept him from sliding down toward the central drain. "I need my duar, and it was strapped to the inside back of my insect suit."

"Try," she urged him. "We've nothing to lose, *verdad?* You don't need instrumental accompaniment to sing."

"No, but I can't make magic without it."

"Give 'er a shot anyway, guv'nor," said Mudge. "It can't make us any worse than we are, wot?"

"All right." He thought a moment, then sang. It had to be something to fit his mood. Something somber and yet hopeful.

He was fonder of rock than country-western, but there was a certain song about another prison, a place called Folsom, where blues of a different kind had also been vanquished through music. It was full of hope, anticipation, whistles, and thoughts of freedom.

Mudge obligingly let out a piercing whistle. It faded to freedom through the bars of their cell, but whistler and singer did not. No train appeared to carry them away. Not even a solitary, curious gneechee.

"You see?" He smiled helplessly, and spread his hands. "I need the duar. I sing and it spells. Can't have one without the other." The question he'd managed to suppress until now could no longer rest unsatisfied.

"We know what probably happened to Clothahump." He looked at the floor, remembering the descending iron bottle. "Where's Talea?"

"That *puta!*" Flor spit on the moss. "If we get a chance before we die I'll disembowel her with my own hands." She held up sharp nailed fingers.

"I couldn't believe it meself, mate." Mudge sounded more tired than Jon-Tom had ever heard him. Something had finally smashed his unquenchable spirit. "It don't make no bloomin' *sense*, dam it! I've known that bird off an' on for years. For 'er t' do somethin' like this t' save 'er own skin, t' go over t' the likes o' these . . . I can't believe it, mate. I can't!"

Jon-Tom tried to erase the memory. That would be easier than forgetting the pain. It wasn't his head that was hurting.

"I can't believe it either, Mudge."

"Why not, friend?" Bribbens crossed one slick green leg over the other. "Allegiance is a temporary thing, and expediency the hallmark of survival."

"Probably what happened," said Caz more gently, "was that she saw what was going to happen, that we were going to be overwhelmed, and decided to cast her lot with the Plated Folk. We know from firsthand experience, do we not, that there are human allies among them. I can't condemn her for choosing life over death. You shouldn't either."

Jon-Tom sat quietly, still not believing it despite the sense in Caz's words. Talea had been combative, even contemptuous at times, but for her to turn on companions she'd been through so much with . . . Yet she'd apparently done just that. Better face up to facts, Jon boy. "Poor boy, you're goin' t' die," as the song lamented.

"What do you suppose they'll do with us?" he asked Mudge. "Or maybe I'd be better just asking 'how'?"

"I over'eard the soldiers talkin'. I was 'alf conscious when they carried us down 'ere." Mudge smiled slightly. "Seems we're t' be the bloody centerpiece at the Empress' evenin' supper, the old dear. 'Eard the ranks wagerin' on 'ow we was goin' t' be cooked."

"I sincerely hope they do cook us," Caz said. "I've heard tales that the Plated Folk prefer their food alive." Flor shuddered, and Jon-Tom felt sick.

It had all been such a grand adventure, marching off to save civilization, overcoming horrendous obstacles and terrible difficulties. All to end up not as part of an enduring legend but a brief meal. He missed the steady confidence of Clothahump. Even if unable to save them through wizardly means, he wished the turtle were present to raise their spirits with his calm, knowledgeable words.

"Any idea what time it's to be?" The windowless walls shut out time as well as space.

"No idea." Caz grinned ruefully at him. "You're the spellsinger. You tell me."

"I've already explained that I can't do anything without the duar."

"Then you ought to have it, Jon-Tom." The voice came from the corridor outside the cell. Everyone faced the bars.

Talea stood there, panting heavily. Flor made an inarticulate sound and rushed the barrier. Talea stepped back out of reach.

"Calm yourself, woman. You're acting like a hysterical cub."

Flor smiled, showing white teeth. "Come a little closer, sweet friend, and I'll show you how hysterical I can be."

Talea shook her head, looked disgusted. "Save your strength, and what brains you've got left. We haven't got much time." She held up a twisted length of wrought iron: the key.

Caz had left his sitting position to move up behind Flor. He put furry arms around her and wrestled her away from the bars.

"Use your head, giantess! Can't you see she's come to let us out?"

"But I thought . . ." Flor finally took notice of the key and relaxed.

"You knocked me out." Jon-Tom gripped the bars with both hands as Talea fumbled with the key and the awkward lock. "You hit me with a metal bottle."

"I sure did," she snapped. "Somebody had to keep her wits about her."

"Then you haven't gone over to the Plated Folk?"

"Of course I did. You're not thinking it through. I forgive you, though."

She was whispering angrily at them, glancing from time to time back up the corridor. "We know that some humans have joined them, right? But how could the locals know which humans in the warmlands are their allies and which are not? They can't possibly, not without checking with their spies in Polastrindu and elsewhere.

"When the fighting began I saw we didn't have a chance. So I grabbed a hunk of iron and started attacking you alongside the guards. When it was finished they accepted my story about being sent along to spy on you and keep track of the expedition. That Eejakrat was suspicious, but he was willing to accept me for now, until he can check with those warmland sources. He figured I couldn't do any harm here." She grinned wickedly.

"His own thoughts are elsewhere. He's too concerned with how much Clothahump knows to worry about me." She nodded up the corridor. "This guard's dead, but I don't know how often they change 'em."

There was a groan and a metallic *snap*. She pushed and the door swung inward. "Come on, then."

They rushed out into the corridor. It was narrow and only slightly better lit than the cell. Several strides further brought them up before a familiar silhouette.

"Clothahump!" shouted Jon-Tom.

"Master, Master!" Pog fluttered excitedly around the wizard's head. Clothahump waved irritably at the famulus. His own attention was fixed on the hall behind him.

"Not now, Pog. We've no time for it."

"Where've they been holding you, sir?" Jon-Tom asked.

Clothahump pointed. "Two cells up from you."

Jon-Tom gaped at him. "You mean you were that close and we could've . . ."

"Could have what, my boy? Dug through the rocks with your bare hands and untied and ungagged me? I think not. It was frustrating, however, to hear you all so close and not be able to reassure you." His expression darkened. "I am going to turn that Eejakrat into mousefood!"

"Not today," Talea reminded him.

"Yes, you're quite right, young lady."

Talea led them to a nearby room. In addition to the expected oil lamps the walls held spears and shields. The furnishings were Spartan and minimal. A broken insect body lay sprawled beneath the table. Neatly piled against the far wall were their possessions: weapons, supplies, and disguises, including Jon-Tom's duar.

They hurriedly helped one another into the insect suits.

"I'm surprised these weren't shattered beyond repair in the fight," Jon-Tom muttered, watching while Clothahump fixed his cracked headpiece.

The wizard finished the polymer spell-repair. "Eejakrat was fascinated by them. I'm sure he wanted me to go into the details of the spell. He has similar interests, you know. Remember the disguised ambassador who talked with you in Polastrindu."

They stepped quietly back out into the corridor. "Where are we?" Mudge asked Talea.

"Beneath the palace. Where else?" It was strange to hear that sharp voice coming from behind the gargoylish face once again.

"How can we get out?" Pog murmured worriedly.

"We walked in," said Caz thoughtfully. "Why should we not also walk out?"

"Indeed," said Clothahump. "If we can get out into the square we should be safe."

XIV

They were several levels below the surface, but under Talea's guidance they made rapid progress upward.

Once they had to pause to let an enormous beetle pass. He waddled down the stairs without seeing them. A huge ax was slung across his back and heavy keys dangled from his belts.

"I don't know if he's the relief for our level or not," Talea said huskily, "but we'd better hurry."

They increased their pace. Then Talea warned them to silence. They were nearing the last gate.

Three guards squatted around a desk on the other side of the barred door. A steady babble of conversation filtered into the corridor from the open door on the far side of the guard room as busy workers came and went. Jon-Tom wondered at the absence of a heavier guard until it came to him that escape would be against orders, an action foreign to all but deranged Plated Folk.

But there was still the barred doorway and the three administrators beyond.

"How did you get past them?" Caz asked Talea.

"I haven't been past them. Eejakrat believed my story, but only to a point. He wasn't about to give me the run of the city. I had a room, not a cell, on the level below this one. If I wanted out, I had to send word to him. We haven't got time for that now. Pretty soon they'll be finding the body I left."

Mudge located a small fragment of loose black cement. He tossed it down the stairs they'd ascended. It made a gratifyingly loud clatter.

"Nesthek, is that you?" one of the administrators called toward the doorway. When there was no immediate reply he rose from his position at the desk and left the game to his companions.

The escapees concealed themselves as best they could. The administrator sounded perplexed as he approached the doorway.

"Nesthek? Don't play games with me. I'm losing badly as it is."

"Bugger it," Mudge said tensely. "I thought at least two of them would come to check."

"You take this one," said Clothahump. "The rest of us will *quietly* rush the others."

"Nesthek, what are you . . . ?" Mudge stabbed upward with his sword. He'd been lying nearly hidden by the lowest bar of the doorway. The sword went right into the startled guard's abdomen. At the same instant Caz leaped out of the shadows to bring his knife down into one of the great compound eyes. The guard-administrator slumped against the bars. Talea fumbled for the keys at his waist.

"Partewx?" Then the other querulous guard was half out of his seat as his companion ran to give the alarm. He didn't make it to the far door. Pog landed on his neck and began stabbing rapidly with his stiletto at the guard's head and face. The creature swung its four arms wildly, trying to dislodge the flapping dervish that clung relentlessly to neck and head. Flor swung low with her sword and cut through both legs.

The other who had turned and drawn his own scimitar swung at Bribbens. The boatman hopped halfway to the ceiling, and the deadly arc passed feet below their intended target.

As the guard was bringing back his sword for another cut, Jon-Tom swung at him with his staff. The guard ducked the whistling club-head and brought his curved blade around. As he'd been taught to, Jon-Tom spun the long shaft in his hands as if it were an oversized baton. The guard jumped out of range. Jon-Tom thumbed one of the hidden studs, and a foot of steel slid directly into the startled guard's thorax. Caz's sword decapitated him before he hit the floor.

"Hold!"

Everyone looked to the right. There was a waste room recessed into that wall. It had produced a fourth administrator guard. He was taller than Jon-Tom, and the insect shape struggling in the three-armed grasp looked small in comparison.

The insect head of Talea's disguise had been ripped off. Her red hair cascaded down to her shoulders. Two arms held her firmly around neck and waist while the third held a knife over the hollow of her throat.

"Move and she dies," said the guard. He began to edge toward the open doorway leading outside, keeping his back hard against the wall.

"If he gives the alarm we're finished, mates," Mudge whispered.

"Let's rush them," said Caz.

"No!" Jon-Tom put an arm in front of the rabbit. "We can't. He'll—"

Talea continued to struggle in the unrelenting grip. "Do something, you idiots!"

Seeing that no one was going to act and that she and her captor were only a few yards from the doorway, she put both feet on the floor and thrust convulsively upward. The knife slid through her throat, emerging from the back of her neck. Claret spurted across the stones.

Everyone was too stunned to scream. The guard cursed, let the limp body fall as he bolted for the exit. Pog was waiting for him with a knife that went straight between the compound eyes. The guard never saw him. He'd had eyes only for his grounded opponents and hadn't noticed the bat hanging above the portal.

Caz and Mudge finished the giant quickly. Jon-Tom bent over the tiny, curled shape of Talea. The blood flowed freely but was already beginning to slow. Major arteries and veins had been severed.

He looked back at Clothahump but the wizard could only shake his head. "No time, no time, my boy. It's a long spell. Not enough time."

Weak life looked out from those sea-green eyes. Her mouth twisted into a grimace and her voice was faint. "One of . . . these days you're going to have to make . . . the important decisions without help, Jon-Tom." She smiled faintly. "You know . . . I think I love you. . . ."

The tears came in a flood, uncontrollable. "It's not fair, Talea. Damn! It's not fair! You can't tell me something like that and then leave me! You can't!"

But she died anyway.

He found he was shaking. Caz grabbed his shoulders, shook him until it stopped.

"No time for that now, my friend. I'm sorry, too, but this isn't the place for being sorry."

"No, it is not." Clothahump was examining the body. "She'll stop bleeding soon. When she does, clean her chitin and put her head back on. It's over in the corner there, where the guard threw it."

Jon-Tom stood, looked dazedly down at the wizard. "You can't . . . ?"

"I'll explain later, Jon-Tom. But all may not be lost."

"What the hell do you mean, 'all may not be lost'?" His voice rose angrily. "She's *dead,* you senile old . . ."

Clothahump let him finish, then said, "I forgive the names because I understand the motivation and the source. Know only that sometimes even death can be forgiven, Jon-Tom."

"Are you saying you can bring her back?"

"I don't know. But if we don't get out of here quickly we'll never have the chance to find out."

Flor and Bribbens slipped the insect head back into place over the pale face and flowing hair. Jon-Tom wouldn't help.

"Now everyone look and act official," Clothahump urged them. "We're taking a dead prisoner out for burial."

Bribbens, Mudge, Caz, and Flor supported Talea's body while Pog flew formation overhead and Jon-Tom and Clothahump marched importantly in front. A few passing Plated Folk glanced at them when they emerged from the doorway, but no one dared question them.

One of the benefits of infiltrating a totalitarian society, Jon-Tom thought bitterly. Everyone's afraid to ask anything of anyone who looks important.

They were on the main floor of the palace. It took them a while to find an exit (they dared not ask directions), but before long they were outside in the mist of the palace square.

The sky was as gray and silent as ever and the humidity as bad, but for all except the disconsolate Jon-Tom it was as though they'd suddenly stepped out onto a warm beach fronting the southern ocean.

"We have to find transport again," Clothahump was murmuring as they made their way with enforced slowness across the square. "Soon someone will note either our absence or that of our belongings." He allowed himself a grim chuckle.

"I would not care to be the prison commandant when Eejakrat learns of our escape. They'll be after us soon enough, but they should have a hell of a time locating us. We blend in perfectly, and only a few have seen us. Nevertheless, Eejakrat will do everything in his power to recapture us."

"Where can we go?" Mudge asked, shifting slightly under the weight of the body. "To the north, back to Ironcloud?"

"No. That is where Eejakrat will expect us to go."

"Why would he suspect that?" asked Jon-Tom.

"Because I made it a point to give him sufficient hints to that effect during our conversations," the wizard replied, "in case the opportunity to flee arose."

"If he's as sly as you say, won't he suspect we're heading in another direction?"

"Perhaps. But I do not believe he will think that we might attempt to return home through the entire assembled army of the Greendowns."

"Won't they be given the alarm about us also?"

"Of course. But militia do not display initiative. I think we shall be able to slip through them."

That satisfied Jon-Tom, but Clothahump was left to muse over what might have been. So close, they'd been so close! And still they did not know what the dead mind was, or how Eejakrat manipulated it. But while willing to take chances, he was not quite as mad as Jon-Tom might have thought. I have no death wish, young spellsinger, he thought as he regarded the tall insect shape marching next to him. We tried as no other mortals could try, and we failed. If fate wills that we are to perish soon, it will be on the ramparts of the Jo-Troom Gate confronting the foe, not in the jaws of Cugluch.

Once among the milling, festering mob of city dwellers they could relax a little. It took a while to locate an alley with a delivery wagon and no curious onlookers. Clothahump could not work the spell under the gaze of kibbitzers.

The long, narrow wagon was pulled by a single large lizard. They waited. No one else entered the alley. Eventually the driver emerged from the back entrance of a warren. Clothahump confronted him and while the others kept watch, hastily spelled the unfortunate driver under.

"Climb aboard then, citizens," the driver said obligingly when the wizard had finished. They did so, carefully laying Talea's body on the wagon bed between them.

They were two-thirds of the way to the Pass, the hustle of Cugluch now largely behind them, when the watchful Jon-Tom said cautiously to the driver, "You're not hypnotized, are you? You never were under the spell."

The worker looked back down at him with unreadable compound eyes as hands moved toward weapons. "No, citizen. I have not been magicked, if that is what you mean. Stay your hands." He gestured at the roadway they were traveling. "It would do you only ill, for you are surrounded by my people." Swords and knives remained reluctantly sheathed.

"Where are you taking us, then?" Flor asked nervously. "Why haven't you given the alarm already?"

"As to the first, stranger, I am taking you where you wish to go, to the head of the Troom Pass. I can understand why you wish to go there, though I do not think you will end your journey alive. Yet perhaps you will be fortunate and make it successfully back to your own lands."

"You know what we are, then?" asked a puzzled Jon-Tom.

The driver nodded. "I know that beneath those skins of chitin there are others softer and differently colored."

"But how?"

The driver pointed to the back of the wagon. Mudge looked uncomfortable. "Well now wot the bloody 'ell were I supposed to do? I thought 'is mind had been turned to mush and I 'ad to pee. Didn't think 'e saw anyway, the 'ard-shelled pervert!"

"It does not matter," the driver said.

"Listen, if you're not magicked and you know who and what we are, why are you taking us quietly where we wish to go instead of turning us over to the authorities?" Jon-Tom wanted to know.

"I just told you: it does not matter." The driver made a two-armed gesture indicative of great indifference. "Soon all will die anyway."

"I take it you don't approve of the coming war."

"No, I do not." His antennae quivered with emotion as he spoke. "It is so foolish, the millennia-old expenditure of life and time in hopes of conquest."

"I must say you are the most peculiar Plated person I have ever encountered," said Clothahump.

"My opinions are not widely shared among my own people," the driver admitted. He chucked the reins, and the wagon edged around a line of motionless carts burdened with military supplies. Their wagon continued onward, one set of wheels still on the roadway, the other bouncing over the rocks and mud of the swampy earth.

"But perhaps things will change, given time and sensible thought."

"Not if your armies achieve victory they won't," said Bribbens coldly. "Wouldn't you be happy as the rest if your soldiers win their conquest?"

"No, I would not," the driver replied firmly. "Death and killing never build anything, for all that it may appear otherwise."

"A most enlightened outlook, sir," said Clothahump. "See here, why don't you come with us back to the warmlands?"

"Would I be welcomed?" asked the insect. "Would the other warm-landers understand and sympathize the way you do? Would they greet me as a friend?"

"They would probably, I am distressed to confess," said a somber Caz, "slice you into small chitinous bits."

"You see? I am doomed whichever way I chose. If I went with you I would suffer physically. If I stay, it is my mind that suffers constant agony."

"I can understand your feelings against the war," said Flor, "but that still doesn't explain why you're risking your own neck to help us."

The driver made a shruglike gesture. "I help those who need help. That is my nature. Now I help you. Soon, when the fighting starts, there will be many to help. I do not take sides among the needy. I wish only that such idiocies could be stopped. It seems though that they can only be waited out."

The driver, an ordinary citizen of the Greendowns, was full of surprises. Clothahump had been convinced that there was no diver-gence of opinion among the Plated Folk. Here was loquacious proof of a crack in that supposed unity of totalitarian thought, a crack that might be exploited later. Assuming, of course, that the forthcoming invasion could be stopped.

Several days later they found themselves leaving the last of the cultivated lowlands. Mist faded behind them, and the friendly silhou-ettes of the mountains of Zaryt's Teeth became solid.

No wagons plied their trader's wares here, no farmers waded pa-tiently through knee-deep muck. There was only military traffic. Ac-cording to Clothahump they were already within the outskirts of the Pass.

Military bivouacs extended from hillside to hillside and for miles to east and west. Tens of thousands of insect troops milled quietly, ex-pectantly, on the gravelly plain, waiting for the word to march. From the back of the wagon Jon-Tom and his companions could look out upon an ocean of antennae and eyes and multiple legs. And sharp iron, flashing like a million mirrors in the diffuse light of a winter day.

No one questioned them or eyed the wagon with suspicion until they reached the last lines of troops. Ahead lay only the ancient riverbed of the Troom Pass, a dry chasm of sand and rock which in the previous ten millennia had run more with blood than ever it had with water.

The officer was winged but flightless, slim, limber of body and thought. He noted the wagon and its path, stopped filling out the scroll in his charge, and hurried to pace the vehicle. Its occupants gave every indication of being engaged in reasonable business, but they ought not to have been where they were. The quality of initiative, so lacking in Plated Folk troops, was present in some small amount in this particular individual officer.

He glanced up at the driver, his tone casual and not hostile. "Where are you going, citizen?"

"Delivering supplies to the forward scouts," said Caz quickly.

The officer slackened his pace, walked now behind the wagon as he inspected its occupants. "That is understandable, but I see no supplies. And who is the dead one?" He gestured with claws and antennae at the limp shape of Talea, still encased in her disguise.

"An accident, a most unforgivable brawl in the ranks," Caz informed him.

"Ranks? What ranks? I see no insignia on the body. Nor on any of you."

"We're not regular army," said the driver, much to the relief of the frantic Caz.

"Ah. But such a fatal disturbance should be reported. We cannot tolerate fighting among ourselves, not now, with final victory so soon to come."

Jon-Tom tried to look indifferent as he turned his head to look past the front of the wagon. They were not quite past the front-line troops. Leave us alone, he thought furiously at the persistent officer. Go back to your work and leave this one wagon to itself!

"We already have reported it," said Caz worriedly. "To our own commandant."

"And who might that be?" came the unrelenting, infuriating question.

"Colonel Puxolix," said the driver.

"I know of no such officer."

"How can one know every officer in the army?"

"Nevertheless, perhaps you had best report the incident to my own command. It never hurts one to be thorough, citizen. And I would still like to see the supplies you are to deliver." He turned as if to signal to several chattering soldiers standing nearby.

"Here's one of 'em!" said Flor. Her sword lopped off the officer's head in the midst of a never-to-be-answered query.

For an instant they froze in readiness, hands on weapons, eyes on the troops nearest the wagon. Yet there was no immediate reaction, no cry of alarm. Flor's move had been so swift and the body had fallen so rapidly that no one had yet noticed.

While their driver did not believe in divine intervention, he had the sense to make the decision his passengers withheld.

"Hiiii-criiickk!" he shouted softly, simultaneously snapping his odd whip over the lizard's eyes. The animal surged forward in a galloping waddle. Now soldiers did turn from conversation or eating to stare uncertainly at the fleeing wagon.

The last few troops scrambled out of the wagon's path. There was nothing ahead save rock and promise.

Someone stumbled over the body of the unfortunately curious officer, noted that the head was no longer attached, connected the perfidy with the rapidly shrinking outline of the racing wagon, and finally thought to raise the alarm.

"Here they come, friends." Caz knelt in the wagon, staring back the way they'd come. His eyes picked out individual pursuers where Jon-Tom could detect only a faint rising of dust. "They must have found the body."

"Not enough of a start," said Bribbens tightly. "I'll never see my beloved Sloomaz-ayor-le-Weentli and its cool green banks again. I regret only not having the opportunity to perish in water."

"Woe unto us," murmured a disconsolate Mudge.

"Woe unto ya, maybe," said the lithe black shape perched on the back of the driver's seat. Pog lifted into the air and sped ahead of the lumbering wagon.

"Send back help!" Jon-Tom yelled to the retreating dot.

"He will do so," Clothahump said patiently, "if his panic does not overwhelm his good sense. I am more concerned that our pursuit may catch us before any such assistance has a chance to be mobilized."

"Can't you make this go any faster?" asked Flor.

"The lanteth is built for pulling heavy loads, not for springing like a zealth over poor ground such as this," said the driver, raising his voice in order to be heard above the rumble of the wheels.

"They're gaining on us," said Jon-Tom. Now the mounted riders coming up behind were close enough so that even he could make out individual shapes. Many of the insects he didn't recognize, but the long, lanky, helmeted Plated Folk resembling giant walking sticks were clear enough. Their huge strides ate up long sections of Pass as they closed on the escapees. Two riders on each long back began to notch arrows into bows.

"The Gate, there's the Gate, by Rerelia's pink purse it is!" Mudge shouted gleefully.

His shout was cut off as he was thrown off his feet. The wagon lurched around a huge boulder in the sand, rose momentarily onto two wheels, but did not turn over. It slammed back down onto the riverbed with a wooden crunch. Somehow the axles held. The spokes bent but did not snap.

Ahead was the still distant rampart of a massive stone wall. Arrows began to zip like wasps past the wagon. The passengers huddled low on the bed, listening to the occasional *thuck* as an arrow stuck into the wooden sides.

A moan sounded above them, a silent whisper of departure, and another body joined Talea. It was their iconoclastic, brave driver. He lay limply in the wagon bed, arms trailing and the color already beginning to fade from his ommatidia. Two arrows protruded from his head.

Jon-Tom scrambled desperately into the driver's seat, trying to stay low while arrows whistled nastily around him. The reins lay draped across the front bars of the seat. He reached for them.

They receded. So did the seat. The rolling wagon had struck another boulder and had bounced, sending its occupants flying. It landed ahead of Jon-Tom, on its side. The panicky lizard continued pulling it toward freedom.

Spitting sand and blood, Jon-Tom struggled to his feet. He'd landed on his belly. Duar and staff were still intact. So was he, thanks to the now shattered hard-shelled disguise. As he tried to walk, a loose piece of legging slid down onto his foot. He kicked it aside, began pulling off the other sections of chitin and throwing them away. Deception was no longer of any use.

"Come on, it isn't far!" he yelled to his companions. Caz ran past, then Mudge and Bribbens. The boatman was assisting Clothahump as best he could.

Flor, almost past him, halted when she saw he was running toward the wagon. "Jon-Tom, *muerte es muerte.* Let it be."

"I'm not leaving without her."

Flor caught up with him, grabbed his arm. "She's dead, Jon-Tom. Be a man. Leave it alone."

He did not stop to answer her. Ignoring the shafts falling around them, he located the spraddled corpse. In an instant he had Talea's body in a fireman's carry across his shoulders. She was so small, hardly seemed to have any weight at all. A surge of strength ran through him, and he ran light-headed toward the wall. It was someone else running, someone else breathing hard.

Only Mudge had a bow, but he couldn't run and use it. It wouldn't matter much in a minute anyway, because their grotesque pursuit was almost on top of them. It would be a matter of swords then, a delaying of the inevitable dying.

A furry shape raced past him. Another followed, and two more. He slowed to a trot, tried to wipe the sweat from his eyes. What he saw renewed his strength more than any vitamins.

A fuzzy wave was funneling out of a narrow crack in the hundred-foot-high Gate ahead. Squirrels and muskrats, otters and possums, an isolated skunk, and a platoon of vixens charged down the Pass.

The insect riders saw the rush coming and hesitated just long enough to allow the exhausted escapees to blend in with their saviors. There was a brief, intense fight. Then the pursuers, who had counted on no more than overtaking and slaughtering a few renegades, turned and ran for the safety of the Greendowns. Many did not make it, their mounts cut out from under them. The butchery was neat and quick.

Soft paws helped the limping, panting refugees the rest of the way in. A thousand questions were thrown at them, not a few centering on their identity. Some of the rescuers had seen the discarded chitin disguises, and knowledge of that prompted another hundred queries at least.

Clothahump adjusted his filthy spectacles, shook sand from the inside of his shell, and confronted a minor officer who had taken roost on the wizard's obliging shoulders.

"Is Wuckle Three-Stripe of Polastrindu here?"

"Aye, but he's with the Fourth and Fifth Corps," said the raven. His kilt was yellow, black, and azure, and he wore a thin helmet. Two throwing knives were strapped to his sides beneath his wings, and his claws had been sharpened for war.

"What about a general named Aveticus?"

"Closer, in the headquarters tent," said the raven. He brushed at the yellow scarf around his neck, the insignia of an arboreal noncommissioned officer. "You'd like to go there, I take it?"

Clothahump nodded. "Immediately. Tell him it's the mad doom-sayers. He'll see us."

The raven nodded. "Will do, sir." He lifted from the wizard's shell and soared over the crest of the Gate.

They marched on through the barely open doorway. Jon-Tom had turned his burden over to a pair of helpful ocelots. The Gate itself, he saw, was at least a yard deep and formed of massive timbers. The stonework of the wall was thirty times as thick, solid rock. The Gate gleamed with fresh sap, a substance Caz identified as a fire-retardant.

The Plated Folk might somehow pierce the Gate, but picks and hatchets would never breech the wall. His confidence rose.

It lifted to near assurance when they emerged from the Pass. Spread out on the ancient river plain that sloped down from the mountains were thousands of camp fires. The warmlanders had taken Clothahump's warning to heart. They would be ready.

He repositioned his own special burden, taking it back from the helpful soldiers. With a grimace he unsnapped the insect head and kicked it aside. Red hair hung limply across his shoulder. He stroked the face, hurriedly pulled his hand away. The skin was numbingly cold.

There were two arrows in her back. Even in death, she had protected him again. But it would be all right, he told himself angrily. Clothahump would revive her, as he'd promised he would. Hadn't he promised? Hadn't he?

They were directed to a large three-cornered tent. The banners of a hundred cities flew above it. Squadrons of brightly kilted birds and bats flew in formation overhead, arrowhead outlines full of the flash and silver of weapons. They had their own bivouacs, he noted absently, on the flanks of the mountains or in the forest that rose to the west.

Wuckle Three-Stripe was there, still panting from having ridden through the waiting army to meet them. So was Aveticus, his attitude and eyes as alert and ready as they'd been that day so long ago in the council chambers of Polastrindu. He was heavily armored, and a crimson sash hung from his long neck. Jon-Tom could read his expression well enough: the marten was eager to be at the business of killing.

There were half a dozen other officers. Before the visitors could say anything a massive wolverine resplendent in gold chain mail stepped forward and asked in a voice full of disbelief, "Have ye then truly been to Cugluch?" Rumor then had preceded presence.

"To Cugluch an' back, mate," Mudge admitted pridefully. " 'Twas an epic journey. One that'll long be spoken of. The bards will not 'ave words enough t' do 'er justice."

"Perhaps," said Aveticus quietly. "I hope there will be bards left to sing of it."

"We bring great news." Clothahump took a seat near the central table. "I am sorry to say that the great magic of the Plated Folk remains as threatening as ever, though not quite as enigmatic.

"However, for the first time in recorded history, we have powerful allies who are not of the warmlands." He did not try to keep the pleasure from his voice. "The Weavers have agreed to fight alongside us!"

Considerable muttering rose from the assembled leadership. Not all of it was pleased.

"I have the word of the Grand Webmistress Oll herself, given to us in person," Clothahump added, dissatisfied with the reaction his announcement produced.

When the import finally penetrated, there were astonished murmurs of delight.

"The Weavers . . . We canna lose now. . . . Won't be a one of the Plated Bastards left! . . . Drive them all the way to the end of the Greendowns!"

"That is," said Clothahump cautioningly, "they will fight alongside us if they can get here in time. They have to come across the Teeth."

"Then they will never reach here," said a skeptical officer. "There is no other pass across the Teeth save the Troom."

"Perhaps not a Pass, but a path. The Ironclouders will show them the way."

Now derision filled the tent. "There is no such place as Ironcloud," said the dubious Wuckle Three-Stripe. "It is a myth inhabited by ghosts."

"We climbed inside the myth and supped with the ghosts," said Clothahump calmly. "It exists."

"I believe this wizard's word is proof enough of anything," said Aveticus softly, dominating the discussion by sheer strength of presence.

"They have promised to guide the Weaver army here," Clothahump continued to his suddenly respectful audience. "But we cannot count on their assistance. I believe the Plated Folk will begin their attack any day. We confronted and escaped from the wizard Eejakrat.

While he does not know that we know little about his Manifestation, he will not assume ignorance on our part, and thus will urge the assembled horde to march. They appeared ready in any case."

That stimulated a barrage of questions from the officers. They wanted estimates of troop strength, of arboreals, weapons and provisioning, of disposition and heavy troops and bowmen and more.

Clothahump impatiently waved the questions off. "I can't answer any of your queries in detail. I am not a soldier and my observations are attuned to other matters. I can tell you that this is by far the greatest army the Plated Folk have ever sent against the warmlands."

"They will be met by more warmlanders than ever they imagined!" snorted Wuckle Three-Stripe. "We will reduce the populating of the Greendowns to nothing. The Troom Pass shall be paved with chitin!" Cries of support and determination came from those behind him.

The badger's expression softened. "I must say we are pleased, if utterly amazed, to find you once again safely among your kind. The world owes you all a great debt."

"How great, mate?" asked Mudge.

Three-Stripe eyed the otter distastefully. "In this time of crisis, how can you think of mere material things?"

"Mate, I can always th—" Flor put a hand over the otter's muzzle.

The mayor turned to a subordinate. "See that these people have anything they want, and that they are provided with food and the best of shelter." The weasel officer nodded.

"It will be done, sir." He moved forward, saluted crisply. His gaze fell on the form lying limply across Jon-Tom's back. "Shall she be requiring medical care, sir?"

Red hair tickled Jon-Tom's ear. He jerked his head to one side, replied almost imperceptibly.

"No. She's dead."

"I am sorry, sir."

Jon-Tom's gaze traveled across the tent. Clothahump was conversing intently with a cluster of officers including the wolverine, Aveticus, and Wuckle Three-Stripe. He glanced up for an instant and locked eyes with the spellsinger. The instant passed.

The relief Jon-Tom had sought in the wizard's eyes was not there, nor had there been hope.

Only truth.

XV

The meeting did not take long. As they left the tent the tension of the past weeks, of living constantly on the edge of death and disappointment, began to let go of them all.

"Me for a 'ot bath!" said Mudge expectantly.

"And I for a cold one," countered Bribbens.

"I think I'd prefer a shower, myself," said Flor.

"I'd enjoy that myself, I believe." Jon-Tom did not notice the look that passed between Caz and Flor. He noticed nothing except the wizard's retreating oval.

"Just a minute, sir. Where are you going now?"

Clothahump glanced back at him. "First to locate Pog. Then to the Council of Wizards, Warlocks, and Witches so that we may coordinate our magicking in preparation for the coming attack. Only one may magic at a time, you know. Contradiction destroys the effectiveness of spells."

"Wait. What about . . . you know. You promised."

Clothahump looked evasive. "She's dead, my boy. Like love, life is a transitory thing. Both linger as long as they're able and fade quickly."

"I don't want any of your fucking wizardly platitudes!" He towered over the turtle. "You said you could bring her back."

"I said I might. You were despondent. You needed hope, something to sustain you. I gave you that. By pretending I might help the dead I helped the living to survive. I have no regrets."

When Jon-Tom did not respond the wizard continued, "My boy,

your magic is of an unpredictable quality and considerable power. Many times that unpredictability could be a drawback. But the magic we face is equally unpredictable. You may be of great assistance . . . if you choose to.

"But I feel responsibility for you, if not for your present hurt. If you elect to do nothing, no one will blame you for it and I will not try to coerce you. I can only wish for your assistance.

"I am trying to tell you, my boy, that there is no formula I know for raising the dead. I said I would try, and I shall, when the time is right and other matters press less urgently on my knowledge. I must now try my best to preserve many. I cannot turn away from that to experiment in hopes of saving one." His voice was flat and unemotional.

"I wish it were otherwise, boy. Even magic has its limits, however. Death is one of them."

Jon-Tom stood numbly, still balancing the dead weight on his shoulders. "But you said, you told me . . ."

"What I told you I did in order to save you. Despondency does not encourage quick thinking and survival. You have survived. Talea, bless her mercurial, flinty little heart, would be cursing your self-pity this very moment if she were able."

"You lying little hard-shelled—"

Clothahump took a cautious step backward. "Don't force me to stop you, Jon-Tom. Yes, I lied to you. It wasn't the first time, as Mudge is so quick to point out. A lie in the service of right is a kind of truth."

Jon-Tom let out an inarticulate yell and rushed forward, blinded as much by the cold finality of his loss as by the wizard's duplicity. No longer a personality or even a memory, the body on his shoulders tumbled to the earth. He reached blindly for the impassive sorcerer.

Clothahump had seen the rage building, had taken note of the signs in Jon-Tom's face, in the way he stood, in the tension of his skin. The wizard's hands moved rapidly and he whispered to unseen things words like "fix" and "anesthesia."

Jon-Tom went down as neatly as if clubbed by his own staff. Several soldiers noted the activity and wandered over.

"Is he dead, sir?" one asked curiously.

"No. For the moment he wishes it were so." The wizard pointed toward the limp form of Talea. "The first casualty of the war."

"And this one?" The squirrel gestured down at Jon-Tom.

"Love is always the second casualty. He will be all right in a while.

He needs to rest and not remember. There is a tent behind the head-quarters. Take him and put him in there."

The noncom's tail switched the air. "Will he be dangerous when he regains consciousness?"

Clothahump regarded the softly breathing body. "I do not think so, not even to himself."

The squirrel saluted. "It will be done, sir."

There are few drugs, Clothahump mused, that can numb both the heart and the mind. Among them grief is the most powerful. He watched while the soldiers bore the lanky, youthful Jon-Tom away, then forced himself to turn to more serious matters. Talea was gone and Jon-Tom damaged. Well, he was sorry as sorry could be for the boy, but they would do without his erratic talents if they had to. He could not cool the boy's hate.

Let him hate me, then, if he wishes. It will focus his thoughts away from his loss. He will be forever suspicious of me hereafter, but in that he will have the company of most creatures. People always fear what they cannot understand.

Makes it lonely though, old fellow. Very lonely. You knew that when you took the vows and made the oaths. He sighed, waddled off to locate Aveticus. Now there was a rational mind, he thought pleas-antly. Unimaginative, but sound. He will accept my advice and act upon it. I can help him.

Perhaps in return he can help me. Two hundred and how many years, old fellow?

Tired, dammit. I'm so tired. Pity I took an oath of responsibility along with the others. But this evil of Eejakrat's has got to be stopped.

Clothahump was wise in many things, but even he would not ad-mit that what really kept him going wasn't his oath of responsibility. It was curiosity. . . .

Red fog filled Jon-Tom's vision. Blood mist. It faded to gray when he blinked. It was not the ever present mist of the awful Greendowns, but instead a dull glaze that faded rapidly.

Looking up, he discovered multicolored fabric in place of blue sky. As he lay on his back he heard a familiar voice say, "I'll watch him now."

He pushed himself up on his elbows, his head still swimming from the effects of Clothahump's incantation. Several armed warmlanders were exiting the tent.

"Ya feeling better now?"

He raised his sight once more. An upside-down face stared anxiously into his own. Pog was hanging from one of the crosspoles, wrapped in his wings. He spread them, stretching, and yawned.

"How long have I been out?"

" 'Bout since dis time yesterday."

"Where's everyone else?"

The bat grinned. "Relaxing, trying ta enjoy demselves. Orgy before da storm."

"Talea?" He tried to sit all the way up. A squat, hairy form fluttered down from the ceiling to land on his chest.

"Talea's as dead as she was yesterday when you tried ta attack da master. As dead as she was when dat knife went into her t'roat back in Cugluch, an dat's a fact ya'd better get used ta, man!"

Jon-Tom winced, looked away from the little gargoyle face confronting him. "I'll never accept it. Never."

Pog hopped off his chest, landed on a chair nearby, and leaned against the back. It was designed for a small mammalian body, but it still fit him uncomfortably. He always preferred hanging to sitting but given Jon-Tom's present disorientation, he knew it would be better if he didn't have to stare at a topsy-turvy face just now.

"Ya slay me, ya know?" Pog said disgustedly. "Ya really t'ink you're something special."

"What?" Confused, Jon-Tom frowned at the bat.

"You heard me. I said dat ya tink you're something special, don't ya? Ya tink you're da only one wid problems? At least you've got da satisfaction of knowing dat someone loved ya. I ain't even got dat.

"How would ya like it if Talea were alive and every time ya looked at her, so much as smiled in her direction, she turned away from ya in disgust?"

"I don't—"

The bat cut him off, raised a wing. "No, hear me out. Dat's what I have ta go trough every day of my life. Dat's what I've been going trough for years. 'It don't make sense,' da boss keeps tellin' me." Pog sniffed disdainfully. "But he don't have ta experience it, ta live it. 'Least ya know ya was loved, Jon-Tom. I may never have dat simple ting. I may have ta go trough da rest of my life knowin' dat da one I love gets the heaves every time I come near her. How would you like ta live wid dat? I'm goin' ta suffer until I die, or until she does.

"And what's worse," he looked away momentarily, sounding so miserable that Jon-Tom forgot his own agony, "she's here!"

"Who's here?"

"Da falcon. Uleimee. She's wid da aerial forces. I tried ta see her once, just one time. She wouldn't even do dat for me."

"She can't be much if she acts like that toward you," said Jon-Tom gently.

"Why not? Because she's reactin' to my looks instead of my wondaful personality? Looks are important. Don't let anybody tell ya otherwise. And I got a real problem. And dere's smell, and other factors, and I can't do a damn ting about 'em. Maybe da boss can, eventually. But promises don't do nuthin' for me now." His expression twisted.

"So don't let me hear any more of your bemoanings. You're alive an' healthy, you're an interesting curiosity to da females around ya, an you've got plenty of loving ahead of ya. But not me. I'm cursed because I love only one."

"It's kind of funny," Jon-Tom said softly, tracing a pattern on the blanket covering his cot. "I thought it was Flor I was in love with. She tried to show me otherwise, but I couldn't . . . wouldn't, see."

"Dat wouldn't matter anyhow." Pog fluttered off the chair and headed for the doorway.

"Why not?"

"Blind an' dumb," the bat grumbled. "Don't ya see anyting? She's had da hots for dat Caz fellow ever since we fished him outa da river Tailaroam." He was gone before Jon-Tom could comment.

Caz and Flor? That was impossible, he thought wildly. Or was it? What was impossible in a world of impossibilities?

Bringing back Talea, he told himself.

Well, if Clothahump could do nothing, there was still another manipulator of magic who would try: himself.

Troops gave the tent a wide berth during the following days. Inside a tall, strange human sat singing broken love songs to a corpse. The soldiers muttered nervously to themselves and made signs of protection when they were forced to pass near the tent. Its interior glowed at night with a veritable swarm of gneechees.

Jon-Tom's efforts were finally halted not by personal choice but by outside events. He had succeeded in keeping the body from decomposing, but it remained still as the rock beneath the tent. Then on the tenth day after their hasty retreat from Cugluch, word came down from aerial scouts that the army of the Plated Folk was on the march.

So he slung his duar across his back and went out with staff in hand. Behind he left the body of one who had loved him and whom he could love in return only too late. He strode resolutely through the camp, determined to take a position on the wall. If he could not give life, then by God he would deal out death with equal enthusiasm.

Aveticus met him on the wall.

"It comes, as it must to all creatures," the general said to him. "The time of choosing." He peered hard into Jon-Tom's face. "In your anger, remember that one who fights blindly usually dies quickly."

Jon-Tom blinked, looked down at him. "Thanks, Aveticus. I'll keep control of myself."

"Good." The general walked away, stood chatting with a couple of subordinates as they looked down the Pass.

A ripple of expectancy passed through the soldiers assembled on the wall. Weapons were raised as their wielders leaned forward. No one spoke. The only noise now came from down the Pass, and it was growing steadily louder.

As a wave they came, a single dark wave of chitin and iron. They filled the Pass from one side to the other, a flood of murder that extended unbroken into the distance.

A last few hundred warmlander troops scrambled higher into the few notches cut into the precipitous canyon. From there they could prevent any Plated Folk from scaling the rocks to either side of the wall. They readied spears and arrows. A rich, musky odor filled the morning air, exuded from the glands of thousands of warmlanders. An aroma of anticipation.

The great wooden gates were slowly parted. There came a shout followed by a thunderous cheer from the soldiers on the ramparts that shook gravel from the mountainsides. Led by a phalanx of a hundred heavily armored wolverines, the warmlander army sallied out into the Pass.

Jon-Tom moved to leave his position on the wall so he could join the main body of troops pouring from the Gate. He was confronted by a pair of familiar faces. Caz and Mudge still disdained the use of armor.

"What's wrong?" he asked them. "Aren't you going to join the fight?"

"Eventually," said Caz.

"If it proves absolutely necessary, mate," added Mudge. "Right now we've a more important task assigned to us, we do."

"And what's that?"

"Keepin' an eye on yourself."

Jon-Tom looked past them, saw Clothahump watching him speculatively.

"What's the idea?" He no longer addressed the wizard as "sir."

The sorcerer walked over to join them. His left hand was holding a thick scroll half open. It was filled with words and symbols.

"In the end your peculiar magic, spellsinger, may be of far more use to us than another sword arm."

"I'm not interested in fighting with magic," Jon-Tom countered angrily. "I want to spill some blood."

Clothahump shook his head, smiled ruefully. "How the passions of youth do alter its nature, if not necessarily maturing it. I seem to recall a somewhat different personality once brought confused and gentle to my Tree."

"I remember him also," Jon-Tom replied humorlessly. "He's dead too."

"Pity. He was a nice boy. Ah well. You are potentially much more valuable to us here, Jon-Tom. Do not be so anxious. I promise you that as you grow older you will be presented with ample opportunities for participating in self-satisfying slaughter."

"I'm not interested in—"

Sounding less understanding, Clothahump cut him off testily. "Consider something besides yourself, boy. You are upset because Talea is dead, because her death personally affects *you.* You're upset because I deceived *you.* Now you want to waste a potentially helpful talent to satisfy *your* personal blood lust." He regarded the tall youth sternly.

"My boy, I am fond of you. I think that with a little maturation and a little tempering, as with a good sword, you will make a fine person. But for a little while at least, try thinking of something besides *you.*"

The ready retort died on Jon-Tom's lips. Nothing penetrates the mind or acts on it so effectively as does truth, that most efficient but foul-tasting of all medicines. Clothahump had only one thing in his favor: he was right. That canceled out anything else Jon-Tom could think of to say.

He leaned back against the rampart, saw Caz and Mudge, friends both, watching him warily. Hesitantly, he smiled.

"It's okay. The old bastard's right. I'll stay." He turned from them to study the Pass. After a pause and a qualifying nod from Clothahump, Mudge and Caz moved to join him.

The wolverine wedge struck the center of the Plated Folk wave like a knife, leaving contorted, multilated insect bodies in their wake. The rest of the warmlander soldiers followed close behind.

It was a terrible place for a battle. The majority of both armies could only seethe and shift nervously. They were packed so tightly in the narrow Pass that only a small portion of each force could actually confront one another. It was another advantage for the outnumbered warmlanders.

After an hour or so of combat the battle appeared to be going the way of all such conflicts down through the millennia. Led by the wolverines the warmlanders were literally cutting their way up the Pass. The Plated Folk fought bravely but mechanically, showing no more initiative in individual combat than they did collectively. Also, though they possessed an extra set of limbs, they were stiff-jointed and no match for the more supple, agile enemies they faced. Most of the Plated Folk were no more than three and a half feet tall, while certain of the warmlanders, such as the wolverines and the felines, were considerably more massive and powerful. And none of the insects could match the otters and weasels for sheer speed.

The battle raged all that morning and on into the afternoon. All at once, it seemed to be over. The Plated Folk suddenly threw away their weapons, broke, and ran. This induced considerable chaos in the packed ranks behind the front. The panic spread rapidly, an insidious infection as damaging as any fatal disease.

Soon it appeared that the entire Plated Folk army was in retreat, pursued by yelling, howling warmlanders. The soldiers at the Gate broke out in whoops of joy. A few expressed disappointment at not having been in on the fight.

Only Clothahump stood quietly on his side of the Gate, Aveticus on the other. The wizard was staring with aged eyes at the field of battle, squinting through his glasses and shaking his head slowly.

"Too quick, too easy," he was murmuring.

Jon-Tom overheard. "What's wrong . . . sir?"

Clothahump spoke without looking over at him. "I see no evidence of the power Eejakrat commands. Not a sign of it at work."

"Maybe he can't manipulate it properly. Maybe it's beyond his control."

" 'Maybes' kill more individuals than swords, my boy."

"What kind of magic are you looking for?"

"I don't know." The wizard gazed skyward. "The clouds are innocent of storm. Nothing hints at lightning. The earth is silent, and we've naught to fear from tremorings. The ether flows silently. I feel no discord in any of the levels of magic. It worries me. I fear what I cannot sense."

"There's a possible storm cloud," said Jon-Tom, pointing. "Boiling over the far southern ridge."

Clothahump peered in the indicated direction. Yes, there was a dark mass back there, which had materialized suddenly. It was blacker than any of the scattered cumulo-nimbus that hung in the afternoon sky like winter waifs. The cloud foamed down the face of the ridge, rushing toward the Pass.

"That's not a cloud," said Caz, seeking with eyes sharper than those of other creatures. "Plated Folk."

"What kind?" asked Clothahump, already confident of the reply.

"Dragonflies, a few large beetles. All with subsidiary mounted troops, I fear. Many other large beetles behind them."

"They should be no trouble," murmured Clothahump. "But I wonder."

Aveticus crossed the Gate and joined them.

"What do you make of this, sir?"

"It appears to be the usual aerial assault."

Aveticus nodded, glanced back toward the plain. "If so, they will fare no better in the air than they have on the ground. Still . . ."

"Something troubling you then?" said Clothahump.

The marten eyed the approaching cloud confusedly. "It is strange, the way they are grouped. Still, it would be peculiar if they did not at least once try something different."

Yells sounded from behind the Gate. The warmlanders own aerial forces were massing in a great spiral over the camp. They were of every size and description. Their kilts formed a brilliant quiltwork in the sky.

Then the spiral began to unwind as the line of bats and birds flew over the Gate to meet the coming threat. They intercepted the Plated Folk fliers near the line of combat.

As soon as contact was made, the Plated Folk forces split. Half moved to meet the attack. The second half, consisting primarily of powerful but ponderous beetles, dipped below the fight. With them went a large number of the more agile dragonflies with their single riders.

"Look there," said Mudge. "Wot are the bleedin' buggerers up to?"

"They're attacking ground troops!" said Aveticus, outraged. "It is not done. Those in the sky do not do battle with those on the ground. They fight only others of their own kind."

"Well, somebody's changed the rules," said Jon-Tom, watching a tall amazonian figure moving across the wall toward them.

Confusion began to grip the advance ranks of warmlanders. They were not used to fighting attack from above. Most of the outnumbered birds and bats were too busy with their own opponents to render any assistance to those below.

"This is Eejakrat's work," muttered Clothahump. "I can sense it. It is magic, but of a most subtle sort."

"Air-ground support," said the newly arrived Flor. She was staring tight-lipped at the carnage the insect fliers were wreaking on the startled warmlander infantry.

"What kind of magic is this?" asked Aveticus grimly.

"It's called tactics," said Jon-Tom.

The marten turned to Clothahump. "Wizard, can you not counter this kind of magic?"

"I would try," said Clothahump, "save that I do not know how to begin. I can counter lightning and dissipate fog, but I do not know how to assist the minds of our soldiers. That is what is endangered now."

While bird and dragonfly tangled in the air above the Pass and other insect fliers swooped again and again on the ranks of puzzled warmlanders, the sky began to rain a different sort of death.

The massive cluster of large beetles remained high out of arrowshot and began to disgorge hundreds, thousands of tiny pale puffs on the rear of the warmlander forces. Arrows fell from the puff shapes as they descended.

Jon-Tom recognized the familiar round cups. So did Flor. But Clothahump could only shake his head in disbelief.

"Impossible! No spell is strong enough to lift so many into the air at once."

"I'm afraid this one is," Jon-Tom told him.

"What is this frightening spell called?"

"Parachuting."

The warmlander troops were as confused by the sight as by the substance of this assault on their rear ranks. At the same time there was a chilling roar from the retreating Plated Folk infantry. Those who'd abandoned their weapons suddenly scrambled for the nearest canyon wall.

From the hidden core of the horde came several hundred of the largest beetles anyone had ever seen. These huge scarabaeids and their cousins stampeded through the gap created by their own troops.

The startled wolverines were trampled underfoot. Massive chitin horns pierced soldier after soldier. Each beetle had half a dozen bowmen on its back. From there they picked off those warmlanders who tried to cut at the beetle's legs.

Now it was the warmlanders who broke, whirling and scrambling in panic for the safety of the distant Gate. They pressed insistently on those behind them. But terror already ruled their supposed reinforcements. Instead of friendly faces those pursued by the relentless beetles found thousands of Plated Folk soldiers who had literally dropped from the sky.

The birds and their riders, mostly small squirrels and their relatives, fought valiantly to break through the aerial Plated Folk. But by the time they had made any headway against the dragonfly forces confronting them the great, lumbering flying beetles had already dropped their cargo. Now they were flying back down the Pass, to gather a second load of impatient insect parachutists.

Glee turned to dismay on the wall as badly demoralized troops streamed back through the open Gate. Behind them was sand and gravel-covered ground so choked with corpses that it was hard to move. The dead actually did more to save the warmlander forces from annihilation than the living.

When the last survivor had limped inside, the great Gate was swung shut. An insectoid wave crested against the barrier.

Now the force of scarabaeids who'd broken the warmlander front turned and retreated. They could not scale the wall and would only hinder its capture.

Strong-armed soldiers carrying dozens, hundreds of ladders took their places. The ladders were thrown up against the wall in such profusion that several defenders, while trying to spear those Plated Folk raising one ladder, were struck and killed by another. The ladders were so close together they sometimes overlapped rungs. A dark tide began to swarm up the wall.

Having no facility with a bow, Jon-Tom was heaving spears as fast as the armsbearers could supply them. Next to him Flor was firing a large longbow with deadly accuracy. Mudge stood next to her, occasionally pausing in his own firing to compliment the giantess on a good shot.

The wall was now crowded with reinforcements. Every time a warmlander fell another took his place. But despite the number of ladders pushed back and broken, the number of climbers killed, the seemingly endless stream of Plated Folk came on.

It was Caz who pulled Jon-Tom aside and directed his attention far, far up the canyon. "Can you see them, my friend? They are there, watching."

"Where?"

"There . . . can't you see the dark spots on that butte that juts out slightly into the Pass?"

Jon-Tom could barely make out the butte. He could not discern individuals standing on it. But he did not doubt Caz's observation.

"I'll take your word for it. Can you see who 'they' are?"

"Eejakrat I recognize from our sojourn in Cugluch. The giant next to him must be, from the richness of attire and servility of attendants, the Empress Skrritch."

"Can you see what Eejakrat is doing?" inquired a worried Clothahump.

"He looks behind him at something I cannot see."

"The dead mind!" Clothahump gazed helplessly at his sheaf of formulae. "It is responsible for this new method of fighting, these 'tactics' and 'parachutes' and such. It is telling the Plated Folk how to fight. It means they have found a new way to attack the wall."

"It means rather more than that," said Aveticus quietly. Everyone turned to look at the marten. "It means they no longer have to breach the Jo-Troom Gate. . . ."

XVI

"Is it not clear?" he told them when no one responded. "These 'parachute' things will enable them to drop thousands of soldiers *behind* the Gate." He looked grim and turned to a subordinate.

"Assemble Elasmin, Toer, and Sleastic. Tell them they must gather a large body of mobile troops. No matter how bad the situation here grows these soldiers must remain ready behind the Gate, watching for more of these falling troops. They must watch only the sky, for, if we are not prepared, these monsters will fall all over our own camp and all will be lost."

The officer rushed away to convey that warning to the warmlander general staff. Overhead, birds and riders were holding their own against the dragonfly folk. But they were fully occupied. If the beetles returned with more airborne Plated Folk troops, the warmlander arboreals would be unable to prevent them from falling on the underdefended camp. Attacked from the front and from behind, the Jo-Troom Gate would change from impregnable barrier to mass grave.

Once out on the open plains the Plated Folk army would be able to engulf the remnants of the warmlander defenders. In addition to superior numbers, which they'd always possessed, the attackers now had the use of superior tactics. Eejakrat had discovered the flexibility and imagination dozens of their earlier assaults had lacked.

Not that it would matter soon, for the inexorable pressure on the Gate's defenders was beginning to tell. Now an occasional Plated Folk warrior managed to surmount the ramparts. Isolated pockets of fighting were beginning to appear on the wall itself.

" 'Ere now, wot d'you make o' that, mate?" Mudge had hold of Jon-Tom's arm and was pointing northward.

On the plain below the foothills of Zaryt's Teeth a thin dark line was snaking rapidly toward the Gate.

Then a familiar form was scuttling through the milling soldiers. It wore light chain-mail top and bottom and a strange helmet that left room for multiple eyes. Despite the armor both otter and man identified the wearer instantly.

"Ananthos!" said Jon-Tom.

"yes." The spider put four limbs on the wall and looked outward. He ducked as a tiny club glanced off his cephalothorax.

"i hope sincerely we are not too late."

Flor put aside her bow, exhausted. "I never thought I'd ever be glad to greet a spider. Or that to my dying day I'd ever be doing this, *compadre.*" She walked over and gave the uncertain arachnid a brisk hug.

Disdaining the wall, the modest force of Weavers divided. Then, utilizing multiple limbs, incredible agility, and built-in climbing equipment, they scrambled up the sheer sides of the Pass flanking the Gate. They suspended themselves there, out of arrow range, and began firing down on the Plated Folk clustered before the Gate.

This additional firepower enabled the warmlanders on the wall to concentrate on the ladders. Nets were spun and dropped. Sticky, unbreakable silk cables entangled scores of insect fighters.

Dragonflies and riders broke from the aerial combat to swoop toward the new arrivals clinging to the bare rock. The Weavers spun balls of sticky silk. These were whirled lariatlike over their heads and flung at the diving fliers with incredible accuracy. They glued themselves to wings or legs, and the startled insects found themselves yanked right out of the sky.

Now the birds and bats began to make some progress against their depleted aerial foe. There was a real hope that they could now prevent any returning beetles from dropping troops behind the Gate.

While that specific danger was thus greatly reduced, the most important result of the arrival of the Weaver force was the effect it had on the morale of the Plated Folk. Until now all their new strategies and plans had worked perfectly. The abrupt and utterly unexpected appearance of their solitary ancient enemies and their obvious rapport with the warmlanders was a devastating shock. The Weavers were the last people the Plated Folk expected to find defending the Jo-Troom Gate.

Directing the Weavers' actions from a position on the wall by re-laying orders and information, via tiny sprinting spiders colored bright red, yellow and blue, was a bulbous black form. The Grand Webmistress Oll was decked out in silver armor and hundreds of feet of crimson and orange silk.

Once she waved a limb briskly toward Jon-Tom and his compan-ions. Perhaps she saw them, possibly she was only giving a command.

The warmlanders, buoyed by the arrival of a once feared but now welcomed new ally, fought with renewed strength. The Plated Folk forces faltered, then redoubled their attack. Weaver archers and retia-rii wrought terrible destruction among them, and the warmlander bowmen had easy targets helplessly ensnared in sticky nets.

A new problem arose. There was a danger that the growing moun-tain of corpses before the wall would soon be high enough to elimi-nate the need for ladders.

All that night the battle continued by torchlight, with fatigue-laden warmlanders and Weavers holding off the still endless waves of Plated Folk. The insects fought until they died and were walked on emo-tionlessly by their replacements.

It was after midnight when Caz woke Jon-Tom from an uneasy sleep.

"Another cloud, my friend," said the rabbit. His clothing was torn and one ear was bleeding despite a thick bandage.

Wearily Jon-Tom gathered up his staff and a handful of small spears and trotted alongside Caz toward the wall. "So they're going to try dropping troops behind us at night? I wonder if our aerials have enough strength left to hold them back."

"I don't know," said Caz with concern. "That's why I was sent to get you. They want every strong spear thrower on the wall to try and pick off any low fliers."

In truth, the ranks of kilted fighters were badly thinned, while the strength of their dragonfly opponents seemed nearly the same as be-fore. Only the presence of the Weavers kept the arboreal battle equal.

But it was not a swarm of lumbering Plated Folk that flew out of the moon. It was a sea of sulfurous yellow eyes. They fell on the insect fliers with terrible force. Great claws shredded membranous wings, beaks nipped away antennae and skulls, while tiny swords cut with incredible skill.

It took a moment for Jon-Tom and his friends to identify the new combatants, cloaked as they were by the concealing night. It was the size of the great glowing eyes that soon gave the answer.

"The Ironclouders," Caz finally announced. "Bless my soul but I never thought to see the like. Look at them wheel and bank, will you? It's no contest."

The word was passed up and down the ranks. So entranced were the warmlanders by the sight of these fighting legends that some of them temporarily forgot their own defensive tasks and thus were wounded or killed.

The inhabitants of the hematite were better equipped for night fighting than any of the warmlanders save the few bats. The previously unrelenting aerial assault of the Plated Folk was shattered. Fragmented insect bodies began to fall from the sky. The only reaction this grisly rain produced among the warmlanders beneath it was morbid laughter.

By morning the destruction was nearly complete. What remained of the Plated Folk aerial strength had retreated far up the Pass.

A general council was held atop the wall. For the first time in days the warmlanders were filled with optimism. Even the suspicious Clothahump was forced to admit that the tide of battle seemed to have turned.

"Could we not use these newfound friends as did the Plated Folk?" one of the officers suggested. "Could we not employ them to drop our own troops to the rear of the enemy forces?"

"Why stop there?" wondered one of the exhilarated bird officers, a much-decorated hawk in light armor and violet and red kilt. "Why not drop them in Cugluch itself? That would panic them!"

"No," said Aveticus carefully. "Our people are not prepared for such an adventure, and despite their size I do not think our owlish allies have the ability to carry more than a single rider, even assuming they would consent to such a proposition, which I do not think they would.

"But I do not think they would object to duplicating the actions of the Plated Folk fliers in assailing opposing ground forces. As our own can now do."

So the orders went out from the staff to their own fliers and thence to those from Ironcloud. It was agreed. Wearing dark goggles to shield their sensitive eyes from the sun, the owls and lemurs led the rejuvenated warmlander arboreals in dive after dive upon the massed, confused ranks of the Plated Folk army. The result was utter disorientation among the insect soldiers. But they still refused to collapse, though the losses they suffered were beginning to affect even so immense an army.

And when victory seemed all but won it was lost in a single heart-rending and completely unexpected noise. A sound shocking and new to the warmlanders, who had never heard anything quite like it before. It was equally shocking but not new to Flor and Jon-Tom. Though not personally exposed to it, they recognized quickly enough the devastating thunder of dynamite.

As the dust began to settle among cries of pain and fear, there came a second, deeper, more ominous rumble as the entire left side of the Jo-Troom wall collapsed in a heap of shattered masonry and stone. It brought the great wooden gates down with it, supporting timbers splintering like firecrackers as they crashed to the ground.

"Diversion," muttered Flor. "The aerial attack, the parachutists, the beetles . . . all a diversion. *Bastardos;* I should have remembered my military history classes."

Jon-Tom moved shakily to the edge of the wall. If they'd been on the other side of the Gate they'd all be dead or maimed now.

Small white shapes were beginning to emerge from the ground in front of the ruined wall. Waving picks and short swords they cut at the legs of startled warmlander soldiers. Like the inhabitants of Iron-cloud they too wore dark goggles to protect them from the sunlight.

"Termites," Jon-Tom murmured aloud, "and other insect burrowers. But where did they get the explosives?"

"Little need to think on that, boy," Clothahump said sadly. "More of Eejakrat's work. What did you call the packaged thunder?"

"Explosives. Probably dynamite."

"Or even gelignite," added Flor with suppressed anger. "That was an intense explosion."

Sensing victory, the Plated Folk ignored the depradations of the swooping arboreals overhead and swarmed forward. Nor could the hectic casting of spears and nets by the Weavers hold them back. Not with the wall, the fabled ancient bottleneck, tumbled to the earth like so many child's blocks.

It must have taken an immense quantity of explosives to undermine that massive wall. It was possible, Jon-Tom mused that the Plated burrowers had begun excavating their tunnel weeks before the battle began.

Without the wall to hinder them they charged onward. By sheer force of numbers they pushed back those who had desperately rushed to defend the ruined barrier. Then they were across, fighting on the other side of the Jo-Troom Gate for the first time in recorded memory. Warmlander blood stained its own land.

Jon-Tom turned helplessly to Clothahump. The Plated Folk soldiers were ignoring the remaining section of wall and the few arrows and spears that fell from its crest. The wizard stood quietly, his gaze focused on the far end of the Pass and not on the castastrophe below.

"Can't you do something," Jon-Tom pleaded with him. "Bring fire and destruction down on them! Bring . . ."

Clothahump did not seem to be listening. He was looking without eyes. "I almost have it," he whispered to no one in particular. "Almost can . . ." He broke off, turned to stare at Jon-Tom.

"Do you think conjuring up lightning and floods and fire is merely a matter of snapping one's fingers, boy? Haven't you learned anything about magic since you've been here?" He turned his attention away again.

"Can almost . . . yes," he said excitedly, "I can. I believe I can see it now!" The enthusiasm faded. "No, I was wrong. Too well screened by distortion spells. Eejakrat leaves nothing to chance. Nothing."

Jon-Tom turned away from the entranced wizard, swung his duar around in front of him. His fingers played furiously on the strings. But he could not think of a single appropriate song to sing. His favorites were songs of love, of creativity and relationships. He knew a few marches, and though he sang with ample fervor nothing materialized to slow the Plated Folk advance.

Then Mudge, sweaty and his fur streaked with dried blood, was shaking him and pointing westward. "Wot the bloody 'ell is that?" The otter was staring across the widening field of battle.

"It sounds like . . ." said Caz confusedly. "I don't know. A rusty door hinge, perhaps. Or high voices. Many high voices."

Then they could make out the source of the peculiar noise. It was singing. Undisciplined, but strong, and it rose from a motley horde of marchers nearing the foothills. They were armed with pitchforks and makeshift spears, with scythes and knives tied to broom handles, with woodcutters' tools and sharpened iron posts.

They flowed like a brown-gray wave over the milling combatants, and wherever their numbers appeared the Plated Folk were overwhelmed.

"Mice!" said Mudge, aghast. "Rats an' shrews in there, too. I don't believe it. They're not fighters. Wot be they doin' 'ere?"

"Fighting," said Jon-Tom with satisfaction, "and damn well, too, from the look of it."

The rodent mob attacked with a ferocity that more than compensated for their lack of training. The flow of clicking, gleaming death from the Pass was blunted, then stopped. The rodents fought with astonishing bravery, throwing themselves onto larger opponents while others cut at warrior's knees and ankles.

Sometimes three and four of the small warmlanders would bring down a powerful insect by weight alone. Their makeshift weapons broke and snapped. They resorted to rocks and bare paws, whatever they could scavenge that would kill.

For a few moments the remnants of the warmlander forces were as stunned by the unexpected assault as the Plated Folk. They stared dumbfounded as the much maligned, oft-abused rodents threw themselves into the fray. Then they resumed fighting themselves, alongside heroic allies once held in servitude and contempt.

Now if the warmlanders prevailed there would be permanent changes in the social structure of Polastrindu and other communities, Jon-Tom knew. At least one good thing would come of this war.

He thought they were finished with surprises. But while he selected targets below for the spears he was handed, yet another one appeared.

In the midst of the battle a gout of flame brightened the winter morning. There was another. It was almost as if . . . yes! A familiar iridescent bulk loomed large above the combatants, incinerating Plated Folk by the squadron.

"I'll be damned!" he muttered. "It's Falameezar!"

"But I thought he was through with us," said Caz.

"You know this dragon?" Bribbens tended to a wounded leg and eyed the distant fight with amazement. It was the first time Jon-Tom had seen the frog's demeanor change.

"We sure as hell do!" Jon-Tom told him joyfully. "Don't you see, Caz, it all adds up."

"Pardon my ignorance, friend Jon-Tom, but the only mathematics I've mastered involves dice and cards."

"This army of the downtrodden, of the lowest mass of workers. Who do you think organized them, persuaded them to fight? Someone had to raise a cry among them, someone had to convince them to fight for their rights as well as for their land. And who would be more willing to do so, to assume the mantle of leadership, than our innocent Marxist Falameezar!"

"This is absurd." Bribbens could still not quite believe it. "Dragons

do not fight *with* people. They are solitary, antisocial creatures who
. . ."

"Not this one," Jon-Tom informed him assuredly. "If anything,
he's *too* social. But I'm not going to argue his philosophies now."

Indeed, as the gleaming black and purple shape trudged nearer
they could hear the great dragon voice bellowing encouragingly
above the noise of battle.

"Onward downtrodden masses! Workers arise! Down with the in-
vading imperialist warmongers!"

Yes, that was Falameezar and none other. The dragon was in his
sociological element. In between thundering favorite Marxist homi-
lies he would incinerate a dozen terrific insect warriors or squash a
couple beneath massive clawed feet. Around him swirled a bedraggled mob of tiny furry supporters like an armada of fighter craft
protecting a dreadnought.

The legions of Plated Folk seemed endless. But now that the surprise engendered by the destruction of the wall had passed, their
offensive began to falter. The arrival of what amounted to a second
warmlander army, as ferocious if not as well trained as the original,
started to turn the tide.

Meanwhile the Weavers and fliers from Ironcloud continued to
cause havoc among the packed ranks of warriors trying to squeeze
through the section of ruined wall to reach the open plain where their
numbers could be a factor. The diminutive lemur bowmen fired and
fired until their drawstring fingers were bloody.

When the fall came it was not in a great surge of panic. A steady
withering of purpose and determination ate through the ranks of the
Plated Folk. In clusters, and individually, they lost their will to fight
on. A vast sigh of discouragement rippled through the whole exhausted army.

Sensing it, the warmlanders redoubled their efforts. Still fighting,
but with intensity seeping away from them, the Plated Folk were
gradually pressed back. The plain was cleared, and then the destroyed section of wall. The battle moved once again back into the
confines of the Pass. Insect officers raged and threatened, but they
could do nothing to stop the steady slow leak of desire that bled their
soldiers' will to fight.

Jon-Tom had stopped throwing spears. His arm throbbed with the
efforts of the past several days. The conflict had retreated steadily up
the Pass, and the Plated combatants were out of range now. He was
cheering tiredly when a hand clamped on his arm so forcefully that

he winced. He looked around. It was Clothahump. The wizard's grip was anything but that of an oldster.

"By the periodic table, I can see it now!"

"See what?"

"The deadmind." Clothahump's tone held a peculiar mixture of confusion and excitement. "The deadmind. It is not in a body."

"You mean the brain itself's been extracted?" The image was gruesome.

"No. It is scattered about, in several containers of differing shape."

Jon-Tom's mind shunted aside the instinctive vision and produced only a blank from the wizard's description. Flor listened intently.

"It talks to Eejakrat," Clothahump continued, his voice far away, distant, "in words I can't understand."

"Several containers . . . the mind is several minds?" Jon-Tom struggled to make sense of a seeming impossibility.

"No, no. It is one mind that has been split into many parts."

"What does it look like? You said containers. Can you be more specific?" Flor asked him.

"Not really. The containers are mostly rectangular, but not all. One inscribes words on a scroll, symbols and magic terms I do not recognize." He winced with the strain of focusing senses his companions did not possess.

"There are symbols over all the containers as well, though they mostly differ from those appearing on the scroll. The mind also makes a strange noise, like talking that is not. I can read some of the symbols . . . it is strangely inscribed. It changes as I look at it." He stopped.

Jon-Tom urged him on. "What is it? What's happening?"

Clothahump's face was filled with pain. Sweat poured down his face into his shell. Jon-Tom didn't know that a turtle could sweat. Everything indicated that the wizard was expending a massive effort not only to continue to see but to understand.

"Eejakrat . . . Eejakrat sees the failure of the attack." He swayed, and Jon-Tom and Flor had to support him or he would have fallen. "He works a last magic, a final conjuration. He has . . . has delved deep within the deadmind for its most powerful manifestation. It has given him the formula he needs. Now he is giving orders to his assistants. They are bringing materials from the store of sorceral supplies. Skrritch watches, she will kill him if he fails. Eejakrat promises her the battle will be won. The materials . . . I recognize some. No, many. But I do not understand the formula given, the purpose. The purpose is to . . . to . . ." He turned a frightened face upward. Jon-Tom shivered. He'd never before seen the wizard frightened. Not when confronted by the Massawrath, not when crossing Helldrink.

But he was more than frightened now. He was terrified.

"Must stop it!" he mumbled. "Got to stop him from completing the formula. Even Eejakrat does not understand what he does. But he . . . I see it clearly . . . he is desperate. He will try anything. I do not think . . . do not think he can control . . ."

"What's the formula?" Flor pressed him.

"Complex . . . can't understand . . ."

"Well then, the symbols you read on the deadmind containers."

"Can read them now, yes . . . but can't understand . . ."

"Try. Repeat them, anyway."

Clothahump went silent, and for a moment the two humans were afraid he wouldn't speak again. But Jon-Tom finally managed to shake him into coherence.

"Symbols . . . symbols say, 'Property.' "

"That's all?" Flor said puzzledly. "Just 'property'?"

"No . . . there is more. Property . . . property restricted access. U.S. Army Intelligence."

Flor looked over at Jon-Tom. "That explains everything; the parachutes, the tactics, the formula for the explosives to undermine the wall, maybe the technique for doing it as well. *Los insectos* have gotten hold of a military computer."

"That's why Clothahump tried to find an engineer to combat Eejakrat's 'new magic,' " Jon-Tom muttered. "And he got me instead. And you." He gazed helplessly at her. "What are we going to do? I don't know anything about computers."

"I know a little, but it's not a matter of knowing anything about computers. Machine, man or insect, it has to be destroyed before Eejakrat can finish his new formula."

"What the fuck could that devil have dug out of its electronic guts?" He looked back down at Clothahump.

"Don't understand . . ." murmured the wizard. "Beyond my ken. But Eejakrat knows how to comply. It worries him, but he proceeds. He knows if he does not the war is lost."

"Someone's got to get over there and destroy the computer and its mentor," Jon-Tom said decisively. He called to the rest of their companions.

Mudge and Caz ambled over curiously. So did Bribbens, and Pog fluttered close from his perch near the back of the wall. Hastily, Jon-Tom told them what had to be done.

"Wot about the Ironclouders, wot?" Mudge indicated the diving shapes of the great owls working their death up the Pass. "I don't think they'd 'old you, mate, but I ought to be able to ride one."

"I could go myself, boss." Clothahump turned a startled gaze on the unexpectedly daring famulus.

"No. Not you, Pog, nor you, otter. You would never make it, I fear. Hundreds of bowmen, a royal guard of the Greendowns' most skilled archers, surround Eejakrat and the Empress. You could not get within a quarter league of the deadmind. Even if you could, what would you destroy it with? It is made of metal. You cannot shoot an arrow through it. And there may be disciples of Eejakrat who could draw upon its evil knowledge in event of his death."

"We need a plane," Jon-Tom told them. "A Huey or some other attack copter, with rockets."

Clothahump looked blankly at him. "I know not what you describe, spellsinger, but by the heavens if you can do anything you must try."

Jon-Tom licked his lips. The Who, J. Geils, Dylan: none sang much about war and its components. But he had to try something. He didn't know the Air Force song. . . .

"Try something, Jon-Tom," Flor urged him. "We don't have much time."

Time. Time's getting away from us. There's your cue, man. Get there first. Worry about how to destroy the thing then.

Trying to shut the sounds of fighting out of his thoughts, he ran his fingers a couple of times across the duar's strings. The instrument had been nicked and battered by arrows and spears, but it was still playable. He struggled to recall the melody. It was simple, smooth, a Steve Miller hallmark. A few adjustments to the duar's controls. It *had* to work. He turned tremble and mass all the way up. Dangerous, but whatever materialized had to carry him high above the combat, all the way to the end of the Pass.

Anyway, Clothahump's urgency indicated that there was little time left now either for finesse or fine tuning.

Just get me to that computer, he thought furiously. Just get me there safely and I'll find some way to destroy it. Even pulling a few wires would do it. Eejakrat couldn't repair the damage with magic . . . could he?

And if he was killed and the attempt a failure, what did it matter?

Talea was dead and so was much of himself. Yes, that was the answer. Crash whatever carries you and yourself into the computer. That should do it.

Time was the first crucial element. Though he did not know it, he was soon to learn the other.

Time . . . that was the key. He needed to move fast and he didn't have *time* to fool with machines that might or might not work, might or might not appear. Time and flight. What song could possibly fill the need?

Wait a minute! There was something about time and flight slipping, slipping into the future.

His fingers began to fly over the strings as he threw back his head and began to sing with more strength than ever he had before.

There was a tearing sound in the sky, and his nostrils were filled with the odor of ozone. It was coming! Whatever he'd called up. If not the sung-for huge bird, perhaps the British fighter nicknamed the Eagle, bristling with rockets and rapid-fire cannon. Anything to get him into the air.

He sang till his throat hurt, his fingers a blur above the strings. Reverberant waves of sound emerged from the quivering duar and the air vibrated in sympathy.

A deep-throated crackling split the sky overhead, a sound no kin to any earthly thunder. It seemed the sun had drawn back to hide behind the clouds. The fighting did not stop, but warmlander and insect alike slowed their pace. That ominous rumble echoed down the walls of the Pass. Something extraordinary was happening.

Vast wings that were of starry gases filled the air. The winter day turned warm with a sudden eruption of heat. Hot air blew Jon-Tom against the rampart behind him and nearly over, while his companions scrambled for something solid to cling to.

Atop the wall the remaining warmlander defenders scattered in terror. On the cliffsides the Weavers scuttled for hiding places in the crevices and crannies as a monstrous fiery form came near. It touched down on the mountainside where the remaining half of the wall was worked into the naked rock, and twenty feet of granite melted and ran like syrup.

"WHAT HAVE YOU DONE!" roared a voice that could raise a sunspot. The remaining stones of the wall trembled, as did the cells of those still standing atop it. "WHAT HAVE YOU WROUGHT, LITTLE HUMAN!"

"I . . ." Jon-Tom could only gape. He had not materialized the plane he'd wished for or the eagle he'd sung to. He had called up something best left undisturbed, interrupted a journey measurable in billions of years. It was all he could do to gaze back into those vast, infinite eyes, as M'nemaxa, barely touching the melting rock, fanned thermonuclear wings and glared down at him.

"I'm sorry," he finally managed to gasp out, "I was only trying . . ."

"LOOK TO MY BACK!" bellowed the sun horse.

Jon-Tom hesitated, then took a cautious step forward and craned his neck. Squinting through the glare, he made out a dark metallic shape that looked suspiciously like a saddle. It was very small and lost on that great flaming curve of a spine.

"I don't . . . what does this mean?" he asked humbly.

"IT MEANS A TRANSFORMATION IN MY ODYSSEY; A SHORTCUT. LITTLE MAN BENEATH THE STARS, YOU HAVE CREATED A SHORTCUT! I CAN SEE THE END OF MY JOURNEY NOW. NO LONGER MUST I RACE AROUND THE RIM OF THE UNIVERSE. ONLY ANOTHER THREE MILLION YEARS AND I WILL BE FINISHED. ONLY THREE MILLION, AND I WILL KNOW PEACE. AND YOU, MAN, ARE TO THANK FOR IT!"

"But I don't know what I did, and I don't know how I did it," Jon-Tom told him softly.

"CONSEQUENCE IS WHAT MATTERS, CAUSATION IS BUT EPHEMERAL. EMPYREAN RESULTS HAVE BEEN ACHIEVED, LITTLE MAN OF NOTHINGNESS.

"AS YOU HAVE HELPED ME, SO I WILL HELP YOU. BUT I CAN DO ONLY WHAT YOU DIRECT. YOUR MAGIC PUTS THIS SHIELD ON MY BACK, SO MOUNT THEN, GUARDED BY ITS SUBSTANCE AND BY YOUR OWN MAGIC, AND RIDE. SUCH A RIDE AS NO CREATURE OF MERE FLESH AND BLOOD HAS EVER HAD BEFORE NOR WILL HENCE!"

Jon-Tom hesitated. But eager hands were already urging him toward the equine inferno.

"Go on, Jon-Tom," said Caz encouragingly.

"Yes, go on. It must be the spellsong magic that's protecting us," said Flor, "or the radiation and heat would have fried all of us by now."

"But that little lead saddle, Flor . . ."

"The magic, Jon-Tom, the magic. The magic's in the music *and the music's in you*. Do it!"

It was Clothahump who finally convinced him. "It is all or nothing now, my boy. We live or we die on what you do. This is between you and Eejakrat."

"I wish it wasn't. I wish to God I was home. I wish...ahhh, fuck it. Let's go!"

He could not see a barrier shielding the streaming nuclear material that was the substance of M'nemaxa, but one had to be present, as Flor had so incontrovertibly pointed out. He cradled the battered duar against his chest. That barrier had momentarily lapsed when M'nemaxa had touched down, and a thousand tons of solid rock had run like butter. If it lapsed again, there would not even be ashes left of him.

A series of stirrups led to the saddle, which was much larger up close than it had appeared from a distance. He mounted carefully, feeling neither heat nor pain but watching fascinated as tiny solar prominences erupted from M'nemaxa's epidermis only inches from his puny human skin.

It was little different in the saddle, though he could feel some slight heat against his face and hands.

"Just a minim, guv'," said a voice. A small gray shape had bounded into the saddle behind him.

"Mudge? It's not necessary. Either I'll make it or I won't."

"Shove it, mate. I've been watchin' you ever since you stuck your nose int' me business. You don't think I could let you go off on your own now, do you? Somebody's got t' watch out for you. This great flippin' flamin' beastie can't be 'urt, but a good archer might pick you off 'is back like a farmer pluckin' a bloomin' apple." He notched an arrow into his bowstring and grinned beneath his whiskers.

Jon-Tom couldn't think of anything else to say: "Thanks, Mudge. Mate."

"Thank me when we get back. I've always wanted t' ride a comet, wot? Let's be about the business, then."

The serpentine fiery neck arched, and the great head with its bottomless eyes stared back at them. "COMMAND, MAN!"

"I don't know . . ." Mudge was prodding him in the ribs. "Shit . . . giddy up! To Eejakrat!"

Whether the message was conveyed by the word or the mental imagery connected with it no one knew. It didn't matter. The vast wings seared the earth and a warm hurricane blasted those who were beneath. Those wings stretched from one side of the canyon to the other, and the Ironclouders, seeing it race toward them, scattered like gnats.

A swarm of dragonfly fighters rose to meet them, the Empress' private aerial guard. They attacked with the mindless but admirable courage of their kind.

Mudge's bow began its work. The soldiers riding the dragonflies fell from their mounts and none of their arrows reached the sun riders. Those that were launched impacted on the body or wings or neck of M'nemaxa and were vaporized with the briefest of sizzling sounds.

"Fly past them!" Jon-Tom ordered. "Down, over there!" He gestured toward the blunt butte rising fingerlike near the rear of the Pass. Beyond lay the mists of the Greendowns.

Jon-Tom's attention shifted to concentrate on a single figure standing before a pile of materials and a semicircle of metal forms. Dragonflies and riders tried to break through to do battle with swords, but wings and hooves touched them, and their charred remnants fell earthward like so many sizzling lumps of smoking charcoal.

The imperial bodyguard sent a storm of arrows upward. Not one passed the belly of that flaming body. Jon-Tom was watching Eejakrat. He held his own spear-staff tightly, ready to pierce the sorcerer through.

Then his attention was diverted. In the air above the computer floated two faintly glowing pieces of stone. They were so tiny he noticed them only because of their glow. Behind the sorcerer danced the fearful, iridescent green shape of the Empress Skrritch.

What devastating magic so terrified the imperturbable Clothahump? What was Eejakrat about to risk in hopes of winning a lost war?

"Down," he ordered M'nemaxa. "Down to the one surrounded by maggots and evil, down to destroy!"

A whispery sorceral mumbling, rapid and desperate, sounded from the crest of the butte. Eejakrat had panicked. He was rushing the incantation, as others had done before him, though he knew nothing of them. The two glowing shards of stone moved through the air toward the onrushing spirit fire and its mortal riders, and toward each other. Stones and spirit would meet at the same point in the sky.

They were no more than fifty yards from it and as many more from the butte's summit when M'nemaxa suddenly gave forth a thunderous whinny. The infinite eyes glowed more brightly than the stones as the two came almost together a couple of yards in front of them.

There was a faint, hopeless scream from Eejakrat below, a desperate croaking Jon-Tom deciphered: "Not yet . . . too near, too close, not *yet!*"

Then the world was spinning farther and farther below them like a flower caught in a whirlpool.

Gone was the Troom Pass. So too was the butte where Eejakrat had gesticulated frantically before the Empress Skrritch. So were the milling mob of Plated Folk plunging to war and the insistent battle cries of the warmlanders.

Gone were the mists of the distant Greendowns and noisome distant Cugluch, gone too the mountain crags that towered above insignificant warriors. Soon the blue sky itself vanished behind them.

They still rode the spine of the furiously galloping M'nemaxa, but they rode now through the emptiness of convergent eternity. Stars gleamed bright as morning around them, unwinking and cold and so close it seemed you could reach out and touch them.

You *could* touch them. Jon-Tom reached out slowly and plucked a red giant from its place in the heavens. It was warm in his palm and shone like a ruby. He cast it spinning back free into space. A black hole slid past his left foot and he pulled away. It was like quicksand. He inhaled a nebula, which made him sneeze. Behind him Mudge the otter seemed a distant, diffuse shape in the stars.

He breathed infinity. The wings and hooves of M'nemaxa moved in slow motion. A swarm of motile, luminescent dots gathered around the runners, millions of lights pricking the blackness. They danced and swirled around the great horse and its riders.

Where the world had no meaning and natural law was absent, these too finally became real. Gneechees, Jon-Tom thought ponderously. Only now I can see them, I can see them.

Some were people, some animals, others unrecognizable; the afterthoughts, the memories, the souls and shadows of all intelligent life. They were all the colors of the rainbow, a spectrum filled with life, both mysterious and familiar.

He began to recognize some of the forms and faces. He saw Einstein, he saw his own grandfather. He saw the moving lips of now dead singers he had loved, and it was as if their music swelled around him in the ultimate concert. He noted that the faces he saw were not old, and showed no trace of death or suffering. In fact the famous physicist's eyes glittered like a child's. Einstein had his violin with him. Hendrix was there, too, and they played a duet, and both smiled at Jon-Tom.

Then he saw a face he knew well, a face full of fire and light. He concentrated on that face with all his strength, trying to pull it into his brain through his eyes. The face was distinct and warm; it seemed to float toward him instinctively. His whole being glowed with love as it neared him, and suddenly when it touched his lip a flame ignited inside him and he almost lost his seat. It was the Talea gneechee, he knew, and he surrounded it with his entire will.

"We must go back. Now!" he roared at the fiery stallion.

"YOU MUST KNOW THE WORDS, LITTLE MAN, OR REMAIN WITH ME UNTIL THE END OF MY JOURNEY."

What song? Jon-Tom thought. There seemed no music equal to the immensity of space and stars all around him. Every song he had ever heard dried up on his tongue.

The Talea gneechee seemed to stir someplace deep inside him, and he looked out at the cold blue distance ahead. It was time to go back where he belonged. He couldn't be specific, but he suddenly had a real sense of where he belonged in life and he knew he could get there.

His mouth opened and his fingertips caressed the duar. A new sound rose, a new voice came both from the duar and from his mouth, and though he had never heard it before he knew it was, finally, his true voice.

Stars spun faster around him, the universe seemed wrenched for an instant. His head throbbed and his throat burned with the strange wordless song that poured from him like a river a million times stronger than any earthly river.

Now blue sky hurried toward them, then the snowy caps of mountains. The boundary was back—the luscious, palpable limit of existence. He felt more alive than he had ever in his life.

"Cor, wot a friggin' ride!" Mudge's joyous voice came from behind him.

"Love you, Mudge!" screamed Jon-Tom, ecstatic to hear that familiar sound.

"You're crazy—where the 'ell we been?"

Everywhere, Jon-Tom thought, but there was no way to say it.

"THE COURSE OF MY JOURNEY HAS BEEN FOREVER CHANGED," bellowed M'nemaxa. "I HAVE HAD TO CHANGE MY DIRECTION BECAUSE OF THE EVIL IN YOUR WORLD AND NOW MY ROUTE IS ALMOST THROUGH. COME WITH ME TO THE OUTSIDE, LITTLE MAN, YOUR WORLD IS FULL OF DOOM. I WILL SHOW SUCH THINGS AS NO MORTAL SHALL EVER AGAIN SEE."

"Wot's 'e talkin' about, guv'nor?"

"Eejakrat's magic, Mudge. Clothahump knew that they could not control it, and it has created devastation so utter that even M'nemaxa had to detour around it. It's happened before, but in my world. Not here. Look."

The mushroom cloud that billowed skyward from the far end of the Troom Pass was not large, but it was considerably darker and denser than any of the mists behind it.

Below them now the last of the Plated Folk army, those who'd been lucky enough to be trapped in the middle of the Pass, were surrendering, turning over their weapons and going down on all sixes to plead for mercy.

Beneath the now fading mushroom cloud that marked the failure of Eejakrat's imported magic, the butte he'd stood upon had vanished. In its place there was only an empty, radioactive crater. The bomb Eejakrat had been in the process of creating had been a relatively clean one. What remained would serve as a warning to future generations of Plated Folk. It would block the Pass far more effectively than had the Jo-Troom Gate.

Flaming wings slowed. Mudge was deposited gently back on top of the wall. Jon-Tom thanked the flaming being but would not return with him.

"THREE MILLION YEARS!" M'nemaxa boomed, his neighing shaking boulders from the cliffsides of the canyon.

"ONLY THREE MILLION. THANK YOU, LITTLE HUMAN. YOU ARE A WIZARD OF UNKNOWN WISDOM. FAREWELL!"

The vast fiery form rose into the air. There was an earsplitting explosion that rent the fabric of space-time. The gap closed quickly and M'nemaxa had gone, gone back to resume his now truncated journey, gone back to the everywhere otherplace.

Bodies, furred and otherwise, swarmed around the returnees—Caz, Flor, Bribbens holding his bandaged right arm where he'd taken a sword thrust. Pog fluttered excitedly overhead, and warmlander soldiers mixed queries with congratulations.

The battle had ended, the war was over. Those Plated Folk who had not perished in the modest thermonuclear explosion at the far end of the Pass were being herded into makeshift corrals.

Jon-Tom was embarrassed and nervous, but Mudge glowed like M'nemaxa himself from the adulation of the crowd.

When the excitement had died down and the soldiers had gone to join their companions below, Clothahump managed to make his way up to Jon-Tom.

"You did well, my boy, well! I'm quite proud of you." He smiled as much as he could. "We'll make a wizard of you yet. If you can only learn to be a bit more specific and precise in your formulations."

"I'm learning," Jon-Tom admitted without smiling back. "One of the things I've learned is to pay attention to what lies *behind* a person's words." He and the wizard stared into each other's eyes, and neither gave ground.

"I did what I had to do, boy. I'd do it again."

"I know you would. I can't blame you for it anymore, but I can't like you for it, either."

"As you will, Jon-Tom," said the wizard. He looked past the man and his eyes widened. "Though it may be that you condemn me too quickly."

Jon-Tom turned. A petite, slightly baffled redhead was walking toward them. He could only stare.

"Hello," Talea said, smiling slightly. "I must have been unconscious for days."

"You've been dead," said a flabbergasted Mudge.

"Oh, cut it out. I had the strangest dream." She looked down at the canyon. "Missed all the fighting, I see."

"I saw you . . . out there," Jon-Tom said dazedly. "Or a part of you. It came to me and I knew it was you."

"I wouldn't know about that," she said sharply. "All I know is that I woke up in a tent surrounded by corpses. It scared the shit out of me." She chuckled. "Did worse to the attendants. Bet they haven't stopped running.

"Then I asked around for you and got directions. Is it true what everyone's saying about you and M'nemaxa and . . ."

"Everything's true, nothing's false," Jon-Tom said. "Not anymore. Whatever entered me I sent back to you, but it doesn't matter. What is is what matters, and what is, is you."

"You've gotten awfully obscure all of a sudden, Jon-Tom."

He put his hands on her shoulders. "I suppose we have to stay together now." He smiled shyly, not able to explain what had happened in Elsewhere. She looked blank. "Don't you remember what you said to me back in Cugluch?" he asked.

She frowned at him. "I don't know what you're talking about, but that's nothing new, is it? You always did talk too much. But you're wrong about one thing."

"What's that?"

"I do remember what I said back in Cugluch," and she proceeded to give him the deepest, longest, richest kiss he'd ever experienced.

Eventually she let him go. Or was it the other way around? No matter.

Caz and Flor sat on the ramparts nearby, hand in paw. Jon-Tom shook his head, wondering at that blindness that conceals what is most obvious. Bribbens had disappeared, doubtless to make arrangements for reaching the nearest river. Falameezar was able to help the boatman with that, being a river dragon. That is, he was when he wasn't too busy reeducating his rodent charges about their responsibilities and rights as members of the downtrodden proletariat. Clothahump had gone off to discuss the matters of magic with the other warmlander wizards.

"What now, Jon-Tom?" Talea looked at him anxiously. "I guess now that you've mastered your spellsinging you'll be returning to your own world?"

"I don't know." He studied the masonry underfoot. "I'm not so sure you could say I've *mastered* spellsinging." He plucked ruefully at the duar. "I always seem to get what I need, not what I want. That's nice, but not necessarily reassuring.

"And for some reason being a rock star or a lawyer doesn't seem to hold the attraction it once did. I guess you could say I've had my horizons somewhat expanded." Like to include infinity, he told himself.

She nodded knowingly. "You've grown up some, Jon-Tom."

He shrugged. "If experiences can age you, I ought to be the equivalent of Methuselah by now."

"I'll see what I can do about keeping you young. . . ." She ran fingers through his hair. "Does that mean you'll be staying?" She added quietly, "With me, maybe? If you can stand me, that is."

"I've never known a woman like you, Talea."

"That's because there aren't any women like me, idiot." She moved to kiss him again. He edged away from her, preoccupied with a new thought.

"What's the matter? Not coy enough for you?"

"Nothing like that. I just remembered something that's been left undone, something that I promised myself I'd try to do if given the chance."

They found Pog hanging from a spear rack in the middle of the remaining wall. The warmlanders were beginning to disperse, those not remaining behind to guard the Plated Folk forming into their respective companies and battalions preparatory to beginning the long march home. Some were already on their way, too tired or filled with memories of dead companions to sing victory songs. They were traveling west toward Polastrindu or southward to where the river Tailaroam tumbled fresh and clear from the flanks of the Teeth.

The sun was setting over the fringes of the Swordsward. The poisonous silhouette of the mushroom cloud had long since been carried away by the wind. Their kilts flashing as brightly as their wings, squads of aerial warmlanders in arrowhead formations were winging back toward their home roosts. A distant line of silk-clad shapes showed where the Weavers were wending their way northward along the foothills, and a dark mass was just disappearing over the northern crest of the mountains in the direction of fabled Ironcloud.

"Hello, Pog."

"Hi, spellsinger." The bat's voice was subdued, but Jon-Tom no longer had to ask why. "Some job ya did. I'm proud ta call ya my friend."

Jon-Tom sat down on a low bench near the spear rack. "Why aren't you out there celebrating with the rest of the army?"

"I attend to da needs of my master, you know dat. I wait for his woid on what ta do next."

"You're a good apprentice, Pog. I hope I can learn as well as you."

"What's dat supposed ta mean?" The upside-down face turned to stare curiously at him.

"I'm hoping that Clothahump will accept me as an apprentice wizard." The duar rested in his lap and he strummed it experimentally. "Magic seems to be the only thing I have any talent for hereabouts. I'd damn well better learn how to discipline it before I kill myself. I've just been lucky so far."

"Da master, da old fart-face, says dere's no such ting as luck."

"I know, I know." He was slowly picking out a tune on the duar. "But I'm going to have to work like hell if I'm going to attain half the wisdom of that senile little turtle." He started to hum the song that had come to him back in the tent on that day of fury not long ago, when a certain famulus had been thoughtful enough to comfort him and lay down the life laws.

"I appreciated what you said to me that time in the tent, when I came out of the stupor Clothahump was forced to put me into. You see, Pog, Clothahump cared about me because he knew I might be able to help him. Caz and Flor and Bribbens cared about me because we were dependent on one another.

"But the only ones who cared about me personally, really cared, turned out to be Talea, and you. We've got a lot in common, you and

I. A hell of a lot in common. I never saw it before because I couldn't. You were right about love, of course. I thought I wanted Flor." Talea said nothing. "What I really wanted was someone to want me. That's all I've ever wanted. I know that's what you want, too."

Now he began to sing out, loud and clear. Suddenly there was a shimmering in the air around the bat. It was evening now, and the wall was growing dark. Camp fires were beginning to spring up on the plain where Plated Folk and warmlander for the first time in thousands of years were beginning to talk to one another.

"Hey, what's going on?" The bat dropped from his perch, righted himself, and flapped nervous wings.

The bat shape was flowing, shifting in the evening air.

"That was my falcon song, Pog. I've got to get my spellsinging specific, Clothahump says. So I'm giving you the transformation you wanted from him."

Talea clung tight to Jon-Tom's arm, watching. "He's changing, Jon-Tom."

"It's what he wants," he told her softly, also watching the transformation. "He gave me understanding when I needed it most. This is what I'm giving in return. The song I just sang should turn him into the biggest, sleekest falcon that ever split a cloud."

But the shape wasn't right. It was all wrong. It continued to change and glow as Jon-Tom's expression widened in disbelief.

"Oh God. I should've waited. I should've held off and waited for Clothahump's advice. I'm sorry, Pog!" he yelled at the indistinct, alien outline.

"Wait," said Talea gently. Her grip tightened on his arm and she leaned into him. "True, it's no falcon he's becoming. But look—it's incredible!"

The metamorphosis was complete, finished, irrevocable.

"Never mind, never mind, never mind!" sang the transformed thing that had been Pog the bat. The voice was all quicksilver and light. "Never mind, friend Talea. Be true to Clothahump, Jon-Tom. You'll get a wing on it, you will."

A flock of fighters, eagles perhaps, crossed the darkling sky from east to west. A few falcons were scattered among them. Perhaps one was Uleimee.

"Meanwhile you've made me very happy," Pog-that-once-was assured the spellsinger.

Jon-Tom realized he'd been holding his breath. The transformation had stunned him. Talea called to him softly and he turned and found her waiting arms.

Above them the change which had been Pog searched with keen eyes among the winged shapes soaring toward the distant reaches of the warmlands. It saw a particular female falcon emerging with others of her kind from a thick cloud, saw with eyes far sharper than those of any bat, or owl, or falcon.

Leaving the two humans to their own destinies, and rising on suddenly massive wings, the golden phoenix raced for that distant cloud, the sun setting on its back like a rare jewel.

THE DAY
OF THE DISSONANCE

For my cousin Adam Carroll,
An idle evening's read to sandwich in between
Business Week and *Forbes*.
With much affection.

"I'm dying," Clothahump wheezed. The wizard glanced to his left. "I'm dying and you stand there gawking like a virginal adolescent who's just discovered that his blind date is a noted courtesan. With your kind of help I'll never live to see my three-hundredth birthday."

"With your kind of attitude it's a wonder you've managed to live this long." Jon-Tom was more than a little irritated at his mentor. "Listen to yourself: two weeks of nonstop griping and whining. You know what you are, turtle of a wizardly mien? You're a damned hypochondriac."

Clothahump's face did not permit him much of a frown, but he studied the tall young human warily. "What is that? It sounds vaguely like a swear word. Don't toy with me, boy, or it will go hard on you. What is it? Some magic word from your own world?"

"More like a medical word. It's a descriptive term, not a threat. It refers to someone who thinks they're sick all the time, when they're not."

"Oh, so I'm imagining that my head is fragmenting, is that what you're saying?" Jon-Tom resisted the urge to reply, sat his six-feet-plus frame down near the pile of pillows that served the old turtle for a bed.

Not for the first time he wondered at the number of spacious rooms the old oak tree encompassed. There were more alcoves and chambers and tunnels in that single trunk than in a termite's hive.

He had to admit, though, that despite his melodramatic moans and wails, the wizard didn't look like himself. His plastron had lost its normal healthy luster, and the old eyes behind the granny glasses were rheumy with tears from the pain. Perhaps he shouldn't have been so abrupt. If Clothahump couldn't cure himself with his own masterly potions and spells, then he was well and truly ill.

"I know what I am," Clothahump continued, "but what of you? A fine spellsinger you've turned out to be."

"I'm still learning," Jon-Tom replied defensively. He fingered the duar slung over his shoulder. The peculiar instrument enabled him to sing spells, to make magic through the use of song. One might think it a dream come true for a young rock guitarist-cum-law student, save for the fact that he didn't seem to have a great deal of control over the magic he made.

Since the onslaught of Clothahump's pains, Jon-Tom had sung two dozen songs dealing with good health and good feelings. None had produced the slightest effect with the exception of his spirited rendition of the Beach Boys' "Good Vibrations." That bit of spellsinging caused Clothahump to giggle uncontrollably, sending powders and potions flying and cracking his glasses.

Following that ignominious failure, Jon-Tom kept his hands off the duar and made no further attempts to cure the wizard.

"I didn't really mean to imply that you're faking it," he added apologetically. "It's just that I'm as frustrated as you are."

Clothahump nodded, his breath coming in short, labored gasps. His poor respiration was a reflection of the constant pain he was suffering, as was his general weakness.

"I did the best I could," Jon-Tom murmured.

"I know you did, my boy. I know you did. As you say, there is much yet for you to learn, many skills still to master."

"I'm just bulling my way through. Half the time I pick the wrong song and the other half it has the wrong result. What else can I do?"

Clothahump looked up sharply. "There is one chance for me, lad. There is a medicine which can cure what ails me now. Not a spell, not a magic. A true medicine."

Jon-Tom rose from the edge of the pile of pillows. "I think I'd better be going. I haven't practiced yet today and I need to . . ."

Clothahump moaned in pain and Jon-Tom hesitated, feeling guilty. Maybe it was a genuine moan and maybe it wasn't, but it had the intended effect.

"You *must* obtain this medicine for me, my boy. I can't trust the task to anyone else. Evil forces are afoot."

Jon-Tom sighed deeply, spoke resignedly. "Why is it whenever you want something, whether it's help making it to the bathroom or a snack or someone to go on a dangerous journey for you, that evil forces are always afoot?"

"You ever see an evil force, boy?"

"Not in the flesh, no."

"Evil forces always go afoot. They're lousy fliers."

"That's not what I meant."

"Doesn't matter what you meant, my boy. You have to run this errand for me. That's all it is, a little errand."

"Last time you asked me to help you run an errand we ended up with the fate of civilization at stake."

"Well, this time it's only my fate that hangs in the balance." His voice shrank to a pitiful whisper. "You wouldn't want me to die, would you?"

"No," Jon-Tom admitted. "I wouldn't."

"Of course you wouldn't. Because if I die it means the end of your chances to return to your own world. Because only I know the necessary, complicated, dangerous spell that can send you back. It is in your own interest to see that I remain alive and well."

"I know, I know. Don't rub it in."

"Furthermore," the wizard went on, pressing his advantage, "you are partly to blame for my present discomfort."

"What!" Jon-Tom whirled on the bed. "I don't know what the hell you've got, Clothahump, but I certainly didn't give it to you."

"My illness is compounded of many factors, not the least of which are my current awkward living conditions."

Jon-Tom frowned and leaned on his long ramwood staff. "What are you talking about?"

"Ever since we returned from the great battle at the Jo-Troom Gate my daily life has been one unending litany of misery and frustration. All because you had to go and turn my rude but dutiful famulus Pog into a phoenix. Whereupon he promptly departed my service for the dubious pleasures his falcon ladylove could bestow on him."

"Is it my fault you've had a hard time replacing him? That's hardly a surprise, considering the reputation you got for mistreating Pog."

"I did not mistreat Pog," the wizard insisted. "I treated him exactly as an apprentice should be treated. It's true that I had to discipline him from time to time. That was due to his own laziness and incompetence. All part of the learning process." Clothahump straightened his new glasses.

"Pog spread the details of your teaching methods all over the Bellwoods. But I thought the new famulus you finally settled on was working out okay."

"Ha! It just goes to show what can happen when you don't read the fine print on someone's résumé. It's too late now. I've made him my assistant and am bound to him, as he is to me."

"What's wrong? I thought he was brilliant."

"He can be. He can be studious, efficient, and eager to learn."

"Sounds good to me."

"Unfortunately, he has one little problem."

"What kind of problem?"

Clothahump's reply was interrupted by a loud, slurred curse from the room off to the left. The wizard gestured with his head toward the doorway, looked regretful.

"Go see for yourself, my boy, and understand then what a constant upset my life has become."

Jon-Tom considered, then shrugged and headed under the arched passageway toward the next chamber, bending low to clear the sill. He was so much taller than most of the inhabitants of this world that his height was an ever-present problem.

Something shattered and there was another high-pitched curse. He held his ramwood staff protectively in front of him as he emerged into the storeroom.

It was as spacious as Clothahump's bedroom and the other chambers which somehow managed to coexist within the trunk of the old oak. Pots, tins, crates, and beakers full of noisome brews were carefully arranged on shelves and workbenches. Several bottles lay in pieces on the floor.

Standing, or rather weaving, in the midst of the breakage was Sorbl, Clothahump's new famulus. The young great horned owl stood slightly over three feet tall. He wore a thin vest and a brown and yellow kilt of the Ule Clan.

He spotted Jon-Tom, waved cheerily, and fell over on his beak. As he struggled to raise himself on flexible wingtips, Jon-Tom saw that the vast yellow eyes were exquisitely bloodshot.

"Hello, Sorbl. You know who I am?"

The owl squinted at him as he climbed unsteadily to his feet, staggered to port, and caught himself on the edge of the workbench.

"Shure I remember you," he said thickly. "You . . . you're that spielsunger . . . spoilsanger. . . ."

"Spellsinger," Jon-Tom said helpfully.

"Thas what I said. You're that what I said from another world that the master brought through to hulp him against the Pleated Filk."

"The master is not feeling well." He put his staff aside. "And you're not looking too hot either."

"Hooo, me?" The owl looked indignant, walked away from the bench wavering only slightly. "I am perfectly fine, thank you." He glanced back at the bench. "Is just that I was looking for a certain bottle."

"What bottle?"

"Not marked, thish one." Sorbl looked conspiratorial and winked knowingly with one great bloodshot eye. "Medicinal liquid. Not for his ancientness in there. *My* bottle," he finished, suddenly belligerent. "Nectar."

"Nectar? I thought owls liked mice."

"What?" said the outraged famulus. For an instant Jon-Tom had forgotten where he was. The rodents hereabouts were as intelligent and lively as any of the other citizens of this world. "If I tried to take a bite out of a mouse, his relatives would come string me up. I'll stick to small lizards and snakishes. Listen," he continued more softly, "it's hard working for this wizard. I need a lil' lubrication now and then."

"You get any more lubricated," Jon-Tom observed distastefully, "and your brains are going to slide out your ass."

"Nonshensh. I am in complete control of myself." He turned back toward the bench, staggered over to the edge, and commenced a minute inspection of the surface with eyes that should have been capable of spotting an ant from a hundred yards away. At the moment, however, those huge orbs were operating at less than maximum efficiency.

Jon-Tom shook his head in disgust and returned to the wizard's bedside.

"Well," asked Clothahump meaningfully, "what is your opinion of my new famulus?"

"I think I see what you're driving at. I didn't notice any of the qualities you said he possesses. I'm pretty sure he was drunk."

"Really?" said Clothahump dryly. "What a profound observation. We'll make a perceptive spellsinger out of you yet. He is like that too much of the time, my boy. I am blessed with a potentially brilliant famulus, a first-rate, worthy assistant. Sadly, Sorbl is also a lush. Do you know that I have to make him take a cart into town to buy supplies because every time he tries to fly in he ends up by running head-first into a tree and the local farmers have to haul him back to me in a wagon? Do you have any idea how embarrassing that is for the world's greatest wizard?"

"I can imagine. Can't you cure him? I'd think an anti-inebriation spell would be fairly simple and straightforward."

"It is a vicious circle, my boy. Were I not so sick I could do so, but as it stands I cannot concentrate. Past two hundred the mind loses some of its resilience. I tried just that last week. All those methyl ethyl bethels in the spell are difficult enough to get straight when you're at the top of your form. Sick as I was, I must have transposed an -yl somewhere. Made him throw up for three days. Cured his drinking, but made him so ill the only way he could cure himself was by getting falling-down-drunk again.

"I must have that medicine, lad, so that I can function properly again. Otherwise I'm liable to try some complex spell, slip an incantation, and end up with something dangerous in my pentagram. It's hard enough making sure that idiot in there passes me the proper powders. Once he substituted lettuce for liverwort, and I ended up with a ten-foot-tall saber-toothed rabbit. Took me two hasty retraction spells to bunny it down."

"Why don't you just conjure the stuff up?"

"I do not possess the necessary ingredients," Clothahump explained patiently. "If I did, I could just take them, now, couldn't I?"

"Beats me. I've seen you make chocolate out of garbage."

"Medicine is rather more specific in its requirements. Everything must be so precise. You can make milk chocolate, bittersweet chocolate, white chocolate, semisweet chocolate: it's still all chocolate. Alter the composition of a medicinal spell ever so slightly and you might end up with a deadly poison. No, it must be brought whole and ready, and you must bring it to me, my boy." He reached out with a trembling hand. Jon-Tom moved close, sitting down again on the edge of the soft bed.

"I know I did a bad thing when I reached out into the beyond and plucked you hence from your own comfortable world, but the need was great. In the end, you vindicated my judgment, though in a fashion that could not have been foreseen." He adjusted his glasses. "You proved yourself in spite of what everyone thought."

"Mostly by accident." Jon-Tom realized that the wizard was flattering him in order to break down his resistance to making the journey. At the same time he felt himself succumbing to the flattery.

"It need not be by accident any longer. Work at your new profession. Study hard, practice your skills, and heed my advice. You can be more than a man in this world. I don't know what you might have been in your own, but here you have the potential to be a master. *If* you can wrestle your strengths and talent under control."

"With your instruction, of course."

"Why not learn from the best?" said Clothahump with typical immodesty. "In order for me to train you I need many years. One does not master the arcane arts of spellsinging in a day, a week, a year. If you do not fetch this medicine that can cure this bedamned affliction, I will not be around much longer to help you.

"I need only a small quantity. It will fit easily into a pocket of those garish trousers or that absurd purple shirt that foppish tailor Carlemot fashioned for you."

"It's not purple, it's indigo," Jon-Tom muttered, looking down to where it tucked into the pants. His iridescent green lizard-skin cape hung on a wall hook. "From what I've seen, this qualifies as subdued attire here."

"Go naked if you will, but go you must."

"All right, all right! Haven't you made me feel guilty enough?"

"I sincerely hope so," the wizard murmured.

"I don't know how I let you talk me into these things."

"You have the misfortune to be a decent person, a constant burden in any world. You suffer from knowing right from wrong."

"No I don't. If I knew what was right, I'd be long gone from this tree. But you did take me in, help me out, even if you did use me for your own ends. Not that I feel used. You used everyone for your own ends."

"We saved the world," Clothahump demurred. "Not bad ends."

"You're also right about my being stuck here unless you can work the spell to send me home someday. So I suppose I have no choice but to go after this special medicine. It's not by any chance available from the apothecary in Lynchbany?"

"I fear not."

"What a lucky guess on my part."

"Tch. Sarcasm in one so young is bad for the liver." Clothahump raised himself slowly, turned to the end table that doubled as a bed-side desk. He scribbled with a quill pen on a piece of paper. A moment passed, he cursed, put a refill cartridge in the quill, and resumed writing.

When he finished, he rolled the paper tight, inserted it into a small metal tube which hung from a chain, and handed it to Jon-Tom.

"Here is the formula," he said reverently. "She who is to fill it will know its meaning."

Jon-Tom nodded, took the chain, and hung it around his neck. The tube was cool against his chest.

"That is all you need to know."

"Except how to find this magician, or druggist, or whatever she is."

"A store. Nothing more." Clothahump's reassuring tone immediately put Jon-Tom on his guard. "The Shop of the Aether and Neither. It lies in the town of Crancularn."

"I take it this Crancularn isn't a hop, skip, and a jump from Lynchbany?"

"Depends on your method of locomotion, but for most mortals, I would say not. It lies well to the south and west of the Bellwoods."

Jon-Tom made a face. He'd been around enough to have picked up some knowledge of local geography. "There isn't anything well to the southwest of here. The Bellwoods run down to the River Tailaroam which flows into . . ." he stopped. "Crancularn's a village on the shore of the Glittergeist?"

Clothahump looked the other way. "Uh, not exactly, my boy. Actually it lies on the other side."

"The other side of the river?"

"Noooo. The other side of the ocean."

Jon-Tom threw up his hands in despair. "And that's the last straw."

"Actually, lad, it's only the first straw. There are many more to pass before you reach Crancularn. But reach it you must," he finished emphatically, "or I will surely perish from the pain, and any chance you have of returning home will perish with me."

"But I don't even know how big the Glittergeist is."

"Not all that big, as oceans go." Clothahump strove to sound reassuring. "It can be crossed in a few weeks. All you have to do is book passage on one of the many ships that trade between the mouth of the Glittergeist and distant Snarken."

"I've heard of Snarken. Big place?"

"A most maginficent city. So I have been told, never having visited there myself. Grander than Polastrindu. You'd find it fascinating."

"And dangerous."

"No journey is worthwhile unless it is dangerous, but we romanticize. I do not see any reason for anticipating trouble. You are a tourist, nothing more, embarked on a voyage of rest, relaxation, and discovery."

"Sure. From what I've seen of this world it doesn't treat tourists real well."

"That should not trouble an accomplished spellsinger like you."

The wizard was interrupted by the sound of another crash from the nearby storeroom, followed by a few snatches of drunken song.

"You also have your ramwood staff for protection, and you no longer are a stranger to our ways. Think of it as a holiday, a vacation."

"Why do I have this persistent feeling you're not telling me everything?"

"Because you are a pessimist, my boy. I do not criticize. That is a healthy attitude for one embarked on a career in magic. I am not sending you after trouble this time. We do not go to battle powerful invaders from the east. I am asking you only to go and fetch a handful of powder, a little medicine. That is all. No war awaits. True, it is a long journey, but there is no reason why it should be an arduous one.

"You leave from here, proceed south to the banks of the Tailaroam, book passage downstream. At its mouth where the merchant ships dock you, board a comfortable vessel heading for Snarken. Thence overland to Crancularn. A short jaunt, I should imagine."

"Imagine? You mean you don't know how far it is from Snarken to Crancularn?"

"Not very far."

"For someone who deals in exact formulas and spells, you can be disconcertingly nonspecific at times, Clothahump."

"And you can be unnecessarily verbose," the turtle shot back.

"Sorry. My pre-law training. Never use one word where five will fit. Maybe I would've ended up a lawyer instead of a heavy-metal bass player."

"You'll never know if you don't return to your own world, which you cannot do unless . . ."

"I know, I know," Jon-Tom said tiredly. "Unless I make the trip to this Crancularn and bring back the medicine you need. Okay, so I'm stuck."

"I would rather know that you had undertaken this journey with enthusiasm, willingly, out of a desire to help one who only wishes you well."

"So would I, but you'll settle for my going because I haven't got any choice, won't you?"

"Yes," said Clothahump thoughtfully, "I expect that I will."

II

He wasn't in the best frame of mind the morning he set off. Not that anything was keeping him occupied elsewhere, he told himself sourly. He had no place in this world and certainly no intention of setting himself up in practice as a professional spellsinger.

For one thing, that would put him in direct competition with Clothahump. Although the wizard thought well of him, Jon-Tom didn't think Clothahump would take kindly to the idea. For another, he hadn't mastered his odd abilities to the point where he could guarantee services for value received, and might never achieve that degree of expertise. He preferred to regard his spellsinging as a talent of last resort, choosing to rely instead on his staff and his wits to keep him out of trouble.

In fact, the duar provided him with far more pleasure when he simply played it for fun, just like his battered old Fender guitar back home. Now he played it to ease his mind as he walked into town, strumming a few snatches of very unmagical Neil Diamond while wishing he had Ted Nugent's way with strings. At the same time he had to be careful in his selections. Diamond was innocuous enough. If he tried a little Nugent—say, "Cat Scratch Fever" or "Scream Dream"—there was no telling what he might accidentally conjure up.

At least the weather favored his journey. It was early spring. Deep within the Bellwoods, so named for the bell-shaped leaves which produced a tinkling sound when the wind blew through them, there was the smell of dew and new blossoms on the air. Glass butterflies flew everywhere, their stained-glass wings sending shafts of brilliant color twinkling over the ground. Peppermint bees striped in psychedelic hues darted among the flowers.

One hitched a ride on his indigo shirt. Perhaps it thought he was some kind of giant ambulatory flower. Jon-Tom examined it with interest. Instead of the yellow-and-black pattern he was accustomed to, his visitor's abdomen was striped pink, lemon yellow, orange, chocolate brown, and bright blue. Man and insect regarded one another thoughtfully for a long moment. Deciding he was neither a source of pollen nor enlightenment, the bee droned off in search of sweeter forage.

Lynchbany Towne was unchanged from the first time Jon-Tom had seen it, on that rainy day when he, a stranger to this world, had entered it accompanied by Mudge the otter. It was Mudge he sought now. He had no intention of striking out across the Glittergeist alone, no matter how much confidence Clothahump vested in him. There was still far too much of the ways and customs of this place he was ignorant of.

Mudge's knowledge was of the practical and nonintellectual variety. Too, nothing was more precious to the otter than his own skin. He was sort of a furry walking alarm, ready to jump or take whatever evasive action the situation dictated at the barest suggestion of danger. Jon-Tom intended to use him the way the allies had used pigeons in World War I to detect the presence of poison gas.

Mudge would have considered the analogy unflattering, but Jon-Tom didn't care what the otter thought. Despite his questionable morals and wavering sense of loyalty, the otter had been a great help in the past and could be so again.

Luck wasn't with Jon-Tom, however. There was no sign of Mudge in the taverns he normally frequented, nor word of him in the eating establishments or gambling dens. He hadn't been seen in some time in any of his usual haunts.

Jon-Tom finally found mention of him in one of the more reputable rooming houses on the far side of town, where the stink from the central open sewer was less.

The concierge was an overweight koala in a bad mood. A carved pipe dangled from her lips as she scrubbed the floor near the entrance.

"Hay, I've seen him," she told Jon-Tom. Part of her right ear was missing, probably bitten off during a dispute with an irate customer. "I'd laik to know where he gone to much as you, man. He skip away owing me half a week's rent. That not bad as some have dun me, but I work hahd to run this place and every silver counts."

"Only a few days' rent, is it?" Jon-Tom squatted to be at eye level with the koala. "You know where he is, don't you? You're feeding me some story old Mudge paid you to tell anyone who came looking for him because he paid you to do so, because he probably owes everyone *but* you."

She wrinkled her black nose and wiped her paws on her apron. Then she broke out in a wide grin. "You a clever one, you are, man, though strange of manner and talk."

"I'm not really from around here," Jon-Tom confessed. "Actually my home lies quite a distance from Lynchbany. Nor am I a creditor or bill collector. Mudge is my friend."

"Is he now?" She dropped her scrub brush in the pail of wash water and rose. Jon-Tom did likewise. She reached barely to his stomach. That wasn't unusual. Jon-Tom was something of a giant in this world where humans barely topped five and a half feet and many others stood shorter.

"So you his friend, hay? That make you sort of unique. I wasn't aware the otter had any friends. Only acquaintances and enemies."

"No matter. I am his friend, and I need to get in touch with him."

"What for?"

"I am embarked on a journey in the service of the great wizard Clothahump."

"Ah, that old fraud."

"He's not a fraud. Haven't you heard of the battle for the Jo-Troom Gate?"

"Yea, yea, I heard, I heard." She picked up the bucket of wash water, the scrub brush sloshing around inside. "I also know you never believe everything you read in the papers. This journey you going on for him. It going be a hard one, where someone might get deaded?"

"Possibly."

"Hay, then I tell you where the otter is and you make sure he go with you?"

"That's the idea."

"Good! Then I tell you where he is. Because I tell you true, man, he owe me half a week's rent. I just don't want to tell anyone else because maybe they get to him before me. But this is better, much better. Worth a few days' rent."

"About that rent," Jon-Tom said, jiggling the purse full of gold

Clothahump had given him to pay for his passage across the Glittergeist.

The concierge waved him off. "Hay nay, man. Just make sure he go with you on this dangerous journey. More better I dream of him roasting over some cannibal's spit in some far-off land. That will give me more pleasure than a few coins."

"As you wish, madame." Jon-Tom put the purse aside.

"Only, you must be sure promise to come back here someday and regale me with the gory details. For that I pay you myself."

"I'll be sure to make it my business," Jon-Tom said dryly. "Now, where might I find my friend."

"Not here. North."

"Oglagia Towne?"

"Hay nay, farther west. In Timswitty."

"Timswitty," Jon-Tom repeated. "Thanks. You know what business he has there?"

She let out a short, sharp bark, a koalaish laugh. "Same business that otter he have any place he go: thievery, deception, debauchery, and drunkenness. I wager you find him easy enough you keep that in mind."

"I will. Tell me. I've never been north of Lynchbany. What's Timswitty like?"

She shrugged. "Like heah. Like Oglagia. Like any of the Bellwoods towns. Backward, crowded, primitive, but not bad if you willing stand up for your rights and work hard."

"Thank you, madame. You're sure I can't pay you anything for the information you've given me?"

"Keep you money and make you journey," she told him. "I look forward to hearing about the otter's slow and painful death upon you return."

"Don't hold your breath in expectation of his demise," Jon-Tom warned her as he turned to leave. "Mudge has a way of surviving in the damndest places."

"I know he do. He slip out of heah without me smelling his going. I tell you what. If he don't get himself killed on this journey of yours, you can pay me his back rent when you return."

"I'll do better than that, madame. I'll make him pay it himself, in person."

"Fair enough. You have good traveling, man."

"Good day to you too, madame."

Jon-Tom had no intention of walking all the way to Timswitty.

Not since Clothahump had provided him with funds for transport. The local equivalent of a stagecoach was passing through Lynchbany, and he bought himself a seat on the boxy contraption. It was pulled by four handsome horses and presided over by a couple of three-foot-tall chipmunks who cursed like longshoremen. They wore dirty uniforms and scurried about, wrestling baggage and cartons into the rear of the stage.

Jon-Tom had the wrong notion of who was in charge, however. As he strolled past the team of four, one of the horses cocked an eye in his direction.

"Come on, bud, hurry it up. We haven't got all day."

"Sorry. The ticket agent told me you weren't leaving for another fifteen minutes."

The mare snorted. "That senile bastard. I don't know what the world's coming to when you can't rely on your local service people anymore."

"Tell me about it," said the stallion yoked to her. "Unfortunately we were born with hooves instead of hands, so we still have to hire slow-moving fools with small brains to handle business details for us."

"Right on, Elvar," said the stallion behind him.

The discussion continued until the stage left the depot.

"All aboard?" asked the mare second in harness. "Hold on to your seats, then."

The two chipmunks squatted in the rear along with the luggage, preening themselves and trying to catch their breath. There was no need for drovers, since the horses knew the way themselves. The chipmunks were loaders and unloaders and went along to see to the needs of the team, who, after all, did the real work of pulling the stage.

This would have been fine as far as Jon-Tom and the other passengers were concerned except that the horses had an unfortunate tendency to break into song as they galloped, and while their voices were strong and clear, not a one of them could carry a tune in a bucket. So the passengers were compelled to suffer a series of endless, screeching songs all the way through to Timswitty.

When one passenger had the temerity to complain, he was invited to get out and walk. There were two other unscheduled stops along the way as well, once when the team got hungry and stopped to graze a lush meadow through which the road conveniently cut, and again when the two mares got into a heated argument about just who boasted the daintier fetlocks.

It was dark when they finally pulled into Timswitty.

"Come on," snapped the lead stallion, "let's get a move on back there. Our stable's waiting. I know you're all stuck with only two legs, but that's no reason for loafing."

"Really!" One of the outraged travelers was an elegantly attired vixen. Gold chains twined through her tail, and her elaborate hat was badly askew over her ears from the jouncing the stage had undergone. "I have never been treated so rudely in my life! I assure you I shall speak to your line manager at first opportunity."

"You're talking to him, sister," said the stallion. "You got a complaint, you might as well tell me to my face." He looked her up and down. "Me, I think you ought to thank us for not charging you for the extra poundage."

"Well!" Her tail swatted the stallion across the snout as she turned and flounced away to collect her luggage.

Only the fact that his mate restrained him kept him from taking a bite out of that fluffy appendage.

"Watch your temper, Dreal," she told him. "It doesn't do to bite the paying freight. Rotten public relations."

"Bet all her relations have been public," he snorted, pawing the ground impatiently. "What's slowing up those striped rats back there? I need a rubdown and some sweet alfalfa."

"I know you do, dear," she said as she nuzzled his neck, "but you have to try and maintain a professional attitude, if only for the sake of the business."

"Yeah, I know," Jon-Tom overheard as he made his way toward the depot. "It's only that there are times when I think maybe we'd have been better off if we'd bought ourselves a little farm somewhere out in the country and hired some housemice and maybe a human or two to do the dirty work."

He was the only one in the office. The fox and the other passengers already had destinations in mind.

"Can I help you?" asked the elderly marten seated behind the low desk. With his long torso and short waist, the clerk reminded Jon-Tom of Mudge. The marten was slimmer still, and instead of Mudge's jaunty cap and bright vest and pantaloons he wore dark shorts and a sleeveless white shirt, a visor to shade his eyes, and bifocals.

"I'm a stranger in town."

"I suspect you're a stranger everywhere," said the marten presciently.

Jon-Tom ignored the comment. "Where would a visitor go for a little harmless fun and entertainment in Timswitty?"

"Well now," replied the marten primly, "I am a family man myself. You might try the Golden Seal. They offer folksinging by many species and occasionally a string trio from Kolansor."

"You don't understand." Jon-Tom grinned insinuatingly. "I'm looking for a good time, not culture."

"I see." The marten sighed. "Well, if you will go down the main street to Born Lily Lane and follow the lane to its end, you will come to two small side streets leading off into separate cul-de-sacs. Take the north close. If the smell and noise isn't enough to guide you further, look for the small sign just above an oil lamp, the one with the carving of an Afghan on it."

"As in canine or cloth?"

The marten wet his lips. "The place is called the Elegant Bitch. No doubt you will find its pleasures suitable. I wouldn't know, of course. I am a family man."

"Of course," said Jon-Tom gravely. "Thanks."

As he made his solitary way down the dimly lit main street, he found himself wishing Talea was at his side. Talea of the flame-red hair and infinite resourcefulness. Talea of the blind courage and quick temper. Did he love her? He wasn't sure anymore. He thought so, thought she loved him in return. But she was too full of life to settle down as the wife of an itinerant spellsinger who had not yet managed to master his craft.

Not long after the battle of the Jo-Troom Gate, she had regretfully proposed they go their separate ways, at least for a little while. She needed time to think on serious matters and suggested he do likewise. It was hard on him. He did miss her. But there was the possibility she was simply too independent for any one man.

He held to his hopes, however. Perhaps someday she would tire of her wanderings and come back to him. There wasn't a thing he could do but wait.

As for Flor Quintera, the cheerleader he'd inadvertently brought into this world, she had turned out to be a major disappointment. Instead of being properly fascinated by him, it developed that she lusted after a career as a sword-wielding soldier of fortune and had gone off with Caz, the tall, suave rabbit with the Ronald Colman voice and sophisticated manners. Jon-Tom hadn't heard of them in months. Flor was a dream that had brought him back to reality, and fast.

At least this was a fit world in which to pursue dreams. At the moment, though, he was supposed to be pursuing medicine. He clung to that thought as he turned down the tiny side street.

True to the marten's information he heard sounds of singing and raucous laughter. But instead of a single small oil lamp there were big impressive ones flanking the door, fashioned of clear beveled crystal.

Above the door was a swinging sign showing a finely coiffed hound clad in feathers and jewels. She was gazing back over her furry shoulder with a distinctly come-hither look, and her hips were cocked rakishly.

There was a small porch. Standing beneath the rain shield, Jon-Tom knocked twice on the heavily oiled door. It was opened by a three-foot-tall mouse in a starched suit. Sound flooded over Jon-Tom as the doormouse looked him over.

"Step inside and enjoy, sir," he finally said, moving aside.

Jon-Tom nodded and entered. The doormouse closed the door behind him.

He found himself in a parlor full of fine furniture and a wild assortment of creatures representing several dozen species. All were cavorting without a care as to who they happened to be matching up with. There were several humans in the group, men and women. They moved freely among their intelligent furry counterparts.

Jon-Tom noted the activity, listened to the lascivious dialogue, saw the movement of hands and paws, and suspected he had not entered a bar. No question what kind of place this was. He was still surprised, though he shouldn't have been. It was a logical place to look for Mudge.

Still, he didn't want to take the chance of embarrassing himself. First impressions could be wrong. He spoke to the doormouse.

"I beg your pardon, but this is a whorehouse, isn't it?"

The mouse's voice was surprisingly deep, rumbling out of the tiny gray body. "All kinds we get in here," he muttered dolefully, "all kinds. What did you think it was, jack? A library?"

"Not really. There aren't any books."

The doormouse showed sharp teeth in a smile. "Oh, we have books, too. With pictures. Lots of pictures, if that's to your taste, sir."

"Not right now." He was curious, though. Maybe later, after he'd found Mudge.

"You look like you've been a-traveling, sir. Would you like something to eat and drink?"

"Thanks, I'm not hungry. Actually, I'm looking for a friend."

"Everyone comes to the Elegant Bitch in search of a friend."

"You misunderstand. That's not the way I mean."

"Just tell me your ways, sir. We cater to all ways here."

"I'm looking for a buddy, an acquaintance," Jon-Tom said in exasperation. The doormouse had a one-track mind.

"Ah, now I understand. No divertissements, then? This isn't a meeting house, you know."

"You're a good salesman." Jon-Tom tried to placate him. "Maybe later. I have to say that you're the smallest pimp I've ever seen."

"I am not small and I am not a pimp," replied the doormouse with some dignity. "If you wish to speak to the madam . . ."

"Not necessary," Jon-Tom told him, though he wondered not only what she'd look like but what she'd be. "The fellow I'm after wears a peaked cap with a feather in it, a leather vest, carries a longbow with him everywhere he goes, and is an otter. Name of Mudge."

The doormouse preened a whisker, scratched behind one ear. For the first time Jon-Tom noticed the small earplugs. Made sense. Given the mouse's sensitivity to sound, he'd need the plugs to keep from going deaf while working amid the nonstop celebration.

"I recognize neither name nor attire, sir, but there is one otter staying with us currently. He would be in room twenty-three on the second floor."

"Great. Thanks." Jon-Tom almost ran into the mouse's outstretched palm. He placed a small silver piece there and saw it vanish instantly.

"Thank you, sir. If there is anything I can do for you after you have met with this possible friend, please let me know. My name is Whort and I'm the majordomo here."

"Maybe later," Jon-Tom assured him as he started up the carved stairway.

He had no mention of taking the doormouse up on his offer. Not that he had anything against the house brand of entertainment. His long separation from Talea plagued him physically as well as mentally, but this wasn't the place to indulge in any lingering fancies of the flesh. It looked fancy and clean, but you never could tell where you might pick up an interesting strain of VD, and not only the human varieties. In the absence of modern medicine he didn't want to have to count on curing a good dose of the clap with a song or two.

So he restrained his libido as he mounted the second-floor landing and hunted for the right door. He was interrupted in his search by a sight that reminded him this was a real place and not a drug-induced excursion into a dreamland zoo.

A couple of creatures had passed him, and he'd paid them no mind. Coming down the hall toward him now was an exceptionally proportioned young woman in her early twenties. She was barely five feet tall and wore only a filmy peach-colored peignoir. The small pipe she smoked did little to blur the image of prancing, bouncing femininity.

"Well, what are you staring at, tall-skinny-and-handsome?"

It occurred to Jon-Tom this was not intended as a rhetorical question, and he mumbled a reply that got all caught up in his tongue and teeth. Somehow he managed to shamble past her. Only the fact that Clothahump lay dying in his tree along with any chance Jon-Tom had of returning home kept him moving. His head rotated like a searchlight, and he followed the perfect vision with his eyes until she'd disappeared down the stairs.

As he forced himself down the hall, that image lingered on his retinas like a bright light. Sadly, he found the right door and knocked gently, sparing a last sorrowful glance for the now empty landing.

"Mudge?" He repeated the knock, was about to repeat the call, when the door suddenly flew open, causing him to step back hastily. Standing in the opening was a female otter holding a delicate lace nightgown around her. Her eyebrows had been curled and painted, and the tips of her whiskers dipped in gold. She was sniffling, an act to which Jon-Tom attached no particular significance. Otters sniffled a lot.

She took one look at him before dashing past his bulk down the hallway, short legs churning.

Jon-Tom stared after her, was about to go in when a second fur of the night came out, accompanied by an equally distraught third otter. They followed their sister toward the stairs. Shaking his head, he entered the dark room.

Faint light flickered from a single chandelier. Golden shadows danced on the flocked wallpaper. Nothing else moved. Two curved mirrors on opposing walls ran from floor to ceiling. An elegant china washbasin rested on a chellow-wood dresser. The door to the john stood half-agape.

A wrought-iron bed decorated with cast grapevines and leaves stood against the far wall. The headboard curved slightly forward. A pile of sheets and pillows filled the bed, an eruption of fine linen. Jon-Tom guessed this was not the cheapest room in the house.

From within the silks and satins came a muffled but still familiar voice. "Is that you, Lisette? Are you comin' back to forgive me, luv? Wot I said, that were only a joke. Meant nothin' by it, I did."

"That would be the first time," Jon-Tom said coolly.

There was silence, then the pile of sheets stirred and a head emerged, black eyes blinking in the darkness. "Cor, I'm 'aving a bloody nightmare, I am! Too much bubbly."

"I don't know what you've had," Jon-Tom said as he moved toward the bed, "but this is no nightmare."

Mudge wiped at his eyes with the backs of his paws. "Right then, mate, it is no nightmare. You're too damned big to be a nightmare. Wot the 'ell are you doin' 'ere, anyways?"

"Looking for you."

"You picked the time for it." He vanished beneath the linens. "Where's me clothes?"

Jon-Tom turned, searched the shadows until he'd located the vest, cap, pants and boots. The oversized bow and quiver of arrows lay beneath the bed. He tossed the whole business onto the mattress.

"Here."

"Thanks, mate." The otter began to flow into the clothes, his movements short and fast. " 'Tis a providence, it is, wot brings you to poor ol' Mudge now."

"I don't know about that. You actually seem glad to see me. It's not what I expected."

Mudge looked hurt. "Wot, not 'appy to see an old friend? You pierce me to the quick. Now why wouldn't I be glad to see an old friend?"

Something funny going on here, Jon-Tom mused warily. Where were the otter's usual suspicious questions, his casual abusiveness?

As if to answer his questions the door burst inward. Standing there backlit by the light from the hall was a sight to give an opium eater pause.

The immensely overweight lady badger wore a bright red dress fringed with organdy ruffles. Rings dripped from her manicured fingers, and it was hard to believe that the massive gems that encircled her neck were real. They threw the light back into the room.

A few curious customers crowded in behind her as she raised a paw and pointed imperiously at the bed.

"*There* he is!" she growled.

"Ah, Madam Lorsha," said Mudge as he finished his dressing in a hurry, "I 'ave to compliment you on the facilities of your establishment."

"That will be the last compliment you ever give anyone, you deadbeat. Your ass is a rug." She snapped her fingers as she stepped into the room. "Tork."

Bending to pass under the lintel was the largest intelligent warmlander Jon-Tom had yet encountered. It was a shock to see someone taller than himself. The grizzly rose at least seven and a half feet, wore black-leather pants and shirt. He also wore what appeared in the bad light to be heavy leather gloves. Their true nature was revealed all too quickly.

Now, Jon-Tom did not know precisely what had transpired in the elegant room or beyond its walls or between his furry friend who was slipping on his boots in a veritable frenzy and the badger who was clearly the owner of the house of ill repute, but he suspected the sight of the full-grown grizzly adjusting the brass knuckles over his immense paws did not bode well for the future.

"I understand your concern, luv," said Mudge as he casually recovered his bow and quiver, "but now that me mate's 'ere everything will be squared away."

"Will it, now?" she said. The grizzly stood rubbing one palm with a massive fist and grinning. His teeth were very white. The badger eyed Jon-Tom. "Does he mean to say that you'll pay his bill?"

"Pay his bill? What do you mean, pay his bill?"

"He's been up here for three days without coming down, enjoying my best liquor and girls, and now he tells them he hasn't got a silver to his bastard name."

Jon-Tom glared back at Mudge. The otter shrugged, didn't appear in the least embarrassed. "Hey, at least I was honest about it, mate. I told 'em I was broke. But it's all right, ain't it? You'll pay for me, won't you?"

"You *are* his friend?" inquired the badger.

"Well, yeah." He brought out the purse Clothahump had given him and jiggled it. The gold inside jingled musically, and the badger and the bear relaxed.

She smiled at him. "Now that's more like it . . . sir. I can see that you are a gentleman, though I don't think much of your choice of friends." Mudge looked wronged.

"How much does he owe you?"

She didn't even have to think. "Two hundred and fifty, sir. Plus any damages to the linen. I'll have to check."

"I can cover it," Jon-Tom assured her. He turned to look darkly at Mudge, hefting his ramwood staff. "If you'd be kind enough to give me a moment alone with him, I intend to take at least some of it out of his hide."

The badger's smile widened. "Your pleasure is mine, sir." Again she snapped her fingers. The grizzly let out a disappointed grunt, turned, and ducked back through the doorway.

"Take your time, sir. If you need anything helpful—acid, some thin wooden slivers, anything at all—the house will be delighted to supply it."

The door closed behind her. As soon as they were alone, Jon-Tom began to search the room. There was only one window, off to the left. He tried to open it, found it wouldn't budge.

"'Ere now, mate," said Mudge, ambling over, "wot's the trouble? Just pay the old whore and let's be gone from 'ere."

"It's not that simple, Mudge. That money is from Clothahump, to pay for our passage at least as far as Snarken. And I lied about the amount. No way is there two hundred and fifty there."

Mudge took a step backward as Jon-Tom strove to puzzle out the window. "Just a minute there, mate. Wot's that about payin' *our* way? Snarken, you said? That's all the way across the Glittergeist, ain't it?"

"That's right." Jon-Tom squinted at the jamb. "I think this locks from the outside. Clever. Must be a way to break through it."

Mudge continued backing toward the bed. "Nice of you to come lookin' for me, mate, but I'm afraid I can't go with you. And you say 'is wizardship is behind it?"

"That's right. He's sick and I have to go get him some medicine."

"Right. Give the old reptile me best wishes, and I 'ope he makes a speedy recovery. As for me, I've some travelin' to do for me 'ealth, and salt air doesn't agree with me lungs."

"You're not going anywhere unless it's with me," Jon-Tom snapped at him. "You take one step out that door and I'll call the madam. I saw the look in her eyes. She'd enjoy separating your head from the rest of you. So would that side of beef that came in with her."

"I ain't afraid of no bag of suet wot communicates in grunts," Mudge said.

Jon-Tom turned from the window. "Then maybe I ought to call them. I can always find someone else to accompany me."

Mudge rushed at him. "Take it easy, mate, 'old on. To Snarken, you say?"

"Maybe beyond."

"Ain't no place beyond Snarken."

"Yes there is. Little town not too far inland from there." He fumbled between the windowpanes, was rewarded by a double clicking sound. "Ah."

He lifted the window slowly. Halfway up, something loud and brassy began to clang inside the building.

"Shit! There's an alarm spell on this thing!" The sounds of pounding feet came from the hall.

"No time for regrets, mate, and you'd best not stand there gawkin'." Mudge was over the sill in a flash and shinnying down the rainpipe outside. Jon-Tom followed more slowly, envying the otter his agility.

By the time they reached the pavement, faces had appeared at the open window.

"You won't get away from me, otter!" Madam Lorsha yelled, shaking her fist at them as they ran up the side street. At any moment Jon-Tom expected to hear the grizzly's footsteps behind them, feel huge paws closing around his throat. "I'll hunt you to the ends of the world! No one runs out owing Madam Lorsha!"

"Funny what she said about the ends of the world," Jon-Tom murmured as he followed the otter down endless alleyways and turns. He was sure Mudge had memorized this escape route before stepping inside the brothel. "That's where we're going."

"There you go again, mate," said Mudge, "usin' them words like *we* and *us*."

"I need your help, Mudge."

They reached a main street and slowed to a walk as they joined the crowd of evening strollers. Timswitty was a good-sized town, much bigger than Lynchbany. It was unlikely Madam Lorsha's thugs would be able to find them. Jon-Tom tried to hunch over and mask his exceptional height.

"Clothahump is deathly ill, and we must have this medicine. I'm not any happier about making this trip than you are."

"You must be, mate, because I'm not goin' to make it. Don't get me wrongo. You just 'elped me clear out of a bad spot. I am grateful,

I am, but she weren't worth enough to make me put me life on the line for you, much less for that old word-poisoner."

They edged around a strolling couple. "I need someone who knows the way, Mudge."

"Then you needs some other bloke, mate. I ain't never been to Snarken."

"I mean someone who knows the ways of the world, Mudge. I've learned a lot since I've been here, but that's nothing compared to what I don't know. I need your good advice as well as your unconventional knowledge."

"Sure you do." Mudge puffed up importantly in spite of knowing better. "You think you can flatter me into goin', is that it? Or did you think I'd forgotten your intentions to be a solicitor in your own world? Don't take me for a fool, mate."

"I have to have someone along I can trust," Jon-Tom went on. The otter's expression showed that was one ploy he wasn't expecting.

"Now that ain't fair, guv'nor, and you knows it."

"There will also," Jon-Tom added, saving the best for last, "be a good fee for helping me."

That piqued the otter's interest. " 'Ere now, why didn't you come out and say that t' begin with instead of goin' on with all this twaddle about 'ow 'is poor old 'ardheaded curmudgeonly 'oliness was 'aving an attack of the gout or whatever, or 'ow badly you need me unique talents." He moved nearer and put a comradely arm around Jon-Tom's waist, as high as he could comfortably reach.

"You 'ave a 'ell of a lot to learn about life, guv'nor." He rambled on as the evening fog closed in comfortingly around them, explaining that though he didn't know how it was in Jon-Tom's world, here it was gold that spoke clearest and bought one's trust. Not words.

Jon-Tom allowed as how things indeed were different, deferring to the otter's claims while privately disagreeing. It did not matter who was right, however. All that mattered was that Mudge had agreed to join him.

Mudge managed to steer them into a tavern in a high-class district. Having already flashed Clothahump's gold, Jon-Tom couldn't very well claim he didn't have the wherewithal to pay. So he went slowly through his own meal while the otter devoured a gigantic banquet more suitable to the appetite of Madam Lorsha's bouncer. As Mudge explained between mouthfuls, he'd burned up a lot of energy this past week and wanted to make certain he embarked on their long journey at full strength.

Only when the otter had finished the final morsel did he lean contentedly back in his chair.

"So you say we're goin' to distant Snarken, wot, and beyond, and I say there's nothin' beyond. Wot did 'is nibs say it would be like?"

"He didn't exactly say." Jon-Tom picked at a sweet dessert. "Just the town where the store with the medicine is kept."

"Yeah, I 'eard you say somethin' about a town. 'As it got a name?"

Jon-Tom decided the bittersweet berry dessert was to his taste, finished the last of it. "Crancularn."

"WOT?" Mudge suddenly was sitting bolt upright, dribbling the last traces of wrinklerry jelly from his lips as he gaped at the man sitting across the table from him. A few curious diners spared him a glance, returned to their business when they saw no fighting was involved.

Mudge wiped at his sticky whiskers and spoke more softly, eyeing Jon-Tom sideways. "Wot did you say the name o' this dump was, guv'nor?"

"Crancularn. I see you've heard of it."

" 'Eard of it, you're bloody well right I've 'eard of it. That's a place o' the dead, mate."

"I thought there wasn't anything beyond Snarken."

"Not supposed to be, mate, but then, nobody knows where this Crancularn is supposed to be either, except that it moves about from time to time, like lice, and that anyone who ever gets there never comes back. 'Tis the entrance to 'ell itself, mate. Surely you don't mean to go there."

"Not only do I mean to go there, I intend to make a small purchase and return safely with it. And you're coming with me. You promised."

" 'Ere now, mate, when I made this 'ere bargain, weren't nothin' said about Crancularn. I'm out." He stepped off the chair and discovered he was straddling the far end of Jon-Tom's ramwood staff, which had been slipped under the table earlier.

"Sit down," Jon-Tom ordered him. Gingerly, the otter resumed his seat. "You made a promise, Mudge. You agreed to accompany me. In a sense, you accepted the proffered fee. Where I come from an oral contract is enforceable when the details are known to both parties, and in this case the details are now known."

"But *Crancularn*, mate. Can't this medicine be got anywheres else?"

Jon-Tom shook his head. "I pressed Clothahump on that point

repeatedly, and he never wavered. The only place it can be bought is Crancularn." He leaned over the table, spoke almost angrily. "Look, do you think I want to go gallivanting halfway across a strange world in search of some old fart's pills? I like Clothahump, sure, but I have my own life to live. What's left of it. If he dies leaving me stuck here, I might as well be dead. It's interesting enough, your world, but I want to go *home*, damn it! I miss Westwood on the opening night of a Steven Spielberg movie, and I miss the bookstores on Hollywood Boulevard, and the beach, and bagels at the deli, and take-out Chinese food, and—"

"All right, mate, I believe you. Spare me your memories. So it's a contract, is it? At least you're learnin' 'ow to stick up for your rights." He smiled and tapped the staff.

Jon-Tom was taken aback. He'd acted almost exactly the way Mudge would have if their situations had been reversed. The thought was more than a little appalling.

"You'll keep your end of the bargain, then?"

"Aye." Mudge spoke with obvious reluctance. "I gave me word, so I'm stuck with it. Well, a short life but a happy one, they say. 'Tis better than dyin' in one's bed. Alone, anyway."

"There's no need for all this talk of dying." Jon-Tom sipped at the mug of cold cider in front of him. "We are going to get to Crancularn, obtain the necessary medication, and return here. All we're doing is running an errand."

"That's right, mate. Just an errand." He belched derisively, to the unconcealed disgust of the well-dressed diners nearby. "Wot a day it was for me when you tumbled into that glade where I was huntin' so peaceful. Why couldn't you 'ave settled on some other poor bloke besides old Mudge?"

"You were just lucky. As for your ill fortune, we don't know yet who's the fool in this play: you for agreeing to come with me or me for wanting you to."

"You singe me privates, mate," said Mudge, looking wounded, an expression he had mastered.

"A wonder there's anything left to singe, after three days in that brothel. Finish up and let's find a place to sleep. I'm bushed."

III

It took six tries to finally wake Mudge. After three days of nonstop debauchery and the huge meal of the previous night, the otter had to be helped to the bathroom. He got his pants on backwards and his boots on opposite feet. Jon-Tom straightened him out and together they worked their way through Timswitty in search of transportation.

From a nervous dealer badly in need of business they rented a low wooden wagon pulled by a single aged dray lizard, promising to drop it off at the port of Yarrowl at the mouth of the Tailaroam. From Yarrowl it should be a simple matter to book passage on a merchantman making the run across the Glittergeist to Snarken.

They succeeded in slipping quietly out of town without catching the eye of Madam Lorsha or her hirelings and were soon heading south along the narrow trade road. Once within the forest Mudge relaxed visibly.

" 'Peers we gave the old harridan the slip, mate."

Jon-Tom's eyebrows lifted. "We?"

"Well now, guv'nor, since 'tis we who are goin' on this little jaunt and we who are goin' to risk our lives for the sake o' some half-dotty ol' wizard, I think 'tis fair enough for me to say that 'tis we who escaped the clutches of her haunches."

"Plural good and plural bad, it that it?" Jon-Tom chucked the reins, trying to spur the ancient lumbering reptile to greater speed. "I guess you're right."

"Nice of you to agree, mate," said Mudge slyly. "So 'ow's about lettin' me 'ave a looksee at *our* money?"

"I'll keep an eye on our travel expenses, thanks. I need your help with several matters, Mudge, but counting coin isn't one of them."

"Ah well, then." Mudge leaned back against the hard back of the bench, put his arms behind his head, and gazed through the tinkling branches at the morning sun. "If you don't trust me, then to 'ell with you, mate."

"At least if I end up there it'll be with *our* money intact."

They stopped for lunch beneath a tree with bell leaves the size of quart jars. Mudge unpacked snake jerky and fruit juice. The appearance of the fruit juice made the otter shudder, but he was intelligent enough to know that he'd overdone his alcoholic intake just a hair the past week and that the percentage in his blood could not be raised much higher without permanent damage resulting. He poured himself a glass, wincing as he did so.

Something glinted in the glass and he looked sharply to his right. Nothing amiss. Bell leaves making music with the morning breezes, flying lizards darting from branch to branch in pursuit of a psychedelic bee.

Still . . . Carefully he set down his glass next to the wagon wheel. The dray lizard snoozed gratefully in a patch of sunlight, resting its massive head on its forelegs. Jon-Tom lay in the shade of the tree. All seemed right with the world.

But it wasn't.

"Back in a sec, mate." Mudge reached into the back of the wagon. Instead of food and drink he grabbed for his bow and quiver. The crossbow bolt that rammed into the wood between his reaching hands gave him pause. He withdrew them slowly.

"A wise decision," said a voice from the trees.

Jon-Tom sat up fast. "Who said that?"

He found himself staring at the business ends of an assortment of pikes and spears, wielded by an unpleasant-looking assortment of furry assailants.

"Me fault," Mudge muttered, angry at himself. "I 'eard 'em comin', I did, but not quite soon enough."

"It wouldn't have mattered," said the voice which had spoken a moment before. "There are too many of us anyway, and though we are instructed to bring you in alive, it wasn't specified in what condition."

Stepping through the circle of armed warmlanders was a coatimundi nearly as tall as Mudge. His natural black striping had been enhanced with brown decorations painted on muzzle and tail. One front canine was missing, and the remainder of the long, sharp teeth were stained yellow. He rested one paw on the hilt of a thick, curved dagger belted at his waist. The dagger was also stained, but not yellow.

Jon-Tom thought rapidly. Like Mudge's bow, his own duar and ramwood staff lay in the bed of the wagon. If he could just get to them. . . . Well, what if he could? As this apparent leader of their captors had said, they were badly outnumbered.

"Right. Wot is it you want with us?" Mudge asked. "We're just a couple of innocent travelers, poor prospects for thieves."

The coati shook his head and glared at them over his long snout out of bright black eyes. "I'm not interested in your wordly possessions, whatever they might be. I've been ordered by my master to bring you in."

"So Lorsha found us out anyway," the otter muttered. He sounded wistful. "Well, them three days were almost worth dyin' for. You should've been with me, mate."

"Well, I wasn't, and they're not worth dying for from my viewpoint."

"Calm yourselves," said the coati. "No one's speaking of dying here. Cooperate and give me no trouble, and I'll give none back to you." He squinted at Mudge. "And what's all this chattering about someone named Lorsha?"

Mudge came back from his memories and made a face at the coati. "You ain't 'ere to take us back to Madam Lorsha of Timswitty?"

"No. I come from Malderpot."

"Malderpot?" Jon-Tom gaped at him.

"Big town," Mudge informed him, "full of dour folk and little pleasure."

"*We* like it," said a raccoon hefting a halberd.

"No offense," Mudge told him. "Who wants us in Malderpot?"

"Our master Zancresta," said the coati.

"Who's this Zancresta?" Jon-Tom asked him.

A few incredulous looks showed on the faces of their captors, including the coati.

"You mean you've never heard of the Master of Darkness and Manipulator of the Secret Arts?"

Jon-Tom shook his head. " 'Fraid not."

The coati was suddenly uncertain. "Perhaps we have made a mistake. Perhaps these are not the ones we were sent to fetch. Thile, you and Alo check their wagon."

Two of the band rushed to climb aboard, began going through the supplies with fine disregard for neatness. It took them only moments to find Jon-Tom's staff and duar, which Thile held up triumphantly.

"It's the spellsinger, all right," said the muskrat.

"Keep a close watch on his instrument and he'll do us no harm," the coati instructed his men.

"I mean you no harm in any case," said Jon-Tom. "What does your Zancresta want with us?"

"Nothin' good. You can be certain o' that, mate," said Mudge.

"So one of you, at least, has heard of our master."

"Aye, I've 'eard of 'im, though I don't mean to flatter 'is reputation by it." He turned to Jon-Tom. "This 'ere Zancresta chap's the 'ead wizard not only for the town of Malderpot but for much of the northern part o' the Bellwoods. See, each town or village 'as its own wizard or sorcerer or witch, and each o' them claims to be better than 'is neighbor at the arts o' magickin'."

"Zancresta *is* the best," said the coati. "He is the master."

"I ain't goin' to argue the point with you," said Mudge. "I 'ave no interest whatsoever in wizardly debates and functions, for all that I seem to be gettin' repeatedly screwed by 'em.

"Now, if it's the spellsinger 'ere you're come after, take 'im and let me go. I'm only a poor traveler tryin' 'is best to make it down the windy road o' life, and I've 'ad a 'ard enough time makin' ends meet as it is without gettin' caught up again in the world's troubles."

"It may be true," said the coati, eyeing him unflatteringly. "But I have my orders. They say I am to bring back the spellsinger known as Jon-Tom and any who travel with him. You will have the chance to plead your case before the master. Perhaps he will let you go."

"And if 'e don't?"

The coati shrugged. "That's not my affair."

"Easy for you to say," Mudge grumbled.

Spears prodded Jon-Tom and Mudge into the back of the wagon, where they sat with their hands tied behind their backs. A couple of the coati's henchmen took over the reins. The little procession swung back northward, slightly west of Timswitty but also in the opposite direction form Lynchbany and the River Tailaroam.

"This Zancresta 'as a bad reputation, mate," Mudge whispered to his companion. "Mind now, I'm not denyin' 'is abilities. From wot I've 'eard 'e ain't bad at sorcerin', but 'e's unscrupulous as 'ell. Cheats on 'is spells and short-changes 'is incantations, but 'e's too powerful for anyone to go up against. I've 'ad no dealin's with 'im meself, and I stay clear o' folk from Malderpot. As I said, they ain't much for partyin'."

"From what you tell me about their chief wizard, I can see why they aren't."

"Right." Mudge nodded past the drivers. "Now, 'tis clear this 'ere ringtail knows nothin' o' wot 'is master wants with us. That may be somethin' we can turn to our advantage. So somehow we 'ave to get clear o' this charmin' bunch o' throat-slitters before we're brought up before Zancresta himself. If that 'appens, I 'ave this funny feelin' that we'll never see the shores o' the Glittergeist or any other calm water."

"Don't underestimate this one." Jon-Tom indicated the coati, who strolled along in the lead, talking with a couple of his band. "He seems more than the usual hired thug."

"Fancy clothes can't hide one's origin," said Mudge.

"No harm in trying." He raised his voice. "Hey, you, leader!"

"Shut up," snapped the muskrat from the driver's bench. He showed a short sword. "Or you will eat your own tongues for breakfast and can see how your words taste then."

"I just want a word with your chief. Surely one as illustrious as he can spare a prisoner a few minutes of his time."

Evidently the coati's ears were as sensitive as his nose, because he slowed his pace until he was walking alongside the wagon.

"I bear you no hatred, spellsinger. What do you wish to talk about? By the way, my name is Chenelska."

"Don't you have any idea what your master wants with us? What use has so great and powerful a wizard for a mere spellsinger like me?"

Chenelska considered a moment, then glanced past Jon-Tom to Mudge. "Tell me, water rat, is this tall human as ignorant as he appears or is he making fun of me?"

"No." Mudge spoke with sufficient conviction to persuade the coati that he was telling the truth. " 'E's as dumb as he looks."

"Thanks, Mudge. Nice to know I can rely on your good opinion."

"Don't mention it, mate."

"Can it be," said the dumbfounded Chenelska, "that you have never heard of the rivalry between our master and the one that you serve?"

"The one I serve? You mean Clothahump? I don't serve him. I'm not an apprentice or anything like that. He has another who serves him. We're just friends."

"Indeed. Good enough friends that you undertake a long, dangerous mission on his behalf when he lies too ill to travel himself. A mission to cross the Glittergeist in search of a rare and precious medicine he requires to cure himself."

"How the hell do you know that?" Jon-Tom said angrily.

The coati grinned and laughed, a single sharp barking. "It seems that this Clothahump does have another who serves him. A true famulus. A fine, intelligent, hardworking apprentice who serves faithfully and well. Except when he's been treated to a few stiff sips of good bellywarmer."

"Sorbl! That stupid big-eyed sot!"

The coati nodded, still grinning. "Not that we had to work hard at it, you understand. The poor little fellow merely wanted companionship, and other servants of my master provided it, whereupon the turtle's servant grew extremely talkative."

"I'll bet he did," Jon-Tom mumbled disconsolately.

"It has always been a matter of great contention in this part of the world," the coati explained, "as to who the greater wizard is. Clothahump of the tree or my master Zancresta. It didn't bother my master when opinion was divided and drifted back and forth. But it has lately become apparent that outside the immediate environs of Malderpot, the consensus is that your Clothahump is the greater." He moved closer to the wagon and lowered his voice so that his band could not overhear.

"It's true that saving the whole world is a tough act to follow. When word came of the victory over the Plated Folk at the Jo-Troom Gate, and the part of your master Clothahump played in it, there was very little my master could do to counteract the great shift in public opinion, and he has been in a murderous mood ever since."

"As if Clothahump saved all the warmlands just to spite him," Jon-Tom said disgustedly.

"Be that as it may, wizards can be very touchy about such things. Zancresta dwells on evil spells and prepares toxic presents and calls down all who cross him. He has been dangerous to approach ever since this happened. The only way for him to regain his self-respect and cancel his shame is to do something to make himself again be considered the equal of the turtle of the tree. Yet he sees no way to do this. This Clothahump refuses all challenges and duels."

"Clothahump," Jon-Tom explained politely, "doesn't think much of games."

"Word travels that he does not because he is getting senile."

Jon-Tom didn't reply. There was nothing to be gained by arguing with Chenelska and angering him.

"Therefore, my master is badly frustrated, since there is no way he can prove that he is truly the most skilled in the wizardly arts.

"Word arrived recently about this severe sickness Clothahump is suffering from and that he cannot cure with his own magic, that he needs medicine obtainable only from a land beyond Snarken. My master was delighted by it."

"When we get out of this," Jon-Tom whispered to Mudge, "I'm going to string Sorbl up by his feet and hang him beak-first over an open bottle of brandy."

"Mate, I truly 'ope you get that opportunity," said Mudge.

"Thanks to the information the wizard's famulus provided, we were able to locate and intercept you," said Chenelska.

"What does your master intend doing with us?"

"I do not know, man. For now, it would seem sufficient to prevent you from carrying out your mission and returning with the necessary medicine. Perhaps after he has weakened enough my master will take pity on him and travel south to allow him the privilege of begging for his help."

"Clothahump would never do that," Jon-Tom assured the coati. "He'll spit in Zancresta's face before he asks his help."

"Then I imagine he will die." The coati spoke without emotion. "It is of no import to me. I only serve my master."

"Yes, you're a good slave."

The coati moved closer to the wagon and slapped the sideboard angrily. "I am no slave!"

"A slave is one who unquestioningly carries out the orders of his master without considering the possible consequences."

"I know the consequences of what I do." Chenelska glowered at him, no longer friendly. "Of one consequence I am sure. I will emerge from this little journey far better off than you. You think you're smart, man? I was instructed in all the tricks a spellsinger can play. You can make only music with your voice and not magic without your instrument. If I choose to cut your throat, I will be safer still.

"As for the water rat that accompanies you, it may be that the master will free him. If he does so, I will be waiting for him myself, to greet him as is his due." With that, the coati left them, increasing his stride to again assume his place at the head of the little procession.

"I'm beginnin' to wish you'd left me at Madam Lorsha's," the otter said later that night.

"To Tork's tender mercies?" Jon-Tom snorted. "You'd be scattered all over Timswitty by now if I hadn't shown up to save you, and you know it."

"Better to die after three days o' bliss than to lie in some filthy cell in Malderpot contemplatin' a more mundane way o' passin'."

"We're not dead yet. That's something."

"Is it now? You're a fine one for graspin' at straws."

"I once saw a man start a fire with nothing more than a blade of dry grass. It kept both of us warm through a night in high mountains."

"Well 'e ain't 'ere and neither is 'is fire."

"You give up too quickly." Jon-Tom looked ahead, to where Chenelska strode proudly at the head of his band. "I could put in for a writ of habeas corpus after we arrive, but somehow I don't think it would have much sway with this Zancresta."

"Wot's that, mate? Some kind of otherworldly magic?"

"Yes. We're going to need something like it to get out of this with our heads in place. And let's not forget poor Clothahump for worrying about our own skins. He's depending on us."

"Aye, and see 'ow well 'is trust is placed."

They kept to back roads and trails, staying under cover of the forest, avoiding intervening communities. Chenelska intended to avoid unnecessary confrontations as well as keep his not always reliable troops clear of civilization's temptations. So they made good time and after a number of days arrived on the outskirts of a town too small to be a city but too large to be called a village.

A crudely fashioned but solid stone wall encircled it, in contrast to the open city boundaries of Lynchbany and Timswitty. It wasn't a very high wall, a fact Jon-Tom commented on as they headed west.

A small door provided an entrance. The prisoners were hustled quickly down several flights of stone stairs, past crackling torches smelling of creosote, and thrust into a dark, odiferous cell. An obese porcupine turned the large key in the iron lock and departed, leaving them alone in the near blackness.

"Still optimistic, mate?" Mudge leaned against a dank wall and sniffed. "Cast into a dungeon without hope of rescue to spend our last hours talkin' philosophy."

Jon-Tom was running his fingers speculatively over the mossy walls. "Not very well masoned or mortared."

"I stand corrected," said Mudge sardonically. "Talkin' about architecture."

"Architecture's an interesting subject, Mudge. Don't be so quick to dismiss it. If you know how something is put together, you might learn how to take it apart."

"That's right, guv'nor. You find us a loose stone in the wall, take it out, and bring the whole stinkin' city down on top o' us. Then we'll be well and truly free." He slunk off toward a corner.

"Not even a chamber pot in this cesspool. I 'ope they kill us fast instead o' leavin' us to die with this smell." He moved back to grab the bars of the cell, shouted toward the jailer.

"Hey mate, get your fat ass over 'ere!"

In no hurry, the porcupine ambled across the floor from his chair. When he reached the bars he turned his back, and Mudge backed hastily away from the two-foot-long barbed quills.

"I will thank you to be a little more polite."

"Right, sure, guv. Take 'er easy. No offense. You can imagine me state o' mind, chucked in 'ere like an old coat."

"No, I cannot," said the jailer. "I do my job and go home to my family. I do not imagine your state of mind."

"Excuse me," said Jon-Tom, "but have you any idea how long we are to be held in here?"

"Ah, no."

Slow. Their jailer was a little slow in all areas. It was a characteristic of all porcupines, and this one was no exception. That didn't mean he was a moron. Tread slowly, Jon-Tom warned himself.

"Our possessions have become separated from us," he went on. "Do you know what was done with them?"

Lazily, the porcupine pointed upward. "They are in the main guard chamber, to be taken out and sent along with you when word comes for you to be moved."

"Do you know what's going to happen to us?"

The porcupine shook his head. "No idea. None of my business. I do my job and stay out of other people's business, I do."

Mudge instantly divined his companion's intentions, said sadly, "We were searched before we were sent down here. I wonder if they found your sack o' gold, mate?"

"Sack of gold?" Evidently the porcupine wasn't all that slow. For the first time the half-lidded eyes opened fully, then narrowed again.

"You are trying to fool me. Chenelska would never leave a sack of gold in a place where others could find it and steal it."

"Yeah, but wot if 'e didn't think to look for somethin' like that?" Mudge said insinuatingly. "We just don't want 'im to get 'is 'ands on it, after 'im throwin' us down 'ere and all. If you wanted to find out if we were lyin' or not, all you'd 'ave to do is go look for yourself, mate. You 'ave the keys, and we ain't 'ardly goin' to dig our way out o' this cell while you're gone."

"That is true." The jailer started for the stairs. "Do not get any funny ideas. You cannot cut through the bars, and there is no one else here but me."

"Oh, we ain't goin' anywhere, we ain't," Mudge insisted.

"By the way," Jon-Tom added offhandedly, "as long as you're going upstairs, maybe you could do something for us? This is an awfully dank and somber place. A little music would do a lot to lighten it up. Surely working down here day after day, the atmosphere must get pretty depressing after a while."

"No, it does not," said the porcupine as he ascended the stairs. "I like it dank and somber and quiet, though I would be interested in hearing the kind of music you could play. You see, Chenelska told me you were a spellsinger."

Jon-Tom's heart sank. "Not really. I'm more of an apprentice. I don't know enough yet to really spellsing. I just like to make music."

"Nonetheless, I cannot take the chance."

"Wait!" Jon-Tom called desperately. "If you know what spellsinging's all about, then surely you know that a spellsinger can't make magic without his instrument."

"That is so." The porcupine eyed him warily.

"Well then, how about this? You bring down my duar, my instrument, but after you give it to me you chain my hands so I can't pull them back through these bars. That way if I tried to sing anything that sounded dangerous to you, you could yank the duar away from me before I could finish and I couldn't do a thing to stop you from doing so."

The jailer considered, wrestling with unfamiliar concepts. Jon-Tom and Mudge waited breathlessly, glad of the darkness. It helped to conceal their anxiety.

"Yes, I think that would be safe enough," the jailer said finally. "And I *am* curious to hear you sing. I will see if your instrument is with your other possessions. While I look for the sack of gold."

"You won't regret it!" Jon-Tom called after him as he disappeared up the stairway. As soon as he'd left, Mudge looked excitedly at his friend.

"Cor, mate, can you really do anythin' tied like that?"

"I don't know. I have to try. It's clear he wasn't just going to hand me the duar without some kind of safeguard. I just don't know what I could sing that could help us out of here before he decided it sounded threatening and took the duar away from me. Not that I ever know what to sing. I had the same problem in my own world. But it was all I could think of."

"You better think o' somethin', mate, or it'll be two worlds that'll be missin' you permanent. I don't know what this Zancresta has planned for us, but as much as 'e hates Clothahump, I don't figure on 'im bein' overly polite to a couple o' the turtle's servants."

"We're not his servants. At least, you're not."

"Aye, an' you saw 'ow far that got me with Chenelska. I'm stuck with the bedamned label just like you are, like it or not. So *think* of somethin'. Somethin' effective, and fast."

"I don't *know.*" Jon-Tom fought with his memory. "Practically everything I know is hard rock."

Mudge gestured at the walls. "Strikes me as damned appropriate."

"Not like that," Jon-Tom explained impatiently. "It's a name for a kind of popular music. You've heard me sing it."

"Aye, an' I don't pretend to understand a word o' it."

"Then you have something in common with my parents."

Footsteps coming down the stairs interrupted them momentarily.

"You'd better think up somethin' quick, mate."

"I'll try." He stuck his arms out between the bars, waiting expectantly. His spirits were boosted by the sight of the undamaged duar dangling from one of the jailer's paws.

"There was no gold," the porcupine declared sourly.

"Sorry." Mudge sighed fitfully. "About wot one would expect from a snurge like Zancresta. Still, 'tweren't no 'arm in lookin', were there?"

"What were you two talking about while I was gone? I heard you talking." The porcupine looked suspicious.

"Nothin' much, mate. Just makin' conversation. We talk while you're right 'ere, too, don't we?"

"Yes, that is so. Very well." He stepped forward and made as if to hand the duar to Jon-Tom, then hesitated. "I do not know."

"Oh, come on," Jon-Tom urged him, a big smile frozen on his face.

"A little music would be nice. Not everyone has the chance to hear an apprentice spellsinger make music just for pleasure."

"That is what concerns me." The jailer stepped back and rummaged through a wooden chest. When he returned it was to clap a pair of thick leather cuffs on Jon-Tom's wrists. They were connected to one another by a chain. He also, to Jon-Tom's dismay, tied a thick cord around the neck of the duar.

"There," he said, apparently satisfied, and handed over the instrument. Jon-Tom's fingers closed gratefully over the familiar wooden surface, lightly stroked the double set of strings.

The porcupine returned to his chair, keeping a firm grip on his end of the cord. "Now if you try anything funny I don't even have to run over to you. All I have to do is pull this rope." He gave the cord an experimental yank, and Jon-Tom had to fight to hold onto the duar.

"I need a little slack," he pleaded, "or I won't be able to play at all."

"All right." The jailer relaxed his grip slightly. "But if I think you are trying to trick me I will pull it right out of your hands and smash it against the floor."

"Don't worry. I wouldn't try anything like that. Would I, Mudge?"

"Oh, no, sor. Not after you've all but given this gentlebeing your word." The otter assumed an air of mock unconcern as he settled down on the floor to listen. "Play us a lullaby, Jon-Tom. Somethin' soothin' and relaxin' to 'elp us poor ones forget the troubles we face and the problems o' the world."

"Yes, play something like that," asked the porcupine.

Jon-Tom struggled with himself. Best to first play a couple of innocuous ditties to lull this sod into a false sense of security. The trouble was, being mostly into heavy metal, he knew about as many gentle tunes as he did operatic arias. Somehow something by Ozzy Osbourne or Ted Nugent didn't seem right, nor did anything by KISS. He considered "Dirty Deeds Done Dirt Cheap" by AC/DC, decided quickly that one stanza would cost him control of the duar permanently.

He decided to take a chance with some golden oldies. Maybe a few of Roy Orbison's songs, even if his voice wasn't up to it. It seemed to work. The porcupine lazed back in his chair, obviously content, but still holding tight to the cord.

Jon-Tom segued into the part of one song where the lyrics went "the day you walked out on me" and the jailer didn't stir, but neither did the walls part to let them through. Discouraged, he moved on to

"America" by Neil Diamond. A few faint images of the Statue of
Liberty and Ellis Island flickered fitfully in the cell, but Jon-Tom did
not find himself standing safe at either location.

Then he noticed Mudge. The otter sat back in the shadows making
long pulling and throwing motions. It took Jon-Tom a moment to
understand what his companion was driving at. In the middle of
humming "Won't Get Fooled Again," he figured the otter's movements out.

The porcupine had tied the cord to the duar in order to be able to
jerk it quickly out of Jon-Tom's hands. If they could somehow gain
control of the rope, they might be able to make a small lasso and cast
it toward a weapon or even the big keyring lying on the table.

In order to try that, of course, they had to somehow incapacitate
their jailer. Since he seemed half-asleep already, Jon-Tom softened his
voice as much as possible and sang the sweetest ballads he could
think of, finishing with "Sounds of Silence" by Simon and Garfunkel.
That particularly apt selection set the porcupine to snoozing. To
make sure, he added a relaxing rendition of "Scarborough Fair."

Carefully, he tugged gently on the cord. Two half-witted eyes
popped wide open and the line went taut.

"I told you not to try anything," the porcupine growled.

For an instant Jon-Tom was sure they'd lose the duar along with
their last hope. "I didn't mean anything!" he said desperately. "It's
only that playing in the same position all the time hurts my arms. I
wasn't doing anything else."

"Well . . ." The jailer slumped back in his chair. "See that you
don't do it no more. Please play another song. I never heard anything
like them. Pretty."

Despairingly, Jon-Tom simply sang the first thing that came to
mind, the theme song from one of the *Rocky* films. Maybe it was his
frustration, perhaps his sudden indifference. Whatever the reason, he
almost thought he could feel the power running through him. He
tried to focus on it, really working himself into the useless song in the
hope it might lead to something better.

A faint smell of ozone began to filter into the air of the dungeon.
Something crackled near the ceiling. Mudge scrambled warily back
into the farthest corner of the cell. Jon-Tom jumped as an electric
shock ran up his wrists. He tried to pull back into the cell, found he
was trapped against the bars by the leather wristcuffs and linking
chain.

Oh, shit, he mumbled silently. I've gone and done something weird again.

Only this time he was trapped up against whatever it was. Something was materializing in the air next to him. He tugged futilely at the leather cuffs, dropping the duar in the process. The instrument was glowing brightly as it bounced around on the floor like a toad at a disco.

The slow-moving porcupine was on his feet and staring. He'd abandoned the cord in favor of edging 'round toward the rack of weapons. Selecting a long spear, he aimed it at the cell. Jon-Tom was uncomfortably aware of the fact that if the jailer so chose, he could run him through where he stood.

"What are you doing, spellsinger? Stop it!"

"I'm not doing anything!" Jon-Tom prayed his hysteria was as convincing as it was heartfelt. "Untie my hands!"

The jailer ignored him, gazing in stupefied fascination at the slowly rotating cylinder of fluorescent gas that had gathered inside the cell. "Don't lie to me. Something is happening. Something is happening!"

"I know something's happening, you moron! Let me loose!" He wrenched uselessly at his bonds.

The jailer continued to keep his distance. "I am warning you, spellsinger. Put an end to this magic right now!" Keeping his thorny back against the walls, he edged around until he was standing close to the bars. From there he was able to prod the prisoner with the tip of his spear. It was extremely sharp.

"I can't stop it! I don't know what I did and I don't know what's happening."

"I do not believe you." The jailer's voice had turned shrill and he was jabbing seriously with the spear.

Suddenly a loud *bang* came from the cloud of gas. The glowing cylinder dissipated to reveal a massive, powerful form at least seven feet tall standing in the center of the jail cell. It had to crouch to keep from bumping its head against the ceiling.

Mudge quailed back against the wall while Jon-Tom thought wildly about his last song. The indifferently sung song which apparently had been far more effective than all its anxiety-laden predecessors. The theme song from that *Rocky* film . . . what was it?

Oh, yeah. The "Eye of the Tiger."

IV

Actually there were two of them, and they glared around in bewilderment. Jon-Tom had never seen a white tiger before, much less one that wore armor and stood on two legs. Leather and brass strips made a skirt which covered the body from waist to the knees. Additional armor protected the back of arms and legs, was secured over the legs with crisscrossing leather straps. A finely worked brass helmet shielded the head, and an intricate inscription covered the thin nose guard. Holes cut in the top of the helmet allowed the ears to protrude.

The huge furry skull glanced in all directions, taking in unanticipated surroundings. White and black ears flicked nervously as a quarter ton of tiger tried to orient itself. Paws dropped to sheaths, and in an instant each one held a five-foot-long sword with razor-sharp serrated edges.

"By all the nine feline demons, what's going on heah? I declare I'll have some answers right quick or there'll be hell to pay." Slitted eyes fixed on the bars. She took a step forward and glared down at the quivering porcupine. "You! What is this place? Why am ah locked up? Y'all answer me fast or ah'll make a necklace out of yo backbone!"

"G-g-g-guards," the porcupine stammered. It came out as a whisper. Aware his cry wasn't reaching very far, he raised his voice. "Guards!"

"Quit stahling and talk to me," Feminine, Jon-Tom decided. Thunderous, but undeniably feminine. The conjuration was a she. She turned to eye Mudge. "Yo theah. Why won't he talk to me?"

"You talkin' to me, m'dear?" Mudge inquired reluctantly.

She reached down and lifted him easily off the floor with one paw, setting her second sword aside but within easy reach. Fully extended, her claws were nearly as long as Mudge's fingers.

"Now, who else would ah be talking to, you little sponge?"

"Blimey, m'dear, I ain't considered the possibility."

"Guards!" Suddenly it occurred to the porcupine that since he wasn't having much luck obtaining help with his voice, it might be efficacious to employ his feet. He raced up the stairs with unexpected speed. "Guards, help me!"

"Hey, yo!" The tigress dropped Mudge, who promptly retreated to the back of the cell. "Come back heah! Yo heah me?"

"He thinks you're a threat to him."

"What's that?" For the first time she focused her attention on Jon-Tom."

"I said, he thinks you're a threat to him. Because you're in here with us."

"Y'all are awfully big fo a human."

"And you're awfully big period." He continued struggling with the cuffs that bound him to the bars of the cell.

"What is this place?" She turned slowly to make a more careful inspection of the prison. She did not appear frightened. Only irritated.

"We're in a dungeon in a town called Malderpot."

"Nevah heard of it," said the feline amazon. "A dungeon, you say. I can see that fo mahself, honey." She eyed his restraints. "Why ah yo tied up like that?"

"I'm a spellsinger," he explained. "I've been doing a little singing and I think I accidently brought you here."

"So that's it!" Jon-Tom did his best not to cower away from those burning yellow eyes. She stepped back and hefted both her swords. "Well then, y'all can just send me back."

He squirmed against the bars. "I, uh, I'm afraid I can't do that. I don't know how I brought you here. I can try later, maybe. But not without my duar." He pointed into the room. "And I can't play it with my hands tied like this."

"Well, that much is obvious. Ah've got eyes, yo know."

"Very pretty eyes, too."

"Huh," she said, a little more softly. "Spellsingah, yo say? Yo sound moah like a solicitah to me." Jon-Tom didn't inform her about his legal training, not being sure of her opinion of solicitors.

One sword suddenly cut forward and down. Mudge let out a half moan, half squeak, and Jon-Tom closed his eyes. But the sword passed between the bars to delicately cut the chain linking his wrist cuffs. A couple of quick twists of a clawed paw and his hands were free. He spoke as he rubbed the circulation back into his wrists.

"I still need the duar." Loud noises reached them from somewhere on the level above, and he hurried his introductions. "That's Mudge, I'm Jon-Tom Meriweather." He recalled the song he'd sung prior to "Eye of the Tiger." "By any chance would your name be Sage, Rosemary, or Thyme?" Somehow Scarborough didn't seem a possibility.

"Close enuf. Ah am called Roseroar."

Jon-Tom nodded to himself. Once again his songs and his desires had gotten themselves thoroughly mixed. He took a deep breath, repeated the gist of a by now familiar story.

"We're trying to help a wizard who is dying. Because of that a jealous wizard is trying to prevent us from doing so. He had us captured, brought here, and locked up."

"That's no business of mine," said the tigress. "Yo really think mah eyes are pretty?"

"Extremely so." Why didn't Mudge chip in with a word or two? he wondered. He was better at this sort of thing. But the otter hugged his corner of the cell and kept his mouth shut. Jon-Tom plunged on. "Like topaz."

"Yo have a gift of words as well as music, don't yo? Well, let me tell yo, ah am not subject to the simple flattery of the male of any species!"

"Of course you're not. I didn't mean for you to think I was intentionally flattering you, or anything like that. I just made a simple statement of fact."

"Did y'all, now? Where do yo have to go to help this dying friend of yours?"

"Across the Glittergeist Sea."

"So ah'm that fah west, am ah?" She shook her head in wonder. "It's a peculiah world we live in."

"You don't know the half of it," Jon-Tom muttered.

"Ah've nevah been to an ocean, much less the Glittergeist." She looked out through the bars. "So that's yo instrument fo making magic?"

"It is. Also, the keys are on the table nearby. If we could get ahold of the rope attached to the duar, we could maybe drag the keys over here." He eyed the stairwell. "But I don't think we've got much time."

"Well, sugah, if it's the keys you want . . ." Roseroar put one paw on a bar to the left, the other on the bar immediately opposite, inhaled mightily, and pushed. Muscles rippled beneath the armor.

There was a groan and the metal bent like spaghetti. The tigress stepped through the resultant gap, walked over to the table, and picked up the keyring.

"Yo still want these?"

Mudge was already out in the corridor. Jon-Tom was right on his heels. He snatched the duar and slung it over his shoulder.

"I think we'll be able to manage without them. Roseroar, you're quite a lady."

"Aye, with a delicate and ladylike touch," Mudge added.

"Ah think ah like you two," she said thoughtfully, staring at Mudge, "though ah can't decide if y'all are trying to be funny or flattering." She gestured with the two heavy swords. "Ah hope fo yo sake y'all are trying to be funny."

Jon-Tom hastened to reassure her. "You've got to take whatever Mudge says with a grain of salt. Comments like that are part of his nature. Sort of like a disease." He turned to bestow a warning look on the otter.

"Ah can see that," said the tigress. "Well, ah don't know how ah'm going to get home, but ah sure don't fancy this hole. Let's go somewhere quiet and talk."

"Suits me," said Jon-Tom agreeably.

At that moment the porcupine appeared at the top of the stairs, preceded by a pair of big, heavily armed wolves. They saw Roseroar about the time she saw them. She emitted a battle cry, a mixture of roar and curse, that shook moss from the ceiling. Waving both swords like propellers, she charged the stairway, which cleared with astonishing speed.

Mudge executed a little bow and gestured with his right hand. "After you, master o' magic and spellsinger extraordinaire."

Jon-Tom made a face at him, hurried to follow Roseroar upward. From ahead sounded shouts, screams, frantic cries, and yelps. Above all rose the tigress's earthshaking growls.

"Don't be so quick to compliment me," Jon-Tom told the otter. "She's not what I was trying to conjure up."

"I know that, guv'nor," said Mudge, striding along happily in his companion's wake. "It never is, wot? But even though you never get wot you're after with your spellsingin', wotever you gets always seems to work out."

"Tell me that again when she finds out there's no way I can send her home."

"Now, mate," Mudge told him as they started up to the next level, "wot's the use o' creatin' worry where there ain't none? Besides," he went on, his grin widening, "if she turns quarrelsome, you can tell 'er 'ow beautiful 'er eyes are."

"Oh, shut up."

They emerged into the main guardroom, which looked as if a modest typhoon had thundered through it. Every table was overturned and broken furniture littered the floor. Broken spears and pikes sopped up spilled liquid from shattered jugs. A couple of the guards remained, decoratively draped over the broken furniture. None offered a protest as Jon-Tom and Mudge began to search the still intact chests and drawers.

One yielded Mudge's longbow and arrows, another Jon-Tom's ramwood fighting staff. There was no sign of the full purse Clothahump had given him, nor did he expect to find it. Mudge was more disappointed than his companion at the absence of the gold.

"Bloody bedamned stinkin' thieves," he mumbled, ignoring the fact that he'd lifted a purse or two in his own time.

"Be quiet." Jon-Tom led him up the next flight of stairs. "From the way you're carrying on, you'd think this was the first time you'd ever been penniless."

"I'm not sayin' that, mate," replied Mudge, putting a leash on his lamentations, "but when I gets friendly with a bit o' gold or silver and it ups and disappears on me, I feel as if I've lost a good friend. The loss strikes me to the quick."

"One of these days it'd be nice to see you get so emotional over something besides money."

"You do me an injustice, mate." Mudge carried his bow in front of him, a hunting arrow notched and ready to fire. If the fates were kind they'd give him one clear shot at Chenelska or his bullyboys. Nothing would please him more than to be able to give the coati the shaft.

"You want emotional?" he continued as they climbed. "You should've seen me at Madam Lorsha's."

"I'm talking about honest emotion, about caring. Not lust."

"Cor, you mean there's a difference?"

The third landing was the last. They emerged into a small open square lit by torches and oil lamps. To their left was the city wall, to the right the outermost buildings of the town. The light danced wildly as sources of illumination were hastily moved to different positions. Shouts and yells filled the air.

Jon-Tom ducked as a wolf whizzed over his head. It pinwheeled once before striking the wall with a sickening thud.

Roseroar's efforts threw everything into confusion. Horns and shouts were beginning to rouse a whole section of the community. Lights were starting to appear in nearby windows as residents were awakened by the commotion.

Mudge bounced gleefully up and down, pointing at the evidence of the chaos the tigress was causing. "Wot a show! The poor buggers must think the 'ole bloomin' city is under attack."

"Maybe they're right." Jon-Tom started forward.

"Hey, you two!" Roseroar called to them as she idly batted aside a large rat armed with a short sword who had tried to sneak under her guard. The rodent went skidding across the paving stones, shedding bits and pieces of armor and flesh as he went. "Ovah heah! This way!"

They ran toward her. Jon-Tom placed his staff in front of him while Mudge ran backward to guard their rear, his short legs a blur. As they ran they dodged spears and arrows. Mudge responded to each attack individually, and they were rewarded as one figure after another fell from the wall above.

Snarling, a hyena draped in heavy chain mail headed right for Jon-Tom, swinging a viciously studded mace over his head. Jon-Tom blocked it with his staff, and the ramwood held as the mace's chain wrapped around it. He pulled and twisted in one motion, bringing the knobbed end of the staff down on his assailant's helmet. The hyena dropped like a stone. They ran on, Jon-Tom unwrapping the chain from his staff.

Then they were up against the thick wooden door in the city wall. Crossbow bolts thudded into the wood or splintered against the rock as the wall's garrison struggled to regroup.

Mudge inspected it rapidly. "Locked, damn it, from the other side!"

"Pahdon me," said Roseroar. While they covered her she put her back against the door, dug her feet into the pavement, and shoved. The door broke with a snap, the wood holding but not the iron hinges. It fell with a crash. The trio ran out, pursued by yells and weapons. No one chose to pursue beyond the city wall in person. The tigress had demonstrated what she could do at close range, and Malderpot's soldiery had taken the lesson to heart. They held back, waiting for someone higher up to give the necessary orders, and praying those directions would take their time arriving.

Before they did, the fugitives were deep within the concealment offered by the Bellwoods and the night. Eventually they located a place where several giant trees had fallen, forming a natural palisade, and settled in behind the wooden barricade nature had so thoughtfully provided.

The long run hadn't troubled Jon-Tom, who was a good distance runner, nor Mudge, who was blessed with inexhaustible energy, but Roseroar was tired. They waited while she caught her breath.

There in the moonlight she pulled off her helmet, undid the thick belt that held both swords, and put it aside. Then she leaned back against one fallen trunk. Her bright yellow eyes seemed to glow in the darkness. Physically she was unharmed by the fighting, though her armor showed plenty of cuts and dents.

"We owe you our lives," he finally told her.

"Yes, ah expect that's so. Damned if ah know how ah'm going to collect on that debt. Yo told me yo didn't mean to conjuh me up in the first place?"

"That's right," he confessed. "It was an accident. I was trying to put our jailer to sleep. When it didn't work I got upset and spellsang the first thing that came to mind and—poof—there you were."

"Ah was the first thing that came to yo mind?"

"Well, not exactly. Matter of fact, I've never seen anybody like you. This kind of thing happens to me a lot when I try to spellsing."

She nodded, turned to look to where Mudge was already searching the bushes for something edible. "Is he telling the truth, squirt?"

"Me name is Mudge, lady o' the long tooth," said the voice in the bushes, "and I'll make you a deal right now. You can like me o' not, but you don't call me names and I'll respond likewise."

"Ah favor politeness in all things, being a lady of refined tastes," she replied evenly.

Mudge restrained the first reply that came to mind, said instead, "Aye, 'e's tellin' you the truth. A powerful spellsinger 'e is. Maybe the most powerful ever, though we ain't yet sure o' that. 'E certainly ain't. See, 'e 'as this bad 'abit o' tryin' to do one thing and 'e ends up doin' something total unexpected."

Jon-Tom spread his hands in a gesture of helplessness. "It's true. I have this ability but I don't seem able to control it. And now it's caused me to go and inconvenience you."

"That's a fine, politic way of putting it, suh. Going to the Glittergeist, yo said?"

"And across it. We have to get to Snarken."

"Ah've heard of Snahken. It's supposed to be an interesting place, rich in culture." She thought a long moment, then sighed. "Since yo say y'all can't send me home, ah guess ah maht as well tag along with y'all. Besides, ah kind of like the way you have with words, man." Her eyes glittered and Jon-Tom felt suddenly uncomfortable, though he wasn't sure why.

"Oh, 'e's a fine one with words 'e is, luv," Mudge said as he reappeared. He was carrying an armful of some lime-green berries. Jon-Tom took a few, bit into one, and found the taste sweet. More out of politeness than any expectation of acceptance, the otter offered some to the tigress.

"Bleh!" she said as she pulled back. She smiled widely, displaying an impressive array of cutlery. "Suh, do ah look like the kind to enjoy weeds?"

"No you don't, luv, but I thought I'd be polite, since you place such store by it."

She nodded thankfully as she scanned the surrounding woods. "Come the morning ah'll find mahself something to eat. This appeahs to be good game country. Theah should be ample meat about."

Jon-Tom was glad she wasn't looking at him when she said that. "I'm sure we'll run across something edible." He turned to the otter. "What about our pursuit, Mudge?"

The otter responded with his ingratiating, amused bark. "Why, them sorry twits will be all night just tryin' t' get their stories straight. From wot I saw on our way out, most of 'em were your typical city guard and likely ain't in Zancresta's personal service. It'd be that arse'ole Chenelska who'd be put in charge o' organizin' any kind o' formal chase. By the time 'e gets the word, gets 'is conflictin' reports sorted out, and puts together anythin' like a formal pursuit, we'll be well out o' it."

"Then you don't think they'll be able to track us down?"

"I've been seein' to the coverin' o' our tracks ever since we left that cesspool o' a town, mate. They won't find a sign o' us."

"What if they do come after us, though? We can't conceal all of Roseroar's petite footprints."

Mudge assumed a crafty mien. "Aye, that they might, guv. They'll likely comb a wide front to the south, knowin' that we're to be headin' for the ol' Tailaroam. They can run up every tree in the Bellwoods without findin' sign o' us, because we ain't goin' t' go south. We'll fool 'em inside out by goin' west from 'ere. We're so far north o' the river we might as well do it anyhows."

Jon-Tom struggled to recall what he'd been taught of the local geography. "If you go far enough west of here, the forest disappears and you're into the Muddletup Moors."

"You got it, mate. No one would think t'ave a looksee for us there."

"Isn't that because no one ever does go in there?"

"That's right. Wot better place o' safety t' flee to?"

Jon-Tom looked doubtful as he sat back against a fallen trunk. "Mudge, I don't know about your thinking."

"I'm willin' enough to entertain alternative suggestions, m'lord warbler, but you're 'ardly in shape for some straight arguin'."

"Now, that I won't argue. We'll discuss it in the morning."

"In the mornin', then. Night to you, mate."

The thunder woke Jon-Tom. He blinked sleepily and looked up into a gray sky full of massive clouds. He blinked a second time. White clouds were common enough in this world, just as they were in his own. But not with black stripes.

He tried to move, discovered he could not. A huge furry arm lay half on and half off his chest while another curved behind his head to form a warm pillow. Unfortunately, it was also cutting off the circulation to his throbbing left arm.

He tried to disengage himself. As he did so the thunder of Roseroar's purring was broken by a coughing snarl. She stirred, but her arms did not budge.

Another shape moved nearby. Mudge was sitting up on the bed of leaves he'd fashioned for himself. He looked over toward Jon-Tom as he stretched.

"Well, don't just sit there, damn it. Give me a hand here!"

"Wot, and interrupt a charmin' domestic tableau like that?"

"Don't try to be funny."

"Funnier than that?" He pointed at the helpless spellsinger. "Couldn't be if I tried, mate."

Glaring at him, Jon-Tom tried again to disengage himself, but the weight was too much for him. It was like trying to move a soft mountain.

"Come on, Mudge. Have a heart."

"Who, me? You know me better than that, mate." As he spoke Roseroar moved in her sleep, rolling partly across Jon-Tom's midsection and chest. He gasped and kicked his legs in a frantic attempt to extricate himself. The tigress purred thunderously atop him.

Mudge took his time getting to his feet, ambled lazily over to eye the arrangement thoughtfully. "Our dainty lady friend sounds 'appy enough. Best not to disturb 'er. I don't see wot you're fussin' about. It's not like she's got a 'and over your mouth. From where I stands it looks almost invitin', though I can't say as 'ow I'd trade places with you. I'd be lost under 'er."

Jon-Tom put a hand on the tigress's face and pushed. She stirred, moved slightly, and nearly bit his fingers off. He withdrew his hand quickly. She'd moved enough for him to breathe again, anyway.

"Any signs of pursuit?"

"'Aven't smelled or 'eard a thing, mate. I think they're still too disorganized. If they are lookin' for us, you can be sure 'tis to the south o' Malderpot and not 'ere. Still, the sooner we're on our way, the better." He turned, began gathering up his effects.

"Come on now, lad. No time to waste."

"That's real funny, Mudge. How am I supposed to get her off me?"

"Wake 'er up. Belt 'er one, mate."

"No thanks. I like my head where it is. On my shoulders. I don't know how'd she react to something like that in her sleep."

Mudge's eyes twinkled. "Be more interestin' to see wot she might do while she's awake."

There was no need to consider extreme action, however. All the talking had done its job. Roseroar snorted once and opened those bottomless yellow eyes.

"Well, good morning, man."

"Good morning yourself. Roseroar, I value your friendship, but you're breaking my arm."

Her expression narrowed. "Suh, are you insinuatin' that ah am too heavy?"

"No, no, nothing like that." Somewhere off in the bushes Mudge was attending to necessary bodily functions while trying to stifle his laughter. "Actually, I think you're rather svelte."

"Svelte." Roseroar considered the word. "That's nice. Ah like that. Are you saying I have a nice figure?"

"I never saw a tiger I didn't think was attractive," he confessed, honestly enough.

She looked mildly disappointed as she rolled off him. "What the fuzz-ball said is true. Yo ah at least half solicitah."

Jon-Tom rolled over and tried shaking his left arm, trying to restore the circulation at the same time as he was dreading its return. Pins and needles flooded his nerves and he gritted his teeth at the sensation.

"I did study some law in my own world. It might be my profession someday."

"Spellsinging's better," she rumbled. "Svelte?"

"Yeah." He sat up and began pulling on his boots.

"Nice. Ah think ah like yo, man."

"I like you, too, Roseroar."

"Svelte." She considered the new word thoughtfully. "Want to know mah word fo yo?" She was putting on her armor, checking to make sure each catch and strap was fastened securely. She grinned at him, showing six-inch fangs. "Cute. Yo ah kind o' cute."

"Gee." Jon-Tom kept his voice carefully neutral as he replied. "That's nice."

Mudge emerged from the woods, buttoning his shorts. "Gee, I always thought you were cute, too, mate."

"How'd you like your whiskers shoved up your ass?" Jon-Tom asked him softly.

"Calm down, mate." Somehow Mudge stifled his laughter. "Best we get goin' westward. We've given 'em the slip for the nonce, but sooner o' later the absence o' tracks o' mention of us south o' 'ere will hit 'im as distinctly peculiar and they'll start 'untin' for us elsewhere."

Jon-Tom slung the duar over his shoulder and hefted his staff. "Lead on."

Mudge bowed, his voice rich with mock servility. "As thy exalted cuteness decrees."

Jon-Tom tried to bash him with the staff, but the otter was much too fast for him.

V

It took several days for them to reach the outskirts of the Moors, a vast and, as far as anyone knew, uninhabited land which formed the western border of the Bellwoods and reached south all the way to the northern coast of the Glittergeist Sea. After a day's march into the Moors' depths, Mudge felt safe enough to angle southward for the first time since fleeing the city.

Transportation across the ocean was going to present a problem. No ports existed where the ocean met the southern edge of the Moors, and Jon-Tom agreed with the otter that it would be a bad idea to follow the shoreline back eastward toward the mouth of the Tai-laroam. Chenelska would be sure to be looking for them in ports like Yarrowl.

As for the Moors themselves, they looked bleak but hardly threatening. Jon-Tom wondered how the place had acquired its widespread ominous reputation. Mudge could shed little light on the mystery, explaining only that rumor insisted anyone who went into the place never came out again, a pleasant thought to mull over as they hiked ever deeper into the foggy terrain.

It was a sorry land, mostly gray stone occasionally stained red by iron. There were no trees, few bushes, a little grass. The sky was a perpetual puffy, moist gray.

Fog and mist made them miserable, except for Mudge. Nothing appeared to challenge their progress. A few mindless hoots and mournful howls were the only indications of mobile inhabitants, and nothing ever came close to their camps.

They marched onward into the heart of the Muddletup, where none penetrated. As they moved ever deeper into the Moors the landscape began to change, and not for the better. The last stunted trees disappeared. Here, in a place of eternal dampness and cloud cover, the fungi had taken over.

Enormous mushrooms and toadstools dripped with moisture as Jon-Tom and his companions walked beneath spore-filled canopies. Some of the gnarled, ugly growths had trunks as thick as junipers, while others thrust delicate, semi-transparent stems toward the sodden sky. There were no bright, cheerful colors to mitigate the depressing scene, which was mostly brown and gray. Even the occasional maroon or unwholesomely yellow specimen was a relief from the monotonous parade of dullness.

Some of the flora was spotted, some striped. One displayed a checkerboard pattern that reminded Jon-Tom of a non-Euclidian chessboard. Liverworts grew waist-high, while lichens and mosses formed a thick, cushiony carpet into which their boots sank up to the ankles. Clean granite was disfigured by crawling fungoid corruption growing on its surface. And over this vast, wild eruption of thallophytic life there hung a pervasive sense of desolation, of waste and fossilized hope.

The first couple of days had seen no slowing of their progress. Now their pace began to degenerate. They slept longer and spent less time over meals. It didn't matter what food they took from their packs or scavenged from the land: everything seemed to have lost its flavor. Whatever they consumed turned flat and tasteless in their mouths and sat heavy in their bellies. Even the water which fell fresh from the clouds had acquired a metallic, unsatisfying aftertaste.

They'd been in the Moors for almost a week when Jon-Tom tripped over the skeleton. Like everything else lately its discovery provoked little more than a tired murmur of indifference from his companions.

"So wot?" muttered Mudge. "Don't mean a damn thing."

"Ah'm sitting down," said Roseroar. "Ah'm tired."

So was Jon-Tom, but the sight of the stark white bone peeping out from beneath the encrusting rusts and mildews roused a dormant concern in his mind.

"This is all wrong," he told them. "There's something very wrong going on here."

"No poison, if that's wot you're thinkin', mate." Mudge indicated the growths surrounding them. "I've been careful. Everythin' local we've swallowed 'as been edible, even if it's tasted lousy."

"Lucky yo," said Roseroar. "No game at all fo me. Ah find mah-self reduced to eating not just weeds, but this crap. Ah declah ah've nevah been so bored with eating in all mah life."

"Boring, tired, tasteless . . . don't you see what's happening?" Jon-Tom told them.

"You're gettin' worked up over nothin', mate." The otter was lying on a mound of soft moss. "Settle yourself down. 'Ave a sip o' some-thin'."

"Yes." Roseroar slipped off her swordbelt. "Let's just sit heah and rest awhile. There's no need to rush. We haven't seen a sign of pursuit since we left that town, and ah don't think we're likely to encounter any now."

"She's right, mate. Pull up a soft spot and 'ave a sit."

"Both of you *listen* to me." Jon-Tom tried to put some force into his voice, was frightened to hear it emerge from his lips flat and curiously empty of emotion. He felt sad and utterly useless. Some-thing had begun to afflict him from the day they'd first set foot in the Moors. It was something more than just boredom with their sur-roundings, something far more penetrating and dangerous. It was a grayness of the heart, and it was digging its insidious way deeper and deeper into their thoughts, killing off determination and assurance as it went. Eventually, it would ruin their bodies as well. The skeleton was proof enough of that. Whatever was into them was patient and clever, much too calculating, it occurred to Jon-Tom, to be an acci-dent of the environment.

He tried to find the enthusiasm to fight back as he turned to scream at the landscape. "Who are you? Why are you doing this to us? What is it you *want?*"

He felt like a fool. Worse, he knew his companions might think he was becoming unhinged. But they said nothing. He would've wel-comed some outcry of skepticism. Instead, the sense of hopelessness settled ever deeper around them.

Nothing moved within the Moors. Of one thing he was fairly confi-dent: this wasn't wizardry at work. It was too slow. He had to do something, but he didn't know what. All he could think of was how ironic it would be if, after surviving Malderpot, they were to perish here from a terminal case of the blahs.

So he was startled when a dull voice asked, "Don't you understand it all by now?"

"Who said that?" He whirled, trying to spot the speaker. Nothing moved.

"I did."

The voice came from an eight-foot-tall mushroom off to his left. The cap of this blotchy ochre growth dipped slightly toward him.

"Not that I couldn't have," said another growth.

"Nor I," agreed a third.

"Mushrooms," Jon-Tom said unsteadily, "don't talk."

"What?" said the first growth. "Sure, we're not loquacious, but that's a natural function of our existence. There isn't much to talk about, is there? I mean, it's not just a dull life, man, it's boring. B-o-r-i-n-g."

"That's about the extent of it," agreed the giant toadstool against which Roseroar rested. She moved away from it hastily, showing more energy than she had in the previous several days, and put a hand to the haft of each sword.

"I mean, give it some thought." The first mushroom again, which was taking on something of the air of a fungoid spokesman. Jon-Tom saw no lips or mouth. The words, the thoughts, came fully formed into his mind through a kind of clammy telepathy. "What would we talk about?"

"Nothing worth wasting the time discussing," agreed another mushroom with a long, narrow cap in the manner of a morrel. "I mean, you spend your whole existence sitting in the same spot, never seeing anything new, never moving around. So what's your biggest thrill? Getting to make spores?"

"Yeah, big deal," commented the toadstool. "So we don't talk. You never hear us talk, you think fungoids don't talk. Ambulatories are such know-it-alls."

"It doesn't matter," said the second mushroom. "Nothing matters. We're wasting our efforts."

"Wait." Jon-Tom approached the major mushroom, feeling a little silly as he did so. "You're doing something to us. You have been ever since we entered the deep moors."

"What makes you think we're doing anything to you?" said the spokesthing. "Why should we make the effort to do anything to anyone?"

"We've changed since we entered this land. We feel different."

"Different how, man?" asked the toadstool.

"Depressed. Tired, worn-out, useless, hopeless. Our outlook on life has been altered."

"What makes you think we're responsible?" said the second mushroom. "That's just how life is. It's the normal state of existence. You can't blame us for that."

"It's *not* the normal state of existence."

"It is in the Moors," argued the first mushroom.

Jon-Tom held his ground. "There's some kind of telepathy at work here. We've been absorbing your feelings of hopelessness, your idea that nothing's worth much of anything. It's been eating at us."

"Look around you, man. What do you see?"

Jon-Tom turned a slow circle. Instead of the half-hoped-for revelation, his gaze swept over more of what they'd seen the past dreary days—rocks, mushrooms, lichens and mosses, mist and cloud cover.

"Now, I ask you," sighed the first mushroom, "is that depressing or what? I mean, it is de-press-ing."

Jon-Tom could feel his resolve slipping dangerously. Mudge and Roseroar were half-asleep already. He had the distinct feeling that if he joined them, none of them would ever wake up again. The sight of white bone nearby revitalized him. How long had it taken the owner of that skeleton to become permanently depressed?

"I guess you *might* consider your existence here depressing."

"Might consider?" moaned the toadstool. "It *is* depressing. No maybes about it. Like, I'm a *fungus,* man. That's depressing all by itself."

"I've eaten some mushrooms that were downright exciting," Jon-Tom countered.

"A cannibal, too," said the tall toadstool tiredly. "How depressing." It let out a vast telepathic sigh, a wave of anxiety and sadness that rolled over Jon-Tom like a wave.

He staggered, shook off the cobwebs that threatened to bind his mind. "Stop that."

"Stop what? Why sweat it? Just relax, man. You're full of hurry, and desire, and all kinds of useless mental baggage. Why knock yourself out worrying about things that don't matter? Nothing matters. Lie down here, relax, take it easy. Let your foolish concerns fly bye-bye. Open yourself to the true blandness of reality and see how much better you'll feel for it."

Jon-Tom started to sit down, wrestled himself back to an upright stance. He pointed toward the skeleton.

"Like that one?"

"He was only reacting sensibly," said the toadstool.

"He's dead." Jon-Tom's voice turned accusing. "You killed him. At least, this place killed him."

"Life killed him. Slain by dullness. Murdered by monotony. He did what comes naturally to all life. He decayed."

"Decayed? You flourish amidst decay, don't you? You thrive on it."

"He calls this thriving," mumbled another toadstool. "He went the way of all flesh, that's all. Sure, we broke down his organic components. Sometimes I wonder why we bother. It's all such a waste. We live for death. Talk about dull, man. It's, like, numbsville."

Jon-Tom turned and walked over to shake Roseroar, shoving hard against the enormous shoulder. "Wake up, Roseroar. Come on, wake up, damn it!"

"Why bother?" she murmured sleepily, eyeing him through half-closed eyes. "Let me sleep. No, don't let me sleep." The feeble plea hit him like a cry for help.

"Don't worry, I won't. Wake up!" He continued to shake her until she sat up and rubbed at her eyes.

He moved over to where Mudge lay sprawled on his side, kicked the otter ungently. "Move it, water rat! This isn't like you. Think about where we're going. Think of the ocean, of clear salt air."

"I'd rather not, mate," said the otter tiredly. "No point to it, really."

"True, true, true," intoned the fungoid chorus of doom.

"I'll get up in a minute, guv'nor. There's no rush, and we're in no 'urry. Let me be."

"Like hell, I will. Think of the food we've enjoyed. Think of the good times ahead, of the money to be made. Think," he said with sudden alacrity, "of the three days you spent at the Elegant Bitch."

The otter opened his eyes wide, smiling weakly. "Aye, now that's a memory t' 'old tight to."

"Useless, useless, useless," boomed the a cappella ascomycetes.

" 'Tis kind o' pointless, mate," said the otter. For an instant Jon-Tom despaired, fearing he'd lost his friend for good. Then Mudge sprang to his feet and glared at the surrounding growth. "But 'tis also one 'ell of a lot o' fun!"

"Help Roseroar," Jon-Tom ordered him, a great relief surging through him. He turned his attention back to their subtle, even indifferent, assailants.

"Look, I can't help what you are and I can't help it if you find your existences so depressing."

"It's not how we find them," said the first mushroom. "It's how they are. Don't you think we'd change it if we could? But we can't. This is life: boring, dull, unchanging, gray, depressing, decay . . ."

"But it doesn't have to be that way. It's you who let it remain so." Unslinging the duar, he launched into the brightest, cheeriest song he could think of: John Denver's "Rocky Mountain High." He finished with Rick Springfield's "We All Need the Human Touch." The gray sky didn't clear, the mist didn't lift, but he felt a lot better.

"There! What did you think of that?"

"Truly depressing," said the toadstool. "Not the songs. Your voice."

Eighty million mushrooms in the Muddletup Moors, Jon-Tom mused, and I have to get a music critic. He laughed at the absurdity of it, and the laughter made him feel better still.

"Isn't there anything that can lighten your existence, make your lives more bearable so you'll leave us alone?"

"We can't help sharing our feelings," said the second mushroom. "We're not laying all this heavy stuff on you to be mean, man. We ain't mean. We're indifferent. What's bringing you down is your own knowledge of life's futility and your own inability to do anything about it. Face it, man: the cosmos is a downer."

Hopeless. These beings were hopeless, Jon-Tom told himself angrily. How could you fight something that didn't come at you with shields and swords and spears? What could he employ against a broadside of moroseness, a barrage of doubt?

They sounded so sure of themselves, so confident of the truth. All right then, he'd show them the truth! If he couldn't fight them by differing with them, maybe he could win by agreeing with them.

He took a deep breath. "The trouble with you is that you're all manic-depressives."

A long silence, an atmosphere of consideration, before the toadstool inquired, "What are you talking about, man?" In the background a couple of rusts whispered to one another, "Talk about a *weird* dude."

"I haven't had that much psychology, but pre-law requires some," Jon-Tom explained. "You know, I'll bet not one of you has ever considered psychoanalysis for your problems."

"Considered what?" asked the first mushroom.

Jon-Tom found a suitable rock—a hard, uncomfortable one sure to keep him awake. "Pay attention now. Anybody here ever heard of Franz Kafka?"

Several hours passed. Mudge and Roseroar had time to reawaken completely, and the mental voices surrounding them had become almost alive, though all were still flat and tinged with melancholy.

". . . And another thing," Jon-Tom was saying as he pointed upward, "that sky you're all always referring to. Nothing but infantile anal-retentive reinforcement. Well, maybe not exactly that," he corrected himself as he reminded himself of the rather drastic anatomical differences between himself and his audience, "but it's the same idea."

"We can't do anything about it," said the giant toadstool. "The mist and clouds and coolness are always with us. If they weren't, we'd all die. That's depressing. And what's even more depressing is that we don't particularly *like* perpetual mist and clouds and fog."

Jon-Tom struggled desperately for a reply, feeling victory slipping from his grasp. "It's not the fact that it's cloudy and damp all the time that matters. What matters is your outlook on the fact."

"What do you mean, our outlook?" asked a newcomer, an interested slime mold. "Our outlook is glum and miserable and pointless."

"Only if you think of it that way," Jon-Tom informed it. "Sure, you can think of yourselves as hopeless. But why not view your situation in a positive light? It's just a matter of redirecting your outlook on life. Instead of regarding your natural state as depressing, think of the constancy of climate and terrain as stabilizing, reassuring. In mental health, attitude is everything."

"I'm not sure I follow you, man," said another mushroom.

"Me neither, mate."

"Be quiet, Mudge. Listen, existence is what you make of it. How you view your surroundings will affect how you feel about them."

"How can we feel anything other than depressed in surroundings like these?" wondered the liverworts.

"Right, then. If you feel more comfortable, go with those thoughts. There's nothing wrong with being depressed and miserable all the time, so long as you feel *good* about it. Have you ever felt bright and cheery?"

"No, no, no," was the immediate and general consensus.

"Then how do you know that it's any better than feeling depressed and miserable? Maybe one's no better than the other."

"That's not what the other travelers who come our way say," murmured the toadstool, "before they relax, see it our way, and settle down for a couple of months of steady decomposition."

Jon-Tom shivered slightly. "Sure, that's what they say, but do they look any better off, act any more contented, any more in tune with their surroundings than you do?"

"Naturally they're not as in tune with their surroundings," said the first mushroom, "but these surroundings are . . ."

". . . Damp and depressing," Jon-Tom finished for it. "That's okay if you accept it. It's all right to feel depressed all the time if you feel good about it. Why can't it be fun to feel depressed? If that's how your environment makes you feel, then if you feel that way it means you're in tune with your environment, and that should make you feel good, and secure, and confident."

Roseroar's expression reflected her confusion, but she said nothing. Mudge just sat quietly, shaking his head. But they were thinking, and it kept them from growing dangerously listless again.

"Hey," murmured a purple toadstool, "maybe it is okay to feel down and dumpy all the time, if that's what works for you."

"That's it," said Jon-Tom excitedly. "That's the point I'm trying to make. Everything, every entity, is different. Just because one state of mind works for us ambulatories doesn't mean it ought to work the same way for you. At least you aren't confused all the time, the way most of my kind are."

"Far fucking out," announced one enlightened truffle from beneath a clump of shelf fungi. "Existence is pointless. Life is decrepit. Consciousness sucks. And you know what? I feel *good* about it! It all fits."

"Beautiful," said Jon-Tom. "Go with that." He put his hands on his hips and turned a circle. "Anybody else here have any trouble dealing with that?"

"Well, we do," said a flotilla of mushrooms clinging to a scummy pile of dead weeds near a small pool.

"Tell me about it," said Jon-Tom coaxingly.

"It started when we were just spores. . . ."

It went on like that all through the night. By morning, Jon-Tom was exhausted, but the fungoid forest surrounding him was suffused with the first stages of exhilaration . . . in a maudlin manner, of course. But by and large, the group-therapy session had been wildly successful.

Mudge and Roseroar had recovered completely from their insidiously induced lethargies and were eager to set out again. Jon-Tom held back. He wanted to make certain the session would have at least a semipermanent effect, or it wouldn't last them through the Moors to the Glittergeist.

"You've certainly laid a heavy trip on us, man," said the large mushroom that served as speaker for the rest of the forest.

"I'm sure that if you hold to those thoughts, go with the flow, make sure you leave yourselves enough mental space, you'll find that you'll always feel better about your places in existence," Jon-Tom assured it.

"I don't know," said the big toadstool, and for an instant the veil of gloom which had nearly proved lethal descended about Jon-Tom all over again. "But just considering it makes me more inclined to accept it."

The cloud of despair dissipated. "That's it." Jon-Tom grew aware of just how tired he was. "I'd like to stay and chat some more, but we need to be on our way to the Glittergeist again. You wouldn't happen to know in which direction it lies?"

Behind him, the shapes of three giant amanitas crooked their crowns into the mist. "This way, friend. Pass freely from this place . . . though if you'd like to join us in our contented dissolution, you're more than welcome to remain and decompose among us."

"Couldn't think of it," Jon-Tom replied politely, falling in behind Mudge and Roseroar as they started southward. "See, I'm not into decomposition."

"Tell us about it," several rusts urged him.

Worrying that he might be leaving behind a forest full of fungoid Frankensteins, Jon-Tom waved it off by saying, "Some other time."

"Sure, that's it, go on and leave," snapped the toadstool. "We're not worth talking to."

"I've just spent a whole night talking to you. Now you're bringing out new feelings of insecurity."

"No I'm not," said the toadstool, defensive. "It's the same thing as depression."

"Isn't. Why don't you discuss it for a while?" A rising mental susurration trailed in his wake as he hastened after his companions.

Word of the therapy session preceded them through the Muddletup. The intensity of the depression around them varied considerably in strength according to the success of Jon-Tom's therapy. They detoured around the worst areas of despair, where the mental aura bordered on the comatose, and as a result they were never again afflicted with the urge to lie down and chuck it all.

Eventually the fungi gave way to blossoming bushes and evergreens. The morning they emerged from the woods onto a wide, gravelly beach formed of wave-polished agates and jade was one of the happiest of Jon-Tom's life.

Pushing his ramwood staff into the gravel, he hung his backpack from the knobbed end, sat down, and inhaled deeply of the sea air. The sharp salty smell was heartbreakingly familiar.

Mudge let out a whoop; threw off his bow, quiver, pack, and clothes; and plunged recklessly into the warm surf. Jon-Tom felt the urge to join him, but he was just too damn tired. Roseroar sat down next to him. Together they watched the gleeful otter porpoise gracefully through the waves.

"I wish I had my board," Jon-Tom murmured.

"Yo what?" Roseroar looked down at him.

"It's a flat piece of fiberglass and epoxy resin. It floats. You stand on it and let the waves carry you toward shore."

Roseroar considered, decided. "That sounds like fun. Do y'all think yo could teach me?"

He smiled apologetically. "Like I said, I don't have my board with me."

"How big a board do yo need?" Rising, she started stripping off her armor. "Surely not biggah than this?"

"Now, wait a minute, Roseroar. I thought cats hated the water."

"Not tigahs, sugah. Come on. Ah'll race yo to the beach."

He hesitated, glanced up and down the gravel as though someone might appear on this deserted section of shore.

What the hell, he told himself.

The clean tropical salt water washed away the last lingering feelings of depression. Though Roseroar's back wasn't as even as waxed fiberglass, his toes found plenty of purchase in the thick white fur. The tigress's muscles shifted according to his instructions as she steered easily through the waves with powerful arms and legs. It took no time at all to discover that surfing on the back of a tiger was far more exhilarating than plying the waves on a hunk of inanimate resin.

As the afternoon drew to a close, they lay on the warm beach and let the sun dry them. Clean and refreshed, Jon-Tom made a fire and temporary shelter of driftwood while Mudge and Roseroar went scavenging. Life in abundance clung to the shore.

The two unlikely hunters returned with a load of crustaceans the size of king crabs. Three of these—killed, cracked, and cooked over an open fire—were sufficient to fill even the tigress's belly. This time Jon-Tom didn't even twitch as he snuggled up against the amazon's flank. Mudge curled up on the far side of the fire. For the first time since they'd fled Malderpot, they all slept peacefully.

VI

As usual, Mudge woke first. He sat up, stretched, and yawned, his whiskers quivering with the effort. The sun was just up and the last smoke fleeing the firepit. Something, some slight noise, had disturbed the best night's rest he'd had in weeks.

He heard it again, no mistake. Curious, he dressed quickly and tiptoed past his still somnolent companions. As he made his way over a sandy hillock flecked with beach grass, he slowed. A cautious glance over the crest revealed the source of the disturbance.

They were not alone on the beach. A small single-masted sailing craft was grounded on the gravel. Four large, ugly-looking specimens of varying species clustered around a single, much smaller individual. Two of them were arguing over a piece of clothing. Mudge shrugged mentally and prepared to retreat. None of his business. What had awakened him was the piteous cry for help of the person trapped among the ruffians. It was an elderly voice but a strong one.

There was a touch on his shoulder. Inhaling sharply, he rolled and reached for his short sword, then relaxed. It was Jon-Tom, with Roseroar close behind.

"What's happening?"

"Nothin', mate. None o' our business, wot? Let's leave it be. I'm ready for breakfast."

"Is that all you ever think of? Food, money, and sex?"

"You do me a wrong, guv'nor. Sometimes 'tis sex, food, and money. Then again at times 'tis—"

"Never mind," said the exasperated Jon-Tom.

"Foah against one," muttered Roseroar angrily, "and the one looks none too strong. Not very gallant."

"We've got to do something," Jon-Tom murmured. "Mudge, you sneak around behind the trees off to the left and cover them from there. I'll make a frontal assault from here. Roseroar, you . . ." But the tigress was already over the hill and charging down the slope on the other side.

So much for careful tactics and strategy, Jon-Tom thought.

"Come on, Mudge!"

"Now wait a minim, mate." The otter watched Jon-Tom follow in Roseroar's wake, waving his staff and yelling at the top of his lungs. "Bloody fools!" He notched an arrow into his bow and followed.

But there was to be no fight. The assailants turned to see all seven feet and five hundred pounds of white tigress bearing down on them, waving twin swords and bellowing fit to shake the leaves off the nearby trees. There was a concerted rush for the boat.

The four paddled like fiends and were out of sword range before she entered the water in angry pursuit, throwing insults and challenges after them. Mudge might have reached the boat with an arrow or two, but saw no point in meaningless killing or antagonizing strangers. As far as he was concerned, the best battle was the one that never took place.

Meantime Jon-Tom was bending solicitously over the exhausted subject of their rescue. He put an arm beneath the slim furry neck and helped it sit up. It was a ferret, and an old one, distant kin to Mudge's line but thinner still. Much of the normally brown fur was tipped with silver. So was the black mask that ran across the face.

The stranger was clad in beige shorts and vest and wore sandals instead of boots. A plain, floppy hat lay trampled in the sand nearby, next to a small leather sack. Several other similar sacks lay scattered along the beach. All looked empty.

Gradually the elderly ferret's breathing slowed. He opened his eyes, saw Jon-Tom, then looked around wildly.

"Easy, easy, friend. They're gone. We saw to that."

The ferret gave him a disbelieving look, then turned his gaze toward the beach. His eyes settled on the scattered leather sacks.

"My stock, my goods!" He broke away from Jon-Tom, who watched while the oldster went through each sack, one at a time. Finally he sat down on the sand, one sack draped across his lap. He sighed listlessly, threw it aside.

"Gone." He shook his head sadly. "All gone."

"Wot's all gone, senior?" Mudge prodded one of the sacks with a boot.

The ferret didn't look up at him. "My stock, my poor stock. I am . . . I was, a humble trader of trinkets, plying my trade along the shores east of here. I was set upon by those worthless brigands"—he nodded seaward, to where the retreating boat had raised sail and was disappearing toward the horizon—"who stole everything I have managed to accumulate in a short, unworthy life. They kept me and forced me to do their menial work, to cook and clean and wash for them while they preyed upon other unsuspecting travelers.

"They said they would let me go unharmed. Finally they tired of me, but instead of returning me to a place of civilization they brought me here to this empty, uninhabited shore, intending to maroon me in an unknown land where I might starve. They stole what little I had in this world, taunted me by leaving my stock bags, and would have stolen my life as well at the last moment had you not come along, for I was refusing to be abandoned."

"Don't give us too much credit," Jon-Tom advised him. "Our being in a position to rescue you was an accident."

"You can say that again, mate," growled the disgusted Mudge as he slung his bow back over his shoulder.

Jon-Tom ignored the otter. "We're glad we could help. I don't like seeing anyone taken advantage of, especially senior citizens."

"What?"

"Older people."

"Ah. But how can I thank you, sir? How can I show my gratitude? I am destitute."

"Forget it." The ferret's effusiveness was making Jon-Tom uncomfortable. "We're glad we could help."

The ferret rose, wincing and putting one hand against his back. "I am called Jalwar. To whom do I owe my salvation?"

"I'm Jon-Tom. I'm a spellsinger. Of sorts."

The ferret nodded gravely. "I knew at once you were mighty ones."

Jon-Tom indicated the disgruntled Mudge. "That ball of fuzzy discontent is my friend Mudge." The otter grunted once. "And this tower of cautionless strength is Roseroar."

"I am honored to be in your presence," said the ferret humbly, proceeding to prostrate himself on the beach and grasping Jon-Tom's boots. "I have nothing left. My stock is gone, my money, everything save the clothes I wear. I owe you my life. Take me into your service and let me serve you."

"Now, wait a minute." Jon-Tom moved his boots out of the ferret's paws. "I don't believe in slavery."

" 'Ere now, mate, let's not be 'asty." Mudge was quick to intervene. "Consider the poor suck—uh, this poor unfortunate chap. 'E's got nothin', 'e 'asn't. 'E'll need protection, or the next bunch 'e runs into will kill 'im for sure, just for 'is clothes." He eyed the ferret hopefully. "Wot about it, guv? Can you cook?"

"I have some small talent in the kitchen, good sir."

"Mudge . . ." Jon-Tom said warningly. The otter ignored him.

"You said you washed clothes."

"That I did, good sir. I have the ability to make even ancient attire smell sweet as clover again, with the slightest of cleansing materials. I am also handy at repairing garments. Despite my age, I am not a weakling. I can more than carry my weight."

Mudge strutted about importantly. " 'Ere then, friend, I think we should take pity on you and admit you to our company, wot?"

"Mudge, you know how I feel about servants."

"It wouldn't be like that at all, Jon-Tom. 'E *does* need our protection, and 'e'll never get out o' this place without our 'elp, and 'e's more than willin' to contribute 'is share."

The ferret nodded enthusiastically. "Please accept my service, good sir . . . and madame. Allow me to accompany you. Perhaps being proximate to such mighty ones as yourselves will improve my own ill fortune."

"I'll bet you were a good trader," Jon-Tom commented. "Okay, you can come with us, but as an equal. Not as a servant or slave. We'll pay you a decent wage." He remembered the purse filled with gold, stolen by Zancresta's thugs. "As soon as we can afford it, that is."

"Food and shelter and protection is all I ask, great sir."

"And stop calling me sir," said Jon-Tom. "I've introduced you to everyone by name."

"As you wish, Jon-Tom." The ferret turned to look down the beach. "What do we now? I presume you are bound to the east, for if one walks long enough one will come 'round again to the lands bordering the Bellwoods and the River Tailaroam, where civilization is to be encountered."

"Don't I wish," Mudge grumbled.

Jon-Tom shook his head. "We don't go to the east, Jalwar. We go southwest, to Snarken."

"Across the Glittergeist? Sir . . . Jon-Tom . . . I have lived long and seen much. The voyage to Snarken is long and fraught with danger and difficulty. Better to begin the long trek to the mouth of the Tailaroam. Besides, how could one take ship from this deserted land? And north of here lie the Muddletup Moors, where none may penetrate."

"*We* penetrated," said Mudge importantly.

"Did you? If you say it so, I doubt it not. Still, this far north places us well away from the east–west trade routes. We will encounter no vessels here."

"You won't get any arguments from me on that score, mate," said Mudge. "Best to do as you say, go back to the Bellwoods and the Tailaroam and start over. Likely Chenelska's give up on us by now."

"No," said Jon-Tom firmly. "I am not going back and I am not starting over. We've come too far."

Mudge squinted up at him. "Well now, you've just 'eard this wise old chap. 'Ow do you propose to get us across that?" He pointed to the broad, sailless expanse of the Glittergeist. "I like to swim, lad, but I prefer swimmin' across water I can cross."

"What can yo do, Jon-Tom?" Roseroar asked him.

He stood fuming silently for a moment before blurting out, "I can damn well conjure us up a boat, that's what!"

"Uh-oh." Mudge retreated toward the trees, searching for a boulder of appropriate size to conceal himself behind. " 'Is nibs is pissed off and 'e's goin' to try spellsingin' again."

Roseroar eyed the otter curiously. "Isn't that his business, fuzzball?"

"That may be wot some calls it. Me, I'd as soon brush a crocodile's teeth than 'elp 'im with 'is work."

"Ah don't understand. Is he a spellsinger or not?"

" 'E is," Mudge admitted. "Of that there's no longer any doubt. 'Tis just that 'e 'as this disconcertin' tendency to misfire from time to time, and when it 'appens, I don't want to be in the line o' fire."

"Go on, Roseroar," Jon-Tom told her. "Get back there and hide behind a rock with him." He was mad at the otter. Hadn't he, Jon-Tom, helped to bring about the great victory at the Jo-Troom Gate? Purely by accident of course, but still . . .

"No suh," said the tigress, offended. "If'n y'all don't mind, I'll stand right heah."

"Good for you." Jon-Tom unlimbered his duar, turned away to confront the open sea, where soon he hoped to see a proper ship riding empty at anchor. Turning also kept Roseroar from seeing how nervous he was.

Once before on a far-distant river he'd tried to bring forth a boat to carry himself and his companions. Instead, he'd ended up with Falameezar, the Marxist dragon. That misplaced conjuration had produced unexpectedly benign results, but there was no guarantee he'd be as fortunate if he fouled up a second time.

It was too late to back down now. He'd already made his boast. He felt Roseroar's gaze on the back of his neck. If he backed down now he'd prove himself an incompetent to Mudge and a coward to the tigress. He had to try.

He considered several songs and discarded them all as unsuitable. He was beginning to grow frantic when a song so obvious, so simple, offered what seemed like an obvious way out.

His fingers tested the duar's strings and he began to sing.

Flecks of light sprang to instant life around him. It was as though the sand underfoot had come to glowing life. The lights were Gneechees, those minute ultrafast specks of existence that were drawn irresistibly to magic in motion. They coalesced into a bright, dancing cloud around him, and as usual, when he tried to look straight at any of them, they vanished. Gneechees were those suggestions of something everyone sees out of the corner of an eye but aren't there when you turn to look at them.

But he sensed their presence. So did Roseroar and the others. It was a good sign, an indication that the spellsinging was working. Certainly the tune he played seemed harmless enough, even to the wary Mudge, whose opinion of Jon-Tom's musical tastes differed little from that of the average PTA president.

The otter had to admit that for a change the otherworldly ditty Jon-Tom was reciting was easy on the ears, even if the majority of the words, as was true of all of Jon-Tom's songs, were quite incomprehensible.

Jon-Tom had chosen the song as much out of desperation as need. The song was "Sloop *John B.,*" by the Beach Boys. Given their present needs, it was a logical enough choice.

Nothing happened right away. But before long, Jalwar was making protective signs over his face and chest while cowering close to Mudge for protection, while the otter waited nervously for the unexpected to manifest itself. Despite her own awe at what was taking place on the beach, Roseroar stood her ground.

Mudge was worrying needlessly. For once, for the very first time, it looked like Jon-Tom's efforts were to be rewarded with success. For once it appeared that his spellsong was going to produce only what he wanted. The otter moved hesitantly out from behind the shelter of the boulder, while simultaneously holding himself ready to rush for the trees at the first hint of trouble.

"Bugger me for a blue-eyed bandicoot," he muttered excitedly. "The lad's gone an' done it!"

Rocking gently in the waves just beyond the breaking surf was a single-masted sloop. The stern faced shoreward and on the name-plate everyone could clearly make out the words JOHN B.

Jon-Tom let the last words of the song trail away. With it went the Gneechees and the cloud of blue fog from which the boat had emerged. It bobbed gently at anchor, awaiting them.

Roseroar put a proud paw on Jon-Tom's shoulder. "Sugah, bless mah soul if it isn't a spellsingah yo are. That's a fine-looking ship, for all that her lines are strange to me, and ah've sailed many a craft."

Jon-Tom continued to pluck fitfully at the duar as if fearful that the sloop, solid as she looked, might disappear at any moment in a rush of fog.

"Glad you think so. Me, I've never been on anything bigger than a surfboard in my life."

"Not to worry. Ah don't recognize the mannah of ship, but if she sails, ah can handle her."

"So can I." Jalwar appeared behind them. "In my youth I spent much time sailing many kinds of ships."

"See?" said Mudge, joining them on the beach. "The old fur's provin' 'imself valuable already."

"Okay." Jon-Tom nodded reluctantly. "Let's see what she's like on board."

Mudge led them out to the boat, as at home in the water as he was on land. The others followed. By the time Jon-Tom reached the bottom of the boarding ladder, the otter had completed a preliminary inspection.

"She's fully stocked, she is, though the packin's bloody strange."

"Let me have a look." Jon-Tom went first to the galley.

Cans and packages bore familiar labels like Hormel, Armor, Oscar Mayer, and Hebrew National. There was more than enough food for an extensive journey, and they could fish on the way. The tank for the propane stove read full. Jon-Tom tried a burner, was rewarded with a blast of blue flame that caused Roseroar to pull back.

"Ah don't see no source of fire."

"The ship arrives already fully spelled for traveling," Jalwar murmured appreciatively. "Impressive."

"In the song she's supposed to be on a long voyage," Jon-Tom explained.

There was a diesel engine meant to supplement the sails. Jon-Tom didn't try it. Let it wait until they were becalmed. Then he could dazzle them with new magic.

"Roseroar, since you're the most experienced sailor among us, why don't you be captain?"

"As you wish, Jon-Tom." She squeezed through the hatchway back onto the deck and began familiarizing herself with the unusual but not unfathomable rigging. As with any modern sailing ship, the sloop would almost run the sails up and down the masts all by itself. It didn't take the tigress long to figure it out.

An electric winch made short work of the anchor. Roseroar spun the wheel, the sloop hove around with a warm breeze filling its sails, and they headed out to sea. Within an hour they had left the gravel beach and the Muddletup Moors with its confused fungoid inhabitants far behind.

"Which way to Snarken?" she asked as she worked the wheel and a hand winch simultaneously. The mainsail billowed in the freshening wind.

"I don't know. You're the sailor."

"Sailor ah confess to, but ah'm no navigator, man."

"Southwest," Mudge told her. "For now that's good enough.

Roseroar adjusted their heading, brought it in line with the directions supplied by the compass. "Southwest it is." The sloop changed directions smoothly, responding instantly to the tigress's light touch on the wheel.

Feeling reasonably confident that at last all was right with the world, Jon-Tom reprised the song and for good measure added a chorus of the Beach Boys' "Sail On, Sail On, Sailor." The sun was warm, the wind steady, and Snarken seemed just over the near horizon.

Putting up the duar, he escorted Jalwar down to the galley, there to explain the intricacies of the propane stove and such otherworldly esoterica as Saran Wrap and can openers to their designated chef.

That and the rest of a fine day well done, he allowed himself to be first to bed.

To be awakened by rough hands shaking him violently.

"Get up, get up, spellsinger!"

Feeling very strange, Jon-Tom rolled over, to find himself staring into the worried face of the ferret.

"What . . . whash wrong?" He was startled by the sound of his own voice, unnaturally thick and slurred. And the boat seemed to be rolling in circles.

"We are in bad trouble, spellsinger. Bad trouble." Jalwar disappeared.

Jon-Tom sat up. It took three tries. Then he tried to get out of the bunk and discovered he couldn't tell the floor from the ceiling. The floor found him.

"Wot was that?" said a distant voice.

He struggled to get up. "I don't . . ." He reached for the railing of the lower bunk and tried to pull himself upright. "Wheresh the . . . ?" Somehow he managed to drag himself to a standing position. He stood there on shaky knees that felt determined to go their own way, exclusive of any contrariwise instructions from his brain.

"Whash wrong with me?" he moaned.

Two faces appeared in the doorway, one above the other. Both were blurred.

"Shee-it," said Roseroar. "He's drunk! Ah didn't see him get into any liquor."

"Nor did I," said Mudge, trying to push past her. "Give me room, you bloody great amazon!" He put his hands on Jon-Tom's shoulders and gripped hard. Jon-Tom staggered backward.

"Blister me for a brown vole if you're not. Where'd you find the hootch, guv'nor?"

"What hoosh?" Jon-Tom replied thickly. "I didn't . . ." The floor almost went out from under him. "Say, whoosh driving thish bush?"

A disgusted Mudge stepped back. "Can't abide anyone who can't 'old 'is booze."

"Leave him fo now," said Roseroar. "We'll have to handle this ourselves." They turned to leave.

"Hey, wait!" Jon-Tom yelled. He took a step forward, and the boat, sly and tricky craft that it was, deliberately yanked the floor out from under him. He slammed into the door, hung on for dear life.

Mudge was right, he realized through the glassy haze that had formed over his eyeballs. I *am* drunk. Try as he might, he couldn't remember imbibing anything stronger than orange juice at supper. After reprising a couple of choruses of "Sloop *John B.*" to make sure the boat didn't dematerialize out from beneath them in the middle of the night, he'd gone to bed. Jalwar was awake and alert. Everyone was except him.

Suddenly he found himself in desperate need of a porthole, barely located one in time to stick his face out and throw his guts all over the equally upset ocean. When he finally finished puking he was soaking wet from the spray. He felt a little less queasy but not any soberer.

Somehow he managed to slam the porthole shut and refasten it. He staggered toward the gangway, pulled himself toward the deck.

Wind hit him hard the instant he stepped out on the teak planking, and rain filled his vision. Roseroar was holding the wheel steady with grim determination, but Mudge and Jalwar were having a terrible time trying to wrestle the mainsail down.

"Hurry it up!" the tigress roared, her voice barely audible above the storm, "or we'll lose it fo sure!"

"I don't care if we do," Jon-Tom moaned, putting both hands to the sides of his head, "just let's not shout about it, shall we?"

"Tell it to the sky, spellsinger," pleaded Jalwar.

"Yeah, use your magic, mate," added Mudge. "Turn this bloomin' weather back to normal!" Jon-Tom noticed that both of them were soaked. "Get rid of this bloody bedamned storm!"

"Anything, anything," he told them, "if you'll just stop shouting." He staggered and nearly went careening overboard, just managed to save himself by grabbing on to a stay. "I don't unnershtand. It wash so calm when I went to bed."

"Well 'tis not calm now, mate," snapped Mudge, wrestling with the heavy, wet sail.

"Ah've nevah seen a storm like this come up so quickly." Roseroar continued fighting with the wheel.

"The words," Jalwar muttered. "The words of the spellsinging! Don't you remember?" He looked straight at Jon-Tom. "Don't you remember the words?"

"But ish just the chorush," Jon-Tom groaned. "Jusht the chorush." He mumbled them again. " 'Thish ish the worsht trip, I've ever been on.' I didn't mean that part of the shong."

The ferret was nodding. "So you sang. The spirits cannot distinguish between what you sing and mean and what you sing and do not mean. They have a way of taking everything literally."

"But ish *not* the worsht trip I've ever been on!" Jon-Tom stood away from the rail on rubbery legs and screamed his protest at the skies that threatened to swamp them. "Ish *not!*"

The skies paid him no heed.

For hours they battled the winds. Twice they were in danger of being swamped. They were saved only by the unmagical efforts of the sloop's pump. Somehow Jon-Tom got it started, though the effort made him upchuck all over the engine room. That wouldn't happen again, though. His stomach was empty.

If only it would *feel* empty.

Soon after they pumped out the second holdful of water, the storm began to abate. An hour later the mountainous seas started to subside. And still there was no real relief, because thunder and lightning gave way to a thick, impenetrable fog.

Mudge was leaning on the rail, grumbling. "We'd better not be near any land, mates." He glanced upward. A faint glow suffused the upper reaches of the fog bank, which had not thinned in the slightest. "I know you're up there, you great big ugly yellow bastard! Why don't you burn this driftin' piss off so we can see to be on our way!"

"The words of the song," Jalwar murmured. Mudge snarled at him.

"And you pack in it, guv'nor, or I'll do it for you."

It was morning. Somewhere the sun was up there, probably laughing at them. The compass still showed the way, but the wind had vanished with the storm, and none of Jon-Tom's feeble coaxing could induce the shiny new diesel engine to perform.

The restored sail hung limp against the mast. The sloop was floating through glassy, smooth, shallow water. A sandy bottom occasionally rose dangerously close to the keel, only to fall away again into pale blue depths each time it looked like they were about to ground. Roseroar steered as best she could, and with an otter and a ferret aboard there was at least no shortage of sharp eyesight.

But as the day wore on and the fog clung tenaciously to them, it began to look as if Jon-Tom's song was to prove their simultaneous salvation and doom. The wind remained conspicuous by its absence. Sooner or later the shallows would close in around them and they would find themselves marooned forever in the midst of a strange sea.

The tension was taking its toll on everyone, even Roseroar. Their spellsinger, who had conjured up this wonderful craft, was of no use to anyone, least of all himself. Thankfully he no longer threw up. Yet despite his unarguable abstinence from any kind of drink, he remained falling-down drunk. Smashed. Potted.

If anything, his condition had worsened. He strolled about the deck muttering songs so incomprehensible and slurred none of his companions could decipher them.

Just as a precaution, Mudge had sequestered Jon-Tom's duar in a safe place. He'd gotten them into this situation while sober. It was terrifying to contemplate what might happen if he started spellsinging while drunk.

"We have one chance," Jalwar finally declared.

"Wot's that, guv'nor?" Mudge sat on the port side of the bow, keeping his eyes on the threatening shallows.

"To turn around. We aren't that far yet from the beach where this unfortunate turn of events began. We can return there, land, or use this craft, provided the wind will return, to take us back to the mouth of the Tailaroam and civilization."

"I'm tempted, guv, but 'e'll never stand for it." He nodded back to where Jon-Tom lay sprawled on his back on the deck, alternately laughing and hiccuping at the fog.

"How can he object to stop us?" wondered Jalwar. "He has the gift, but no control over it."

"That may be, guv. I'm sure as 'ell no expert on spellsingin', but this I do know. 'E's me friend, and I promised 'im that I'd see 'im through this journey to its end, no matter wot 'appens."

Besides which, the otter reminded himself, if they returned without the medicine, there would be no rich reward from a grateful Clothahump. Mudge had endured too much already to throw that promise away now.

"But what else can we do?" Jalwar moaned. "None of us is a wizard or sorcerer. We cannot cure his odd condition, because it is the result of his own spellsinging."

"Maybe it'll cure itself." Mudge tried to sound optimistic. He watched sadly as Jon-Tom rolled over on the center cabin and tried to puke again. "I feel sorry for 'im. 'Tis clear 'e ain't used to liquorish effects." As if to reinforce the otter's observation, Jon-Tom rolled over again and fell off the cabin, nearly knocking himself out on the deck. Lifting himself to a sitting position, he burst out laughing. He was the only one on the boat who found the situation amusing.

Mudge shook his head. "Bleedin' pitiful."

"Yes, it is sad," Jalwar agreed.

"Cor, but not the way you think it is, mate. 'Ere 'e is, sufferin' from one o' the finest binges I've ever seen anybody on, and 'e ain't even had the pleasure o' drinkin' the booze. Truly pitiful." A glance downward showed sand looming near.

"Couple o' degrees to starboard, luv!" he called sternward.

"Ah heah y'all." Roseroar adjusted the boat's heading. The sandy bottom fell away once again.

"It'll wear off," the otter mumbled. "It 'as to. Ain't nobody can stay drunk this long no matter 'ow strong a spell's been laid on 'is belly. I wonder when 'e did it?"

"The same time he did everything else," Jalwar explained. "Don't you remember the song?"

"You mean that part about it bein' 'the worst trip I've ever been on'?"

"Not just that. Remember that he made the tigress captain because she was the best sailor among us? That would leave him as next in command, would it not?"

"Beats me, mate. I'm not much on ships and their lore."

"He reduced himself to first mate," Jalwar said positively. "That was in the song, too. A line that went something like 'The first mate, he got drunk.' "

"Aye, now I recall." The otter nodded toward the helpless spellsinger, who remained enraptured by a hysteria perceptible only to himself. "So 'e spellsung 'imself into this condition without even bein' aware o' doin' it."

"I fear that is the case."

"Downright pitiful. Why couldn't 'e 'ave made me first mate? I'd 'andle a long drunk like this ten times better than 'e would. 'E's got to come out of it sometime."

"I hope so," said Jalwar. He glanced at the sky. "Perhaps we will lose this infernal fog, anyway. Then we might pick up a wind enabling us to turn back."

"Now, I told you, guv," Mudge began, only to be interrupted by a shout.

What stunned him to silence, however, was not the fact of the shout but its origin. It came from the water off to starboard.

It was repeated. "Ahoy, there! You on the sloop! What's happenin'!"

"What's happenin'?" Roseroar frowned, tried to see into the fog. "Jon-Tom, wake up!" The sails continued to luff against the mainmast.

"Huh? Wash?" Jon-Tom laughed one more time, then struggled to stand up.

"Ahoy, aboard the sloop!" A new voice this time, female.

"Wash . . . whosh that?" He stumbled around the center cabin and tried to squint into the fog. Neither his eyesight nor his brain was functioning at optimum efficiency at the moment.

A second boat materialized out of the mist. It was a low-slung outboard with a pearlescent fiberglass body. Three . . . no, four people lounged in the vinyl seats. Two couples in their twenties, all human, all normal size.

"What's happenin', *John B.?*" asked the young man standing behind the wheel. He didn't look too steady on his feet himself. A cooler sat between the front seats, full of ice and aluminum cans. The cans had names like Coors and Lone Star on them.

Jon-Tom swayed. He was hallucinating, the next logical step in his mental disintegration. He leaned over the rail and tried to focus his remaining consciousness on the funny cigarette the couple in the front of the boat were passing back and forth. The other pair were exchanging hits on a glass pipe.

The big outboard was idling noisily. One girl leaned over the side to clean her Foster Grants in the ocean. Next to the beer cooler was a picnic basket. A big open bag of pretzels sat on top. The twisted, skinny kind that tasted like pure fried salt. Next to the bag was a two-pound tin of Planter's Redskin Peanuts, and several brightly colored tropical fruits.

He tried to will himself sober. If anything could have cleared his mind, it should have been the sight of the boat and its occupants. But the uncontrollable power of his own spellsinging held true. Despite everything he tried, the self-declared first mate still stayed drunk. He swallowed the words on his tongue and tried a second time.

"Who . . . who are you?"

"I'm Charlie MacReady," said the boat's driver cheerily, through a cannabis-induced fog of his own. He smiled broadly, leaned down to speak to his girlfriend. "Dig that getup that guy's got on. Must've been a helluva party!"

Jon-Tom briefly considered his iridescent lizard-skin cape, his indigo shirt, and the rest of his attire. Subdued clothing . . . for Clothahump's world.

The girl in the front was having a tough time with her sunshades. Maybe she didn't realize that the glasses were clean and that it was her eyes that needed washing out. She leaned over again and nearly tumbled into the water.

Her boyfriend grabbed the strap of her bikini top and pulled hard enough to hold her in the boat. Unfortunately, it was also hard enough to compress certain sensitive parts of her anatomy. She whirled to swing at him, missed badly thanks to the effects of what the foursome had been smoking all morning. For some unknown reason this started her giggling uncontrollably.

Jon-Tom wasn't laughing anymore. He was battling his own sozzled thoughts and magically contaminated bloodstream.

"Who *are* you people?"

"I told you." The boat's driver spoke with pot-induced ponderousness. "MacReady's the name. Charles MacReady. I am a stockbroker from Manhattan. Merrill Lynching. You know, the bull?" He rested one hand on the shoulder of the suddenly contemplative woman seated next to him. She appeared fascinated by the sheen of her nail polish.

"This is Buffy." He nodded toward the front of the boat. "The two kids up front are Steve and Mary-Ann. Steve works in my office. Don't you, Steve?" Steve didn't reply. He and Mary-Ann were giggling in tandem now.

The driver turned back to Jon-Tom. "Who are you?"

"One hell of a good question," Jon-Tom replied thickly. He glanced down at his outrageous costume. Is this what happens when you get the DTs? he wondered. Somehow he'd always imagined having the DTs would involve stronger hallucinations than a quartet of happily stoned vacationers loaded down with pot and pretzels.

"My name . . . my name . . ." For one terrible instant there was a soft, puffy blank in his mind where his name belonged. The kind of disorientation one encounters in a cheap house of mirrors at the state fair, where you have to feel your way through to the exit by putting your hands out in front of you and pushing through the nothingness of your own reflections.

Meriweather, he told himself. Jonathan Thomas Meriweather. I am a graduate law student from UCLA. The University of California at Los Angeles. He repeated this information slowly to the driver of the boat.

"Nice to meet you," said MacReady.

"But you, you, you, where are you? Where are you from?" Jon-Tom was aware he was half crying, but he couldn't stop himself. His desperation overwhelmed any suggestion of self-control.

The song, the song, that seemingly innocuous song so full of un-foreseen consequences. First the boat, then the storm and his drunk-enness, and now . . . where in the song had the sloop *John B.* been going?

The stockbroker from Manhattan pointed to his right. "Just out for the afternoon from the Nassau Club Med. You know, man. The Bahamas? You lost out of Miami or what?" He jiggled the chain of polyethelene beads that hung from his neck.

"Wanna come back in with us?"

"It can't be," Jon-Tom whispered dazedly. "It can't be this easy." The song he'd repeated over and over, what was the phrasing? "Around Nassau Town we did roam . . . I wanna go home, I wanna go home . . . this is the worst trip, I've ever been on."

"I wanna go home," Jon-Tom sang in his mind. *"Around Nassau Town.* Yes . . . yes, we'll follow you back! We'll follow you back." He clung to the rail for dear life, his eyes locked on the big Evinrude rumbling at the stern of the ski boat.

"You coming over here or you just going to follow us in?"

"We'll follow you," Jon-Tom mumbled. "We'll follow." He turned to the helm. "Roseroar, put on all sail . . . no, wait." It was still windless. "The engine. I'll get that engine started and we'll follow them in!" He took a wild step toward the hatchway, felt himself going backward over the rail, tumbling toward a waiting pane of glass that wasn't there.

An immense paw had hold of him, was pulling him back on deck. "Watch yourself, sugah," Roseroar told him quietly. She'd cleared the distance to him from her position at the wheel in one leap.

Now she stared across the water. "Who are these strange folk? Ah declare, ah can't make top no bottom of their words."

"Tell them," Jon-Tom moaned weakly toward the ski boat, "tell them who you are, tell them where we are!"

But Charles MacReady, stockbroker on vacation, seven days, six nights, $950 all-inclusive from LaGuardia, not counting the fact that he expected to get laid tonight, did not reply. He was staring at the boat where seven feet of white tigress dressed in leather and brass armor stood on hind legs staring back at him.

Giggling rose from the floorboards in the front of the boat. MacReady's girlfriend had progressed from an intimate examination of her nails to her toes, which she was regarding now with a Buddha-like glassy stare.

MacReady dazedly flipped the butt of the sansemilla stick over the side as though it had been laced with cyanide and said clearly, "Holy shit." Then he sat down hard in the driver's seat and fired up the big outboard.

"No wait," Jon-Tom screamed, "wait!" He tried to dive over the side, and it took all of Roseroar's considerable strength to prevent him from drowning himself. In his current state he couldn't float, much less swim.

"Easy there, Jon-Tom. What's gotten into y'all?"

He wrenched away from her, tore down the hatchway into the hold, and fumbled with the diesel. It took three tries but this time it started up. Then he was running, crawling back up the stairs and flying for the steering wheel console. The compass rocked. He stabbed a button. A gargling came from underneath the ship, hesitated, died. He jabbed the button again. This time the sound was a *whir, whir.*

Mudge raced back from the bow. "Wot the bloody 'ell is goin' on back 'ere?"

Roseroar stood aside, guarding the railing, and eyed the otter uncertainly. "There ah people in a boat. We must be neah some land."

"I 'eard. That's bloody marvelous. They goin' to lead us in?"

"I think they're frightened of something," Roseroar told him.

Jon-Tom was crying, crying and jabbing away at the starter. "You don't understand, you don't understand!" The sound of the ski boat's outboard was fading with distance. Still the engine refused to turn over.

Then there was a deep growl. Roseroar jumped and grabbed the rail as the boat began to move.

"Where are they?" Jon-Tom cried, trying to steer and search the fog at the same time. "Which way did they go?"

"I do not know, Jon-Tom," said Jalwar helplessly. "I did not see." He pointed uncertainly into the fog off the bow. "That way, I think."

Jon-Tom increased their speed and the diesel responded efficiently. They couldn't be far from the town of Nassau. The foursome from New York had been out for the afternoon only. Hadn't the stockbroker said so? Besides, they wore only swim suits and carried little in the way of supplies. Surely he was near enough to hit the island! And from Nassau it would be a short flight to the Florida coast. To home, to Miami, Disneyworld, hotels, and soap operas on TV in the afternoon. Images shoved purposefully into the back of his mind sprang back to the fore: home.

He was home.

So crazed was he with hope and joy that he didn't think what the reaction would be to his arriving in Nassau with the likes of Mudge and Jalwar and Roseroar in tow. But none of that mattered. None.

Unintentionally and quite without intending to do so, he'd spell-sung himself home.

VII

He clung desperately to that thought as day gave way to night. Still no sign of Nassau or any of the Bahamas. No hint of pleasure boats plying the placid Caribbean. No lights on shore to guide them in. Only the ever-present fog and an occasional glimpse of a half-moon glittering on high, keeping a watchful silver eye on his waning hopes.

He was still at the wheel the next morning. The fog had fled from the sky only to settle heavily inside his heart. You could see for miles in every direction. None yielded a glimpse of a coconut palm, a low-lying islet, or the warm glass-and-steel face of a Hilton Hotel. Only when the diesel finally sputtered to a halt, out of fuel, did he sit away from the helm, exhausted.

Worst of all, he was sober. Desperation and despair had driven the spellsong-induced drunkenness from his body. It was sour irony: he had regained the use of his senses when he no longer had need of them.

Roseroar assumed the wheel again, said nothing. With the disappearance of the fog had come the return of the wind. The sails filled.

"Wheah shall I set course for, Jon-Tom?" she asked gently. He didn't reply, stared blankly over the side.

Mudge watched him closely. "Snarken, luv. You know the way." Roseroar nodded, swung the wheel over.

"What's wrong with him?"

Mudge replied thoughtfully. " 'E believed for a few minutes last night 'e might 'ave been 'ome, back in 'is own world. Now, me, I don't believe we went from one world to another that simple, even if that was a peculiar boat full of mighty odd-lookin' 'umans. The birds were sharp enough lookin', though. I'll give 'em that."

Roseroar gave him a look of distaste. "Y'all are disgustin'. Yo friend is heartsick and all yo can thank of, yo scummy little degenerate pervert, is intercourse."

"Blow it out your striped arse, you self-righteous bitch! I'd swear on me mother's 'ead that 'alf an army's done proper work under that tail."

Roseroar lunged for the otter. A ghost of a voice made her pause.

"Don't. Please." For the first time in days a familiar face swung around to face both of them. "It's not worth it. Not on my behalf."

Roseroar reluctantly returned to her station behind the wheel. "Blimey, mate," said Mudge softly, "you really do think we went over into your world, don't you?"

He nodded. "It was in the song. I didn't mean it to happen that way, but yes, I think we crossed over. And I was too drunk to do anything about it."

"Maybe we're still in yo world," said Roseroar.

Mudge noticed movement in the water. "'Ang on. I think I know 'ow to find out." He headed toward the bow.

Jon-Tom rose, swayed slightly. Roseroar put out a hand to steady him but he waved her off with a smile. "Thanks. I'm okay now. Stone-cold sober."

"Yo drunkenness did come from yo song, then?"

"Something else I didn't plan on. It's worn off. That's why I don't think we're still in my world. The good wears off along with the bad." His voice fell to a whisper. "I was *home*, Roseroar! Home."

"Ah am sorry fo yo, Jon-Tom. Ah really and truly am."

"You've got a big heart, Roseroar. Along with everything else." He smiled at her, then walked toward the front of the boat. Maybe he was wrong. Maybe there was still a chance, however faint that seemed now.

The otter was leaning over the side. "How are you going to find out where we are?" Jon-Tom asked.

Mudge glanced up at him. "That's easy enough, guv'nor. All you 'ave to do is ask." He turned his face to the water racing past the prow and shouted, "Hey, you, where are we?"

Jon-Tom peered over the railing to see the playful, smooth, gray-backed shapes sliding easily through the water, hitching a free ride on the boat's bow-wave. One of them lifted its bottle-nose clear of the surface and squeaked a reply.

"You're at half past a quarter after." Giggles rose from around the speaker as the rest of the dolphins vented their appreciation of the little joke.

Mudge gave Jon-Tom an apologetic look. "Sorry, mate, but tain't easy gettin' a straight answer out o' this bunch o' sea-goin' comedians."

"Never mind," Jon-Tom sighed. "The fact that it answered at all is proof enough of which world we're in."

"Hey-ya," said another of the slim swimmers, "have you guys heard the one about the squid and the Third Mistress of Pack Thirty?"

"No." Mudge leaned forward, interested.

The dolphin now speaking sidled effortlessly up to the side of the speeding sloop. "It seems she . . ." Jon-Tom abandoned the ongoing display of oceanic vulgarity and climbed the central cabin to contemplate the horizon.

No, he wasn't home anymore. Maybe he'd hallucinated the whole incident. Maybe there'd been no ski boat full of stoned stockbrokers from New York. Maybe the entire episode was nothing more than the result of his drunkenness.

Except that Mudge and Roseroar and Jalwar had seen them also.

The last vestiges of inebriation left him frighteningly cold inside. It was bad enough that fate had dumped him in this alien otherworld. Now it had chosen to tease him with a glimpse of reality, of home. He felt like a poor kid forced to stand in front of the main display window at F.A.O. Schwarz the night before Christmas.

Slipping the duar around in front of him, he tried the song again, tried altering the inflection in his voice, the volume of each stanza. Tried until his throat was dry and he could hardly speak. Nothing worked. The song remained a song and nothing more.

He tried other songs, with the same result. He sang everything he could remember that alluded however vaguely to going home, to returning home, to longing for home. The sloop *John B.* cut cleanly through the waves, running southwestward under Roseroar's expert guidance. There was no sign of land to cheer him. Only the dolphins with their endless corny jokes.

"Sail ahead!" Jalwar yelled from the top of the mainmast. Jon-Tom shoved his own concerns aside as he joined Mudge near the bowsprit. Stare as he might, he saw only empty horizon. Mudge had no difficulty in matching the ferret's vision.

"I see 'er, mate."

"What does she look like?"

"Rigged normal, not like this thing." The last of Jon-Tom's hopes vanished. Not a speedboat, then. "Big, two rows of oars. That I don't like."

"Why not?"

"Think about it, mate. Only a fool would try rowin' across an ocean. Only a fool . . . and them that's given no choice in the business."

The visitor was bearing down on them fast. Soon Jon-Tom could make out the silhouette. "Can you see a flag?"

Mudge stared hard. Then he began to shake. "That's all she wrote, mate. There's a 'eart with a knife through it flyin' from the yardarm. Pirates." He raced sternward, Jon-Tom hurrying after him.

"I thought only traders traveled the Glittergeist."

"Aye, traders and them that preys on 'em." The otter was dancing frantically around Roseroar. "Do somethin', you bloody great caricature of a courtesan!"

Roseroar put the wheel hard over, said evenly, "They've probably seen us already."

"Jon-Tom, spellsing us out o' 'ere!" By now the huge, swift shape of the pirate ship was bearing down on their stern. Strange figures lined the rails and the double rows of oars dipped in unison.

"There's not enough wind," Roseroar observed. "What there is, is at our back, but they're supplementin' their own sails with those oahs."

Jon-Tom was trying to untangle his duar from around his neck. "Our engine's out of diesel." He found himself eyeing the approaching behemoth in fascination. "Interesting lines."

"Interestin' my arse!" Mudge was saying frantically. "You'll see 'ow interestin' it can be if they take us!"

"I'm afraid I don't know many songs about boats," Jon-Tom muttered worriedly, trying to concentrate, "and none at all about pirates. See, where I come from they're a historical oddity. Not really a valid subject for contemporary songwriters."

"Screw wot's contemporary!" the otter pleaded with him. "Sing something!"

Jon-Tom tried a couple of hasty, half-remembered tunes, none of which had the slightest effect on the *John B.* or the approaching vessel. It was hard to remember anything, what with Jalwar moaning and genuflecting to the north and Mudge hopping hysterically all over the boat when he wasn't screaming in Jon-Tom's face.

Then there was no time left to think as Roseroar rumbled, "Stand by to repel boarders, y'all!"

Jon-Tom put the duar aside. No time for playing. The upper deck of the pirate ship loomed over them. Arrayed along the rail was the oddest assortment of creatures he'd encountered since finding himself in this world.

One massive dirty-furred polar bear missing an ear stood alongside three vicious-looking pikas armed with four-foot-long lances. A pair of lynxes caressed chipped battle-axes and prepared to swing down on ropes dangling from a boom. Next to them a tarsier equipped with oversized sunglasses aimed a bow at the sloop.

"Take 'em!" snarled a snaggle-toothed old bobcat. He leaped boldly over the side, swinging a short scimitar over his ears, and landed on the club end of Jon-Tom's ramwood staff. He made a strangled sound as the breath went out of him and there was a cracking sound as a rib went.

As the bobcat slid over the side a coyote came down a rope dangling above Roseroar, intent on splitting her skull with a mace. The tigress's swords flashed in unison. Four limbs went their separate ways as the coyote's limbless torso landed soundlessly on the deck, spraying blood in all directions. It twitched horribly.

Jon-Tom fought for control of his stomach as the attackers began swarming over the side in earnest. He found himself backing away from a couple of armored sloths whose attitudes were anything but slothful and, rather shockingly, a middle-aged man. The sloths carried no weapons, relying instead on their six-inch-long foreclaws to do damage. They didn't move as fast as the others, but Jon-Tom's blows glanced harmlessly off their thick leather armor.

They forced him back toward the railing. The man jumped between the two sloths and tried to decapitate Jon-Tom with his axe. Jon-Tom ducked the blow and lunged, catching one of the sloths square on the nose with the end of his staff. He heard the bone snap, felt the cartilage give under his weight. As the sloth went down, its face covered with blood, its companion moved in with both paws.

Jon-Tom spun the staff, touched the hidden switch set in the wood, and six inches of steel emerged from the back end of the shaft to slide into the sloth's throat. It looked at him in surprise before crumpling. The man with the axe backed off.

Jalwar and Mudge were trying to hack loose the grappling hooks that now bound the sloop to the larger vessel, but they couldn't do that and defend themselves as well. Both went down under a wave of attackers. Roseroar had been backed up to the stern. She stood there, enclosed by a picket line of spears and lances. Every time someone made a move to get under her guard, they ended up with their insides spilling all over the deck.

Finally one of the mates barked an order. The spearmen backed off, yielding their places to archers. Arrows were aimed at the tigress. Being a brave warrior but not a suicidal one, she nodded and handed over her weapons. The pirates swarmed over her with chains and steel bands, binding her in such a way that if she tried to exert pressure on her bonds she would only end up choking herself. They were much more casual in tying up Jon-Tom.

A towline was attached to the sloop as the prisoners were marched up a gangplank onto the capturing craft. They formed a sullen quartet as they were lined up for review. The rest of the crew stood aside respectfully as an unbloodied figure stepped forward and regarded the captives.

The leopard was as tall as Jon-Tom. His armor was beautiful as well as functional, consisting of intricately worked leather crisscrossed with silver metal bands. His tail emerged from a hole in the back of the armor. The last half of the tail looked like a prosthesis, but Jon-Tom decided it would be impolitic to inquire about it just now. Four long knives were attached to the belt that ran around the upper part of the big cat's waist. No armor covered the muscular arms.

Leather gloves with the tips cut out to permit the use in battle of sharp claws showed many patches and deep cuts from previous fights. A deep gash across the black nose had healed imperfectly. Jon-Tom took all this in as the leopard strutted silently past them. The rest of the crew murmured restlessly.

"You fought well," their inspector finally growled. "Very well. Too well, thinks I." He glanced significantly toward the sloop which bobbed astern of the bigger ship.

"Too many shipmates lost in taking such a small prize." Green eyes flashed. "I don't believe in trading good mates for scum, but we were curious about your strange craft. Where do you come from and how come you by such a peculiar vessel? 'Tis not fashioned of wood. I'm sure of that."

"It's fiberglass."

The leopard's eyes snapped toward Jon-Tom. "Are you the owner of the craft?"

Jon-Tom nodded affirmatively. "I am."

Something stung his face and he staggered, temporarily blinded. His hand went instinctively to his face and came away with blood. He could feel the four parallel cuts the leopard's claws had made. They were shallow, if messy. A little lower and he would have lost both eyes.

Roseroar made a dangerous noise deep in her throat while Mudge muttered a particularly elegant curse. The leopard ignored them both as it stepped forward. Its nose was almost touching Jon-Tom's.

"I am . . . *sir,*" it said dangerously. Mudge mumbled something else, and immediately the leopard's gaze flashed toward the otter. "Did you say something, dung-eater?"

"Wot, me? Just clearin' me throat . . . sir. Dried out it were by a hot fight."

" 'Tis going to get hotter for you, thinks I." The big cat returned his attention to Jon-Tom, who stood bleeding silently. "Any complaints?"

Jon-Tom lowered his gaze from the leopard's face, feeling the blood trickling down his face and wondering if the scarring would be permanent.

"No, sir. No complaints, sir."

The leopard favored him with a thin smile. "That's better."

"Are you the captain of this ship . . . sir?"

The leopard threw back his head and roared. "I am Sasheem, first mate." He looked to his right, stepped aside. "Here comes the captain now."

Jon-Tom didn't know what to expect. Another bear, perhaps, or some other impressive figure. He forgot that captains are fashioned of brain as well as brawn, mind as much as muscle. The sight of the captain surprised but did not shock him. It seemed somehow perversely traditional.

Captain Corroboc was a parrot. Bright green, with patches of blue and red. He stood about four feet tall. The missing right leg had been replaced with one of wood. Metal springs enabled it to bend at the knee. A leather patch covered the one empty eye socket.

As was the fashion among the feathered citizens of this world, Corroboc wore a kilt. It was unpatterned and blood red, a perfect match to his crimson vest. The absence of a design showed that he had abandoned his clanship. Unlike many of the other fliers Jon-Tom had encountered, he wore no hat or cap. A narrow bandolier crossed the feathered breast. Sun glinted off the dozen tiny stilettos it held.

A member of the crew later informed them that the captain could throw four of the deadly little blades at a time: one with each flexible wingtip, one with his beak, and the last with his remaining foot. All this with lethal accuracy while balancing on the artificial leg.

The remaining bright blue eye flicked back and forth between the prisoners. Above and below the eye patch the skin showed an unwholesome yellow where feathers were missing.

"These be all the crew of our prize?" He looked up at the first mate, and Jon-Tom was surprised to see the powerful leopard flinch back. Corroboc made eye contact with each of his own crew in turn.

"A brave bunch you are. A bloodthirsty death-dealing collection . . . of infants!" His tail quivered with his anger. "Infants, the lot of you!" Not only Sasheem, but the rest of the cutthroats were completely cowed by this battered green bird. Jon-Tom determined not to cross him.

"Four against nearly a hundred, was it? A fine lot you are!" He cocked his head sideways to gaze at the prisoners. "Now then. Where be you four bound?"

"Just a few days out from the Tailaroam," Mudge volunteered ingratiatingly. "We were just on a little fishin' trip, we were, and—"

The wooden leg was a blur. It caught the otter between his short legs. Mudge turned slightly the color of the captain as he grabbed himself and collapsed on the deck. Corroboc eyed him indifferently.

"The Emir of Ezon has a tradition of employing eunuchs to guard his palace. I haven't decided what to do with any of you yet, but one more lie like that and you'll find yourself a candidate for the knife o' the ship's doctor."

Jon-Tom tried to pick a likely candidate for ship's physician out of the surrounding collection of cutthroats and failed, though he imagined that whoever that worthy might be, he hadn't taken his internship at the Mayo Clinic.

Mudge held his peace, along with everything else. The blue eye fastened on Jon-Tom. "Perhaps you be smarter than your sourwhiskered companion. Where be you bound, man?"

"Snarken," Jon-Tom replied without hesitation.

Corroboc nodded. "Now, that makes sense. A sensible one. You be a strange specimen, tall man. Be you from the region o' the Bellwoods?"

"I am." He had to risk the falsehood. It was true enough now, anyway.

The parrot blew his nose on the deck, sniffed. "Fortunately for you I am in a good humor this morning." Jon-Tom decided he did not want to encounter him when he was in a bad mood. "You two"—he indicated Mudge and Jalwar—"can start cleaning out the bilges. That's a job long overdue and one I am certain you'll find to your liking. Won't you?"

Uncertain whether to say yes sir, no sir, or nothing at all, Jalwar stood and shook in terror. Mudge wasn't up to commenting. Corroboc was apparently satisfied, because he nodded absently before moving down to stare fearlessly up at the towering Roseroar.

"As for you, I'd be pleased to make you one of my crew. 'Tis plain enough to see you're no stranger to a life of fighting. You'd make a valuable addition."

"Ah'll think it ovah, suh."

Good girl, Jon-Tom thought. There was no point in making the pirate parrot mad with an outright refusal, though he found himself wishing her reply hadn't been quite so convincing. Surely she wasn't seriously considering the offer? But why not? Nothing bound her to Jon-Tom. In fact, she had reason enough to abandon him. Hadn't he yanked her unwillingly from her homeland and involved her in dangers in which she had no interest? If she were forced to throw in with some stranger, why not this captain as easily as some unsteady, homesick spellsinger?

Spellsinger! He'd almost forgotten his own abilities. Not a one of this band of murderers knew of his avocation. He prayed his companions would keep the secret and not blurt it out in a thoughtless moment. He was particularly worried about the elderly Jalwar, but the trader stood petrified and volunteered nothing.

As if reading his thoughts, the pirate captain turned his attention back to him. "And you, tall man. What be you good for?"

"Well, I can fight, too." Corroboc glanced toward his first mate.

Sasheem muttered an opinion, reluctantly. "Passing well."

Corroboc grunted and Jon-Tom added, "I am also an entertainer, a troubadour by trade."

"Huh! Well, 'tis true we could do with a bit o' song on this scow from time to time." He gave his crew a look of disgust. "I gets tired o' listening to the drunken prattling o' this uncultured bunch."

Fighting to conceal his anxiety, Jon-Tom went on. "My instrument's on board our ship, along with the rest of our personal effects."

"Is it, now?" Corroboc was sweating him with that one piercing eye. "I expect we'll find it in due course. You in a rush to demonstrate your talents?"

"At your leisure, sir." Jon-Tom felt the back of his indigo shirt beginning to cling damply to his skin. "It's only that it's a fine instrument. I'd hate to see one of your refined crew reduce it to kindling in hopes of finding gold or jewels inside. They wouldn't."

Corroboc snorted. "Rest assured they'll mind their stinking manners." He addressed the leopard. "Take 'em below and lock 'em in the brig. Let them stew there for a bit."

"These two also?" Sasheem pointed to Jalwar and Mudge.

"Aye, the bilges will wait. Let them share each other's filth for a while. By the time I decide to let them out they'll be clamorin' to get to work."

This sophisticated sally brought appreciative laughter from the crew as they sloughed away to their posts. The pirate ship turned westward with the sloop trailing obediently behind it.

As they were herded below, Jon-Tom had his first glimpse of the rowers. Most were naked save for their own fur. They were a cross section of species, from humans to rodents. All exhibited the last stages of physical and mental degeneration.

That's where we'll all end up, on the rowing benches, he thought tiredly. Unless we can figure out some way out of this.

At the moment, entry into paradise seemed the more likely route. If he could only get his hands on his duar, there might be a chance. However fickle his spellsinging, however uncertain he was of what he might sing, he was sure of one thing: he'd fashion *some* kind of magic. And the first try would be his last. He was sure of that much. Corroboc wasn't stupid, and the captain would give him no second chance to try his hand at wizardry.

Roseroar suddenly twisted to look back over her shoulder, one paw going to her rump. The first mate was grinning back at her.

"Put yo hands on me like that again, cub, and ah'll make music with yo bones."

"Gentle now, big one," said the amused leopard. "I have no doubt you'd do just that if given the chance. But you won't be given the chance. It'll go easier on you in the long run if you mind your manners and be nice to Sasheem. If not, well, we have an ample supply of chain on this boat, we do. Your heart may be made of iron, but the rest of you is only flesh and bone. Nice flesh it is, too. Think over your options."

"If I ask him nicely, Corroboc will give you to me."

She glared back at him. "Ah won't be a comforting gift."

Sasheem shrugged. "Comforting or unforgiving, it won't matter. I aim to have you. Willingly if possible, otherwise if not. You may as well settle your mind to that." They were herded into a barred cell. Sasheem favored Roseroar with a departing smirk as he joined the rest of his companions in mounting the gangway.

Roseroar sat down heavily, her huge paws clenching and unclenching. "That furred snake. Ah'd like to get my claws into his—"

"Not yet, Roseroar," Jon-Tom cautioned her. "We've got to be patient. They don't know that I'm a spellsinger. If I can just get my hands on my duar, get one chance to play and sing, we'll have a chance."

"A chance at wot, mate?" Mudge slumped dispiritedly in a corner. "For you to conjure up some poor dancin' girl to take Roseroar's place? To bury this slimy tub in flowers?"

"I'll do *something*," Jon-Tom told him angrily. "You see if I don't."

"I will that, guv." The otter rolled over, ignoring the fact that the floor of their cage was composed of rank straw stained dark by the urine of previous captives.

"What are you doing?"

"I'm goin' to 'ave a sleep, mate."

"How can you sleep now?"

"Because I'm tired, mate." The otter glanced up at him. "I am tired of fightin', tired with fear, and most of all I'm tired o' listenin' to wot a wonderful spellsinger you are. When you're ready to magic us out o' this 'ole and back to someplace civilized, wake me. If not, maybe I'll be lucky and not wake up meself."

"One should never ride the wave of pessimism," Jalwar chided him.

"Close your cake 'ole, you useless old fart. You don't know wot the 'ell you're talkin' about." Hurt, the old ferret lapsed into silence.

Jon-Tom had moved to the barrier and held a cell bar in each hand. They were fixed deep into the wood of the ship. Small scavenger lizards and dauntingly big bugs skittered about in the dark sections of the hold while others could be heard using the rafters for pathways.

Then he turned to walk over to Roseroar and put a comforting hand on her head, stroking her between the ears. She responded with a tired, halfhearted purr.

"Don't worry, Roseroar. I got you into this. Maybe I can't get myself home, but I can damn well get you out of it. I owe you that much. I owe all of you that much."

Mudge was already asleep and didn't hear the promise. Jalwar squatted in another corner picking resignedly at strands of hay.

I just don't know *how* I'm going to get you all out of this, Jon-Tom mused silently.

VIII

Somehow the concept of "swabbing the deck" was tinged with innocence; a reflection of childhood memories of stories about wooden ships and iron men.

The reality of it was something else.

You rested on your hands and knees on a rough planked deck, stripped to the waist beneath a hot sun that blistered your neck and set the skin to peeling off your back. Sweat flowed in streams from under your arms, from your forehead and your belly. Anything small and solid, be it a speck of dust or one of your own hairs, that slipped into your eye made you want to run screaming for the railing to throw yourself over the side.

Salt air worsened your situation, exacerbating the sore spots, making them fester and redden faster. Splinters stung the exposed skin of hands and ankles while your palms were raw from pushing the wide brushes soaked with lye-based cleaning solution.

Meanwhile you advanced slowly the length of the deck, making sure to remove each bloodstain lest some laughing member of the crew remind you of its presence by pressing a heavy foot on your raw fingers.

By midday Jon-Tom no longer cared much if they were rescued or if he were thrown over the rail to be consumed by whatever carnivorous fish inhabited this part of the Glittergeist. He didn't have much hope left. Already he'd forgotten about Clothahump's illness, about returning home, forgotten about everything except surviving the day.

By late afternoon they'd finished scrubbing every square foot of the main deck and had moved up to the poop deck. The helmsman, a grizzled old warthog, ignored them. There was no sign of the captain, for which Jon-Tom was unremittingly grateful.

A crude, temporary shelter had been erected off to the left, close by the captain's perch. Huddled beneath the feeble shade this provided was a girl of sixteen, maybe a little older. Once she might have been pretty. Now her long blonde hair was so much pale seaweed clinging to her face. She was barely five feet tall. Her eyes were a washed-out blue. Excepting the heavy steel manacle that encircled her neck and was attached to a chain bolted to the deck, she was stark naked.

It provided her with a radius of movement of about ten feet. No more. Just enough to get from the shelter to the rail, where she would have to perform any personal bodily functions in full view of the crew. Jon-Tom had no trouble following the whip welts, casual burns, and bruises that covered most of her body.

She sat silently within the shelter, her legs extended to one side, and said nothing as they approached. She just stared.

Jon-Tom used a forearm to wipe the sweat from around his lips. They were alone on the deck except for the old helmsman. He risked whispering.

"Who are you, girl?" No reply. Only those empty blue eyes, staring. "What's your name?"

"Leave 'er be, mate," said Mudge softly. "Can't you see there's not much left o' 'er? She's mad or near enough, or maybe they cut out 'er tongue to keep 'er from screamin'."

"None of those," said the helmsman. He spoke without taking his eyes from the ship's course. "That's Folly, the captain's toy. He took her off a ship that sank several months ago. She's been nuthin' but trouble since. Uncooperative, unappreciative when the captain tried bein' nice to her. I don't know why he doesn't throw her overboard and be done with it. It was folly to bring her aboard, and folly to keep her, so Folly's been her name."

"But what's her real name?"

A thin, barely audible reply came from within the shelter. "I have no name. Folly's as good as any."

"You can talk. They haven't broken you yet."

She glared bitterly at Jon-Tom. "What do you know about anything? I've been watching you." Her mouth twisted. "You're hurting now. I watched when they took your boat and brought you aboard. The tigress will be around awhile. The old one won't last two weeks. The otter a little longer, if he keeps his mouth shut.

"As for you," she eyed Jon-Tom contemptuously, "you'll say the wrong thing and lose your tongue. Or worse."

"What happened to you?" Jon-Tom was careful to keep his voice down and his arms moving lest Sasheem or one of the other mates take note of the conversation.

"What does it matter?"

"It matters to me. It should matter to you, because we're going to get off this ship." If the helmsman overheard he gave no sign.

The girl laughed sharply. "And you thought I'd gone mad." She glanced at Roseroar. "The man is crazy, isn't he?" Roseroar made no reply, bending to her work.

"And you'll come with us," he went on. "I wouldn't leave you here."

"Why not? You've got your own business to attend to. Why not leave me here? You don't know me, you don't owe me." She spat at the deck. "This is a stupid conversation. You're not going anywhere."

"What happened?" he prodded gently.

A tiny bit of the hardness seemed to go out of her, and she looked away from him. "My family and I were on a trading packet bound from Jorsta to the Isles of Durl when we ran afoul of these bastards. They killed my father along with the rest of the males and later, my mother. Since my little sister was too young to be of any use to them, they threw her overboard. They killed everyone, except for me. For some reason that unmentionable thing they call their captain took a fancy to me. I imagine he saw future profit in me." She shrugged. "I've taken care to give them nothing but trouble since. Hence my name, a gift of the crew."

"Been less troublesome lately," grunted the helmsman significantly.

"Have you tried to escape?"

"Escape to where? Yes, I tried anyway. Better drowning or sharks than this. At least, I tried before they put this chain on me. I only tried once. There are worse things than being beaten. As you may find out."

He lowered his voice to make certain the helmsman couldn't over-hear. "I don't intend to. We're getting off this ship. Will you come with us when we do?"

"No." She stared straight back at him. "No. I won't. I don't want to be hurt anymore."

"That's why I'm taking you with us." She turned away from him. "What's wrong?"

Mudge gave him a gentle nudge. "Watch your mouth, lad. 'Tis the captain, may 'e rot in 'is own excrement."

"How goes she, Pulewine?" Corroboc inquired of his helmsman.

"Steady on course, Captain."

Jon-Tom kept his attention on his scrub brush, heard the *thunk* of the captain's wooden leg move nearer.

"And how be our fine cleaning crew this bright morning? Are they working like the elegant fighters we brought aboard?"

"No, Captain." The helmsman allowed himself a grunting laugh. "As anyone can see, they're working like the scum that they are."

"That's good." Corroboc walked around Jon-Tom until the parrot was standing between him and Folly's shelter. He turned his good eye on the man. "Now then, mayhap we each understand our place in the order o' things, har?"

"Yes, Captain," murmured Jon-Tom readily enough.

"Aye, that be the way to answer. Keep that tone about you and you'll live to do more service." He cast a glance into the shelter and Jon-Tom went cold as he saw the look that came over Folly's face as she drew back into the shadows.

"Chatting with the young she, have you?"

Since the helmsman had been privy to much of their conversation, Jon-Tom could hardly deny it had taken place.

"A word or two, sir. Harmless enough."

"Har, I be sure o' that! A cute little specimen of her species, though not marketable in her present condition, fears I. A consequence of noncooperation." Jon-Tom said nothing, scrubbed harder, trying to push the brush through the wood.

"That's it, boy. Scrub well and we'll see to giving you a chance to entertain us when you've finished." He shared a laugh with the helmsman. "Though not the kind you think, no. The two of you can entertain us together."

"I wouldn't get under that whey-faced stringbean if you shot me with pins," Folly snapped.

Corroboc turned that merciless eye on his prisoner. "Now, what make you think you'd be having any choice in the matter, Folly? It'll be a pleasant thing to work out the geometry of it." He lashed out suddenly with his one good foot. The sharp claws cut twin bloody gouges up her thigh and she let out a soft cry.

Jon-Tom dug his fingernails into the wood of the brush.

"That be better now, and we'll be having no more arguments, will we?" Folly clung to the shadows and whimpered, holding her injured leg. "You've been disappointment enough to me. As soon as we make land I'll rid myself of you, and I'll make certain your buyer is of a similar mind when it comes to staging entertainments. Then perhaps you'll yearn for the good old days back aboard Corroboc's ship, har?" He turned back to the deck cleaners.

"Keep at it, slime." He addressed his helmsman. "When they've finished the deck, run them forward and set them to scrubbing the sides. Sling them over in nets. If one of them falls through, it will serve as a fine lesson to the others."

"Aye, Captain," said the helmsman.

Corroboc rose on bright green wings to glide down to the main deck. The warthog cast a wizened eye at Jon-Tom.

"Watch thy tongue and mind thy manners and thee might live as much as a year." This admonition was finished off with a thick, grunting laugh. "Still going to escape?"

You bet your porcine ass we are, Jon-Tom thought angrily as he attacked the decking. The wood was the only thing he could safely take out his fury on. We'll get out of this somehow and take that poor battered girl with us.

Without his realizing it, the sight of Folly had done something their own desperate situation had not: it forced him to realize how selfish he'd been these past hours, moping around bemoaning his fate. He wasn't the only one who had problems. Everyone else was depending on him—Mudge and Jalwar and Roseroar, and Clothahump sick and hurt back in his tree, and now Folly.

So he hadn't made it back to his own world. Tough. Self-pity wouldn't get him any closer to L.A. He had friends who needed him.

Mudge noticed the change in his friend's attitude immediately. He scrubbed the deck with renewed enthusiasm.

"Work 'ard and 'ave confidence, mates," he whispered to Jalwar and Roseroar. "See that look on me pal's face? I've seen it afore. 'E may be 'alf bonkers, but sometimes 'tis the 'alf bonkers, part crazy part that sees a way out where none's to be seen."

"I pray it is so," whispered Jalwar, "or we are well and truly doomed."

"'Alf a chance," Mudge muttered. "That's all 'e needs is 'alf a chance."

"They may not give it to him," commented Roseroar.

While his companions slept the sleep of the exhausted that night, Jon-Tom planned and schemed. Corroboc was going to let him sing, out of curiosity if naught else. Songs would have to be chosen carefully, with an eye toward suppressing any suspicions the captain might have. Jon-Tom had no doubt that the homicidal parrot would watch him carefully.

His recital should be as bland and homogenous as possible. Somehow he would have to find an effective tune that would have the hoped-for results while sounding perfectly innocent. The lyrics would have to be powerful but nonthreatening.

Only when he'd arranged a program in his mind did he allow himself to fall into a troubled, uneasy sleep.

The first mate had them scrubbing the base of the mainmast the next morning. Corroboc strolled past without looking at the work, and Jon-Tom turned slowly toward him, keeping his tone deferential.

"Your pardon, Captain."

The parrot turned, wingtips resting on slim bird hips. "Don't waste my time, boy. You've plenty to do."

"I know that, Captain sir, but it's very much the wrong kind of work. I miss my chosen avocation, which is that of minstrel. My knowledge of songs of far lands is unsurpassed."

"Be that so, boy?"

Jon-Tom nodded vigorously. "I know wondrous chords and verse of great beauty, can bring forth the most mellifluous sounds from my instrument. You would find that they fall lightly on the ears and sometimes, I am embarrassed to say it, risquely." He risked a knowing wink.

"I see," was all Corroboc said at first. Then, "Can it be that after only a day you know where your true interests lie? Har, truth and a little sun can do that to one. You'd rather sing for your supper now than scrub for it, har?"

"If you would allow me, Captain." Jon-Tom tried to look hopeful and compliant at the same time.

"Far lands, you say? 'Tis been a longish time since there's been any music aboard this tub other than the screaming of good citizens as they made their way over the side." He glanced to his left. Mudge, Jalwar, and Roseroar had been set to varnishing the railings.

"And what of your mates? How do you think they'll react if they have to do your labor as well as their own?"

Licking his lips, Jon-Tom stepped forward and smiled weakly, concealing his face from sight of his companions. "Look, sir, I can't help what they think, but my back's coming apart. I don't have any fur to protect me from the sun the way they do, and they don't seem to care. So why should I care what they think?"

"That be truth, as 'tis a poor naked-fleshed human you be. Not that it matters to me. However—" he paused, considering, while Jon-Tom held his breath, "we'll give you a chance, minstrel. Har. But," he added dangerously, "if you be lying to me to get out of a day's work, I'll put you to polishing the ship's heads from the inside out."

"No, Captain, I wouldn't lie to you, no sir!" He added disingenuously, "If I weren't a minstrel, what would I be doing carrying a musical instrument about?"

"As a master practitioner of diverse perversions I might suggest any number of things, har, but I can't see you haven't the necessary imagination." He turned and shouted. "Kaskrel!" A squirrel with a ragged tail hurried to obey. "Get belowdecks and fetch the instrument from my cabin. The one we took from this man's prize."

"Aye sir!" the squirrel squeaked, disappearing down a hatch.

"Come with me, tall man." Jon-Tom followed Corroboc up onto the poop deck. There the captain settled himself into a wicker chair that hung from a crossbeam. The top of the basket chair doubled as a perch, offering the captain a choice of resting positions. This time he chose to sit inside the basket.

The squirrel appeared momentarily, carrying Jon-Tom's duar. He tried not to look at the instrument with the longing he felt, particularly since a curious Sasheem had followed the sailor up the ladder. The squirrel handed it over and Jon-Tom caressed it lovingly. It was undamaged.

He was about to begin playing when a new voice interrupted him.

At first he thought both of the dog's ears had been cropped. Then he saw that they were torn and uneven, evidence of less refined surgery. The dog limped and leaned on a crutch. Unlike Corroboc he still had the use of both legs. It was just that one was a good foot shorter than the other. Jowls hung loosely from the canine face.

"Don't do it, Cap'n."

Corroboc eyed the arrival quizzically. "Now what be your objection, Macreeg?"

The old dog looked over at Jon-Tom. "I don't like it, sir. Better to keep this one swabbing the decks."

Corroboc kicked out with his wooden leg. It caught the sailor's crutch and sent him stumbling in pursuit of new support, only to land sprawling on his rump, accompanied by the derisive laughter of his fellow sailors.

"Har, where be your sense of refinement, Macreeg? Where be your feeling for culture?"

Neither perturbed nor intimidated, the old sailor slowly climbed back to his feet, stretching to his full four and a half feet of height.

"I just don't trust him, Cap'n. I don't like the look of him and I don't like his manner."

"Well, I be not in love with his naked features either, Mister Macreeg, but they don't upset me liver. As for his manner"—he threw Jon-Tom one of his disconcertingly penetrating glances— "what of your manner, man?"

"Anything you say, Captain sir," replied Jon-Tom as he dropped his eyes toward the deck.

The parrot held the stare a moment longer. "Har, that be adequate. Not quite servile enough yet, but that will come with time. You see?" He looked toward the old sailor. "There be nothing wrong in this. Music cannot harm us. Can it, tall man? Because if I were to think for one instant that you were trying to pull something peculiar on me . . ."

"I'm just a wandering minstrel, sir," Jon-Tom explained quickly. "All I want is a chance to practice the profession for which I was trained."

"Har, and to save your fragile skin." Corroboc grunted. "So be it." He leaned back in the gently swaying basket chair. Sasheem stood nearby, cleaning his teeth with what looked like a foot-long icepick. Jon-Tom knew if he sang anything even slightly suggestive of rebellion or defiance, that sharp point would go through his offending throat.

He plucked nervously at the duar, and his first words emerged as a croak. Fresh laughter came from the crew. Corroboc obviously enjoyed his discomfiture.

"Sorry, sir." He cleared his throat, wishing for a glass of water but not daring to chance the request. "This . . . this particular song is by a group of minstrels who called themselves the Eagles."

Corroboc appeared pleased. "My cousins in flight, though I chose to fly clanless. Strong, but weak of mind. I never cared much for their songmaking, as their voices be high and shrill."

"No, no," Jon-Tom explained. "The song is not by eagles, but by men like myself who chose to call themselves that."

"Strange choice of names. Why not call themselves the Men? Well, it be of no matter. Sing, minstrel. Sing, and lighten the hearts of my sailors and myself."

"As you command, Captain sir," said Jon-Tom. And he began to sing.

The duar was no Fender guitar, but the words came easily to him. He began with "Take It Easy." The long high notes rolled smoothly from his throat. He finished, swung instantly into the next song he'd carefully chosen. Corroboc's eye closed and the rest of the crew started to relax. They were enjoying the music. Jon-Tom moved on to "Best of My Love," then a medley of hits by the Bee Gees.

Nearby, Mudge blinked as he slapped varnish on wind-scoured wood. "Wot's 'e tryin' to do?"

"Ah don't know," said Roseroar. "Ah heah no mention of powerful demons oah spirits."

Only Jalwar was smiling as he worked. "You aren't supposed to, and neither are the ruffians around us. Listen! Don't you see what he's up to? Were he to sing of flight or battle that leopard would lay open his throat in an instant. He knows what he's doing. Don't listen to the words. They're doing as he intends. Look around you. Look at the crew."

Mudge peered over his shoulder. His eyes widened.

"Blimey, they're fallin' asleep!"

"Yes," said Jalwar. "They wait ready for the slightest hint of danger, and instead he lulls them with lullabies. Truly he is a master spellsinger."

"Don't say that, mate," muttered Mudge uneasily. "I've seen 'is nibs go wrong just when 'e thought 'e 'ad it right." But though he hardly dared believe, it was looking more and more as if Jon-Tom was going to bring it off.

The spellsinger was now wending his lilting way through "Peaceful Easy Feeling." "See," whispered Jalwar excitedly through clenched, sharp teeth, "even the armpit of a captain begins to go!"

No question but that Corroboc was slumped in the chair. Sasheem yawned and sat down beside him. They made an unlovely couple.

All around the deck the crewmembers were blinking and yawning and falling asleep where they stood. Only the three prisoners remained awake.

"We are aware of what he is doing," Jalwar explained, "and in any case the magic is not directed at us."

"That's good, guv'nor." Mudge had to work to stifle a yawn, blinked in surprise. "Strong stuff 'e's workin'."

By the time Jon-Tom sang the final strains of "Peaceful Easy Feeling," the pirate ship was sailing aimlessly. Its bloodthirsty crew lay snoring soundly on the deck, in the hold below, and even up in the rigging. He took a step toward Corroboc and ran his eyes over the captain's attire without finding what he was hunting for. Then he joined his friends.

"Did any of you see where he put his keyring?"

"No, mate," Mudge whispered, "but we'd best find 'em fast."

Jon-Tom started for the door leading to the captain's cabin, then hesitated uncertainly. Once inside, where would he look? There might be a sealed chest, many drawers, a hidden place beneath a nest or mattress, and the keyring might not even be kept in the cabin. Maybe Sasheem had charge of the keys, or maybe one of the other ship's officers.

He couldn't go looking for them and still sing the sleep spell. Already some of the somnolent crew were beginning to stir impatiently. And he didn't have the slightest idea how long the spellsong would remain in effect.

"Do somethin', mate!" Mudge was tugging uselessly on his own ankle chains.

"Where should I look for the keys? They're not on the captain." Suddenly words in his mind, suggestive of something once remembered. Not suggestions of a place to hunt for keys, but snatches of a song.

A song about steel cat eyes and felines triumphant. About "The Mouse Patrol That Never Sleeps," a lethal little bloodthirsty ditty about an ever-watchful carnivorous kitty. Or so he'd once described it to a friend.

He sang it now, wishing Ian Anderson were about to accompany him on the flute, the words pouring rapidly from his lips as he tried to concentrate on the tune while keeping a worried eye on the comatose crew.

The section of anchor chain that had been used to bind Roseroar suddenly cracked and fell away. She looked in amazement at the broken links, then up at Jon-Tom. Wordlessly, she went to work on the much thinner chains restraining her companions. Mudge and Jalwar were freed quickly as immense biceps strained. They vanished below-decks as she worked on Jon-Tom's bindings. By the time she'd finished freeing him, the otter and ferret had reappeared. Mudge's longbow was slung over his shoulder and his face was almost hidden by the burden of the tigress's armor. Jalwar dragged her heavy swords behind him, panting hard.

They turned and raced for the tow rope attached to the *John B.* Only Jon-Tom lingered.

"Come on," Roseroar called to him. "What ah yo waitin' fo?"

He whispered urgently back to her. "The girl! I promised."

"She don't care what yo do. She'll only be trouble."

"Sorry, Roseroar." He turned and rushed for the nearest open hatch.

"Damn," the tigress growled. She pushed past him, vanished below. While he waited he sang, but the spellsong was beginning to surrender its potency. Several sailors rolled over in their sleep, snuffling uneasily.

Then a vast white-and-black shape was pushing past him, the limp naked form of Folly bouncing lightly on one shoulder like a hunting trophy. Jon-Tom's heart stopped for a second, until he saw that her condition was no different from that of the rest of the ship's complement. His spellsinging had put Folly to sleep also.

"Satisfied?" Roseroar snarled.

"Quite." He muffled a grin as he raced her to the stern.

Mudge and Jalwar were just boarding the sloop, Mudge having negotiated the short swim with ease, while Jalwar displayed typical ferret agility by walking the swaying tow rope all the way down to the boat. Roseroar was about to step over the side when she saw Jon-Tom hesitate for the second time.

"*Now* what's the mattah?"

"I've done a lot of running, Roseroar, and I'm a pretty good swimmer, but the sea's rough and my shoulders are so sore from pushing that damn scrub brush that I'm not sure if I can make it. You go on. I'll try and catch up. When you cast off the line you can swing her 'round and pick me out of the water."

She shook her head. "Ah declah, ah nevah heard anyone, not even a human, talk so damn much. Grab hold." She turned her back to him.

Deciding this wasn't the time to salvage whatever remained of his already bruised male ego, he put both arms around her neck, using one to help balance Folly. Roseroar ignored her double burden as she went hand over hand down the towrope until all of them were standing safe on the deck of the *John B.*

"Cast off!" Jon-Tom shouted at Mudge as he ran for the stern. "I'll take the wheel. Roseroar, you run the sails up."

"With pleasure." She dumped Folly's unconscious form onto the deck. Jon-Tom winced as it hit, decided that one more black and blue mark wouldn't show up against the background of bruises that covered the girl's entire body.

Roseroar worked two winches at once while Mudge hacked away

with his short sword at the thick hauser linking them to the pirate ship. In seconds the sloop swung clear. Her sails climbed the mast, caught the wind. Jon-Tom turned her as confused shouts and cries of outrage began to sound from the deck of the larger vessel.

"Not a moment too soon." Jalwar spoke admiringly from his position atop the center cabin. "You have the gift, it is certain."

Jon-Tom shrugged off the compliment and concentrated on catching as much wind as possible. "I didn't study for it and I didn't plan on it. It's just a lucky combination of my musical training and something I've picked up in this world."

"Nonetheless, it cannot be denied. You have the gift."

For an instant it was as if the years had left the ferret and a different being entirely was standing next to the mainmast looking down at Jon-Tom. He blinked once, but when he looked again it was just the same Jalwar, aged and stooped and tired. The ferret turned away and stumbled toward the bow to see if he could help Mudge or Roseroar.

The tigress had the rigging well in hand, and at Jon-Tom's direction, Mudge was breaking out the sloop's spinnaker. Behind them, furious faces lined the port side of the pirate ship. Rude gestures and and bloodthirsty curses filled the air. Above all sounded a thunderous cackling from Corroboc. The faces fled the railing, to reappear elsewhere on the ship as the crew swarmed up the masts. Oars began to dip as dull-eyed galley slaves took up the cue provided by whip and drum. The big ship began to come about.

But this time the sloop was sailing with the wind to port. The square-rigged pirate craft could not tack as well as the modern, fore-rigged sloop, nor could it overtake them on oar power. Still, with the galley slaves driven to collapse, it looked for a moment as if Corroboc might still close the distance between vessels. Then Mudge finally puzzled out the rigging that lifted the spinnaker. The racing sail ballooned to its full extent, filled with wind, and the sloop fairly leaped away from its pursuers.

"We made it, we're away!" Jon-Tom shouted gleefully. Mudge joined him in the stern. The otter balanced precariously on the bobbing aft end railing, turned his back to the pirate ship, and pulled down his pants. Bending over, he made wonderfully insulting faces between his legs. The pirates responded with blood-chilling promises of what they'd do if they caught the sloop, but their words, like their ship, were rapidly falling astern.

"Yes, we made it." Jalwar glanced speculatively up at the billowing sails. "If the wind holds."

As soon as his audience had dropped out of sight, Mudge ceased his contortions and jumped to the deck, buttoning his shorts.

"We'll make it all right, guv'nor." He was smiling broadly as he gave Jon-Tom a friendly whack on the back. "Bake me for a brick, mate, but you sure 'ad me fooled! 'Ere I was expectin' you to conjure up somethin' like a ten-foot-tall demon to demolish them bastards, and instead you slickered me as well as them."

"I knew that if I tried anything overt, Corroboc would have me riding a pike before the day was out." Jon-Tom adjusted their heading.

"Aye, that 'e would. Crikey but that were a neat slip o' thought, puttin' 'em all gentle to beddy-bye like you did, and then freein' up the monster missus there." He nodded in Roseroar's direction.

"Actually I'd intended to go looking for the key," Jon-Tom told him, trying to hide his embarrassment. "When I realized I didn't have the slightest idea where Corroboc's keyring was hidden I knew the only chance we had left was to free Roseroar."

The tigress stepped down from the mast to join them, staring back over the stern. "Ah only wish ah'd had a few minutes to mahself on that boat." Her eyes narrowed and she growled low enough to chill the blood of her companions. "That fust mate, fo example. Wouldn't he have been surprised when he'd woke up without his—"

"Roseroar," Jon-Tom chided her, "that's no way for a lady to talk."

She showed sharp teeth, huge fangs. "That depends on the lady, don't it, Jon-Tom?" Suddenly she pushed past him, frowning as she squinted into the distance.

"What's wrong?" he asked, turned to look aft.

She spoke evenly, unafraid, and ready.

"Looks like we ain't finished with ol' Corroboc yet."

IX

"Get below, Jalwar," Jon-Tom told the ferret. "You'll be of no use to us on deck."

"I must disobey, sir." The oldster had picked up a long fishing gaff and was hefting it firmly. "I am not going back onto that floating purgatory. I'd rather die here."

Jon-Tom nodded, held his staff ready in front of him. In planning and executing their subtle flight from the pirate ship he'd forgotten one thing. Forgotten it because he'd been in this strange world so long he'd come to think of it as normal. So when he'd planned their escape he hadn't considered that they might have to deal with the fact that Corroboc and several of his crew could fly.

There were only six of them. The captain must have threatened all of them with dismemberment to force so small a group to make the attack. Behind the parrot flew a couple of ravens, a hawk, and a small falcon. They were armed with thin spears and light swords.

Jon-Tom set the sloop on automatic pilot, which left him free to join the fight. Jalwar thought the flashing red light of this new magic fascinating.

The fliers were fast and agile. Corroboc in particular might be short an eye and a leg, but there was nothing wrong with his wings. He dove and twisted as he thrust, keeping just out of range of his former prisoner's weapons. Nevertheless, it soon became clear that the pirates were overmatched.

Corroboc's strategy was good. It called for his crew to stay just beyond sword range while striking with their needlelike spears. It might even have worked except for the one joker in the sloop's deck. With his longbow, Mudge gleefully picked off first the falcon and then wounded one of the ravens.

This forced the attackers to close with their quarry, and their agility couldn't compensate for their relatively small size. One of Roseroar's spinning swords sliced the wounded raven in half. Then another of Mudge's arrows pierced the hawk's thin armor. When he saw that he couldn't hope to win either at long range or in close, Corroboc ordered a retreat.

"Have a care for your gullets, scum!" the parrot shouted at them as he danced angrily in the air just out of arrow range. "I swear your fate be sealed! The oceans, nay, the whole world be not big enough to hide you from me. Wherever you run to old Corroboc will find you, and when he do, you'll wish you'd never been borned!"

"Blow it out your arse, mate!" Mudge followed this with a long string of insulting comments on the captain's dubious ancestry. Roseroar listened with distaste.

"Such uncouthness! Ah do declah, it makes me queasy all ovah. Ah do so long fo the refined conversation of civilized company."

The otter overheard and cast a dignified eye back at her. "Cor! I'll 'ave you know, me elephantine kitten, that me language is as fucking refined as anyone's!"

"Yes," she agreed sweetly. "Ah surely don't know how ah could have thought otherwise."

Jon-Tom stepped between them. "What are you two arguing about this time? We won, and we're safely on course again."

A shaky, no longer cocky voice came from the gangway. "What . . . what did we win? Who won?"

Jon-Tom remembered Folly. "Take the wheel, Roseroar."

"Jon-Tom, if'n yo want mah opinion, ah think—!"

He disengaged the autopilot. The boat heeled sharply to port, and Roseroar was forced to grab the wheel to keep it from spinning wildly.

Jon-Tom searched the gangway, finally discovered Folly huddled far back in a lower bunk. Within the sloop's clean, quiet confines she looked suddenly fragile. The iron collar was an ugly dark stain around her pale neck.

He studied it thoughtfully. The sloop was well stocked. If he searched, he was certain he could find a hacksaw or something with which to cut the metal.

"Relax, calm yourself." He spoke gently, soothingly. "You're free.

Just as I promised. Well, not completely free," he corrected himself, smiling encouragingly. "You're still stuck with us. But you can forget about Corroboc. You'll never have to worry about him again. I spellsang them to sleep. You too. While they all slept, we escaped."

Her reply was halting. "Then . . . you are a wizard. And I doubted you."

"Forget it. Sometimes I doubt it myself." She was swaying on the bunk and he was suddenly concerned. "Hey, you don't look so good."

"I'm so tired. . . ." She put her hand to her forehead and fell over into his arms. He was acutely aware of her nakedness. Not to mention her smell. Corroboc's ship was no paragon of good hygiene. Folly likely hadn't bathed since she'd been taken captive.

He slipped a supportive arm around her back. "Come with me." He helped her stumble toward the ship's head. "We'll let you get cleaned up. Then we'll find some way to get that chunk of iron off you. While you're showering I'll see if I can find something for you to wear. There must be clothes in one of the ship's storage lockers."

"I thank you for your kindness, sir."

He smiled again. "That's better. Just call me Jon-Tom." She nodded, leaning against him. For a minute he thought she was going to break down in his arms. She didn't. Not then, and not later. The first thing she'd lost on Corroboc's ship was the ability to cry.

While she washed, he searched the ship's cabinets. One contained familiar clothing. Familiar to him, but not to any of his companions. He made a few selections and left them outside the shower, along with a hacksaw and a file.

He'd expected to see an improvement, but he was still shocked when she reappeared on deck later that afternoon.

She'd removed the iron collar. Her hair was combed out and pulled back behind her. She stood there and looked down at herself uneasily.

"I must look passing strange in these peculiar garments."

"You'll get no argument on that from me, luv." The flabbergasted Mudge moved closer to inspect the odd attire. "Strange sort o' material." He ran a paw over one leg, reached higher. " 'Ere too."

"That's not material," she said angrily, knocking his questing fingers away.

Mudge grinned as he dodged. "Fine-feelin' material to me, luv."

"You try that again, water rat, and I'll . . ."

Jon-Tom ignored them. The argument wasn't serious. Mudge was being his usual obnoxious self, and he thought Folly realized it. Besides which he was busy enough trying to sort out his own jumbled feelings.

Folly was gorgeous. There was no other word for it. Young, but beautiful, standing there on the deck in old Levi's and a worn sweat-shirt that had SLOOP JOHN B. printed across the back. She looked so achingly normal, so much like any girl he might encounter on the beach back home, that for a moment he was afraid he would be the one to cry.

Only the fading but still visible bruises on her face and the ring the collar had left around her neck reminded him of where he'd found her. He would have to hunt for the sloop's first-aid kit. Or maybe he could think of a good healing song, something more effective here than bandages and ointments.

Roseroar gave the new arrival a cursory once-over and snorted. "Skinny little thing. Yo humans . . ." She turned her gaze to the stars that were coming out. Jalwar was already asleep somewhere below, the poor old ferret exhausted by the strenuous events of the past few days. The horizon astern was clear, the pirate ship having dropped out of sight long ago. The wind off the waves still blew them steadily toward Snarken, a goal temporarily lost and now within reach again.

Snarken itself proved easy to locate. As soon as they sailed within fifty miles of the city there was a perceptible increase in the volume of surface traffic around the sloop. All they had to do was hail a couple of merchant ships bound for the same destination and follow them in.

A long range of hills that rolled down to the sea was split by a wide but crowded inlet. Once through they found themselves in a spacious bay ringed by lush green slopes that climbed several hundred feet above the harbor. Still higher land was visible off in the distance.

Wharves and docks crowded together on the far side of the bay. These were home to dozens of vessels that docked here from lands known and alien. Snarken was the principal port on the Glittergeist's southwestern shore.

Jon-Tom steered them through the merchantmen, in search of an empty dock. Many of the wharves were constructed of stone. The rocks were smooth and rounded, evidence that they had been carried down to the beach by glaciers some time far in the past. The stones were cemented tightly together and topped with planks.

They finally located an open slip. Mudge dickered with the dockmaster until a fee was settled on. This brought up the matter of their Malderpot-induced impecuniousness. A solution was found in the form of several stainless steel hammers taken from the sloop's toolbox. These the avaricious dockmaster eagerly accepted in payment.

"What do you think, Mudge?" Jon-Tom asked the otter as they walked up the pier. "Will he leave the ship alone?"

"An 'onest bloke's easy enough to spot, bein' a rare sort o' bird. She'll be safe in our absence. For one thing, the greedy bugger's terrified of 'er."

Jon-Tom nodded, paused as they stepped off the pier onto the cobblestone avenue that fronted the harbor. Lizard-drawn wagons piled high with goods clanked and rumbled all around them. Strange accents and aromas filled the air.

"That bit o' business do bring one problem to mind, mate."

"What's that, Mudge?"

"Wot are we goin' to do for money? We can't keep tradin' away ship's tools."

Jon-Tom rubbed his chin thoughtfully. "Right you are. We're going to have to buy supplies for the trek to Crancularn, too. We're going to need a lot."

"I'll say!" said Folly impatiently. "I need some real clothes. I can't walk around in this silly otherworldly stuff. People will laugh at me. Besides"—she ran her hands over the too-tight seat of her jeans—"it binds me most strangely."

Mudge stepped toward her. " 'Ere now, luv, let me 'ave a looksee. Might be we could loosen this 'ere. . . ."

She jumped away from his outstretched fingers. "Keep your hands to yourself, water rat, or you're liable to lose them."

Mudge pursed his lips hurtfully, turned to Jon-Tom. "Now, 'ere's an idea, mate. Why don't we sell 'er? That were probably the best idea that ever occurred to that rancid bag o' feathers Corroboc. Now that she's cleaned up 'alfway decent, she'd likely bring a nice bit o' change. It would solve two of our problems at once, wot?"

Despite his speed, the otter barely succeeded in ducking under Jon-Tom's swing. The chase shifted to a cluster of big wooden barrels, but Jon-Tom was unable to run the tireless otter down. He wore him out pretty good, though.

"Take it easy, mate." Both man and otter fought to catch their breath. Mudge looked out from behind a barrel. "Let's not kill each other over it. It were just a thought."

"Okay. But let's not have any more idiotic talk about selling Folly or anyone else."

The object of this exhausted discussion gazed curiously up at her rescuer. "Why don't you sell me? I'm nothing to you. I'm nothing to anyone except myself. Don't think I'm being ungrateful. I wouldn't have lived another month on that ship. I want to help you. I can't think of any other way to repay you for your kindness." She threw a warning glance the otter's way. Wisely, Mudge said nothing.

"All I have, though, is myself. If you need money so badly, selling me should solve your problem. I'm worth something." She turned away, unable to meet his eyes. "Even after the way I've been used."

He tried hard not to be angry with her. "Where I come from, Folly, we don't sell people."

"You don't?" She looked genuinely puzzled. "Then what do you do with people who have nothing else to do?"

"We put 'em on welfare, social security."

She shook her head. "Those words mean nothing to me."

He tried to explain. "We see to it that everyone is guaranteed some sort of minimum income, some kind of sustenance."

"Even if they're no good at anything?"

"Even if they're no good at anything."

"That doesn't seem very efficient."

"Maybe it's not efficient, but it's human."

"Brock's blocks, now there you 'ave it, luv. That explains it all. Sounds like the sort o' bizarre scheme a bunch o' 'umans would dream up."

"Nobody gets sold," Jon-Tom announced with finality.

"Right then, mate. Wot do you propose we do for funds?" He indicated the rows of buildings lining the harborfront. "We need food and a place to sleep and supplies."

Jon-Tom glanced up at the heretofore silent Roseroar. "You wouldn't sell her, would you?"

The tigress turned away. "It ain't fo me to say." She sniffed toward the girl. "Perhaps she's just tryin' to tell yo she wants to go her own way."

Jon-Tom posed the question. "Is that true, Folly?"

"No. I have no place to go, but I don't want to cause trouble or be in the way, and I do want to help."

"Sensibly put," said Mudge brightly. "If you'll allow me, mate, I'll begin searchin' out the likely markets, and we can—"

"Wait a minute." Jon-Tom was nodding to himself. "We can sell the sloop."

"The magic boat?" Jalwar looked doubtful. "Is that wise?"

"Why not? From what Clothahump told me, Crancularn lies overland from Snarken. We've no further need for a boat, magic or not. As for returning home, I hope to be able to pay our way. I'm tired of sailing. I'd like to be a passenger for a while." He put a hand on Mudge's shoulder.

"You saw the way the wharfmaster jumped at the chance to get those two hammers. Think what some rich local would pay for the whole boat. There's nothing like it anywhere around here."

"I'd rather sell the girl," he murmured, "but the boat would fetch more. You're right about that, guv. I'm no yacht broker, but I'll do me best to strike us the best bargain obtainable."

"Mudge, with you doing the dealing, I know we'll come out well."

The otter concluded a sale that very afternoon. Payment was made in gold. They left behind a delighted trader in ships and a wharfmaster greedily counting out his commission. Jon-Tom had no regrets. He'd obtained the sloop for a song.

By nightfall they were established in a clean, moderately priced harborfront inn.

"Wot now, mate?" Mudge dug into his dinner and talked around mouthfuls of food. Jalwar displayed refined table manners, while Roseroar ate with precision and unexpected delicacy. Folly gobbled down everything set before her and still finished well ahead of the others. Confident she could take care of herself, Jon-Tom parceled out a pocketful of coin and sent her off in search of attire more suited to her new surroundings.

"We need to find out which way Crancularn lies," he told the otter as he sipped at his own tankard, "acquire sufficient supplies, and be on our way. Clothahump is waiting on us, and much as I'd like to, we can't linger here."

"Ah'm ready fo some clean countryside," agreed Roseroar. "Ah've had enough o' the ocean to last me fo a while."

"You're bound and determined to see this insanity through to the bitter end, aren't you, mate?"

"You know that I am, Mudge. I gave my word."

"I was afraid you'd say somethin' like that." He sighed, wiped gravy from his lips. "Wait 'ere."

The otter vanished into the main dining room of the inn, returned moments later. He was not alone. With him was a finely coiffed orangutan. This individual was dressed in old but well-cared-for clothing. Lace ruffles billowed from collar and sleeves. His orange beard was trimmed short and he puffed on a long, curved pipe. One earring of silver and garnet dangled from his left ear.

"So you weesh to traveel eenland?" There was an odd lilt to his voice that reminded Jon-Tom of the other orang he'd met, the venerable Doctor Nilanthos of Lynchbany. That reminded him of the mugging victims the good doctor had worked on, and of the mugger, the flame-haired Talea. He forced his thoughts back to the present. Talea was far away.

"That's right. We need a certain medicine."

The primate nodded once. "Weel, you'll find no better place to seek eet than here een Snarken. Eet's the beegest city on the western shore of the Gleetergeist, and eef what you seek ees not to be found here, eet ees not to be found anywhere."

"You see, lad," said Mudge hopefully. "Wot did I tell you? Might as well start lookin' for 'is sorcerership's fix right 'ere."

"Sorry, Mudge."

"C'mon, mate. Couldn't we at least try a local chemist's shop?"

"What ees thee problem, stranger?" asked the orang. The aroma drifting from the bowl at the end of the thin pipe was fragrant and powerful. Jon-Tom suspected it contained more than merely tobacco. Evidently the orang noticed Jon-Tom's interest, because he turned the pipe about. "Care for a heet?"

Jon-Tom forced himself to decline. "Thanks, but not until we get this business straightened out."

"Hey guv, 'ow about me?" Mudge eyed the pipe hungrily.

"You were not offered," said the orang imperturbably.

"The medicine we seek," Jon-Tom said hastily, before Mudge could comment, "is available only from a certain shop. In the town of Crancularn."

The orang started ever so slightly, puffed furiously on his pipe. "Crancularn, ai?"

"In the Shop of the Aether and Neither."

"Weel now." The orang banged his pipe on the side of the table, knocking out the dottle while making certain not to stain his silk-and-satin attire. "I have neever been to Crancularn. But I have heard rumor of theese shop you seek. Some say eet ees no more than that, a device of the veelagers of theese town to breeng attention upon themselves. Others, they say more."

"But you've never been there," said Roseroar.

"No. I don't know anyone who's actually been there. But I do know where eet ees supposed to lie."

"Where?" Jon-Tom leaned forward anxiously.

The orang lifted a massive, muscular arm and pointed westward. "There. That way."

Mudge tugged irritably at his whiskers. "Precise directions, why can't any of these helpful blokes we run into ever give us precise directions?"

"Don't worry." The orang smiled. "Eef you want to find eet badly enough, you weel. People know where eet ees.They just don't go there, that's all."

"Why not?"

The orang shrugged, smacked thick lips around the stem of his pipe. "Beats mee, stranger. I've neever had the desire to go and find out. Thee fact that no one else goes there strikes mee as reeson enough not to go. Eef you are bound to go, I weesh you thee best of luck." He stepped back from the table. The main room of the inn's restaurant was jammed with diners now, and his table lay on the other side of the floor. He reached up, grabbed the nearest chandelier, and made his way across the ceiling gracefully, without disturbing any of the other customers.

"It doesn't make any sense," Jon-Tom was muttering. "If no one knows of any specific danger in Crancularn, why doesn't anyone go there?"

"I could think of several reasons," said Jalwar thoughtfully.

"Can you really, baggy-nose?" said Mudge. "Why don't you enlighten us then, guv'nor?"

"There may be dangers there that remain little known."

"He would have told us anything known," Jon-Tom argued. "No reason to keep it from us. What else, Jalwar?"

"There may be nothing there at all."

"I'll take Clothahump's word that there is. Go on."

The ferret spread his hands. "This shop you speak of so hopefully. It may be less than you wish for. Many such establishments never live up to their reputations."

"We'll find out," Jon-Tom said determinedly, "because no matter what anyone says, we're going there." His expression altered suddenly as he stared past the ferret.

"Wot is it, mate?" asked Mudge, abruptly alert. "Wot do you see?"

"Darkness. Nighttime. It's been night out for a long time. Too long. Folly should have returned by now." He whirled angrily on the otter. "Damn it, Mudge, did you . . . ?"

"Now 'old on a minim, mate." The otter raised both paws defensively. "I said my piece and you said you didn't want to sell 'er. I wouldn't do anythin' like that behind your back."

"If you were offered the right price you'd sell your own grandmother without *her* permission."

"I never knew me grandmum, mate, so I couldn't guess at 'er worth, but I swears on me works that as far as I know the girl's done only wot you said she could do: gone shoppin' for some respectable coverin' for that skinny naked body o' 'ers. Well, not all that skinny."

Jon-Tom had a sudden thought, turned on the largest member of their party. "Roseroar?"

The massive torso shaded the table as the tigress daintily set down half a roast lizard as big as the duar. She picked with maddening slowness at her teeth before replying.

"Ah will pretend ah didn't heah that insult, suh. Ah think it's obvious enough what has happened."

"What's obvious?" He frowned.

"Why, you gave her some gold. As she told yo herself, you owe her nothing and she owes you little, since you turned down her offah to sell herself. It's cleah enough to me that she's gone off to seek her own fortune. We've given her her freedom. She held no love fo us and ah must admit the feelin's mutual."

"She wouldn't think of it like that," Jon-Tom muttered worriedly. "She isn't the type."

Mudge let out a sharp, barking laugh. "Now, wot would you know about 'er type, mate? I didn't know wot 'er 'type' was, and I've forgotten more about women of more species than you'll ever think on."

"She's just not the type, Mudge," Jon-Tom insisted. "This city's as new to her as it is to us, and we're the only friends or security she's got."

"A type like that," said Roseroar disdainfully, "can find friends wherevah she goes."

"She just wouldn't run off like that, without saying anything. Maybe you're right, Mudge. Maybe she does want to strike off on her own, but she'd have told us first."

"Wot for?" wondered Mudge sarcastically. "To spare you from worryin' about 'er? Maybe she don't like long good-byes. Not that it matters. You've seen 'ow big this town is. Wot can we do about it?"

"Wait until morning," Jon-Tom said decisively. "We can't do much without sleep, and it'll be good to sleep on something that doesn't roll and pitch."

"Me sentiments exactly, mate."

"In the morning we'll make some inquiries. You're good at making inquiries, Mudge. Like finding that orang to tell us the way to Crancularn."

"Cor, some 'elp 'e was." He pointed wildly backward. "That way! 'Ow 'elpful! That may be the most I can find out about the girl. I don't know why you bother, mate. I thought the main thing was gettin' that dope back to Clothy-wothy."

"Check on the girl first. She may be in some kind of trouble. I'll let her go her own way, but I want to make sure that's what she wants. I want her to say it to me."

Mudge looked disgusted. "It's your funeral, mate. Just don't make it mine, too."

They slept soundly. In the morning they began checking the clothing stores in the area. Yes, a girl of that description had been into several of the shops and then had moved on. The trail halted abruptly at the eighth shop. Beyond it, Folly had not been seen.

"Face it, mate, she's gone off on 'er lonesome."

"One last try." Jon-Tom nodded toward the corner, where a pair of uniformed skunks were lounging. Civil patrol, just as in Lynchbany, where their particular anatomical capabilities made them the logical candidates for the police service. It was simple for them to control an angry mob or recalcitrant prisoner through nonviolent means. Jon-Tom would much rather be beaten up.

The cops turned as he approached, taking particular note of the heavily armed Roseroar.

"Trouble, strangers?" one of the police inquired.

"No trouble." Both striped tails relaxed, for which Jon-Tom was grateful. "We're looking for someone. A companion, human female of about mid-to-late adolescence. Attractive, blonde fur. She was shopping in this area last night."

The cops looked at each other. Then the one on the left raised a hand over his head, palm facing the ground. "About so tall?"

"Yes!" Jon-Tom said excitedly.

"Wearing funny sort of clothes, dark blue pants?"

"That's her!" Suddenly he remembered who he was talking to. "What happened to her?"

"Not much, as far as I know. We were just coming on duty." He turned to gesture up a steep street. "Was about four blocks up that way, two to the left. She was out cold when we stumbled over her. Friend of yours, you say?"

Jon-Tom nodded.

"Well, we tried to bring her around and didn't have much luck. It was pretty plain what had happened to her. The pockets of her pants and blouse had been ripped open and she had a lump here," he touched his head near his left ear, "about the size of a lemon."

"Somebody rolled 'er," said Mudge knowledgeably.

"My fault," said Jon-Tom. "I thought she'd be okay." He stared at Mudge.

"Hey, don't be mad at me, mate. I didn't slug 'er."

"She kept saying she could take care of herself."

"I thought 'er mouth was bigger than 'er brain," the otter commented sourly. "Take care o' 'erself, wot? Not by 'alf." He turned to the cop. "Wot 'appened to 'er, then?"

"We relayed it in." He glanced at his partner. "Do you know what headquarters did with her afterwards?" The other skunk shrugged and the first looked thoughtful. "Let me think."

"Hospital," Jon-Tom suggested. "Did they send her to a hospital?"

"Not that bad a bump, stranger. She was half-conscious by the time we got her into the station. Kept moaning about her mother or something. She didn't have a scrap of identification on her, I remember that. Also kept mumbling for someone named—" he fought to recall, "Pompom?"

"Jon-Tom. That's me."

"She couldn't tell us where you were . . . that sock on the head rattled her pretty good, I'd think . . . and the name meant nothing to us. Weird as it was, we thought she was still off her nut. Mid-adolescent, you said?" He nodded. "I thought she looked underage for a human. Now I remember what happened to her. Social Services took her in. Several groups put in a claim and the Friends of the Street won."

"Yeah, that's right," said his partner. "I saw that on the report sheet."

"Who are the Friends of the Street?" Jon-Tom asked.

"Kind of like an orphanage, stranger," the cop explained. He turned and pointed. "They're up on Pulletgut Hill there. Never been there myself. No reason. But that's where she was taken. I expect she'll be okay. From what I hear it's a well-run, sober, clean place."

Mudge put a consoling paw on Jon-Tom's arm. "See, mate? 'Tis all worked out for the best."

"Yes," growled Roseroar. "Let's get on with this quest of yours, Jon-Tom. The girl's in the kind of place best suited to helpin' her."

Jon-Tom listened to all of them, surprised Jalwar by asking for his opinion.

"Since you request the thoughts of a humble servant, I have to say that I agree with your friends. Undoubtedly the young woman is now among those her own age, being cared for by those whose business it is to succor such unfortunates. We should be about our business."

Jon-Tom nodded. "You're probably right, Jalwar." He looked at Mudge and Roseroar. "You're probably all right." He eyed the senior of the two cops. "You're sure this is a decent place?"

"The streets of Snarken are full of homeless youth. We bag 'em all the time. So there are many orphanages. Some are supported by taxes, others are private. If I remember aright, the Friends of the Street are among the private organizations."

"Okay, okay," Jon-Tom grumbled, out-reasoned as well as out-voted.

"So when do we leave, mate?"

"Tomorrow morning, I suppose, if you think you can lay in enough supplies by tonight."

"Cor, can a fish fry? Leave 'er to me, mate. You and the cat-mountain and the old bugger get yourselves back to the inn. Relax and suck in the last o' the sea air. Leave everythin' to ol' Mudge."

Jon-Tom did so, and was rewarded that evening by the sight of not one but two large, comfortable wagons tied up outside the inn. They were piled high with supplies and yoked to two matched horned lizards apiece, the kind of dray animals who could handle smooth roads or rough trails with ease.

"You've done well," Jon-Tom complimented the otter.

Mudge appeared to be undergoing the most indescribable torture as he reached into a pocket and handed over three gold coins. "And 'ere's the change, mate."

Jon-Tom hardly knew what to say. "I didn't think there'd be this much. You're changing, Mudge."

"Please don't say anythin', mate," said the tormented otter. "I'm in pain enough as it is."

"Did you ever think of setting yourself up as a legitimate merchant, Mudge."

"Wot, *me?*" The otter staggered. "Why, I'd lose me self-respect, not to mention me card in the Lynchbany Thieves' Guild! It'd break me poor mother's 'eart, it would."

"Sorry," Jon-Tom murmured. "I won't mention it again."

Roseroar was giving the loads a professional inspection. "Ah take back everything ah said about yo, ottah. Yo've done a fine job o' requisitionin'." She turned to Jon-Tom. "Theah's mo than enough heah to last us fo a journey of many months. He spent the gold well."

Mudge executed a low bow. "Thanks, tall, luscious, and unattainable. Now 'ow about a last decent meal before we're back to eatin' outdoor cooking?" He headed for the inn entrance.

Jon-Tom held back, spoke sheepishly. "Look, I understand how you all feel and I respect your opinions, and you're probably all right as rain and I'm probably wrong. I'll understand if you all want to go in and eat and go to bed, but I'm not tired. I know it doesn't make any sense, but I'm going up to this Friends of the Street place to make a last check on Folly."

Mudge threw up his hands. " 'Umans! Now, wot do you want to go and waste your time with that for, mate? The girl's a closed chapter, she is."

"A closed chapter," Jalwar agreed, "with a happy ending. Leave it be. Why aggravate yourself?"

"I won't aggravate myself. It'll just take a minute." He plucked one string of his duar. "I owe her a farewell song and I want to let her know that we'll probably be coming back this way, in case she wants to see us or anything."

"Pitiful," Mudge mumbled. "Plumb pitiful. Right then, mate, come on. Let's get it over with."

"You don't have to come," Jon-Tom reminded him. "What about your big supper?"

"It'll keep." He took the man's arm and urged him up the street. They climbed the first hill.

"Look at it, mate. The night's as black as the inside of a process-server's 'eart." He stared up the narrow, winding avenue. "You sure we can find this place?"

Jon-Tom nodded. "It's atop a hill. We can always ask directions. We're not helpless."

"No," said a new voice, startling them, "not now you're not."

"Roseroar . . . you're not hungry either?"

"Ah've got a bellyfull of thunder," she shot back, "but ah figured ah'd better come along to make sure you two don't end up in an alley somewheres. Those muggahs may still be working this area."

"We can take care of ourselves, luv," said Mudge.

"Ah'm sure you can, but you can take better care o' yourselves with me around."

Jon-Tom looked past her. She noticed the direction of his gaze.

"Jalwah wanted to come, too, bless his heart, but there's climbing to do and he's more than a little worn out. He'll wait fo us and keep a watch on our supplies."

"Fine," said Jon-Tom, turning and starting to climb again. "We'll be back soon enough."

"Aye, right quick," Mudge agreed.

But they were both wrong.

X

The Friends of the Street occupied a complex of stone-and-mortar buildings atop a seaward-facing hillside. It was located in an area of comfortable individual homes and garden plots instead of the slum Jon-Tom expected.

"Whoever endowed this place," he told his companions as they approached the main entrance, "had money."

"And plenty o' it," Mudge added.

Several long, narrow, two-story structures were linked together by protective walls. Blue tile roofs gleamed in the moonlight. Dim illumination flickered behind a couple of windows, but for the most part the complex was dark. That wasn't surprising. It was late and the occupants should be in bed. Flowery wrought-iron trellises blocked the front doorway, but there was a cord to be pulled. Jon-Tom tugged on it, heard the faint echo of ringing from somewhere inside. Leaves shuffled in tall trees nearby. The thousand bright stars of Snarken electrified the shoreline far below.

The door opened and a curious lady squirrel peeked out at them. She was elderly and clad entirely in black. Black lace decorated the cuffs of her sleeves. Hanging from her gray neck was a single golden medallion on a gold chain. Several letters had been engraved on it, but they were too small for Jon-Tom to make out.

"Yes, what is it?"

"Are you the master of this orphanage?" Jon-Tom asked.

"Me?" She did not smile. "No. What do you wish with the Headmaster?" She was watching Roseroar carefully.

"Just a couple of quick questions." He put on his most ingratiating grin.

"Office hours are from mid-morning to nightfall." She moved to shut the door.

Jon-Tom took a step forward, still wearing his grin. "We have reason to believe that an acquaintance of ours was recently—" he searched for the right word, "enrolled at the orphanage."

"You mean you don't know for certain?"

"No. It would have been within the last day."

"I see. Visiting hours are at nightfall only." Again the attempt to close the door, again Jon-Tom rushed to forestall her.

"Please, ma'am. We have to depart on a long difficult journey tomorrow. I just want a moment to assure myself that your institution is as admirable on the inside as it is from without."

"Well," she murmured uncertainly, "wait here. The Headmaster is at his late-eve devotions. I will ask if he can see you."

"Thanks."

The wait that ensued was long, and after a while he was afraid they'd been given a polite brushoff. He was about to use the bell-pull a second time when she reappeared trailing an elderly man.

As always, Jon-Tom was surprised to see another human in a position of authority, since they didn't seem to be among the more prolific groups here. In Clothahump's world mankind was just one of dozens of intelligent species.

The man was only a few inches shorter than Jon-Tom, which made him unusually tall for a local. With the exception of a radically different cut, his attire was identical with that of the much smaller squirrel: all black with lace cuffs and the same golden medallion. He held his hands clasped in front of his chest. His gray hair was combed neatly back at sides and forehead. A gray goatee protruded from his chin, and he wore thin wire glasses with narrow lenses. To Jon-Tom he resembled a cross between Colonel Sanders and a contrabassoon.

His smile and words both spoke of kindly concern, however. "Greetings. Welcome, strangers, to Friends of the Street." He gestured toward the squirrel. "Ishula tells me you have a friend among our flock?"

"We think so. Her name's Folly."

The Headmaster frowned. "Folly. I don't know that we have anyone staying with us by that . . . oh, yes! The young woman who was brought in the previous evening. She told us her terrible tale of being captured by pirates on the high seas. You are the ones she described as her rescuers, are you not?"

"That's right."

"To think that such awfulness is abroad in the world." The Headmaster shook his head regretfully. "The poor girl has endured more than any intelligent creature should suffer."

Jon-Tom had to admit that so far all of his concerns and fears looked unjustified. Still, he couldn't leave satisfied without at least a fast look at the facilities.

"I know it's late, and it's cold out here. We have to leave on a long trip tomorrow, as I told your assistant. Could we come in for a moment and have a look around? We just want to make sure that Folly's going to be well looked after. We place no claim on her and I'm sure she'll be much better off here than with us."

"Why, certainly, do come in," said the Headmaster. "My name is Chokas, by the way. Ishula, the gate."

The squirrel unlocked the iron grille as Jon-Tom made his own introductions.

"Delighted, ah am sure," said Roseroar as she ducked through the opening.

They found themselves in a long white hallway. Chokas led them down the tiled corridor, chatting effusively and not at all upset by their presence or the lateness of the hour. The squirrel trailed behind, occasionally pausing to dust a bench or vase with her tail.

Jon-Tom made polite responses to the Headmaster's conversation, but he was only paying partial attention. The rest of him searched for indications of subterfuge or concealed maleficence. He was not rewarded.

The corridor and the rooms branching off it were spotless. Decorative plants occupied eaves and niches or hung in planters from the beamed ceiling. There were skylights to admit the warmth of day. Without being asked, Chokas volunteered a further tour of the Friends of the Street. Beginning to relax, Jon-Tom accepted.

Padded benches paralleled clean tables in the dining room, and the kitchen was as shiny as the hallway.

"We pride ourselves on our hygiene here," the Headmaster informed him.

The larder was filled to overflowing with foodstuffs of every kind, suitable for sustaining the energetic offspring of many races. Beyond, the reason for the interlocking architecture became apparent. It circled to enclose a broad courtyard. Play areas were marked out beneath several bubbling fountains, and tall trees shaded the grounds.

Roseroar bent to whisper to him. "Come, haven't y'all seen enough? The girl will be well cared fo heah."

"I have to admit it's not the kind of place I expected," he confessed. "Hell, I'd be half-tempted to move in myself." He raised his voice as he spoke to the Headmaster. "Terrific-looking place you run here, Chokas."

The man nodded his thanks. "We are privileged to serve as guardians and protectors of the homeless and those who have lost their way at a tender age. We take our responsibilities seriously."

"What sort o' schooling do they get?" Roseroar asked.

"Histories, geographies, mathematics, training in the social verities, domestic subjects such as cooking and sewing. Physical education. Instruction in discipline and courtesy. A well-rounded curriculum, we believe."

"I've seen enough." Jon-Tom glanced toward the second-floor dormitories. "So long, Folly. It was interesting knowing you. Have a full and happy life and maybe we'll meet again someday." He turned back toward the entry hall. "Thanks again for the tour, Chokas."

"My pleasure. Please come visit us anytime, sir. The Friends of the Street encourages visitation."

The front door closed quietly behind them, leaving the trio standing on the cobblestone avenue outside. Roseroar started down the hill.

"That's done. Now we can get down to mo important business."

"I admit she's better off here than with us," Jon-Tom said. "Certainly it's a more stable environment than any alternative we could come up with."

"Hang on a minim, you two." Jon-Tom and Roseroar turned, to see Mudge inspecting the entrance.

"What's the matter, Mudge?" Come to think of it, Jon-Tom hadn't heard a single comment from the otter during the tour. "I'd think that you, of any of us, would be anxious to get back to the inn."

"That I am, mate."

"Come on, then, ottah," said Roseroar impatiently. "Don't tell me you miss the cub? You liked her no mo than did ah."

"True enough, mistress of massive hindquarters. I thought 'er obstinate, ignorant, and nothin' but trouble, for all that she went through. Life's tough and I ain't me sister's keeper. But I wouldn't leave a slick, slimy salamander who'd ooze all over me in a place like this."

"You saw something, Mudge?" Jon-Tom moved to stand next to him. "I thought it was neat, clean, and well-equipped."

"Bullocks," snapped the otter. "We saw what they wanted us to see, nothin' more. That Chokas chap's as slick as greased owl shit and I'd trust 'im about as far as I can piss." He turned to face them both. "I don't suppose either o' you sharp-eyed suckers 'appened to note that there are no windows on the first floor anywheres facin' the streets?"

Jon-Tom looked left, then right, and saw that the otter was correct. "So? I'm sure they have their reasons."

"I'll bet they do. Notice also that all the second-story windows are barred?"

"More decorative wrought iron," murmured Jon-Tom, his eyes roving over the upper floors.

"Decorative is it, mate?"

"This is a rough city," said Roseroar. "Orphans are vulnerable. Perhaps the bahs are to keep thieves from breakin' in and stealing youngsters to sell into slavery."

"If that's the case then the 'Friends' of the Street 'ave done a mighty professional job o' protectin' their charges from the outside. Observe that none of these trees overhang any part of any of the buildin's."

That was true. A cleared expanse of street formed an open barrier between the nearest orchard and the outermost structures.

"But what does all of it prove?" Jon-Tom asked the otter.

"Not a bloody thing, mate. But I've been around a bit, and I'm tellin' you that my gut tells me somethin' 'ere ain't right. Me, I'd be curious to 'ave a little chat with one or two o' the occupants without that piranha-faced squirrel o' our charmin' guide Chokas about. I've 'eard descriptions o' orphanages, and this place makes the best o' them look like that dungeon we fled in Malderpotty. That's wot bothers me, mate." He gazed up at the silent walls. "It's *too* sweet."

"I'm not sure I follow you."

"Look, guv. Cubs is dirty. They make filth the way I makes sweat. 'Tis natural. This place is supposed to be full o' cubs and it's as clean as milady's intimates."

Roseroar spoke softly as she studied the barred upper windows. "Ah did think it uncommon neat fo such an establishment. Almost like a doctah's office."

"You too, Roseroar?" Jon-Tom said in surprise.

"Me too what? What the ottah says makes sense. Ain't no secret ah've little love fo the cub, but ah'd sleep easier knowin' she's been properly cared fo."

"If you both feel that way, then we need to talk with her before we go." Jon-Tom started back for the entrance. Mudge held him by an arm.

"Slow there, spellsinger. Ol' Chokas were friendly enough because we didn't ask no awkward questions or try to poke into places 'e didn't want us to see. If 'e'd wanted us to meet any o' 'is kids 'e'd 'ave brought 'em down to us. I don't think 'e'll be likely to accede to our little request."

"He has a good reason. They're likely to all be asleep. It's late."

"All of 'em?" wondered Mudge. "I doubt it. Wot about those off-spring of the night-lifers? The gophers and the moles?"

"Maybe they have separate quarters so they can be active at night without disturbing the others," Jon-Tom suggested. "If they're nocturnal, they wouldn't need lights in their rooms."

"There'd still be some hint o' activity. Remember, mate, we're talkin' about a bunch o' young cubs."

Jon-Tom chewed his lower lip. "It was awfully quiet in there, wasn't it?"

"Like a tomb, mate. Tell you wot. Why don't you spellsing the lot o' them to sleep the way you did that bunch on the pirate ship?"

"Wouldn't work. On the ship, everyone was within range of the duar and of my voice. Too many walls here."

Mudge nodded. "Right then. My turn to perform a little magic."

"You?"

The otter grinned, his whiskers twitching. "You ain't the only master o' strange arts around 'ere, mate."

They followed him around the side, until they were far from the entrance. As they walked Jon-Tom noted that no other doors were visible in the complex. There was only the single entrance. Still, there might be other doors around the back. And the Friends of the Street were not constrained by, say, the Los Angeles Fire Code.

Mudge halted near a tree that grew closer to the buildings than any of the others.

"Now then, my petite purr-box, I 'ave a little job for you." He pointed up into the tree. "See that branch there? The second one up?" She nodded. "Can you climb up there and then climb out along it?"

She frowned. "What foah? It won't hold mah weight."

"That's precisely the idea, luv."

Jon-Tom immediately divined the otter's intent. "It's no good, Mudge. That branch'll throw you headfirst into the wall. I'll end up with a furry Frisbee on my hands instead of a valuable friend."

"Don't worry about me, guv. I knows wot I'm about. We otter folk are born acrobats. Most o' the time there's nothin' more to it than play, but we can get serious with it if we need too. Let me give 'er a try."

"One try is all you'll get." He swung the duar around until it rested against his chest. "Why don't I try spellsinging you onto the roof?"

Mudge looked unwilling. "That would work fine, wouldn't it, mate? With you standin' 'ere below these barred windows caterwaulin' fit to shiver a bat's ears."

"Ah resent the comparison, watah rat." Roseroar advanced up the tree trunk.

Mudge shrugged. "Don't matter 'ow you describe it. You'd wake the 'ole place."

"I could try singing quietly."

"Aye, and likely catapult . . . sorry again, Roseroar . . . me into the middle o' some far ocean. No offense, mate, but you know well as I that there be times when your spellsingin' don't quite strike the mark. So if it's all the same, I'd rather take me chances with the tree."

"Thanks for the vote of confidence," Jon-Tom muttered. A glance showed Roseroar already crawling carefully out onto the chosen limb. "Go ahead, but I think you're nuts."

"Why, guv, I didn't think me mental condition were a matter o' dispute anymore. An' the proof of it's that I'm standin' 'ere askin' you to let me catapult meself toward a stone wall instead o' lying in a soft bed somewhere back in the Bellwoods."

He moved aside as the thick branch began to bend toward the ground beneath Roseroar. She kept crawling along it until she couldn't advance any more, then swung beneath and continued advancing toward the end of the limb hand-over-hand. Seconds later the leaves were brushing the street.

Mudge nestled himself into a crook between two smaller branches near the end. "Wot's your opinion o' this, luv?"

Roseroar had to use all her weight to hold the branch down. She studied the distant roof speculatively. "A lot to miss and little to land on. Wheah do y'all wish the remains sent?"

"Two optimists I'm blessed with," the otter mumbled. "I thank the both o' you for your encouragin' words." He patted the wood behind him. "Wortyle wood. I thought she'd bend without breakin'. They make ship's ribs out o' this stuff." He glanced back at Roseroar. "Any time you're ready, lass."

"Yoah sure about this?"

"No, I'm not, but I ain't doin' no good sittin' 'ere on me arse talkin' about it."

"That ain't the part that's goin' to get smashed," she said as she stepped away from the quivering branch.

The wortyle wood whipped upward so fast the air vibrated in its wake. Mudge was thrown with tremendous force into the night sky. The otter did a single flip and described an elegant arc as he began to descend.

As it developed, his judgment was only slightly off. He didn't reach the roof, but neither did he smash into the side of the building. He fell only a little short.

At first it looked as if he was going to land hard on the cobblestones, but at the last instant he grabbed with his right hand. Short, powerful muscles broke his fall as his fingers locked onto the iron grating barring one window. He hung there for a long moment, catching his breath. Then he reached up with the other hand and pulled himself on to the iron.

His companions stood beneath the window, staring up at him. "Can you get in?" Jon-Tom asked softly.

Mudge responded with a snort of contempt, fiddled with the grate. Seconds later a metallic click reached Jon-Tom and Roseroar.

"He's very clevah, yo friend."

"He's had a lot of experience with locks," Jon-Tom informed her dryly. Another click from above signified the opening of the window.

They waited below, feeling exposed standing there on the otherwise empty, moonlit street. Minutes passed. A pink rope snaked down from the open window. Jon-Tom reached up to take hold of the chain of knotted bedsheets.

"They'll support me," he told Roseroar. "I don't think they'll hold you."

"Nevah mind. Y'all are just goin' to spend a few minutes talkin' to the girl-cub anyways." She nodded toward the nearby grove. "Ah'll wait foah y'all up in the same tree. Ain't nobody goin' to spot me up theah. If I see anyone comin' this way and it looks tricky, I'll whistle y'all a warnin'."

As she stood there in the pale light Jon-Tom was conscious of her strength and power, but her words struck him as odd. "I didn't know tigers could whistle."

"Well, ah'll let ya'all know somehow." She turned and loped toward the trees.

Jon-Tom braced his feet against the wall and pulled himself up. Mudge was waiting to help him inside.

Jon-Tom found himself standing in near blackness. "Where are we?" he whispered.

"Some sort o' storage closet, mate." Mudge's night vision was several cuts above his friend's."

But as they moved cautiously through the darkness Jon-Tom's eyes adjusted to the weak illumination, and he was able to make out buckets, pails, piles of dust rags, curry combs, and other cleaning supplies. Mudge stopped at the door and tried the handle.

"Locked from the other side." The otter hunted through the darkness, came back holding something that looked like an awl. He inserted it into the door lock and jiggled delicately. Though Jon-Tom heard nothing, the otter was apparently satisfied by some sound. He put the awl aside and pushed.

The door opened silently. Mudge peered into a dark dormitory. Against opposite walls stood beds, cots, mats, and diverse sleeping stations for children of different species. On the far wall windows looked down into the courtyard with the trees and fountains. Unlike those on the outside, these were not barred.

They tiptoed out of the closet and found themselves walking between rows of silent youngsters. All of them appeared to be neatly groomed and squeaky clean. There wasn't a hair or patch of fur out of place. The dormitory itself was comfortably cool and as spotless as the dining room and entry hall had been.

"I don't see any indications of abuse here," Jon-Tom whispered as they went from bed to bed.

Mudge was shaking his head doubtfully. "Too neat, mate. Too perfect." They reached the end of the long chamber without finding Folly. The door at the end was also locked from the outside. "And another thing, mate. Too many locks 'ere." He used the tool to pick it.

Beyond was a short hall. A stairway led downward off the left. Mudge picked the lock on the door across the hall and they entered a second dorm.

Grunts and whistles and snores covered their footsteps as they commenced an inspection of the new group of beds. Halfway down the line they found Folly. Jon-Tom shook her gently awake. She rolled over, woke up.

She was gasping with fright. There was no mistaking the look in her eyes, the tenseness of her body, the expression on her face. It reminded Jon-Tom a little of the look she'd displayed on the pirate ship whenever Corroboc appeared.

As soon as she recognized him she threw her arms around him and started sobbing.

"Jon-Tom, Jon-Tom. And Mudge too. I thought you'd forgotten me. I thought you'd go off and leave me here!"

"I didn't forget you, Folly." Acutely conscious of her curves beneath the thin black nightdress, he gently pushed her away. "What's wrong?"

She looked around wildly. "You've got to get me out of here! Quickly, before the night patrol shows up."

"Night patrol? You mean, someone looks in on you?"

"No, I mean *patrol.* No one's allowed out of bed after dark. If they catch you, they beat you. Bad. Not like Corroboc, but bad enough."

"But we were here earlier, and we didn't see any implications of—"

"Don't be a fool, mate," said Mudge tightly. "D'you think these servants o' the downtrodden would be stupid enough to hit their charges where it'd show?"

"No, I guess not. They beat you here?"

Folly spat on the floor. "Only out of love, of course. Every time they beat you it's out of love. They beat you if you don't learn your lessons, they beat you if you don't hold your knife right at mealtime, they beat you for not saying yes sir and no ma'am, and sometimes I think they beat you for the fun of it, to remind you how bad the world outside is." Her nails dug into his arms.

"You've got to get me out of here, Jon-Tom!" How much truth there was to her accusations, he couldn't tell, but the desperation in her voice was genuine enough.

Mudge kept a paw on the hilt of his short sword. "Let's make up our feeble minds, mate. Some o' these cubs are startin' to move around."

"I'm awake." Jon-Tom turned to the bed next to Folly's. It was occupied by a young margay. She sat up rubbing at her eyes. She wore the same black nightdress.

"Is what Folly says true?" he asked the young cat.

"Who . . . who are you?" asked the now wide-awake youngster. Folly hastened to reassure her.

"It's okay. They're friends of mine."

"Who're you?" Jon-Tom countered.

"My name's Myealn." To his surprise she began to sniffle. He'd never seen a feline cry before. "Pu-please, sir, can you help me get away from this place, too?"

Then he was being assailed by a volley of anxious whispers.

"Me too, sir . . . and me . . . me also . . . !"

The whole dorm was awake and crowding around Folly's bed, pawing at the adults, pleading in a dozen dialects for help. Tails twitched nervously from the backsides of dozens of nightclothes, all black.

"I don't understand," he muttered. "This looks like such a nice place. But it's not right if they beat you all the time."

"That's not all they do," said Folly. "Haven't you noticed how perfect this place is?"

"You mean, clean?"

She shook her head. "It's not just clean. It's sterile. Woe unto any of us caught with a dirt smudge or piece of lint on us. We're supposed to be perfect at mealtime, perfect at study, and perfect at devotions, so we can be perfect citizens when we're old enough to be turned out on the street again.

"A bunch of the supervisors here were raised here and this is the only home they know. They're the worst. We wear only black because a perfect person can't have any distractions and color is distracting. There're no distractions of any kind. No dancing, no singing, no merriment at all. Maybe all the jokes the pirates told were brutal and crude, but at least they had a sense of humor. There's no humor in this place."

Myealn had slipped out of her bed. Now she leaned close to Folly. "The other thing," she whispered urgently. "Tell them about the other thing."

"I was getting to that." Nervously, Folly glanced at the doorway at the far end of the room. "Since a perfect person doesn't need silly things like merriment and pleasure, one of the first things they do here is make sure you're made perfect in that regard."

Mudge frowned. "Want to explain that one, luv?"

"I mean, they see to it that no pleasurable diversions of any kind remain to divert you from the task of becoming perfect." The otter gaped at her, then waved to take in the shuffling crowd of anxious, black-clad youngsters.

"Wot a bloody 'ouse o' devils we stumbled into! You mean every one o' these . . . ?"

Folly nodded vigorously. "Most of them, yes. The males are neutered and the females spayed. To preserve their perfection by preventing any sensual distractions. They're going to operate on me tomorrow."

"Against your will?" Jon-Tom struggled to come to grips with this new, coldly clinical horror.

"What could we do?" Myealn sobbed softly. "Who would object on our behalf? We're all orphans, none of us even have guardians. And the Friends of the Street have a wonderful reputation with the people who run the city government because there's never any trouble here."

"And the Friends of the Street put model citizens back into the population," Folly added. "People who never give the city any trouble.

Jon-Tom was so furious he was shaking. "If you got out of this place," he asked the trembling, altered youngsters, "where would you go?"

Again a flurry of desperate pleas. "Anywhere . . anyplace . . . the waterfront, I want to be a sailor . . I can sew, be a seamstress . . . I'm good with paints . . . I want to be . . . !"

He shushed them all. "We'll get you out. Somehow. Mudge, what about the dorm we came through? Can we risk going back that way with all these kids?"

"Fuck the risk, mate." Jon-Tom had never seen the otter so mad. "Not only are we goin' back into the other dorm, we're goin' to break every cub out o' this pit o' abomination. Come on, you lot," he told them. "Quiet-like." Jon-Tom followed behind, making sure no one was left and shepherding them along like a giraffe among a flock of sheep.

The hallway and the stairs were silent. Once in the other dorm those awake went from bed to bed waking their friends and explaining what was happening. When they were through, the center aisle was full of milling, anxious young faces.

Mudge opened the door to the supply closet. At the same time the door at the other end of the dorm burst open. Standing in the opening was the powerful figure of a five-foot-tall adult lynx. Green eyes flashed.

"What's going on in here?" He started in. "By the Eight Levels of Purity, I will have the hide off whoever is responsible!" Then he caught sight of Jon-Tom standing like a pale tower above the heads of the youngsters. "How did you get in here?"

Jon-Tom faced him with a broad, innocent smile. "Just visiting. A little late, I know. Special dispensation from Chokas."

"Just visiting be damned! Where's your pass? These are not visiting times."

Jon-Tom kept smiling as the cubs crowded close around him. "Like I said, friend, it's a special occasion."

The monitor carried a short, ugly black whip which he now drew back threateningly. "You're coming with me to see the Headmaster, whoever you are. I do not know how you got in here, or you either," he added as he espied Mudge, "but you are not leaving without making proper explanation. The rest of you," he roared, "back to your beds!"

The youngsters milled around uncertainly. Many of them were starting to bawl.

" 'Ere now, guv'nor, there's no reason to get upset." Mudge toddled toward him, smiling broadly.

The whip cracked just in front of the otter's nose. The children started to scatter for their beds, whimpering loudly.

"Now, hold on there, friend." Jon-Tom put his ramwood staff in front of his chest. "Let's be careful with that whip, shall we?"

"Cute little gimcrack, snake master," said Mudge, still grinning and walking toward the monitor. The lynx eyed his approach warily.

"That is far enough, trespasser. Take another step toward me and I'll have one of your eyes out."

Mudge halted, threw up both hands and gaped at the lynx in mock horror. "Wot, and mar me perfection? Crikey, why would you want to muss up me perfect self?" He started to turn, abruptly leaped at the monitor.

The lynx wasn't slow, but Mudge was a brown blur in the dim light. The whip snapped down and cut across the back of the otter's neck. Mudge's sword was faster still, slicing through the whip handle just above the big cat's fingers.

The monitor bolted for the open door. "Mudge, no!" Jon-Tom yelled, but Mudge didn't hear him in time. Or perhaps he did. The short sword spun end over end. It was the hilt that struck the lynx in the back of the head with a gratifying loud *thump*. The monitor dropped as if poleaxed.

Jon-Tom breathed a sigh of relief. "Smart throw, Mudge. We don't need a murder complicating our departure."

Mudge retrieved his sword. "That's right, mate, but I can't take the credit. I was *tryin'* to separate 'is 'ead from 'is shoulders."

"Quick now!" Jon-Tom instructed the youngsters as he headed for the storage closet. "Everyone out, before someone else shows up to check on you." He led them through the storage closet. "Don't push, everyone's going to get out . . . don't shove in the back. . . ."

Roseroar strained to see better as shadows moved against the open window. So far no one had appeared to spot the dangling rope of pastel linen, but it would take only one passing pedestrian to give the alarm.

She expected to see Jon-Tom or Mudge or even the girl. What she did not expect to see was the silent column of cubs who began descending the sheets. Some species were built for climbing and climbed down quickly and gracefully, while others had a more difficult time with the descent, but all made it safely. She dropped clear of the tree and rushed toward the building. The cubs largely ignored her as they ran off in different directions, small dark shapes swallowed by the shadows.

The prepubescent exodus continued for some time. Finally Jon-Tom, Mudge, and Folly appeared at the open window.

At the same time, lights began to wink on throughout the orphanage complex.

XI

So the otter's suspicions had been well founded, she decided. That was the only possible explanation for the mass escape in progress. She waited anxiously as Mudge slipped down the rope. Folly followed closely.

Jon-Tom had just stepped through the window opening and was climbing over the iron grate when something whizzed past his head. It struck the street below. Roseroar picked it up, found herself inspecting a small club. The knobbed end was studded with nails. Not the kind of disciplinary device one would expect a dormitory supervisor or teacher to carry.

The last fleeing cub vanished down a narrow alleyway. Within the orphanage, bells were clanging violently. Mudge reached the bottom of the rope and jumped clear. Folly slipped, fell the last five feet, and almost broke an ankle. The reason for her fall was clear; a pile of pink linen spiraled down on top of her.

"Bloody 'ell!" The otter looked upward and cursed. "I 'ad the other end tied to a bedpost. Someone must 'ave cut it." He could see Jon-Tom hanging on to the grating with one hand while trying to defend himself with his staff. From within the storage closet outraged shouts were clearly audible down on the street. The grating creaked loudly as it bent on its hinges.

"They'll 'ave 'im in a minute," the otter muttered helplessly, "if that old iron doesn't break free first."

Neither happened. Someone inside the supply room jabbed outward with a spear. Jon-Tom leaned back to dodge the deadly point, lost his grip, and fell. The staff dropped from his fingers as he tumbled head over heels, wrapped up in his lizard skin cape. Folly screamed. Lesser wails came from dark shadows nearby as those few children who'd paused to catch their breath saw their benefactor fall.

But there was no sickening thud of flesh meeting stone. Roseroar grunted softly. It was the only hint of any strain as she easily caught the plunging Jon-Tom in both arms. He pushed away the cape which had become wrapped around his head and stared up at her.

"Thanks, Roseroar." She grinned, set him down gently. He adjusted his attire and recovered his staff. The duar, still slung across his back, had survived the fall unscathed.

" 'Ell of a catch, luv!" Mudge gave the tigress a complimentary whack on the rump, darted out of reach before her paw could knock him silly. There were several faces staring down at them from the open window, yelling and issuing dire promises. Jon-Tom ignored them.

"Y'all okay?" Roseroar inquired solicitously.

"Fine." He slung the cape back over his shoulders, brushed at his face. "If you hadn't caught me, Clothahump would have a longer wait for his medicine."

"And y'all brought out the girl, ah see."

Folly stepped toward her. "I am *not* a girl! I'm as grown-up as you are."

Roseroar lifted her eyebrows as she regarded the skimp of a human. "Mah deah, no one is as grown-up as ah am."

"Depends on whether someone prefers quality to quantity."

" 'Ere now, wot's all this?" Mudge stepped between the ladies. "Not that I mind if you two want to 'ave a go at each other. Just give me a ten-minute 'ead start before the fireworks commence, yes?" He gestured to his right. "I don't think now's the time for private digressions, though."

At least a dozen black-clad adult shapes had appeared near the main entrance. Jon-Tom couldn't see if Chokas was among them, but he had no intention of hanging around to find out.

They headed off in the opposite direction, and Jon-Tom saw they needn't worry about pursuit. The black-clad gestapo maintained by the Friends of the Street wasn't after them. They were fanning out toward the alleys and side streets in search of their escaped flock.

Jon-Tom considered intercepting them. It was difficult not to, but he had to tell himself that they'd done everything possible for the children. Most, if not all, of them ought to make it to the safety of the crowded city below, and he suspected they were wise enough to discard their incriminating black-and-lace night clothes at the first opportunity.

One of their own was faced with the same dilemma. "You've got to get out of that nightdress, Folly," he told her. Obediently, she started to pull it over her head, and he hastened to restrain her. "No, no, not yet!"

They were racing down a steep street that led back toward the harbor area. It had begun to drizzle. He was grateful for the rain. It should aid the fleeing children in their escape.

"Why not yet?" Folly eyed him curiously. Curiosity gave way rapidly to a coy smile. "When you first saw me on Corroboc's boat I wasn't wearing anything but an iron collar. Why should my nakedness bother you now?"

"It doesn't bother me," he lied. "It's raining and I don't want you contracting pneumonia." Citizens of Snarken out for an evening stroll watched the flight with interest.

"I don't mind if you see me naked," she said innocently. "You like me a little, don't you, Jon-Tom?"

"Of course I like you."

"No. I mean you *like* me."

"Don't be silly. You're still a child, Folly."

"You don't look at me the way you'd look at a child."

"She ain't built like no cub, mate."

Jon-Tom glared over at the otter. "Stay out of this, Mudge."

"Excuse me, guv'nor. None o' me business, right?" He skittered along next to Roseroar, running fluidly on his stubby legs and trying to hide a grin.

"I'm concerned for your welfare, Folly." Jon-Tom struggled to explain. "I don't like to see anyone taken advantage of. You noticed that we freed everyone from the orphanage and not just you."

"I know, but you didn't come to free everyone. You came because I was there."

"Of course. You're a friend, Folly. A good friend."

"Is that all?" As she ran there was a lot of movement beneath the damp nightdress. Jon-Tom was having a difficult time concentrating on the street ahead. "Just a good friend?"

Roseroar listened with one ear to the infantile dialogue while trying her best to ignore it. Idiot humans! She made certain to inspect every side street they passed. Surely, as soon as the Friends of the

Street finished rounding up as many escapees as they could, they'd contact the police about the break-in.

Besides worrying about that new problem, she had to endure the banalities mouthed by the adolescent human female who was flirting shamelessly with Jon-Tom.

So what? She considered her discomfiture carefully. Why, she asked herself, should she find such harmless chatter so aggravating? Admirable the spellsinger might be, but he wasn't even a member of a related species. Any relationship besides mutual respect and strong friendship was clearly out of the question. The very thought was absurd! The man was a skinny, furless thing less than half her size. It made no sense for her to concern herself with his personal business.

She assured herself her interest was only natural. Jon-Tom was a friend, a companion now. It was just as he'd said to the girl: it hurt to see anyone taken advantage of. Roseroar wasn't about to let this scheming adolescent take advantage of him. And take advantage of him Folly would, if given half a chance. Roseroar was sure of that much. She shook her head as Jon-Tom allowed himself to be smothered with verbal pap, astonished at the naiveté displayed during courtship by the human species. She'd thought better of him.

She ignored it for as long as she could, until she was unable to stand the veiled remarks and coy queries any longer.

"Ah think we can slow down some now." Jon-Tom and Mudge agreed with her. Everyone slowed to a fast walk. Roseroar moved close to the girl. "And ah also think it would be a good ideah if we all kept quiet foah a while. We don't want to attract any undue attention. In addition to which, if ah'm forced to listen to any moah o' yoah simperin', girl, ah may vomit."

Folly eyed the tigress. "Something bothering you?"

"Nothin' much, little female. It's just that ah have a great respect foah the language. Hearin' it used so foolishly always upsets mah digestion."

Folly turned to Jon-Tom. She flashed blue eyes and blonde hair in the reflected light from storefronts and street lamps. Her skin, wet with drizzle, sparkled.

"Do you think I'm talking foolish, Jon-Tom?"

"Maybe just a little, yes."

She responded with a much practiced and perfectly formed pout. Roseroar sighed and turned away, wondering why she went to the trouble. The spellsinger had shown himself to be a man of intelligence and insight. It distressed her to see him so blatantly manipulated. She increased her stride so she wouldn't have to listen to any more of it.

"You don't like me," Folly murmured to Jon-Tom.

"Of course I like you."

"I knew you did!" She turned and threw her arms around him, making him stagger. "I knew you liked me!"

"Please, Folly." Jon-Tom reluctantly worked to disengage himself. Roseroar would have been happy to help, though she might have broken both of the girl's arms in the process. "Folly, I already have a woman." Her expression fell abruptly. She moved away from him, once more concentrating on the street ahead.

"You never told me that."

"It was never necessary to tell you. Her name's Talea. She lives near a town called Lynchbany, which lies far across the Glittergeist."

Otter ears overheard and Mudge fell back to join them. "O' course, she ain't really 'is woman," he said conversationally, thoroughly delighting in Jon-Tom's discomfort. "They're just friends is all."

Folly's delight returned upon hearing this disclosure. "Oh, that's all right, then!"

"Besides, you're much too young for what you're thinking," Jon-Tom told her, impaling Mudge with a stare promising slow death.

"Too young for what?"

"Just too young." Strange. The right words had been there on his lips just a moment earlier. Odd how they vanished the instant you needed them.

"Bet I could convince you otherwise," she said coquettishly.

"Here's the right cross street," he said hastily, lengthening his stride. "We'll be back at the inn in a couple of minutes."

A short furry shape jumped from an alcove ahead of him. Roseroar reached for her swords. Folly hid behind Jon-Tom as Mudge put a hand to his bow.

They relaxed when the shape identified itself.

"Jalwar!" Jon-Tom couldn't conceal his surprise. "What are you doing out here?" He tried to see past the ferret.

The oldster put a finger to his lips and beckoned for them to follow. They crept along behind him, turned down a long narrow alley. It was ripe with moldering garbage. Jalwar pointed to the main street beyond.

Both of their heavily laden wagons were still hitched to the rails outside the inn. Idling around the wagons were at least two dozen uniformed skunks and civet cats from Snarken's olfactory constabulary. Several well-dressed civilians lounged next to the front wagon and chatted amiably with the officer in charge of the cops.

Jalwar drew back into the shadows. "I saw them arrive," he whispered. "Many have stayed outside with our wagons. Others went upstairs searching for us. I was drinking and overheard in time to sneak away. I listened when they came back down and talked to others and to the innkeeper." The ferret's gaze shifted from Jon-Tom to Mudge. "They were talking about you."

"Me?" Mudge squeaked, suddenly sounding defensive. "Now, why would they be talkin' about me?"

"Because," Jalwar replied accusingly, "it seems you spent some time playing at dice with several of them."

"So wot's wrong with a friendly little game o' dice. Blimey, you'd think one o' them caught me in the sack with 'is bleedin' daughter."

It came to Jon-Tom in a rush: the finely fashioned wagons, the handsome dray animals, the new harnesses, the mountainous stock of supplies.

"Mudge . . ." he said dangerously.

The otter retreated. There was little room to maneuver in the alley, a fact he was acutely conscious of.

"Now, mate, take it easy. We needed them supplies, now, didn't we? 'Tis in a good cause, ain't it? Think o' 'is poor sickly wizardship lyin' and waitin' for us way back in Lynchbany and all the folks who need 'im well and 'ealthy again."

"How did you manage it, Mudge? How did you cheat so many of them at the same time?"

"Well, we otter folk are known for our quickness, and I've always been quick as any."

"Y'all must've been a little too quick this time." Roseroar peered toward the inn. "Judgin' from the number o' police about, ah'd say you defrauded moah than a few idle sailors."

"Wouldn't be much point in defrauding poor folks, now, would there, luv? Wot we got from sellin' the ship weren't near enough to buy supplies an' equipment for a proper expedition, but 'twere plenty to buy me into a handsome game o'chance with a few leadin' citizens."

"Fat lot of good those supplies do us now," Jon-Tom muttered.

Jalwar was rummaging through a pile of broken crates. "Here." He dragged out their backpacks. "I was able to throw these from our rooms while they were still searching for us below. It was all I had time to save."

Jon-Tom wiped grime from his own pack. "Jalwar, you're a wonder. Thanks."

"A small service, sir." Jon-Tom didn't bother to correct the ferret anymore. Let him say "sir" if it pleased him. "I only wish I could have informed you sooner, but I could not follow your path quickly enough." He smiled apologetically. "These aged legs of mine."

"It wouldn't have mattered. We were occupied with saving Folly."

"What now?" Roseroar wondered as she hefted her own massive pack.

Jon-Tom considered. "We can't hang around here. Now the cops have two reasons for picking us up. They might go easy on us over the Friends of the Street business, but not about this. For one thing, that officer in charge is a little too chummy with the citizens Mudge cheated. I'm not anxious to tour the inside of Snarken's prison."

"Give me a break, mate," whined the otter. "If you 'adn't been so set on goin' after 'er"—he pointed toward Folly—"we'd 'ave cleared this dump 'ours ago." He glared disgustedly at the girl. "I blame meself for it, though. Should've kept me concerns to meself." He added hopefully, "We could still sell 'er."

"No." Jon-Tom put an arm around her shoulders. "Folly stays with us until we can find her a safe haven."

"I could suggest something," she murmured softly. He moved his arm.

"Right then," he said briskly. "No point in hanging around here waiting for the cops to find us." He started back the way they'd come. Mudge followed, kicking at the garbage.

"Suits me, mate. Looks now like we're goin' to 'ave to walk all the way to this bleedin' Crancularn. Might as well get going. Only don't let's go spend the 'ole trip blamin' poor ol' Mudge for the fact that we ain't ridin' in comfort."

"Fair enough. And you don't blame me for this." So saying, he booted the otter in the rump so hard it took Roseroar's strength to extract him from the pile of barrels where he landed.

They slunk out of Snarken on foot—tired, anxious, and broke. Mudge grumbled every step of the way but acknowledged his mistake (sort of) by assuming the lead. It was also a matter of self-defense, since it kept him well out of range of Jon-Tom's boot.

Mudge also partly redeemed himself by returning from one short disappearance with an armful of female clothing, a bit of doubtful scavenging which Jon-Tom forced himself to rationalize.

"Lifted it from a drunken serval," the otter explained as Folly delightedly traded her black nightdress for the frilly if somewhat too-small attire. "The doxy I took it off won't miss it, and we've need of it."

They moved steadily through the city's outskirts. By the time the sun rose over the horizon to illuminate the now distant harbor, they were crossing the highest hill westward. There they traded some goods from Jon-Tom's pack for breakfast at a small inn, as he wanted to try and hold on to their three remaining gold pieces for an emergency. Midday saw them far from the city, hiking between rows of well-tended fruit trees.

Mudge was rubbing his belly. "Not bad for foreign cookin', mate."

"No, but we're going to have to eat lightly to conserve what money we have left."

"We could sell the girl's favors."

"Not a bad idea," Jon-Tom said thoughtfully.

Mudge looked at him in surprise. "Wot's that? You agrees?"

"Sure, if it's okay with her." He called ahead. "Hey, Roseroar! Mudge here has a suggestion about how you can help us raise some cash."

"No, no, no, mate!" said the suddenly panicky otter. "I meant the girl, the *girl.*"

Jon-Tom shrugged. "Big girl, little girl, what's the difference?" He started to call out to the tigress a second time. Mudge slammed a muffling paw over Jon-Tom's mouth, having to stand on tiptoes to manage it.

"Okay, guv'nor. I get your point. I'll keep me ideas to meself."

"See that you do, or I'll repeat your suggestion to Roseroar."

"I'd deny 'avin' anything to do with it."

"Sure you will, but who do you think she'll believe, me or you?"

"That'd be a foul subterfuge, mate."

"In which inventions I have an excellent teacher."

Mudge wasn't flattered by the backhanded compliment.

They marched steadily westward. As the days passed the character of the country grew increasingly rural. Houses were fewer and far between. Semitropical flora made way for coniferous forest that reminded Mudge of his beloved Bellwoods. The palms and thin-barked trees of the coast fell behind them.

They asked directions of the isolated travelers they encountered. All inquiries were met with expressions of disbelief or confessions of ignorance. Everyone seemed to know that Crancularn lay to the west. Exactly where to the west, none was able to say with certainty.

Besides, there was naught to be found in Crancularn but trouble, and the country folk had no need of more of that. They were busy enough avoiding the attentions of Snarken's predatory tax collectors.

In short, Crancularn was well-known, by reputation if not by sight, and that reputation was not enticing to potential visitors.

Two days after the road had become a mere trail, they settled down to enjoy the bright sunshine. A clear stream followed the track, tumbling glassily on its course down to the now distant Glittergeist. An octet of commune spiders were busy building a six-foot-square web between two trees. They would share equally in any catch.

Jon-Tom studied the pinecone that had fallen near his feet. It was long and slim, and the scales shone like bronze. Mudge had slipped out of his boots and was wading the stream, wishing it were deep enough for him to have a swim, while Jalwar had wandered into the woods in search of berries and edible roots to supplement their meager diet. Roseroar catnapped beneath an evergreen whose trunk grew almost parallel to the ground, while Folly, as always, stayed as close to Jon-Tom as he would allow.

"Don't look so discouraged," she said. "We'll get there."

Jon-Tom was picking at the cone, tossing the pieces into the stream and watching the little triangular brown boats until they disappeared over slick stones.

"How can we get there if nobody can give us directions? 'West' isn't good enough. I thought it would be easy once we got out of Snarken. I thought at least a few of the country folk would know the way to Crancularn. From what Clothahump told me, this store of the Aether and Neither is supposed to be pretty famous."

"Famous enough to avoid," Folly murmured.

"Some of them must be lying. They *must* be. I can't believe not a soul knows the way. Why won't they tell us?"

Folly looked thoughtful. "Maybe they're concerned and want to protect us from ourselves. Or maybe none of them really does know the way."

"Mebbee they don't know the way, boy, because it moves around."

"What?" Jon-Tom looked back to see an old chipmunk standing next to a botherbark bush. He pressed against the small of his back with his left paw and gripped the end of a curved cane with the other. Narrow glasses rested on the nose, and an ancient floppy hat nearly covered his head down to his eyes. A gray shirt hung open to the waist, and below he wore brown dungarees held up by suspenders. He also had very few teeth left.

"What do you mean, it moves around?" Roseroar looked up interestedly and moved to join them. The chipmunk's eyes went wide at the sight and Jon-Tom hurried to reassure him.

"That's Roseroar. She's a friend."

"That's good," said the chipmunk prosaically. Mudge turned to listen but was reluctant to abandon the cool water.

The oldster leaned against the tree for support and waved his cane. "I mean, it moves around, sonny. It never stays in the same place for very long."

"That's crazy," said Folly. "It's just another town."

"Oh, it's a town, all right, but not like any other, lass. Not Crancularn." He peered out from beneath the brim of his hat at Jon-Tom. "Why thee want to go there, tall man?"

"We need something from there. From a store."

The chipmunk nodded. "Aye, the Shop of the Aether and Neither."

"Then you've heard of it!" Jon-Tom said excitedly. "We need something, a certain medicine, that can only be purchased in that store."

The oldster grunted, though it came out as more of a rusty squeak. "Well, that's thy business."

"Please, we've come a long way. From across the Glittergeist. We need directions. *Specific* directions."

Another grunt-squeak. "Long way to come to make fools of thyselves."

"It's not for us. A friend of mine, a teacher and a great wizard, is very sick and badly needs this medicine. If you can tell us how to get to Crancularn, we'll pay you, somehow."

The oldster shook his head sadly. "I'd tell thee if I could, boy, but I can't help you. I don't know where Crancularn is." Jon-Tom slumped. "But there's them that do. Only, I wouldn't be the one to go asking them."

"Let us worry about that," said Jon-Tom eagerly. "Who are they?"

"Why, the enchanted ones, of course. Who else?"

"Enchanted ones?"

"Aye, the little people of the magic. The fairy folk. You know."

Folly's eyes were wide with childlike wonder. "When I was a little girl, I used to hear stories of the fairy folk. My mother used to tell me." She went very quiet and Jon-Tom tried to rush the conversation to take her thoughts off more recent memories.

"Where would we find these fairy folk?" The thought of meeting real honest-to-Tinker Bell fairies was enough to motivate him. Getting directions to Crancularn would be a bonus.

"I wouldn't advise anyone to risk such an encounter, sonny, but I can see that thee art determined." He indicated the steep slope behind them. "They hide in the wet ravines and steep canyons of these hills, keeping to themselves. Don't much care for normal folk such as us. But thee art human, and it is said that they take human form. Perhaps thee will have better luck than most. Seek the places where the water runs deep and clear and the rocks are colored so dark they are almost black, where the moss grows thick above the creeks and . . ."

" 'Ere now, grandpa." Mudge spoke from his rocky seat out in the stream. "This 'ere moss, it don't 'ave no mental problems now, do it?"

The chipmunk frowned at him. "How could mere moss have mental problems?"

Mudge relaxed. Their near-disastrous experience in the Muddletup Moors was still fresh in his mind. "Never mind."

The chipmunk gave him an odd look, turned back to Jon-Tom. "Those are the places where thee might encounter the fairy folk. If thee must seek them out."

"It seems we've no choice." Rising, Jon-Tom turned to inspect the tree-fringed hillside.

The elderly chipmunk resumed his walk. "I wish thee luck, then. I wish thee luck. Thee will need it to locate the enchanted ones, and thee will need it even more if thee do."

The ridge above gave way to a heavily wooded slope on the far side that grew progressively steeper. Soon they were fighting to maintain their balance as they slipped and slid down the dangerous grade.

At least, Jon-Tom and Roseroar were. With their inherent agility and lower centers of gravity, Jalwar and Mudge had no difficulty at all with the awkward descent, and Folly proved lithe as a gibbon.

A stream ran along the bottom of the narrow gorge. It was broader than the one they'd left behind, but not deep enough to qualify as a river. Moss and many kinds of ferns clung to logs and boulders. Insects hummed in the cool, damp air while dark granite and schist soaked up the rays of the sun.

They spent most of the day searching along the creek before deciding to move on. An insurmountable waterfall forced them to climb up the far side of the gorge. They topped the next ridge, climbed down still another slope where they camped for the night.

By the afternoon of the following day they were exploring their fourth such canyon. Jon-Tom was beginning to think that the fairy folk were a myth invented by an especially garulous old rodent to amuse himself at the expense of some gullible travelers.

They were finishing up a late meal when Mudge suddenly erupted from his seat on a thick patch of buttery yellow flowers. His bark of surprised pain echoed down the creek.

Everyone jumped. Roseroar automatically reached for her swords. Folly crouched ready to run while Jalwar's fur bristled on his neck. Jon-Tom, who was more familiar with the otter's overreactions, left his staff alone.

"What the hell bit you?"

Mudge was trying to inspect his backside. "Somethin' sure as 'ell did. 'Ere, Folly, be a good girl and see if I'm bleedin'?" He turned to her and bent slightly.

She examined the area dominated by the short, stubby tail and protected by leather shorts. "I don't see anything."

" 'Ave a close look."

"You fuzzy pervert." She gave him a look of disgust as she moved away.

"No, really. Not that I deny the accusation, luv, but somethin' took a chunk out o' me backside for sure."

"Liar! What would I do with a chunk of you?"

The voice was high but firm and came from the vicinity of the flowerbed. Jon-Tom crawled over for a close look, searching for the source of the denial.

Tiny hands parted the stalks, which were as yellow as the thick-petaled flowers, and he found himself staring at something small, winged, feminine, and drastically overweight.

"I'll be damned," he murmured. "A fat fairy."

"Watch your mouth, buster," she said as she sort of lumbered out lightly until she was standing on a broken log. The log was brown with red longitudinal stripes running through the bark. "I know I've got a small personal problem, and I don't need some big-mouthed human reminding me of the fact."

"Sorry." Jon-Tom tried to sound contrite. "You are a fairy, aren't you? One of the enchanted folk?"

"Nah," she snapped back, "I'm a stevedore from Snarken."

Jon-Tom studied her closely. Her clothing resembled wisps of spun gossamer lavender candy. A miniature tiara gleamed on her head. Long hair trailed below her waist. The tiara had been knocked askew and covered one eye. She grunted as she struggled to straighten it. In her right hand she clutched a tiny gold wand. Her wings were shards of cellophane mottled with thin red stripes.

"We were told," Folly said breathlessly, "that you could help us."

"Now, why would I want to do that? We've got enough problems of our own." She stared at Jon-Tom. "That's a nice duar. You a musician, bright boy?"

" 'e's a spellsinger, and a right powerful one, too," Mudge informed her. "Come all the way from across the Glittergeist to fetch back medicine for a sick sorcerer."

"He's a right powerful fool," she snapped. She sat down heavily on the log, her legs spread wide in a most casual and unladylike manner. Jon-Tom estimated her to be about four inches high and almost as wide.

"I'm called Jon-Tom." He introduced his companions. An uneasy silence ensued and he finally asked, "What's your name?"

"None of your business."

"Come on," he said coaxingly. "Whether you help us or not is up to you, but can't we at least be polite to one another?"

"What's this? A polite human? That doesn't make any sense, bald-body." She shrugged. "What the hell. My name's Grelgen. Want to make something of it?"

"Uh, no." Jon-Tom decided he was going to have to tread very carefully with this pint-size package of enchanted belligerence.

"Smart answer. You got anything to eat?"

Jalwar started to rummage through his pack. "I think we have some snake jerky, and there are a few hard rolls."

"Ptui!" She spat to her right. "I mean *real* food. Fruit tarts, cream cups, nectar custard, whipped honey rolls."

Jon-Tom said carefully, "I think I am beginning to see what your problem is."

"Oh, you are, are you, fungus-foot? You think everything's cut and dried, don't you? It's all so obvious to you." She was pacing now, back and forth atop the log, waving her tiny hands to punctuate her words.

"Say, you can't fly, can you?"

She turned to face him. "Of course I can fly, dumbutt." She wiggled her diaphanous wings. "What do you think these are for? Air-conditioning?"

"All right, then let's see you fly. Come on, fly."

"Feh! You'd think I didn't have anything better to do than put on a show for a bunch of pituitary freaks."

"You can't fly!" Jon-Tom said triumphantly. *"That's* your big problem. You've gotten so . . ."

"Watch it, jack," she said warningly.

". . . so healthy that you can't lift off anymore. I wouldn't think it would make a difference. A bumblebee's too heavy for flight, but it manages, and without enchantment."

"I'm a fairy, one of the enchanted folk," Grelgen informed him, speaking as one would to an idiot child. "Not a bumblebee. There are structural, aerodynamic, and metabolic differences you wouldn't understand. As for problems, you're the ones who are stuck with the biggie." She stabbed the wand at Mudge. "That turkey tried to assassinate me!"

Mudge gaped in surprise. "Wot, me? I did nothin' o' the kind, your shortness."

"You sat on me, rat-breath."

"Like 'ell I did! You crawled underneath me. Anyways, 'ow was I supposed to see you or anything else under all them flowers?"

Grelgen crossed her arm. "I was sitting there minding my own business, having a little afternoon snack of nectar and pollen, and you deliberately dropped your rat-butt right on top of me."

"You expect me to inspect every patch o' ground I sit down on?"

"In our lands, yes."

"We didn't know it were your lands." Mudge was fast losing patience with this infinitesimal harridan.

"Ah-*ha!* So, a casual assassin. The worst kind." She put two fingers to her lips and let out a sharp, piercing whistle. Jon-Tom listened admiringly. The sound was loud enough to attract an empty cab from two blocks down a Manhattan street.

What it did attract, from beneath mushrooms and flowers, from behind moss beds and tree roots, was a swarm of enchanted folk, several hundred of them. A few carried wands resembling Grelgen's, but most hefted miniature bows and arrows, crossbows, and spears. Jon-Tom put a hand out to restrain Roseroar from picking up her swords, even though the tigress weighed more than all the enchanted folk combined.

"Magic," he whispered warningly.

Roseroar yielded, but not to his admonition. "Magic or no, the tips of their weapons are moistened. I suspect poison. An ungallant way to fight."

"I guess if you're four inches tall you have to use every advantage you can think of."

Jalwar moved close, whispered to him. "Move carefully here, spellsinger, or we may vanish in an arrogant conjuration. These folk have a deserved reputation for powerful magic."

"That's how I figure it," he replied. "Maybe they're not all as obnoxious or combative as our friend there."

"What's that, what did you say?"

"I said," he told Grelgen, "that it's nice of you to invite us to meet all your friends and relatives."

"When one of us is threatened, buster, all spring to the rescue."

Jon-Tom noted that none of the fairies surrounding them was in any condition to fly. Every one of them waddled about with obvious difficulty, and the slimmest was a candidate for the enchanted branch of Weight Watchers.

"You're our prisoners," she finished.

"I see," said Mudge. "And wot if we decide not to be your prisoners?"

"Then you'll be dead," she assured him unpleasantly.

Mudge studied the array of glistening little weapons. " 'Ospitable folk, wot?"

"Watch 'em," said Grelgen to her relations. She turned and sauntered to the end of the branch, hopped off, and landed with a wheeze in the grass below. There she entered into a mumbling conversation with several other wandbearers. Most of them were clad only in rags and tatters.

Mudge *would* have to sit on someone of importance, thought Jon-Tom angrily. The conference broke up moments later.

"This way," said one of the other armed fairies, gesturing upstream. Surrounded by miniuscule guards, they were marched off up the creek.

"You sure you didn't see her, Mudge?" Jon-Tom asked the otter.

"Would I 'ave been stupid enough to sit on 'er if I 'ad, mate? Use your 'ead. It were those bloody flowers."

"You weren't looking, then," Jon-Tom said accusingly.

"So I weren't lookin'. Should I 'ave been lookin'?"

"No, I guess not. It's nobody's fault."

"Pity I didn't flatten 'er," the otter murmured, careful to keep his voice down.

"It might not have mattered, sir," Jalwar murmured. "The fairy folk are known for their resilience."

"I can see that," said Mudge, studying their obese escort. "The one with the mouth looks like she could bounce."

"Be quiet," said Jon-Tom. "We're in enough trouble already. She'll hear you."

"Damned if I care if she does, guv." The otter had his hands shoved in his pockets and kicked disgustedly at pebbles as they walked along the side of the creek. "If she ain't got common sense to see that—"

A paw the size of his head covered his mouth and, incidently, most of his face. "Watch yo mouth, ottah," Roseroar told him. "Yo heard Jon-Tom. Let's not irritate these enchanted folk any moah than we already have."

"I'd like to irritate 'em," said the otter when she'd removed her paw. But his voice had become a whisper.

The stream narrowed. Canyon walls closed in tight around the marchers, all but shutting out the sun. Trees and bushes grew into one another, forming a dense, hard-to-penetrate tangle. The captives had to fight their way through the thickening undergrowth.

Dusk brought them to the outskirts of the enchanted folk's village. In appearance it was anything but enchanted. Tiny huts and homes were scattered around a natural amphitheater. Evidence of disrepair and neglect abounded. Some of the buildings were falling down, and even those cut into massive tree roots had piles of trash mounded up against the doorways. To Jon-Tom all this was clear proof of a loss of pride among the inhabitants.

Tiny lights flickered to life behind many of the miniature windows, and smoke started to curl from minute chimneys. Off to one side of the community a circular area was surrounded by a stone wall pierced by foot-high archways. The six-inch high wall ended at both ends against a sheer cliff of gray granite.

The four captives filled this arena. Once they were inside the insignificant walls, Grelgen and two other fairies stood within the archways waving their wands and murmuring importantly. When the invocation was finished, she stepped back and retreated toward the village with her cronies.

Folly took a step toward the minuscule barrier and tried to step over. She gasped and drew back as if bitten, holding her right hand.

"What is it?" Jon-Tom asked anxiously.

"It's *hot*. The air's hot."

Experimentally, Jon-Tom waved at the emptiness above the tiny stone wall. An invisible wall of flame now enclosed them. He shook his hand and blew on his fingers to cool them, deciding they weren't going to blister. Escape wouldn't be easy.

Roseroar sighed and settled herself on the hard ground. "An ironic conclusion to yoah expedition, Jon-Tom. Captured and imprisoned by a bunch of disgruntled, not to mention uncouth, enchanted folk."

"Don't be so quick to give up. They may decide to let us go yet. Besides," he swung his duar around, "we have magic of our own."

Mudge looked imploringly heavenward. "Why me, wot?"

"I do not know that spellsinging will work against the fairy folk, sir," said Jalwar. "In my travels I have heard that they are immune to all forms of magic except their own. It may be that yours will have no effect on them, and may even be turned against you."

"You don't say." Jon-Tom's fingers fell from the duar's strings, together with what remained of his confidence. "I didn't know that."

"It may not be so, but it is what I have heard many times."

"We'll hold it as a last resort, then."

"Wot difference does it make, mate? 'Alf the time it backfires on you anyhows. If it doubles back on us I wouldn't want it to 'appen while I'm stuck in this clearin'."

"Neither would I, Mudge." He looked out toward the winking lights of the village. "We may not have any choice. They don't seem much inclined to listen to reason."

"I think they'll all crazy," commented Folly.

In the fading light she looked healthy and beautiful. The impermanent bruises and scars Corroboc had inflicted on her were healing fast. She was resilient, tough, and growing more feminine by the day. She was also making Jon-Tom increasingly uneasy.

He turned to Mudge, saw the otter standing as close as possible to the invisible barrier enclosing them.

"What's up, Mudge?"

The otter screwed up his face, his whiskers twitching. "Can't you smell it, too, mate? Garbage." He nodded toward the town. "It's everywhere. Maybe they're enchanted, but that's not the word I'd use to describe their sewage system."

"Ah saw their gardens when we came in," said Roseroar thoughtfully. "They appeahed to be untended."

"So fairy town's gone to hell," Jon-Tom murmured. "Something's very wrong here."

"Wot difference do it make to us, mate? We 'ave our own problems. Dealin' with 'Er Grossness, for one thing."

"If we could figure out what's wrong here," Jon-Tom argued, "maybe we could ingratiate ourselves with our captors."

"You ingratiate yourself, mate. Me, I'm for some sleep."

Jon-Tom didn't doubt that the otter could sleep on the bare rock. If Mudge were tossed out of a plane at twenty thousand feet, the otter could catch twenty winks before awakening to open his parachute. It was a talent he often envied.

"Sleeping won't solve our problem."

"It'll solve me immediate one, mate. I'm pooped."

"Perhaps yoah magic will work against the enchanted folk," Roseroar said hopefully.

"I don't know." Jon-Tom tapped the wood of the duar, was rewarded with a melodious thumping sound. The moon was shining down into the narrow defile, illuminating the dense woods surrounding them. "I'm going to hold off till the last possible moment to find out."

The tigress was slipping out of her armor and using it to make a crude pillow. "Ah don't know." She rested her massive head on black and white paws. "It seems to me that we're already theah."

Grelgen and the rest of the fairy council came for them in the morning. Their principal nemesis had changed into a flowing gown of orange chiffon. The bright pastel attire had not softened her disposition, however.

"We've been considering what to do with you bums most of the night," she informed them brusquely.

Jon-Tom stretched, pushed at his lower back, and wished he'd had the sense to use Roseroar for a cushion. He was stiff and sore from spending the night on the hard ground.

"All I can tell you is that we're innocent of any charges you discussed. So what are you going to do now?"

"Eat," she informed him. "Talk more later."

"Well now, I could do with a spot o' breakfast!" Mudge tried to muster some enthusiasm. Maybe Jon-Tom was right after all, and these cute little enchanted bastards were finally going to act in a civilized manner. "Where do we eat?"

"Wrong pronoun," Grelgen said. She turned to point with her wand.

Jon-Tom followed it into the brush. What the poor light of evening had kept hidden from view was now revealed by the bright light of day. Up the creek beyond the town, thick peeled branches spanned a shallow excavation. The firepit showed signs of recent use.

Mudge saw it, too, and his initial enthusiasm vanished. "Uh, wot's on the menu, luv?"

"Fricasseed water rat," she told him, with relish.

"Wot, *me?*" Mudge squeaked.

"Give the main course a bottle of elf dust. What better end for a guilty assassin?"

Up till now Jon-Tom had considered their predicament as nothing more than a matter of bad communication. This new vision of a bunch of carnivorous fairies feasting on Mudge's well-done carcass shoved everything over the edge into the realm of the surreal.

"Listen, you can't eat any of us."

Grelgen rested pudgy hands on soft hips. "Why not?"

Jon-Tom struggled for a sensible reply. "Well, for one thing, it just doesn't fit your image."

She squinted sideways at him. "You," she said decisively, "are nuts. I'm going to have to consult with the Elders to make sure it's okay to eat crazy people."

"I mean, it just doesn't seem right. What about your honey rolls and custards and like that?"

Grelgen hesitated. When she spoke again, she sounded slightly embarrassed.

"Actually, you're right. It's only that every once in a while we get this craving, see? Whoever's unlucky enough to be in the neighborhood at the time ends up on the village menu." She glanced over at Folly and tried to regain some of her former arrogance. "We also find it helpful now and then to bathe in the blood of a virgin."

Folly digested this and collapsed, rolling about on the ground while laughing hysterically. Grelgen saw the tears pouring down the helpless girl's cheeks, grunted, and looked back over a shoulder. Jon-Tom followed her gaze.

On the far side of fairy town a bunch of muscular, overweight enchanted folk were sliding an oversized wooden bowl down a slope. At the sound of Grelgen's voice they halted.

"Right! Cancel the bathing ceremony!"

Cursing under their breath, the disappointed bowl movers reversed their efforts and began pushing their burden back into the bushes.

"So you think it's funny, do you? Right then, you're first on the fire instead of the water rat."

That put a clamp on Folly's laughter.

"Why her?" Jon-Tom demanded to know.

"Why not her? For one thing she's already depelted."

"Oh, no you don't." Folly braced herself against the bare granite wall, as far from Grelgen as she could get. "You just try and touch me! I'll squash you like a bug."

Grelgen looked disgusted, waved her wand almost indifferently, and whispered something under her breath. Folly leaped away from the wall, clutching her backside. The stone had become red-hot.

"Might as well resign yourself to it, girl," said Grelgen. "You're on this morning's menu and that's all there is to it. If there's anything that gets my gall it's an uncooperative breakfast."

"Please," Jon-Tom pleaded with her, dropping to his knees to be nearer eye level with their tormentor. "We mean you no harm. We only came into your lands to ask you for some information."

"Sorry. Like I said, we've got the craving, and when it comes upon us we've got to have meat."

"But why us?" Mudge asked her. "These woods must be full o' lizards and snakes enough to supply your 'ole village."

"Food doesn't wander into our custody," she snapped at him. "We don't like hunting. And the forest creatures don't stage unprovoked assaults on our person."

"Blimey," Mudge muttered. " 'Ow can such small 'eads be so bloomin' dense? I told you that were an accident!"

Grelgen stared silently at him as she tapped one tiny glass slipper with her wand. Jon-Tom absently noted that the slipper was three sizes too small for her not-so-tiny foot.

"Don't give me any trouble. I'm in a disagreeable mood as it is." She whistled up a group of helpers and they started through one archway toward Folly. Her initial defiance burned out of her, she hid behind Roseroar. Jon-Tom knew that wouldn't save her.

"Look," he said desperately, trying to stall for time as he swung the duar into playing position and tried to think of something to sing, "you said that meat isn't usually what you eat, that you only have this craving for it occasionally?"

"What about it?" Grelgen snapped impatiently.

"What do you eat normally? Besides what you told me earlier."

"Milk and honey, nectar and ambrosia, pollen and sugar sap. What else would fairy folk eat?"

"So *that's* it. I had a hunch." A surge of hope rushed through him.

"What's it?" she asked, frowning at him.

He sat down and crossed his legs, set the duar aside. "I don't suppose there are any professional dieticians in the village?"

"Any what?"

"No, of course not. See, all your problems are diet-related. It not only explains your unnatural craving for protein, it also explains your, uh, unusually rotund figures. Milk's okay, but the rest of that stuff is nothing but pure sugar. I mean, I can't even *imagine* how many calories there are in a daily dose of amborsia. You probably use a lot of glucose when you're flying, but when you stop flying, well, the problem only compounds itself."

One of the Elder fairies waiting impatiently behind Grelgen now stepped forward. "What is this human raving about?"

Grelgen pushed him back. "It doesn't matter." She turned back to Jon-Tom. "What you say makes no sense, and it wouldn't matter if it did, because we still have our craving." She started to aim her wand at the trembling Folly. "No use in trying to hide, girl. Step out here where I can see you."

Jon-Tom leaned sideways to block her aim. "Wait! You've got to listen to me. Don't you see? If you'd only change your eating habits you'd lose this craving for protein."

"We're not interested in changing our eating habits," said another of the Elders. "We *like* nectar and honey and ambrosia."

"All right, all right!" Jon-Tom said frantically. "Then there's only one way out. The only other way to reduce your craving for protein is for you to start burning off all these extra ounces you've been accumulating. You've got to break the cycle." He picked up the duar. "At least give me a chance to help you. Maybe I can't do it with spellsinging, but there are all kinds of magic."

"Consider carefully, man," Grelgen warned him. "Don't you think we're aware that we have a little problem? Don't you think we've tried to use our own magic to solve it?"

"But none of you is a spellsinger."

"No. That's not our kind of magic. But we've tried *everything*. We're stuck with what we are. Your spellsinging can't help us. Nothing can help us. We've experimented with every type of magic known to the enchanted folk, as well as that employed by the magic-workers of the greater world. We're trapped by our own metabolisms." She rolled up her sleeves. "Now let's get on with this without any more bullshitting, okay?" She raised the wand again.

"Just one chance, just give me one chance!" he pleaded.

She swung the wand around to point it at him, and he flinched. "I'm warning you, buster, if this is some sort of trick, you'll cook before her."

"There's one kind of magic I don't think you've tried."

She made a rude noise. "Worm dung! We've tried it all."

"Even aerobics?"

Grelgen opened her mouth, then closed it. She turned to conference with the Elders. Jon-Tom waited nervously.

Finally she stuck her head out of the pile and inquired almost
reluctantly, "What strange sort of magic is this?"

Jon-Tom took a deep breath and rose. Putting aside the duar, he
began stripping to the waist.

Roseroar came over to whisper in his ear. "Suh, are yo preparin'
some trick ah should know about? Should ah be ready with mah
swords?"

"No, Roseroar. No tricks."

She shrugged and moved away, shaking her head.

Jon-Tom started windmilling his arms, loosening up. Grelgen immediately retreated several steps and raised the wand threateningly.
"All you need is to learn this magic," he said brightly. "A regular
program of aerobics. Not only will it reduce your unnatural craving
for protein, it should bring back your old aerodynamic figures."

"What does that mean?" asked one of the younger fairies.

"It means we'll be able to fly again, stupid," replied one of the
Elders as he jabbed the questioner in the ribs.

"Fly again." The refrain was taken up by the rest of the crowd.

"It's a trick!" snapped Grelgen, but the weight of opinion (so to
speak) was against her.

"All right." She tucked her wand under one arm and glared up at
Jon-Tom. "You get your chance, man. If this is a trick to buy time, it
better be good, because it's going to be your last one."

"It's no trick," Jon-Tom assured her, feeling the sweat starting to
trickle from beneath his arms. And he hadn't even begun yet.

"Look, I'm no Richard Simmons, but I can see we need to start
with the basics." He was aware he had the undivided attention of
several hundred sets of eyes. He took a deep breath, thankful for the
morning runs which kept him in decent condition. "We're going to
start with some deep knee-bends. Hands on hips . . . watch those
wings, that's it. Ready." He hesitated. "This would work better if we
had some music."

Grelgen grunted, turned, and barked a command. There was a
brief delay. Several small figures made their way through the enchanted mob and took up positions atop the stone wall. Each carried
a delicate instrument. There were a couple of flutes, a set of drums,

and something that resembled a xylophone which had been in a bad traffic accident.

"What should we play?" piped one of the minuscule musicians.

"Something lively."

"A dance or roundelet?" They discussed the matter among themselves, then launched into a lively tune with faintly oriental overtones. Jon-Tom waited until he was sure of the rhythm, then smiled at his attentive if uncertain audience.

"Ready? Let's begin! Imitate me." He dipped. "Come on, it's not hard. One, two, three, and bend; one, two, three, and *bend;* . . . that's it!"

While Jon-Tom's companions looked on, several hundred fairy folk struggled to duplicate the human's movements. Before too long, groans and moans all out of proportion to the size of the throats they came from filled the air.

Grelgen was gasping and sweating. Her orange chiffon gown was soaked. "You're sure that you're not actually trying to murder us?"

"Oh, no." Jon-Tom was breathing a little hard himself. "See, this isn't an instantaneous kind of magic. It takes time." He sat down and put his hands behind his neck, wondering how far he could go before Grelgen gave up. "Now, this kind of magic is called situps. Up, down, up, down . . . you in the back there, no slacking, now . . . up, down . . ."

He worried constantly that Grelgen and her colleagues would become impatient before the new exercise regimen had time to do its work. He needn't have worried. The enchanted folk took weight off as rapidly as they put it on. By the second day the most porcine of the villagers could boast of shrunken waistlines. By the third the effects were being felt by all, and by the fourth even Grelgen could stay airborne for short flights.

"I don't understand, mate," said Mudge. "You said it 'tweren't magic, yet see 'ow quick-like they're shrinkin' down!"

"It's their metabolic rate. They burn calories much faster than we do, and as soon as they get down to where they can fly again, the burning accelerates."

The results were reflected in Grelgen's changing attitude. As the exercises did their work, her belligerence softened. Not that she became all sweetness and light, but her gratitude was evident.

"A most wondrous gift you have given us, man. A new kind of magic." It was the morning of the fifth day of their captivity and a long time since any of the enchanted folk had suggested having one of their guests for supper.

"I have a confession to make. It's not magic. It's only exercise."

"Call it by whatever name you wish," she replied, "it is magic to us. We are starting to look like the enchanted folk once more. Even I," she finished proudly. She did a deep knee-bend to prove it, something she couldn't have imagined doing five days earlier. Of course, she did it while hovering in midair, which made it somewhat easier. Still, the accomplishment was undeniable.

"You are free to go," she told them.

Roseroar stepped forward and cautiously thrust out a paw. The invisible wall of fire which had kept them imprisoned had vanished, leaving behind only a little lingering heat. The tigress stepped easily over the tiny stone wall.

"Our gratitude is boundless," Grelgen went on. "You said you came to us for help." She executed a neat little pirouette in the air, delighting in her rediscovered mobility. "What is it you wish to know?"

"We need directions to a certain town," he told her. "A place called Crancularn."

"Ah. An ambiguous destination. Not mine to wonder why. Wait here." She flew toward the village, droning like a wasp, and returned several minutes later with four newly slimmed Elders. They settled on the wall. Between them, the four Elders held a piece of parchment six inches square. It was the biggest piece of writing material the village could produce.

"Crancularn, you said?" Jon-Tom nodded at her.

She rolled up the sleeves of her burgundy-and-lime dress, waved the wand over the parchment as she spoke. The parchment twisted like a leaf in the wind. It continued to quiver as a line of gold appeared on its surface, tracing the outlines of mountains and rivers, trails, and paths. None of them led directly toward the golden diamond that shone brightly in the upper-lefthand corner of the parchment.

Grelgen finished the incantation. The parchment ceased its shaking, allowing the concentrating Elders to relax their grip. Jon-Tom picked the freshly inscribed map off the grass. It was warm to the touch. One tiny spot not far from a minor trail fluoresced brightly.

"The glow shows you where you are at any time," Grelgen informed him. "It will travel as you travel. Hold fast to the map and you will never be lost." She rose on diaphanous wings to hover near his shoulder and trace over the map with her wand. "See? No easy journey from here and no trails directly to the place."

"We're told Crancularn moves about."

"So it does. It has that characteristic. But the map will take you there, never fear. This is the cartography of what will be as well as of what is. A useful skill which we rarely employ. We like it where we are."

Jon-Tom thanked her as he folded the map and slipped it carefully into a pocket of his indigo shirt.

Grelgen hovered nearby. "Tell me, man. Why do you go to Crancularn?"

"To shop for something in the Shop of the Aether and Neither." She nodded, a grave expression on her tiny face. "We've heard many rumors," he went on. "Is there something dangerous about the shop?"

"Indeed there is, man. Included among its usual inventory is a large supply of the Truth. That is something most travelers seek to avoid, not to find. Beware what purchases you make. There are bonuses and discounts to be had in that place you may not find to your liking."

"We'll watch our step," he assured her.

She nodded solemnly. "Watch your hearts and souls as well. Good luck to you, man, and to your companions. Perhaps if you return by a similar route we can show you the Cloud Dance." She looked wistful. "I may even participate myself."

"Dancing in the air isn't as difficult as dancing on the ground," said Folly.

Grelgen grinned at her. "That depends on what you're doing in the air, infant." With great dignity she pivoted and led the four Elders back to the village.

They were free, Jon-Tom knew, and so again were the enchanted folk.

XII

The map led them out of the narrow defile that was the enchanted canyon. Music and rhythmic grunts followed them as they left behind a village full of fairies aerobicizing like mad. Grelgen had a long way to go before she looked like Jane Fonda but she was determined to out perform her subjects, and Jon-Tom didn't doubt she had the willpower to do so.

Several days' march through game-filled country brought them over the highest mountain pass and down onto the western slopes. Despite Grelgen's insistence that the journey the rest of the way to Crancularn would not be easy, they were beginning to relax. Since leaving behind the enchanted village they had encountered no dangerous animals or sapients, and food was plentiful.

Ahead lay the desert. Jon-Tom felt certain they could cross it in a couple of days. All was well.

No more bad dreams bothered him, and he awoke refreshed and at ease. Fallen leaves had made a comfortable, springy bed. They were now back into deciduous forest, having left most of the evergreen woods behind.

He pushed his cape aside. A few wisps of smoke still rose from the remains of last night's fire. Roseroar snored softly on the far side of the embers while Mudge dozed nearby. That in itself was unusual. Normally the otter woke first.

Jon-Tom scanned the rest of the camp and sat up fast.

"Jalwar? Folly!"

The woods did not answer, nor did anyone else.

He climbed to his feet, called again. His shouts roused Mudge and Roseroar.

"Wot's amiss, mate?"

Jon-Tom gestured at the campsite. "See for yourself."

Mudge inspected the places where the missing pair had slept. "They aren't off 'untin' for breakfast berries. All their gear's gone."

"Could they have been carried off?" Jon-Tom muttered.

"Why would anybody bother to sneak in softly and steal that pair away while leavin' us snug and in dreamland?" Roseroar said. "Makes no sense."

"You're right, it doesn't. So they left on their own, and with a stealthiness that implies premeditation."

"What?" she growled in confusion.

"Sorry. My legal training talking. It means they planned to sneak out. Don't ask me why."

"Which way would they go?"

"Maybe there's a town nearby. I'll check the map." He reached into his pocket, grasped air. A frantic, brief search proved that the map was well and truly gone.

"Mudge, did you . . . ?"

The otter shook his head, his whiskers bristling in anger. "You never gave it to me, guv'nor. I saw you put it up yourself." He sighed, sat down on a rock, and adjusted his cap, leaning the feather down at its usual rakish angle. "Can't say as 'ow I'm surprised. That Corroboc might 'ave been a class-one bastard, but 'e knew wot 'e were about when 'e named that girl."

"Ah've been suspicious of her motives from the beginning," Roseroar added. "We should have sold the little bitch in Snarken, when we had the chance."

Jon-Tom found himself staring northwestward, through the thinning forest toward the distant desert. "It doesn't make sense. And what about Jalwar? He's gone, too, and that makes even less sense. How can he get anywhere without our help and protection?"

Mudge came and stood next to his friend, put a comforting paw on his shoulder. "Ah, lad. 'Ave you learned so little o' life since you've been in this world? Who knows wot old Jalwar promised the girl? 'E's a trader, a merchant. Obviously 'e made 'er a better offer than anything we 'ave. Maybe 'e were bein' marooned on that beach by 'onest folk 'e'd cheated. This ain't no world for takin' folks on faith, me friend. For all we know Jalwar's a rich old bugger in 'is 'ome town."

"If he wanted Folly to help him, why would they take the map? They wouldn't need it to retrace the trail back to Snarken."

"Then it's pretty clear they ain't 'eadin' for Snarken, mate." He turned and stared down the barely visible path. "And we ought to be able to prove it."

Sure enough, in the dew-moistened earth beyond the campsite the two sets of footprints stood out clearly, the small, almost dainty marks of Jalwar sharp beside Folly's sandalprints. They led downslope toward the desert.

" 'Tis plain wot they're about, mate. They're 'eading for Crancularn. That's why they stole the map."

"But why? Why not go theah with the rest of us?" Roseroar was shaking her head in puzzlement.

"You're as dense as 'e is, luv. Ain't it plain enough yet to both of you? Jalwar's a *trader.* They're goin' to try and buy up the 'ole supply o' this medicine 'is sorcerership needs so badly and 'old it for ransom." He stared at Jon-Tom. "We told the old fart too much, mate, and now 'e's bent on doin' us dirty."

"Jalwar, maybe . . ." Jon-Tom mumbled unhappily, "but I can't believe that Folly . . ."

"Why not, mate? Or did you think she were in love with you? After wot she went through, she's just lookin' out after 'erself. Can't blame 'er for that, wot?"

"But we were taking care of her, good care."

Mudge shrugged. "Not good enough, it seems. Like I said, no tellin' wot old Jalwar promised 'er in return for 'elpin' 'im."

"What now, Jon-Tom?" asked Roseroar gently.

"We can't turn back. Map or no map. I suppose we could go back to the village of the enchanted folk and get another one, but that would put us weeks behind them. We can't lose that much time if Mudge's suspicions are correct. They'd beat us to the medicine easily. I studied that map pretty intensively after Grelgen gave it to us. I can remember some of it."

"That ain't the 'ole of it, mate." Mudge bent and put his nose close to the ground. When he stood straight again, his whiskers were twitching. "An otter can follow a scent on land or through water if there's just enough personal perfume left to tickle 'is nostrils. This track's fresh as a new whore. Until it rains we've got a trail to follow, and there's desert ahead. Maybe if we pee on the run we can overtake the bloody double-crossers."

"Ah second the motion, suh. Let's not give up, Jon-Tom."

"I wasn't thinking of giving up, Roseroar. I was thinking about what we're going to do when we do catch up with them."

"That's the spirit!" She leaned close. "Leave the details to me." Her teeth were very white.

"I'm not sure that would be the civilized thing to do, Roseroar." Despite the deception, the thought of Folly in Roseroar's paws was not a pleasant one.

"All mah actions are dictated by mah society's code of honah, Jon-Tom," she said stiffly. She frowned at a sudden thought. "Don't tell me that after what's happened heah yo still feel fo the little bitch?"

He was shouldering his backpack. "We still don't know that she went with Jalwar voluntarily. Maybe he forced her."

Mudge was waiting at the edge of the campsite, anxious to get moving. "Come on now, mate. Even if you exclude age as a consideration, the girl was bigger and stronger than that old ferret. And she could always have screamed."

"Not necessarily. Not if Jalwar had a knife at her throat. Look, I admit it looks like she went with him voluntarily, but I won't condemn her until we know for sure. She's innocent until proven guilty."

Mudge spat on the ground. "Another o' your otherworldly misconceptions."

"It's not otherworldly. It's a universal truism," Jon-Tom argued.

"Not in this universe it ain't."

Roseroar let them argue while she assumed the lead, glancing occasionally at the ground to make sure they were still on the trail, scanning the woods for signs of ambush. For the moment she preferred to ignore both of her argumentative companions.

From time to time Mudge would move up alongside her to dip his nose to the earth. Sometimes the footprints of their quarry would disappear under standing water or mix with the tracks of other creatures. Mudge always regained the trail.

"Must 'ave took off right after the last o' us fell asleep," the otter commented that afternoon. "I guess them to be at least six hours ahead of us, probably more."

"We'll catch them." Jon-Tom was covering the ground easily with long, practiced strides.

"Maybe that ferret weren't so old as 'e made 'imself out to be," Mudge suggested.

"We'll still catch them."

But the day went with no sign of girl and ferret. They let Roseroar lead them on through the darkness, until accumulating bumps and bruises forced Jon-Tom to call a halt for the night. They slept fitfully and were up again before the dawn.

By afternoon the last trees had surrendered to scrub brush and bare rock. Ahead of them a broad, hilly plain of yellow and brown mixed with the pure white of gypsum stretched from horizon to horizon. It was high desert, and as such, the heat was not as oppressive as it might have been. It was merely dauntingly hot. The air was still and windless, and the shallow sand clearly showed the tracks of Jalwar and Folly.

It was a good thing, because the sand did not hold their quarry's spoor as well as damp soil, and Mudge had increasing difficulty distinguishing it from the tracks of desert dwellers as they started out across the plain.

"I 'ope you remember that map well, mate."

"This is the Timeful Desert, as I remember it."

Mudge frowned. "I thought deserts were supposed to be timeless, not timeful."

"Don't look at me. I didn't name it." He pointed toward a low dune. "The only sure source of water is a town in the middle of the desert called Redrock. The desert's not extensive, but it's plenty big enough to kill us if we lose our way."

"That's a comfortin' thought to be settin' out with." The otter looked up at Roseroar. "Any sign o' our friends, tall tail?"

Roseroar's extraordinary eyesight scanned the horizon. "Nothing but sand. Nothing moves."

"Can't say as 'ow I blame it." He kicked sand from his boots.

By the morning of the next day the mountains had receded far behind them. Jon-Tom busied himself by searching for a suggestion of green, a hint of moisture. It seemed impossible that the land could be utterly barren. Even a stubby, tired cactus would have been a welcome sight.

They saw nothing, which did not mean nothing existed in the Timeful Desert. Only that if any life did survive, it did not make itself known to the trio of travelers.

He felt sure they would overtake Jalwar and Folly, but they did not. Not all that day nor the next.

It was on that third day that Mudge had them halt while he knelt in the sand.

" 'Ere now, 'ave either of you two noticed this?"

"Noticed what?" The sweat was pouring down Jon-Tom's face, as much in frustration at finding no sign of their quarry as from the heat.

Mudge put a paw flat on the ground. "This 'ere sand. 'Ave a close look."

Jon-Tom knelt and stared. At first he saw nothing. Then one grain crept from beneath Mudge's fingers. A second, a third, moving from west to east. Mudge's paw hadn't moved them, nor had the wind. There was no wind.

At the same time as loose grains were shifting from beneath the otter's paw, a small rampart of sand was building up against the other side of his thumb. The sand was moving, without aid of wind, from east to west.

Jon-Tom put his own hand against the hot sand, watched as the phenomenon repeated itself. All around them, the sand was shifting from east to west. He felt the small hairs on the back of his neck stiffen.

" 'Tis bloody creepy," the otter muttered as he rose and brushed sand from his paws.

"Some underground disturbance," Jon-Tom suggested. "Or something alive under the surface." That was not a pleasant thought, and he hastened to discard it. They had no proof that anything lived in this land, anyway.

"That's not all." Mudge gestured back the way they'd come. "There's somethin' else mighty funny. See that 'ill we passed the other day?" Jon-Tom and Mudge strained to see the distant relative of a Serengeti kopje. " 'Tis lower than it were."

"Nothing unnatural about that, Mudge. It's just shrinking into the distance as we walk."

The otter shook his head insistently. " 'Tis shrinkin' too bloomin' fast, mate." He shouldered his pack and resumed the march. "One more thing. Don't it seem to either o' you that we're walkin' downhill?"

Jon-Tom didn't try to hide his confusion. He gestured at the western horizon. "We're on level ground. What are you talking about?"

"I dunno." The otter strained to put his feelings into words. " 'Tis just that somethin' don't feel right 'ere, mate. It just don't feel right."

That night the otter's nose proved of more help than his sense of balance. They dug a hole through a dark stain in the sand and were rewarded with a trickle of surprisingly clear water. Patience enabled them to top off their water skins and relieve their major anxiety. It was decided unanimously to spend the night by the moisture seep.

Jon-Tom felt someone shaking him awake, peered sleepily into still solid darkness. Mudge stared anxiously down at him.

"Got somethin' for you to 'ave a looksee at, mate."

"At this hour? Are you nuts?"

"I 'ope so, mate," the otter whispered. "I sincerely 'ope so."

Jon-Tom sighed and unrolled himself. As he did so he found himself spitting out sand. The full moon gleamed brightly on their campsite, to reveal packs, weapons, and Roseroar's feet partially buried in sand.

"The wind came up during the night, that's all." He found he was whispering, too, though there seemed no reason for it.

"Feel any wind now, mate?"

Jon-Tom wet a finger, stuck it into the air. "No. Not a breeze."

"Then 'ave a look at your own feet, mate."

Jon-Tom did so. As he stared he saw sand flowing over his toes. There was no wind at all, and now the sand was moving much faster. He drew his feet up as if the pulverized silica might bite him.

"Look all around, lad."

The sand was crawling westward at an ever more rapid pace. It seemed to accelerate even as he watched. In addition to the steady movement there came the first murmurs of a dry, slithery, rasping sound as grains tumbled over one another.

The discussion finally woke Roseroar. "What's goin' on heah?"

"I don't know," Jon-Tom muttered, eyeing the crawling ground. "The sand is moving, and much faster now than it was yesterday. I'm not sure I want to know what's making it move."

"Should we go back?" The tigress was slipping on her sandals, shaking the grains from the leather.

"We can't go back." He pulled on his boots. "If we go back now, we lose Jalwar, Folly, and likely as not, Clothahump's medicine. But I won't force either of you to stay with me. Roseroar, are you listening to me?"

She wasn't. Instead, she was pointing southward. "Ah think we might get ourselves a second opinion. We have company, y'all."

The line of camels the tigress had spotted was slightly behind them but moving in the same direction. Hastily gathering their equipment, the trio hurried to intercept the column of dromedaries. As they ran the sun began to rise, bringing with it welcome light and unwelcome heat. And all around them, the sand continued to crawl inexorably westward.

Mounted on the backs of the camels was an irregular assortment of

robed rodents—pack rats, kangaroo rats, field mice, and other desert
dwellers of related species. They looked to Jon-Tom like a bunch of
midget bewhiskered bedouins. He loped alongside the lead camel,
tried to bow slightly, and nearly tripped over his own feet.

"Where are you headed in such a hurry?" The pack rat did not
reply. The camel did.

"We go to Redrock. Everyone goes now to Redrock, man. Everyone who lives in the desert." The camel's manner was imperious and
wholly typical of his kind. He spat a glob of foul-smelling sputum to
his left, making Jon-Tom dodge.

"Who are you people?" inquired the pack rat in the front. There
was room on the camel's back for several.

"Strangers in this land."

"That is obvious enough," commented the camel.

"Why is everyone going to Redrock?" Jon-Tom asked.

The camel glanced back up at its lead rider and shook its head
sadly. The rat spoke. "You really don't know?"

"If we did, would we be askin' you, mate?" said Mudge.

The rat gestured with both paws, spreading his arms wide. "It is
the Conjunction. The time when the threads of magic that bind together this land reach their apogee. The time of the time inversion."

"What does that mean?"

The rat shrugged. "Do not ask me to explain it. I am no magician.
This I do know. If you do not reach the safety of Redrock by the time
the next moon begins to rise, you never will." He slapped the camel
on the side of its neck. The animal turned to gaze back up at him.

"Let's have none of that, Bartim, or you will find yourself walking.
I am measuring my pace, as are the rest of the brethren."

"The time is upon us!"

"No less so upon me than thee," said the camel with a pained
expression. He turned to glance back to where Jon-Tom was beginning to fall behind. "We will see you in Redrock, strangers, or we will
drink the long drink to your memory."

Panting hard in the rising light, Jon-Tom slowed to a walk, unable
to maintain the pace. On firm ground he might have kept up, but not
in the soft sand. Roseroar and Mudge were equally winded.

"What was that all about, Jon-Tom?" asked Roseroar.

"I'm not sure. It didn't make much sense."

"Ah you not a spellsingah?"

"I know my songs, but not other magic. If Clothahump were here
. . ."

"If 'is wizardship were 'ere we wouldn't be, mate."

"What do you think of their warning?"

Sand was building up around the otter's feet, and he kicked angrily at it. "They were both scared. Wot of I couldn't say, but scared they were. I think we'd better listen to 'em and get a move on. Make Redrock by nightfall, they said. If they can do it, so can we. Let's get to it."

They began to jog, keeping up a steady pace and taking turns in the lead. They barely paused to eat and made lavish use of their water. The more they drank, the less there was to carry, and if the warning was as significant as it had seemed, they would have to drink in Redrock that night or not drink at all.

As for the nature of the menace, that began to manifest itself as they ran.

It was evening, and still no sign of the city, nor of the caravan, which had far outdistanced them. The sand was moving rapidly now, threatening to engulf their feet every time they paused to catch their breath.

At first he thought he was sinking. A quick glance revealed the truth. The ground behind them was rising. It was as if they were running inland from a beach and the beach was pursuing, a steadily mounting tidal wave of sand. He thought about turning and trying to scramble to the crest of the granular wave. What stopped him was the possibility that on the other side they might find only another, even higher surge.

So they ran on, their lungs heaving, legs aching. Once Mudge stumbled and they had to pull him to his feet while the sand clutched eagerly at his legs.

When he fell a second time, he tried to wave them off. It was as if his seemingly inexhaustible energy had finally given out.

" 'Tis no use, lad. I can't go on anymore. Save yourselves." He fluttered weakly with a paw.

Jon-Tom used the pause to catch his wind. "You're right, Mudge," he finally declared. "That's the practical thing to do. I'll always remember how nobly you died." He turned to go on. Roseroar gave him a questioning look but decided not to comment.

A handful of sand struck Jon-Tom on the back of the neck. "Noble, me arse! You *would've* left me 'ere, wouldn't you? Left poor old Mudge to die in the sand!"

Jon-Tom grinned, took care to conceal it from the apoplectic otter.

"Look, *mate*. I'm tired, too, and I'm damned if I'm going to carry you."

The otter staggered after his companions. "I suppose you think it's funny, don't you, you 'ypocritical, angular bastard?"

Jon-Tom fought not to laugh. For one thing, he couldn't spare the wind. "Come off it, Mudge. You know we wouldn't have left you."

"Oh, wouldn't you, now? Suppose I 'adn't gotten up to follow you, eh? Wot then? 'Ow do I knows you would've come back for me?"

"It's a moot point, Mudge. You were just trying to hitch a ride."

"I admit nothin'." The otter pushed past him, taking the lead, his short, stubby legs moving like pistons.

"A strange one, yoah fuzzy little friend," Roseroar whispered to Jon-Tom. She matched her pace to his.

"Oh, Mudge is okay. He's a lazy, lying little cheat, but other than that he's a prince."

Roseroar considered this. "Ah believes the standards o' yoah world must be somewhat different from mine."

"Depends on what part of my culture you come from. Mudge, for example, would be right at home in a place called Hollywood. Or Washington, D.C. His talents would be much in demand."

Roseroar shook her head. "Those names have no meanin' fo me."

"That's okay. They don't for a lot of my contemporaries, either."

The sand continued to rise behind them, mounting toward the darkening sky. At any moment the wave might crest, to send tons of sand tumbling over them, swallowing them up. He tried not to think of that, tried not to think of anything except lifting his legs and setting one foot down ahead of the other. When the angle of the dune rising in their wake became sharper than forty-five degrees the sand would be rushing at them so rapidly they would be hard put to keep free of its grasp.

All around them, in both directions as far as they could see, the desert was climbing for the stars. He could only wonder at the cause. The Conjunction, the pack rat had said. The moon was up now, reaching silvery tendrils toward the panting, desperate refugees. At moonrise, the rat told him. But when would the critical moment come? Now, in minutes, or at midnight? How much time did they have left?

Then Roseroar was shouting, and a cluster of hills became visible ahead of them. As they ran on, the outlines of the hills sharpened, grew regular and familiar: Redrock, so named for the red sandstone of which its multistoried towers and buildings had been constructed.

In the first moonlight and the last rays of the sun the city looked as if it were on fire.

Now they found themselves among other stragglers—some on foot, others living in free association with camels and burros. Some snapped frantic whips over the heads of dray lizards.

Several ostrich families raced past, heavy backpacks strapped to their useless wings. They carried no passengers. Nor did the family of cougars that came loping in from the north, running on hind legs like Roseroar. Bleating and barking, honking and complaining, these streams of divergent life came together in pushing, shoving lines that struggled to enter the city.

"We're going to make it!" he shouted to his companions as they merged with the rear of the mob. He was afraid to look back lest an avalanche of brown-and-yellow particles prove him a fatal liar. His throat felt like the underside of the hood of a new Corvette after a day of drag-racing, but he didn't dare stop for a drink until they were safely inside the city walls.

Then the ground fell away beneath him.

They were on a bridge, and looking down he could see through the cracks in the wood. The lumber to build it must have come from distant mountains. There was no bottom to the moat, a black ring encircling the city.

His first thought was that Redrock had been built on a hill in the center of some ancient volcanic crater. A glance at the walls of the moat proved otherwise. They were too regular, too smooth, and too vertical to have been fashioned by hand. *Something* had dug the awesome ring. Who or what, he could not imagine.

Thick smells and heavy musk filled the air around him. The bridge seemed endless, the gaps between the heavy timbers dangerously wide. If he missed a step and put a leg through, he wouldn't fall, but he would be trampled by the anxious mass of life crowding about him.

Once within the safety of the city walls, the panic dissipated. Lines of tall guards clad in yellow shepherded the exhausted flow of refugees into the vast courtyard beyond the gate. There were no buildings within several hundred yards of the wall and the moat just beyond. A great open space had been provided for all who sought shelter from the rising sands. How often did this phenomenon take place? The camel and the pack rat hadn't said, but it was obviously a regular and predictable occurrence.

"I have to see what's going on outside," he told Roseroar. She nodded, towering above most of the crowd.

Tents had been set up in expectation of the flood of refugees. Jon-Tom and his companions were among the last to enter, but they had interests other than shelter.

"This way," the tigress told him. She took his hand and pulled him bodily through the milling, swarming crowd, a striped iceberg breasting a sea of fur. Somehow Mudge managed to keep up.

Then they found themselves by the city wall, followed it until they came to stone stairs leading upward. Jon-Tom let loose of Roseroar's paw and led the way.

Would the sand wave fill the moat? If so, what would happen afterward?

A few others already stood watching atop the wall. They were calm and relaxed, so Jon-Tom assumed there was no danger. Everyone in the city was handling the situation too well for there to be any danger.

One blasé guard, a tall serval wearing a high turban to protect his delicate ears, stood aside to let them pass. "Mind the vibration, visitors," he warned them.

They reached the top and stared out over the desert. Beyond the moat, the world was turning upside down.

There was no sign of the far mountains they had left many days ago. No sign of any landmark. Not a rock protruded from the ground. There was only the sand sea rising and rushing toward the city in a single wave two hundred feet high, roaring like a billion pans of frying bacon. Jon-Tom wanted to reach back and put his hand on the guard, to ask what was going to happen next. Since none of the other onlookers did so, he held his peace and like them, simply stood and gaped.

The massive wave did not fall forward to smash against the puny city walls. It began to slide into the dark moat, pouring in a seemingly endless waterfall into the unbelievable excavation. The wave was endless, too. As they watched it seemed to grow even higher, climbing toward the clouds as its base disappeared into the moat.

The thunder was all around him, and he could feel the sandstone blocks quivering underfoot. Jon-Tom turned. Across the roofs of the city, in all directions, he could see the wave. The city was surrounded by rushing sand hundreds of feet high and inestimable in volume, all of it cascading down into the depths which surrounded Redrock.

Thirty minutes passed. The wave began to shrink. Uncountable tons of sand continued to pour into the moat, which still showed no sign of filling up. Another thirty minutes and the torrent had slowed to a trickle. A few minutes more and the last grains tumbled into the abyss.

Beyond, the moon illuminated the skeleton of the desert. Bare rock stood revealed, as naked as the surface of the moon. Between the city and the mountains, nothing lived, nothing moved. A few hollows showed darkly in the rock, ancient depressions now emptied of sand and gravel.

A soft murmur rose from the onlookers as they turned away from the moat and the naked desert to face the center of the city. Jon-Tom and his companions turned with them.

In the exact center of Redrock a peculiar glassy tower stood apart from the sandstone buildings. All eyes focused on the slim spire. There was a feeling of expectation.

He was about to give in to curiosity and ask the guard what was going to happen when he heard something rumble. The stone under his feet commenced quivering. It was a different tremor this time, as though the planet itself were in motion. The rumbling deepened, became a roaring, then a constant thunder. Something was happening deep inside the earth.

"What is it, what's going on?" Roseroar yelled at him. He did not reply and could not have made himself heard had he tried.

Sudden, violent wind blew hats from heads and veils from faces. Jon-Tom's cape stretched out straight behind him like an iridescent flag. He staggered, leaned into the unexpected hurricane as he tried to see the tower.

The sands of the Timeful Desert erupted skyward from the open mouth of the glass pillar, climbing thousands of feet toward the moon. Reaching some predetermined height, the silica geyser started to spread out beneath the clouds. Jon-Tom instinctively turned to seek shelter, but stopped when he saw that none of the other pilgrims had moved.

As though sliding down an invisible roof, the sand did not fall anywhere within the city walls. Instead, it spread out like a cloud, to fall as yellow rain across the desert. It continued to fall for hours as the tower blasted it into the sky. Only when the moon was well past its zenith and had begun to set again did the volume decrease and finally peter out.

Then the geyser fell silent. The chatter of the refugees and the cityfolk filled the air, replacing the roar of the tower. A glance revealed that the bottomless moat was empty once again.

Beyond the wall, beyond the moat, the Timeful Desert once more was as it had been. All was still. The absence of life there despite the presence of water was now explained.

"Great magic," said Roseroar solemnly.

"Lethal magic." Mudge twitched his nose. "If we'd been a few minutes longer we'd be out there somewhere with our 'earts stopped and our guts full o' sand."

Jon-Tom stopped a passing fox. "Is it over? What happens now?"

"What happens now, man," said the fox, "is that we sleep, and we celebrate the end of another Conjunction. Tomorrow we return to our homes." She pushed past him and started down the stairs.

Jon-Tom resorted to questioning one of the guards. The muskrat was barely four feet tall and wore his fur cut fashionably short.

"Please, we're strangers here." He nodded toward the desert. "Does this happen every year?"

"Twice a year," the guard informed him, bored. "A grand sight the first time, I suppose."

"What's it for? Why does it happen?"

The muskrat scratched under his chin. "It is said that these are the sands of time. All time. When they have run their course, they must be turned to run again. Who turns them, or why, no one knows. Gods, spirits, some great being somewhere else who is bored with the task, who knows? I am no sorcerer or scholar, visitor." He turned to leave.

"Let 'im go, mate," said Mudge. "I don't care wot it's about. Runnin' for me life always tires me out. Me for a spot o' sleep and somethin' to drink." He started down the stairs. Jon-Tom and Roseroar followed.

"What do yo think happens heah?" the tigress asked him.

"I imagine it's as the guard told us. The desert is some kind of hourglass, holding all time within it." He gazed thoughtfully at the sky. "I wonder: if you could stop the mechanism somehow, could you stop time?" He turned toward the glassy tower. "I'd sure like to have a look inside that."

"Best not to," she told him. "Yo might find something. Yo might find your own time."

He nodded. "Anyway, we have other fish to fry."

"Ah beg yo pahdon?"

"Jalwar and Folly. If everyone else is forced to seek sanctuary here from the Conjunction, they would also. If they weren't caught by the sand, they should be somewhere here in the city."

"Ah declah, Jon-Tom, ah hadn't thought o' that!" She scanned the courtyard below.

"Unless," he went on, "they were far enough ahead of us to have already crossed the desert."

"Oh." She looked downcast, then straightened. "No mattah. We'll find them." She began looking for an empty place among the crowds. Probably the few city inns were already full to overflowing with the wealthy among the refugees. The city gates were open and some were already filing back out into the desert.

"Yo know, somethin' just occurred to me, Jon-Tom. This old Jalwah, ah'm thinkin' we've been underestimatin' him all along. Do yo suppose he deliberately led us out heah into this desert knowin' we didn't know about this comin' Conjunction thing, and hopin' we might get oahselves killed?"

Jon-Tom considered only a moment. "Roseroar, I think that's a very good possibility, just as I think that the next time we meet up with our ferret friend, we'd better watch our step very carefully indeed."

XIII

Inquiries in the marketplace finally unearthed mention of Folly and Jalwar's passing. They were indeed several days ahead of their pursuers, and yet they had rented no riding animals. Apparently Jalwar was not only smarter than they'd given him credit for, he was also considerably stronger. The merchant who provided the information did not know which way the ferret and the girl had gone, but Jon-Tom remembered enough of the map to guess.

The desert reaches were much more extensive to north and south. There was no way back to Snarken except via Redrock. Therefore their earlier suppositions still held true. Jalwar was making for Crancularn as fast as possible.

Roseroar's search for nighttime lodging was terminated. There was no time to waste. Jon-Tom reluctantly allowed Mudge to scavenge for supplies, and the travelers then beat a hasty retreat from Redrock before their unwilling victualers could awaken to the discovery of their absent inventory.

"Of course, we'll pay for these supplies on our way back," Jon-Tom said.

"And 'ow do you propose we do that?" Mudge labored under his restocked pack. The desert was oddly cool underfoot, the sand stable and motionless once again. It was as though the grains had never been displaced, had never moved.

"I don't know, but we have to do something about this repeated steali—"

"Watch it, mate."

"About this repeated foraging of yours. Why do you insist on maintaining the euphemisms, Mudge?"

The otter grinned at him. "For appearances' sake, mate."

"It troubles me as well," Roseroar murmured, "but we must make use of any means that we can to see this thing through."

"I know, but I'll feel better about it if we can pay for what we've 'borrowed' on our way back."

Mudge sighed, shook his head resignedly. " 'Umans," he muttered.

Despite Jon-Tom's expectations, they did not catch up to their quarry. They did encounter occasional groups of nomads returning to their campsites, sometimes sharing their camps for the night. All expressed ignorance when asked if they had seen any travelers fitting Jalwar's or Folly's description.

On the third day they had their first glimpse of the foothills which lay beyond the western edge of the Timeful Desert. On the fourth they found themselves hiking among green grass, cool woodlands, and thick scrub. Mudge luxuriated in the aroma and presence of running water, while Roseroar was able to enjoy fresh meat once more.

On their first day in the forest she brought down a monitor lizard the size of a cow with one swordthrust. Mudge joined her in butchering the carcass and setting the steaks to cook over a blaze of thin, white-barked logs.

"Smells mighty good," commented a strange voice.

Roseroar rose to a sitting position. Mudge peered around the cookfire while Jon-Tom put aside the duar he'd been strumming.

Standing at the edge of their little clearing in the trees was a five-foot-tall cuscus, a bland expression on his pale face. He was dressed in overlapping leather strips and braids, snakeskin boots of azure hue, and short brown pants. A single throwing knife was slung on each hip, and he was scratching himself under the chin with his furless, prehensile tail. As he scratched he leaned on the short staff he carried. Jon-Tom wondered if, like his own, the visitor's also concealed a short, deadly length of steel in the unknobbed end. The visitor's fur was pale beige mottled with brown.

He was also extraordinarily ugly, a characteristic of the species, though perhaps a female cuscus might have thought otherwise of the newcomer. He made no threatening gestures and waited patiently.

"Come on in and have a seat." Jon-Tom extended the invitation only after Roseroar had climbed to her feet and Mudge had moved close to his bow.

"That is right kind of you, sir. I am Hathcar." Jon-Tom performed introductions all around.

Roseroar was sniffing the air, glanced accusingly down at the visitor. "You are not alone."

"No, large she, I am not. Did I forget to mention it? I am sorry and will now remedy my absentmindedness." He put his lips together and emitted a sharp, high-pitched whistle.

With much rustling of bushes a substantial number of creatures stepped out into clear view, forming a line behind the cuscus. They were an odd assortment, from the more familiar rats and mice to bandicoots and phalangers. There was even a nocturnal aye-aye, who wore large, dark sunglasses and carried a short, sickle-shaped weapon.

Their clothes were on the ragged side, and their boots and sandals showed signs of much usage. Altogether not a prosperous-looking bunch, Jon-Tom decided. The presence of so many weapons was not reassuring. These were not kindly villagers out for a daily stroll.

Still, if all they wanted was something to eat. . . .

"You're welcome to join us," he told Hathcar. "There's plenty for all."

Hathcar looked past him, to where Mudge was laboring with the cooking. His tongue licked black lips.

"You are kind. Those of us who prefer meat haven't made such a grand catch in many a day." He smiled as best he could.

Jon-Tom gestured toward Roseroar. "Yes, she's quite the huntress."

"She sizes the part. Still, there is but one of her and many of us. How is it that she has been so successful and we have not?"

"Skill is more important than numbers." One huge paw caressed the hilt of a long sword.

Hathcar did not seem impressed. "Sometimes that can be so, unless you are a hundred against one lizard."

"Sometimes," she agreed coolly, "but not always."

The cuscus changed the subject. "What seek you strangers in this remote land?"

"We're on a mission of importance for a great and powerful wizard," Jon-Tom told him. "We go to the village of Crancularn."

"Crancularn." Hathcar looked back at his colleagues, who were hard-pressed to restrain their amusement. "That's a fool's errand."

Jon-Tom casually let his fingers stray to his staff. He'd had just about enough of this questioning, enigmatic visitor. Either they wanted something to eat or they didn't, and double-talk wasn't on the menu.

"Maybe you think we look like fools," Hathcar said. All hints of laughter fled from the gang standing behind him. Jon-Tom didn't reply, waited for what might come.

The cuscus's smile returned, and he moved toward the fire. "Well, you have offered us a meal. That's a wise decision. Certainly not one to be made by fools." He pulled a throwing knife. "If I might try a bite? It looks well done. My compliments to the cook." Mudge said nothing.

Jon-Tom watched the visitor closely. Was he going to cut meat with it . . . or throw it? He couldn't decide.

Something came flying through the air toward him. He ducked and rolled, ending up on his feet holding the ramwood staff protectively in front of him. Mudge picked up his bow and notched an arrow into the string. Roseroar's longswords flashed as they were drawn. All within a couple of seconds.

Hathcar was careful not to raise the knife he now held. Behind him, his colleagues gripped their own weapons threateningly. But the cuscus was not glaring at Jon-Tom. His gaze was on the creature who had come flying through the air to land heavily next to the tall human.

The mongoose was clad entirely in black. It lay on its belly, moaning. Strange marks showed on its narrow backside.

"Faset," Hathcar hissed, "what happened?" The mongoose rolled to look at him, yelped when its bruised pelvis made contact with the ground.

"I happened." Everyone turned toward the voice.

The unicorn strolled casually into the clearing. It was gold. Not the light gold of a palomino but a pure metallic gold like the color of a coin or ring, except for white patches on its forehead and haunches. It might have risen from a vat of liquid gold except that Jon-Tom could clearly see that the color was true, down to the shortest hair.

In its mouth it carried a small crossbow. This it dropped at Jon-Tom's feet. Then it nodded meaningfully toward the still groaning mongoose. Jon-Tom now recognized the marks on the mongoose's pants. They were hoofprints.

Hathcar was beside himself as he glared furiously at the unicorn. "Who the hell are you, four-foot? And who asked you to interfere? This is none of your business."

The unicorn gazed at him out of lapis eyes, said coolly, "I am making it my business." He smiled at Jon-Tom. "My name's Drom. I was grazing back in the woods when I heard the talk. Ordinarily I would have ignored it, as I ignored your presence." He nodded toward the mongoose, who was trying to crawl back to its comrades while avoiding Hathcar.

"However, I happened to chance upon this ebon worm as he was aiming his little toy at your back." Drom raised a hoof, brought it down on the crossbow. There was a splintering sound. "The unpleasant one there," and he nodded toward Hathcar, "was right. This was none of my business. I don't trouble to involve myself in the affairs of you social types. But I can't stand to see anyone backshot." He turned his magnificent head, the thin golden goatee fluttering, and glared back at Hathcar.

"Yo ah a true gentlemale, suh," said Roseroar approvingly.

"You should have stayed out of this, fool." Hathcar moved quickly to join his gang. "Anyway, he lies. No doubt this insect," and he kicked at the miserable Faset, "was trying to put a bolt through you. But that has nothing to do with me."

"You called him by name," Jon-Tom said accusingly.

"A casual acquaintance." Hathcar continued to retreat. His backers muttered uneasily.

"Glad you don't know 'im, friend." Mudge's arrow followed the cuscus's backpedaling. "I'd 'ate to think you 'ad anything to do with 'is little ambushcade."

"What about your invitation?" Hathcar wanted to know.

"I think we'd rather dine alone." Jon-Tom smiled thinly. "At least until we can sort things out."

"That's not very friendly of you. It's not polite to withdraw an invitation once extended."

"My back," the mongoose blubbered. "I think my back is broken."

"Shut up, asshole." Hathcar kicked him in the mouth and blood squirted. The cuscus tried to grin at the tall man. "Really, this thing has nothing to do with me." His band was beginning to melt into the forest. "Always hanging around, looking for sympathy. Sorry our visit upset you. I understand." Then he too was gone, swallowed by the vegetation.

Roseroar's ears were cocked forward. "They're still movin' about," she murmured warily.

"Where?" Jon-Tom asked her.

"Back among the trees."

"They are spreading out in an attempt to encircle you," said the one-horned stallion.

"Permit me to congratulate you on your timely arrival, mate." Mudge's eyes searched the woods as he spoke. "I never sensed 'im."

"Nor did I," said Roseroar, sparing a glance for the remains of the crossbow.

"I don't understand," Jon-Tom murmured. "We offered them all the food they could eat."

"It wasn't just your food they were after." Drom kicked the crossbow fragments aside. "I know that bunch by reputation. They were after your weapons and armor, your fine clothes and your money."

Mudge let out a barking laugh. "Our money! Now that's amusin'. We haven't a copper to our names," he lied.

"Ah, but they thought you did." The unicorn nodded toward the forest. "Small comfort that would have been to you if they had learned that afterwards."

"You're right there."

Roseroar was turning a slow circle, keeping the roasting carcass at her back as much as possible. "They're still out theah. Probably they think we can't heah them, but ah can." She growled deep in her throat, a blood chilling sound. "Our friend here is right. They're trying to get behind us."

"And to surprise you. Hathcar did not show his full strength. Many more of his band remained concealed while he spoke to you."

Jon-Tom eyed the silent trees in alarm. "How many more?"

"A large number, though, of course, I am only guessing based on what I could observe during my approach."

"We appreciate your help. You might as well take off now. Our problems aren't yours."

"They are now," the unicorn told him. "These are indifferent murderers, full of false pride. I have embarrassed their leader in front of his band. Now he must kill me or lose face and possibly his status as leader."

Roseroar strode toward the back of the clearing. "Move in heah, where theah's some covah."

The unicorn shook his head, the mane of gold rippling in the filtered light. "It will not be good enough, tigress. I can see that you are powerful as well as well-versed in war, but there are too many of them, and you will be fighting in very close quarters. If they come at you from all directions simultaneously you won't have a chance. You require a more defensible position."

"You know of one?" Jon-Tom asked him.

"It is not far from here. I think if we can get there we will be able to stand them off."

"Then let's get the hell out of here," he muttered as he shouldered his pack.

Mudge held back, torn between common sense and the effort he'd put into their supper. Roseroar saw his hesitation.

"A full belly's small consolation to someone with his guts hangin' out. Ah declah, short-whiskahs, sometimes ah wondah about yo priorities."

"Sometimes I wonder meself, lass." He looked longingly back at the lost roast as they hurried through the woods, following the stallion's lead.

Drom maintained a steady but slow pace to enable his newfound friends to keep up with him. Everyone watched the surrounding woods. But it was Roseroar's ears they relied on most.

"Stayin' carefully upwind of us, but I can heah them movin' faster. They're still behind us, though. Must think we're still in the camp."

"Wait a minute!" Jon-Tom called a halt. "Where's Mudge?"

Roseroar cursed under her breath. "Damn that ottah! Ah knew ah should've kept a closer watch on him. He's gone back fo some of that meat. Yoah friend is a creature of base instincts."

"Yes, but he's not stupid. Here he comes."

Mudge appeared, laboring beneath a section of roast nearly as big as himself. "Sorry, mates. I worked all day on this bloody banquet, and I'm damned if I was goin' to leave it all for those bastards."

"You're damned anyway," snapped Jon-Tom. "How are you going to keep up, hauling that on your back?"

The otter swung the heavy, pungent load off his shoulders. "Roseroar?"

"Not me, ottah. Yo stew in yoah own stew."

"We're wasting time," said Drom. "Here." He dipped his head forward. "Hold it still."

A quick jab and the roast was impaled on the spiral horn. "Now let's be away from here before they discover our flight." He turned and resumed his walk. "Disgusting."

"What is?" Jon-Tom asked as he jogged alongside.

"The smell of cooked flesh, the odiferous thought of consuming the body of another living creature, the miasma of carbonized protein, what else?"

Suddenly Jon-Tom wasn't so hungry anymore.

Creepers and vines strangled the entrance to the ancient structure. Roseroar was reluctant to enter. The strangely slitted windows and triangular doorways bespoke a time and people who had ruled the world long before the warmblooded.

"Sulolk used this place," murmured Drom as he trotted inside.

Distant shouts of outrage came from behind them, deciding the tigress. She bent beneath the low portal and squeezed in.

The single chamber beyond had a vaulted ceiling that enabled her to stand easily. There was more than enough room for all of them. Mudge was admiring the narrow windows, fashioned by a forgotten people for reasons of unknown aesthetics but admirably suited to the refugees' present needs. He notched an arrow into his bow and settled himself behind one thin gap.

Jon-Tom took up a stance to the left of the opening, ready to use his steel-tipped staff on anyone who tried to enter. A moment later he was able to move to a second window as Roseroar jammed a massive stone weighing at least three hundred pounds into the doorway, blocking it completely.

"This is a good place to fight from." Drom used a hoof to shove the cooling roast from his horn onto clean rock. "A small spring flows from the floor of a back room. Cracks in the ceiling allow fresh air to circulate. I have often slept here in safety." He indicated the damp grass growing from the floor. "There is food as well."

"For you," admitted Jon-Tom, watching the woods for signs of their pursuers. "Well, we have what's in our packs and the roast we saved." He glanced to his right, toward the other guarded window. "You shouldn't have done that, Mudge."

"Cor, it ain't no fun fightin' on an empty stomach, mate." He leaned forward; his black nose twitched as he sampled the air. "If they try chargin' us, I can pick 'em off easy. Our 'orny friend's right. This is a damn good place."

Roseroar was eyeing the wall carvings uneasily. "This is a very old place. I smell ancient feahs." She had drawn both longswords.

There was a thump as Drom settled down to wait. "I smell only clean grass and water."

Threatening shouts began to emanate from the trees. Mudge responded with some choice comments about Hathcar's mother, whom he had never met but whom thousands of others undoubtedly had. This inspired a rain of arrows which splintered harmlessly against the thick stone walls. One flew through Jon-Tom's window to stick in the earth behind him.

"Here they come!" he warned his companions.

There was nothing subtle about the bandits' strategy. While archers tried to pin down the defenders, an assortment of raccoons, foxes, and cats rushed at the entrance, carrying a big log between them. But Roseroar braced her massive shoulders against the boulder from behind and kept it from being pushed inward, while Mudge put arrows in the log wielders as fast as they could be replaced.

"Another bugger down!" the otter would yell each time an arrow struck home.

This continued for several minutes while Mudge reduced the number of Hathcar's band and Roseroar kept the boulder from moving so much as an inch inward. No martyrs to futility, those hefting the battering ram finally gave up and fled for the safety of the woods with the otter's deadly shafts urging them on.

No one had approached Jon-Tom's window during the fight. Mudge and Roseroar had done all the work and he felt pretty useless.

"What now? I don't think they'll try that again."

"No, but they'll bloody well try somethin' else," murmured the otter. "Say, mate, why don't you 'ave a go at 'em with your duar?"

Jon-Tom blinked. "I hadn't thought of that. Well, I had, but it's hard to think and sing when you're running."

"Why make music? To aggravate them?" asked Drom interestedly.

"Nope. 'E's a spellsinger, 'e is," said Mudge, "and a right good one, too. When 'e can control it," he added by way of afterthought.

"A spellsinger. I am impressed," said the unicorn. Jon-Tom felt a little better, though he wished the golden stallion would quit staring at him so intensely.

"What do you think they'll try next?" Jon-Tom asked the otter.

Mudge eyed the trees. "This bunch bein' about as imaginative as a pile o' cow flop, I'd expect them to try smokin' us out. If four legs there is right about the cracks in the roof lettin' air in, they'll be wastin' their time."

"Are yo certain theah's no back way in?"

"None that I was ever able to discover," Drom told the tigress.

"Not that you'd fit places where some o' the rest of us might," observed Mudge thoughtfully. He handed his bow and quiver to Jon-Tom. "I'd better check out the nooks and crannies, mate. We don't want some nasty surprises to show up and stick us in the behind when we ain't lookin'." He headed for the crumbling back wall.

Jon-Tom eyed the bow uncertainly. "Mudge, I'm not good at this."

"Just give a shout if they come at us again. It ain't 'ard, mate. Just shove an arrow through the window there. *They* don't know you can't shoot." He bent, crawled under a lopsided stone and disappeared.

Jon-Tom awkwardly notched an arrow, rested it on the window sill as Roseroar took up a position behind the one the otter had vacated.

"Ah don't understand," she murmured, squinting at the forest. "We all ain't worth the trouble we're causin' this Hathcar. That ottah brought down five or six o' them. If ah was this fella ah'd give up and go in search of less deadly prey."

"That would be the reasonable thing to do," said Drom, nodding, "except that as chief he has lost face already before his band. He will not give up, though if he suffers many more losses his own fighters may force him to quit." The unicorn climbed to his feet and strolled over to Roseroar's window. She made room for him.

"Hathcar!" he shouted.

A reluctant voice finally replied. "Who calls? Is that you, meddler with a spike in his brain?"

"It is I." Drom was unperturbed by the bandit leader's tone. "Listen to me! These travelers are poor. They have no money."

Cuscus laughter rang through the trees. "You expect me to believe that?"

"It's true. In any case, you cannot defeat them."

"Don't bet on that."

"You cannot break in here."

"Maybe not, but we'll force you out. It may take time, but we'll do it."

"If you do, then I will only lead them to another place of safety, one even harder to assault than this one. I know these woods, and you know I speak the truth. So why not depart now before suffering any more senseless losses? It's a stupid leader who sacrifices his people for no gain."

Muttering came from different places in the trees, proof that Drom's last words had hit home. Hathcar hastened to respond.

"No matter if you lead them elsewhere. We'll track you down no matter where you go."

"Perhaps you will. Or perhaps you'll find yourselves led into a trap. We of the forest have ways of defending ourselves against you lovers of civilization. There are hidden pits and tree-mounted weapons scattered throughout my territory. Follow me and find them at your peril."

This time the woods were silent. Drom nodded to himself. "Good.

They're thinking it over, probably arguing about it. If they come to their senses, we may be able to get out of here without any more violence."

Jon-Tom peered through the narrow slit in the stone. "You think they'll really react that sensibly?"

"I don't know, but he knows I'm talking truth," said the unicorn softly. "I know this section of forest better than he does, and he knows that I know that."

"But how could we slip out of here and get past them?"

Drom chuckled. "I did fudge on that one a bit. Yet for all he knows there are a dozen secret passages out of here."

"If they are, they're bloody well still secret." Mudge emerged from the crawlspace he'd entered and wiped limestone dust from his shirt and whiskers. "Tight as a teenage whore. Nothin' bigger than a snake could get out the back way. We're safe enough here, all right." Jon-Tom gladly handed back the otter's bow and found himself a soft place on the floor.

"Then I guess we wait until they attack again or give up and leave us alone. I suppose we ought to stand watch tonight."

"Allow me, suh," said Roseroar. "Ah'm as comfortable with the night as ah am with the day."

"While we wait to see what they'll do," said Drom, "perhaps now you'll tell me what you people are doing in this country, so far from civilization."

Jon-Tom sighed. "It's a long story," he told the unicorn, and proceeded to relate it yet again. As he spoke, the sun set and the trees blended into a shadowy curtain outside. An occasional arrow plunked against the stone, more for nuisance value than out of any hope of hitting any of the defenders inside.

Hathcar had indeed lost too many in the futile attack to try it again. He knew that if he continued to fling his followers uselessly against an impregnable position they would melt quietly away into the woods. That night he moved away from the main campfire and sought counsel from an elderly rat and wolf, the two wisest of his band.

"So how do we pry those stinking bastards out of there?"

The rat's hair was tinged with white and his face and arms were scarred. He picked at the dirt with one hand. "Why bother? Why not let them rot in there if they so desire? There are easier pickin's elsewhere."

Hathcar leaned toward him, glaring in the moonlight. "Do you know what happened today? Do you? They made a fool of me. Me, Hathcar! Nobody makes a fool of Hathcar and walks away to boast of it, nobody! Not on their own legs, they don't."

"It was just a thought," the rat mumbled. "It had to be said."

"Right. It's been said. It's also been forgotten." The rat said nothing.

"How about smoking them out?" suggested the wolf.

The cuscus let out a derisive snort. "Don't you think they've already thought of that? If they haven't tried to break out, it means they aren't worried about smoke; and if they aren't worried about it, it probably means it won't work if we try it."

"Could we," suggested the rat, "maybe force our way in through the roof?"

Hathcar sighed. "You're all looking at the obvious, all of you. I'm the only one who can see beyond the self-evident. That cursed four-legs led them straight here, so he's probably telling the truth when he says he knows it well. He wouldn't box himself into a situation he wasn't comfortable with. He say they can slip out anytime and hide somewhere else twice as strong. Maybe he's lying, but we can't take that chance. We have to take them here, while we know what we're up against. That means our first priority is to get rid of that horned meddler."

"How about moving a couple of archers in close? Those with good night vision. If they can sneak up against the wall they might get a clear shot inside."

Hathcar considered. "Not bad, except that if they don't snuff the unicorn right away that fucking water rat's likely to get 'em both. I've never seen anybody shoot like that." He shook his head.

"No, it's not good enough, Parsh. I'm sure they've got a guard up, and I won't send any more of the boys against that otter's bow. No, we have to bring the unicorn out somehow, far enough so we can get a clear shot at him. By himself, if possible."

The rat spat on the ground. "That's likely, isn't it?"

"You know, there may be a way."

Hathcar frowned at the wolf. "I was only half-serious, Brungunt."

"I'm wholly serious. All we need is the right kind of bait."

"That blow you took in Ollorory village has addled your brains," said Parsh. "Nothing's going to bring that unicorn out where we can get at him."

"Go on, Brungunt," said the thoughtful Hathcar.

The wolf leaned close. "It should be done when most of them

sleep. We must watch and smell for when the stallion takes his turn as sentry. If they post only the one guard, we may have a chance. Great care must be taken, for it will be a near thing, a delicate business. Bait or no bait, if the meddler senses our presence, I do not think he can be drawn out. So after we set the bait we must retreat well out of range. It will work, you'll see. So powerful is the bait, it will draw our quarry well out where we can cut off his retreat. Then if won't matter if he bolts into the woods. The important thing is that we'll be rid of him, and the ones we really want will be deprived of his advice and aid."

"No," said Hathcar, his eyes gleaming, "no. I want that four-legs, too. I want him dead. Or better yet, we'll just hamstring him." He grinned viciously in the dark. "Yes, hamstring him. That's better still." He forced himself from contemplation of pleasures to come. "This bait? Where do we get it?"

Brungunt scratched an ear and even the skeptical Parsh looked interested. "First we must find a village or farm that numbers humans among its occupants." He was nodding to himself as he spoke. "This is an old, old magic we will work tonight, but you don't have to be a sorcerer to work it. It works itself. It is said by those who may know that a unicorn may not be taken by force, but only by stealth and guile."

"Get to the point," said Hathcar impatiently.

The wolf hurried his words. "We don't have to sneak up on him. He'll come to us. He'll follow a maiden fair and true. It is said."

Hathcar looked doubtful. "What kind of maiden? A coltish mare?"

"No, no. It must be a human maiden."

Parsh the rat was thoroughly shocked. "You expect to find a virgin around here? Species notwithstanding."

"There is a town not far from this place."

"Crestleware." Hathcar nodded.

"We can but try," said the wolf, spreading his paws.

"A virgin. Are you certain about this, Brungunt?"

"The bond is supposed to be most powerful. The girl need only lead him far enough for us to get behind him before he picks up our scent. Do not ask me to explain this thing. I only relate what I have heard told."

"Wouldn't cost us a one. You'd better be right about this, Brungunt, or I'll see your ears decorating my spear."

"That's not fair!" protested the wolf. "I am only relating a legend."

"Look to your ears, wolf." Hathcar rose. "And tell the others to look to theirs. Parsh, you come with me." He glared at Brungunt. "We will return as quickly as possible. This magic sounds to me like it works better in the dark, and I don't want to give that four legs another day to think of a better place." He glanced through the trees toward the moonlit ruins. "Hamstring him, yes. I'll see that damned meddler crawling to me on his knees, and then we'll break those as well."

XIV

Hathcar crouched low as he pointed toward the clearing in front of the silent fortress. The slim girl who stood next to him watched closely, her eyes wide. She had been awakened in the middle of the night by her mother and sent off in the company of this ugly stranger. She hadn't wanted to go, but her mother had insisted, assuring her it would only be until sunrise and that everything was all right, everything had been arranged. Then she would be brought home and allowed to sleep all day. And they had promised her candy.

"There is the place, little one."

"Don't call me little," she snapped. "I'm as grown up as you are! And my name's Silky."

"Sorry," Hathcar growled softly, restraining himself. He wasn't very fond of cubs, but he needed this one's cooperation.

"You're going to pay my daddy two gold pieces for luring out this unicorn to you. What makes you think he'll come out and follow me?"

"He'll come," Hathcar assured her. "Just be nice to him, tell him how strong and beautiful he is."

She stared warily at the cuscus and his two companions out of eyes that were not as innocent as her parents insisted they were. "You're sure this is a unicorn you're sending me after?"

"Are you sure you're a virgin?"

"Yes, I'm sure," she said tiredly. She'd heard this stranger discussing the matter with her mother.

Hathcar turned and pointed back through the woods. "Back this way there's a pool in a little hollow. Bring him there. We'll be waiting."

"What happens when we get there?" she asked curiously.

"None of your business, lit . . . Silky. Your daddy's being paid for your services. You do what I want you to and you don't ask questions."

"Okay." She hesitated. "You're not going to hurt him, are you? I've never seen a unicorn, but I've been told they're real pretty."

"Oh, no, no, we won't hurt him," said Hathcar smoothly. "We just want to surprise him. We're his friends, and we want to surprise him, and you won't tell him about us because that would ruin the surprise, wouldn't it?"

"I guess so." She smiled brightly. "I like surprises, too. Can I watch when you surprise him?"

"Sure you can," Hathcar assured her innocently. "I think you'll be surprised, too." He turned to leave her, Brungunt and Parsh following.

"It's dark," she said uncertainly.

"You'll be okay," Brungunt told her. "Didn't you say you were a big girl?"

"That's right, I am."

"Fine. Just bring the four-legs down to the pool."

"Why didn't we just abduct the little bitch?" Parsh wanted to know as they made their way through the woods to rejoin the rest of the waiting band.

"Big village," Hathcar told him. "A good place to buy supplies. The price hurts, but it'll be worth it. Besides, Brungunt here said the girl had to act voluntarily or the magic wouldn't work."

"That's so," the wolf agreed, nodding. "It is so told."

"So it's better all around this way," Hathcar finished.

Silky stood waiting, counting away the minutes to allow the unicorn's friends time to ready their surprise. Then she strolled out into the small clearing in front of the broken old building. She was wearing her best dress. It clung to her budding figure as she moved. Her mother had spent fifteen minutes combing out the long auburn hair to make certain her daughter looked her best. The old wolf had insisted on it.

Two gold pieces. That would buy a lot of things for the family, including candy. She determined to do exactly as the cuscus ordered, even if he'd been lying to her about the surprise he was planning. After all, the horned one was nothing to her.

Still, she was trembling slightly at the prospect of actually meeting a unicorn as she stepped out into the silvery moonlight. There were many stories told about the shy, solitary four-legs. They kept to themselves in the deep forest, shunning civilization and intelligent company.

The ancient stones before her were silent. Should she cry out? If she did, what could she say? "Here, unicorn"? There was no one to advise her, since Hathcar had joined the rest of his friends far back in the trees, out of sight and scent. The old wolf had assured her she had only to approach the ruins and the unicorn would come to her. Would come and would follow back to the pool. And the surprise waiting there.

She stood before the ruins and waited.

Within, there was movement she could not see. Drom's head lifted, his nostrils twitching. He blinked at the bodies sleeping soundly around him. It was his turn on watch.

Trotting silently so as not to disturb his newfound friends, he moved to one window slit and peered out. Standing alone in the moonlight was a small, slim figure. A human figure, young and pure. Ancient emotions began to pluck at him.

Nodding at no one in particular, he quietly began pushing at the boulder which blocked the entryway. He worked with care, wanting to make positive identification of the beckoning shape outside without waking his companions.

When the stone had been edged to one side he walked through the opening and stepped out onto the grass, sniffing at the air, which was heavy with the girl's clean, sweet-smelling scent. She was alone. The night was still, and there was no wind to mask concealed odors.

He walked over to the girl, who eyed him nervously and took a step backward.

"Hello. You're . . . awfully pretty." She licked her lips, glanced over a shoulder once, then said confidently, "Won't you come and walk with me? It's a nice night in the forest."

"In a minute, little one. There's something I have to do first." Turning, he moved back to the ruins and stuck his head inside, let out a soft whinny. "Wake up."

There were stirrings on the floor. Lightest of sleepers, Roseroar sat up fast when she saw that the boulder defending them had been moved.

"Now what?" She stared at the unicorn. "Explain yoself, suh." She

was on her feet and heading for the boulder. Drom cut her off. "If
they come at us now . . ." she began warningly.

"Relax, cat-a-mountain. They're not coming. They're not even
watching us." Behind them, Jon-Tom and Mudge were also awakening.

"How do yo know?" Roseroar was peering cautiously out. She saw
and smelled the girl immediately, but no one else.

"Because they've decided to try something else." He let out a soft,
whinnying laugh. "By the time they realize this latest ploy has failed,
it will be too late. We'll be long gone from this place and beyond their
reach. Who among you is the fleetest of foot?"

"Roseroar over the long distance, me over the short. I think," Jon-
Tom told him sleepily, still not sure just what was going on.

"Good. You and the otter climb onto my back and ride."

A sweet but anxious voice sounded from outside. "Who are you
talking to? Why don't you come out and talk with me?"

"Who the 'ell is *that?*" Mudge rushed to a window. "Blimey, 'tis a
girl!"

"What?" Jon-Tom joined him, gaped at the figure standing in the
clearing. "What's she doing here?"

"Tempting me." Drom chuckled again. "Hathcar and his curs
have moved out of scent range, no doubt to lie in wait to ambush me
as I am drawn helplessly to them by this irresistibly pure young
female."

"I'm not sure I follow you."

"It's part of an ancient legend, a very old magic."

"Lousy magic," said Jon-Tom.

"Oh, no, it's very good magic, and very true. Only not in my case.
We're wasting time." He turned his flank to Jon-Tom, tilted his head
low. "Can you mount by yourself? Use my mane for a grip if you
need one."

Jon-Tom climbed onto the broad, strong back easily, pulled Mudge
up behind him.

"Leave some room," Drom instructed him. "We're not leaving the
girl here for Hathcar." He trotted outside, Roseroar pacing him easily while restlessly searching the woods for signs of their enemies.

Silky watched them approach. Hathcar and the old wolf hadn't
said anything about the unicorn's companions. She stared worriedly
at the big cat loping alongside the four legs. The tigress could swallow her in one gulp.

Then the unicorn was standing close and smiling down at her over his goatee. "Do not be afraid, little one. All is well. How came you into this business?"

She hesitated before replying. "They paid my mother and father. They paid them two gold pieces for me to come with them for the night and help them surprise you."

"Surprise me. I see," murmured Drom, nodding knowingly.

"You were supposed to follow me." She turned and pointed. "That way, to a hollow full of water so your friends could surprise you."

"And a fine surprise that would've been, wot?" growled Mudge softly.

"There's been a change in plans," Drom informed her. "Get onto my back, in front of this handsome gentleman. We're taking you back to your parents. You did as requested and drew me out of my refuge. We're just going to take a little detour, that's all. So you've fulfilled your end of the contract, at least in part, and your parents should be entitled to keep whatever payment they've already received for your service."

"I don't know." She scuffed the ground with one foot. "I didn't bring you to the pool."

"Is that your fault?" Drom leaned close. "You don't really like those people out there, do you?"

"No," she said suddenly. "No, I don't. But I had to do it. I had to."

"You are a true innocent, as you would have to be. You have done all you could."

"What about my candy?" she asked petulantly.

Jon-Tom reached down a hand. The girl took it reluctantly and he swung her up in front of him. Her nearness reminded him uncomfortably of Folly.

Drom turned and exploded into a wild gallop, restraining himself only enough to allow Roseroar to keep pace. Jon-Tom felt confident the unicorn could carry three fully grown men with ease. He, the girl, and Mudge were no burden at all.

After they'd covered several kilometers, the stallion slowed. Roseroar was panting hard and they had made a clean escape from the ruins.

"Wish I could see those bastards' faces when they come lookin' for us," Mudge commented.

"They'll be looking for this one, too." Jon-Tom smiled down at the other passenger. "Where's your village, little girl?"

"I am *not* a little girl!"

"Sorry, young lady. Where do you live?"

She stared into the woods. Her sense of direction was superb. A hand gestured to the north. "That way."

Drom nodded and changed direction as he headed down a gentle slope. He called back to Jon-Tom. "Will you continue on to Crancularn in search of your medicine, now that you have escaped the attentions of Hathcar's band?"

"We must," Jon-Tom told him. "You're welcome to accompany us if you like."

"Aye, mate," said Mudge. "We'd be glad of your help."

"I have never been to Crancularn, though I know of it. I would be delighted to accompany you."

"It's settled, then," said a pleased Jon-Tom. Not only was the unicorn a welcome addition to their trio, it had to be admitted that riding was more fun than walking.

By morning they were at the outskirts of the girl's village. Cultivated fields surrounded the town. Jon-Tom let her down gently.

"I didn't do all I was supposed to do," she muttered uneasily.

"You did all you could. It's not your fault that their plan didn't work."

The town was enclosed by a strong wooden palisade and looked more than capable of withstanding an attack by any angry bunch of bandits. He didn't think Hathcar would try to take revenge for his failure against the girl or her parents.

"I still think you're pretty," the girl said to Drom. "Can I kiss you good-bye? That's supposed to be good luck."

Drom smacked his lips with evident distaste. "I'd prefer you didn't, but if you must." He dropped his head, stood still for a buss just below the right eye.

"Geh!" he muttered as she pulled away. "Now be on your way, human, and count yourself fortunate this night."

"Good-bye, unicorn. Good-bye, strangers." She was still waving at them as they disappeared back into the forest.

No armed mob of angry, frustrated bandits materialized to interrupt their progress as they swung back to the west. With luck it would be midday before Hathcar finally realized his plans had fallen through and ventured to check on the ruins.

"I think I understand what was going on," Jon-Tom murmured. "The girl was a virgin."

" 'Ere now, mate," Mudge protested, "I've been around meself, but even I can't tell for certain just by lookin'."

"She'd have to have been for it to fit." He glanced down at their mount. "She was a virgin, wasn't she, Drom?" Roseroar looked on curiously.

"The sight and scent of her suggested so," the stallion replied.

"I read something somewhere about the attentions of a virgin girl being irresistible to a unicorn."

"An ancient and more-or-less accurate notion, which Hathcar was counting on to draw me out. They would have succeeded with their plan except for ignorance of one fact."

"Wot fact, mate?" Mudge asked.

Drom turned to look back at the otter. "I'm gay." He increased his pace.

"Uh, 'ere now, mate, maybe we'd all be better off walkin' after all."

"Nonsense. We are still not far enough away from Hathcar's troop to chance slowing down."

"That's debatable. Besides, there's no need for you to keep on carryin' us about like this. Don't want to make you uncomfortable or nothin'."

"It sounds to me as though you are the one who is feeling uneasy, otter."

"Wot, me? Not me, guv'nor. It's just that I—"

"What's wrong with you, Mudge?" Jon-Tom asked him. "I thought you'd be glad of the chance to rest your precious feet."

"Relax, otter," the stallion said. "You are not my type. Now if you happened to be a Percheron, or a Clydesdale, or maybe a shire . . ." He let the images trail off.

"If you have to worry about something, think about Hathcar," Jon-Tom instructed the otter.

Mudge did so, though he still kept a wary eye on their mount. Later, his confusion was broken by the sound of distant thunder. Or perhaps it was only a bellow of outrage.

Silky's parents kept the money already paid to them by Hathcar, and as Jon-Tom surmised, the cuscus did not try to take it back by force from the heavily defended town. There seemed no way for him to vent his rage and frustration until it occurred to him that since the girl had truly done her best, if anything she actually deserved a bonus.

So it was that while Silky did not get her much-desired candy, she was the only girl in the village who could look forward to the coming winter confidently, clad as she was in her brand-new wolfskin coat.

The travelers stopped in late afternoon. The roast that Mudge had risked his life to salvage was almost gone, but Roseroar soon brought in enough fresh food for all. Drom nibbled contentedly at a nearby field of petal pedals. Each blue-and-pink flower produced a different musical note when it was munched.

Mudge ate close to Jon-Tom. "Don't it bother you, mate?"

"Don't . . . doesn't what bother me?"

The otter nodded toward the unicorn. " 'Im."

Jon-Tom bit into his steak. The meat was succulent and rich with flavor. "He saved us once and might save us again. As for his personal sexual preferences, I could care less. He'd be downright inconspicuous on Hollywood Boulevard."

"Well, maybe you're right. Now, me, I knew it from the first. The way 'e minced out of the woods toward us."

Drom overheard, lifted his muzzle, and said with dignity, "I do not mince, otter. I prance." He looked at Jon-Tom. "You really believe your former acquaintances will beat you to Crancularn and to the medicine you have come for?"

"I hope not, but I fear it. They stole our only map."

"That is a small loss. Do not regret it." The unicorn crunched a clump of purple *ormods* with petals the shade of enameled amethyst. The flowers hummed as they were consumed. "I can guide you there."

"We were told it moves around."

"Only in one's imagination. There are those who stumble through it without seeing it, or circle 'round it as if blind. So they say it has moved. It does not move, but to find it you must wish to. I know. I was told by those who could know. I will lead you to Crancularn."

"That's bleedin' wonderful," Mudge confessed aloud. He was mad at himself. There was no reason for him to be nervous or wary in the unicorn's presence. Drom was a likable chap, wasn't he, and Mudge didn't look in the least like a shire horse, did he? And hadn't he always been told never to look a gift unicorn in the mouth? He was upset with himself.

Hadn't the four-legs carried himself and Jon-Tom all this way from Hathcar's territory without complaining? Why, with him galloping along and the rest of them taking turns riding him, they might yet overtake that prick Jalwar and his whore of a helpmate Folly.

They made rapid progress westward, but still there was no sign of their former friends.

When they finally found themselves on the outskirts of Crancularn itself, Jon-Tom found it hard to believe. He'd half come to think of the town as existing only in Clothahump's imagination. Yet there it was.

Yes, there it was, and after too many close calls with death, after crossing the Muddletup Moors and the Glittergeist Sea and innumerable hills and vales, he was more than a little discouraged by the sight of it.

The setting was impressive enough: a heavily forested slope that climbed the flank of a slowly smoking volcano. The town itself, however, was about as awe-inspiring as dirty, homey Lynchbany. Tumble-down shacks and ramshackle two- and three-story buildings of wood and mud crowded close to one another as if fearful of encountering the sunlight. A dirty fog clung to the streets and the angular, slate-roofed structures. As they headed toward the town, a familiar odor made his nostrils contract: the thick musk of the unwashed of many species mixed with the stink of an open sewer system. His initial excitement was rapidly fading.

Massive oaks and sycamores grew within the town itself, providing more shade where none was required and sometimes even shouldering buildings aside. Jon-Tom was about to ask Drom if perhaps they might have come to the wrong place when the unicorn reared back on its hind hooves and nearly dumped him and Mudge to the ground. Roseroar snarled as she assumed a defensive posture.

Coming straight at them, belching smoke and bellowing raggedly, was a three-footed demon. A rabbit rode the demon's back. This individual wore a wide-brimmed felt hat; a long-sleeved shirt of muslin, open halfway; and a short mauve skirt similar to the kilts favored by the intelligent arboreals of this world. His enormous feet were unshod.

The demon slowed as it approached. Jon-Tom drew in a deep breath as it stopped in front of him and hastened to reassure his companions. "It's all right. It can't harm you."

"How do yo know, Jon-Tom?" Roseroar kept her hands on her sword hilts.

"Because I know what it is. It's a Honda ATC Offroad Threewheeler." He admired the red-painted demon. "Automatic too. I didn't know Honda made an ATC with automatic."

"Funny name for a demon," Mudge was muttering.

"Hiya," said the rabbit cheerfully, revving the engine. "Can I help you folks?"

"You sure can." Jon-Tom pointed at the ATC. "Where'd you get that?"

The rider raced the motor and Drom shied away. "From the Shop of the Aether and Neither. Where else?"

Jon-Tom felt a burst of excitement. Maybe Clothahump was right. The inexplicable presence of the ATC in this world was proof enough that powerful magic was at work here.

"That's where we want to go."

"Figures," said the rabbit. "Nice of you to drop in. We don't get a lot of visitors here in Crancularn. For some reason, travelers avoid us."

"Might be your wonderful reputation," Mudge told him.

The rabbit eyed them appraisingly. "Strangers. Don't know if Snooth will serve you. She don't get much business from outsiders." He shrugged. "Ain't none of my business, your business."

"Who's Snooth?" Jon-Tom asked him.

"The proprietress. Of the Shop of the Aether and Neither." He looked back over his shoulder, pointed. "Go through town and stay on the north trail that winds around the base of the mountain. Snooth's place is around the side a ways." He turned back to inspect them a last time.

"You're a weird-looking bunch. I don't know what you've come to buy, but you'll need all the luck you can muster to pry anything out of Snooth's stock. And no, you can't have one of my feet to help you." He put the all-terrain vehicle in gear and roared off into the woods, the ATC popping and growling.

"I still say it were a demon," Mudge muttered.

"No demon, just a machine. From my world."

"Ah'd dislike being a resident o' yoah world, then, Jon-Tom." Roseroar made a face. "Such noise. And that smell!"

It had to have been conjured, Jon-Tom knew. Conjured by a magic even more powerful than Clothahump's. His heart raced. If this Snooth could bring something as solid as the ATC into this world, something lifted from a dealership in Kyoto or L.A. or Toronto, then perhaps she could also send things back to such places.

Things like himself.

He didn't dare dwell on that possibility as they made their way through town. For the most part, the busy, bored citizenry ignored them. Many of them were using or playing with otherworldly devices. Jon-Tom began to have second thoughts about his chances of being sent home. Maybe this Snooth was no sorceress but just some local shopkeeper who happened to have stumbled onto some kind of one-way transdimensional gate or something.

Mudge pointed out a traveling minstrel. The diminutive musical mouse was plinking out a very respectable polka not on a duar or handlebar lyre or bark flute but on a Casiotone 8500 electronic keyboard. Jon-Tom wondered what the mouse was using for batteries.

Not all the devices in use were recognizably from his own world. The sign over a fishmonger's stall was a rotating globe of red and white lambent light that spelled out the shop's name and alternated it with that of the owner. There appeared to be nothing supporting the globe. As they stared, the globe twisted into the shape of a fish, then into the outlines of females of various species in provocative poses. Sex sells, Jon-Tom reminded himself. Even fish. He walked over to stand directly underneath the globe. There was no source of support or power, much less a visible explanation for its photonic malleability. One thing he was sure of: it hadn't come from his own world.

Neither had the device they saw an old mandrill using to cut wood. It had a handle similar to that of a normal metal saw, but instead of a length of serrated steel the handle was attached to a shiny bar no more than a quarter-inch in diameter. The baboon would hitch up his gloves, choose a piece of wood, put both hands on the handle and touch the thin bar to the log. It would cut through like butter.

There were other worlds, then, and this Snooth apparently had access to goods from many of them. As they made their way through the town, he thought back to his companions' reaction to the ATC. To someone unfamiliar with internal combustion devices on a world where magic held sway, it certainly must have looked and sounded like a demon. Crancularn was full of such alien machines. No wonder it had acquired an unwholesome reputation.

But the townsfolk themselves were open and friendly enough. In that they were no different from the inhabitants of the other cities and villages Jon-Tom had visited. As for their blasé acceptance of otherworldly devices, there was nothing very extraordinary about that. People, no matter their shape or size or species, were infinitely adaptable. Only a hundred years ago in his own world, a hand-held television or calculator watch would have seemed like magic even to sophisticated citizens, who nonetheless would have made use of them enthusiastically.

For that matter, how many of his contemporaries actually understood what made a computer tick or instant replay possible? People had a way of just accepting the workings of everyday machinery they didn't understand, whether it was powered by alkaline batteries or arcane spells.

Then they were leaving the town again, fog drifting lazily around them. They had attracted no more than an occasional cursory glance from the villagers. Huge trees hugged the fertile lower slopes of the volcano, which simmered quietly and unthreateningly above them.

Inquiries in town had produced no mention of visitors resembling Jalwar or Folly. Either the two had lost their way or else with Drom's aid they had already passed the renegade pair in the woods. Jon-Tom experienced a pang of regret. He still wasn't completely convinced of Folly's complicity in the theft of the map.

No time for that now. The rabbit on the ATC implied they might have trouble purchasing what they wanted from this Snooth. Jon-Tom struggled to compose a suitably effective speech. All they needed was a little bit of medicine. Nothing so complex as a malleable globe or toothless saw. His hand went to the tiny vial dangling from the chain around his neck. Inside was the formula for the desperately needed medicine. He hadn't brought it this far to be turned away empty-handed.

There was no sign, no posted proclamations to advertise the shop's presence. They turned around a cluster of oaks, and there it was, a simple wooden building, one story high. It was built up against the rocks. A single wooden door was set square in the center of the storefront, which was shaded by a broad, covered porch.

A couple of high-backed rocking chairs sat on the porch, unoccupied. Wooden shingles in need of repair covered the sloping roof that likewise ran up into the rocks. Jon-Tom estimated the entire building enclosed no more than a thousand square feet of space. Hardly large enough for store and home combined.

As they drew close, a figure emerged from inside and settled into the farther rocking chair. The chair creaked as it rocked. The tall kangaroo wore a red satin vest which blended with her own natural rust color and, below, a kilt similar in style to the rabbit's. There were pockets and a particularly wide one directly in front to permit the owner access to her pouch. Jon-Tom stared at the lower belly but was unable to tell if the female was carrying a joey, though once he thought he saw something move. But he couldn't be sure, and since he was ignorant of macropodian etiquette, he thought it best not to inquire.

She also wore thick hexagonal granny glasses and a heavy necklace of turquoise, black onyx, and malachite. A matching bracelet decorated her right wrist, and she puffed slowly on a corncob pipe which was switched periodically from one side of her mouth to the other.

He halted at the bottom of the porch steps. "Are you the one they call Snooth?"

"I expect I am," the kangaroo replied, "since I'm the only one around here by that name." She took her pipe from her lips and regarded them thoughtfully. "You folks aren't from around here. What can I do for you?"

"We've undertaken one hell of a shopping trip," Jon-Tom told her.

She sighed. "I was afraid of that. Just when I got myself all nice and comfortable. Well, that's par for the course."

Jon-Tom's eyes grew wide. "That's an expression of my world."

"Is it? I traffic with so many I sometimes get confused. Sure as the gleebs are on the fondike."

Jon-Tom decided to tread as lightly as possible, bearing the rabbit's admonition in mind. "We don't want to disturb you. We could come back tomorrow." He tried to see past her, into the store. "You haven't by any chance had a couple of other out-of-town customers in recently, have you? An old ferret, maybe accompanied by a human female?" He held his breath.

The kangaroo scratched under her chin with her free hand. "Nope. No one of that description. In fact, I haven't had any local out-of-town customers stop by in some time."

Forbearing to inquire into the nature of a local out-of-towner, which seemed to Jon-Tom to be a contradiction in terms, he permitted himself a moment of silent exultation. They'd done it! With Drom's help they'd succeeded in beating Jalwar to Crancularn. Now he could relax. The object of their long, arduous journey was almost in his grasp.

He turned to leave. "We don't want to upset your siesta. We'll come back tomorrow."

A small brown shape pushed past him. Mudge took up an aggressive stance on the lowest step. "Now let's 'old on a minim 'ere, guv'nor." The otter fixed the proprietress with a jaundiced eye. "This 'ere dump is the place I've been 'earin' about for weeks? This cobbled-together wreck is the marvelous, the wondrous, the magnificent Shop o' the Aether and Neither? And you're the owner?"

The kangaroo nodded.

"Well," announced Mudge in disgust, "it sure as 'ell don't look like much to me."

"Mudge!" Jon-Tom angrily grabbed the otter by his shoulder.

The kangaroo, however, did not appear upset. "Appearances can be deceiving, my fuzzy little cousin." She turned to face Jon-Tom as she stood on enormous, powerful feet. She was as tall as he was. The rickety porch boards squeaked under her weight.

"I can tell just by looking at you that you've come a long ways to do your shopping. Except for the Crancularnians, most of my customers travel far to buy from me, some by means most devious. Some I sell to, others I do not." She turned and pointed toward a thin scrawl on a worn piece of wood that was nailed over the doorway. The sign said:

WE RESERVE THE RIGHT TO REFUSE SERVICE TO ANYTHING

"It's not for ourselves that we come seeking your help," Jon-Tom told her. "We're here at the behest of a great wizard who lives in the forest of the Bellwoods, far across the Glittergeist Sea. His name's Clothahump."

"Clothahump." Eyes squinted in reflection behind the granny glasses. She put out a hand, palm facing downward, and positioned it some four feet above the porch. "Turtle, old gentleman, about yea high?"

Jon-Tom nodded vigorously. "That's him. You've met him?"

"Nope. But I know of him by reputation. As wizards go, he's up near the top." This revelation impressed even the skeptical Mudge, who'd always thought of Clothahump as no better than a talented fakir verging on senility who just happened to get lucky once in a while. "What's wrong with him?"

Jon-Tom fumbled with the vial around his neck, removed the small piece of paper from within. "He says he's dying, and he's in terrible pain. He says this can cure him."

Snooth took the fragment, adjusted her glasses, and read. Her lips moved as she digested the paper's information. "Yes, yes . . . I believe I have this in stock." She glanced back at Jon-Tom. "Your devotion to your mentor does you credit."

Which made him feel more than a little guilty, since the main reason he'd undertaken the journey was to protect his only chance of returning home by ensuring Clothahump's continued good health.

"You overpraise my altruism."

"I think not." She stared at him in the most peculiar fashion. "You are better than you give yourself credit for. That is why you would make a good adjudicator. Your good instincts outweigh your common sense."

For the second time since arriving at the store Jon-Tom's eyes widened. "How did you know that I was studying to be a lawyer?"

"Lucky guess," said Snooth absently, dismissing the matter despite Jon-Tom's desire to pursue it further. She held out the paper with the formula written on it. "May I hold on to this?"

Jon-Tom shrugged. "Why not? It's the medicine we need."

Snooth tucked the paper neatly into her pouch. Again Jon-Tom thought he saw something moving about within. If Snooth was carrying a joey, it was evidently either too immature or too shy to show itself.

"Come on in." She turned and pushed wide the door.

Her visitors mounted the steps and crossed the porch. The front room of the building was furnished in simple kaleidoscopic style. To one side was another rocking chair, only instead of being fashioned of wood it was composed of transparent soap bubbles clinging to a thin metal frame. The bubbles were moving in slow motion and looked fragile and ready to burst.

"Surely you don't sit in that?" Roseroar said.

"Wouldn't be much use for anything else. Like to try it?"

"Ah couldn't," the tigress protested. "Ah'd bust it as well as mah tail end."

"Maybe not," said the kangaroo with quiet confidence.

Reluctantly, Roseroar accepted the challenge, turning to set herself gently into the chair. The soap bubbles gave under her weight but did not break, nor did the thin metal frame. And the bubbles kept moving, massaging the chair's new occupant with a gentle sliding motion. A rich throbbing purr filled the room.

"How much?" Roseroar inquired.

"Sorry. That's a demo model. Not for sale."

"Come on, Roseroar," Jon-Tom told her. "That's not what we came for." She abandoned the caressing chair sadly.

As they crossed the room, Jon-Tom had time to notice a circular recording device, a heatless stove, and a number of utterly alien machines scattered among the familiar. Snooth led them through another doorway barred by opaque ceramic strips that hung in midair and into a back store room filled with broken, jumbled goods. A bathroom was visible off to the left.

A second suspended curtain admitted them to the store.

Jon-Tom's brain went blank. He heard Roseroar hiss next to him and even the always voluble Mudge was at a loss for words. Drom inhaled sharply in surprise.

As near as they could tell, the shop filled the whole inside of the mountain.

XV

Ahead of them was an aisle flanked by long metal shelves. The multiple shelving rose halfway to the forty-foot-high ceiling and was crammed with boxed, crated, and clear-packaged goods. Jon-Tom saw only a few empty slots. The shelving and the aisle between ran away into the distance until all three seemed to meet at some distant vanishing point.

He turned and stared to his left. Shelves and aisles marched off into the distance as far as he could see. He looked right and saw a mirror image of the view on his left.

"I never dreamed . . ." he began, only to be interrupted by the proprietress.

"Oh, but you have dreamed, shopper. Everyone dreams." She gestured with a negligent wave. "There are a lot of worlds in the plenum. Some produce a lot of goods for sale, others only a few. I try to keep up with what the major dimensions are doing. It isn't an easy job, being a shopkeeper. There's one place where time runs backwards. Plays hell with my inventory."

Jon-Tom continued to gape at the endless rows. "How do you know what you've got here, let alone where it's located?"

"Oh, we're very up-to-date in the store." From a side pocket she extracted a length of bright blue metal six inches long and two and half an inches thick. A transparent facing ran the length of it. There were no buttons or switches visible.

"Pocket computer." She showed it to Jon-Tom. As he watched, words scrolled rapidly across the face. Languages and script changed as he stared. Twice Snooth turned it vertically and the words scrolled from top to bottom. Several times they reversed and traveled from right to left. Once there were no letters at all, only colors changing in sequence. Once there was only music.

"Thought-activated. Handy little gadget. Bought it from a place whose location can't be determined, only inferred. Very talented folks there. See?"

A chemical formula appeared on the transparent facing and froze in position. A long numerical sequence appeared below it.

"Down this way." Snooth hopped off to her left, eventually turned down an aisle.

Roseroar stared at the endless ranks of goods. "How many shelves do y'all have down heah?"

"Can't really say," the kangaroo replied. "It changes all the time."

"You run this whole place by yourself?" Jon-Tom asked her.

She nodded. "You get used to it. I like stockwork, and the perks are good."

"How far is the medicine?"

"Not far. Only about half a day's hop. Any longer and I'd have paused to pack us a meal or dig out a scooter."

"Is that anything like the Honda ATC we saw one of your customers riding around outside of town?"

"That'd be Foharfa's toy. He's going to break his neck on that thing one of these days. No, a scooter's just an inertialess disc. You guide it by sensing your relationship to the local planetary magnetic field."

Jon-Tom swallowed. "I'm afraid I don't have a license to drive anything like that."

"No matter. I'm enjoying the walk."

"Can we buy one to get us 'ome, maybe?" Mudge asked hopefully.

"Sorry. I've none in general stock. Besides, I make it a rule not to let certain goods travel beyond Crancularn. The world's a complicated enough place as it is. You can overtechnologize magic if you're not careful."

"Looks like your business is rather slow," observed Drom.

Snooth shrugged in mid-hop. "I'm not looking to get rich, unicorn. I just like the business, that's all. Besides, it's a good way to keep up with what's going on in the greater cosmos. Goods are better than gossip and more honest reflections of what's happening elsewhere than official news pronouncements and zeeways."

"Must be 'ard on profits," Mudge commented.

"That depends on what kind of profit you're trying to make, otter."

Jon-Tom eyed the kangaroo uneasily. "That's a funny thing for a shopkeeper to say. Are you sure you aren't some kind of sorceress yourself?"

"Who, me?" Snooth appeared genuinely shocked. "Not I, sir. Too many responsibilities, too many regulations attached to the profession. I prefer my present employment, thank you. And the cost-of-living in Crancularn is low." A pause, then, "What about this ferret and girl you referred to earlier?"

"They were traveling with us," Jon-Tom explained. "We had an unfortunate parting of the ways."

"Unfortunate, 'ell!" Mudge rumbled. "The dirty buggers stole our map, they did, and it were only by dint o' good luck and this spellsinger's determination and this one-horn's knowledge o' the lay o' the land that we . . . !"

Snooth interrupted him, smiling at Jon-Tom. "So you are a spellsinger? I noticed the duar you carry right off, but I imagined you to be no more than a traveling musician."

"I'm still an amateur," Jon-Tom confessed. "I'm still learning how to control my abilities."

"I think one day you will, though I sense you still have a long way to go."

"It's just that it's so new to me. The magic, not the music. Everything's so new to me. I'm not of this world."

"I know. You smell of elsewhere. Do not let your transposition faze you. Newness is life's greatest pleasure and delight." She indicated the shelves walling them in. "Every new product I encounter is a source of wonderment to me."

"I wish I could share your enthusiasm. But I can't help my homesickness. You can't, by any chance, send me home by the same means you use to stock your goods?" he asked hopefully.

"I am truly sorry," Snooth told him softly, and it struck him that she was. "This is only a receive-and-disperse operation. I can only ship products, not people."

Jon-Tom slumped. "Well, it's no more than what I expected. Clothahump said as much."

"You must tell me about your travels. Oddly, I know more about many other worlds than about this one. The result of being tied to my business."

So partly to please her and partly to help relieve his own disappointment, Jon-Tom regaled her with a recitation of the adventures they had experienced during their long journey. It took at least the half day Snooth had claimed before she finally called the march to a halt. Jon-Tom looked down the aisle. They still were not in sight of its end.

Strange medications filled bottles and jars and containers of unfamiliar material. The twenty-foot-high shelves they had halted before represented a cosmological pharmacopia. Jon-Tom made out pills and drops, salves and unguents, bandages and bindings, scattered among less recognizable items.

Snooth regarded the shelving for a moment, consulted her blue metal bar, and hopped a few yards farther down the aisle. Then she climbed one of the motorized ladders that ran from the topmost shelf to tracks cut in the stone floor and ascended the shelving halfway.

"Here we are," she said, sounding gratified. She opened an ordinary cardboard box and removed a small plastic container. "Only one. I'll have to restock this item. I don't have the room to keep more than one of any item on the shelves. There are instructions on the side which I presume your wizard will know how to interpret."

"I'm sure he will," Jon-Tom said, reaching relievedly for the container.

"Stop right there, please."

Jon-Tom whirled. Roseroar growled and reached for her swords as Mudge tried to ready his longbow.

"Don't!"

A figure emerged from behind a translucent crate containing frozen flowers and came toward them. In his hands Jalwar held something resembling a multiple crossbow. At least three dozen lethal-looking little darts were clustered in concentric circles at the tip of the weapon.

"Poison. Enough to kill all of you at once. Even you, mistress of long teeth." Roseroar continued to glower at the new arrival, but let her paws fall slowly from the hilts of her swords.

"A wise decision," Jalwar told her.

Jon-Tom was staring past him. "Folly. Where's Folly?" When the ferret did not immediately reply, Jon-Tom felt a surge of excitement despite the precariousness of the situation. "So she *didn't* go with you voluntarily, did she!"

"No." Jalwar made the admission indifferently. "But she came, and that was all I required. I needed assistance in hauling rudimentary supplies, and she struck me as the easiest of all of you to manipulate. As a beast of burden she proved adequate." He smiled thinly, enjoying himself. "Then, too, the destruction of innocence has always appealed to me, and she still had a little left."

Jon-Tom struggled to restrain himself. He didn't for a second doubt the lethality of those multiple darts or Jalwar's willingness to employ them.

"Where is she? What have you done with her?"

"In good time I will tell you, my impetuous blind friend." The ferret cocked an eye toward Snooth. "So that is the precious medicine our friend Clothahump requires so desperately. How interesting. I suddenly feel the need for some medication myself. You, proprietress! I'll take that container, if you don't mind."

"Take a 'elluva lot more than that to cure wot ails you, mate," said Mudge insultingly.

"You think so, do you? Yet I am not so sick that I have failed to outwit you all. I did not think you would make it here without the map, and in my confidence I slowed my approach. I thought in any event that with the aid of my help I would always know your location. Indeed, without that help I would not have been able to rush in close on your heels and track your progress within this place from two aisles over."

"What help?" Jon-Tom asked warily.

"Now, be that the right tone with which to greet an old comrade, man?" said a voice Jon-Tom had hoped never to hear again. He turned to his right.

"Corroboc."

The parrot executed a half bow. "It be right good of you to remember me name. That singing magic you worked on me ship, that be my fault for not guessing you had more than entertainment for old Corroboc in mind. But I'm not the one to dwell on old regrets. No, not I, even though me worthless crew chose a new captain and set me adrift barely within flying range o' the mainland.

"There I found your strange boat and picked up your trail. I knew o' your aims and thought somehow to follow until I found a way o' repayin' you all for your kindnesses to me. In the forest I saw two of you leave from the rest." He nodded toward Jalwar.

"When I saw the respect with which he were treatin' me old friend Folly, I thought to meself, now here be one after me own heart. So I settled down for a chat, and after an exchange of pleasantries me and the good ferret here, we came to an understandin', har."

"That bird will cut out our hearts and dance on them," Roseroar whispered to Jon-Tom. "We might as well rush them now."

"Steady on, you oversized bit o' fluff," Mudge warned her. "All the cards 'aven't been dealt yet, wot?"

"Whisper all you want," snapped Jalwar. "It will avail you naught."

Corroboc pulled a short, thin sword from the flying scabbard slung at his waist. Holes in the blade made it light and strong. He caressed the flat side of the blade lovingly.

"Many days have I had to anticipate the pleasures of our reunion. I beg you not to provoke me new friend lest he put an end to you all too quick. I want our meeting to be a memorable experience for all. Aye, memorable! You see, I've no ship, no crew anymore. All I have left to me be this moment, which I don't want to hurry."

Realization rushed in on Jon-Tom as he turned on Jalwar. "You work for Zancresta, don't you? You've been working for Zancresta from the first! Running into you on the northern shore of the Glittergeist was no coincidence. Those brigands weren't attacking you. It was all a ploy to let you worm yourself into our company."

"An apt metaphor, Jon-Tom," said Roseroar.

"Tell me something," Jon-Tom went on quietly. "How much is Zancresta paying you to keep this medicine from Clothahump?"

The ferret burst out laughing, though the business end of the strange weapon he held did not waver. "Paying me? You idiots! Spellsinger? Pah! *I* am Zancresta! Wizard of Malderpot, supreme master of the arcane arts, diviner of the unknown and parter of the shrouds! Fools, beggars of a humble knowledge, you are blinder than the troglodytes of Tatrath and dumber than the molds that grub out an existence in the cracks between the stones."

The ferret seemed to swell in their eyes as they stared, though neither his size nor shape actually changed. But the curved spine stiffened, the voice was no longer shaky, and an inner unholy light emanated from suddenly bottomless eyes while a barely perceptible dark aura sprang to malevolent life around him.

"I didn't think you'd get this far, none of you! But where a spellsinger, however inept, is involved, there are never any assurances. So when you escaped from Malderpot and my servants lost you in the woods, I determined to find you myself. Your bold and unforeseen move into the Muddletup Moors confused me, I must admit. But only for a time, and I was just able to intercept you on the shores of the Glittergeist and execute my little charade.

"I did not think I would be with you long, but luck and false fortune seemed to follow you wherever you went. Across the ocean, on this kindred spirit's vessel, even into the land of the bellicose enchanted folk. When you not only managed your release from their hands but induced them to assist you with a map, I determined to press on ahead on my own to seek out this Shop of the Aether and Neither and buy up all the necessary medicine before you could arrive.

"And again you surprised me, not out of cleverness or insight, but through blind luck. So Corroboc and I paralleled your progress through this bloated emporium of useless goods, he flying above to check periodically on your position, until you kindly located the object of the quest for me. Which I will now take possession of." He glanced up at Snooth.

"I do not think she has in hand a device or medicine that can save her from the fast-acting effects of hruth venom. Once that container has been handed over I will relieve you of your weapons and leave you to the tender attentions of my patient friend. Perhaps he will grow bored before all of you are dead." Corroboc made neat, thin slices in one of his own feathers with the razor-sharp sword while Zancresta looked suddenly wistful.

"Ah, the day that I stand at that fat fraud's bedside, holding the precious medicine he so desperately requires just beyond his feeble reach, making him plead and beg for it, that will be a day of triumph indeed."

"What have you done with Folly!"

Zancresta came back from his private reverie. "Ah, my pack animal and my insurance. I have never feared you, spellsinger, but your talents act in ways wayward and unpredictable. Sometimes it is awkward to deal with such implausibilities, and I do worry some on the impetuous nature of your companions.

"Knowing of your insipidly tender nature, I took care to keep the girl tightly under my control, lest she foolishly try to run to you for misguided salvation."

"You hypnotized her?"

"I am unfamiliar with the term, but if you mean did I blur her simple mind in order to make her compliant, yes. I no longer have need of her as crude labor or as insurance against your actions, however." He pointed down the aisle.

"These shelves reach far back into the mountain, which you may have noticed is of volcanic origin. I would presume that each aisle ends in a fairly hot place. Perhaps the proprietress stores goods back there that require constant heat. Being of a warm nature myself, I dismissed the girl and bade her wander down to the end of the aisle. She acquired on Corroboc's ship a dark coloration which I venture to say will change rapidly to red as she stumbles into the hot center of this mountain."

Jon-Tom took a step backward and Zancresta raised his peculiar multiple dart-thrower. "Let her go. She is nothing."

There was a flash of gold from behind Roseroar. Again Zancresta raised the weapon, but a feathery hand came down on his arm.

"Nay, let the horned one go," snarled Corroboc. "I've no real quarrel with him. He won't be in time to save the girl and I want these three left alive and conscious." He started toward the ladder, sword in one hand, the other outstretched toward Snooth. "The medicine, if you please, hag."

"As you wish."

"No!" Jon-Tom shouted. "Don't give it to him!"

The kangaroo's reply was firm. "I am not a party to what is a private quarrel. This is between you and him." She handed over the precious container. "Here, catch." At the last instant she tossed it toward the pirate captain.

Corroboc grabbed for the small plastic cylinder and missed. It struck the floor, vaporizing instantly and spitting out a thick cloud of black smoke.

Jon-Tom threw himself sideways and down. The dart-thrower twanged and something struck his boot while others thunked harmlessly into the back of his thick snakeskin cape. He heard no screams of pain and prayed that his friends had also managed to dodge Zancresta's weapon. He started to rise, preparing to do battle with his staff, when it occurred to him that in a hand-to-hand fight Roseroar's swords and Mudge's bow would be more effective, and that, in any case, they had a sorcerer to deal with now. So he put the ramwood aside and fumbled with the duar. An old Moody Blues tune came to mind, suitable for combating evil. He played and sang.

It had its intended effect. As the smoke began to dissipate he could hear the ferret moan, see him staggering backwards clutching at his head.

But Zancresta was not to be so simply vanquished. Gathering his strength, he glared at Jon-Tom and began to recite:

"Nails of rails and coils of toil,
Come to me now, rise to a boil,
Become with strength my herpetological foil!"

The sorcerer's fingers stretched, elongated, became powerful constrictors that writhed and curled toward Jon-Tom.

Whether it was out of fear for Folly or for himself or sheer anger, he couldn't say, but now the music flowed easily through him. Without missing a bar he segued straight into a slithering song by Jefferson Airplane. The snakes shriveled and shrank to become ferret fingers once more.

A second time Zancresta threw out his hands toward Jon-Tom.

"Xyleum, phylum, cellulose constrained,
Hypoblastic hardwood rise up now unrestrained.
Chlorophyllic transformation make thyself known.
Long and strong and sharp and straight
And solid as a stone!"

The wooden stake that materialized to leap at Jon-Tom's chest was the size of a small tree. A few branches erupted from its trunk, and it continued to grow even as it flew toward him, sending out roots and leaves. He barely had time enough to switch to a throaty rendition of Def Lepard's "Pyromania."

The huge, growing spear blew up in a ball of fire. The force of it knocked Zancresta backward to the floor.

It gave Jon-Tom a moment to check on his companions. They were unhurt, but there was plenty of blood on the floor of the aisle. It all came from the same source, and was sticky with green and blue feathers. A beaked skull lay sightless in one place, a leg elsewhere, a pair of wings on a half-empty shelf. More blood stained Roseroar's muzzle and claws. Her swords were still sheathed and clean. She hadn't needed to use them, having dismembered Corroboc as neatly as Jon-Tom would have a fried chicken.

Mudge stepped forward to fire a single arrow at Zancresta. The sorcerer raised a hand, uttered one contemptuous word. The arrow turned rotten before it crumpled against the ferret's hip. Meanwhile Jon-Tom wondered and worried about Folly. If only Drom had time enough to reach her before . . . !

Sensing his opponent's lapse of concentration, Zancresta waved a hand over his head and declaimed stentoriously. A small black cloud appeared in the air between them. Thunder rolled ominously.

Jon-Tom barely had the presence of mind to shout the right words from Procol Harum's "In Held I Was" and hold up the duar in front of him in time to intercept the single bolt of lightning that emerged from the cloud. The instrument absorbed the bolt, though the impact sent him stumbling. The cloud disintegrated.

Now, for the first time, there was a hint of fear in Zancresta's eyes. Fear, but not surrender. Not yet. He stood staring at his opponent, making no effort to draw his torn and ragged clothes tighter about him.

"Not accident, then," he muttered as he stood there. "Not just luck. I worried about that, but in the end gave it little credence. Now I see that I was wrong. You think you've won, don't you? You think you've beaten me?" He looked up at the ladder. Snooth stood on it holding the original container of medicine. Zancresta had been so busy watching Jon-Tom that he hadn't seen the proprietress switch it for the smoke bomb.

"You all think you've beaten me. Well, you haven't. Not Zancresta, you haven't. Because you see, I came prepared to deal with every possibility, no matter how remote or unlikely. Yes, I even came prepared to deal with the chance that this stripling spellsinger might possess some small smidgen of talent."

"Go ahead and try something." Jon-Tom felt ten feet tall. He could feel the power surging inside him, could feel the music fighting to get out. His fingers tingled and the duar was like a third arm. He was riding high, on the same kind of high the stars got when they sang in front of thousands in the big halls and arenas. He stopped just short of levitating.

"Come on, Zancresta," he taunted the sorcerer, "trot out anything you can think of, bring forth all your nastiness! I've got a song for every one of 'em, and when you're finished"—he was already humming silently the last song he planned to sing this day—"when you're finished, Jalwar-Zancresta, I've got a final riff for you."

The ferret pursed his lips and shook his head sadly. "You poor, simple, unwilling immigrant, do you think I'm so easily beaten? I know a hundred powerful conjurations to throw at you, remember a thousand curses. But you are correct. I know that your music could counter them." Something was wrong, Jon-Tom thought. Zancresta ought to have been begging for mercy. Instead, he sounded as confident as ever.

"Your music is strong, spellsinger, but you are feeble here." He tapped his head. "You see, as I said, I came prepared to deal with anything." He looked to his right.

"Charrok, I need you now."

From behind a partly vacant shelf, a new shape appeared. Jon-Tom braced himself for anything, his fingers ready on the duar, his mind full of countering songs. The figure that emerged did not inspire any fear in him, however. In fact, it was singularly unimpressive.

The mockingbird stood barely three feet tall, shorter even than Corroboc. He wore an unusually plain kilt of black on beige and yellow, a single matching yellow vest devoid of adornment, and a single yellow cap.

Zancresta gestured at Jon-Tom. "That's the one I told you about. Do what I paid you to do!"

The mockingbird carefully shook out his wings, then the rest of his feathers, put flexible wingtips on his hips and cocked his head sideways to eye Jon-Tom.

"I hear tell from Zancresta here that you're the best."

"The best what?"

The mockingbird reached back over a shoulder. Roseroar and Mudge tensed, but the bird produced not an arrow or spear but a thin wooden box overlaid with three sets of strings.

"A syreed," murmured Roseroar.

Charrok nestled the peculiar instrument under one wing and flexed the strong feathers of the other. "Now we're going to learn who's really the best."

"Bugger me for a mayor's mother!" Mudge gasped. "The bloody bastard's a spellsinger 'imself!"

XVI

"That," said the mockingbird with obvious pride, "is just what I am."

"Now, look," said Jon-Tom even as he made sure the duar was resting comfortably against his ribs, "I don't know you and I've no reason to fight you. If you've been listening to what's been going on you know who's on the side of right here and who on the side of evil."

"Evil-schmieval," said the mockingbird. "I'm just a country spellsinger. I don't go around making moral judgments. I just make music. The other I leave to solicitors and judges." Feathers dipped toward multiple strings. "Let's get to it, man."

The voice that emerged from that feathered throat was as sweet and sugary as Jon-Tom's was harsh and uneven, and it covered a range of octaves no human could hope to match.

Well then, Jon-Tom decided grimly as he saw the smile that had appeared on the ferret's face, it was up to him to respond with musical inventiveness, sharper lyrics, and better playing. If nothing else, he could at least match the mockingbird in enthusiasm and sheer volume.

The mountain rattled and the shelving shook. The floor quivered underfoot and stone powder fell from the ceiling as the two spellsingers threw incisive phrases and devastating rhymes at each other. Charrok sang of acid tongues and broken hearts, of mental anguish and crumbling self-esteem. Jon-Tom countered with appropriate verses by Queen and the Stones, by Pat Benatar and Fleetwood

Mac. Charrok's clashing chords smashed violently against Jon-Tom's chords by the Clash. The mockingbird even resorted to calling up the defeated warriors of the Plated Folk, and Jon-Tom had to think fast to fight back with the pounding, sensual New Wave of Adam Ant.

As the two singers did battle, Mudge struggled to get a clear shot at Zancresta. The wizard had witnessed several demonstrations of the otter's prowess with the longbow, however, and was careful not to provide him with a decent target.

Jon-Tom was finally forced to pause, no matter the consequences. He was panting hard and his fingers were numb and bloody from nonstop strumming. Worse, his throat stung like cracked suede and he feared creeping hoarseness.

But the arduous duel had taken its toll on his opponent as well. Charrok no longer fluffed out his feathers proudly between songs, nor did he appear quite as confident as he had when the battle had begun.

At which point Jon-Tom thought to try another line of attack entirely.

"That last tune, the one about the drunken elephant with the knife? That was pretty sharp. You got some good riffs in there. I couldn't do that."

"Sometimes," Charrok croaked, "it's harder with fingers than with feathers." He held up his right wing and wiggled the flexible tips for emphasis. "You're not doing too badly yourself, though. What was that bit about dirty deeds done dirt cheap?"

"AC/DC," Jon-Tom replied tiredly. "I thought it might conjure me up a few berserk assassins. No such luck."

"Good try, though," Charrok complimented him. "I could almost feel the knife at my throat."

Zancresta stepped forward, careful to keep the body of his hired instrument between himself and Mudge.

"What is this? I am not paying you to indulge in casual conversation with this man. I am paying you to kill him!"

Charrok turned. His gaze narrowed as he stared up at the sorcerer. "You hold on a minute there, Mr. Zancresta, sir. You hired my spellsinging, not my soul."

"Don't get existential with me, you warbling bumpkin! You'll do as you're told!"

Charrok was unperturbed by the sorcerer's outburst. "That's what I've been doing." He nodded toward Jon-Tom. "This fella's mighty damn good. He might, just might, be better than me."

"I don't know who's best and I don't care," Jon-Tom said hastily, "but you sing like a storm and you play like a fiend. I'd appreciate it a lot if you could show me that last song." He strummed an empty chord on the duar. "Maybe I've only got five fingers here, but I'd damn sure like to give it a try."

"I don't know . . . a duar only has two sets of strings and my syreed three. Still, if you dropped a note here and there. . . ." He started to walk over. "Let's have a looksee."

"No fraternizing with the enemy," Zancresta snapped, putting a restraining paw on the mockingbird's shoulder. Charrok shook it off.

"Maybe he ain't my enemy."

"Of course I'm not," said Jon-Tom encouragingly, moving forward himself. "A gig's a gig, but that shouldn't come between a couple of professionals." When Charrok was near enough, Jon-Tom put a comradely arm around the bird's shoulders, having to bend over to do so. "This isn't your fight, singer. Two musician-magicians of our caliber shouldn't be trying to destroy each other. We should be collaborating. Imagine the wizardry we could work! This shouldn't be a duel, it should be a jam session."

"I'd like that," said Charrok. He searched the aisle beyond. "Where are the berries?"

"Not that kind of jam. I mean we should play together, make music and magic together."

A hand reached out and clutched in frustration at the mockingbird's vest. "I won't have this!" The ferret was jumping up and down on short legs. "I tell you, I won't have it! I've paid you well to serve me in this matter. We have a contract! There is too much at stake here."

"Yeah, including my reputation," Charrok told him frostily. "But," he glanced up at Jon-Tom, "that can always be settled between friends. As for your money, you can have it back. I've decided I don't want . . ."

"Look out, mate!" Mudge yelled. The otter threw himself forward, hit Zancresta just in time to make the subtle knife thrust the ferret had been aiming at Jon-Tom beneath Charrok's wing miss. The two went rolling over together on the floor.

"Hold him, suh!" Roseroar thundered as she advanced, ready to remove Zancresta's head from his neck as easily as she would a stopper from a bottle.

But the ferret was scrambling to his feet, leaving a bleeding Mudge lying on the floor. Displaying incredible agility, the sorcerer dodged under Roseroar's wild rush and started climbing up the nearest shelf.

ing free. "I am glad to have been of assistance, madame, but leave us not get carried away with our emotions."

"But I thought . . ." Folly looked hurt and Jon-Tom hastened to reassure her.

"Drom's not being unfriendly, Folly. He's just being himself. I'll explain later." He looked at the unicorn. "It was a fine bit of rescue work, Drom."

"I try." The unicorn searched the aisle. "Where is the evil one? And the great feline? Did you defeat him during my absence?"

"No." Jon-Tom smiled at the mockingbird. "This is Charrok. When Zancresta discovered that he couldn't defeat me with his own magic, he tried to do it with another spellsinger. Charrok and I conjured up quite a musical storm before we came to the conclusion that harmony is better than dissonance. As for Roseroar, she's gone after Zancresta."

"I should pity the ferret, then."

"That's the truth, mate," said Mudge. "That's some broad. If she were only a fourth 'er size."

"You have to learn to think big, Mudge." Jon-Tom became serious. "Zancresta's as fast on his feet as he is with his mind. He might give her the slip in here."

" 'E can't get out, though, mate," Mudge commented. "Unless there's another way in, and I'd bet me tool there's only the one. I'd say the best we can do now is find that oversized she-rat who runs the place. She 'ad the medicine when the fight started, and I'd wager she's kept it with 'er."

It was a long hike back to the entryway, and Jon-Tom's appraisal of the ferret as being fleet of foot turned out to be accurate, for when they turned up the last aisle Zancresta was already there.

"Ah just missed him in a side aisle," Roseroar rumbled angrily, having rejoined them only moments earlier. "He won't get away this time."

Zancresta's clothes were shredded, and he looked very unwizardly as he stood panting heavily before the exit. A glance down the side aisle showed his tormentors approaching rapidly. There was nothing, however, to prevent his escaping to plot against them from the outside. Nothing except an old female kangaroo.

"Get out of my way, hag! My time is precious and I have none to waste in argument."

"I'm not here to argue with you." Snooth spoke calmly, the pipe dangling from her lips. Her right hand was extended, palm upward. "You owe me payment."

"Payment? Payment for what?" Zancresta snarled impatiently. His enemies were hurrying now, the ferocious tigress in the lead. He did not have much time.

"For damage done to stock and fixtures."

"I was trying to escape from that insane female who even now approaches. You can't hold me responsible for that."

"I hold you responsible for everything," she replied darkly. "You initiated conflict. You interrupted a sale. I forgive you all that, but you must pay for the damage you've caused. I'm not running a philanthropic organization here. This is a business." She gestured with the palm. "Pay up."

"Fool! I said I've no time to argue with you. This little store you have here is a very clever piece of work, I'll admit that. But I am Zancresta of Malderpot and I am not impressed. I give you one chance to get out of my way."

Snooth did not move. The wizard's paw dipped into an intact pocket and he flung something small and round at her as the kangaroo's hands went to her belly. There was a *crump!* as the small round thing exploded, filling the portal with angry red smoke. Jon-Tom had tried to shout a warning. It came too late.

"Now I will leave over you, hag!"

But there was something else in the doorway now, something besides the uninjured and glowering Snooth. It rose from her pouch, the pouch where Jon-Tom thought he had detected hints of movement before. It rose and grew and it was immediately clear it was no joey, no infant kangaroo. It was far larger, and it expanded as Jon-Tom and his companions slowed to a halt.

Zancresta backed slowly away from the apparition. It enlarged until it reached the roof forty feet overhead, and still it grew, until it could only fit in the cavern by bending low against the rock ceiling.

It had the shape of a red kangaroo, but its face was not the face of a gentle vegetarian like Snooth. The ears were immense, sharply pointed, and hung with thick gold rings. The long snout was full of scimitarlike teeth, and sulfurous eyes centered on tiny black pupils glared downward. Gray smoke encircled and obscured the behemoth's waist, rising lazily from Snooth's pouch. Gorillalike arms hung to the floor, where backturned knuckles rested on the smooth stone.

A bright crimson band encircled the huge forehead. It was inscribed with glowing symbols drawn from an ancient place and time. A thin silken vest flapped in an unfelt wind against the mountainous chest.

And there was the voice. Not gentle and matronly like Snooth's, but awesome in its depth and richness. The apparition spoke, and the earth trembled.

"BEHOLD, ODIOUS IMP, TOILER IN OBSCURITY, MEDDLER IN IN-EFFECTUALITY: I AM HARUN AL-ROOJINN, MASTER OF ALL THE SPIRITS OF TIME PAST AND TIME FUTURE WHERE MARSUPIALS RULE AND ALL OTHERS ARE BUT TINY SCURRYING THINGS THAT HIDE IN ROCKS AND FEED ON WORMS! BEHOLD, AND BE AFRAID!" A hand big enough to sail the Glittergeist if fitted out with sails and rigging reached for Zancresta.

The sorcerer cowered back against the shelving. His expression was desperate as he sought refuge and found none. He dropped to his knees and begged.

"Forgive me, forgive me, I did not know!"

"IGNORANCE IS THE EXCUSE OF THE CONTEMPTUOUS," bellowed the djinn. "ABUSERS OF KNOWLEDGE RARELY SEEK ENLIGHTEN-MENT FROM OTHERS. THOSE WHO TRAMPLE CONVENTION DESERVE NO PITY. THOSE WHO DO NOT PAY WHAT THEY OWE DESERVE TO PERISH."

"I'm sorry!" Zancresta screamed, utterly frantic now. "I was blinded by anger."

"YOU WERE BLINDED BY EGO, WHICH IS FAR WORSE."

"It is a terrible thing to feel inferior to another. I can't stand it. I was overcome with the need to redeem myself, to restore my standing as the greatest practitioner of the mystic arts. All I have done was only for love of my profession." He prostrated himself, arms extended. "I throw myself on your mercy."

"YOU LOVE ONLY YOURSELF, WORM. MERCY? YOU WOULD HAVE SLAIN MY MORTAL TO SAVE A FEW COINS, TO SHOW YOUR DOMI-NANCE. MERCY? YEA, I WILL GRANT YOU MERCY." The ferret's head lifted, and there was a hopeful look on his tormented face.

"THIS IS MY MERCY: THAT YOU SHALL DIE QUICKLY INSTEAD OF SLOWLY!"

Zancresta shrieked and dodged to his left, but he wasn't fast enough to escape that immense descending hand. The fingers contracted once, and the shriek was not repeated. There was only a quick echo of bones crunching. Jon-Tom and his companions stared numbly.

The hand opened and dropped the jellied smear that had been Jalwar-Zancresta, Wizard of Malderpot.

"I ASK YOU," the djinn muttered in slightly less deafening tones, "YOU TRY TO RUN A LITTLE BUSINESS DOWN THROUGH THE AGES AND YOU FIND ETERNITY FULL OF WELCHERS. SPEAKING OF WHICH"—the massive toothy skull and burning yellow eyes lifted to regard Jon-Tom—"THERE IS MORE YET TO DO."

"Hey, wait a minute," said Jon-Tom, starting to back away, "we're ready to pay for what we want. We didn't come here to stiff anybody." He glanced toward Snooth, who only shrugged helplessly. Apparently now that the djinn had been called, she was powerless to control it.

"PAY FOR YOUR GOODS YOU MAY, BUT NOW I HAVE BEEN CALLED FORTH, AND I MUST ALSO BE PAID. HOW WILL YOU DO THAT, PALE WORM? I HAVE NO NEED OF YOUR MONEY. PERHAPS YOU WILL SING ME A SONG SO THAT I MAY LET YOU LEAVE?" Volcanic laughter filled the Shop of the Aether and Neither.

Jon-Tom felt a hand pushing at him. "Well come on, then, mate," Mudge whispered urgently, "go to it. I'm right 'ere behind you if you need me 'elp."

"You're such a comfort." Still, the otter was right. It was up to him to somehow placate this djinn and get them out of there. But he was exhausted from his duel with Charrok and Zancresta, and worn out from thinking up song after song. He was also more than a little irritated. Not the most sensible attitude to take, perhaps, but he was too tired to care.

"You listen to me, Hargood ali rooge."

The djinn glowered. "I DON'T LIKE MORTALS WHO GET MY NAME WRONG."

"Okay, I can go with that," Jon-Tom replied, "but you'll have to excuse me. I've had a helluva couple of weeks. We came here to get some medicine for a sick friend. If that old fart hadn't intruded," and he gestured at the smear on the floor, "we'd be out of here and on our way by now. We didn't have a damn thing to do with his actions."

"TRULY YOU WOULD HAVE BEEN ON YOUR WAY, BUT WHICH WAY IS RIGHT AND PROPER FOR YOU TO GO, LITTLE MORTAL?"

"Do you still have the medicine, Snooth?" The kangaroo nodded, opened a fist to show the precious container. A hand the size of a bus lowered to block her from Jon-Tom's sight.

"THE MEDICINE YOU MAY TAKE. IF YOU CAN SATISFY ME. AND

YOU HAVE SEEN WHAT HAPPENS TO MERE MORTALS WHO DIS-
PLEASE ME."

Jon-Tom was beginning to understand why Crancularn had acquired a less than favorable reputation among travelers in this part of
the world, in spite of the miracles it offered for sale.

"YOU THINK LONG, MORTAL. DO NOT THINK TO TRICK ME BY
SOME FOOLISHNESS SUCH AS ASKING ME TO SHRINK MYSELF INTO A
BOTTLE." A hand hovered above them and Folly flinched. "I DON'T
NEED TO CHANGE MY SIZE TO SHOW MY POWER. ALL I NEED TO DO
IS PUT MY THUMB ON YOUR HEAD."

"Whatever happened to the customer's always right?" Jon-Tom
shot back.

The djinn hesitated. "WHAT OTHERWORLDLY IDIOCY IS THAT?"

"Just good business practice."

"A MORTAL WITH A KNACK FOR BUSINESS." The djinn looked
interested. "I WILL LET YOU PAY WITH YOUR BUSINESS, THEN, AND
PERHAPS YOU AND YOUR FRIENDS WILL LEAVE HERE WITH YOUR
BONES INTACT. YOU ARE A SPELLSINGER. I HAVE HEARD MANY
SPELLSINGERS, BUT NONE THAT PLEASED ME. I DO NOT THINK I
KNOW OF ONE FROM YOUR WORLD. SING ME A SPELLSONG OF YOUR
WORLD, WORM. SING ME A SONG THAT WILL AMUSE ME, INTRIGUE
ME. SING ME SOMETHING DIFFERENT. THEN, AND ONLY THEN,
WILL I LET YOU TAKE THE MEDICINE AND GO!" The djinn folded
arms with thick muscles like the trunks of great trees.

"THINK CAREFULLY ON WHAT YOU WILL SING. I GROW IMPA-
TIENT QUICKLY AND WILL NOT ALLOW YOU A SECOND CHANCE."

Jon-Tom stood sweating and thinking furiously. What song could
he possibly sing that would interest this offspring of magic, who had
access to the goods of thousands of worlds? What did he know that
might be offbeat and just weird enough to have some effect on a
djinn?

Off to his left Roseroar stood watching him quietly. Mudge was
muttering something like a prayer. Folly paced anxiously behind him
while Drom pawed at the floor and wished he were outside where
he'd at least have a running chance.

Feathers caressed his neck. "You can do it, colleague." Charrok
was smiling confidently at him.

Mystical. It had to be overtly mystical, yet not so specific as to
anger the djinn into thinking Jon-Tom was trying to trick him. What
did he know that fit that description? He was just a hard rocker when

he wasn't studying law. All he knew were the hits, the platinum songs.

There was only one possibility, one choice. A song full of implications instead of accusations, mysterious and not readily comprehended. Something to make the djinn think.

He let his fingers slide over the duar's strings. His throat was dry but his hoarseness was gone.

"Watch it, mate," Mudge warned him.

To his surprise Jon-Tom found he could smile down at the otter. "No sweat, Mudge."

"Wot can you sing for 'im 'e don't already 'ave, guv'nor?" The otter waved a hand at the endless shelves crammed with goods from dimensions unknown. "Wot can you give 'im in song 'e don't already own?"

"A different state of mind," Jon-Tom told him softly, and he began to sing.

He was concerned that the duar would not reproduce the eerie chords correctly. He need not have worried. That endlessly responsive, marvelously versatile instrument duplicated the sounds he drew from memory with perfect fidelity, amplifying them so that they filled the chamber around him. It was a strange, quavering moan, a galvanizing cross between an alien bass fiddle being played by something with twelve hands and the snore of a sleeping brontosaurus. Only one man had ever made sounds quite like that before, and Jon-Tom strained hands and lips to reproduce them.

"If you can just get your mind together," he crooned to the djinn, "and come over to me, we'll watch the sunrise together, from the bottom of the sea."

The words and sounds made no sense to Roseroar, but she could sense they were special. Bits and pieces of broken light began to illuminate the chamber around her. Gneechees, harbingers of magic, had appeared and were swarming around Jon-Tom in all their unseeable beauty.

It was a sign the song was working, and it inspired Jon-Tom to sing harder still. Harun al-Roojinn leaned forward as if to protest, to question, and hesitated. Behind the fiery yellow eyes was a first flicker of uncertainty. Jon-Tom sang on.

"First, have you ever been experienced? Have you ever been experienced?" The djinn drifted back on nonexistent heels. His great burning eyes began to glaze over slightly, as if someone were drawing wax paper across them.

"Well, I have," Jon-Tom murmured. The notes bounced off the walls, rang off the ears of the djinn, who seemed to have acquired a pleasant indifference to those around him.

Jon-Tom's own expression began to drift as he continued to sing, remembering the words, remembering the chords. A brief eternity passed. It was Mudge who reached up to break the trance.

"That's it, mate," he whispered. He shook Jon-Tom hard. "C'mon, guv, snap out o' it." Jon-Tom continued to play on, a beatific expression on his face. The djinn hovered before him like some vast rusty blimp, hands folded over his chest, great claws interlocked, whispering.

"BEAUTIFUL . . . Beautiful . . . beautiful . . ."

"Come *on,* mate!" The otter turned to Roseroar, who was swaying slowly in time to the music, her eyes blank. A thin trickle of drool fell from her mouth. Mudge tried to kick her in the rump, but his foot wouldn't reach that high. So he settled for slapping Folly.

"What . . . what's happening?" She blinked. "Stop hitting me." She focused on the drifting djinn. "What's happened to him? He looks so strange."

" 'E ain't the only one," Mudge snapped. " 'Elp me wake the rest of 'em up."

They managed to revive Drom and Charrok and Roseroar, but Jon-Tom stubbornly refused to return to reality. He was as locked into the deceptively langorous state of mind he'd conjured up as was the target of his song.

"Wake *up!*" Roseroar demanded as she shook him. He turned to her, still playing, and smiled broadly.

"Wake up? But why? Everything's so beautiful." He looked half through her. "Did I ever tell you how beautiful you are?"

Roseroar was taken aback by that one, but only for a moment. "Tell me later, suh." She threw him over her left shoulder and started for the door, keeping a wary eye on the stoned djinn.

"Just a second." Drom paused at the portal and snatched the container of medicine from Snooth's fingers.

"Hey, what about my payment, sonny?"

"You've already been paid, madame." The unicorn used his horn to point at Harun al-Roojinn. "Collect from him." Drom trotted out, through the storeroom of broken devices, through the living area, and out the front door to join his friends.

Snooth watched him go, hands on hips, her expression grim.

"Tourists! I should've known they'd be more trouble than they're worth." She stomped out onto the porch and watched until they'd vanished into the woods. Then she reached inside, found the sign she wanted, hung it on the door, and slammed it shut. The message on the sign was clear enough.

OUT TO LUNCH
BACK IN TEN THOUSAND YEARS

Jon-Tom bounced along on Roseroar's powerful shoulder. Mudge kept pace easily alongside, Folly rode atop the reluctant but soft-hearted Drom, and Charrok scouted their progress from above.

As the Shop of the Aether and Neither receded behind them, Jon-Tom gradually began to emerge from the mental miasma into which he'd plunged both himself and Harun al-Roojinn. Fingers moved less steadily over the duar's strings, and his voice fell to a whisper. He blinked.

" 'E's comin' round," Mudge observed.

"It's about time," said Folly. "What did he do to himself?"

"Some wondrous magic," muttered Drom. "Some powerful other-worldly conjuration."

Mudge snorted and grinned. "Right, mate. What 'e did to the monster was waste 'im. Unfortunately, 'e did 'imself right proud in the process."

Jon-Tom's hand went to his head. "Ooooo." Shifting outlines resolved themselves into the running figure of Mudge.

" 'Angover, mate?"

"No. No, I feel okay." He looked up suddenly, back toward the smoking mountain. "Al-Roojinn?"

"Zonked, skunked, blown-away. A fine a piece o' spellsingin' as was ever done, mate."

"It was the song," Jon-Tom murmured dazedly. "A good song. A special song. Jimi's best. If anything could dazzle a djinn, I knew it would be that. You can put me down now, Roseroar." The tigress set him down gently.

"Come on, mate. We'd best keep movin' fast before your spellsong wears off."

"It's all right, I think." He looked back through the forest toward the mountain. "It's not a restraining song. It's a happy song, a re-laxing song. Al-Roojinn didn't seem either happy or relaxed. Maybe he's happy now."

They followed the winding trail back toward Crancularn and discovered a ghost town populated by slow-moving, nebulous inhabitants who smiled wickedly at them, grinning wraiths that floated in and out of reality. "It's there but some don't see it," Drom had said. Now Jon-Tom understood the unicorn's meaning. The real Crancularn was as insubstantial as smoke, as solid as a dream.

They forced themselves not to run as they left the town behind, heading for the familiar woods and the long walk back to far-distant Lynchbany. Somewhere off to the right came the grind of the ATC, but this time the helpful rabbit, be he real or wraith, did not put in an appearance. Once Jon-Tom glanced back to reassure himself that he'd actually been in Crancularn, but instead of a crumbling old town, he thought he saw a vast bubbling cauldron alive with dancing, laughing demons. He shuddered and didn't look back again.

By evening they were all too exhausted to care if Al-Roojinn and a dozen vengeful cousins were hot on their trail or not. Mudge and Roseroar built a fire while the others collapsed.

"I think we're safe now," Jon-Tom told them. He ran both hands through his long hair, suddenly sat up sharply. "The medicine! What about the—!"

"Easy, mate." Mudge extracted the container from a pocket. " 'Ere she be, nice and tidy."

Jon-Tom examined the bottle. It was such a small thing on which to have expended so much effort, barely an inch high and half again as wide. It was fashioned of plain white plastic with a screw-on cap of unfamiliar design.

"I wonder what it is." He started to unscrew the top.

"Just a minim, mate," said Mudge sharply, nodding at the container. "Do you think that's wise? I know you're a spellsinger and all that, but maybe there's a special reason for that little bottle bein' tight-sealed the way it is."

"Any container of medicine would be sealed," Jon-Tom responded. "If there was any danger, Clothahump would have warned me not to open it." Another twist and the cap was off, rendering further argument futile.

He stared at the contents, then held the bottle under his nose and sniffed.

"Well," asked Drom curiously, "do you have any idea what it is?"

Jon-Tom ignored the unicorn. Frowning, he turned the bottle upside down and dumped one of several tablets into his palm. He eyed it uncertainly, and before anyone could stop him, licked it. He sat and smacked his lips thoughtfully.

Abruptly his face contorted and his expression underwent a horrible, dramatic change. His eyes bugged and a hateful grimace twisted his mouth. As he rose his hands were trembling visibly and he clutched the bottle so hard his fingers whitened.

"It's got him!" Folly stumbled back toward the bushes. "Something's got him!"

"Roseroar!" Mudge shouted. "Get 'im down! I'll find some vines to tie 'im with!" He rushed toward the trees.

"No," Jon-Tom growled tightly. "No." His face fell as he stared at the bottle. Then he drew back his hand and made as if to fling the plastic container and its priceless contents into the deep woods. At the last instant he stopped himself. Now he was smiling malevolently at the tablet in his hand.

"No. We're going to take it back. Take it back so that Clothahump can see it. Can see what we crossed half a world and nearly died a dozen times to bring him." He stared at his uneasy companions. "This is the medicine. This will cure him. I'm sure it will. Then, when the pain has left his body and he is whole and healthy again, I'll strangle him with my bare hands!"

"Ah don't understand yo, Jon-Tom. What's wrong if that's the right medicine?"

"What's wrong? I'll tell you what's wrong." He shook the bottle at her. "It's acetylsalicylic acid, that's what's wrong!" Suddenly the anger went out of him, and he sat back down heavily on a fallen tree. "Why didn't I think that might be it? Why?"

Mudge fought to pronounce the peculiar, otherworldly word, failed miserably. "You mean you know wot the bloody stuff is?"

"Know it?" Jon-Tom lifted tired eyes to the otter. "You remember when I arrived in this world, Mudge?"

"Now, that would be a 'ard day to forget, mate. I nearly spilled your guts all over a field o' flowers."

"Do you remember what I was wearing?"

Mudge's face screwed up in remembrance. "That funny tight shirt and them odd pants."

"Jeans, Mudge, jeans. I had a few things with me when Clothahump accidently brought me over. My watch, which doesn't work anymore because the batteries are dead."

"Spell's worn out, you mean."

"Let's don't get into that now, okay? My watch, a lighter, a few keys in a small metal box, and another small box about this big." He traced an outline in the air in front of him.

"The second box held a few little items I always carried with me for unexpected emergencies. Some Pepto-Bismol tablets for an upset stomach, a couple of Band-Aids, a few blue tablets whose purpose we won't discuss in mixed company, and some white tablets. Do you remember the white tablets, Mudge?"

The otter shook his head. "I wouldn't 'ave a looksee through your personal things, mate." Besides, he'd been interrupted before he could get the two boxes opened.

"Those tablets were just like these, Mudge. Just like these." He stared dumbly at the bottle he held. "Acetylsalicylic acid. Aspirin, plain old ordinary everyday aspirin."

"Ah guess it ain't so ordinary hereabouts," said Roseroar.

"Now, mate," said Mudge soothingly, " 'is wizardship couldn't 'ave known you 'ad some in your back pocket all along, now could 'e? It were a sad mistake, but an 'onest one."

"You think so? Clothahump knows *everything.*"

"Then why send us across 'alf the world to find somethin' 'e already 'ad in 'is 'ouse?"

"To test me. To test my loyalty. He's grooming me to take his place someday if he can't send me home, and he has to make sure I'm up to the reputation he's going to leave behind. So he keeps testing me."

"Are you tellin' me, mate," muttered Mudge carefully, "that this 'ole damn dangerous trip was unnecessary from the beginnin'? That this 'ere glorious quest could've been left undone and we could've stayed comfy an' warm back in the Bellwoods, doin' civilized work like gettin' laid an' drunk?"

Jon-Tom nodded sadly. "I'm afraid so."

Mudge's reaction was not what Jon-Tom expected. He anticipated a replay of his own sudden fury, at least. Instead, the otter clasped his hands to his belly, bent over, and fell to the ground, where he commenced to roll wildly about while laughing uncontrollably. A moment later Drom's own amused, high-pitched whinny filled the woods, while Roseroar was unable to restrain her own more dignified but just as heartfelt hysteria.

"What are you laughing about? You idiots, we nearly got killed half a dozen times on this journey! So what are you laughing about?" For some reason this only made his companions laugh all the harder.

Except for one. Soft hands were around his neck and still softer flesh in his lap as Folly sat down on his thighs.

"I understand, Jon-Tom. I feel sorry for you. I'll always understand and I'll never laugh at you."

He struggled to squirm free of her grasp. This was difficult since she was seated squarely in his lap and had locked her hands tightly behind his neck.

"Folly," he said as he wrestled with her, "I've told you before that there can't be anything between us! For one thing, I already have a lady, and for another, you're too young."

She grinned winsomely. "But she's half a world away from here, and I'm getting older every day. If you'll give me half a chance, I'll catch up to you." By now the unicorn was lying on his back kicking weakly at the air, and Mudge was laughing hard enough to cry. Jon-Tom fought to free himself and failed each time he tried, because his hands kept contacting disconcerting objects.

Mudge looked up at his friend. Tears ran down his face and formed droplets on the ends of his whiskers. " 'Ow are you going to magic your way out o' *this* one, spellslinger?" Something nudged him from behind, and he saw that the unicorn had crawled over close to him.

"Small you may be, otter, but you are most admirable in so many ways. I look forward to joining you on your homeward journey. It will give us the chance to get to know each other better. And it is said that where there is a will, there is a way." He nuzzled the wide-eyed otter's haunches.

Then it was Jon-Tom's turn to laugh. . . .

Timeful Desert

Crestleware

Crancularn

Redrock

Village of the
Enchanted Folk

Snarken

Orangel

Cities   Forest   Hills